12-9-84

To Stuart —
Given with love
     on   your birthday,
          Jill

FRANK HERBERT

FOUR COMPLETE NOVELS

ABOUT THE AUTHOR

FRANK HERBERT was born in Washington State in 1920. He was educated in his home state and spent thirty years as a newspaper reporter and editor on the West Coast, including a ten-year stint with the *San Francisco Examiner*. Herbert's interest in various fields has led him to do special research in psychology, arid lands, ecology, and alternative energy, among others, which has stood him in good stead as a writer of deeply interesting and fully realized novels.

In 1963 Herbert achieved worldwide fame with the publication of *Dune*, which became a best-seller and which has, to date, sold more than ten million copies all over the world. Herbert's other Dune novels, *Dune Messiah, Children of Dune, God Emperor of Dune,* and *Heretics of Dune,* have all served to widen his reputation as a novelist of unsurpassable skill and imagination; the last three books have all appeared on national best-seller lists and the latest, *Heretics of Dune*, became a best-seller even before its official publication date.

In addition to the Dune novels, Frank Herbert is the author of some twenty other books, both fiction and nonfiction, including *The Jesus Incident, The Eyes of Heisenberg*, and, recently, *The White Plague*, also a best-seller.

Herbert lives in Washington State and Maui, Hawaii.

FRANK HERBERT

FOUR COMPLETE NOVELS

WHIPPING STAR

THE DOSADI EXPERIMENT

THE SANTAROGA BARRIER

SOUL CATCHER

AVENEL BOOKS / NEW YORK

CONTENTS

WHIPPING STAR

*To Lurton Blassingame, who helped buy the time for this book,
dedicated with affection and admiration*

A BuSab agent must begin by learning the linguistic modes and action limits (usually self-imposed) of the societies he treats. The agent seeks data on the functional relationships which derive from our common universe and which arise from interdependencies. Such interdependencies are the frequent first victims of word-illusions. Societies based on ignorance of original interdependencies come sooner or later to stalemate. Too long frozen, such societies die.

—BuSab Manual

FURUNEO WAS his name. Alichino Furuneo. He reminded himself of this as he rode into the city to make the long-distance call. It was wise to firm up the ego before such a call. He was sixty-seven years old and could remember many cases where people had lost their identity in the sniggertrance of communication between star systems. More than the cost and the mind-crawling sensation of dealing with a Taprisiot transmitter, this uncertainty factor tended to keep down the number of calls. But Furuneo didn't feel he could trust anyone else with this call to Jorj X. McKie, Saboteur Extraordinary.

It was 8:08 A.M. local at Furuneo's position on the planet called Cordiality of the Sfich system.

"This is going to be very difficult, I suspect," he muttered, speaking at (but not to) the two enforcers he had brought along to guard his privacy.

They didn't even nod, realizing no reply was expected.

It was still cool from the night wind which blew across the snow plains of the Billy Mountains down to the sea. They had driven here into Division City from Furuneo's mountain fortress, riding in an ordinary groundcar, not attempting to hide or disguise their association with the Bureau of Sabotage, but not seeking to attract attention, either. Many sentients had reason to resent the Bureau.

Furuneo had ordered the car left outside the city's Pedestrian Central, and they had come the rest of the way on foot like ordinary citizens.

Ten minutes ago they had entered the reception room of this building. It was a Taprisiot breeding center, one of only about twenty known to exist in the universe, quite an honor for a minor planet like Cordiality.

The reception room was no more than fifteen meters wide, perhaps thirty-five long. It had tan walls with pitted marks in them as though they had been soft once and someone had thrown a small ball at them according to some random whim. Along the right side across from where Furuneo stood with his enforcers was a high bench. It occupied three-fourths of the long wall. Multi-faceted rotating lights above it cast patterned shadows onto the face of the bench and the Taprisiot standing atop it.

Taprisiots came in odd shapes like sawed-off lengths of burned conifers, with stub limbs jutting every which way, needlelike speech appendages fluttering even when they remained silent. This one's skidfeet beat a nervous rhythm on the surface where it stood.

For the third time since entering, Furuneo asked, "Are you the transmitter?"

No answer.

5

Taprisiots were like that. No sense getting angry. It did no good. Furuneo allowed himself to be annoyed, though. Damned Taprisiots!

One of the enforcers behind Furuneo cleared his throat.

Damn this delay! Furuneo thought.

The whole Bureau had been in a state of jitters ever since the max-alert message on the Abnethe case. This call he was preparing to make might be their first real break. He sensed the fragile urgency of it. It could be the most important call he had ever made. And directly to McKie, at that.

The sun, barely over the Billy Mountains, spread an orange fan of light around him from the windowed doorway through which they had entered.

"Looks like it's gonna be a long wait for this Tappy," one of his enforcers muttered.

Furuneo nodded curtly. He had learned several degrees of patience in sixty-seven years, especially on his way up the ladder to his present position as planetary agent for the Bureau. There was only one thing to do here: wait it out quietly. Taprisiots took their own time for whatever mysterious reasons. There was no other *store*, though, where he could buy the service he needed now. Without a Taprisiot transmitter, you didn't make real-time calls across interstellar space.

Strange, this Taprisiot talent—used by so many sentients without understanding. The sensational press abounded with theories on how it was accomplished. For all anyone knew, one of the theories could be right. Perhaps Taprisiots *did* make these calls in a way akin to the data linkage among Pan Spechi crèche mates—not that this was understood, either.

It was Furuneo's belief that Taprisiots distorted space in a way similar to that of a Caleban jumpdoor, sliding between the dimensions. If that was really what Caleban jumpdoors did. Most experts denied this theory, pointing out that it would require energies equivalent to those produced by fair-sized stars.

Whatever Taprisiots did to make a call, one thing was certain: It involved the human pineal gland or its equivalent among other sentients.

The Taprisiot on the high bench began moving from side to side.

"Maybe we're getting through to it," Furuneo said.

He composed his features, suppressed his feelings of unease. This was, after all, a Taprisiot breeding center. Xenobiologists said Taprisiot reproduction was all quite tame, but Xenos didn't know everything. Look at the mess they'd made of analyzing the Pan Spechi Con-Sentiency.

"Putcha, putcha, putcha," the Taprisiot on the bench said, squeaking its speech needles.

"Someting wrong?" one of the enforcers asked.

"How the devil do I know?" Furuneo snapped. He faced the Taprisiot, said, "Are you the transmitter?"

"Putcha, putcha, putcha," the Taprisiot said. "This is a remark which I will now translate in the only way that may make sense to ones like yourselves of Sol/Earth ancestry. What I said was, 'I question your sincerity.' "

"You gotta justify your sincerity to a damn Taprisiot?" one of the enforcers asked. "Seems to me . . . "

"Nobody asked you!" Furuneo cut him off. Any probing attack by a Taprisiot was likely a greeting. Didn't the fool know this?

Furuneo separated himself from the enforcers, crossed to a position below the bench. "I wish to make a call to Saboteur Extraordinary Jorj X. McKie," he said.

"Your robogreeeter recognized and identified me and took my creditchit. Are you the transmitter?"

"Where is this Jorj X. McKie?" the Taprisiot asked.

"If I knew, I'd be off to him in person through a jumpdoor," Furuneo said. "This is an important call. Are you the transmitter?"

"Date, time, and place," the Taprisiot said.

Furuneo sighed and relaxed. He glanced back at the enforcers, motioned them to take up stations at the room's two doors, waited while they obeyed. Wouldn't do to have this call overheard. He turned then, gave the required local coordinates.

"You will sit on floor," the Taprisiot said.

"Thank the immortals for that," Furuneo muttered. He'd once made a call where the transmitter had led him to a mountainside in wind and driving rain and made him stretch out, head lower than feet, before opening the overspace contact. It had had something to do with "refining the embedment," whatever that meant. He'd reported the incident to the Bureau's data center, where they hoped one day to solve the Taprisiot secret, but the call had cost him several weeks with an upper respiratory infection.

Furuneo sat.

Damn! The floor was cold!

Furuneo was a tall man, two meters in bare feet, eighty-four standard kilos. His hair was black with a dusting of grey at the ears. He had a thick nose and wide mouth with an oddly straight lower lip. He favored his left hip as he sat. A disgruntled citizen had broken it during one of his early tours with the Bureau. The injury defied all the medics who had told him, "It won't bother you a bit after it's healed."

"Close eyes," the Taprisiot squeaked.

Furuneo obeyed, tried to squirm into a more comfortable position on the cold, hard floor, gave it up.

"Think of contact," the Taprisiot ordered.

Furuneo thought of Jorj X. McKie, building the image in his mind—squat little man, angry red hair, face like a disgruntled frog.

Contact began with tendrils of cloying awareness. Furuneo became in his own mind a red flow sung to the tune of a silver lyre. His body went remote. Awareness rotated above a strange landscape. The sky was an infinite circle with its horizon slowly turning. He sensed the stars engulfed in loneliness.

"*What the ten million devils!*"

The thought exploded across Furuneo. There was no evading it. He recognized it at once. Contactees frequently resented the call. They couldn't reject it, no matter what they were doing at the time, but they could make the caller feel their displeasure.

"*It never fails! It never fails!*"

McKie would be jerked to full inner awareness now, his pineal gland ignited by the long-distance contact.

Furuneo settled himself to wait out the curses. When they had subsided sufficiently, he identified himself, said, "I regret any inconvenience I may have caused, but the max-alert failed to say where you could be located. You must know I would not have called unless it were important."

A more or less standard opening.

"How the hell do I know whether your call's important?" McKie demanded. "Stop babbling and get on with it!"

This was an unusual extension of anger even for the volatile McKie. "Did I interrupt something important?" Furuneo ventured.

"I was just standing here in a telicourt getting a divorce!" McKie said, "Can't you imagine what a great time everyone here's having, watching me mubble-dubble to myself in a sniggertrance? Get to the business!"

"A Caleban Beachball washed ashore last night below Division City here on Cordiality," Furuneo said. "In view of all the deaths and insanity and the max-alert message from the Bureau, I thought I'd better call you at once. It's still your case, isn't it?"

"Is this your idea of a joke?" McKie demanded.

In lieu of red tape, Furuneo cautioned himself, thinking of the Bureau maxim. It was a private thought, but McKie no doubt was catching the mood of it.

"Well?" McKie demanded.

Was McKie deliberately trying to unnerve him? Furuneo wondered. How could the Bureau's prime ·function—to slow the processes of government—remain operative on an internal matter such as this call? Agents were duty bound to encourage anger in government because it exposed the unstable, temperamental types, the ones who lacked the necessary personal control and ability to think under psychic stress, but why carry this duty over to a call from a fellow agent?

Some of these thoughts obviously bled through the Taprisiot transmitter because McKie reflected them, enveloping Furuneo in a mental sneer.

"You lotsa time unthink yourself," McKie said.

Furuneo shuddered, recovered his sense of self. Ahhh, that had been close. He'd almost lost his ego! Only the veiled warning in McKie's words had alerted him, allowing recovery. Furuneo began casting about in his mind for another interpretation of McKie's reaction. Interrupting the divorce could not account for it. If the stories were true, the ugly little agent had been married fifty or more times.

"Are you still interested in the Beachball?" Furuneo ventured.

"Is there a Caleban in it?"

"Presumably."

"You haven't investigated?" McKie's mental tone said Furuneo had been entrusted with a most crucial operation and had failed because of inherent stupidity.

Now fully alert to some unspoken danger, Furuneo said, "I acted as my orders instructed."

"Orders!" McKie sneered.

"I'm supposed to be angry, eh?" Furuneo asked.

"I'll be there as fast as I can get service—within eight standard hours at the most," McKie said. "Your *orders*, meanwhile, are to keep that Beachball under constant observation. The observers must be hopped up on *angeret*. It's their only protection."

"Constant observation," Furuneo said.

"If a Caleban emerges, you're to detain it by any means possible."

"A Caleban . . . detain it?"

"Engage it in conversation, request it's cooperation, anything," McKie said. His mental emphasis added that it was odd a Bureau agent should have to ask about throwing a monkey wrench into someone's activities.

"Eight hours," Furuneo said.

"And don't forget the angeret."

A Bureau is a life form and the Bureaucrat one of its cells. This analogy teaches us which are the more important cells, which in greatest peril, which most easily replaced, and how easy it is to be mediocre.

—LATER WRITINGS OF BILDOON IV

MCKIE, ON the honeymoon planet of Tutalsee, took an hour to complete his divorce, then returned to the float-home they had moored beside an island of love flowers. Even the nepenthe of Tutalsee had failed him, McKie thought. This marriage had been wasted effort. His ex hadn't known enough about Mliss Abnethe despite their reported former association. But that had been on another world.

This wife had been his fifty-fourth, somewhat lighter of skin than any of the others and more than a bit of a shrew. It had not been her first marriage, and she had shown early suspicion of McKie's secondary motives.

Reflection made McKie feel guilty. He put such feelings aside savagely. There was no time for nicety. Too much was at stake. Stupid female!

She had already vacated the float-home, and McKie could sense the living entity's resentment. He had shattered the idyll which the float-home had been conditioned to create. The float-home would return to its former affability once he was gone. They were gentle creatures, susceptible to sentient irritation.

McKie packed, leaving his toolkit aside. He examined it: a selection of stims, plastipicks, explosives in various denominations, raygens, multigoggles, pentrates, a wad of uniflesh, solvos, miniputer, Taprisiot life monitor, holoscan blanks, rupters, comparators . . . all in order. The toolkit was a fitted wallet which he concealed in an inner pocket of his nondescript jacket.

He packed a few changes of clothing in a single bag, consigned the rest of his possessions to BuSab storage, left them for pickup in a sealpack which he stored on a couple of chairdogs. They appeared to share the float-home's resentment. They remained immobile even when he patted them affectionately.

Ah, well. . . .

He still felt guilty.

McKie sighed, took out his S'eye key. This jump was going to cost the Bureau megacredits. Cordiality lay halfway across their universe.

Jumpdoors still seemed to be working, but it disturbed McKie that he must make his journey by a means which was dependent upon a Caleban. Eerie situation. S'eye jumpdoors had become so common that most sentients accepted them without question. McKie had shared this common acceptance before the max-alert. Now he wondered at himself. Casual acceptance demonstrated how easily rational thought could be directed by wishful thinking. This was a common susceptibility of all sentients. The Caleban jumpdoor had been fully accepted by the Confederated Sentients for some ninety standard years. But in that time, only eighty-three Calebans were known to have identified themselves.

McKie flipped the key in his hand, caught it deftly.

Why had the Calebans refused to part with their gift unless everyone agreed to call it a "S'eye"? What was so important about a name?

I should be on my way, McKie told himself. Still he delayed.

Eighty-three Calebans.

The max-alert had been explicit in its demand for secrecy and its outline of the problem: Calebans had been disappearing one by one. Disappearing—if that was what the Caleban manifestation could be called. And each *disappearance* had been accompanied by a massive wave of sentient deaths and insanity.

No question why the problem had been dumped in BuSab's lap instead of onto some police agency. Government fought back wherever it could: Powerful men hoped to discredit BuSab. McKie found his own share of disturbance in wondering about the hidden possibilities in the selection of himself as the sentient to tackle this.

Who hates me? he wondered as he used his personally tuned key in the jumpdoor. The answer was that many people hated him. Millions of people.

The jumpdoor began to hum with its aura of terrifying energies. The door's vortal tube snapped open. McKie tensed himself for the syrupy resistance to jumpdoor passage, stepped through the tube. It was like swimming in air become molasses—perfectly normal-appearing air. But molasses.

McKie found himself in a rather ordinary office: the usual humdrum whirldesk, alert-flicker light patterns cascading from the ceiling, a view out one transparent wall onto a mountainside. In the distance the rooftops of Division City lay beneath dull gray clouds, with a luminous silver sea beyond. McKie's implated brainclock told him it was late afternoon, the eighteenth hour of a twenty-six-hour day. This was Cordiality, a world 200,000 light-years from Tutalsee's planetary ocean.

Behind him, the jumpdoor's vortal tube snapped closed with a crackling sound like the discharge of electricity. A faint ozone smell permeated the air.

The room's standard-model chairdogs had been well trained to comfort their masters, McKie noted. One of them nudged him behind the knees until he dropped his bag and took a reluctant seat. The chairdog began massaging his back. Obviously it had been instructed to make him comfortable while someone was summoned.

McKie tuned himself to the faint sounds of normality around him. Footsteps of a sentient could be heard in an outer passage. A Wreave by the sound of it: that peculiar dragging of the heel on a favored foot. There was a dim conversation somewhere, and McKie could make out a few Lingua-galach words, but it sounded like a multilingual conversation.

He began fidgeting, which set the chairdog into a burst of rippling movements to soothe him. Enforced idleness nagged at him. Where was Furuneo? McKie chided himself. Furuneo probably had many planetary duties as BuSab agent here. And he couldn't know the full urgency of their problem. This might be one of the planets where BuSab was spread thin. The gods of immortality knew the Bureau could always find work.

McKie began reflecting on his role in the affairs of sentiency. Once, long centuries past, con-sentients with a psychological compulsion to "do good" had captured the government. Unaware of the writhing complexities, the mingled guilts and self-punishments, beneath their compulsion, they had eliminated virtually all delays and red tape from government. The great machine with its blundering power over sentient life had slipped into high gear, had moved faster and faster. Laws had been conceived and passed in the same hour. Appropriations had flashed into being and were spent in a fortnight. New bureaus for the most improbable purposes had leaped into existence and proliferated like some insane fungus.

Government had become a great destructive wheel without a governor, whirling with such frantic speed that it spread chaos wherever it touched.

In desperation, a handful of sentients had conceived the Sabotage Corps to slow that wheel. There had been bloodshed and other degrees of violence, but the wheel had been slowed. In time, the Corps had become a Bureau, and the Bureau was whatever it was today—an organization headed into its own corridors of entropy, a group of sentients who preferred subtle diversion to violence . . . but were prepared for violence when the need arose.

A door slid back on McKie's right. His chairdog became still. Furuneo entered, brushing a hand through the band of grey hair at his left ear. His wide mouth was held in a straight line, a suggestion of sourness about it.

"You're early," he said, patting a chairdog into place across from McKie and seating himself.

"Is this place safe?" McKie asked. He glanced at the wall where the S'eye had disgorged him. The jumpdoor was gone.

"I've moved the door back downstairs through its own tube," Furuneo said. "This place is as private as I can make it." He sat back, waiting for McKie to explain.

"That Beachball still down there?" McKie nodded toward the transparent wall and the distant sea.

"My men have orders to call me if it makes any move," Furuneo said. "It was washed ashore just like I said, embedded itself in a rock outcropping, and hasn't moved since."

"Embedded itself?"

"That's how it seems."

"No sign of anything in it?"

"Not that we can see. The Ball does appear to be a bit . . . banged up. There are some pitting and a few external scars. What's this all about?"

"No doubt you've heard of Mliss Abnethe?"

"Who hasn't?"

"She recently spent some of her quintillions to hire a Caleban."

"Hire a . . . " Furuneo shook his head. "I didn't know it could be done."

"Neither did anyone else."

"I read the max-alert," Furuneo said. "Abnethe's connection with the case wasn't explained."

"She's a bit kinky about floggings, you know," McKie said.

"I thought she was treated for that."

"Yeah, but it didn't eliminate the root of her problem. It just fixed her so she couldn't stand the sight of a sentient suffering."

"So?"

"Her solution, naturally, was to hire a Caleban."

"As a victim!" Furuneo said.

Furuneo was beginning to understand, McKie saw. Someone had once said the problem with Calebans was that they presented no patterns you could recognize. This was true, of course. If you could imagine an *actuality*, a being whose presence could not be denied but who left your senses dangling every time you tried to look at it—then you could imagine a Caleban.

"*They're shuttered windows opening onto eternity*," as the poet Masarard put it.

In the first Caleban days, McKie had attended every Bureau lecture and briefing about them. He tried to recall one of those sessions now, prompted by a nagging sensation that it had contained something of value to his present problem. It had been something about "communications difficulties within an aura of affliction."

The precise content eluded him. Odd, he thought. It was as though the Calebans' crumbled projection created an effect on sentient memory akin to their effect on sentient vision.

Here lay the true source of sentient uneasiness about Calebans. Their artifacts were real—the S'eye jumpdoors, the Beachballs in which they were reputed to live—but no one had ever really *seen* a Caleban.

Furuneo, watching the fat little gnome of an agent sit there thinking, recalled the snide story about McKie, that he had been in BuSab since the day before he was born.

"She's hired a whipping boy, eh?" Furuneo asked.

"That's about it."

"The max-alert spoke of deaths, insanity. . . . "

"Are all your people dosed with *angeret?*" McKie asked.

"I got the message, McKie."

"Good. Anger seems to afford some protection."

"What exactly is going on?"

"Calebans have been . . . vanishing," McKie said. "Every time one of them goes, there are quite a few deaths and . . . other unpleasant effects—physical and mental crippling, insanity. . . . "

Furuneo nodded in the direction of the sea, leaving his question unspoken.

McKie shrugged. "We'll have to go take a look. The hell of it is, up until your call there seemed to be only one Caleban left in the universe, the one Abnethe hired."

"How're you going to handle this?"

"That's a beautiful question," McKie said.

"Abnethe's Caleban," Furuneo said. "It have anything to say by way of explanation?"

"Haven't been able to interview it," McKie said. "We don't know where she's hidden herself—or it."

"Don't know. . . . " Furuneo blinked. "Cordiality's pretty much of a backwater."

"That's what I've been thinking. You said this Beachball was a little the worse for wear?"

"That's odd, isn't it?"

"Another oddity among many."

"They say a Caleban doesn't get very far from its Ball," Furuneo said. "And they like to park 'em near water."

"How much of an attempt did you make to communicate with it?"

"The usual. How'd you find out about Abnethe hiring a Caleban?"

"She bragged to a friend who bragged to a friend who-. . . . And one of the other Calebans dropped a hint before disappearing."

"Any doubt the disappearances and the rest of it are tied together?"

"Let's go knock on this thing's door and find out," McKie said.

Language is a kind of code dependent upon the life rhythms of the species which originated the language. Unless you learn those rhythms, the code remains mostly unintelligible.

—BuSab Manual

MCKIE'S IMMEDIATE ex-wife had adopted an early attitude of resentment toward BuSab. "They use you!" she had protested.

He had thought about that for a few minutes, wondering if it might be the reason he found it so easy to use others. She was right, of course.

McKie thought about her words now as he and Furuneo sped by groundcar toward the Cordiality coast. The question in McKie's mind was, How are they using me this time? Setting aside the possibility that he had been offered up as a sacrifice, there were still many possibilities in reserve. Was it his legal training they needed? Or had they been prompted by his unorthodox approach to interspecies relationships? Obviously they entertained some hope for a special sort of official sabotage—but what sort? Why had his instructions been so incomplete?

"You will seek out and contact the Caleban which has been hired by Madame Mliss Abnethe, or find any other Caleban available for sentient contact, and you will take appropriate action."

Appropriate action?

McKie shook his head.

"Why'd they choose you for this gig?" Furuneo asked.

"They know how to use me," McKie said.

The groundcar, driven by an enforcer, negotiated a sharp turn, and a vista of rocky shore opened before them. Something glittered in the distance among black lava palisades, and McKie noted two aircraft hovering above the rocks.

"That it?" he asked.

"Yes."

"What's the local time?"

"About two and a half hours to sunset," Furuneo said, correctly interpreting McKie's concern. "Will the *angeret* protect us if there's a Caleban in that thing and it decides to . . . disappear?"

"I sincerely hope so," McKie said. "Why didn't you bring us by aircar?"

"People here on Cordiality are used to seeing me in a groundcar unless I'm on official business and require speed."

"You mean nobody knows about this thing yet?"

"Just the coastwatchers for this stretch, and they're on my payroll."

"You run a pretty tight operation here," McKie said. "Aren't you afraid of getting too efficient?"

"I do my best," Furuneo said. He tapped the driver's shoulder.

The groundcar pulled to a stop at a turnaround which looked down onto a reach of rocky islands and a low lava shelf where the Caleban Beachball had come to rest. "You know, I keep wondering if we really know what those Beachballs are."

"They're homes," McKie grunted.

"So everybody says."

Furuneo got out. A cold wind set his hip aching. "We walk from here," he said.

There were times during the climb down the narrow path to the lava shelf when McKie felt thankful he had been fitted with a gravity web beneath his skin. If he

13

fell, it would limit his rate of descent to a non-injurious speed. But there was nothing it could do about any beating he might receive in the surf at the base of the palisades, and it offered no protection at all against the chill wind and the driving spray.

He wished he'd worn a heatsuit.

"It's colder than I expected," Furuneo said, limping out onto the lava shelf. He waved to the aircars. One dipped its wings, maintaining its place in a slow, circling track above the Beachball.

Furuneo struck out across the shelf and McKie followed, jumped across a tidal pool, blinked and bent his head against a gust of windborne spray. The pounding of the surf on the rocks was loud here. They had to raise their voices to make themselves understood.

"You see?" Furuneo shouted. "Looks like it's been banged around a bit."

"Those things are supposed to be indestructible," McKie said.

The beachball was some six meters in diameter. It sat solidly on the shelf, about half a meter of its bottom surface hidden by a depression in the rock, as though it had melted out a resting place.

McKie led the way up to the lee of the Ball, passing Furuneo in the last few meters. He stood there, hands in pockets, shivering. The round surface of the Ball failed to cut off the cold wind.

"It's bigger than I expected," he said as Furuneo stopped beside him.

"First one you've ever seen close up?"

"Yeah."

McKie passed his gaze across the thing. Knobs and indentations marked the opaque metallic surface. It seemed to him the surface variations carried some pattern. Sensors, perhaps? Controls of some kind? Directly in front of him there was what appeared to be a crackled mark, perhaps from a collision. It lay just below the surface, presenting no roughness to McKie's exploring hand.

"What if they're wrong about these things?" Furuneo asked.

"Mmmm?"

"What if they aren't Caleban homes?"

"Don't know. Do you recall the drill?"

"You find a 'nippled extrusion' and you knock on it. We tried that. There's one just around to your left."

McKie worked his way around in that direction, getting drenched by a wind-driven spray in the process. He reached up, still shivering from the cold, knocked at the indicated extrusion.

Nothing happened.

"Every briefing I ever attended says there's a door in these things somewhere," McKie grumbled.

"But they don't say the door opens every time you knock," Furuneo said.

McKie continued working his way around the Ball, found another nippled extrusion, knocked.

Nothing.

"We tried that one, too," Furuneo said.

"I feel like a damn fool," McKie said.

"Maybe there's nobody home."

"Remote control?" McKie asked.

"Or abandoned—a derelict."

McKie pointed to a thin green line about a meter long on the Ball's windward surface. "What's that?"

Furuneo hunched his shoulders against spray and wind, stared at the line. "Don't recall seeing it."

"I wish we knew a lot more about these damn things," McKie grumbled.

"Maybe we aren't knocking loud enough," Furuneo said.

McKie pursed his lips in thought. Presently he took out his toolkit, extracted a lump of low-grade explosive. "Go back on the other side," he said

"You sure you ought to try that?" Furuneo asked.

"No."

"Well—" Furuneo shrugged, retreated around the Ball.

McKie applied a strip of the explosive along the green line, attached a time-thread, joined Furuneo.

Presently, there came a dull thump that was almost drowned by the surf.

McKie felt an abrupt inner silence, found himself wondering, *What if the Caleban gets angry and springs a weapon we've never heard of?* He darted around to the windward side.

An oval hole had appeared above the green line as though a plug had been sucked into the Ball.

"Guess you pushed the right button," Furuneo said.

McKie suppressed a feeling of irritation which he knew to be mostly *angeret* effect, said, "Yeah. Give me a leg up." Furuneo, he noted, was controlling the drug reaction almost perfectly.

With Furuneo's help McKie clambered into the open port, stared inside. Dull purple light greeted him, a suggestion of movement within the dimness.

"See anything?" Furuneo called.

"Don't know." McKie scrambled inside, dropped to a carpeted floor. He crouched, studied his surroundings in the purple glow. His teeth clattered from the cold. The room around him apparently occupied the entire center of the Ball—low ceiling, flickering rainbows against the inner surface on his left, a giant soup-spoon shape jutting into the room directly across from him, tiny spools, handles, and knobs against the wall on his right.

The sense of movement originated in the spoon bowl.

Abruptly, McKie realized he was in the presence of a Caleban.

"What do you see?" Furuneo called.

Without taking his gaze from the spoon, McKie turned his head slightly. "There's a Caleban in here."

"Shall I come in?"

"No. Tell your men and sit tight."

"Right."

McKie returned his full attention to the bowl of the spoon. His throat felt dry. He'd never before been alone in the presence of a Caleban. This was a position usually reserved for scientific investigators armed with esoteric instruments.

"I'm . . . ah, Jorj X. McKie, Bureau of Sabotage," he said.

There was a stirring at the spoon, an effect of radiated meaning immediately behind the movement: "I make your acquaintance."

McKie found himself recalling Masarard's poetic description in *Conversation With a Caleban.*

"Who can say how a Caleban speaks?" Masarard had written. *"Their words come at you like the corruscating of a nine-ribbon Sojeu barber pole. The insensitive way such words radiate. I say the Caleban speaks. When words are sent, is that not speech? Send me your words, Caleban, and I will*

tell the universe of your wisdom."

Having experienced the Caleban's words, McKie decided Masarard was a pretentious ass. The Caleban radiated. Its communication registered in the sentient mind as sound, but the ears denied they had heard anything. It was the same order of effect that Calebans had on the eyes. You felt you were seeing something, but the visual centers refused to agree.

"I hope my . . . ah, I didn't disturb you," McKie said.

"I possess no referent for disturb," the Caleban said. "You bring a companion?"

"My companion's outside," McKie said. *No referent for disturb?*

"Invite your companion," the Caleban said.

McKie hesitated, then, "Furuneo! C'mon in."

The planetary agent joined him, crouched at McKie's left in the purple gloom. "Damn, that's cold out there," Furuneo said.

"Low temperature and much moisture," the Caleban agreed. McKie, having turned to watch Furuneo enter, saw a closure appear from the solid wall beside the open port. Wind, spray, and surf were shut off.

The temperature in the Ball began to rise.

"It's going to get hot," McKie said.

"What?"

"Hot. Remember the briefings? Calebans like their air hot and dry." He could already feel his damp clothing begin to turn clammy against his skin.

"That's right," Furuneo said. "What's going on?"

"We've been invited in," McKie said. "We didn't disturb him because he has no referent for disturb." He turned back to the spoon shape.

"Where is he?"

"In that spoon thing."

"Yeah . . . I, uh—yeah."

"You may address me as Fanny Mae," the Caleban said. "I can reproduce my kind and answer the equivalents for female."

"Fanny Mae," McKie said with what he knew to be stupid vacuity. *How can you look at the damn thing? Where is its face?* "My companion is Alichino Furuneo, planetary agent on Cordiality for the Bureau of Sabotage." *Fanny Mae? Damn!*

"I make your acquaintance," the Caleban said. "Permit an inquiry into the purpose for your visit."

Furuneo scratched his right ear. "How're we hearing it?" He shook his head. "I can understand it, but. . . ."

"Never mind!" McKie said. And he warned himself: *Gently now. How do you question one of these things?* The insubstantial Caleban presence, the twisting way his mind accepted the thing's words—it all combined with the *angeret* in producing irritation.

"I . . . my orders," McKie said. "I seek a Caleban employed by Mliss Abnethe."

"I receive your questions," the Caleban said.

Receive my questions?

McKie tried tipping his head from side to side, wondered if it were possible to achieve an angle of vision where the *something* across from him would assume recognizable substance.

"What're you doing?" Furuneo asked.

"Trying to see it."

"You seek visible substance?" the Caleban asked.

"Uhhh, yes," McKie said.

Fanny Mae? he thought. It would be like an original encounter with the Gowachin planets, the first Earth-human encountering the first froglike Gowachin, and the Gowachin introducing himself as William. *Where in ninety thousand worlds did the Caleban dig up that name? And why?*

"I produce mirror," the Caleban said, "which reflects outward from projection along plane of being."

"Are we going to see it?" Furuneo whispered. "Nobody's ever seen a Caleban."

"Shhh."

A half-meter oval *something* of green, blue, and pink without apparent connection to the empty-presence of the Caleban materialized above the giant spoon.

"Think of this as stage upon which I present my selfdom," the Caleban said.

"You see anything?" Furuneo asked.

McKie's visual centers conjured a borderline sensation, a feeling of distant life whose rhythms danced unfleshed within the colorful oval like the sea roaring in an empty shell. He recalled a one-eyed friend and the difficulty of focusing the attention on that lonely eye without being drawn to the vacant patch. *Why couldn't the damn fool just buy a new eye? Why couldn't . . .*

He swallowed.

"That's the oddest thing I ever saw," Furuneo whispered. "You see it?"

McKie described his visual sensation. "That what you see?"

"I guess so,"Furuneo said.

"Visual attempt fails," the Caleban said. "Perhaps I employ insufficient contrast."

Wondering if he could be mistaken, McKie thought he detected a plaintive mood in the Caleban's words. Was it possible Calebans disliked not being seen?

"It's fine," McKie said. "Now, may we discuss the Caleban who . . . "

"Perhaps overlooking cannot be connected," the Caleban said, interrupting. "We enter state for which there exists no remedy. 'As well argue with the night,' as your poets tell us."

The sensation of an enormous sigh swept out from the Caleban and over McKie. It was sadness, a doom-fire gloom. He wondered if they had experienced an *angeret* failure. The emotional strength carried terror within it.

"You feel that?" Furuneo asked.

"Yes."

McKie felt his eyes burning. He blinked. Between blinks, he glimpsed a flower element hovering within the oval—deep red against the room's purple, with black veins woven through it. Slowly it blossomed, closed, blossomed. He wanted to reach out, touch it with a handful of compassion.

"How beautiful," he whispered.

"What is it?" Furuneo whispered.

"I think we're seeing a Caleban."

"I want to cry," Furuneo said.

"Control yourself," McKie cautioned. He cleared his throat. Twanging bits of emotion tumbled through him. They were like pieces cut from the whole and loosed to seek their own patterns. The *angeret* effect was lost in the mixture.

Slowly the image in the oval faded. The emotional torrent subsided.

"Wheweee," Furuneo breathed.

"Fanny Mae," McKie ventured. "What was . . . "

"I am one employed by Mliss Abnethe," the Caleban said. "Correct verb usage?"

"Bang!" Furuneo said. "Just like that."

McKie glanced at him, at the place where they had entered the Ball. No sign remained of the oval hole. The heat in the room was becoming unbearable. *Correct verb usage?* He looked at the Caleban manifestation. Something still shimmered above the spoon shape, but it defied his visual centers to describe it.

"Was it asking a question?" Furuneo asked.

"Be still a minute," McKie snapped. "I want to think."

Seconds ticked past. Furuneo felt perspiration running down his neck, under his collar. He could taste it in the corners of his mouth.

McKie sat silently staring at the giant spoon. The Caleban employed by Abnethe. He still felt the aftermath of the emotional mélange. Some lost memory demanded his attention, but he couldn't bring it out for examination.

Furuneo, watching McKie, began to wonder if the Saboteur Extraordinary had been mesmerized. "You still thinking?" he whispered.

McKie nodded, then, "Fanny Mae, where is your employer?"

"Coordinates not permitted," the Caleban said.

"Is she on this planet?"

"Different connectives," the Caleban said.

"I don't think you two are talking the same language," Furuneo said.

"From everything I've read and heard about Calebans, that's the big problem," McKie said. "Communication difficulty."

Furuneo wiped sweat from his forehead. "Have you tried calling Abnethe long distance?" he asked.

"Don't be stupid," McKie said. "That's the first thing I tried."

"Well?"

"Either the Taprisiots are telling the truth and can't make contact, or she's bought them off some way. What difference does it make? So I contact her. How does that tell me where she is? How do I invoke a monitor clause with someone who doesn't wear a monitor?"

"How could she buy off the Taprisiots?"

"How do I know? For that matter, how could she hire a Caleban?"

"Invocation of value exchange," the Caleban said.

McKie chewed at his upper lip.

Furuneo leaned against the wall behind him. He knew what inhibited McKie here. You walked softly with a strange sentient species. No telling what might cause affront. Even the way you phrased a question could cause trouble. They should have assigned a Zeno expert to help McKie. It seemed odd that they hadn't.

"Abnethe offered you something of value, Fanny Mae?" McKie ventured.

"I offer judgment," the Caleban said. "Abnethe may not be judged friendly-good-nice-kindly . . . acceptable."

"Is that . . . your judgment?" McKie asked.

"Your species prohibits flagellation of sentients," the Caleban said. "Fanny Mae orders me flagellated."

"Why don't you . . . just refuse?" McKie asked.

"Contract obligation," the Caleban said.

"Contract obligaton." McKie muttered, glancing at Furuneo, who shrugged.

"Ask where she goes to be flagellated," Furuneo said.

"Flagellation comes to me," the Caleban said.

"By flagellation, you mean you're whipped," McKie said.

"Explanation of whipping describes production of froth," the Caleban said. "Not proper term. Abnethe orders me flogged."

"That thing talks like a computer," Furuneo said.

"Let me handle this," McKie ordered.

"Computer describes mechanical device," the Caleban said. "I live."

"He meant no insult," McKie said.

"Insult not interpreted."

"Does the flogging hurt you?" McKie asked.

"Explain hurt."

"Cause you discomfort?"

"Reference recalled. Such sensations explained. Explanations cross no connectives."

Cross no connectives? McKie thought. "Would you choose to be flogged?" he asked.

"Choice made," the Caleban said.

"Well . . . would you make the same choice if you had it to do over?" McKie asked.

"Confusing reference," the Caleban said. "If over refers to repetition, I make no voice in repetition. Abnethe sends Palenki with whip, and flogging occurs."

"A Palenki!" Furuneo said. He shuddered.

"You knew it had to be something like that," McKie said. "What else could you get to do such a thing except a creature without much brain and lots of obedient muscle?"

"But a Palenki! Couldn't we hunt for . . . "

"We've known from the first what she had to be using," McKie said. "Where do you hunt for one Palenki?" He shrugged. "Why can't Calebans understand the concept of being hurt? Is it pure semantics, or do they lack the proper nerve linkages?"

"Understand nerves," the Caleban said. "Any sentience must possess control linkages. But hurt . . . discontinuity of meaning appears insurmountable."

"Abnethe can't stand the sight of pain, you said," Furuneo reminded McKie.

"Yeah. How does she watch the floggings?"

"Abnethe views my home," the Caleban said.

When no further answer was forthcoming, McKie said, "I don't understand. What's that have to do with it?"

"My home this," the Caleban said. "My home contains . . . aligns? Master S'eye. Abnethe possesses connectives for which she pays."

McKie wondered if the Caleban were playing some sarcastic game with him. But all the information about them made no reference to sarcasm. Word confusions, yes, but no apparent insults or subterfuges. Not understand pain, though?

"Abnethe sounds like a mixed-up bitch," McKie muttered.

"Physically unmixed," the Caleban said. "Isolated in her own connectives now, but unified and presentable by your standards—so say judgments made in my presence. If, however, you refer to Abnethe psyche, mixed-up conveys accurate description. What I see of Abnethe psyche most intertwined. Convolutions of odd color displace my vision-sense in extraordinary fashion."

McKie gulped. "You *see* her psyche?"

"I see all psyche."

"So much for the theory that Calebans cannot see," Furuneo said. "All is illusion, eh?''

"How . . . how is this possible?'' McKie asked.

"I occupy space between physical and mental,'' the Caleban said. ''Thus your fellow sentients explain in your terminology.''

"Gibberish,'' McKie said.

"You achieve discontinuity of meaning,'' the Caleban said.

"Why did you accept Abnethe's offer of employment?'' McKie asked.

"No common referent for explanation,'' the Caleban said.

"You achieve discontinuity of meaning,'' Furuneo said.

"So I surmise,'' the Caleban said.

"I must find Abnethe,'' McKie said.

"I give warning,'' the Caleban said.

"Watch it,'' Furuneo whispered. ''I sense rage that's not connected with the *angeret*.''

McKie waved him to silence. "What warning, Fanny Mae?''

"Potentials in your situation,'' the Caleban said. ''I allow my . . . person? Yes, my person. I allow my person to entrap itself in association which fellow sentients may interpret as non-friendly.''

McKie scratched his head, wondered how close they were to anything that could validly be called communication. He wanted to come right out and inquire about the Caleban disappearances, the deaths and insanity, but feared possible consequences.

"Non-friendly,'' he prompted.

"Understand,'' the Caleban said, ''life which flows in all carries subternal connectives. Each entity remains linked until final discontinuity removes from . . . network? Yes, linkages of other entities into association with Abnethe. Should personal discontinuity overtake self, all entities entangled share it.''

"Discontinuity?'' McKie asked, not sure he followed this but afraid he did.

"Tanglements come from contact between sentients not originating in same linearities of awareness,'' the Caleban said, ignoring McKie's question.

"I'm not sure what you mean by discontinuity,'' McKie pressed.

"In context,'' the Caleban said, ''ultimate discontinuity, presumed opposite of pleasure—your term.''

"You're getting nowhere,'' Furuneo said. His head ached from trying to equate the radiant impulses of communication from the Caleban with speech.

"Sounds like a semantic identity situation,'' McKie said. ''Black and white statements, but we're trying to find an interpretation in between.''

"All between,'' the Caleban said.

"Presumed opposite of pleasure,'' McKie muttered.

"Our term,'' Furuneo reminded him.

"Tell me, Fanny Mae,'' McKie said, ''do we other sentients refer to this *ultimate discontinuity* as death?''

"Presumed approximate term,'' the Caleban said. ''Abnegation of mutual awareness, ultimate discontinuity, death—all appear similar descriptives.''

"If you die, many others are going to die, is that it?'' McKie asked.

"All users of S'eye. All in tanglement.''

"All?'' McKie asked, shocked.

"All such in your . . . wave? Difficult concept. Calebans possess label for this concept . . . plane? Planguinity of beings? Surmise proper term not shared. Problem concealed in visual exclusion which clouds mutual association.''

Furuneo touched McKie's arm. "Is she saying that if she dies, everyone who's used a S'eye jumpdoor goes with her?"

"Sounds like it."

"I don't believe it!"

"The evidence would seem to indicate we have to believe her."

"But. . . ."

"I wonder if she's in any danger of going soon," McKie mused aloud.

"If you grant the premise, that's a good question," Furuneo said.

"What precedes your ultimate discontinuity, Fanny Mae?" McKie asked.

"All precedes ultimate discontinuity."

"Yeah, but are you headed toward this ultimate discontinuity?"

"Without choice, all head for ultimate discontinuity."

McKie mopped his forehead. The temperature inside the ball had been going up steadily.

"I fulfill demands of honor," the Caleban said. "Acquaint you with prospect. Sentients of your . . . planguinity appear unable, lacking means of withdrawal from influence of my association with Abnethe. Communication understood?"

"McKie," Furuneo said, "have you any idea how many sentients have used a jumpdoor?"

"Damn near everyone."

"Communication understood?" the Caleban repeated.

"I don't know," McKie groaned.

"Difficult sharing of concepts," the Caleban said.

"I still don't believe it," McKie said. "It squares with what some of the other Calebans said, near as we can reconstruct it after the messes they've left."

"Understand withdrawal of companions creates disruption," the Caleban said. "Disruption equates with mess?"

"That's about it," McKie said. "Tell me, Fanny Mae, is there immediate danger of your . . . ultimate discontinuity?"

"Explain imminent," the Caleban said.

"Soon!" McKie snapped. "Short time!"

"Time concept difficult," the Caleban said. "You inquire of personal ability to surmount flagellation?"

"That's good enough," McKie said. "How many more flagellations can you survive?"

"Explain survive," the Caleban said.

"How many flagellations until you experience ultimate discontinuity?" McKie demanded, fighting down the *angeret*-reinforced frustration.

"Perhaps ten flagellations," the Caleban said. "Perhaps lesser number. Perhaps more."

"And your death will kill all of us?" McKie asked, hoping he'd misunderstood.

"Lesser number than all," the Caleban said.

"You just think you're understanding her," Furuneo said.

"I'm *afraid* I understand her!"

"Fellow Calebans," the Caleban said, "recognizing entrapment, achieve withdrawing. Thus they avoid discontinuity."

"How many Calebans remain in our . . . plane?" McKie asked.

"Single entity of selfness," the Caleban said.

"Just the one," McKie muttered. "That's a damn thin thread!"

"I don't see how the death of one Caleban can cause all that havoc," Furuneo said.

"Explain by comparison," the Caleban said. "Scientist of your planguinity explains reaction of stellar selfdom. Stellar mass enters expanding condition. In this condition, stellar mass engulfs and reduces all substances to other energy patterns. All substances encountered by stellar expansion change. Thus ultimate discontinuity of personal selfdom reaches along linkages of S'eye connectives, repatterns all entities encountered."

"Stellar selfdom," Furuneo said, shaking his head.

"Incorrect term?" the Caleban asked, "Energy selfdom, perhaps."

"She's saying," McKie said, "that use of S'eye doors has tangled us with her life some way. Her death will reach out like a stellar explosion along all these tangled networks and kill us."

"That's what you *think* she's saying," Furuneo objected.

"That's what I have to believe she's saying," McKie said. "Our communication may be tenuous, but I think she's sincere. Can't you still feel the emotions radiating from her?"

"Two species can be said to share emotions only in the broadest way," Furuneo said. "She doesn't even understand what we mean by pain."

"Scientist of your planguinity," the Caleban said, "Explains emotional base for communication. Lack in emotional commonality, sameness of labels uncertain. Emotion concept not certain for Calebans. Communication difficulty assumed."

McKie nodded to himself. He could see a further complication: the problem of whether the Caleban's words were spoken or radiated in some unthinkable manner completed their confusion.

"I believe you're right in one thing," Furuneo said.

"Yes?"

"We have to assume we understand her."

McKie swallowed in a dry throat. "Fanny Mae," he said, "have you explained this ultimate discontinuity prospect to Mliss Abnethe?"

"Problem explained," the Caleban said. "Fellow Calebans attempt remedy of error. Abnethe fails of comprehension, or disregards consequences. Connectives difficult."

"Connectives difficult," McKie muttered.

"All connectives of single S'eye," the Caleban said. "Master S'eye of self creates mutual problem."

"Don't tell me you understand that," Furuneo objected.

"Abnethe employs Master S'eye of self," the Caleban said. "Contract agreement gives Abnethe right of use. One Master S'eye of self. Abnethe uses."

"So she opens a jumpdoor and sends her Palenki through it," Furuneo said. "Why don't we just wait here and grab her?"

"She could close the door before we even got near her," McKie growled. "No, there's more to what this Caleban's saying. I think she's telling us there's only one Master S'eye, the control system, perhaps, for all the jumpdoors . . . and Fanny Mae here is in control of it, or the channel operation or . . ."

"Or something," Furuneo snarled.

"Abnethe control S'eye by right of purchase," the Caleban said.

"See what I mean?" McKie said. "Can you override her control, Fanny Mae?"

"Terms of employment require not interfere."

"But can't you still use your own S'eye doors?" McKie pressed.

"All use," the Caleban said.

"This is insane!" Furuneo snapped.

"Insanity defines as lack of orderly thought progression in mutual acceptance of logical terms," the Caleban said. "Insanity frequent judgment of one species upon other species. Proper interpretation otherwise."

"I think I just had my wrist slapped," Furuneo said.

"Look," McKie said, "the other deaths and insanity around Caleban disappearances substantiate our interpretation. We're dealing with something explosive and dangerous."

"So we find Abnethe and stop her."

"You make that sound so simple," McKie said. "Here are your orders. Get out of here and alert the Bureau. The Caleban's communication won't show on your recorder, but you'll have it all down in your memory. Tell them to scan you for it."

"Right, You're staying?"

"Yes."

"What'll I say you're doing?"

"I want a look at Abnethe's companions and her surroundings."

Furuneo cleared his throat. Gods of the underworld, it was hot! "Have you thought of, you know, just bang?" He made the motion of firing a raygen.

"There's a limit on what can go through a jumpdoor and how fast," McKie chided. "You know that."

"Maybe this jumpdoor's different."

"I doubt it."

"After I've reported in, what then?"

"Sit tight outside there until I call you—unless they give you a message for me. Oh, and start a general search on Cordiality . . . just in case."

"Of course." Furuneo hesitated. "One thing—who do I contact at the Bureau? Bildoon?"

McKie glanced up. Why should Furuneo question whom to call? What was he trying to say?

It dawned on McKie then that Furuneo had hit on a logical concern. BuSab director Napoleon Bildoon was a Pan Spechi, a pentarchal sentient, human only in appearance. Since McKie, a human, held nominal charge of this case, that might appear to confine control of it, excluding other members of the ConSentiency. Interspecies political infighting could take odd turns in a time of stress. It would be best to involve a broad directorate here.

"Thanks," McKie said. "I wasn't thinking much beyond the immediate problem."

"This *is* the immediate problem."

"I understand. All right, I was tapped for this chore by our Director of Discretion."

"Gitchel Siker?"

"Yes."

"That's one Laclac and Bildoon, a Pan Spechi. Who else?"

"Get somebody out of the Legal Department."

"Bound to be a human."

"The minute you stretch it that far, they'll all get the message," McKie said. "They'll bring in the others before making any official decision."

Furuneo nodded. "One other thing."

"What?"

"How do I get out of here?"

McKie faced the giant spoon. "Good question. Fanny Mae, how does my companion leave here?"

"He wishes to journey where?"

"To his home."

"Connectives apparent," the Caleban said.

McKie felt a gush of air. His ears popped to a change in pressure. There was a sound like the pulling of a cork from a bottle. He whirled. Furuneo was gone.

"You . . . sent him home?" McKie asked.

"Correct," the Caleban said. "Desired destination visible. Sent swiftness. Prevent temperature drop below proper level."

McKie, feeling perspiration roll down his cheeks, said, "I wish I knew how you did that. Can you actually *see* our thoughts?"

"See only strong connectives," the Caleban said.

Discontinuity of meaning, McKie thought.

The Caleban's remark about temperature came back to him. What was a proper temperature level? Damn! It was boiling in here! His skin itched with perspiraton. His throat was dry. Proper temperature level?

"What's the opposite of proper?" he asked

"False," the Caleban said.

> *The play of words can lead to certain expectations which life is unable to match. This is a source of much insanity and other forms of unhappiness.*
>
> —WREAVE SAYING

FOR A reflexive time which he found himself unable to measure, McKie considered his exchange with the Caleban. He felt cast adrift without any familiar reference points. How could *false* be the opposite of *proper?* If he could not measure meanings, how could he measure time?

McKie passed a hand across his forehead, gathering perspiration which he tried to wipe off on his jacket. The jacket was damp.

No matter how much time had passed, he felt that he still knew where he *was* in this universe. The beachball's interior walls remained around him. The *unseeable* presence of the Caleban had not become less mysterious, but he could look at the shimmering existence of the thing and take a certain satisfaction from the fact that it spoke to him.

The thought that every sentient who had used a jumpdoor would die if this Caleban succumbed sat on McKie's awareness. It was muscle-numbing. His skin was slick with perspiration, and not all of it from the heat. There were voices of death in this air. He thought of himself as a being surrounded by all those pleading sentients—quadrillions upon quadrillions of them. *Help us!*

Everyone who'd used a jumpdoor.

Damnation of all devils! Had he interpreted the Caleban correctly? It was the logical assumption. Deaths and insanity around the Caleban *disappearances* said he must exclude any other interpretation.

Link by link, this trap had been forged. It would crowd the universe with dead flesh.

The shimmering oval above the giant spoon abruptly waved outward, contracted, flowed up, down, left. McKie received a definite impression of distress. The oval vanished, but his eyes still tracked the Caleban's *unpresence*.

"Is something wrong?" McKie asked.

For answer the round vortal tube of a S'eye jumpdoor opened behind the Caleban. Beyond the opening stood a woman, a figure dwarfed as though seen through the wrong end of a telescope. McKie recognized her from all the newsvisos and from the holoscans he had been fed as background briefing for this assignment.

He was confronting Mliss Abnethe in a light somewhat reddened by its slowed passage through the jumpdoor.

It was obvious that the Beautybarbers of Steadyon had been about their expensive work on her person. He made a mental note to have that checked. Her figure presented the youthful curves of a pleasurefem. The face beneath fairy-blue hair was focused around a red-petal mouth. Large summery green eyes and a sharply cleaving nose conveyed odd contrast—dignity versus hoyden. She was a flawed queen, age mingled with youth. She must be at least eighty standard years, but the Beautybarbers had achieved this startling combination: available pleasurefem and remote, hungry power.

The expensive body wore a long gown of grey rainpearls which matched her, movement for movement, like a glittering skin. She moved nearer the vortal tube. As she approached, the edges of the tube blocked off first her feet, then her legs, thighs, waist.

McKie felt his knees age a thousand years in that brief passage. He remained crouched near the place where he'd entered the Beachball.

"Ahhh, Fanny Mae," Mliss Abnethe said. "You have a guest." Jumpdoor interference caused her voice to sound faintly hoarse.

"I am Jorj X. McKie, Saboteur Extraordinary," he said.

Was that a contraction in the pupils of her eyes? McKie wondered. She stopped with only her head and shoulders visible in the tube's circle.

"And *I* am Mliss Abnethe, private citizen."

Private citizen! McKie thought. This bitch controlled the productive capacity of at least five hundred worlds. Slowly McKie got to his feet.

"The Bureau of Sabotage has official business with you," he said, putting her on notice to satisfy the legalities.

"I am a *private* citizen!" she barked. The voice was prideful, vain, marred by petulance.

McKie took heart at the revealed weakness. It was a particular kind of flaw that often went with wealth and power. He had had experience in dealing with such flaws.

"Fanny Mae, am I your guest?" he asked.

"Indeed," the Caleban said. "I open my door to you."

"Am I your employer, Fanny Mae?" Abnethe demanded.

"Indeed, you employ me."

A breathless, crouching look came over her face. Her eyes went to slits. "Very well. Then prepare to fulfill the obligation of . . . "

"One moment!" McKie said. He felt desperate. Why was she moving so fast?

What was that faint whine in her voice? "Guests do not interfere," Abnethe said.

"BuSab makes its own decisions about interference!" McKie said.

"Your jurisdiction has limits!" she countered.

McKie heard the beginnings of many actions in that statement: hired operatives, gigantic sums spent as bribes, doctored agreements, treaties, stories planted with the visos on how this good and proud lady had been mistreated by her government, a wide enlistment of personal concern to justify—what? Violence against his person? He thought not. More likely to discredit him, to saddle him with onerous misdeeds.

Thought of all that power made McKie wonder suddenly why he made himself vulnerable to it. Why had he chosen BuSab? *Because I'm difficult to please*, he told himself. *I'm a Saboteur by choice*. There was no going back on that choice now. BuSab appeared to walk down the middle of everywhere and always wound up on the high road.

And this time BuSab appeared to be carrying most of the sentient universe on its shoulders. It was a fragile burden perched there, fearful and feared. It had sunk stark claws into him.

"Agreed, we have limits," McKie growled, "but I doubt you'll ever see them. Now, what's going on here?"

"You're not a police agent!" Abnethe barked.

"Perhaps I should summon police," McKie said.

"On what grounds?" She smiled. She had him there and knew it. Her legal staff had explained to her the open association clause in the ConSentient Articles of Federation: *"When members of different species agree formally to an association from which they derive mutual benefits, providing their agreement breaks no law, covenant, or legative article binding upon said contracting parties; provided further that said formal agreement was achieved by voluntary means and involves no breach of the public peace."*

"Your action will bring about the death of this Caleban," McKie said. He didn't hold out much hope for this argument, but it bought a bit more time.

"You'll have to establish that the Caleban concept of discontinuity interprets precisely as death," Abnethe said. "You can't do that, because it's not true. Why do you interfere? This is just harmless play between consenting ad—"

"More than play," the Caleban said.

"Fanny Mae!" Abnethe snapped. "You are *not* to interrupt! Remember our agreement."

McKie stared in the direction of the Caleban's *unpresence*, tried to interpret the spectrum-flare that rejected his senses.

"Discern conflict between ideals and structure of government," the Caleban said.

"Precisely!" Abnethe said. "I'm assured that Calebans cannot suffer pain, that they don't even have a term for it. If it's my pleasure to stage an apparent flogging and observe the reaction of . . . "

"Are you sure she suffers no pain?" McKie asked.

Again a gloating smile came over Abnethe's face. "I've never seen her suffer pain. Have you?"

"Have you seen her do anything?"

"I've seen her come and go."

"Do you suffer pain, Fanny Mae?" McKie asked.

"No referents for this concept," the Caleban said.

"Are these floggings going to bring about your ultimate discontinuity?" McKie asked.

"Explain bring about," the Caleban said.

"Is there any connection between the floggings and your ultimate discontinuity?"

"Total universe connectives include all events," the Caleban said.

"I pay well for my game," Abnethe said. "Stop interfering, McKie."

"How're you paying?"

"None of your business!"

"I make it my business," McKie said. "Fanny Mae?"

"Don't answer him!" Abnethe snapped.

"I can still summon police and the officers of a Discretionary Court," McKie said.

"By all means," Abnethe gloated. "You are, of course, ready to answer a suit charging interference with an open agreement between consenting members of different species?"

"I can still get an injunction," McKie said. "What's your present address?"

"I decline to answer on advice of counsel."

McKie glared at her. She had him. He could not charge her with flight to prevent prosecution unless he had proved a crime. To prove a crime he must get a court to act and serve her with the proper papers in the presence of bonded witnesses, bring her into a court, and allow her to face her accusers. And her attorneys would tie him in knots every step of the way.

"Offer judgment," the Caleban said. "Nothing in Abnethe contract prohibits revelation of payment. Employer provides educators."

"Educators?" McKie asked.

"Very well," Abnethe conceded. "I provide Fanny Mae with the finest instructors and teaching aids our civilization can supply. She's been soaking up our culture. Anything she requested, she's got. And it wasn't cheap."

"And she still doesn't understand pain?" McKie demanded.

"Hope to acquire proper referents," the Caleban said.

"Will you have time to acquire those referents?" McKie asked.

"Time difficult concept," the Caleban said. "Statement of instructor, to wit: 'Relevancy of time to learning varies with species.' Time possesses length, unknown quality termed duration, subjective and objective dimension. Confusing."

"Let's make this official," McKie said. "Abnethe, are you aware that you're killing this Caleban?"

"Discontinuity and death are not the same," Abnethe objected. "Are they, Fanny Mae?"

"Wide disparity of equivalents exists between separate waves of being," the Caleban said.

"I ask you formally, Mliss Abnethe," McKie said, "if this Caleban calling herself Fanny Mae has told you the consequences of an event she describes as ultimate discontinuity."

"You just heard her say there are no equivalents!"

"You've not answered my question."

"You're quibbling!"

"Fanny Mae," McKie said, "have you described for Mliss Abnethe the consequences of . . ."

"Bound by contract connectives," the Caleban said.

"You see!" Abnethe pounced. "She's bound by our open agreement, and you're interfering." Abnethe gestured to someone not visible in the jumpdoor's vortal tube.

The opening suddenly doubled its diameter. Abnethe stepped aside, leaving half her head and one eye visible to McKie. A crowd of watching sentients could now be discerned in the background. Into Abnethe's place darted the turtle form of a giant Palenki. Its hundreds of tiny feet flickered beneath its bulk. The single arm growing from the top of its ring-eyed head trailed a long whip in a double-thumbed hand. The arm thrust through the tube, jerked the whip against jumpdoor resistance, lashed the whip forward. The whip cracked above the spoon bowl.

A crystalline spray of green showered the unseeable region of the Caleban. It glittered for a moment like a fluorescent explosion of fireworks, dissolved.

An ecstatic moan came through the vortal tube.

McKie fought an intense outpouring sensation of distress, leaped forward. Instantly, the S'eye jumpdoor closed, dumping a severed Palenki arm and whip onto the floor of the room. The arm writhed and turned, slower . . . slower. It fell still.

"Fanny Mae?" McKie said.

"Yes?"

"Did that whip hit you?"

"Explain whip hit."

"Encounter your substance!"

"Approximately."

McKie moved close to the spoon bowl. He still sensed distress but knew it could be a side effect of *angeret* and the incident he had just witnessed.

"Describe the flogging sensation," he said.

"You possess no proper referents."

"Try me."

"I inhaled substance of whip, exhaled my own substance."

"You breathed it?"

"Approximately."

"Well . . . describe your physical reactions."

"No common physical referents."

"Any reaction, dammit!"

"Whip incompatible with my glssrrk."

"Your what?"

"No common referents."

"What was that green spray when it hit you?"

"Explain greenspray."

By referring to wavelengths and describing airborne water droplets, with a side excursion into wave and wind action, McKie thought he conveyed an approximate idea of green spray.

"You observe this phenomenon?" the Caleban asked.

"I saw it, yes."

"Extraordinary!"

McKie hesitated, an odd thought filling his mind. *Could we be as insubstantial to Calebans as they appear to us?*

He asked.

"All creatures possess substance relative to their own quantum existence," the Caleban said.

"But do you see our substance when you look at us?"

"Basic difficulty. Your species repeats this question. Possess no certain answer."

"Try to explain. Start by telling me about the green spray."

"Greenspray unknown phenomenon."

"But what could it be?"

"Perhaps interplanar phenomenon, reaction to exhalation of my substance."

"Is there a limit of how much of your substance you can exhale?"

"Quantum relationship defines limitations of your plane. Movement exists between planar origins. Movement changes referential relatives."

No constant referents? McKie wondered. But there had to be! He explored this aspect with the Caleban, questions and answers obviously making less and less sense to both of them.

"But there must be some constant!" McKie exploded.

"Connectives possess aspect of this constant you seek," the Caleban said.

"What are connectives?"

"No . . ."

"Referents!" McKie stormed. "Then why use the term?"

"Term approximates. Tangential occlusion another term expression something similar."

"Tangential occlusion." McKie muttered. Then, "tangential occlusion?"

"Fellow Caleban offers this term after discussion of problem with Laclac sentient possessing rare insight."

"One of you talked this over with a Laclac, eh? Who was this Laclac?"

"Identity not conveyed, but occupation known and understandable."

"Oh? What was his occupation?"

"Dentist."

McKie exhaled a long, held breath, shook his head with bewilderment. "You understand—dentist?"

"All species requiring ingestion of energy sources must reduce such sources to convenient form."

"You mean they bite?" McKie asked.

"Explain bite."

"I thought you understood dentist!"

"Dentist—one who maintains system by which sentients shape energy for ingestion," the Caleban said.

"Tangential occlusion," McKie muttered. "Explain what you understand by occlusion."

"Proper matching of related parts in shaping system."

"We're getting nowhere," McKie growled.

"Every creature somewhere," the Caleban said.

"But where? Where are you, for example?"

"Planar relationships unexplainable."

"Let's try something else," McKie said. "I've heard you can read our writing."

"Reducing what you term writing to compatible connectives suggests time-constant communication," the Caleban said. "Not really certain, however, of time-constant or required connectives."

"Well . . . let's go at the verb to see," McKie said. "Tell me what you understand by the action of seeing."

"To see—receive sensory awareness of external energy," the Caleban said.

McKie buried his face in his hands. He felt dispirited, his brain numbed by the Caleban's radiant bombardment. What would be the sensory organs? He knew such a question would only send them off on another empty label chase.

He might as well be listening to all this with his eyes or with some other organ rude and unfitted to its task. Too much depended on what he did. McKie's imagination sensed the stillness which would follow the death of this Caleban—an enormous solitude. A few infants left, perhaps—but doomed. All the good, the beautiful, the evil . . . everything sentient . . . all gone. Dumb creatures which had never gone through a jumpdoor would remain. And winds, colors, floral perfumes, birdsong—these would continue after the crystal shattering of sentiency.

But the dreams would be gone, lost in that season of death. There would be a special kind of silence: no more beautiful speech strewn with arrows of meaning.

Who could console the universe for such a loss?

Presently he dropped his hands, said, "Is there *somewhere* you could take this . . . your *home* where Mliss Abnethe couldn't reach you?"

"Withdrawal possible."

"Well, do it!"

"Why?"

"Agreement prohibits."

"Break the damned agreement!"

"Dishonorable action brings ultimate discontinuity for all sentients on your . . . suggest *wave* as preferred term. Wave. Much closer than plane. Please substitute concept of wave wherever plane used in our discussion."

This thing's impossible, McKie thought.

He lifted his arms in a gesture of frustration and, in the movement, felt his body jerk as a long-distance call ignited his pineal gland. The message began to roll, and he knew his body had gone into the sniggertrance, mumbling and chuckling, trembling occasionally.

But this time he didn't resent the call.

All definitions, no matter the language, should be considered probationary.

—THE CALEBAN QUESTION
BY DWEL HARTAVID

"GITCHEL SIKER here," the caller said.

McKie imagined the Bureau's Director of Discretion, a suave little Laclac sitting in that nicely tailored environment back at Central. Siker would be relaxed, fighting tendril withdrawn, his face split open, an elite chairdog ministering to his flesh, trained minions a button-push away.

"About time you called," McKie said.

"About time *I* called?"

"Well, you certainly must've gotten Furuneo's message quite a . . . "

"What message?"

McKie felt as though his mind had touched a grinding wheel shooting off ideas like sparks. No message from Furuneo?

"Furuneo," McKie said, "left here long enough ago to . . . "

"I'm calling," Siker interrupted, "because there's been no sign of either of you for too damn long, and Furuneo's enforcers are worried. One of them . . . Where was Furuneo supposed to go and how?"

McKie felt an idea blossoming in his mind. "Where was Furuneo born?"

"Born? On Landy–B. Why?"

"I think we'll find him there. The Caleban used its S'eye system to send him *home*. If he hasn't called yet, better send for him. He was supposed to . . . "

"Landy–B only has three Taprisiots and one jumpdoor. It's a retreat planet, full of recluses and . . . "

"That'd explain the delay. Meanwhile, here's the situation. . . . "

McKie began detailing the problem.

"Do you believe this, this *ultimate discontinuity* thing?" Siker interrupted.

"We have to believe it. The evidence all says it's true."

"Well, maybe . . . but . . . "

"Can we afford a *maybe*, Siker?"

"We'd better call in the police."

"I think she wants us to do just that."

"Wants us. . . . Why?"

"Who'd have to sign a complaint?"

Silence.

"Are you getting the picture?" McKie pressed.

"It's on your head, McKie."

"It always is. But if we're right, that doesn't make any difference, does it?"

"I'm going to suggest," Siker said, "that we contact the top level in the Central Police Bureau—for consultation only. Agreed?"

"Discuss that with Bildoon. Meanwhile, here's what I want done. Assemble a Bureau ConSentient Council, draft another max-alert message. Keep the emphasis on Calebans, but bring in the Palenkis, and start looking into Abnethe's . . . "

"We can't do that, and you know it!"

"We have to do it."

"When you took this assignment, you received a full explanation of why we . . . "

"Utmost discretion doesn't mean hands off," McKie said. "If that's the way you're thinking, then you've missed the importance of . . . "

"McKie, I can't believe . . . "

"Sing off, Siker," McKie said. "I'm going over your head to Bildoon."

Silence.

"Break his contact!" McKie ordered.

"That won't be necessary."

"Won't it?"

"I'll put the agents onto Abnethe at once. I see your point. If we assume that . . . "

"We assume," McKie said.

"The orders will be issued in your name, of course," Siker said.

"Keep your skirts clean any way you like," McKie said. "Now, have our people start probing into the Beautybarbers of Steadyon. She's been there, and recently. Also, I'll be sending along a whip she . . . "

"A whip?"

"I just witnessed one of the flagellations. Abnethe cut the connection while her Palenki still had an arm through the S'eye door. Cut the arm right off. The Palenki will grow another arm, and she can hire more Palenkis, but the whip and arm could give us a lead. Palenkis don't practice gene tagging, I know, but it's the best we have at the moment."

"I understand. What'd you see during the . . . incident?"

"I'm getting to that."

"Hadn't you better come in and put your report directly onto a transcorder?"

"I'll depend on you for that. Don't think I should show at Central for a bit."

"Mmm. See what you mean. She'll try to tie you up with a countersuit."

"Or I miss my guess. Now, here's what I saw. When she opened the door, she practically filled it, but I could see what appeared to be a window in the background. If it was a window, it opened onto a cloudy sky. That means daylight."

"Cloudy?"

"Yes. Why?"

"It's been cloudy here all morning."

"You don't think she's . . . no, she wouldn't."

"Probably not, but we'll have Central scoured just to be sure. With her money, no telling who she might've bought."

"Yeah . . . well, the Palenki. Its shell carried an odd design—triangles, diamonds in red and orange, and a rope or snake of yellow wound all the way around and through it."

"Phylum identification," Siker said.

"Yes, but what Palenki family?"

"Well, we'll check it. What else?"

"There was a mob of sentients behind her during the actual flogging. I saw Preylings, couldn't miss those wire tentacles. There were some Chithers, a few Soborips, some Wreaves . . ."

"Sounds like her usual patch of sycophants. Recognize any of them?"

"I'll try for ID's later, but I couldn't attach any names to this mob. But there was one, a Pan Spechi, and he was stage-frozen or I miss my guess."

"You sure?"

"All I know is what I saw, and I saw the scars on his forehead—ego surgery, sure as I'm sniggering."

"That's against every Pan Spechi legal, moral, and ethical . . . "

"The scars were purple," McKie said. "That checks, doesn't it?"

"Right out in the open, no makeup or anything to cover the scars?"

"Nothing. If I'm right, it means he's the only Pan Spechi with her. Another would kill him on sight."

"Where could she be where there'd be only one Pan Spechi?"

"Beats me. Oh, and there were some humans, too—green uniforms."

"Abnethe house guards."

"That's the way I made it."

"Quite a mob to be hiding away."

"If anyone can afford it, she can."

"One more thing," McKie said. "I smelled yeast."

"Yeast?"

"No doubt about it. There's always a pressure differential through a jumpdoor. It was blowing our way. Yeast."

"That's quite a bag of observations."

"Did you think I was getting careless?"

"No more than usual. Are you absolutely sure about that Pan Spechi?"

"I saw the eyes."

"Sunken, the facets smoothing over?"

"That's the way it looked to me."

"If we can get a Pan Spechi to make an official observation of this fellow, that'd give us a lever. Harboring a criminal, you know."

"Apparently, you haven't much experience with Pan Spechi," McKie said. "How'd you get to be Director of Discretion?"

"All right, McKie, let's not . . ."

"You know damn well a Pan Spechi would blow up if he saw this fellow. Our observer would try to dive through the jumpdoor and . . ."

"So?"

"Abnethe would close it on him. She'd have half of our observer, and we'd have the other half."

"But that'd be murder!"

"An unfortunate accident, no more."

"That woman *does* swing a lot of weight, I admit, but . . ."

"And she'll have our hides if she can make it stick that she's a private citizen and we're trying to sabotage her."

"Messy," Siker agreed. "I hope you made no official sounds in her direction."

"Ah, but I did."

"You what?"

"I put her on official notice."

"McKie, you were told to handle this with dis—"

"Look, we want her to start official action. Check with Legal. She can try a countersuit against me personally, but if she moves against the Bureau, we can ask for a *seratori* hearing, a personal confrontation. Her legal staff will advise her of that. No, she'll try to get at . . ."

"She may not go into court against the Bureau," Siker said, "but she's certain to set her dogs on us. And it couldn't come at a worse time. Bildoon has just about used up his ego-time. He'll be going into the crèche any time now. You know what that means."

"The Bureau Director's chair up for grabs," McKie said. "I've been expecting it."

"Yes, but things'll be in a real uproar around here."

"You're eligible for the seat, Siker."

"So are you, McKie."

"I pass."

"That'll be the day! What I'm worried about is Bildoon. He'll blow when he hears about this ego-frozen Pan Spechi. That might be all it takes to . . ."

"He'll handle it," McKie said, putting more confidence into the statement than he felt.

"And you could be wrong. I hope you know I'm not passing."

"We all know you want the job," McKie said.

"I can imagine the gossip."

"Is it worth it?"

"I'll let you know."

"I'm sure you will."

"One thing," Siker said. "How're you going to keep Abnethe off your back?"

"I'm going to become a schoolteacher," McKie said.

"I don't think I want that explained," Siker said. He broke the contact.

McKie found himself still seated in the purple gloom of the Beachball. Sweat bathed his body. The place was an oven. He wondered if his fat was actually being reduced by the heat. Water loss, certainly. The instant he thought of water, he sensed the dryness in his throat.

"You still there?" he rasped.

Silence.

"Fanny Mae?"

"I remain in my home," the Caleban said.

The sensation that he heard the words without hearing grated on McKie, fed on the *angeret* in his system, stirred a latent rage. *Damn superior stupid Caleban! Got us into a real mess!*

"Are you willing to cooperate with us in trying to stop these floggings?" McKie asked.

"As my contract permits."

"All right. Then you insist to Abnethe that you want me as your teacher."

"You perform functions of teacher?"

"Have you learned anything from me?" McKie asked.

"All mingled connectives instruct."

"Connectives," McKie muttered. "I must be getting old."

"Explain old," the Caleban said.

"Never mind. We should've discussed your contract first thing. Maybe there's a way to break it. Under what laws was it executed?"

"Explain laws."

"What honorable system of enforcement?" McKie blared.

"Under natural honor of sentient connectives."

"Abnethe doesn't know what honor means."

"I understand honor."

McKie sighed. "Were there witnesses, signatures, that sort of thing?"

"All my fellow Calebans witness connectives. Signatures not understood. Explain."

McKie decided not to explore the concept of signatures. Instead he asked, "Under what circumstances could you refuse to honor your contract with Abnethe?"

After a prolonged pause the Caleban said, "Changing circumstances convey variable relationships. Should Abnethe fail in her connectives or attempt redefinition of essences, this could produce linearities open for my disentanglement."

"Sure," McKie said. "That figures."

He shook his head, studied the empty air above the giant spoon. Calebans! You couldn't see them, couldn't hear them, couldn't understand them.

"Is the use of your S'eye system available to me?" McKie asked.

"You function as my teacher."

"Is that a yes?"

"Affirmative answer."

"Affirmative answer," McKie echoed. "Fine. Can you also transport objects to me, sending them where I direct?''

''While connectives remain apparent.''

''I hope that means what I think it does,'' McKie said. ''Are you aware of the Palenki arm and whip over there on your floor?''

''Aware.''

''I want them sent to a particular office at Central. Can you do that?''

''Think of office,'' the Caleban said.

McKie obeyed.

''Connectives available,'' the Caleban said. ''You desire sending to place of examination.''

''That's right!''

''Send now?''

''At once.''

''Once, yes. Multiple sending remains outside our capabilities.''

''Huh?''

''Objects going.''

As McKie blinked, the arm and whip snapped out of his view accompanied by a sharp crack of exploding air.

''Do the Taprisiots work in any way similar to what you do transporting things?'' McKie asked.

''Message transportation minor energy level,'' the Caleban said. ''Beautybarbers even more minor.''

''I guess so,'' McKie said. ''Well, never mind. There's the little matter of my friend, Alichino Furuneo, though. You sent him home, I believe?''

''Correct.''

''You sent him to the wrong home.''

''Creatures possess only one home.''

''We sentients have more than one home.''

''But I view connectives!''

McKie felt the wash of radiant objection from the Caleban, steadied himself. ''No doubt,'' he said. ''But he has another home right here on Coridality.''

''Astonishment fills me.''

''Probably. The question remains, can you correct this situation?''

''Explain situation.''

''Can you send him to his home on Cordiality?''

Pause then, ''That place not his home.''

''But can you send him there?''

''You wish this?''

''I wish it.''

''Your friend converses through a Taprisiot.''

''Ahhh,'' McKie said. ''You can listen in on his conversation, then?''

''Message content not available. Connectives visible. I possess awareness that your friend exchanges communication with sentient of other species.''

''What species?''

''One you label Pan Spechi.''

''What'd happen if you sent Furuneo to . . . his home here on Cordiality right now?''

''Shattering of connectives. But message exchange concludes in this linearity. I send him. There.''

''You sent him?''

"But connectives you convey."

"He's here on Cordiality right now?"

"He occupies place not his home."

"I hope we're together on that."

"Your friend," the Caleban said, "desires presence with you."

"He wants to come here?"

"Correct."

"Well, why not? All right, bring him."

"What purpose arises from friend's presence in my home?"

"I want him to stay with you and watch for Abnethe while I attend to other business."

"McKie?"

"Yes."

"You possess awareness that presence of yourself or other of your kind prolongs impingement of myself upon your wave?"

"That's fine."

"Your presence foreshortens flogging."

"I suspected as much."

"Suspected?"

"I understand!"

"Understanding probable. Connectives indicative."

"I can't tell you how happy that makes me," McKie said.

"You wish friend brought?"

"What's Furuneo doing?"

"Furuneo exchanges communication with . . . assistant."

"I can imagine."

McKie shook his head from side to side. He could sense the morass of misunderstanding around every attempt at communication here. No way to steer clear of it. No way at all. At the very moment when they thought they had achieved closest communication, right then they could be widest of the mark.

"When Furuneo concludes his conversation, bring him," McKie said. He hunched back against the wall. Gods of the underworld! The heat was almost unbearable. Why did Calebans require such heat? Maybe the heat represented something else to a Caleban, a visible wave form, perhaps, serving some function other sentients couldn't begin to understand.

McKie felt then that he was engaged in an exchange of worthless noises here—shadow sounds. Reason had gone, swinging from planet to planet. He and the Caleban were striking false bargains, trying to climb out of chaos. If they failed, death would take away all the innocent and the sinful, the good and the guilty. Boats would drift on countless oceans, towers would fall, balconies crumble, and suns would move alone across unmarked skies.

A wave of relatively cold air told McKie that Furuneo had arrived. McKie turned, saw the planetary agent sprawled beside him and just beginning to sit up.

"For the love of reason!" Furuneo shouted. "What're you doing to me?"

"I needed the fresh air," McKie said.

Furuneo peered at him. "What?"

"Glad to see you," McKie said.

"Yeah?" Furuneo brought himself to a squatting position beside McKie. "You have any idea what's just happened to me?"

"You've been to Landy–B," McKie said.

"How'd you know? Was that your doing?"

"Slight misunderstanding," McKie said. "Landy–B's your home."

"It is not!"

"I'll leave you to argue that with Fanny Mae," McKie said. "Have you started the search on Cordiality?"

"I barely got it going before you . . . "

"Yes, but you've started it?"

"I've started it."

"Good. Fanny Mae will keep you posted on various things and bring your people here for reports and such as you need them. Won't you, Fanny Mae?"

"Connectives remain available. Contract permits."

"Good girl"

"I'd almost forgotten how hot it was in here." Furuneo said, mopping his forehead. "So I can summon people. What else?"

"You watch for Abnethe."

"And?"

"The instant she and one of her Palenki floggers make an appearance, you get a holoscan record of everything that happens. You do have your toolkit?"

"Of course."

"Fine. While you're scanning, get your instruments as close to the jumpdoor as you can."

"She'll probably close the door as soon as she sees what I'm doing."

"Don't count on it. Oh, one thing."

"Yes?"

"You're my teaching assistant."

"Your what?"

McKie explained about the Caleban's agreement.

"So she can't get rid of us without violating the terms of her contract with Fanny Mae," Furuneo said. "Cute." He pursed his lips. "That all?"

"No. I want you and Fanny Mae to discuss connectives."

"Connectives?"

"Connectives. I want you to try finding out what in ten billion devils a Caleban means by connectives."

"Connectives," Furuneo said. "Is there any way to turn down the furnace in here?"

"You might take that as another subject: Try to discover the reason for all this heat."

"If I don't melt first. Where'll you be?"

"Hunting—provided Fanny Mae and I can agree on the connectives."

"You're not making sense."

"Right. But I'll try to make tracks—if Fanny Mae'll send me where the game is."

"Ahhh," Furuneo said. "You could walk into a trap."

"Maybe. Fanny Mae, have you been listening?"

"Explain listening."

"Never mind!"

"But mind possesses ever!"

McKie closed his eyes, swallowed, then, "Fanny Mae, are you aware of the information exchange just concluded between my friend and myself here?"

"Explain conclu . . . "

"Are you aware?" McKie bellowed.

"Amplification contributes little to communication," the Caleban said. "I possess desired awareness—presumably.''

"Presumably," McKie muttered, then, "Can you send me to a place near Abnethe where she will not be aware of me, but where I can be aware of her?''

"Negative."

"Why not?"

"Specific injunction of contract."

"Oh." McKie bent his head in thought, then, "Well, can you send me to a place where I might become aware of Abnethe through my own efforts?"

"Possibility. Permit examination of connectives."

McKie waited. The heat was a tangible thing inside the Beachball, a solid intrusion on his senses. He saw it was already beginning to wilt Furuneo.

"I saw my mother," Furuneo said, noting McKie's attention.

"That's great," McKie said.

"She was swimming with friends when the Caleban dumped me right in the pool with them. The water was wonderful."

"They were surprised, no doubt."

"They thought it was a great joke. I wish I knew how that S'eye system works."

"You and a billion billion others. The energy requirement gives me the chills."

"I could use a chill right now. You know, that's one weird sensation—standing one minute talking to old friends, the next instant yakking at empty air here on Cordiality. What do you suppose they think?"

"They think it's magic."

"McKie," the Caleban said, "I love you."

"You what?" McKie exploded.

"Love you," the Caleban repeated. "Affinity of one person for another person. Such affinity transcends species."

"I guess so, but . . . ''

"Since I possess this universal affinity for your person, connectives open, permitting accomplishment of your request."

"You can send me to a place near Abnethe?"

"Affirmative. Accord with desire. Yes."

"Where is this place?" McKie asked.

He found, with a chill wash of air and a sprawling lurch onto dusty ground, that he was addressing his question to a moss capped rock. For a moment he stared at the rock, regaining his balance. The rock was about a meter tall and contained small veins of yellow-white quartz with flecks of reflective brilliance scattered through them. It stood in an open meadow beneath a distant yellow sun. The sun's position told McKie he'd arrived either at midmorning or midafternoon local.

Beyond the rock, the meadow, and a ring of straggly yellow brushes stretched a flat horizon broken by the tall white spires of a city.

"Loves me?" he asked the rock.

Never underestimate the power of wishful thinking to filter what the eyes see and what the ears hear.

—THE ABNETHE CASE,
BUSAB PRIVATE FILES

WHIP AND severed Palenki arm arrived at the proper BuSab laboratory while it was temporarily unoccupied. The lab chief, a Bureau veteran named Treej Tuluk, a back-bowing Wreave, was away at the time, attending the conference which McKie's report had precipitated.

As with most back-bowers, Tuluk was an odor-id Wreave. He had an average-appearing Wreave body, two and a half meters tall, tubular, pedal bifurcation, vertical face slit with manipulative extensors dangling from the lower corner. From long association with humans and humanoids he had developed a brisk, slouching gait, a predilection for clothing with pockets, and un-Wreavish speech mannerisms of a cynical tone. The four eye tubes protruding from the top of his facial slit were green and mild.

Returning from the conference, he recognized the objects on his lab floor immediately. They matched Sikers's description. Tuluk complained to himself briefly about the careless manner of delivery and was soon lost in the intricacies of examination. He and the assistants he summoned made initial holoscans before separating whip and arm.

As they had expected, the Palenki gene structure offered no comparatives. The arm had not come from one of the few Palenkis on record in the ConSentient Register. Tuluk filed the DNA chart and message sequence, however. These could be used to identify the arm's original owner, if that became necessary.

At the same time study of the whip went ahead. The artifact report came out of the computers as "Bullwhip, copy of ancient earth type." It was made of steerhide, a fact which gave Tuluk and his vegetarian aides a few brief moments of disgust, since they had assumed it was a synthetic.

"A sick archaism," one of Tuluk's Chither assistants called the whip. The others agreed with this judgment, even a Pan Spechi for whom periodic reversion to carnivorous type in his crèche cycle was necessary to survival.

A curious alignment in some of the cell molecules attracted their attention then. Study of the whip and arm continued at their respective paces.

There is no such thing as pure objectivity.

—GOWACHIN APHORISM

MCKIE TOOK the long-distance call while standing beside a dirt road about three kilometers from the rock. He had come this far on foot, increasingly annoyed by the strange surroundings. The city, he had soon discovered, was a mirage hanging over a dusty plain of tall grass and scrubby thornbushes.

It was almost as hot on the plain as it had been in the Caleban's Beachball.

Thus far the only living things he had seen were some distant tawny animals and countless insects—leapers, crawlers, fliers, hoppers. The road contained two parallel indentations and was the rusty red color of abandoned iron. It seemed to originate in a faraway line of blue hills on his right, plunging straight across the plain to the heat-muddled horizon on his left. The road contained no occupant except himself, not even a dust cloud to mark some hidden passage.

McKie was almost glad to feel the sniggertrance grip him.

"This is Tuluk," his caller said. "I was told to contact you as soon as I had anything to report. Hopefully, I intrude at an opportune moment."

McKie, who had a journeyman's respect for Tuluk's competence, said, "Let's have it."

"Not much on the arm," Tuluk said. "Palenki, of course. We can identify the original owner, if we ever get him. There'd been at least one previous regrowth of this member. Sword cut on the forearm, by the look of it."

"What about the phylum markings?"

"We're still checking that."

"The whip?"

"That's something else. It's real steerhide."

"Real?"

"No doubt of it. We could identify the original owner of the skin, although I doubt it's walking around anywhere."

"You've a gruesome sense of humor. What else?"

"The whip's an archaism, too. Bullwhip, ancient earth style. We got an original ID by computer and brought in a museum expert for confirmation. He thought the construction was a bit on the crude side, but close enough to leave little doubt it was a copy of a real original. Fairly recent manufacture, too."

"Where could they get an original to copy?"

"We're checking that, and it may provide a lead. These things aren't too common."

"Recent manufacture," McKie said. "You sure?"

"The animal from which that hide was removed has been dead about two standard years. Intracellular structure was still reactive to catalyzing."

"Two years. Where would they get a real steer?"

"That narrows it down. There are some around for story props in the various entertainment media, that sort of thing. A few of the outback planets where they haven't the technology for pseudoflesh still raise cattle for food."

"This thing gets more confusing the deeper we go into it," McKie said.

"That's what we think. Oh, there's chalf dust on the whip."

"Chalf! That's where I got the yeast smell!"

"Yes, it's still quite strong."

"What would they be doing with that much quick-scribe powder?" McKie asked. "There was no sign of a chalf-memory stick—but that means little, of course."

"It's just a suggestion," Tuluk said, "but they couldn've chalf-scribed that design on the Palenki."

"Why?"

"Give it a false phylum, maybe?"

"Perhaps."

"If you smelled chalf after the whip came through, there'd have to be quite a bit of it around. You thought of that?"

"The room wasn't all that big, and it was hot."

"The heat would explain it, all right. Sorry we didn't have more for you."

"That's all?"

"Well, it might not be any use, but the whip had been stored in a hanging position supported by a thin length of steel."

"Steel? Are you positive?"

"Positive."

"Who still uses steel?"

"It's not all that uncommon on some of the newer planets. R&R has even turned up some where they build with it."

"Wild!"

"Isn't it, though?"

"You know," McKie said, "We're looking for an outback planet, and that's where I seem to be."

"Where are you ?"

"I don't know."

"You don't know?"

McKie explained his predicament.

"You field agents take awful chances sometimes," Tuluk said.

"Don't we just."

"You wear a monitor. I could ask this Taprisiot to identify your location. Want to invoke the monitor clause?"

"You know that's an open payment clause," McKie said. "I don't think this is a sufficient emergency yet that I can risk bankrupting us. Let me see if I can identify this place by other means first."

"What do you want me to do, then?"

"Call Furuneo. Have him allow me another six hours, then get the Caleban to pick up me."

"Pick you up, right. Siker said you were onto some doorless S'eye thing. Can it pick you up anywhere?"

"I think so."

"I'll call Furuneo right away."

Facts can be whatever you want them to be. This is the lesson of relativity.

—BuSab Manual

MCKIE HAD been walking for almost two hours before he saw the smoke. Thin spirals of it stood in the air against the backdrop of distant blue hills.

It had occurred to McKie during his walk that he might have been set down in a place where he could die of thirst or starvation before his legs carried him to the safe companionship of his civilized fellows. A self-accusatory moroseness had overtaken him. It wasn't the first time he had realized that some accident of the machinery he took for granted might prove fatal.

But the *machinery* of his own mind? He cursed himself for using the Caleban's S'eye system this way when he knew the unreliability of communication with the creature.

Walking!

You never thought you might have to walk to safety.

McKie sensed the eternal flaw in sentient relationship with machinery. Reliance on such forces put your own muscles at a disadvantage in a universe where you might have to rely on those muscles at any moment.

Such as right now.

He appeared to be getting nearer to the smoke, although the hills looked as remote as ever.

Walking.

Of all the stupid damn foul-ups. Why would Abnethe pick a place like this to start her kinky little game? If this were the place it had started. If the Caleban hadn't made another communication error.

If love could find a way. What the devil did love have to do with all this?

McKie plodded on, wishing he had brought some water. First the heat of the Beachball, now this. His throat felt as though he'd built a fire in it. The dust kicked up by his feet didn't help. Every step stirred up a puff of pale red from the narrow track. The dust clogged his throat and nostrils. It had a musty taste.

He patted the toolkit in his jacket pocket. The raygen could burn a thin hole in this parched earth, might even strike down to water. But how could he bring the water up to his demanding throat?

Plenty of insects around. They buzzed and flew about, crawled at the edge of the track, attempted at times to alight on his exposed flesh. He finally took to carrying his toolkit's stim like a fan, setting it at medium potency. It cleared the air around his face whenever a swarm approached, dropped jittering patches of stunned insects behind him.

He grew aware of a noise—low, indistinct booming. Something being pounded. Something hollow and resonant. It originated out there in the distance where the smoke stood on the air.

It could be a natural phenomenon, McKie told himself. Could be wild creatures. The smoke might be natural fires. Still, he brought the raygen from his kit, kept it in a side pocket where he could get at it quickly.

The noise became louder in slow stages, as though it were being amplified to mark consecutive positions of his approach. Screens of thornbush and gentle undulations in the plain concealed the source.

McKie trudged up a gentle rise, still following the road.

Sadness transfixed him. He'd been cast away on some poverty-stricken backyard world, a place that stiffened the eyes. He'd been given a role in a story with a moral, a clipped-wing fairy story. He was a burned-out wanderer, his thirst a burnished yearning. Anguish had lodged in him somewhere. He pursued an estranged, plodding dream which would dissolve in the awakening doom of a single Caleban.

The toll that Caleban's death would bring oppressed him. It turned his ego upside down and drained out all the lightness. His own death would be a lost bubble burst in such a conflagration.

McKie shook his head to drive away such thoughts. Fear would pluck him of all sensibility. He could not afford it.

One thing sure now; the sun was setting. It had descended at least two widths toward the horizon since he'd started this stupid trek.

What in the name of the infinite devils was that drumming? It came at him as though riding the heat: monotonous, insistent. He felt his temples throbbing to an irritating counterpoint—beat, throb, beat, throb . . .

McKie topped the low rise, stopped. He stood at the brim of a shallow basin which had been cleared of the thornbush. At the basin's center, a thorn fence enclosed twenty or so conical huts with grass roofs. They appeared to be made of mud. Smoke spiraled from holes in several of the roofs and from pit fires outside others. Black dots of cattle grazed in the basin, lifting their heads occasionally, with stubby whiskers of brown grass protruding from their mouths.

Black-skinned youths carrying long poles watched the cattle. More black-skinned men, women, and children went about various occupations within the thorn enclosure.

McKie, whose ancestry contained blacks from the planet Caoleh, found the scene curiously disturbing. It touched a genetic memory that vibrated to a wrong rhythm. Where in the universe could people be degraded to such primitive living standards? The basin was like a textbook scene from the dark ages of ancient Earth.

Most of the children were naked, as were some of the men. The women wore string skirts.

Could this be some odd return to nature? McKie wondered. The nudity didn't bother him particularly. It was the combination.

The narrow track led down into the basin and through the thorn fence, extending out the other side to disappear over the crest of the opposite side.

McKie began the descent. He hoped they'd let him have water in this village.

The booming noise came from within a large hut near the center of the cluster. A two-wheeled cart with four great two-horned beasts yoked to it waited beside the hut.

McKie studied the cart as he approached. Between its high sidewalls were piled jumbles of strange artifacts—flat, boardlike things, rolls of garish fabric, long poles with sharp metal tips.

The drumming stopped, and McKie noted that he had been seen. Children ran screaming among the huts, pointing at him. Adults turned with slow dignity, studied him.

An odd silence settled over the scene.

McKie entered the village through a break in the thorn fence. Emotionless black faces turned to observe his progress. The place assaulted McKie's nostrils—rotting flesh, dung, acrid stenches whose character he didn't care to explore, woodsmoke and burning meat.

Clouds of black insects swarmed about the beasts yoked to the cart, seeming to ignore the slow switching of their tails.

A red-bearded white man emerged from the larger hut as McKie approached. The man wore a flat-brimmed hat, dusty black jacket, and dun pants. He carried a whip of the same pattern the Palenki had used. Seeing the whip, McKie knew he had come to the right place.

The man waited in the doorway, a mean-eyed, menacing figure, thin lips visible through the beard. He glanced once at McKie, nodded at several of the black men off to McKie's left, motioned toward the cart, returned his attention to McKie.

Two tall black men moved to stand at the heads of the yoked beasts.

McKie studied the contents of the cart. The boardlike objects, he saw, had been carved and painted with strange designs. They reminded him of Palenki carapaces. He didn't like the way the two men at the heads of the yoked beasts stared at him. There was danger here. McKie kept his right hand in his jacket pocket, curled around the raygen tube. He felt and saw the black residents closing in behind him. His back felt exposed and vulnerable.

"I am Jorj X. McKie, Saboteur Extraordinary," he said, stopping about ten paces from the bearded white man. "And you?"

The man spat in the dust, said something that sounded like: "Getnabent."

McKie swallowed. He didn't recognize the greeting. Strange, he thought. He hadn't believed the ConSentiency contained a language completely unfamiliar to him. Perhaps R&R had come up with a new planet here.

"I am on an official mission of the Bureau," McKie said. "Let all men know this." There, that satisfied the legalities.

The bearded man shrugged, said, "Kawderwelsh."

Someone behind McKie said: "Krawl'ikido!"

The bearded man glanced in the direction of the voice, back to McKie.

McKie shifted his attention to the whip. The man trailed the end of it behind him on the ground. Seeing McKie's attention, he flicked a wrist, caught the flexible end of the whip in two fingers which he lifted from the handle. He continued to stare at McKie.

There was a casual proficiency in the way the man handled the whip that sent a shudder through McKie. "Where'd you get that whip?" he asked.

The man looked at the object in his hand. "Pitsch," he said. "Brawzhen-buller."

McKie moved closer, held out a hand for the whip.

The bearded man shook his head from side to side, scowled. No mistaking that answer. "Maykely," he said. He tapped the butt of the whip handle against the side of the cart, nodded at the piled cargo.

Once more, McKie studied the contents of the cart. Handmade artifacts, no doubt of it. There could be a big profit in esoteric and decorative objects, he knew. These could be artifacts that curried to the buyer boredom brought on by the endless, practical, serial duplications from automatic factories. If they were manufactured in this village, though, the whole operation looked to be a slave-labor thing. Or serfdom, which was the same thing for all practical purposes.

Abnethe's *game* might have sicker overtones, but it had more understandable motives.

"Where's Mliss Abnethe?" he asked.

That brought a response. The bearded man jerked his head up, glared at McKie. The surrounding mob emitted an unintelligible cry.

"Abnethe?" McKie asked.

"Seeawss Abnethe!" the bearded man said.

The crowd around them began chanting: "Epah Abnethe! Epah Abnethe! Epah Abnethe!"

"Rooik!" the bearded man shouted.

The chant stopped abruptly.

"What is the name of this planet?" McKie asked. He glanced around at the staring black faces. "Where is this place?"

No one answered.

McKie locked eyes with the bearded man. The other returned his stare in a predatory, measuring manner, nodded once, as though he'd come to some conclusion. "Deespawng!" he said.

McKie frowned, swore under his breath. This damned case presented communication difficulties at every turn! No matter. He'd seen enough here to demand a full-scale investigation by a police agency. You didn't keep humans in this primitive state. Abnethe must be behind this place. The whip, the reaction to her name. The village smelled of Abnethe's sickness. McKie observed some of the people across from him, saw scars on their arms and chests. Whip scars? If they were, Abnethe's money wouldn't save her. She might get off with another reconditioning, but this time there'd be a more thorough . . .

Something exploded against the back of McKie's neck, knocking him forward.. The bearded man raised the whip handle, and McKie saw the thing rushing toward his head. He felt a giant, coughing darkness lurch across his mind as the thing crashed against the side of his head. He tried to bring the raygen out of his pocket, but his muscles disobeyed. He felt his body become a limping, horrified stagger. His vision was a bloody haze.

Again something exploded against his head.

McKie sank into nighmare oblivion. As he sank, he thought of the monitor in his skull. If they had killed him a Taprisiot somewhere would jerk to attention and send in a final report on one Jorj X. McKie.

A lot of good that' ll do me! the darkness said.

Where is the weapon with which I enforce your bondage? You give it to me every time you open your mouth.

—LACLAC RIDDLE

THERE WAS a moon, McKie realized. That glowing thing directly in front of him had to be a moon. The realization told him he'd been seeing the moon for some time, puzzling over it without being fully awake. The moon had lifted itself out of blackness above a paralyzed outline of primitive roofs.

He was still in the village, then.

The moon dangled there, incredibly close.

The back and left side of McKie's head began throbbing painfully. He explored his bruised senses, realized he had been staked out in the open flat on his back, wrists and ankles tightly bound, his face pointed at the sky.

Perhaps it was another village.

He tested the security of his bindings, couldn't loosen them.

It was an undignified position: flat on his back, legs spread, arms outstretched.

For a time, he watched the changing guard of strange constellations move across his field of vision. Where was this place?

Firelight blazed up somewhere off to his left. It flickered, sank back to orange gloom. McKie tried to turn his head toward it, froze as pain stabbed upward from his neck through his skull. He groaned.

Off in the darkness an animal screamed. The scream was followed by a hoarse, grunting roar. Silence. Then another roar. The sounds creased the night for McKie, bent it into new dimensions. He heard soft footsteps approaching.

"I think he groaned," a man said.

The man was speaking standard Galach, McKie noted. Two shadows came out of the night and stood over McKie's feet.

"Do you think he's awake?" It was a female voice masked by a *starter*.

"He's breathing as though he's awake," the man said.

"Who's there?" McKie rasped. His own voice sent agony pinwheeling through his skull.

"Good thing your people know how to obey instructions," the man said. "Imagine him running loose around here!"

"How did you get here, McKie?" the woman asked.

"I walked," McKie growled. "Is that you, Abnethe?"

"He walked!" the man snarled.

McKie, listening to that male voice, began to wonder about it. There was a trace of alien sibilance in it. Was it human or humanoid? Among the sentients only a Pan Spechi could look that human—because they had shaped their flesh to the human pattern.

"Unless you release me," McKie said, "I won't answer for the consequences."

"You'll answer for them," the man said. There was laughter in his voice.

"We must be sure how he got here," the woman said.

"What difference does it make?"

"It could make a great deal of difference. What if Fanny Mae is breaking her contract?"

"That's impossible!" the man snorted.

"Nothing's impossible. He couldn't have got here without Caleban help."

"Maybe there's another Caleban."

"Fanny Mae says not."

"I say we do away with this intruder immediately," the man said.

"What if he's wearing a monitor?" she asked."

"Fanny Mae says no Taprisiot can locate this place!"

"But McKie is here!"

"And I've had one long-distance call since I arrived," McKie said. *No Taprisiot can locate this place?* he wondered. What would prompt that statement?

"They won't have time to find us or do anything about it," the man said. "I say we do away with him."

"That wouldn't be very intelligent," McKie said.

"Look who's talking about intelligence," the man said.

McKie strained to discern details of faces, but they remained blank shadows. What was it about that male voice? The *storter* disguised the woman's voice, but why would she bother?

"I am fitted with a life monitor," McKie said.

"The sooner, the better," the man said.

"I've stood as much of that as I can," the woman said.

"Kill me, and that monitor starts transmitting," McKie said. "Taprisiots will scan this area and identify everyone around me. Even if they can't locate you, they'll know you."

"I shudder at the prospect," the man said.

"We must find out how he got here," the woman said.

"What difference does it make?"

"That's a *stupid* question!"

"So the Caleban broke her contract."

"Or there's a loophole in it we don't know about."

"Well, plug it up."

"I don't know if we can. Sometimes I wonder how much we really understand each other. What are connectives?"

"Abnethe, why're you wearing that storter?" McKie asked.

"Why do you call me Abnethe?" she asked."

"You can disguise your voice, but you can't hide your sickness or your style," McKie said.

"Did Fanny Mae send you here?" she demanded.

"Didn't somebody say that was impossible?" McKie countered.

"He's a brave one," the woman chuckled.

"Lot of good it does him."

"I don't think the Caleban could break our contract," she said. "You recall the protection clause? It's likely she sent him here to get rid of him."

"So let's get rid of him."

"That's not what I meant!"

"You know we have to do it."

"You're making him suffer, and I won't have it!" the woman cried.

"Then go away and leave it to me."

"I can't stand the *thought* of him suffering! Don't you understand?"

"He won't suffer."

"You have to be sure."

It's Abnethe for certain, McKie thought, recalling her conditioning against witnessing pain. *But who's the other one?*

"My head's hurting," McKie said. "You know that, Mliss? Your men practically beat my brains out.

"What brains?" the man snapped.

"We must get him to a doctor," she said.

"Be sensible!" the man snapped.

"You heard him. His head hurts."

"Mliss, stop it!"

"You used my name," she said.

"What difference does it make? He'd already recognized you."

"What if he escapes?"

"From here?"

"He got here, didn't he?"

"For which we can be thankful!"

"He's suffering," she said."

"He's lying!"

"He's suffering. I can tell."

"What if we take him to a doctor, Mliss?" the man asked, "What if we do that and he escapes? BuSab agents are resourceful, you know."

Silence.

"I promise," the man said.

"For sure?"

"Didn't I say it?"

"I'm leaving here," she said. "I don't want to know what happens to him. You're never to mention him again, Cheo. Do you hear me?"

"Yes, my dear, I hear you."

"I'm leaving now," she said.

"He's going to cut me into little pieces," McKie said, "and I'll scream with pain the whole time."

"Shut him up!" she screeched.

"Come away, my dear," the man said. He put an arm around her. "Come along, now."

Desperately, McKie said, "Abnethe! He's going to cause me intense pain. You *know* that."

She began sobbing as the man led her away. "Please . . . please . . . " she begged. The sound of her crying faded into the night.

Furuneo, McKie thought, *don't dally. Get that Caleban moving. I want out of here.*

Now!

He strained against his bindings. They stretched just enough to tell him he'd reached their limits. He couldn't feel the stakes move at all.

Come on, Caleban! McKie thought. *You didn't send me here to die. You said you loved me.*

> *It is because you speak to me that I do not believe in you.*
>
> —QUOTED FROM A CALEBAN

AFTER SEVERAL hours of questioning, counter-questioning, probe, counter-probe, and bootless answers, Furuneo brought in an enforcer assistant to take over the watch on the Caleban. At Furuneo's request Fanny Mae opened a portal and let him out onto the lava ledge for a spell of fresh air. It was cold out on the shelf, especially after the heat in the Beachball. The wind had died down, as it did most days here just before night. Surf still pounded the outer rocks and surged against the lava wall beyond the Beachball. But the tide was going out, and only a few dollops of spray wet the ledge.

Connectives, Furuneo thought bitterly. *She says it's not a linkage, so what is it?* He couldn't recall ever having felt this frustrated.

"That which extends from one to eight," the Caleban had said, "That is a connective. Correct use of verb to be?"

"Huh?"

"Identify verb," the Caleban said. "Strange concept."

"No, no! What did you mean there, one to eight?"

"Unbinding stuff," the Caleban said.

"You mean like a solvent?"

"Before solvent."

"What the devil could *before* have to do with solvents?"

"Perhaps more internal than solvents," the Caleban said.

"Madness," Furuneo said, shaking his head. Then, "Internal?"

"Unbounded place of connectives," the Caleban said.

"We're right back where we started," Furuneo groaned. "What's a connective?"

"Uncontained opening between," the Caleban said.

"Between *what*?" Furuneo roared.

"Between one and eight."

"Ohhh, no!"

"Also between one and *x*," the Caleban said.

As McKie had done earlier, Furuneo buried his face in his hands. Presently he said, "What's between one and eight except two, three, four, five, six, and seven?"

"Infinity," the Caleban said. "Open-ended concept. Nothing contains everything. Everything contains nothing."

"You know what I think?" Furuneo asked.

"I read no thoughts," the Caleban said.

"I think you're having your little game with us," Furuneo said. "That's what I think."

"Connectives compel," the Caleban said. "Does this expand understanding?"

"Compels . . . a compulsion?"

"Venture movement," the Caleban said.

"Venture what?"

"That which remains stationary when all else moves," the Caleban said. "Thus, connective. Infinity concept empties itself without connective."

"Whoooooheee!" Furuneo said.

At this point he asked to be let outside for a rest.

Furuneo was no closer to understanding why the Caleban maintained such a high temperature in the Beachball.

"Consequences of swiftness," the Caleban said, varying this under questioning with "Rapidity convergence." Or "Perhaps concept of generated movement arrives closer."

"Some kind of friction?" Furuneo probed.

"Uncompensated relationship of dimensions possibly arrives at closest approximation," the Caleban answered.

Now, reviewing these frustrating exchanges, Furuneo blew on his hands to warm them. The sun had set, and a chill wind was beginning to move off the bluff toward the water.

Either I freeze to death or bake, he thought. *Where in the universe is McKie?*

At this point Tuluk made long distance contact through one of the Bureau Taprisiots. Furuneo, who had been seeking a more sheltered position in the lee of the Beachball, felt the pineal ignition. He brought down the foot he had been lifting in a step, planted the foot firmly in a shallow pool of water, and lost all bodily sensation. Mind and call were one.

"This is Tuluk at the lab," the caller said. "Apologies for intrusion and all that."

"I think you just made me put a foot in cold water," Furuneo said.

"Well, here's some more cold water for you. You're to have that friendly Caleban pick up McKie in six hours, time elapse measured from four hours and fifty-one minutes ago. Synchronize."

"Standard measure?"

"Of course, standard!"

"Where is he?"

"He doesn't know. Wherever that Caleban sent him. Any idea how it's done?"

"It's done with connectives," Furuneo said.

"Is that right? What are connectives?"

"When I find out, you'll be the first to know."

"That sounds like a temporal contradiction, Furuneo."

"Probably is. All right, let me get my foot out of the water. It's probably frozen solid by now."

"You've the synchronized time coordinate for picking up McKie?"

"I got it! And I hope she doesn't send him home."

"How's that?"

Furuneo explained.

"Sounds confusing."

"I'm glad you figured that out. For a moment there, I thought you weren't approaching our problem with sufficient seriousness."

Among Wreaves seriousness and sincerity are almost as basic as they are with Taprisiots, but Tuluk had worked among humans long enough to recognize the jibe. "Well, every being has its own insanity," he said.

It was a Wreave aphorism, but it sounded sufficiently close to something the Caleban might have said that Furuneo experienced a momentary *angeret*-enforced rage and sensed his ego shimmering away from him. He shuddered his way back to mental solidity.

"Did you almost lose yourself?" Tuluk asked.

"Will you sign off and let me get my foot out of the water?"

"I receive the impression you are fatigued," Tuluk said. "Get some rest."

"When I can. I hope I don't fall asleep in the Caleban hothouse. I'd wake up done just about right for a cannibal dinner."

"Sometimes you humans express yourselves in a disgusting fashion," the Wreave said. "But you'd better remain alert for a while. McKie may require punctuality."

He was the kind of man who created his own death.

—EPITAPH FOR ALICHINO FURUNEO

IT WAS dark, but she needed no light for black thoughts.

Damn Cheo for a sadistic fool! It had been a mistake to finance the surgery that had transformed the Pan Spechi into an ego-frozen freak. Why couldn't he stay the way he'd been when they'd first met? So exotic . . . so . . . so . . . exciting.

He was still useful, though. And there was no doubt he'd been the first to see the magnificent possibilities in their discovery. That, at least, remained exciting.

She reclined on a softly furred chairdog, one of the rare feline adaptives that had been taught to lull their masters by purring. The soothing vibrations moved through her flesh as though seeking out irritations to subdue. So relaxing.

She sighed.

Her apartment occupied the top ring of the tower they had had built on this world, safe in the knowledge that their hiding place lay beyond the reach of any law or any communication except that granted through a single Caleban—who had but a short time to live.

But how had McKie come here? And what had McKie meant, that he'd had a call through a Taprisiot?

The chairdog, sensitive to her mood, stopped purring as Abnethe sat up. Had Fanny Mae lied? Did another Caleban remain who could find this place?

Granted that the Caleban's words were difficult to understand—granted this, yes, there was yet no mistaking the essentials. This world was a place whose key lay in only one mind, that of Madame Mliss Abnethe.

She sat straight on the chairdog.

And there would be death without suffering to make this place forever safe—a giant orgasm of death. Only one door, and death would close it. The survivors, all chosen by herself, would live on in happiness here beyond all . . . connectives . . .

Whatever those were.

She stood up, began pacing back and forth in the darkness. The rug, a creature adapted like the chairdog, squirmed its furry surface at the caress of her feet. An amused smile came over her face.

Despite the complications and the strange timing it required, they'd have to increase the tempo of the floggings. Fanny Mae must be forced to discontinue as soon as possible. To kill without suffering among the victims, this was a prospect she found she could still contemplate.

But there was need for hurry.

Furuneo leaned, half dozing, against a wall within the Beachball. Sleepily he cursed the heat. His mindclock said there was slightly less than an hour remaining until the time for picking up McKie. Furuneo had tried to explain the time schedule to the Caleban, but she persisted in misunderstanding.

"Lengths extend and distend," she had said. "They warp and sift with vague movements between one and another. Thus time remains inconstant."

Inconstant?

The vortal tube of a S'eye jumpdoor snapped open just beyond the Caleban's giant spoon. The face and bare shoulders of Abnethe appeared in the opening.

Furuneo pushed himself away from the wall, shook his head to restore alertness. Damnation, it was hot in here!

"You are Alichino Furuneo," Abnethe said. "Do you know me?"

"I know you."

"I recognized you at once," she said. "I know most of your stupid Bureau's planetary agents by sight. I've found it profitable."

"Are you here to flog this poor Caleban?" Furuneo asked. He felt for the holoscan in his pocket, moved into a position for a rush toward the jumpdoor as McKie had ordered.

"Don't make me close this door before we've had a little discussion," she said.

Furuneo hesitated. He was no Saboteur Extraordinary, but you didn't get to be a planetary agent without recognizing when to disobey a senior agent's orders.

"What's to discuss?" he asked.

"Your future," she said.

Furuneo stared up into her eyes. The emptiness of them appalled him. This woman was ridden by a compulsion.

"My future?" he asked.

"Whether you're to have *any* future," she said.

"Don't threaten me," he said.

"Cheo tells me," she said, "that you're a possibility for our project."

For no reason he could explain, Furuneo knew this to be a lie. Odd how she gave herself away. Her lips trembled when she said that name—Cheo.

"Who's Cheo?" he asked.

"That's unimportant at the moment."

"What's your project, then?"

"Survival."

"That's nice," he said. "What else is new?" He wondered what she would do if he brought out the holoscan and started recording.

"Did Fanny Mae send McKie hunting for me?" she asked.

That question was important to her, Furuneo saw. McKie must have stirred up merry hob.

"You've seen McKie?" he asked.

"I refuse to discuss McKie," she said.

It was an insane response, Furuneo thought. She'd been the one to bring McKie into the conversation.

Abnethe pursed her lips, studied him. "Are you married, Alichino Furuneo?" she asked.

He frowned. Her lips had trembled again. Surely she knew his marital status. If it was valuable for her to recognize him, it was thrice valuable to know his strengths and weaknesses. What was her game?

"My wife is dead," he said.

"How sad," she murmured.

"I get along," he said, angry. "You can't live in the past."

"Ahhh, that is where you may be wrong," she said.

"What're you driving at, Abnethe?"

"Let's see," she said, "your age—sixty-seven standard, if I recall correctly."

"You recall correctly, as you damn well know."

"You're young," she said. "You look even younger. I'd guess you're a vital person who enjoys life."

"Don't we all?" he asked.

It was going to be a bribe offer, then, he thought.

"We enjoy life when we have the proper ingredients," she said. "How odd it is to find a person such as yourself in that stupid Bureau."

This was close enough to a thought Furuneo had occasionally nurtured for himself that he began wondering about this Cheo and the mysterious project with its possibilities. What were they offering?

They studied each other for a moment. It was the weighted assessment of two contestants about to enter a competition.

Would she offer herself? Furuneo wondered. She was an attractive female: generous mouth, large green eyes, a pleasant oval face. He'd seen the holoscans of her figure—the Beautybarbers had done well by her. She'd maintained herself with all the expensive care her money could buy. But would she offer herself to him? He found this difficult to contemplate. Motives and stakes didn't fit.

"What're you afraid of?" he asked.

It was a good opening attack, but she answered him with a peculiar note of sincerity: "Suffering."

Furuneo tried to swallow in a dry throat. He hadn't been celibate since Mada's death, but that had been a special kind of marriage. It had gone beyond words and bodies. If anything remained solid and basic, *connective*, in the universe, their kind of love did. He had but to close his eyes to feel the memory-presence of her. Nothing could replace that, and Abnethe must know it. She couldn't offer him anything unobtainable elsewhere.

Or could she?

"Fanny Mae," Abnethe said, "are you prepared to honor the request I made?"

"Connective appropriate," the Caleban said.

"Connectives!" Furuneo exploded. "What are connectives?"

"I don't really know," Abnethe said, "but apparently I can exploit them without knowing."

"What're you cooking up?" Furuneo demanded. He wondered why his skin felt suddenly chilled in spite of the heat.

"Fanny Mae, show him," Abnethe said.

The jumpdoor's vortal tube flickered open, closed, danced and shimmered. Abruptly, Abnethe no longer was visible in it. The door stood open once more, looking down now onto a sunny jungle shore, a softly heaving ocean surface, an oval stabo-yacht hanging in stasis above a clearing and a sandy beach. The yacht's afterdeck shields lay open to the sun, exposing almost in the center of the deck a young woman stretched out in repose, facedown on a floater hammock. Her body was drinking the rays of a tuned sun filter.

Furuneo stared, unable to move. The young woman lifted her head, stared out to sea, lay back.

Abnethe's voice came from directly over his head, another jumpdoor obviously, but he couldn't take his gaze from that well-remembered scene. "You recognize this?" she asked.

"It's Mada," he whispered.

"Precisely."

"Oh, my god," he whispered. "When did you scan that?"

"It is your beloved, you're sure?" Abnethe asked.

"It's . . . it's our honeymoon," he whispered. "I even know the day. Friends took me to visit the seadome, but she didn't enjoy swimming and stayed behind."

"How do you know the actual day?"

"The flambok tree at the edge of the clearing: It bloomed that day, and I missed it. See the umbrella flower?"

"Oh, yes. Then you've no doubt about the authenticity of this scene?"

"So you had your snoopers staring at us even then?" he rasped.

"Not snoopers. We are the snoopers. This is now."

"It can't be! That was almost forty years ago!"

"Keep your voice down, or she'll hear you."

"How can she hear me? She's been dead for . . . "

"This is now, I tell you! Fanny Mae?"

"In person of Furuneo, concept of now contains relative connectives," the Caleban said. "Nowness of scene true."

Furuneo shook his head from side to side.

"We can pluck her from that yacht and take both of you to a place the Bureau will never find," Abnethe said. "What do you think of that, Furuneo?"

Furuneo wiped tears from his cheeks. He was aware of the sea's ozone smell, the pungency of the flambok blossom. It had to be a recording, though. Had to be.

"If it's now, why hasn't she seen us?" he asked.

"At my direction Fanny Mae masks us from her sight. Sound, however, will carry. Keep your voice down."

"You're lying!" he hissed.

As though at a signal, the young woman rolled over, stood up, and admired the flambok. She began humming a song familiar to Furuneo.

"I think you know I'm not lying," Abnethe said. "This is our secret, Furuneo. This is our discovery about the Calebans."

"But . . . how can . . . "

"Given the proper connectives, whatever they are, even the past is open to us. Only Fanny Mae of all the Calebans remains to link us with this past. No Taprisiot, no Bureau, nothing can reach us there. We can go there and free ourselves forever."

"This is a trick!" he said.

"You can see it isn't. Smell that flower, the sea."

"But why . . . what do you want?"

"Your assistance in a small matter, Furuneo."

"How?"

"We fear someone will stumble on our secret before we're ready. If, however, someone the Bureau trusts is here to watch and report—giving a false report . . .''

"What false report?''

"That there've been no more floggings, that Fanny Mae is happy, that . . . ''

"Why should I do that?''

"When Fanny Mae reaches her . . . ultimate discontinuity, we can be far away and safe—you with your beloved. Correct, Fanny Mae?''

"Truthful essence in statement,'' the Caleban said.

Furuneo stared through the jumpdoor. Mada! She was right there. She had stopped humming and was coating her body with a skin-protective. If the Caleban moved the door a little closer, he knew he'd be able to reach out and touch his beloved.

Pain in Furuneo's chest made him aware of a constriction there. The past!

"Am . . . I down there somewhere?'' he asked.

"Yes,'' Abnethe said.

"And I'll come back to the yacht?''

"If that's what you did originally.''

"What would I find, though?''

"Your bride gone, disappeared.''

"But . . . ''

"It would be thought that some creature of the sea or the jungle killed her. Perhaps she went swimming and . . . ''

"She lived thirty-one years after that,'' he whispered.

"And you can have those thirty-one years all over again,'' Abnethe said.

"I . . . I wouldn't be the same. She'd . . . ''

"She'd know you.''

Would she really? he wondered. Perhaps—yes. Yes, she'd know him. She might even come to understand the need behind such a decision. But he saw quite clearly that she'd never forgive him. Not Mada.

"With proper care she might not have to die in thirty-one years,'' Abnethe said.

Furuneo nodded, but it was a gesture only for himself.

She wouldn't forgive him any more than the young man returning to an empty yacht could forgive him. And that young man had not died.

I couldn't forgive myself, he thought. *The young man I was would never forgive me all those lovely lost years.*

"If you're worried,'' Abnethe said, "about changing the universe or the course of history or any such nonsense, forget it. That's not how it works, Fanny Mae tells me. You change a single, isolated situation, no more. The new situation goes off about its business, and everything else remains pretty much the same.''

"I see.''

"Do you agree to our bargain?'' Abnethe asked.

"What?''

"Shall I have Fanny Mae pick her up for you?''

"Why bother?'' he asked. I can't agree to such a thing.

"You're joking!''

He turned, stared up at her, saw that she had a small jumpdoor open almost directly over his head. Only her eyes, nose, and mouth could be seen through the opening.

"I am not joking.''

Part of her hand became visible as she lifted it, pointed toward the other door.

"Look down there at what you're rejecting. Look, I say! Can you honestly tell me you don't want that back?"

He turned.

Mada had gone back to the hammock, snuggled face-down against a pillow. Furuneo recalled that he'd found her like that when he'd returned from the seadome.

"You're not offering me anything," he said.

"But I am! It's true, everything I've told you!"

"You're a fool," he said, "if you can't see the difference between what Mada and I had and what you offer. I pity . . . "

Something fiercely compressive gripped his throat, choked off his words. Furuneo's hands groped in empty air as he was lifted up . . . up . . . He felt his head go through jumpdoor resistance. His neck was precisely within the boundary juncture when the door was closed. His body fell back into the Beachball.

Body jargon and hormone squirts, these begin to get at communication.

—CULTURE LAG, AN UNPUBLISHED WORK
BY JORJ X. MCKIE

"YOU FOOL, Mliss!" Cheo raged. "You utter, complete, senseless fool! If I hadn't come back when I . . . "

"You killed him!" She rasped, backing away from the bloody head on the floor of her sitting room. "You . . . you killed him! And just when I'd almost . . . "

"When you'd almost ruined everything," Cleo snarled, thrusting his scarred face close to her. "What do you humans use for brains?"

"But he'd . . . "

"He was ready to call his helpers and tell them everything you'd blurted to him!"

"I won't have you talking to me this way!"

"When it's my neck you're putting on the block, I'll talk to you any way I want."

"You made him suffer!" she accused.

"He didn't feel a thing from what I did. You're the one who made him suffer."

"How can you say that?" She backed away from the Pan Spechi face with its frighteningly oversized humanoid features.

"You bleat about being unable to stand suffering," he growled, "but you *love* it. You cause it all around you! You *knew* Furuneo wouldn't accept your stupid offer, but you taunted him with it, with what he'd lost. You don't call *that* suffering?"

"See here, Cheo, if you . . . "

"He suffered right up to the instant I put a stop to it," the Pan Spechi said. "And you *know* it!"

"Stop it!" she screamed. "I didn't! He wasn't!"

"He was and you knew it, every instant of it, you knew it."

She rushed at him, beat her fists against his chest. "You're lying! You're lying! You're lying!"

He grabbed her wrists, forced her to her knees. She lowered her head. Tears ran down her cheeks. "Lies, lies, lies," she muttered.

In a softer, more reasonable tone, he said: "Mliss, hear me. We've no way to know how much longer the Caleban can last. Be sensible. We've a limited number of fixed periods when we can use the S'eye, and we have to make the most of them. You've wasted one of those periods. We can't afford such blunders, Mliss."

She kept her gaze down, refused to look at him.

"You know I don't like to be severe with you, Mliss," he said, "but my way is best—as you've said yourself many times. We've our own ego-integrity to preserve."

She nodded without looking at him.

"Let's join the others now," he said. "Plouty has devised an amusing new game."

"One thing," she said.

"Yes?"

"Let's save McKie. He'd be an interesting addition to . . . "

"No."

"What harm could it do? He might even be useful. It isn't as though he'd have his precious Bureau or anything to enforce his . . . "

"No! Besides, it's probably too late. I've already sent the Palenki with . . . well, you understand."

He released her wrists.

Abnethe got to her feet, nostrils flaring. She looked up at him then, eyes peering through her lashes, her head tilted forward. Suddenly her right foot lashed out, caught Cheo with a hard heel in the left shin.

He danced back, nursed the bruise with one hand. Despite the pain, he was amused. "You see?" he said. "You *do* like suffering."

She was all over him then, kissing him, apologizing. They never did get down to Plouty's new game.

You can say things which cannot be done. This is elementary. The trick is to keep attention focused on what is said and not on what can be done.

—BUSAB MANUAL

As FURUNEO'S life monitor ignited at his death, Taprisiots scanned the Beachball area. They found only the Caleban and four enforcers in hovering guard ships. Reasoning about actions, motives or guilt did not come within the Taprisiot scope. They merely reported the death, its location, and the sentients available to their scanners.

The four enforcers came in for several days of rough questioning as a result. The Caleban was a different matter. A full BuSab management conference was required before they could decide what action to take about the Caleban. Furuneo's death had come under extremely mysterious circumstances—no head, unintelligible responses from the Caleban.

As Tuluk entered the conference room on a summons that had roused him from sleep, Siker was flailing the table. He was using his middle fighting tendril for the gesture, quite un-Laclac in emotional intensity.

"We don't act without calling McKie!" Siker said. "This is too delicate!"

Tuluk took his position at the table, leaned into the Wreave support provided for his species, spoke mildly: "Haven't you contacted McKie yet? Furuneo was supposed to have ordered the Caleban . . . ."

That was as far as he got. Explanation and data came at him from several of the others.

Presently Tuluk said, "Where's Furuneo's body?"

"Enforcers are bringing it to the lab now."

"Have the police been brought in?"

"Of course."

"Anything on the missing head?"

"No sign of it."

"Has to be the result of a jumpdoor," Tuluk said. "Will the police take over?"

"We're not going to allow that. One of our own."

Tuluk nodded. "I'm with Siker, then. We don't move without consulting McKie. This case was handed to him when we didn't know its extent. He's still in charge."

"Should we reconsider that decision?" someone down the table asked.

Tuluk shook his head. "Bad form," he said. "First things first. Furuneo's dead, and he was supposed to have ordered McKie's return some time ago."

Bildoon, the Pan Spechi chief of the Bureau, had watched this exchange with attentive silence. He had been ego holder of his pentarchal life group for seventeen years—a reasonably average time in his species. Although the thought revolted him in a way other species could never really understand, he knew he'd have to give up the ego to the youngest member of his creche circle soon. The ego exchange would come sooner than it might have without the strains of command. Terrible price to pay in the service of sentience, he thought.

The humanoid appearance which his kind had genetically shaped and adopted had a tendency to beguile other humanoids into forgetting the essentially alien character of the Pan Spechi. The time would come, though, when they would be unable to avoid that awareness in Bildoon's case. His friends in the ConSentiency would see the crèche-change at its beginning—the glazing of the eyes, the rictus of the mouth. . . .

Best not think about that, he warned himself. He needed all his abilities right now.

He felt he no longer lived in his ego-self, and this was a sensation of exquisite torture for a Pan Spechi. But the black negation of all sentient life that threatened his universe demanded the sacrifice of personal fears. The Caleban must not be allowed to die. Until he had assured himself of the Caleban's survival, he must cling to any rope which life offered him, endure any terror, refuse to mourn for the almost-death-of-self that lurked in Pan Spechi nightmares. A greater death pressed upon them all.

Siker, he saw, was staring at him with an unspoken question.

Bildoon spoke three words: "Get a Taprisiot."

Someone near the door hurried to obey.

"Who was most recently in contact with McKie?" Bildoon asked.

"I believe I was," Tuluk said.

"It'll be easier for you, then," Bildoon said. "Make it short."

Tuluk wrinkled his facial slit in agreement.

A Taprisiot was led in, was helped up onto the table. It complained that they were being much too rough with its speech needles, that the embedment was imperfect, that they hadn't given it sufficient time to prepare its energies.

Only after Bildoon invoked the emergency clause of the Bureau's special contract would it agree to act. It positioned itself in front of Tuluk then, said, "Date, time, and place."

Tuluk gave the local coordinates.

"Close face," the Taprisiot ordered.

Tuluk obeyed.

"Think of contact," the Taprisiot squeaked.

Tuluk thought of McKie.

Time passed without contact. Tuluk opened his face, stared out.

"Close face!" the Taprisiot ordered.

Tuluk obeyed.

Bildoon said, "Is something wrong?"

"Hold silence," the Taprisiot said. "Disturb embedment." Its speech needles rustled. "Putcha, putcha," it said. "Call go when Caleban permit."

"Contact through a Caleban?" Bildoon ventured.

"Otherwise not available," the Taprisiot said. "McKie isolated in connectives of another being."

"I don't care how you get him, just get him!" Bildoon ordered.

Abruptly, Tuluk jerked as the sniggertrance marked pineal ignition.

"McKie?" he said. "Tuluk here."

The words, uttered through the mumbling of the sniggertrance, were barely audible to the others around the table.

Speaking as calmly as he could, McKie said, "McKie will not be here in about thirty seconds unless you call Furuneo and have him order that Caleban to get me out of here."

"What's wrong?" Tuluk asked.

"I'm staked out, and a Palenki is on its way to kill me. I can see it against the firelight. It's carrying what appears to be an ax. It's going to chop me up. You know how they . . . "

"I can't call Furuneo. He's . . . "

"Then call the Caleban!"

"You know you can't call a Caleban!"

"Do it, you oaf!"

Because McKie had ordered it, suspecting that he might know such a call would be made, Tuluk broke the contact, sent a demand at the Taprisiot. It was against reason: All the data said Taprisiots couldn't link sentients and Calebans.

To the observers in the conference room, the more obvious mumbling and chuckling of the sniggertrance faded, made a brief return, disappeared. Bildoon almost barked a question at Tuluk, hesitated. The Wreave's tubular body remained so . . . still.

"I wonder why the Tappy said he had to call through a Caleban," Siker whispered.

Bildoon shook his head.

A Chither near Tuluk said, "You know, I could swear he ordered the Taprisiot to *call* the Caleban."

"Nonsense," Siker said.

"I don't understand it," the Chither said. "How could McKie go somewhere and not know where he is?"

"Is Tuluk out of the sniggertrance or isn't he?" Siker asked, his voice fearful. "He acts like nobody's there."

Every sentient around the table froze into silence. They all knew what Siker meant. Had the Wreave been trapped in the call? Was Tuluk gone, taken into strange limbo from which the personality never returned?

"NOW!" someone roared.

The assembled sentients jerked back from the conference table as McKie came tumbling out of nowhere in a shower of dust and dirt. He landed flat on his back on the table directly in front of Bildoon, who lifted half out of his chair. McKie's wrists were bloody, his eyes glazed, red hair tangled in a wild mop.

"Now," McKie whispered. He turned onto his side, saw Bildoon, and as though it explained everything, added, "The ax was descending."

"What ax?" Bildoon demanded, sliding back into his chair.

"The one the Palenki was aiming at my head."

"The . . . WHAT?"

McKie sat up, massaged his torn wrists where the bindings had held him. Presently he shifted his ministrations to his ankles. He looked like a Gowachin frog deity.

"McKie, explain what's going on here," Bildoon ordered.

"I . . . ahh, well, the nick of time was almost a fatal nick too late," McKie said. "What made Furuneo wait so long? He was told six hours, no more. Wasn't he?" McKie looked at Tuluk, who remained silent, stiff as a length of gray pipe against the Wreave support.

"Furuneo's dead," Bildoon said.

"Ahhh, damn," McKie said softly. "How?"

Bildoon made the explanation brief, then asked, "Where've you been? What's this about a Palenki with an ax?"

McKie, still sitting on the table, gave a neatly abbreviated chronological report. It sounded as though he were talking about a third person. He wound it up with a flat statement; "I have no idea at all where I was."

"They were going to . . . chop you up?" Bildoon asked.

"The ax was coming down," McKie said. "It was right there." He held up a hand about six centimeters from his nose.

Siker cleared his throat, said, "Something's wrong with Tuluk."

They all turned.

Tuluk remained propped against the support, his face slit closed. His body was there, but he wasn't.

"Is he . . . lost?" Bildoon rasped and turned away. If Tuluk failed to *come back* . . . how like the Pan Spechi ego-loss that would be!

"Somebody down there shake up that Taprisiot," McKie ordered.

"Why bother?" That was a human male from the Legal Department. "They never answer a question about . . . you know." He glanced uneasily at Bildoon, who remained with face averted.

"Tuluk made contact with the Caleban," McKie said, remembering. "I told him . . . it's the only way he could've done it with Furuneo dead." He stood up on the table, walked down its length to stand towering over the Taprisiot.

"You!" he shouted. "Taprisiot!"

Silence.

McKie drew a finger along an arm of speech needles. They clattered like a line of wooden clackers, but no intelligible sound came from the Taprisiot.

"You're not supposed to touch them," someone said.

"Get another Taprisiot in here," McKie ordered.

Someone ran to obey.

McKie mopped his forehead. It required all his reserves to keep from trembling. During the descent of the Palenki ax he had said goodbye to the universe. It had been final, irrevocable. He still felt that he had not returned, that he was watching the antics of some other creature in his own flesh, a familiar creature but a stranger, really. This room, the words and actions around him, were some sort of distorted play refined to blind sterility. In the instant when he had accepted his own death, he had realized there still remained uncounted things he wanted to experience. This room and his duties as a BuSab agent were not among those desires. The odd reality was drowned in selfish memories. Still, this flesh went through the motion. That was what training did.

A second Taprisiot was herded into the room, its needles squeaking complaints. It was hoisted onto the table, objecting all the way. "You *have* Taprisiot! Why you disturb?"

Bildoon turned back to the table, studied the scene, but remained silent, withdrawn. No one had ever been brought back from the long-distance trap.

McKie faced the new Taprisiot. "Can you contact this other Taprisiot?" he demanded.

"Putcha, putcha . . . " the second Taprisiot began.

"I'm sincere!" McKie blared.

"Ahseeda day-day," the second Taprisiot squeaked.

"I'll stack you with somebody's firewood if you don't get cracking," McKie snarled. "Can you make contact?"

"Who you call?" the second Taprisiot asked.

"Not me, you fugitive from a sawmill!" McKie roared. "Them!" He pointed at Tuluk and the first Taprisiot.

"They stuck to Caleban," the second Taprisiot said. "Who you call?"

"What do you mean, *stuck?*" McKie demanded.

"Tangled?" the Taprisiot ventured.

"Can either of them be called?" McKie asked.

"Untangle soon, then call," the Taprisiot said.

"Look!" Siker said.

McKie whirled.

Tuluk was flexing his facial slit. A mandibular extensor came out, withdrew.

McKie held his breath.

Tuluk's facial slit opened wide, and he said, "Fascinating."

"Tuluk?" McKie said.

The slit widened. Wreave eyes stared out. "Yes?" Then, "Ah, McKie. You made it."

"You call now?" the second Taprisiot asked.

"Get rid of him," McKie ordered.

Squeaking protests—"If you not call, why disturb?"—the Taprisiot was removed from the room.

"What happened to you, Tuluk?" McKie asked.

"Difficult to explain," the Wreave said.

"Try."

"Embedment," Tuluk said. "That has something to do with planetary conjunctions, whether the points linked by a call are aligned with each other across open space. There was some problem with this call, discontinuous through a stellar mass, perhaps, And it was contact with a Caleban . . . I don't appear to have the proper words."

"Do *you* understand what happened to you?"

"I think so. You know, I hadn't realized where I lived."

McKie stared at him, puzzled. "What?"

"Something's wrong here," Tuluk said. "Oh, yes: Furuneo."

"You said something about where you lived," McKie prodded.

"Space occupancy, yes," Tuluk said. "I live in a place with many . . . ahh, synonymous? yes, synonymous occupants."

"What're you talking about?" McKie asked.

"I was actually in contact with the Caleban during my call to you," Tuluk said. "Very odd, McKie. It was as though my call went through a pinhole in a black curtain, and the pinhole was the Caleban."

"So you contacted the Caleban," McKie prompted.

"Oh, yes. Indeed I did." Tuluk's mandibular extensors moved in a pattern indicative of emotional disturbance. "I saw! That's it. I saw . . . ahhh, many frames of parallel films. Of course, I didn't really *see* them. It was the eye."

"Eye? Whose eye?"

"That's the pinhole," Tuluk explained. "It's our eye, too, naturally."

"Do you understand any of this, McKie?" Bildoon asked.

"My impression is he's talking like a Caleban," McKie said. He shrugged. "Contaminated, perhaps. Entangled?"

"I suspect," Bildoon said, "that Caleban *communication* can be understood only by the certifiably insane."

McKie wiped perspiration from his lip. He felt he could *almost* understand what Tuluk had said. Meaning hovered right at the edge of awareness.

"Tuluk," Bildoon said, "try to tell us what happened to you. We don't understand you."

"I am trying."

"Keep at it," McKie said.

"You contacted the Caleban," Bildoon said. "How was that done? We've been told it's impossible."

"It was partly because the Caleban seemed to be handling my call to McKie," Tuluk said. "Then . . . McKie ordered me to call the Caleban. Perhaps it heard."

Tuluk closed his eyes, appeared lost in reverie.

"Go on," Bildoon said.

"I . . . it was. . . . " Tuluk shook his head, opened his eyes, stared pleadingly around the room. He met curious, probing eyes on all sides. "Imagine two spiderwebs," he said. "Natural spiderwebs, now, not the kind they spin at our command . . . random products. Imagine that they must . . . contact each other . . . a certain congruity between them, an occlusion."

"Like a *dental* occlusion?" McKie asked.

"Perhaps. At any rate, this necessary congruity, this *shape* required for contact, presumes proper connectives."

McKie expelled a harsh breath. "What the devil are connectives?"

"I go now?" the first Taprisiot interrupted.

"Damn!" McKie said. "Somebody get rid of this thing!"

The Taprisiot was hustled from the room.

"Tuluk, what are connectives?" McKie demanded.

"Is this important?" Bildoon asked.

"Will you all take my word for it and let him answer?" McKie asked. "It's important. Tuluk?"

"Mmmmmm," Tuluk said. "You realize, of course, that artificiality can be refined to the point where it's virtually indistinguishable from original reality?"

"What's that have to do with connectives?"

"It's precisely at that point where the single distinguishing characteristic between original and artificial is the connective," Tuluk explained.

"Huh?" McKie said.

"Look at me," Tuluk said.

"I *am* looking at you!"

"Imagine that you take a food vat and produce in it an exact fleshly duplicate of my person," Tuluk said.

"An exact fleshly . . . "

"You could do it, couldn't you?" Tuluk demanded.

"Of course. But why?"

"Just imagine it. Don't question. An exact duplicate down to and including the cellular message units. This flesh would be imbued with all my memories and responses. Ask it a question you might ask me, and it would answer as I might answer. Even my mates wouldn't be able to distinguish between us."

"So?" McKie said.

"Would there be any difference between us?" Tuluk asked.

"But you said . . . "

"There'd be one difference, wouldn't there?"

"The time element, the . . . "

"More than that," Tuluk said. "One would know it was a copy. Now, that chairdog in which Ser Bildoon sits is a different matter, not so?"

"Huh?"

"It's an unthinking animal," Tuluk said.

McKie stared at the chairdog Tuluk had indicated. It was a product of genetic shaping, gene surgery and selection. What possible difference could it make that a chairdog was an animal—however remotely descended?

"What does the chairdog eat?" Tuluk asked."

"The food tailored for it, what else?" McKie turned back to the Wreave, studied him.

"But neither the chairdog nor its food is the same as their ancestral flesh," Tuluk said. "The vat food is an endless, serial chain of protein. The chairdog is flesh which is ecstatic in its work."

"Of course! That's the way it was . . . made." McKie's eyes went wide. He began to see what Tuluk was explaining.

"The differences, these are the connectives," Tuluk said.

"McKie, do you understand this gibberish?" Bildoon demanded.

McKie tried to swallow in a dry throat. "The Caleban sees only these . . . *refined* differences?" he asked.

"And nothing else," Tuluk said

"Then it doesn't see us as . . . shapes or dimensions or . . . "

"Or even as extensions in time the way we understand time," Tuluk said. "We are, perhaps, nodes on a standing wave. Time, for the Caleban, isn't something squeezed out of a tube. It's more like a line which your senses intersect."

"Hahhhhh," McKie breathed.

"I don't see where this helps us one bit," Bildoon said. "Our major problem is to find Abnethe. Do you have any idea, McKie, where that Caleban sent you?"

"I saw the constellations overhead," McKie said. "Before I leave, we'll get a mindcord on what I saw and have a computer check on the star patterns."

"Provided the pattern's in the master registry," Bildoon said.

"What about the slave culture McKie stumbled on?" one of the legal staff asked. "We could ask for a . . . "

"Haven't any of you been listening?" McKie asked. "Our problem is to find Abnethe. I thought we had her, but I'm beginning to think this may not be that easy. Where is she? How can we go into a court and say, 'At some unknown place in an unknown galaxy, a female believed to be Mliss Abnethe, but whom I didn't really see, is alleged to be conducting . . . ' "

"Then what do we do?" the legal staffer growled.

"With Furuneo dead, who's watching Fanny Mae?" McKie asked.

"We have four enforcers inside, watching . . . where she is, and four outside, watching them," Bildoon said. "Are you sure you've no other clue to where you were?"

"None."

"A complaint by McKie would fail now," Bildoon said. No—a better move might be to charge her with harboring a"—he shuddered—"a Pan Spechi fugitive."

"Do we know who that fugitive is?" McKie asked.

"Not yet. We haven't decided the proper course yet." He glanced at a Legal Department representative, a human female seated near Tuluk. "Hanaman?"

Hanaman cleared her throat. She was a fragile-looking woman, thick head of brown hair in gentle waves, long oval face with soft blue eyes, delicate nose and chin, wide full mouth.

"You think it advisable to discuss this in council now?" she asked.

"I do, or I wouldn't have called on you," Bildoon said.

For an instant McKie thought the reproof might bring real tears to Hanaman's eyes, then he saw the controlled downtwist at the corners of her mouth, the measuring stare she swept around the conference room. She had brains, he saw, and knew there were those here susceptible to her sex.

"McKie," she said, "is it necessary for you to stand on the table? You're not a Taprisiot."

"Thanks for reminding me," he said. He jumped down, found a chairdog opposite her, stared back at her with a bland intensity.

Presently she focused on Bildoon, said, "To bring everyone up to date, Abnethe with one Palenki tried to flog the Caleban about two hours ago. Acting on our orders, an enforcer prevented the flogging. He cut off the Palenki's arm with a raygen. As a result, Abnethe's legal staff is already seeking an injunction."

"Then they were prepared ahead of time," McKie said.

"Obviously," she agreed. "They're alleging outlaw sabotage, misfeasance by a bureau, mayhem, misconduct, malicious mischief, felonious misprision . . . "

"Misfeasance?" McKie demanded.

"This is a robo-legum case, not a Gowachin jurisdiction," Hanaman said. "We don't have to exonerate the prosecutor before entering the . . . " She broke off, shrugged. "Well, you know all that. BuSab is being held to answer for collective responsibility in the consequences of unlawful and wrongful acts committed by its agents in pursuance of the authority permitted them . . . "

"Wait a minute!" McKie interrupted. "This is bolder than I expected from that crowd."

"And they charge," Hanaman went on, "that the Bureau is guilty of a felony by criminal neglect in its failure to prevent a felony from being committed and in not bringing to justice the offender after such commission."

"Have they named names, or is it all John Does?" McKie asked.

"No names."

"If they're this bold, they're desperate," McKie said. "Why?"

"They know we aren't going to sit idly by and allow our people to be killed," Bildoon said. "They know we have copies of the contract with the Caleban, and it gives Abnethe sole control of the Caleban's jumpdoor. No one else could've been responsible for Furuneo's death, and the perpetrator . . . "

"No one except the Caleban," McKie said.

A profound silence settled over the room.

Presently Tuluk said, "You don't seriously believe . . . "

"No, I don't," McKie said. "But I couldn't prove my belief to a robo-legum court. This does present an interesting possibility, though."

"Furuneo's head," Bildoon said.

"Correct," McKie said. "We demand Furuneo's head."

"What if they contend the Caleban sequestered the head?" Hanaman asked.

"I don't intend asking them for it," McKie said. "I'm going to ask the Caleban."

Hanaman nodded, her gaze intent on McKie and with a light of admiration in her eyes. "Clever," she breathed. "If they attempt to interfere, they're guilty. But if we get the head . . . " She looked at Tuluk.

"What about it, Tuluk?" Bildoon asked. "Think you could get anything from Furuneo's brain?"

"That depends on how much time has passed between the death and our key-in," Tuluk said. "Nerve replay has limits, you know."

"We know," Bildoon said.

"Yeah," McKie said. "Only one thing for me to do now, isn't there?"

"Looks that way," Bildoon said.

"Will you call off the enforcers, or shall I?" McKie asked.

"Now, wait a minute!" Bildoon said. "I know you have to go back to that Beachball, but . . . "

"Alone," McKie said.

"Why?"

"I can give the demand for Furuneo's head in front of witnesses," McKie said, "but that's not enough. They *want* me. I got away from them, and they've no idea how much I know abut their hidey hole."

"Exactly what do you know?" Bildoon asked.

"We've already been through that," McKie said.

"So you now see yourself as bait?"

"I wouldn't put it exactly that way," McKie said, "but if I'm alone, they might try bargaining with me. They might even . . . "

"They might even shorten you!" Bildoon snarled.

"You don't think it's worth the try?" McKie asked. He stared around the room at the attentive faces.

Hanaman cleared her throat. "I see a way out of this," she said.

Everyone looked at her.

"We could put McKie under Taprisiot surveillance," she said.

"He's a ready-made victim, if he's sitting there in a sniggertrance," Tuluk said.

"Not if the Taprisiot contacts are minimal every few seconds," she said.

"And as long as I'm not yelling for help, the Tappy breaks off," McKie said. "Good."

"I don't like it," Bildoon said. "What if . . . "

"You think they'll talk openly to me if they see the place full of enforcers?" McKie asked.

"No, but if we can prevent . . . "

"We can't, and you know it."

Bildoon glared at him.

"We must have those contacts between McKie and Abnethe, if we're going to try cross-charting to locate her position," Tuluk said.

Bildoon stared at the table in front of him.

"That Beachball has a fixed position on Cordiality," McKie argued. "Cordiality has a known planetary period. At the instant of each contact, the Ball will be pointing at a position in space—a line of least resistance for the contact. Enough contacts will describe a cone with . . . "

"With Abnethe somewhere in it," Bildoon supplied, looking up. "Provided you're right about this thing."

"The call connectives have to seek their conjunction through open space," Tuluk said. "There must be no large stellar masses between call points, no hydrogen clouds of any serious dimensions, no group of large planetary . . . "

"I understand the theory," Bildoon said. "But there's no theory needed about what they can do to McKie. It'd take them less than two seconds to slip a jumpdoor over his neck and . . . " He drew a finger across his throat.

"So you have the Tappy contact me every two seconds," McKie said. "Work it in relays. Get a string of agents in . . . "

"And what if they don't try to contact you?" Bildoon asked.

"Then we'll have to sabotage them," McKie said.

It is impossible to see any absolute through a screen of interpreters.

—WREAVE SAYING

WHEN YOU came right down to it, McKie decided, this Beachball wasn't as weird a home as some he'd seen. It was hot, yes, but that fitted a peculiar requirement of the occupant. Sentients existed in hotter climates. The giant spoon where the Caleban's *unpresence* could be detected—well, that could be equated with a divan. Wall handles, spools there, lights and whatnot—all those were almost conventional in appearance, although McKie seriously doubted he could understand their functions. The automated homes of Breedywie, though, displayed more outlandish control consoles.

The ceiling here was a bit low, but he could stand without stooping. The purple gloom was no stranger than the vari-glare of Gowachin, where most offworld sentients had to wear protective goggles while visiting friends. The Beachball's floor covering did not appear to be a conventional living organism, but it *was* soft. Right now it smelled of a standard pyrocene cleaner-disinfectant, and the fumes were rather stifling in the heat.

McKie shook his head. The fly-buzz "zzzt" of Taprisiot contact every two seconds was annoying, but he found he could override the distraction.

"Your friend reached ultimate discontinuity," the Caleban had explained. "His substance has been removed."

For *substance* read blood-and-body, McKie translated. He hoped the translation achieved some degree of accuracy, but he cautioned himself not to be too sure of that.

If we could only have a little air current in here, McKie thought. *Just a small breeze.*

He mopped perspiration from his forehead, drank from one of the water jugs he had provided for himself.

"You still there, Fanny Mae?" he asked.

"You observe my presence?"

"Almost."

"That *is* our mutual problem—seeing each other," the Caleban said.

"You're using time-ordinal verbs with more confidence, I note," McKie said.

"I get the hang of them, yes?"

"I hope so."

"I date the verb as a nodal position," the Caleban said.

"I don't believe I want that explained," McKie said.

"Very well; I comply."

"I'd like to try again to understand how the floggings are timed," McKie said.

"When shapes reach proper proportion," the Caleban said.

"You already said that. What shapes?"

"Already?" the Caleban asked. "That signifies earlier?"

"Earlier," McKie said. "That's right. You said that about shapes before."

"Earlier and before and already," the Caleban said. "Yes; times of different conjunction, by linear alteration of intersecting connectives."

Time, for the Caleban, is a position on a line, McKie reminded himself, recalling Tuluk's attempt at explanation. *I must look for the subtly refined differences; they're all this creature sees.*

"What shapes?" McKie repeated.

"Shapes defined by duration lines," the Caleban said. "I see many duration lines. You, oddly, carry visual sensation of one line only. Very strange. Other teachers explain this to self, but understanding fails . . . extreme constriction. Self admires molecular acceleration, but . . . maintenance exchange confuses."

Confuses! McKie thought.

"What molecular acceleration?" he asked.

"Teachers define molecule as smallest physical unit of element or compound. True?"

"That's right."

"This carries difficulty in understanding unless ascribed by self to perceptive difference between our species. Say, instead, molecule perhaps equals smallest physical unit visible to species. True?''

What's the difference? McKie thought. *It's all gibberish.* How had they gotten off onto molecules and acceleration from the proper proportion of undefined shapes?

''Why acceleration?'' he insisted.

''Acceleration always occurs along convergence lines we use while speaking one to another.''

Oh damn! McKie thought. He lifted a water jug, drank, choked on a swallow. He bent forward, gasping. When he could manage it, he said, ''The heat in here! Molecular speedup!''

''Do these concepts not interchange?'' the Caleban asked.

''Never mind that!'' McKie blurted, still spitting water. ''When you speak to me . . . is *that* what accelerates the molecules?''

''Self assumes this true condition.''

Carefully McKie put down the water jug, capped it. He began laughing.

''Not understand these terms,'' the Caleban objected.

McKie shook his head. The Caleban's words still came at him with that non-speech quality, but he detected definite querulous notes . . . overtones. Accents? He gave it up. There was *something* though.

''Not understand!'' the Caleban insisted.

This made McKie laugh all the harder. ''Oh, my,'' he gasped, when he could catch his breath. ''The ancient wheeze was right all along, and nobody knew it. Oh, my. Talk is just hot air!''

Again laughter convulsed him.

Presently he lay back, inhaled deeply. In a moment he sat up, took another swallow of water, capped the jug.

''Teach,'' the Caleban commanded. ''Explain these unusual terms.''

''Terms? Oh . . . certainly. Laughter. It's our common response to non-fatal surprise. No other significant communicative content.''

''Laughter,'' the Caleban said. ''Other nodal encounters with term noted.''

''Other nodal . . . '' McKie broke off. ''You've heard the word before, you mean?''

''Before. Yes. I . . . self . . . I attempt understanding of term, laughter. We explore meaning now?''

''Let's not,'' McKie objected.

''Negative reply?'' the Caleban asked.

''That's correct—negative. I'm much more curious about what you said about . . . maintenance exchange. That was what you said, wasn't it? Maintenance exchange confuses?''

''I attempt define position for you odd one-tracks,'' the Caleban said.

''One-tracks, that's how you think of us, eh?'' McKie asked. He felt suddenly small and inadequate.

''Relationship of connectives one to many, many to one,'' the Caleban said. ''Maintenance exchange.''

''How in the hell did we get into this dead-end conversation?'' McKie asked.

''You seek positional referents for placement of floggings, that begins conversation,'' the Caleban said.

''Placement . . . yeah.''

''You understand S'eye effect?'' the Caleban asked.

McKie exhaled slowly. To the best of his knowledge, no Caleban had ever
before volunteered a discussion of the S'eye effect. The one-two-three of how to
use the mechanism of the jumpdoors—yes, this was something they could (and
did) explain. But the effect, the theory. . . .

"I . . . uh, use the jumpdoors," McKie said. "I know something of how the
control mechanism is assembled and tuned to . . . "

"Mechanism not coincide with effect!"

"Uhhh, certainly," McKie agreed. "The word's not the thing."

"Precisement! We say—I translate, you understand?—we say, 'Term evades
node.' You catch the hanging of this term, self thinks."

"I . . . uh, get the hang of it," McKie agreed.

"Recommend hang-line as good thought," the Caleban said. "Self, I believe
we approach true communication. It wonders me."

"You wonder about it."

"Negative. It wonders about me."

"That's great," McKie said in a flat voice. "That's communication?"

"Understanding diffuses . . . scatters? Yes—understanding scatters when we
discuss connectives. I observe connectives of your . . . psyche. For psyche, I
understand 'other self.' True?"

"Why not?" McKie asked.

"I see," the Caleban said, ignoring McKie's defeated tone, "psyche patterns,
perhaps their colors. Approachments and outreaching touch by awareness. I come,
through this, to unwinding of intelligence and perhaps understand what you mean
by term, stellar mass. Self understands by being stellar mass, you hang this,
McKie?"

"Hang this? Oh, sure . . . sure."

"Good! Comes now an understanding of your . . . wandering? Difficult word,
McKie. Very likely this an uncertain exchange. Wandering equals movement
along one line for you. This cannot exist for us. One moves, all move for Caleban
on own plane. S'eye effect combines all movements and vision. I *see* you to other
place of your desired wandering."

McKie, his interest renewed by this odd rambling, said, "You *see* us . . . that's
what moves us from one place to another?"

"I hear sentient of your plane say sameness, McKie. Sentient say, 'I will see
you to the door.' So? Seeing moves."

Seeing moves? McKie wondered. He mopped his forehead, his lips. It was so
damned hot! What did all this have to do with "maintenance exchange"? Whatever that was!

"Stellar mass maintains and exchanges," the Caleban said. "Not see through
the self. S'eye connective discontinues. You call this . . . privacy? Cannot say.
This Caleban exists alone or self on your plane. Lonely."

We're all lonely, McKie thought.

And this universe would be lonely soon, if he couldn't find a way to escape their
common grave. Why did the problem have to hang on such fumbling communication?

It was a peculiar kind of torment trying to talk to the Caleban under these
pressures. He wanted to speed the processes of understanding, but speed sent all
sentiency hurtling toward the brink. He could feel time flying past him. Urgency
churned his stomach. He marched with time, retreated with it—and he'd started
somehow on the wrong foot.

He thought about the fate of just one baby who'd never passed through a jumpdoor. The baby would cry . . . and there'd be no one to answer.

The awesome totality of the threat daunted him.

Everyone gone!

He put down a surge of irritation at the zzzt-beat of the Taprisiot intrusions. *That*, at least, was companionship.

"Do Taprisiots send our messages across space the same way?" he asked. "Do they *see* the calls?"

"Taprisiot very weak," the Caleban said. "Taprisiot not possess Caleban energy. Self energy, you understand?"

"I dunno. Maybe."

"Taprisiot see very thin, very short," the Caleban said. "Taprisiot not see through stellar mass of self. Sometimes Taprisiot ask for . . . boost? Amplification! Caleban provide service. Maintenance exchange, you hang? Taprisiot pay, we pay, you pay. All pay energy. You call energy demand . . . *hunger*, not so?"

"Oh, hell!" McKie said. "I'm not getting the half of . . ."

A brawny Palenki arm carrying a whip inserted itself into the space above the giant spoon. The whip cracked, sent a geyser of green sparks into the purple gloom. Arm and whip were gone before McKie could move.

"Fanny Mae," McKie whispered, "you still there?"

Silence . . . then, "No laughter, McKie. Thing you call surprise, but no laughter. I break line there. An abruptness, that flogging."

McKie exhaled, noted the mindclock timing of the incident, relayed the coordinates at the next Taprisiot contact.

There was no sense talking about pain, he thought. It was equally fruitless to explore inhaling whips or exhaling substance . . . or maintenance exchanges or hunger or stellar masses or Calebans moving other sentients by energy of *seeing*. Communication was bogged down.

They'd achieved something, though Tuluk had been right. The S'eye contacts for the floggings required some timing or periodicity which could be identified. Perhaps there *was* a line of sight involved. One thing sure: Abnethe had her feet planted on a real planet somewhere. She and her mob of psycho friends—her *psycho-phants!*—all of them had a position in space which could be located. She had Palenkis, renegade Wreaves, an outlaw Pan Spechi—gods knew what all. She had Beautybarbers, too, and Taprisiots, probably. And somehow the Beautybarbers, the Taprisiots, and this Caleban all used the same sort of energy to do their work.

"Could we try again," McKie asked, "to locate Abnethe's planet?"

"Contract forbids."

"You have to honor it, eh? Even to the death?"

"Honor to ultimate discontinuity, yes."

"And that's pretty near, is it?"

"Position of ultimate discontinuity becomes visible to self," the Caleban said. "Perhaps this equates with near."

Again arm and whip flicked into being, showered the air with a cascade of green sparks, and withdrew.

McKie darted forward, stopped beside the spoon bowl. He had never before ventured quite this close to the Caleban. There was more heat near the bowl, and he felt a tingling sensation along his arms. The shower of green sparks had left no mark on the carpeting, no residual substance, nothing. McKie felt the insistent attraction of the Caleban's *unpresence*, a disturbing intensity this near. He forced himself to turn away. His palms were wet with fear.

What else am I afraid of here? he asked himself.

"Those two attacks came pretty close together," McKie said.

"Positional adjacency noted," the Caleban said. "Next coherence more distant. You say 'farther away'? True?"

"Yeah. Will the next flogging be your last?"

"Self not know," the Caleban said. "Your presence lessens flogging intensity. You . . . reject? Ahhh, repel!"

"No doubt," McKie said. "I wish I knew why the end of you means the end of everyone else."

"You transfer self of you with S'eye," the Caleban said. "So?"

"Everyone does!"

"Why? You teach explanation of this?"

"It's centralizing the whole damn universe. It's . . . it's created the specialized planets—honeymoon planets, gynecology planets, pediatrics planets, snow sport planets, geriatrics planets, swim sport planets, library planets—even BuSab has almost a whole planet to itself. Nobody gets by without it, anymore. Last figures I saw, fewer than a fraction of one percent of the sentient population had never used a S'eye jumpdoor."

"Truth. Such use creates connectives, McKie. You must hang this. Connectives must shatter with my discontinuity. Shatter conveys ultimate discontinuity for all who use jumpdoor S'eye."

"If you say so. I still don't understand."

"It occurs, McKie, because my fellows choose me for . . . coordinator? Inadequate term. Funnel? Handler, perhaps. No still inadequate. Ahhh! I, self of I, *am* S'eye!"

McKie backed away, retreating from such a wave of sadness that he felt he could not contain it. He wanted to scream in protest. Tears flowed down his cheeks unbidden. A sob choked him. Sadness! His body was reacting to it, but the emotion came from outside of himself.

Slowly it faded.

McKie blew air soundlessly through his lips. He still trembled from the passage of that emotion. It had been the Caleban's emotion, he realized. But it came out like the waves of heat in this room, swept over and immersed every nerve receptor in its path.

Sadness.

Responsibility for all those impending deaths, no doubt.

I am S'eye!

What in the name of all devils in the universe could the Caleban mean by such a strange claim? He thought of each jumpdoor passage. Connectives? Threads, perhaps. Each being caught by the S'eye effect trailed threads of itself through the jumpdoors. Was that it? Fanny Mae *had* used the word "funnel." Every traveler went through her . . . hands? Whatever. And when she ceased to exist, the threads broke. All died.

"Why weren't we warned about this when you offered us the S'eye effect?" McKie asked.

"Warned?"

"Yes! You offered . . . "

"Not offer. Fellow explain effect. Sentients of your wave expose great joy.

They offer exchange of maintenance. You call this pay, not so?''

"We should've been warned.''

"Why?''

"Well, you don't live forever, do you?''

"Explain this term, forever.''

"Forever . . . always. Infinity?''

"Sentients of your wave seek infinity?''

"Not for individual members, but for . . . ''

"Sentient species, they seek infinity?''

"Of course they do!''

"Why?''

"Doesn't everyone?''

"But what about other species for which yours must make way? You not believe in evolution?''

"Evo—'' McKie shook his head sharply. "What's that have to do with it?''

"All beings have own day and depart,'' the Caleban said. "Day correct term? Day, unit of time, allotted linearity, normal extent of existence—you hang this?''

McKie's mouth moved, but no words came out.

"Length of line, time of existence,'' the Caleban said. "Approximately translated, correct?''

"But what gives you the right to . . . *terminate* us?'' McKie demanded, finding his voice.

"Right not assumed, McKie,'' the Caleban said. "Given condition of proper connectives, another of my fellows takes up S'eye . . . control before self reaches ultimate discontinuity. Unusual . . . circumstance rejects such solution here. Mliss Abnethe and . . . associates shorten your one-track. My fellows leave.''

"They ran for it while they had time; I understand,'' McKie said.

"Time . . . yes, your single-track line. This comparison provides suitable concept. Inadequate but sufficient.''

"And you are definitely the last Caleban in our . . . wave?''

"Self alone,'' the Caleban said. "Terminal end-point Caleban—yes. Self confirms description.''

"Wasn't there any way to save yourself?'' McKie asked.

"Save? Ahhh . . . avoid? Evade! Yes, evade ultimate discontinuity. This you suggest?''

"I'm asking if there wasn't some way for you to escape the way your . . . fellows did.''

"Way exists, but result same for your wave.''

"You could save yourself, but it would end us, that it?''

"You not possess honor concept?'' the Caleban asked. "Save self, lose honor.''

"Touché,'' McKie said.

"Explain touché,'' the Caleban said. "New term.''

"Eh? Oh, that's a very old, ancient term.''

"Linear beginning term, you say? Yes, those best with nodal frequency.''

"Nodal frequency?''

"You say—often. Nodal frequency contains often.''

"They mean the same thing; I see.''

"Not same; similar.''

"I stand corrected.''

"Explain touché. What meaning conveys this term?"

"Meaning conveys . . . yeah. It's a fencing term."

"Fencing? You signify containment?"

McKie explained fencing as best he could with a side journey into swordsmanship, the concept of single combat, competition.

"Effective touch!" the Caleban interrupted, her words conveying definite wonder. "Nodal intersection! Touché! Ahhh-ahhh! This contains why we find your species to fascinate us! This concept! Cutting line: touché! Pierced by meaning: touché!"

"Ultimate discontinuity," McKie snarled. "Touché! How far away is your next *touché* with the whip?"

"Intersection of whip touché!" the Caleban said. "You seek position of linear displacement, yes. It moves me. We perhaps occupy our linearities yet; but self suggests another species may need these dimensions. We leave, outgo from existence then. No so?"

When McKie didn't answer, the Caleban said, "McKie, you hang my meaning?"

"I think I'm going to sabotage you," McKie muttered.

Learning a language represents training in the delusions of that language.

—GOWACHIN APHORISM

CHEO, THE ego-frozen Pan Spechi, stared out across the forest toward sunset over the sea. It was good, he thought, that the Ideal World contained such a sea. This tower Mliss had ordered built in a city of lesser buildings and spires commanded a view which included also the distant plain and far away mountains of the interior.

A steady wind blew against his left cheek, stirred his yellow hair. He wore green trousers and an open-mesh shirt of dull gold and gray. The clothing gave a subtle accent to his humanoid appearance, revealing the odd ripples of alien muscles here and there about his body.

An amused smile occupied his mouth, but not his eyes. He had Pan Spechi eyes, many-faceted, glistening—although the facets were edge-faded by his ego-surgery. The eyes watched the insect movements of various sentients on streets and bridgeways below him. At the same time, they reported on the sky overhead (a faraway flock of birds, streamers of sunset clouds) and told him of the view toward the sea and the nearby balustrade.

We're going to pull it off, he thought.

He glanced at the antique chronograph Mliss had given him. Crude thing, but it showed the sunset hour. They'd had to disengage from the Taprisiot mindclock system, though. This crude device showed two hours to go until the next contact. The S'eye controls would be more accurate, but he didn't want to move.

They can't stop us.

But maybe they can. . . .

He thought about McKie then. How had the BuSab agent found this place? And finding it, how had he come here? McKie sat in the Beachball with the Caleban right now—bait, obviously. Bait!

For what?

Cheo did not enjoy the contradictory emotions surging back and forth through him. He had broken the most basic Pan Spechi law. He had captured his crèche's ego and abandoned his four mates to a mindless existence terminating in mindless death. A renegade surgeon's instruments had excised the organ which united the pentarchal Pan Spechi family across all space. The surgery had left a scar on Cheo's forehead and a scar on his soul, but he had never imagined he would find such delicate relish in the experience.

Nothing could take the ego from him!

But he was alone, too.

Death would end it, of course, but all creatures had that to face.

And thanks to Mliss, he had a retreat from which no other Pan Spechi could extricate him . . . unless . . . but there'd be no other Pan Spechi, very soon. There'd be no other organized sentients at all, except the handful Mliss had brought here to her Ark with its mad Boers and Blacks.

Abnethe came hurrying onto the observation deck behind him. His ears, as multiplanar in discrimination as his eyes, marked the emotions in her footsteps—boredom, worry, the constant fear which constricted her being.

Cheo turned.

She had been to a Beautybarber, he observed. Red hair now crowned her lovely face. McKie had red hair, too, Cheo reminded himself. She threw herself onto a reclining chairdog, stretched her legs.

"What's your hurry?" he asked.

"Those Beautybarbers!" she snapped. "They want to go *home!*"

"Send them."

"But where will I find others?"

"That *is* a proper problem, isn't it?"

"You're making fun of me, Cheo. Don't."

"Then tell them they can't go home."

"I did."

"Did you tell them why?"

"Of course not! What a thing to say!"

"You told Furuneo."

"I learned my lesson. Where are my legal people?"

"They've already gone."

"But I had other things to discuss with them!"

"Won't it wait?"

"You *knew* we had other business. Why'd you let them go?"

"Mliss, you don't really want to know the other matter on their minds."

"The Caleban's to blame," she said. "That's our story, and no one can disprove it. What was the other matter the legal numbheads wanted to discuss?"

"Mliss, drop it."

"Cheo!"

His Pan Spechi eyes glittered suddenly. "As you wish. They conveyed a demand from BuSab. They have asked the Caleban for Furuneo's head."

"His . . . " She paled. "But how did they know we . . . "

"It was an obvious move under the circumstances."

"What did you tell them?" she whispered. She stared at his face.

"I told them the Caleban closed the S'eye jumpdoor just as Furuneo was entering it of his own volition."

"But they know we have a monopoly on that S'eye," she said, her voice stronger. "Damn them!"

"Ahhh," Cheo said, "but Fanny Mae has been moving McKie and his friends around. *That* says we have no monopoly."

"That's exactly what I said before. Isn't it?"

"It gives us the perfect delaying tactic," he said. "Fanny Mae sent the head somewhere, and we don't know where. I've told her, of course, to deny this request."

She swallowed. "Is that . . . what you told them?"

"Of course."

"But if they question the Caleban . . . "

"They're just as likely to get a confusing answer as a usable one."

"That was very clever of you, Cheo."

"Isn't that why you keep me around?"

"I keep you around for mysterious reasons of my own," she said, smiling.

"I depend on that," he said.

"You know," she said, "I'll miss them."

"Miss who?"

"The ones who hunt us."

A basic requirement for BuSab agents is, perhaps, that we make the right mistakes.

—MCKIE'S COMMENTARY ON FURUNEO,
BUSAB PRIVATE FILES

BILDOON STOOD in the doorway to Tuluk's personal lab, his back to the long outer room where the Wreave's assistants did most of their work. The BuSab chief's deep-set eyes held a faceted glitter, a fire that failed to match the composure of his humanoid Pan Spechi face.

He felt weak and sad. He felt he existed in a contracting cave, a place without wind or stars. Time was closing in on everyone. Those he loved and those who loved him would die. All sentient love in the universe would die. The universe would become homeless, enclosed by melancholy.

Mourning filled his humanoid flesh: snows, leaves, suns—eternally alone.

He felt the demands of action, of decision, but feared the consequences of anything he might do. Whatever he touched might crumble, become so much dust falling through his fingers.

Tuluk, he saw, was working at a bench against the opposite wall. He had a length of the bullwhip's rawhide stretched between two clamps. Parallel with the rawhide and about a millimeter below it was a metal pole which lay balanced on air without visible support. Between rawhide and pole could be seen flickers of miniature lightning which danced along the entire length of the gap. Tuluk was bent over, reading meters set into the bench beneath the device.

"Am I interrupting anything?" Bildoon asked.

Tuluk turned a knob on the bench, waited, turned the knob once more. He caught the pole as the invisible supporting force released it. He racked the pole on supports against the back wall above the bench.

"That is a silly question," he said, turning.

"It is, at that," Bildoon said. "We have a problem."

"Without problems, we have no employment," Tuluk said.

"I don't think we're going to get Furuneo's head." Bildoon said.

"It's been so long now, we probably couldn't have gotten a reliable nerve replay, anyway," Tuluk said. He screwed his face slit into an S-curve, an expression he knew aroused amusement among other sentients but which represented intense thought for a Wreave. "What do the astronomers say about the star pattern McKie saw on that mysterious planet?"

"They think there may have been an error in the mindcord."

"Oh. Why?"

"For one thing, there isn't even a hint, not the slightest subjective indication of variation in stellar magnitudes."

"All the visible stars had the same light intensity?"

"Apparently."

"Odd."

"And the nearest pattern similarity," Bildoon said, "is one that doesn't exist anymore."

"What do you mean?"

"Well . . . there's a Big Dipper, a Little Dipper, various other constellations and zodiac similarities, but . . . " He shrugged.

Tuluk stared at him blankly. "I don't recognize the references," he said presently.

"Oh, yes—I forgot," Bildoon said. "We Pan Spechi, when we decided to copy human form, explored their history with some care. These patterns of stars are ones which were visible from their ancient homeworld."

"I see. Another oddity to go with what I've discovered about the material of this whip."

"What's that?"

"It's very strange. Parts of this leather betray a subatomic structure of peculiar alignment."

"Peculiar? How?"

"Aligned. Perfectly aligned. I've never seen anything like it outside certain rather fluid energy phenomena. It's as though the material had been subjected to some peculiar force or stress. The result is, in some ways, similar to neomaser alignment of light quanta."

"Wouldn't that require enormous energy?"

"Presumably."

"But what could cause it?"

"I don't know. The interesting thing is that it doesn't appear to be a permanent change. The structure shows characteristics like plastic memory. It's slowly snapping back into reasonably familiar forms."

Bildoon heard the emphasis which betrayed Tuluk's disturbance. "Reasonably familiar?" he asked.

"That's another thing," Tuluk said. "Let me explain. These subatomic structures and their resultant overstructures of genetic message units undergo slow evolution. We can, by comparing structures, date some samples to within two or three thousand standard years. Since cattle cells form the basic protein for vat culture food, we have fairly complete records on them over a very long time indeed. The strange thing about the samples in this piece of rawhide"—he gestured with a mandibular extensor—"is that its pattern is very ancient."

"How ancient?"

"Perhaps several hundred thousand years."

Bildoon absorbed this for a moment, then, "But you told us earlier that this rawhide was only a couple of years old."

"According to our catalyzing tests, it is."

"Could this alignment stress have mixed up the pattern?"

"Conceivably."

"You doubt it, then?"

"I do."

"You're not trying to tell me that whip was brought forward through time?"

"I'm not trying to tell you anything outside the facts which I've reported. Two tests, previously considered reliable, do not agree as to the dating of this material."

"Time travel's an impossibility," Bildoon said.

"So we've always assumed."

"We *know* it. We know it mathematically and pragmatically. It's a fiction device, a myth, an amusing concept employed by entertainers. We reject it, and we are left without paradox. Only one conclusion remains: The alignment stress, whatever that was, changed the pattern."

"If the rawhide were . . . squeezed through a subatomic filter of some sort, that might account for it," Tuluk said. "But since I have no such filter, nor the power to do this theoretical squeezing, I cannot test it."

"You must have some thoughts about it, though."

"I do. I cannot conceive of a filter which would do this thing without destroying the materials subjected to such forces."

"Then what you're saying," Bildoon said, voice rising in angry frustration, "is that an impossible device did an impossible thing to that impossible piece of . . . of . . . "

"Yes, sir," Tuluk said.

Bildoon noticed that Tuluk's aides in the outer room were turning their faces toward him, showing signs of amusement. He stepped fully into Tuluk's lab, closed the door.

"I came down here hoping you'd found something which might force their hand," Bildoon said, "and you give me conundrums."

"Your displeasure doesn't change the facts," Tuluk said.

"No, I guess it doesn't."

"The structure of the Palenki arm cells was aligned in a similar fashion," Tuluk said. "But only around the cut."

"You anticipated my next question."

"It was obvious. Passage through a jumpdoor doesn't account for it. We sent several of our people through jumpdoors with various materials and tested random cells—living and dead—for a check."

"Two conundrums in an hour is more than I like," Bildoon said.

"Two?"

"We now have twenty-eight positional incidents of Abnethe flogging that

Caleban or attempting to flog it. That's enough to show us they do *not* define a cone in space. Unless she's jumping around from planet to planet, that theory's wrong.''

''Given the powers of that S'eye, she *could* be jumping around.''

''We don't think so. That isn't her way. She's a nesting bird. She likes a citadel. She's the kind who castles in chess when she doesn't have to.''

''She could be sending her Palenkis.''

''She's there with 'em every time.''

''We've collected six whips and arms, in all,'' Tuluk said. ''Do you want me to repeat these tests on all of them?''

Bildoon stared at the Wreave. The question wasn't like him. Tuluk was plodding, thorough.

''What would you rather be doing?'' Bildoon asked.

''We have twenty-eight examples, you say. Twenty-eight is one of the euclidean perfects. It's four times the prime seven. The number strongly indicates randomness. But we're faced with a situation apparently excluding randomness. Ergo, an organizing pattern is at work which is not revealed by analytic numbering as far as we've taken it. I would like to subject the spacing—both in time and physical dimension—to a complete analysis, compare for any similarities we . . .''

''You'd put an assistant on the other whips and arms to check them out?''

''That goes without saying.''

Bildoon shook his head. ''What Abnethe's doing—it's impossible!''

''If she does a thing, how can it be impossible?''

''They have to be somewhere!'' Bildoon snapped.

''I find it very strange,'' Tuluk said, ''this trait you share with humans of stating the obvious in such emphatic fashion.''

''Oh, go to hell!'' Bildoon said. He turned, slammed out of the lab.

Tuluk, racing to the door after him, opened it and called at the retreating back, ''It is a Wreave belief that we already *are* in hell!''

He returned to his bench, muttering. Humans and Pan Spechi—impossible creatures. Except for McKie. Now, there was a human who occasionally achieved analytic rapport with sentients capable of higher logic. Well . . . every species had its exceptions to the norm.

> *If you say, "I understand," what have you done? You have made a value judgment.*
>
> —LACLAC RIDDLE

BY AN effort of communication which he still did not completely understand, McKie had talked the Caleban into opening the Beachball's external port. This permitted a bath of spray-washed air to flow into the place where McKie sat. It also did one other thing: It allowed a crew of watchers outside to hold eye contact with him. He had just about given up hoping Abnethe would rise to the bait. There would have to be another solution. Visual contact with watchers also permitted a longer spacing between Taprisiot guard contacts. He found the new spacing less tiresome.

Morning sunshine splashed across the lip of the opening into the Beachball. McKie put a hand into the light, felt the warmth. He knew he should be moving around, making a poor target of himself, but the presence of the watchers made attack unlikely. Besides, he was tired, drugged to alertness and full of the odd emotions induced by *angeret*. Movement seemed an empty effort. If they wanted to kill him, they were going to do it. Furuneo's death proved that.

McKie felt a special pang at the thought of Furuneo's death. There had been something admirable and likable about the planetary agent. It had been a fumbling, pointless death—alone here, trapped. It had not advanced their search for Abnethe, only placed the whole conflict on a new footing of violence. It had shown the uncertainty of a single life—and through that life, the vulnerability of all life.

He felt a self-draining hate for Abnethe then. That madwoman!

He fought down a fit of trembling.

From where he sat McKie could see out across the lava shelf to the rocky palisades and a mossy carpeting of sea growth exposed at the cliff base by the retreating tide.

"Suppose we have it all wrong," he said, speaking over his shoulder toward the Caleban. "Suppose we really aren't communicating with each other at all. What if we've just been making noises, assuming a communication content which doesn't exist?"

"I fail of understanding, McKie. The hang doesn't get me."

McKie turned slightly. The Caleban was doing something strange with the air around its position. The oval *stage* he had seen earlier shimmered once more into view, disappeared. A golden halo appeared at one side of the giant spoon, rose up like a smoke ring, crackled electrically, and vanished.

"We're assuming," McKie said, "that when you say something to me, I respond with meaningful words directly related to your statement—and that you do the same. This may not be the case at all."

"Unlikely."

"So it's unlikely. What *are* you doing there?"

"Doing?"

"All that activity around you."

"Attempt making self visible on your wave."

"Can you do it?"

"Possible."

A bell-shaped red glow formed above the spoon, stretched into a straight line, resumed its bell curve, began whirling like a child's jump rope.

"What see you?" the Caleban asked.

McKie described the whirling red rope.

"Very odd," the Caleban said. "I flex creativity, and you report visible sensation. You need yet that opening to exterior conditions."

"The open port? It makes it one helluva lot more comfortable in here."

"Comfort—concept self fails to understand."

"Does the opening prevent you from becoming visible?"

"It performs magnetic distraction, no more."

McKie shrugged. "How much more flogging can you take?"

"Explain much."

"You've left the track again," McKie said.

"Correct! That forms achievement, McKie."

"How is it an achievement?"

"Self leaves communicative track, and you achieve awareness of same."

"All right, that's an achievement. Where's Abnethe?"

"Contract . . ."

" . . . prohibits revealing her location," McKie completed. "Maybe you can tell me, then, is she jumping around or remaining on one planet?"

"That helps you locate her?"

"How in fifty-seven hells do I know?"

"Probability smaller than fifty-seven elements," the Caleban said. "Abnethe occupies relatively static position on specific planet."

"But we can't find any pattern to her attacks on you or where they originate," McKie said.

"You cannot see connectives," the Caleban said.

The whirling red rope flickered in and out of existence above the giant spoon. Abruptly, it shifted color to a glowing yellow, vanished.

"You just disappeared," McKie said.

"Not my person visible," the Caleban said.

"How's that?"

"You not seeing person-self."

"That's what I said."

"Not say. Visibility to you not represent sameness of my person. You visible-see effect."

"I wasn't seeing you, eh? That was just some effect you created?"

"Correct."

"I didn't think it was you. You're going to be something more shapely. I do notice something though: There are moments when you use our verb tenses better; I even spotted some fairly normal constructions."

"Self hangs this get me," the Caleban said.

"Yeh, well . . . maybe you're not getting the hang of our language, after all." McKie stood up, stretched, moved closer to the open port, intending to peer out. As he moved, a shimmering silver loop dropped out of the air where he had been. He whirled in time to see it snake back through the small vortal tube of a jumpdoor.

"Abnethe, is that you?" McKie demanded.

There was no answer, and the jumpdoor snapped out of existence.

The enforcers watching from outside rushed to the port. One called, "You all right, McKie?"

McKie waved him to silence, took a raygen from his pocket, held it loosely in his hand. "Fanny Mae," he said, "are they trying to capture or kill me the way they did with Furuneo?"

"Observe theyness," the Caleban said. "Furuneo not having existence, observable intentions unknown."

"Did you see what just happened here?" McKie asked.

"Self contains awareness of S'eye employment, certain activity of employer persons. Activity ceases."

McKie rubbed his left hand across his neck. He wondered if he could bring the raygen into play quickly enough to cut any snare they might drop over his head. That silver thing dropping into the room had looked suspiciously like a noose.

"Is that how they got Furuneo?" McKie asked. "Did they drop a noose over his neck and pull him into the jumpdoor?"

"Discontinuity removes person of sameness," the Caleban said.

McKie shrugged, gave it up. That was more or less the answer they got every time they tried to question the Caleban about Furuneo's death.

Oddly, McKie discovered he was hungry. He wiped perspiration from his jaw and chin, cursed under his breath. There was no real assurance that what he *heard* in the Caleban's words represented real communication. Even granting some communication, how could he depend on the Caleban's interpretations or the Caleban's honesty? When the damn thing *spoke*, though, it radiated such a sense of sincerity that disbelief became almost impossible. McKie rubbed his chin, trying to catch an elusive thought. Strange. Here he was, hungry, angry, and afraid. There was no place to run. They had to solve this problem. He *knew* this for an absolute fact. Imperfect as communication with the Caleban actually was, the warning from the creature could not be ignored. Too many sentients had already died or gone insane.

He shook his head at the fly-buzz of Taprisiot contact. Damn surveillance! This contact, however, failed to break off. It was Siker, the Laclac Director of Discretion. Siker had detected McKie's disturbed emotions and, instead of breaking contact, had locked in.

"No!" McKie raged. He felt himself stiffen into the mumbling sniggertrance. "No, Siker! Break off!"

"But what's wrong, McKie?"

"Break off, you idiot, or I'm done for!"

"Well . . . all right, but you felt . . . "

"Break it!"

Siker broke the contact.

Once more aware of his body, McKie found himself dangling from a noose which had choked off his breath and was pulling him up into a small jumpdoor. He heard scrambling at the open port. There were shouts, but he couldn't respond. Fire encircled his neck. His chest burned. Panic filled his mind. He found he had dropped the raygen during the sniggertrance. He was helpless. His hands clawed futilely at the noose.

Something grabbed his feet. Added weight tightened the noose.

Abruptly, the lifting force gave way. McKie, fell, sprawling in a tangle with whoever had grabbed his feet.

Several things happened at once. Enforcers helped him to his feet. A holoscan held by a Wreave was shoved past his face toward the jumpdoor, which closed with an electric snap. Groping hands and extensors removed the noose from his neck.

McKie inhaled a choking breath, gasped. He would have collapsed without the support of those around him.

Gradually, he became aware that five other sentients had entered the Beachball—two Wreaves, Laclac, a Pan Spechi and a human. The human and one of the Wreaves worked over McKie, clearing away the noose and supporting him. the holoscan operator was a Wreave, who was busy examining his instrument. The others were watching the space all around them, raygens ready. At least three sentients were trying to talk at the same time.

"All right!" McKie husked, shutting off the babble. His throat hurt when he spoke. He grabbed the length of noose from the Wreave's extensors, examined it. The rope was a silvery material which McKie failed to recognize. It had been cut cleanly with a raygen.

McKie looked at the enforcer with the holoscan, said, "What did you get?"

"The attack was made by an ego-frozen Pan Spechi, ser," the Wreave enforcer said. "I got a good record of his face. We'll try for ID."

McKie tossed him the severed length of noose. "Get this thing back to the lab, too. Tell Tuluk to break it down to its basic structure. It may even have some of . . . Furuneo's cells on it. The rest of you . . . "

"Ser?" It was the Pan Spechi among the enforcers.

"Yes?"

"Ser, we have orders. If an attempt is made on your life, we are to stay with you in here." He passed a raygen to McKie. "You dropped this, I believe."

McKie pocketed it with an angry gesture.

Taprisiot contact filled McKie's mind. "Break it!" he snapped.

But the contact firmed. It was Bildoon in a no-nonsense mood. "What's going on there, McKie?"

McKie explained.

"There are enforcers around you right now?"

"Yes."

"Anyone see the attackers?"

"We got a holoscan. It was the ego-frozen Pan Spechi."

McKie felt the emotional shudder from his Bureau chief. The sensation of horror was followed by a sharp command: "I want you back here at Central immediately."

"Look," McKie reasoned. "I'm the best bait we have. They want me dead for some . . . "

"Back, and now!" Bildoon said. "I'll have you brought in forcibly, if you make that necessary."

McKie subsided. He'd never before experienced such a black mood from a caller. "What's wrong?" he asked.

"You're bait wherever you are, McKie—there or here. If they want you, they'll come for you. I want you here, where we can surround you with guards."

"Something's happened," McKie said.

"You're damn right something's happened! All those bullwhips we were examining have disappeared. The lab is a shambles, and one of the Tuluk's assistants dead—decapitated and . . . no head."

"Ahhhhh, damn," McKie said. Then, "I'm on my way."

All the wisdom of the universe cannot match the alert willingness to dodge a violent blow.

—ANCIENT FOLK SAYING

CHEO SAT cross-legged on a bare stretch of floor in the anteroom of his quarters. A sharply defined orange crosslight from windows in the next room stretched his shadow beside him like something lifeless from the night. In his hands he held the length of noose which had remained after it had been cut in the closing of the jumpdoor.

Damnable interference! That big Laclac with the raygen had been fast! And the Wreave with the holoscan had made a record through the jumpdoor—no doubt of that. They'd start hunting back along his trail now, asking questions, showing the holoscan of his face.

Not that it would do them any good.

Cheo's jeweled eyes glittered with shards of light. He could almost hear the BuSab operatives: *"Do you recognize this Pan Spechi?"*

The Pan Spechi equivalent of a chuckle, a rumbling grunt, shook him. Fat lot of good that search would do them! No friend or acquaintance from the old days would be likely to recognize his face, now that the medics had changed it. Oh, the bridge of the nose and the set of the eyes were similar, but . . .

Cheo shook his head. Why was he worrying? No one—absolutely no one—was going to stop him from destroying the Caleban! And after that, all these conjectures would be academic.

He sighed heavily. His hands were gripping the length of rope so tightly that his muscles ached. It took him several heartbeats of effort to release them. He climbed to his feet, threw the severed rope at a wall. A flailing end of it lashed a chairdog, which whimpered sibilantly through its atrophied vocal structure.

Cheo nodded to himself. They had to get the guards away from the Caleban or the Caleban away from the guards. He rubbed the scars on his forehead, hesitated. Was that a sound behind him? Slowly he turned, lowered his hand.

Mliss Abnethe stood in the doorway to the outer hall. The orange light created embers in the pearl sheathing of her gown. Her face held back anger, fear, and the grievous murmurings of her psyche.

"How long have you been there?" he asked, trying to keep his voice steady.

"Why?" She stepped into the room, closed the door. "What've you been doing?"

"Fishing," he said.

She swept the room with her insolent gaze, saw the pile of whips in a corner. They were thrown over something vaguely round and hairy. A wet red stain crept onto the floor from beneath the pile. She paled, whispered, "What's that?"

"Get out of here, Mliss," he said.

"What've you been doing?" she shrieked, whirling on him.

I should tell her, he thought. I should really tell her.

"I've been working to save our lives," he said.

"You've killed someone, haven't you?" she rasped.

"He didn't suffer," Cheo said, his voice tired.

"But you . . . "

"What's one more death among the quadrillions we're planning?" he asked. By all the devils of Gowachin, she was a tiresome bitch!

"Cheo, I'm afraid."

Why did she have to whimper like that?

"Calm yourself," he said. "I've a plan to separate the Caleban from her guardians. When we achieve that, we can proceed with her destruction, and the thing's done."

She swallowed, said, "She suffers. I know she does."

"That's nonsense! You've heard her deny it. She doesn't even know what pain means. No referents!"

"But what if we're wrong? What if it's just a misunderstanding?"

He advanced on her, stood glaring over her. "Mliss, do you have any idea how much *we'll* suffer if we fail?"

She shuddered. Presently, her voice almost normal, she asked, "What's your plan?"

One species can, all by itself, produce infinite varieties of experiences. The interaction between many species creates the illusion that infinity has been enlarged by several orders of magnitude.

> —THE CALEBAN QUESTION
> BY DWEL HARTAVID

MCKIE FELT danger signals from every nerve ending. He stood with Tuluk in the Wreave's lab. The place should have been comfortingly familiar, but McKie felt as though the walls had been removed, opening the lab onto boundless space from which attack could come. No matter which way he turned, his back was exposed to menace. Abnethe and her friends were getting desperate. The fact of desperation said she was vulnerable. If only he could understand her vulnerability. Where was she vulnerable? What was her weakness?

And where had she hidden herself?

"This is very strange material," Tuluk said, straightening from the bench where he had been examining the silvery rope. "Very strange."

"What's strange about it?"

"It cannot exist."

"But it's right there." McKie pointed.

"I can see that, my friend."

Tuluk extruded a single mandible, scratched thoughtfully at the right lip of his face slit. One orange eye became visible as he turned, glanced at McKie.

"Well?" McKie said.

"The only planet where this material could have been grown ceased to exist several millennia ago," Tuluk said. "There was only one place—a peculiar combination of chemistry and solar energy . . . "

"You've got to be mistaken! The stuff's right there."

"The Archer's Eye," Tuluk said. "You recall the story of the nova there?"

McKie cocked his head to one side, thought for a moment, then, "I've read about it, yes."

"The planet was called Rap," Tuluk said. "This is a length of Rapvine."

"Rapvine."

"You've heard of it?"

"I don't believe so."

"Yes, well . . . it's strange stuff. Has a relatively short life span, among its other peculiar characteristics. Another thing: the ends don't fray, even when it's cut. See?" Tuluk plucked several strands from the cut end, released them. They slapped back into position. "It was called *intrinsic attraction*. There's been considerable speculation about it. I'm now in a position to . . . "

"Short life," McKie interrupted. "How short?"

"No more than fifteen or twenty standard years under the most ideal conditions."

"But the planet . . . "

"Millennia ago, yes."

McKie shook his head to clear it. His eyes scanned the length of silvery rope suspiciously. "Obviously, somebody found how to grow the stuff someplace other than Rap."

"Perhaps. But they've managed to keep it a secret all this time."

"I don't like what I think you're thinking," McKie said."

"That's the most convoluted statement I've ever heard you make," Tuluk said. "It's meaning is clear enough, however. You believe I'm considering the possibility of time travel or . . . "

"Impossible!" McKie snapped.

"I've been engaged in a most interesting mathematical analysis of this problem," Tuluk said.

"Number games aren't going to help us."

"Your behavior is most un-McKie," Tuluk said. "Irrational. Therefore, I'll try not to burden your mind with too much of my symbolic construction. It is, however, more than a game for . . . "

"Time travel," McKie said. "Nonsense!"

"Our habitual forms of perception tend to interfere with the thinking process required for analysis of this problem," Tuluk said. "Thus, I discard these modes of thought."

"Such as?"

"If we examine the series relationships, what do we have? We have a number of point-dimensions in space. Abnethe occupies a position on a specific planet, as does the Caleban. We are given the actuality of contact between the two points, a series of events."

"So?"

"We must assume a pattern to these point-contacts."

"Why? They could be random examp—"

"Two specific planets whose movements describe coherent patterns in space. A pattern, a rhythm. Otherwise, Abnethe and her crew would be attacking with more frequency. We are confronted by a system which defies conventional analysis. It had temporal rhythm translatable into point-series rhythm. It is spatial and temporal."

McKie felt the attraction of Tuluk's argument as a force lifting his mind out of a cloud. "Some form of reflection, maybe?" he asked. "It doesn't have to be time trav—"

"This is not a fugue!" Tuluk objected. "A simple quadratic equation achieves no elliptical functions here. Ergo we are dealing with linear relationships."

"Lines," McKie whispered. "Connectives."

"Eh? Oh, yes. Linear relationships which describe moving surfaces across some form or forms of dimension. We cannot be sure of the Caleban's dimensional outlook, but our own is another matter."

McKie pursed his lips. Tuluk had moved into an extremely thin air of abstractions, but there was an inescapable elegance to the Wreave's argument.

"We can treat all forms of space as quantities determined by other quantities," Tuluk said. "We have methods for dealing with such forms when we wish to solve for unknowns."

"Ahhh," McKie murmured. "N-dimension points."

"Precisely. We first consider our data as a series of measurements which define the space between such points."

McKie nodded. "A classic n-fold extended aggregate."

"Now you begin to sound like the McKie familiar to me. An aggregate of n dimensions, to be sure. And what is time in such a problem? Time we know to be an aggregate of one dimension. But we are given, you'll recall, a number of point-dimensions in space *and* time."

McKie whistled soundlessly, admiring the Wreave's logic, then, "We either have one continuous variable in the problem or *n* continuous variables. Beautiful!"

"Just so. And by reduction through the infinity calculus, we discover we are dealing with two systems containing *n*-body properties."

"That's what you found?"

"That's what I found. It can only follow that the point-contacts of our problem have their separate existence within different frameworks of time. Ergo, Abnethe occupies another dimension time from that of the Beachball. Inescapable conclusion."

"We may not be dealing with time travel phenomena in the classic fictional sense," McKie said.

"These subtle differences the Caleban sees," McKie said. "These *connectives*, these threads . . . "

"Spiderwebs embedded in many universes," Tuluk said. "Perhaps. Let's assume individual lives spin these web threads . . . "

"Movements of matter undoubtedly spin them, too."

"Agreed. And they cross. They unite. They intersect. They combine in mysterious ways. They become tangled. Some of the web threads are stronger than others. I have experienced this entanglement, you know, when I placed the call which saved your life. I can imagine some of these threads being rewoven, combined, aligned—what have you—to recreate conditions of long past times in our dimensions. Might be a relatively simple problem for a Caleban. The Caleban might not even understand the recreation the way we do."

"I'll buy that."

"What would it take?" Tuluk mused. "A certain poignancy of experience, perhaps; something which imparts sufficient strength to the lines, threads, webs of the past that they can be picked up, manipulated to reproduce the original setting and its contents."

"We're just tossing words back and forth," McKie objected. "How could you reweave an entire planet or the space around . . . "

"Why not? What do we know of the powers involved? To a crawling insect, three of your strides may be a day's journey."

McKie felt himself being convinced in spite of native caution. "It is true," he agreed, "that the Caleban S'eye gives us the power to walk across light years."

"Such a common exploit that we no longer even wonder at the enormous energies this must require. Think what such a journey would mean to our hypothetical insect! And we may be getting the merest glimpse of Caleban powers."

"We should never have accepted the S'eye," McKie said. "We have perfectly adequate FTL ships and metabolic suspension. We should've told the Calebans to go jump in their collective connectives!"

"And deny ourselves real-time control of our universe? Not on your life, McKie. What we should have done was test the gift first. We should have probed for dangers. We were too bedazzled by it, though."

McKie lifted his left hand to scratch his eyebrow, felt a prickling of danger. It rushed up his spine, exploded in a blow against his arm. He felt pain there; something bit through to the bone. Despite the shock, he whirled, saw a Palenki arm upraised with a glittering blade. The arm came through a narrow vortal tube. Visible through the opening were a Palenki turtle head, beside it, the right side of a Pan Spechi face—purple scar on the forehead, one faceted emerald eye.

For a suspended moment McKie saw the blade begin its descent toward his face, knew it was going to strike before his shocked muscles could respond. He felt metal touch his forehead, saw the orange glow of a raygen beam stab past his face.

McKie stood frozen, locked in stillness. It was a tableau. He saw surprise on the Pan Spechi face, saw a severed Palenki arm begin its tumble to the floor still clutching a shattered metal remnant. McKie's heart was pounding as though he had been running for an hour. He felt hot wetness spread across his left temple. It ran down his cheek, along his jaw, into his collar. His arm throbbed, and he saw blood dripping from his fingertips.

The S'eye jumpdoor had winked out of existence.

Someone was beside him then, pressing a compress against his head where the metal had touched . . .

Touched?

Once more he had prepared himself for sudden death at a Palenki's hand, a descending blade. . . .

Tuluk, he saw, was bending to retrieve the metal remnant.

"That's another nick of time I've escaped," McKie said.

Surprisingly, there was no tremor in his voice.

> *Providence and Manifest Destiny are synonyms often invoked to support arguments founded in wishful thinking.*
>
> —FROM THE WREAVE COMMENTARY

IT WAS midafternoon on Central before Tuluk sent for McKie to return to the lab. Two squads of enforcers accompanied McKie. There were enforcers all around in augmented force. They watched the air, the walls, the floors. They watched each other and the space around their alternate numbers. Every sentient carried a raygen at the ready.

McKie, having spent two hours with Hanaman and five of her aides in Legal, was ready for down-to-dirt facts. Legal was moving to search every Abnethe property, to seize every record they could find—but it was all off there somewhere in the rarefied atmosphere of symbols. Perhaps something would come of it, though. They had a telocourt order, reproduced thousands of times, giving the Bureau's enforcement arm sufficient authority for search on most worlds outside the Gowachin pale. Gowachin officials were moving in their own way to cooperate—exonerating sufficient enforcers, clearing the names of appropriate police agencies.

Crime-One police on Central and elsewhere were assisting. They had provided enforcers, opened files normally not privileged to BuSab, temporarily linked their identification and modus computers to BuSab's core.

It was action, of course, but it struck McKie as too circuitous, too abstract. They needed another kind of line to Abnethe, something connected to her which could be reeled in despite any of her attempts to escape.

He felt now that he lived in a flushed-out spirit.

Nooses, blades, gnashing jumpdoors—there was no mercy in the conflict which engaged them.

Nothing he did slowed the dark hurricane that hurtled toward the sentient universe. His nerves punished him with sensations of rough, grasping inadequacy. The universe returned a glassy stare, full of his own fatigue. The Caleban's words haunted him—*self-energy . . . seeing moves . . . I am S'eye!*

Eight enforcers had crowded into the small lab with Tuluk. They were being very self effacing, apologetic—evidence that Tuluk had protested in that bitingly sarcastic way Wreaves had.

Tuluk glanced up at McKie's entrance, returned to examination of a metal sliver held in stasis by a subtron field beneath a bank of multicolored lights on his bench.

"Fascinating stuff, this steel," he said, lowering his head to permit one of his shorter and more delicate mandibular extensors to get a better grip on a probe with which he was tapping the metal.

"So it's steel," McKie said, watching the operation.

Each time Tuluk tapped the metal, it gave off a shimmering spray of purple sparks. They reminded McKie of something just at the edge of memory. He couldn't quite place the association. A shower of sparks. He shook his head.

"There's a chart down the bench," Tuluk said. "You might have a look at it while I finish here."

McKie glanced to his right, saw an oblong of chalf paper with writing on it. He moved the necessary two steps to reach the paper, picked it up, studied it. The writing was in Tuluk's neat script.

Substance: steel, an iron-base alloy. Sample contains small amts manganese, carbon, sulfur, phosphorus, and silicon, some nickel, zirconium, and tungsten with admixture chromium, molybdenum, and vanadium.

Source comparison: matches Second-Age steel used by human political subunit Japan in making of swords for Samurai Revival.

Tempering: sample hard-quenched on cutting edge only; back of sword remains soft.

Estimated length of original artifact: 1.01 meters.

Handle: linen cord wrapped over bone and lacquered. (See lacquer, bone, and cord analyses: attached.)

*   *   *

McKie glanced at the attached sheet: "Bone from a sea mammal's tooth, reworked after use on some other artifact, nature unknown but containing bronze."

The linen cord's analysis was interesting. It was of relatively recent manufacture, and it displayed the same submolecular characteristics as the earlier samples of rawhide.

The lacquer was even more interesting. It was based in an evaporative solvent which was identified as a coal-tar derivative, but the purified sap was from an ancient *Coccus lacca* insect extinct for millennia.

"You get to the part about the lacquer yet?" Tuluk asked, glancing up and twisting his face slit aside to look at McKie.

"Yes."

"What do you think of my theory now?"

"I'll believe anything that works," McKie growled.

"How are your wounds?" Tuluk asked, returning to his examination of the metal.

"I'll recover." McKie touched the omniflesh patch at his temple. "What's that you're doing now?"

"This material was fashioned by hammering," Tuluk said, not looking up. "I'm reconstructing the pattern of the blows which shaped it." He shut off the stasis field, caught the metal deftly in an extended mandible.

"Why?"

Tuluk tossed the metal onto the bench, racked the probe, faced McKie.

"Manufacture of swords such as this was a jealously guarded craft," he said. "It was handed down in families, father to son, for centuries. The irregularity of the hammer blows used by each artisan followed characteristic patterns to an extent that the maker can be identified without question by sampling that pattern. Collectors developed the method to verify authenticity. It's as definite as an eye print, more positive than any skin-print anomaly."

"So what did you find out?"

"I ran the test twice," Tuluk said, "to be certain. Despite the fact that cell revivification tests on lacquer and cord attachments show this sword to have been manufactured no more than eighty years ago, the steel was fashioned by an artisan dead more thousands of years than I care to contemplate. His name was Kanemura, and I can give you the index referents to verify this. There's no doubt who made that sword."

The interphone above Tuluk's bench chimed twice, and the face of Hanaman from Legal appeared on it. "Oh, there you are, McKie," she said, peering past Tuluk.

"What now?" McKie asked, his mind still dazed by Tuluk's statement.

"We've managed to get those injunctions," she said. "They lock up Abnethe's wealth and production on every sentient world except the Gowachin."

"But what about the warrants?" McKie demanded.

"Of course; those, too," Hanaman said. "That's why I'm calling. You asked to be notified immediately."

"Are the Gowachin cooperating?"

"They've agreed to declaration of a ConSent emergency in their jurisdiction. That allows all Federation police and BuSab agencies to act there for apprehension of suspects."

"Fine," McKie said. "Now, if you could only tell me when to find her, I think we can pick her up."

Hanaman looked from the screen with a puzzled frown. "When?"

"Yeah," McKie snarled. "When."

If you believe yourself sufficiently hungry, you will eat your own thoughts.

— A PALENKI SAYING

THE REPORT on the Palenki phylum pattern was waiting for McKie when he returned to Bildoon's office for their strategy conference. The conference had been scheduled earlier that day and postponed twice. It was almost midnight at Central, but most of the Bureau's people remained on duty, especially the enforcers. *Sta-lert* capsules had been issued along with the *angeret* by the medical staff. The enforcer squad accompanying McKie walked with that edgy abruptness this mixture of chemicals always exacted as payment.

Bildoon's chairdog had lifted a footrest and was ripple-massaging the Bureau Chief's back when McKie entered the office. Opening one jeweled eye, Bildoon said, "We got the report on the Palenki—the shell pattern you holoscanned." He closed his eye, sighed. "It's on my desk there."

McKie patted a chairdog into place, said, "I'm tired of reading. What's it say?"

"Shipsong Phylum," Bildoon said. "Positive identification. Ahhh, friend— I'm tired, too."

"So?" McKie said. He was tempted to signal for a massage from the chairdog. Watching Bildoon made it very attractive. But McKie knew this might put him to sleep. The enforcers moving restlessly around the room must be just as tired as he was. They'd be sure to resent it if he popped off for a nap.

"We got warrants and picked up the Shipsong Phylum's leader," Bildoon said. "It claims every phylum associate is accounted for."

"True?"

"We're trying to check it, but how can you be sure? They keep no written records. It's just a Palenki's word, whatever that's worth."

"Sworn by its arm, too, no doubt." McKie said.

"Of course." Bildoon stopped the chairdog massage, sat up. "It's true that phylum identification patterns can be used illegitimately."

"It takes a Palenki three or four weeks to regrow an arm," McKie said.

"What's that signify?"

"She must have several dozen Palenkis in reserve."

"She could have a million of 'em for all we know."

"Did this phylum leader resent its pattern being used by an unauthorized Palenki?"

"Not that we could see."

"It was lying," McKie said.

"How do you know?"

"According to the Gowachin juris-dictum, phylum forgery is one of the eight Palenki capital offenses. And the Gowachin should know, because they were assigned to educate the Palenkis in acceptable law when R&R brought those one-armed turtles into the ConSent fold."

"Huh!" Bildoon said. "How come Legal didn't know that? I've had them researching this from the beginning."

"Privileged legal datum," McKie said. "Interspecies courtesy and all that. You know how the Gowachin are about individual dignity, privacy, that sort of thing."

"You'll be read out of their court when they find out you spilled this," Bildoon said.

"No. They'll just appoint me prosecutor for the next ten or so capital cases in their jurisdiction. If the prosecutor accepts a case and fails to get a conviction, he's the one they execute, you know."

"And if you decline the cases?"

"Depends on the case. I could draw anything from a one-to-twenty sentence for some of them."

"One-to—you mean standard years?"

"I don't mean minutes," McKie growled.

"Then why'd you tell me?"

"I want you to let me break this phylum leader."

"Break him? How?"

"You any idea how important the mystique of the arm is to the Palenki?"

"Some idea. Why?"

"Some idea," McKie muttered. "Back in the primitive days, Palenkis made criminals eat their arms, then inhibited regrowth. Much loss of face, but even greater injury to something very deep and emotional for the Palenkis."

"You're not seriously suggesting . . . "

"Of course not!"

Bildoon shuddered. "You humans have a basically blood-thirsty nature. Sometimes I think we don't understand you."

"Where's this Palenki?" McKie asked.

"What're you going to do?"

"Question him! What'd you think?"

"After what you just said, I wasn't sure."

"Come off that, Bildoon. Hey, you!" McKie gestured to a Wreave enforcer lieutenant. "Bring the Palenki in here."

The enforcer glanced at Bildoon.

"Do as he says," Bildoon said.

The enforcer looped his mandibles uncertainly but turned and left the room, signaling half a squad to attend him.

Ten minutes later the Palenki phylum leader was herded into Bildoon's office. McKie recognized the snake-weaving pattern on the Palenki's carapace, nodded to himself: Shipsong Phylum, all right. Now that he saw it, he made the identification himself.

The Palenki's multiple legs winked to a stop in front of McKie. The turtle face turned toward him expectantly. "Will you truly make me eat my arm?" it asked.

McKie glanced accusingly at the Wreave lieutenant.

"It asked what kind of human you were," the Wreave explained.

"I'm glad you rendered such an accurate description," McKie said. He faced the Palenki. "What do *you* think?"

"I think not possible, Ser McKie. Sentients no longer permit such barbarities." The turtle mouth rendered the words without emotion, but the arm dangling to the right from its headtop juncture writhed with uncertainty.

"I may do something worse," McKie said.

"What is worse?" the Palenki asked.

"We'll see, won't we? Now! You can account for every member of your phylum, is that what you claim?"

"That is correct."

"You're lying," McKie said, voice flat.

"No!"

"What's your phylum name?" McKie asked.

"I give that only to phylum brothers!"

"Or to the Gowachin," McKie said.

"You are not Gowachin."

In a flat splatting of Gowachin grunts, McKie began describing the Palenki's probable unsavory ancestry, its evil habits, possible punishments for its behavior. He concluded with the Gowachin identification-burst, the unique emotion/word pattern by which he was required to identify himself before the Gowachin bar.

Presently the Palenki said, "You are the human they admitted to their legal concourse. I've heard about you."

"What's your phylum name?" McKie demanded.

"I am called Biredch of Ank," the Palenki said, and there was a resigned tone in its voice.

"Well, Biredch of Ank, you're a liar."

"No!" the arm writhed.

There was terror in the Palenki's manner now. It was a brand of fear McKie had been trained to recognize in his dealings through the Gowachin. He possessed the Palenki's privileged name; he could demand the arm.

"You have compounded a capital offense," McKie said.

"No! No! No!" the Palenki protested.

"What the other sentients in this room don't realize," McKie said, "is that phylum brothers accept gene surgery to affix the identity pattern on their carapaces. The index marks are grown into the shell. Isn't this true?"

The Palenki remained silent.

"It's true," McKie said. He noted that the enforcers had moved into a close ring around them, fascinated by this encounter. "You!" McKie said, snapping an arm toward the Wreave lieutenant. "Get your men on their toes!"

"Toes?"

"They should be watching every corner of this room," McKie said. "You want Abnethe to kill our witness?"

Abashed, the lieutenant turned, barked orders to his squad, but the enforcers were already at their shifty, turning, eye-darting inspection of the room. The Wreave lieutenant shook a mandible angrily, fell silent.

McKie returned his attention to the Palenki. "Now, Biredch of Ank, I'm going to ask you some special questions. I already know the answers to some of them. If I catch you in one lie, I'll consider a reversion to barbarism. Too much is at stake here. Do you understand me?"

"Ser, you cannot believe that . . . "

"Which of your phylum mates did you sell into slave service with Mliss Abnethe?" McKie demanded.

"Slaving is a capital offense," the Palenki breathed.

"I've already said you were implicated in a capital offense," McKie said. "Answer the question."

"You ask me to condemn myself?"

"How much did she pay you?" McKie asked.

"Who pay me what?"

"How much did Abnethe pay you?"

"For what?"

"For your phylum mates?"

"What phylum mates?"

"That's the question," McKie said. "I want to know how many you sold, how much you were paid, and where Abnethe took them."

"You cannot be serious!"

"I'm recording this conversation," McKie said. "I'm going to call your United Phyla Council presently, play the recording for them, and suggest they deal with you."

"They will laugh at you! What evidence could you . . . "

"I've your own guilty voice," McKie said. "We'll get a voicecorder analysis of everything you've said and submit it with the recording to your council."

"Voicecorder? What is this?"

"It's a device which analyzes the subtle pitch and intonation of the voice to determine which statements are true and which are false."

"I've never heard of such a device!"

"Damn few sentients know all the devices BuSab agents use," McKie said. "Now, I'm giving you one more chance. How many of your mates did you sell?"

"Why are you doing this to me? What is so important about Abnethe that you should ignore every interspecies courtesy, deny me the rights of . . . "

"I'm trying to save your life," McKie said.

"Now who's lying?"

"Unless we find and stop Abnethe," McKie said, "damn near every sentient in our universe excepting a few newly hatched chicks will die. And *they'll* stand almost no chance without adult protection. You've my oath on it."

"Is that a solemn oath?"

"By the *egg* of my arm," McKie said.

"Oooooo," the Palenki moaned. "You know even this of the egg?"

"I'm going to invoke your name and force you to swear by your most solemn oath in just a moment," McKie said.

"I've sworn by my arm!"

"Not by the *egg* of your arm," McKie said.

The Palenki lowered its head. The single arm writhed.

"How many did you sell?" McKie asked.

"Only forty-five," the Palenki hissed.

"*Only* forty-five?"

"That's all! I swear it!" Glistening fear oils began oozing from the Palenki's eyes. "She offered so much, and the chosen ones accepted freely. She promised unlimited eggs!"

"No breeding limit?" McKie asked. "How could that be?"

The Palenki glanced fearfully at Bildoon, who sat hunched across the desk, face grim.

"She would not explain, other than to say she'd found new worlds beyond the ConSent jurisdiction."

"Where are those worlds?" McKie asked.

"I don't know! I swear it by the egg of my arm! I don't know!"

"How was the deal set up?" McKie asked.

"There was a Pan Spechi."

"What did he do?"

"He offered my phylum the profits from twenty worlds for one hundred standard years."

"Whoooeee!" someone behind McKie said.

"When and where did this transaction take place?" McKie asked.

"In the home of my eggs only a year ago."

"A hundred years' profits," McKie muttered. "A safe deal. You and your phylum won't be around even a fraction that long if she succeeds in what she's planning."

"I didn't know. I swear I didn't know. What is she doing?"

McKie ignored the question, asked, "Have you any clue at all as to where her worlds may be?"

"I swear not," the Palenki said. "Bring your voicecorder. It will prove I speak the truth."

"There's no such thing as a voicecorder for your species," McKie said.

The Palenki stared at him a moment, then, "May your eggs rot!"

"Describe the Pan Spechi for us," McKie said.

"I withdraw my cooperation!"

"You're in too far now," McKie said, "and my deal's the only one in town."

"Deal?"

"If you cooperate, everyone in this room will forget your admission of guilt."

"More trickery," the Palenki snarled.

McKie looked at Bildoon, said, "I think we'd better call in the Palenki council and give them the full report."

"I think so," Bildoon agreed.

"Wait!" the Palenki said. "How do I know I can trust you?"

"You don't," McKie said.

"But I have no choice, is that what you say?"

"That's what I say."

"May your eggs rot if you betray me."

"Every one of them," McKie agreed. "Describe your Pan Spechi."

"He was ego-frozen," the Palenki said. "I saw the scars, and he bragged of it to show that I could trust him."

"Describe him.

"One Pan Spechi looks much like another. I don't know—but the scars were purple. I remember that."

"Did he have a name?"

"He was called Cheo."

McKie glanced at Bildoon.

"The name signifies new meanings for old ideas," Bildoon said. "It's in one of our ancient dialects. Obviously an alias."

McKie returned his attention to the Palenki. "What kind of agreement did he give you?"

"Agreement?"

"Contract . . . surety! How did he insure the payoff?"

"Oh. He appointed phylum mates of my selection as managers on the chosen worlds."

"Neat," McKie said. "Simple hiring agreements. Who could fault a deal like that or prove anything by it?"

McKie brought out his toolkit, removed the holoscan, set it for projection, and dialed the record he wanted. Presently the scan which the Wreave enforcer had captured through the jumpdoor danced in the air near the Palenki. McKie slowly turned the projection full circle, giving the Palenki a chance to see the face from every angle.

"Is that Cheo?" he asked.

"The scars present the identical pattern. It is the same one."

"That's a valid ID," McKie said, glancing at Bildoon. "Palenkis can identify random line patterns better than any other species in the universe."

"Our phylum patterns are extremely complex," the Palenki boasted.

"We know," McKie said.

"What good does this do us?" Bildoon asked.

"I wish I knew," McKie said.

No language has ever really come to grips with temporal relationships.

—A GOWACHIN OPINION

McKIE AND Tuluk were arguing about the time-regeneration theory, ignoring the squad of enforcers guarding them, although it was obvious their companions found the argument interesting.

The theory was all over the Bureau by this time—about six hours after the session with the Palenki phylum leader, Biredch of Ank. It had about as many scoffers as it had supporters.

At McKie's insistence, they had taken over one of the interspecies training rooms, had set up a datascan console, and were trying to square Tuluk's theory with the subatomic alignment phenomenon discovered in the rawhide and other organic materials captured from Abnethe.

It was Tuluk's thought that the alignment might point toward some spatial vector, giving a clue to Abnethe's hideout.

"There must be some vector of focus in our dimension," Tuluk insisted.

"Even if that's true, what good would it do us?" McKie asked. "She's not in our dimension. I say we go back to the Caleban's . . . "

"You heard Bildoon. You don't go anywhere. We leave the Beachball to enforcers while we concentrate on . . . "

"But Fanny Mae's our only source of new data!"

"Fanny . . . oh, yes; the Caleban."

Tuluk was a pacer. He had staked out an oval route near the room's instruction focus, tucked his mandibles neatly into the lower fold of his facial slit, and left only his eyes and breathing/speech orifice exposed. The flexing bifurcation which served him as legs carried him around a chairdog occupied by McKie, thence to a point near a Laclac enforcer at one extreme of the instruction focus, thence back along a mixed line of enforcers who milled around across from a float-table on which McKie was doodling, thence around behind McKie and back over the same route.

Bildoon found them there, waved the pacing Wreave to a halt. "There's a mob of newspeople outside," he growled. "I don't know where they got the story, but it's a good one. It can be described in a simple sentence: 'Calebans linked to threatened end of universe!' McKie, did you have anything to do with this?"

"Abnethe," McKie said, not looking up from a complicated chalf doodle he was completing.

"That's crazy!"

"I never said she was sane. You know how many news services, 'caster systems, and other media she controls?"

"Well . . . certainly, but . . . "

"Anybody linking *her* to this threat?"

"No, but . . . "

"You don't find that strange?"

"How could any of these people know she . . . "

"How could they *not* know about Abnethe's corner on Calebans?" McKie demanded. "Especially after talking to you!" He got up, hurled his chalf scribe at the floor, started up an aisle between rows of enforcers.

"Wait!" Bildoon snapped. "Where're you going?"

"To tell 'em about Abnethe."

"Are you out of your mind? That's all she needs to tie us up—a slander and libel case!"

"We can demand her appearance as accuser," McKie said. "Should've thought about this earlier. We're not thinking straight. Perfect defense: truth of accusation."

Bildoon caught up with him, and they moved up the aisle in a protective cordon of enforcers. Tuluk brought up the rear.

"McKie," Tuluk called, "you observe an inhibition of thought processes?"

"Wait'll I check your idea with Legal," Bildoon said. "You may have something, but . . ."

"McKie," Tuluk repeated. "do you . . ."

"Save it!" McKie snapped. He stopped, turned to Bildoon. "How much more time you figure we have?"

"Who knows?"

"Five minutes, maybe?" McKie asked.

"Longer than that, surely."

"But you don't know."

"I have enforcers at the Caleban's . . . well, they're keeping Abnethe's attacks to a min—"

"You don't want anything left to chance, right?"

"Naturally, not that I'd . . ."

"Well, I'm going to tell those newsies out there the . . ."

"McKie, that female has her tentacles into unsuspected areas of government," Bildoon cautioned. "You've no idea the things we found in . . . we've enough data to keep us busy for . . ."

"Some really important powers in with her, eh?"

"There's no doubt of it."

"And that's why it's time we took the wraps off."

"You'll create a panic!"

"We need a panic. A panic will set all sorts of sentients trying to contact her—friends, associates, enemies, lunatics. We'll be flooded with information. And we *must* develop new data!"

"What if these illegitimates"—Bildoon nodded toward the outer door— "refuse to believe you? They've heard you spout some pretty strange tales, McKie. What if they make fun of you?"

McKie hesitated. He'd never before seen such ineffectual maundering in Bildoon, a sentient noted for wit, brilliant insight, analytical adroitness. Was Bildoon one of those Abnethe had bought? Impossible! But the presence of an ego-frozen Pan Spechi in this situation must have set up enormous traumatic shock waves among the species. And Bildoon was due for ego-collapse soon. What really happened in the Pan Spechi psyche as that moment neared when they reverted to the mindless crèche-breeder form? Did it ignite an emotional frenzy of rejection? Did it inhibit thought?

In a voice pitched only for Bildoon's ears, McKie asked, "Are you ready to step down as Chief of Bureau?"

"Of course not!"

"We've known each other a long time," McKie whispered. "I think we understand and respect each other. You wouldn't be in the king seat if I'd challenged you. You know that. Now—one friend to another: Are you functioning as well as you should in this crisis?"

Angry contortions fled across Bildoon's face, were replaced by a thoughtful frown.

McKie waited. When it came, the ego-shift would send Bildoon into shambling collapse. A new personality would step forth from Bildoon's crèche, a sentient knowing everything Bildoon knew, but profoundly different in emotional outlook. Had this present shock precipitated the crisis? McKie hoped not. He was genuinely fond of Bildoon, but personal considerations had to be put aside here.

"What are you trying to do?" Bildoon muttered.

"I'm not trying to expose you to ridicule or speed up any . . . natural process," McKie said. "But our present situation is too urgent. I'll challenge you for the Bureau directorship and throw everything into an uproar, if you don't answer truthfully."

"Am I functioning well?" Bildoon mused. He shook his head. "You know the answer to that as well as I do. But you've a few lapses to explain, as well, McKie."

"Haven't we all?" McKie asked.

"That's it!" Tuluk said, stepping close to them. He glanced from Bildoon to McKie. "Forgive me, but we Wreaves have extremely acute hearing. I listened. But I must comment: The shock waves, or whatever we wish to call them, which accompanied the departure of the Calebans and left behind such death and insanity that we must buffer ourselves with *angeret* and other . . . "

"So our thought processes are mucked up," Bildoon said.

"More than that," Tuluk said. "These vast occurrences have left . . . reverberations. The news media will not laugh at McKie. All sentients grasp at answers to the strange unrest we sense. 'Periodic sentient madness,' it's called, and explanations are being sought every . . . "

"We're wasting time," McKie said.

"What would you have us do?" Bildoon asked.

"Several things," McKie said. "First, I want Steadyon quarantined, no access to the Beautybarbers of any kind, no movement on or off the planet."

"That's madness! What reason could we give?"

"When does BuSab have to give reasons?" McKie asked. "We have a *duty* to slow the processes of government."

"You know what a delicate line we walk, McKie!"

"The second thing," McKie said, unperturbed, "will be to invoke our emergency clause with the Taprisiots, get notification of every call made by every suspected friend or associate of Abnethe's."

"They'll say we're trying to take over," Bildoon breathed. "If this gets out, there'll be rebellion, physical violence. You know how jealously most sentients guard their privacy. Besides, the emergency clause wasn't designed for this; it's an identification and delay procedure within normal . . . "

"If we don't do this, we'll die, and the Taprisiots with us," McKie said. "That should be made clear to them. We need their willing cooperation."

"I don't know if I can convince them," Bildoon protested.

You'll have to try."

"But what good will these actions do us?"

"Taprisiots and Beautybarbers both operate in some way similar to the Calebans, but without as much . . . power," McKie said. "I'm convinced of that. They're all tapping the sampe power source."

"Then what happens when we shut down the Beautybarbers?"

"Abnethe won't go very long without them."

"She probably has her own platoons of Beautybarbers!"

"But Steadyon is their touchstone. Quarantine it, and I think Beautybarber activity will stop everywhere."

Bildoon looked at Tuluk.

"Taprisiots understand more than they've indicated about *connectives*," Tuluk said. "I think they will listen to you if you point out that our last remaining Caleban is about to enter ultimate discontinuity. I think they'll realize the significance of this."

"Explain the significance to me, if you don't mind. If Taprisiots can use these . . . these . . . they must know how to avoid the disaster!"

"Has anybody asked them?" McKie asked.

"Beautybarbers . . . Taprisiots . . . " Bildoon muttered. Then, "What else do you have in mind?"

"I'm going back to the Beachball," McKie said.

"We can't protect you as well there."

"I know."

"That room's too small. If the Caleban would come to . . . "

"She won't move. I've asked."

Bildoon sighed, a deeply human emotional gesture. The Pan Spechi had absorbed more than shape when they had decided to copy the human pattern. The differences, though, were profound, and McKie reminded himself of this. Humans could only see dimly into Pan Spechi thoughts. With crèche-reversion imminent for this proud sentient, what was he truly thinking? A crèche mate would come forth presently, a new personality with all the Bildoon crèche's millennial accumulation of data, all the . . .

McKie pursed his lips, inhaled, blew out.

How did Pan Spechi transfer that data from one unit to another? They were always linked, they said, ego holder and crèche mates, dormant and active, slavering flesheater and thinking aesthete. Linked? How?

"Do *you* understand connectives?" McKie asked, staring into Bildoon's faceted eyes.

Bildoon shrugged. "I see the way your thoughts wander," he said.

"Well?"

"Perhaps we Pan Spechi share this power," Bildoon said, "but if so, the sharing is entirely unconscious. I will say no more. You come close to invasion of crèche privacy."

McKie nodded. Crèche privacy was the ultimate defensive citadel of Pan Spechi existence. They would kill to defend it. No logic or reason could prevent the automatic reaction once it was ignited. Bildoon had displayed great friendship in issuing his warning.

"We're desperate," McKie said.

"I agree," Bildoon said, overtones of profound dignity in his voice. "You may proceed as you've indicated."

"Thanks," McKie said.

"It's on your head, McKie," Bildoon added.

"Provided I can keep my head," McKie said. He opened the outer door onto a clamor of newspeople. They were being held back by a harried line of enforcers, and it occurred to McKie, grasping this scene in its first impact, that all those involved in this turmoil were vulnerable from this direction.

Delusions demand reflex reactions (as though they had autonomic roots) where doubts and questioning not only aren't required, but are actively resisted.

—BuSab Manual

CROWDS WERE already forming on the morning-lighted palisades above the Beachball when McKie arrived.

News travels fast, he thought.

Extra squads of enforcers, called in anticipation of this mob scene, held back sentients trying to get to the cliff's edge, barred access to the lava shelf. Aircraft of many kinds were being blocked by a screen of BuSab fliers.

McKie, standing near the Beachball, looked up at the hectic activity. The morning wind carried a fine mist of sea spray against his cheek. He had taken a jumpdoor to Furuneo's headquarters, left instructions there, and used a Bureau flier for the short trip to the lava shelf.

The Beachball's port remained open, he noted. Mixed squads of enforcers milled about in a confused pattern around the Ball, alert to every quarter of their surroundings. Picked enforcers watched through the port where other enforcers shared this uneasy guardianship.

It was quite early in Cordiality's day here, but real-time relationships confused such arbitrary time systems, McKie thought. It was night at Central's headquarters, evening at the Taprisiot council building where Bildoon must still be arguing . . . and only Immutable Space knew what time it was wherever Abnethe had her base of operations.

Later than any of them think, no doubt, McKie told himself.

He shouldered his way through the enforcers, got a boost up through the port, and surveyed the familiar purple gloom inside the Beachball. It was noticeably warmer in here out of the wind and spray, but not as warm as McKie remembered the place.

"Has the Caleban been talking?" McKie asked a Laclac, one of the enforcers guarding the interior.

"I don't call it talking, but the answer is not recently."

"Fanny Mae," McKie said.

Silence.

"You still there, Fanny Mae?" McKie asked.

"McKie? You invoke presence, McKie?"

McKie felt he had registered the words on his eyeballs and relayed them to his hearing centers. They definitely were weaker than he remembered.

"How many floggings has she undergone in the past day?" McKie asked the Laclac.

"Local day?" the Laclac asked.

"What difference does it make?"

"I presumed you were asking for accurate data." The Laclac sounded offended.

"I'm trying to find out if she's been under attack recently," McKie said. "She sounds weaker than when I was here before." He stared toward the giant spoon where the Caleban maintained her *unpresence*.

"Attacks have been intermittent and sporadic but not very successful," the Laclac said. "We've collected more whips and Palenki arms, although I understand they're not being successfully transmitted to the lab."

"McKie invokes presence of Caleban self called Fanny Mae?" the Caleban asked.

"I greet you, Fanny Mae," McKie said.

"You possess new connective entanglements, McKie," the Caleban said, "but *the* pattern of you retains recognition. I greet you, McKie."

"Does your contract with Abnethe still lead us all toward ultimate discontinuity?" McKie asked.

"Intensity of nearness," the Caleban said. "My employer wishes speech with you."

"Abnethe? She wants to talk to me?"

"Correct."

"She could've called me anytime," McKie said.

"Abnethe conveys request through self of me," the Caleban said. "She asks relay among anticipated connective. This connective you perceive under label of 'now.' You hang this, McKie?"

"I hang it," McKie growled. "So let her talk."

"Abnethe requires you send companions from presence."

"Alone?" McKie demanded. "What makes her think I'd do such a thing?" It was getting hotter in the Beachball. He wiped perspiration from his upper lip.

"Abnethe speaks of sentient motive called *curiosity.*"

"I've my own conditions for such a conference," McKie said. "Tell her I won't agree unless I'm assured she'll make no attack on you or on me during our talk."

"I give such assurance."

"*You* give it?"

"Probability in Abnethe assurance appears . . . incomplete. Approximate descriptive. Assurance by self runs intense . . . strong. Direct? Perhaps."

"Why do you give this assurance?"

"Employer Abnethe indicates strong desire for talk. Contract covers such . . . catering? Very close term. Catering."

"You guarantee our safety, is that it?"

"Intense assurance, no more."

"No attack during our talk," McKie insisted.

"Thus propels connective," the Caleban said.

Behind McKie, the Laclac enforcer grunted, said, "Do you understand that gibberish?"

"Take your squad and get out of here," McKie said.

"Ser, my orders . . . "

"Deface your orders! I'm acting under the cartouche of Saboteur Extraordinary with full discretion from the Bureau Chief himself! Get out!"

"Ser," the Laclac said, "during the most recent flogging nine enforcers went mad here despite ingestion of *angeret* and various other chemicals we'd believed would protect us. I cannot be responsible for . . . "

"You'll be responsible for a tide station on the nearest desert planet if you don't obey me at once," McKie said. "I will see you packed off to *boredom* after an official trial by . . . "

"I will not heed your threats, ser," the Laclac said. "However, I will consult Bildoon himself if you so order."

"Consult, then, and hurry it! There's a Taprisiot outside."

"Very well." The Lalac saluted, crawled out the port. His conpanions in the Beachball continued their restive watch, with occasional worried glances at McKie.

They were brave sentients, all of them, McKie thought, to continue this duty in the face of unknown peril. Even the Laclac demonstrated extraordinary courage—with his perversity. Only obeying orders though; no doubt of that.

Although it galled him, McKie waited.

An odd thought struck him: If all sentients died, all power stations of their universe would grind to a halt. It gave him a strange feeling, this contemplation of an end to mechanical things and commercial enterprise.

Green, growing things would take over—trees with golden light in their branches. And the dull sounds of nameless metal devices, things of plastic and glass, would grow muffled with no ears to hear them.

Chairdogs would die, unfed. Protein vats would fail, decompose.

He thought of his own flesh decomposing.

The whole fleshly universe decomposing.

It would be over in an instant, the way universe measured time.

A wild pulse lost on some breeze.

Presently the Laclac reappeared in the port, said, "Ser, I am instructed to obey your orders, but to remain outside in visual contact with you, returning to this place at the first sign of trouble."

"If that's the best we can do, that's it," McKie said. "Get moving."

In a minute McKie found himself alone with the Caleban. The sense that every *place* in this room lay behind him persisted. His spine itched. He felt increasingly that he was taking too much of a risk.

But there was the desperation of their position.

"Where's Abnethe?" McKie asked. "I thought she wanted to talk."

A jumpdoor opened abruptly to the left of the Caleban's spoon. Abnethe's head and shoulders appeared in it, all slightly pink-hazed by the slowdown of all energy within that portal. The light was sufficient, though, that McKie could see subtle changes in Abnethe's appearance. He was gratified to note a harried look to her. Wisps of hair escaped her tight coiffure. Bloodshot veins could be detected in her eyes. There were wrinkles in her forehead.

She needed her Beautybarbers.

"Are you ready to give yourself up?" McKie asked.

"That's a stupid question," she said. "You're alone at my command."

"Not quite alone," McKie said, "There are . . . " He broke off at the sly smile which formed on Abnethe's lips.

"You'll note that Fanny Mae has closed the exterior port of her residence," Abnethe said.

McKie shot a glance to his left, saw that the port was closed. Treachery?

"Fanny Mae!" he called. "You assured me . . . "

"No attack," the Caleban said. "Privacy."

McKie imagined the consternation in the enforcers outside right now. But they would never be able to break into the Beachball. He saved his protests, swallowed. The room remained utterly still.

"Privacy, then," he agreed.

"That's better," Abnethe said. "We must reach agreement, McKie. You're becoming somewhat of a nuisance."

"Oh, more than a nuisance, certainly?"

"Perhaps."

"Your Palenki, the one who was going to chop me up—I found him a nuisance,

too. Maybe even more than a nuisance. Now that I think about it, I recall that I
suffered.''

Abnethe shuddered.

''By the way,'' McKie said, ''we know where you are.''

''You lie!''

''Not really. You see, you're not where you think you are, Mliss. You think
you've gone back in time. You haven't.''

''You lie, I say!''

''I have it pretty well figured out,'' McKie said. ''The place where you are was
constructed from your *connectives*—your memories, dreams, wishes . . . perhaps
even from things you expressly described.''

''What nonsense!'' She sounded worried.

''You asked for a place that would be safe from the apocalypse,'' McKie said.
''Fanny Mae warned you about ultimate discontinuity, of course. She probably
demonstrated some of her powers, showed you various places available to you along
the connectives of you and your associates. That's when you got your big idea.''

''You're guessing,'' Abnethe said. Her face was grim.

McKie smiled.

''You could stand a little session with your Beautybarbers,'' he said. ''You're
looking a bit seedy, Mliss.''

She scowled.

''Are they refusing to work for you?'' McKie persisted.

''They'll come around!'' she snapped.

''When?''

''When they see they've no alternative!''

''Perhaps.''

''We're wasting time, McKie.''

''That's true. What was it you wanted to say to me?''

''We must make an agreement, McKie; just the two of us.''

''You'll marry me, is that it?''

''That's your price?'' She was obviously surprised.

''I'm not sure,'' McKie said. ''What about Cheo?''

''Cheo begins to bore me.''

''That's what worries *me*,'' McKie said. ''I ask myself how long it would be
until *I* bored you?''

''I realize you're not being sincere,'' she said, ''that you're stalling. I think,
however, we can reach agreement.''

''What makes you think that?''''

''Fanny Mae suggested it,'' she said

McKie peered at the shimmering *unpresence* of the Caleban. ''Fanny Mae
suggested it?'' he murmured.

And he thought, *Fanny Mae determines her own brand of reality from what she
sees of these mysterious connectives: a special perception tailored to her particular energy consumption.*

Sweat dripped from his forehead. He rocked forward, sensing that he stood on
the brink of a revelation.

''Do you still love me, Fanny Mae?'' he asked.

Abnethe's eyes went wide with surprise. ''Whaaat?''

''Affinity awareness,'' the Caleban said. ''Love equates with this coherence I
possess of you, McKie.''

"How do you savor my single-track existence?" McKie asked.

"Intense affinity," the Caleban said. "Product of sincerity of attempts at communication. I-self-Caleban love you human-person, McKie."

Abnethe glared at McKie. "I came here to discuss a mutual problem, McKie," she flared. "I did not anticipate standing aside for a gibberish session between you and this stupid Caleban!"

"Self not in stupor," the Caleban said.

"McKie," Abnethe said, voice low, "I came to suggest a proposition of mutual benefit. Join me. I don't care what capacity you choose, the rewards will be more than you could possibly . . . "

"You don't even suspect what's happened to you," McKie said. "That's the strange thing."

"Damn you! I could make an emperor out of you!"

"Don't you realize where Fanny Mae has hidden you?" McKie asked. "Don't you recognize this *safe* . . . "

"Mliss!"

It was an angry voice from somewhere behind Abnethe, but the speaker was not visible to McKie.

"Is that you, Cheo?" McKie called. "Do you know where you are, Cheo? A Pan Spechi must suspect the truth."

A hand came into view, yanked Abnethe aside. The ego-frozen Pan Spechi took her place in the jumpdoor opening.

"You're much too clever, McKie," Cheo said.

"How dare you, Cheo!" Abnethe screamed.

Cheo swirled, swung an arm. There was the sound of flesh hitting flesh, a stifled scream, another blow. Cheo bent away from the opening, came back into view.

"You've been in that place before, haven't you, Cheo?" McKie asked. "Weren't you a mewling, empty-minded female in the crèche at one period of your existence?"

"Much too clever," Cheo snarled.

"You'll have to kill her, you know," McKie said. "If you don't, it'll all be for nothing. She'll digest you. She'll take over your ego. She'll *be* you."

"I didn't know this happened with humans," Cheo said.

"Oh, it happens," McKie said. "That's her world, isn't it, Cheo?"

"Her world," Cheo agreed, "but you're mistaken about one thing, McKie. I can control Mliss. So it's my world, isn't it? And another thing: I can control you!"

The jumpdoor's vortal tube suddenly grew smaller, darted at McKie.

McKie dodged aside, shouted, "Fanny Mae! You promised!"

"New connectives," the Caleban said.

McKie executed a sprawling dive across the room as the jumpdoor appeared beside him. It nipped into existence and out like a ravening mouth, narrowly missing McKie with each attack. He twisted, leaped—dodged panting through the Beachball's purple gloom, finally rolled under the giant spoon, peered right and left. He shuddered. He hadn't realized a jumpdoor could be moved around that rapidly.

"Fanny Mae," he rasped, "shut the S'eye, close it down or whatever you do. You promised—no attack!"

No response.

McKie glimpsed an edge of the vortal tube hovering just beyond the spoon bowl.

"McKie!"

It was Cheo's voice.

"They'll call you long distance in a minute, McKie," Cheo called. "When they do, I'll have you."

McKie stilled a fit of trembling.

They *would* call him! Bildoon had probably summoned a Taprisiot already. They'd be worrying about him—the port closed. And he'd be helpless in the grip of the call.

"Fanny Mae!" McKie hissed. "Close that damn S'eye!"

The vortal tube glittered, shifted up and around to come at him from the side. Cursing, McKie rolled into a ball, kicked backward and over onto his knees, leaped to his feet and flung himself across the spoon handle, scrambled back under it.

The searching tube moved away.

There came a low, crackling sound, like thunder to McKie. He glanced right, left, back over his head. There was no sign of the deadly opening.

Abruptly, something snapped sharply above the spoon bowl. A shower of green sparks cascaded around McKie where he lay beneath it. He slid to the side, brought up his raygen. A Palenki arm and whip had been thrust through the jumpdoor's opening. It was raised to deliver another blow against the Caleban.

McKie sprayed the raygen's beam across the arm as the whip moved. Arm and whip grazed the far edge of the spoon, brought another shower of sparks.

The jumpdoor's opening winked out of existence.

McKie crouched, the afterimage of the sparks still dancing on his retinas. Now—now he recalled what he'd been trying to remember since watching Tuluk's experiment with the steel!

"S'eye removed."

Fanny Mae's voice fell on McKie's forehead, seemed to seep inward to his speech centers. Hunter of Devils! She sounded weak!

Slowly McKie lifted himself to his feet. The Palenki arm and whip lay on the floor where they had fallen, but he ignored them.

Shower of sparks!

McKie felt strange emotions washing through him, around him. He felt happily angry, satiated with frustrations, words and phrases tumbling through his mind like pinwheels.

That perverted offspring of an indecent union!

Shower of sparks! Shower of sparks!

He knew he had to hold that thought and his sanity no matter what the surging waves of emotion from Fanny Mae did to him.

Shower of . . . shower . . .

Was Fanny Mae dying?

"Fanny Mae?"

The Caleban remained silent, but the emotional onslaught eased.

McKie knew there was something he had to remember. It concerned Tuluk. He had to tell Tuluk.

Shower of sparks!

He had it then: *The pattern that identifies the maker! A shower of sparks.*

He felt he'd been running for hours, that his nerves were bruised and tangled. His mind was a bowl of jelly. Thoughts quivered through it. His brain was going to melt and run away like a stream of colored liquid. It would spray out of him— shower on . . .

Shower of . . . of . . . SPARKS!

Louder this time, he called, "Fanny Mae?"

A peculiar silence rippled through the Beachball. It was an emotionless silence, something shut off, removed. It made McKie's skin prickle.

"Answer me, Fanny Mae," he said.

"S'eye absents itself," the Caleban said.

McKie felt shame, a deep and possessive sense of guilt. It flowed over him and through him, filled every cell. Dirty, muddy, sinful, shameful . . .

He shook his head. Why should he feel guilt?

Ahhh. Realization came over him. The emotion came from outside him. It was Fanny Mae!

"Fanny Mae," he said, "I understand you could not prevent that attack. I don't blame you. I understand."

"Surprise connectives," the Caleban said. "You overstand."

"I understand."

"Overstand? Term for intensity of knowledge? Realization!"

"Realization, yes."

Calmness returned to McKie, but it was the calmness of something being withdrawn.

Again he reminded himself that he had a vital message for Tuluk. *Shower of sparks*. But first he had to be certain that that mad Pan Spechi wasn't going to return momentarily.

"Fanny Mae," he said, "can you prevent them from using the S'eye?"

"Obstructive, not preventive," the Caleban said.

"You mean you can slow them down?"

"Explain slow."

"Oh, no," McKie moaned. He cast around his mind for a Caleban way to phrase his question. How would Fanny Mae say it?

"Will there be . . . " He shook his head. "The next attack, will it be on a short connective or long one?"

"Attack series breaks here," the Caleban said. "You inquire of duration by your time sense. I overstand this. Long line across attack nodes, this equates with more intense duration for your time sense."

"Intense duration," McKie muttered. "Yeah."

Shower of sparks, he reminded himself. *Shower of sparks*.

"You signify employment of S'eye by Cheo," the Caleban said. "Spacing extends at this place. Cheo goes farther down your track. I overstand intensely for McKie. Yes?"

Farther down my track, McKie thought. He gulped as realization hit him. What had Fanny Mae said earlier? "See us to the door! I am S'eye!"

He breathed softly, lest sudden motion dislodge this brutal clarity of understanding.

Overstanding!

He thought of energy requirements. Enormous! *"I am S'eye!"* And *"Self-energy—by being stellar mass!"* To do what they did in this dimension, Calebans required the energy of a stellar mass. *She inhaled the whip!* She'd said it herself: they sought energy here. The Calebans fed in this dimension! In other dimensions, too, no doubt.

McKie considered the refined discrimination Fanny Mae must possess even to attempt communication with him. It would be as though he immersed his mouth in water and tried to talk to a single microorganism there!

I should have understood, he thought, *when Tuluk said something about realizing where he lived.*

"We have to go right back to the beginning," he said.

"Many beginnings exist for each entity," the Caleban said.

McKie sighed.

Sighing, he was seized by a Taprisiot contact. It was Bildoon.

"I'm glad you waited," McKie said, cutting off Bildoon's first anxious inquiries. "Here's what I want you to . . . "

"McKie, what's going on there?" Bildoon insisted. "There are dead enforcers all around you, madmen, a riot . . . "

"I seem to be immune," McKie said, "or else Fanny Mae is protecting me some way. Now, listen to me. We don't have much time. Get Tuluk. He has a device for identifying the patterns which originate in the stress of creation. He's to bring that device here—right here to the Beachball. And fast."

Taken in isolated tandem, Government and Justice are mutually exclusive. There must be a third force at work for any society to achieve both government and justice. This is why the Bureau of Sabotage sometimes is called "The Third Force."

—FROM AN ELEMENTARY TEXTBOOK

IN THE hushed stillness within the Beachball, McKie leaned against a curved wall, sipped ice water from a thermocup. He kept his eyes active, though, watching Tuluk set up the needed instruments.

"What's to prevent our being attacked while we work?" Tuluk asked. He rolled a glowing loop on a squat stand into position near the Caleban's *unpresence*. "You should've let Bildoon send in some guards."

"Like those ones who were foaming at the mouth outside?"

"There's a fresh crew outside there now!"

Tuluk did something which made the glowing loop double its diameter.

"They'd only get in the way," McKie said. "Besides, Fanny Mae says the spacing isn't right for Abnethe." He sipped ice water. The room had achieved something approaching sauna temperature, but without the humidity.

"Spacing," Tuluk said. "Is that why Abnethe keeps missing you?" He produced a black wand from his instrument case. The wand was about a meter long. He adjusted a knob on the wand's handle, and the glowing loop contracted. The squat stand beneath the glowing loop began to hum—an itch-producing middle C.

"They miss me because I have a loving protector," McKie said. "It isn't every sentient who can say a Caleban loves him."

"What is that you're drinking?" Tuluk asked. "Is that one of your mind disrupters?"

"You're very funny," McKie said. "How much longer are you going to be fiddling with that gear?"

"I am not fiddling. Don't you realize this isn't portable equipment? It must be adjusted."

"So adjust."

"The high temperature in here complicates my readings," Tuluk complained. "Why can't we have the port open?"

"For the same reason I didn't let any guards in here. I'll take my chances without having them complicated by a mob of insane sentients getting in my way."

"But must it be this hot?"

"Can't be helped," McKie said. "Fanny Mae and I have been talking, working things out."

"Talking?"

"Hot air," McKie said.

"Ahhh, you make a joke."

"It can happen to anyone," McKie said. "I keep asking myself if what we see as a star is all of a Caleban or just part of one. I opt for part." He drank deeply of the ice water, discovered there was no more ice in it. Tuluk was right. It was damnably hot in here.

"That's a strange theory," Tuluk said. He silenced the humming of his instrument case. In the abrupt stillness something else in the case could be heard ticking. It was not a peaceful sound. It had the feeling of a timing device affixed to a bomb. It counted moments in a deadly race.

McKie felt each counted moment accumulate like a congealing bubble. It expanded . . . expanded—and broke! Each instant was death lashing at him. Tuluk with his strange wand was a magician, but he had reversed the ancient process. He was turning golden instants into deadly lead. His shape was wrong, too. He had no haunches. The tubular Wreave shape annoyed McKie. Wreaves moved too slowly.

The damnable ticking!

The Caleban's Beachball might be the last house in the universe, the last container for sentient life. And it contained no bed where a sentient might die decently.

Wreaves didn't sleep in beds, of course. They took their rest in slanted supports and were buried upright.

Tuluk had gray skin.

Lead.

If all things ended now, McKie wondered, which of them would be the last to go? Whose breath would be the final one?

McKie breathed the echoes of all his fears. There was too much hanging on each counted instant here.

No more melodies, no more laughter, no more children racing in play. . . .

"There," Tuluk said.

"You ready?" McKie asked.

"I will be ready presently. Why does the Caleban not speak?"

"Because I asked her to save her strength."

"What does she say of your theory?"

"She thinks I have *achieved truth*."

Tuluk took a small helix from his instrument case, inserted it into a receptacle at the base of the glowing ring.

"Come on, come on," McKie jittered.

"Your urgings will not reduce the necessary time for this task," Tuluk said.

"For example, I am hungry. I came without stopping to break my daily fast. This does not press me to speed which might produce errors, nor does it arouse me to complain."

"Aren't you complaining?" McKie asked. "You want some of my water?"

"I had water two days ago," Tuluk said.

"And we wouldn't want to rush you into another drink."

"I do not understand what pattern you hope to identify," Tuluk said. "We have no records of artisans for a proper comparison of . . ."

"This is something God made," McKie said."

"You should not jest about deities," Tuluk said.

"Are you a believer or just playing safe?" McKie asked.

"I was chiding you for an act which might offend some sentients," Tuluk said. "We have a hard enough time bridging the sentient barriers without raising religious issues."

"Well, we've been spying on God—or whatever—for a long time," McKie said. "That's why we're going to get a spectroscopic record of this. How much longer you going to be at this fiddling?"

"Patience, patience," Tuluk muttered. He reactivated the wand, waved it near the glowing ring. Again the instrument began humming, a higher note this time. It grated on McKie's nerves. He felt it in his teeth and along the skin of his shoulders. It itched inside him where he couldn't scratch.

"Damn this heat!" Tuluk said. "Why will you not have the Caleban open a door to the outside?"

"I told you why."

"Well, it doesn't make this task any easier!"

"You know," McKie said, "when you called me and saved my skin from that Palenki chopper—the first time, remember? Right afterward you said you'd been tangled with Fanny Mae, and you said a very odd thing."

"Oh?" Tuluk had extended a small mandible and was making delicate adjustments to a knob on the case below the glowing ring.

"You said something about not knowing that was where you lived. Remember that?"

"I will never forget it." Tuluk bent his tubular body across the glowing ring, stared back through it while passing the wand back and forth in front of the ring's opening.

"Where was that?" McKie asked.

"Where was what?"

"Where you lived!"

"That? There are no words to describe it."

"Try."

Tuluk straightened, glanced at McKie. "It was a bit like being a mote in a vast sea . . . and experiencing the warmth, the friendship of a benign giant."

"That giant—the Caleban?"

"Of course."

"That's what I thought."

"I will not answer for inaccuracies in this device," Tuluk said. "But I don't believe I can adjust it any closer. Given a few days, some shielding—there's an odd radiation pattern from that wall behind you—and projection dampers, I might, I just *might* achieve a fair degree of accuracy. Now? I cannot be responsible."

"And you'll be able to get a spectroscopic record?"

"Oh, yes."

"Then maybe we're in time," McKie said.

"For what?"

"For the right spacing."

"Ahhh, you mean the flogging and the subsequent shower of sparks?"

"That's what I mean."

"You could not . . . flog her yourself, gently?"

"Fanny Mae says that wouldn't work. It has to be done with violence . . . and the intent to *create intensity of anti-love* . . . or it won't work."

"Oh. How odd. You know, McKie, I believe I could use some of your water, after all. It's the heat in here."

> *Any conversation is a unique jazz performance. Some are more pleasing to the ears, but that is not necessarily a measure of their importance.*
>
> —LACLAC COMMENTARY

THERE WAS a popping sound, a stopper being pulled from a bottle. Air pressure dropped slightly in the Beachball, and McKie experienced the panic notion that Abnethe had somehow opened them onto a vacuum which would rain away their air and kill them. The physicists said this couldn't be done, that the gas flow, impeded by the adjustment barrier within the jumpdoor, would block the opening with its own collision breakdown. McKie suspected they pretended to know about S'eye phenomena.

He missed the jumpdoor's vortal tube at first. Its plane was horizontal and directly above the Caleban's spoon bowl.

A Palenki arm and whip shot through the opening, delivered a lashing blow to the area occupied by the Caleban's *unpresence*. Green sparks showered the air.

Tuluk, bending over his instruments, muttered excitedly.

The Palenki arm drew back, hesitated.

"Again! Again!"

The voice through the jumpdoor was unmistakably that of Cheo.

The Palenki delivered another blow and another.

McKie lifted his raygen, dividing his attention between Tuluk and that punishing whip. Did Tuluk have his readings? No telling how much more of this the Caleban could survive.

Again the whip lashed. Green sparks glimmered and fell.

"Tuluk, do you have enough data?" McKie demanded.

Arm and whip jerked back through the jumpdoor.

A curious silence settled over the room.

"Tuluk?" McKie hissed.

"I believe I have it," Tuluk said. "It's a good recording. I will not vouch for comparison and identification, however."

McKie grew aware that the room was not really silent. The thrumming of

Tuluk's instruments formed a background for a murmur of voices coming through the jumpdoor.

"Abnethe?" McKie called.

The opening tipped, gave him a three-quarter view of Abnethe's face. There was a purple bruise from her left temple down across her cheek. A silver noose held her throat, its end firmly in the grip of a Pan Spechi hand.

Abnethe, McKie saw, was trying to control a rage which threatened to burst her veins. Her face was alternately pale and flushed. She held her mouth tight, lips in a thin line. Compressed violence radiated from every pore.

She saw McKie. "See what you've done?" she shrieked.

McKie pushed himself away from the wall, fascinated. He approached the jumpdoor. "What *I* did? That looks more like Cheo's handiwork."

"It's all your fault!"

"Oh? That was clever of me."

"I tried to be reasonable," she rasped. "I tried to help you, save you. But no! You treated me like a criminal. This is the thanks I got from you."

She gestured at the noose around her throat.

"WHAT DID I DO TO DESERVE THIS?"

"Cheo!" McKie called. "What'd she do?"

Cheo's voice came from a point beyond the arm gripping the noose. "Tell him, Mliss."

Tuluk, who had been ignoring the exchange, busying himself with his instruments, turned to McKie. "Remarkable," he said. "Truly remarkable."

"Tell him!" Cheo roared as Abnethe held a stubborn silence.

Both Abnethe and Tuluk began talking at once. It came through to McKie as a mixed jumble of noises: "Youinterstellferederhydrowithgenlawnmassfulexecufrom . . . ''

"Shut up!" McKie shouted.

Abnethe jerked back, shocked to silence, but Tuluk went right on: " . . . and that makes it quite certain there's no mistaking the spectral absorption pattern. It's a star, all right. Nothing else would give us the same picture."

"But which star?" McKie asked.

"Ahhh, that *is* the question," Tuluk said.

Cheo pushed Abnethe aside, took her place in the jumpdoor. He glanced at Tuluk, at the instruments. "What's all this, McKie? Another way to interfere with our Palenkis? Or did you come back for a new game of ring-around-your-neck?"

"We've discovered something you might like to know," McKie said.

"What could *you* discover that would possibly interest me?"

"Tell him, Tuluk," McKie said.

"Fanny Mae exists somehow in intimate association with a stellar mass," Tuluk said. "She may even *be* a stellar mass—at least as far as our dimension is concerned."

"Not dimension," the Caleban said. "Wave."

Her voice barely reached McKie's awareness, but the words were accompanied by a rolling wave of misery that rocked him and set Tuluk to shuddering.

"Wha-wha-what w-w-was th-th-that?" Tuluk managed.

"Easy, easy," McKie cautioned. He saw that Cheo had not been touched by that wave of emotion. At least, the Pan Spechi remained impassive.

"We'll have Fanny Mae identified shortly," McKie said.

"Identity," the Caleban said, her communication coming through with more strength but with an icy withdrawal of emotion. "Identity refers to unique self-understanding quality as it deals with self-label, self-abode and self-mani-festations. You not me hang yet, McKie. You hang term yet? Self-I overstand your time node."

"Hang?" Cheo asked, jerking the noose around Abnethe's neck.

"A simple old-fashioned idiom," McKie said. "I imagine Mliss gets the hang of it."

"What're you talking about?" Cheo asked.

Tuluk took the question as having been directed to him. "In some way," he said, "Calebans manifest themselves in our universe as stars. Every star has a pulse, a certain unique rhythm, a never-duplicated identity. We have Fanny Mae's pattern recorded now. We're going to run a tracer on that pattern and try to identify her as a star."

"A stupid theory like that is supposed to interest *me?*" Cheo demanded.

"It had better interest you," McKie said. "It's more than a theory now. You think you're sitting in a safe hidey-hole. All you have to do is eliminate Fanny Mae, that's supposed to eliminate our universe and leave you out there the only sentients left at all? Is that it? Ohhh, are you ever wrong."

"Calebans don't lie!" Cheo snarled.

"But I think they can make mistakes," McKie said.

"Proliferation of single-tracks," the Caleban said.

McKie shuddered at the icy wave which accompanied the words. "If we discontinue, will Abnethe and her friends still exist?" he asked.

"Different patterns with short limit on extended connectives," the Caleban said.

McKie felt the icy wave invade his stomach. He saw that Tuluk was trembling, facial slit opening and closing.

"That was plain enough, wasn't it?" McKie asked. "You'll change somehow, and you won't live very long after us."

"No branchings," the Caleban said.

"No offspring," McKie translated.

"This is a trick!" Cheo snarled. "She's lying!"

"Calebans don't lie," McKie reminded him.

"But they can make mistakes!"

"The right kind of mistake could ruin everything for you," McKie said.

"I'll take my chances," Cheo said. "And you can take . . . "

The jumpdoor winked out of existence.

"S'eye alignment difficult," the Caleban said. "You hang difficult? More intense energy requirement reference. You hang?"

"I understand," McKie said. "I hang." He mopped his forehead with a sleeve.

Tuluk extended his long mandible, waved it agitatedly. "Cold," he said. "Cold-cold-cold-cold."

"I think she's holding on by a thin thread," McKie said.

Tuluk's torso rippled as he inhaled a deep breath into his outer trio of lungs. "Shall we take our records back to the lab?" he asked.

"A stellar mass," McKie muttered. "Imagine it. And all we see here is this . . . this bit of nothing."

"Not put something here," the Caleban said. "Self-I put something here and uncreate you. McKie discontinues in presence of I-self."

"Do you hang that, Tuluk?" McKie asked.

"Hang? Oh, yes. She seems to be saying that she can't make herself visible to us because that'd kill us."

"That's the way I read it," McKie said. "Let's get back and start that comparison search."

"You expend substance without purpose," the Caleban said.

"What now?" McKie asked.

"Flogging approaches, and I-self discontinue," the Caleban said.

McKie put down a fit of trembling. "How far away, Fanny Mae?"

"Time reference by single-track difficult, McKie. Your term: soon."

"Right away?" McKie asked and he held his breath.

"Ask you of intensity immediate?" the Caleban inquired.

"Probably," McKie whispered.

"Probability," the Caleban said. "Energy necessity of self-I extends alignment. Flogging not . . . immediate."

"Soon, but not right away," Tuluk said.

"She's telling us she can take one more flogging and that's the last one," McKie said. "Let's move. Fanny Mae, is there a jumpdoor available to us?"

"Available, McKie. Go with love."

One more flogging, McKie thought as he helped Tuluk gather up the instruments. But why was a flogging so deadly to the Caleban? Why a flogging, when other energy forms apparently didn't touch them?

The most common use of abstraction is to conceal contradictions. It must be noted that the abstracting process has been demonstrated to be infinite.

—CULTURE LAG, AN UNPUBLISHED WORK
BY JORJ X. MCKIE

AT SOME indeterminate moment, and that soon, the Caleban was going to be lashed by a whip, and it would die. The half-mad possibility was about to become apocalyptic reality, and their sentient universe would end.

McKie stood disconsolately in Tuluk's personal lab, intensely aware of the mob of enforcer guards around them.

"Go with love."

The computer console above Tuluk's position at the bench flickered and chittered.

Even if they identified Fanny Mae's star, what could they do with that new knowledge? McKie asked himself. Cheo was going to win. They couldn't stop him.

"Is it possible," Tuluk asked, "that the Calebans created this universe? Is this their 'garden patch'? I keep remembering Fanny Mae saying it would *uncreate* us to be in her presence."

He leaned against his bench, mandibles withdrawn, face slit open just enough to permit him to speak.

"Why's the damn computer taking so long?" McKie demanded.

"The pulse problem's very complicated, McKie. The comparison required special programming. You haven't answered my question.''

"I don't have an answer! I hope those numbies we left in the Beachball know what to do.''

"They'll do what you told them to do,'' Tuluk chided. "You're a strange sentient, McKie. I'm told you've been married more than fifty times. Is it a breach of good manners to discuss this?''

"I never found a woman who could put up with a Saboteur Extraordinary,'' McKie muttered. "We're hard creatures to love.''

"Yet the Caleban loves you.''

"She doesn't know what we mean by love!'' He shook his head. "I should've stayed at the Beachball.''

"Our people will interpose their own bodies between the Caleban and any attacks,'' Tuluk said. "Would you call that love?''

"That's self-preservation,'' McKie snarled.

"It's a Wreave belief that all love is a form of self-preservation,'' Tuluk said. "Perhaps this is what our Caleban understands.''

"Hah!''

"It's a probability, McKie, that you've never been overly concerned about self-preservation, thus have never really loved.''

"Look! Would you stop trying to distract me with your babbling nonsense?''

"Patience, McKie. Patience.''

"Patience, he says!''

McKie jerked himself into motion, paced the length of the lab, the guardian enforcers dodging out of his way. He returned to Tuluk, stooped. "What do stars feed on?''

"Stars? Stars don't feed.''

"She inhales something here, and she feeds here,'' McKie muttered. He nodded. "Hydrogen.''

"What's this?''

"Hydrogen,'' McKie repeated. "If we opened a big enough jumpdoor. . . . Where's Bildoon?''

"He's conferring with the ConSent representative over our high-handed actions in quarantining the Beautybarbers. It's also a distinct possibility that our dealings with the Taprisiots have leaked out. Governments do not like this sort of action, McKie. Bildoon is trying to save your skin and his own.''

"But there's plenty of hydrogen,'' McKie said.

"What is this of jumpdoors and hydrogen?''

"Feed a cold and starve a fever,'' McKie said.

"You are not making sense, McKie! Did you take your *angeret* and normalizers?''

"I took 'em!''

The computer's readout chamber made a chewing sound, spewed forth a quadruple line of glowing characters which danced in the chamber and resolved themselves into legible arrangements. McKie read the message.

"Thyone,'' Tuluk said, reading over his shoulder.

"A star in the Pleiades,'' McKie said.

"We call it Drnlle,'' Tuluk said. "See the Wreave characters in the third row? Drnlle.''

"Any doubt of this identification?''

"You joke.''

"Bildoon!" McKie hissed. "We have to try it!"

He spun around, pounded out of the lab, dodged through Tuluk's assistants in the outer area. Tuluk darted in his wake, drawing their enforcer guardians into a thin line close behind.

"McKie!" Tuluk called. "Where are you going?"

"To Bildoon . . . then back to Fanny Mae.

The value of self government at an individual level cannot be overestimated.

—BuSab Manual

NOTHING COULD stop him now, Cheo told himself.

Mliss could die in a few minutes, deprived of air in the Beautybarber tank where he'd confined her. The others on their refuge world would have to follow him, then. He would control the S'eye and the threads of power.

Cheo stood in his quarters with the S'eye controls near at hand. It was night outside, but all things remained relative, he reminded himself. Dawn would be breaking soon where the Caleban's Beachball rested above the surf on Cordiality.

The Caleban's ultimate dawn . . . the dawn of ultimate discontinuity. That dawn would slip into eternal night on all the planets which shared a universe with the doomed Caleban.

In just a few minutes, this planet-of-the-past where he stood would reach its point of proper connectives with Cordiality. And the Palenki waiting across the room there would do what it had been commanded to do.

Cheo rubbed the scars on his forehead.

There'd be no more Pan Spechi then to point accusing fingers at him, to call him with ghostly voices. Never again would there be a threat to the ego which he had secured to himself.

No one could stop him.

Mliss could never come back from death to stop him. She must be gasping in the sealed tank by now, straining for the oxygen which did not exist there.

And that stupid McKie! The Saboteur Extraordinary had proved to be elusive and annoying, but no way remained for him to stop the apocalypse.

Just a few more minutes now.

Cheo looked at the reference dials on the S'eye controls. They moved so slowly it was difficult to detect any change while you kept your eyes on them. But they moved.

He crossed to the open doors onto the balcony, drew a questioning stare from the Palenki, and stepped outside. There was no moon, but many stars shone in patterns alien to a Pan Spechi. Mliss had ordered a strange world here with its bits of ancient history from her Terran past, its odds and ends of esoterica culled from the ages.

Those stars, now. The Caleban had assured them no other planets existed here . . . yet there were stars. If those were stars. Perhaps they were only bits of glowing gas arranged in the patterns Mliss had requested.

It would be a lonely place here after the other universe was gone, Cheo realized.

And there would be no escaping those starry patterns, reminders of Mliss.

But it would be safe here. No pursuit, because there would be no pursuers.

He glanced back into the lighted room.

How patiently the Palenki waited, eyes lidded, motionless. The whip dangled limply from its single hand. Crazy anachronism of a weapon! But it worked. Without that wild conjunction of Mliss and her kinky desires, they would never have discovered the thing about the weapon, never have found this world and the way to isolate it forever.

Cheo savored the thought of *forever*. That was a very long time. Too long, perhaps. The thought disturbed him. Loneliness . . . forever.

He cut off these thoughts, looked once more at the S'eye dials. The pointers had moved a hair closer to the curtained moment. They would coincide presently.

Not looking at the pointers, not looking anywhere, really, Cheo waited. Night on the balcony was full of the odors Mliss had gathered—exotic blooms, scents and musks of rare life forms, exhalations of a myriad species she had brought to share her Ark.

Ark. That was an odd name she'd given this place. Perhaps he'd change that . . . later. Crèche? No! That carried painful reminders.

Why were there no other planets? he wondered. Surely the Caleban could have provided other planets. But Mliss had not ordered them created.

Only the thinnest of lines separated the pointers on the S'eye dials.

Cheo went back into the room, called the Palenki.

The squat turtle shape stirred itself to action, came to Cheo's side. The thing looked eager. Palenkis enjoyed violence.

Cheo felt suddenly empty, but there was no turning back. He put his hands to the controls—humanoid hands. They would remind him of Mliss, too. He turned a knob. It felt oddly alien beneath his fingers, but he stifled all uneasiness, all regrets, concentrated on the pointers.

They flowed into each other, and he opened the jumpdoor.

"Now!" he commanded.

If words are your symbols of reality, you live in a dream world.

—WREAVE SAYING

MCKIE HEARD the Pan Spechi's shouted command as the jumpdoor's vortal tube leaped into existence within the Beachball. The opening dominated the room, filled the purple gloom with bright light. The light came from behind two figures revealed by the opening: a Palenki and the Pan Spechi, Cheo.

The vortal tube began swelling to dangerous dimensions within the confined room. Wild energies around its rim hurled enforcer guardians aside. Before they could recover, the Palenki arm thrust into the room, lashed out with its whip.

McKie gasped at the shower of green and golden sparks around the Caleban. Golden! Again the whip struck. More sparks glittered, fell, shimmered into nothingness.

"Hold!" McKie shouted as the enforcers recovered and moved to attack. He wanted no more casualties from a closing jumpdoor. The enforcers hesitated.

Once more the Palenki lashed out with its whip.

Sparks glowed, fell.

"Fanny Mae!" McKie called.

"I reply," the Caleban said. McKie felt the abrupt rise in temperature, but the emotion with the words was calm and soothing . . . and powerful.

The enforcers jittered, their attention darting from McKie to the area where the Palenki arm continued its vicious play with the whip. Each stroke sent a shower of golden sparks into the room.

"Tell me of your substance, Fanny Mae," McKie said.

"My substance grows," the Caleban said. "You bring me energy and goodness. I return love for love and love for hate. You give me strength for this, McKie."

"Tell me of discontinuity," McKie said.

"Discontinuity withdraws!" There was definite elation in the Caleban's words. "I do not see node of connectives for discontinuity! My companions shall return in love."

McKie inhaled a deep breath. It was working. But each new flow of Caleban words brought its blast from the furnace. That, too, spoke of success. He mopped his forehead.

The whip continued to rise and fall.

"Give up, Cheo!" McKie called. "You've lost!" He peered up through the jumpdoor. "We're feeding her faster than you can rob her of substance."

Cheo barked an order to the Palenki. Arm and whip withdrew.

"Fanny Mae!" the Pan Spechi called.

There was no answer, but McKie sensed a wave of pity.

Does she pity Cheo? McKie wondered.

"I command you to answer me, Caleban!" Cheo roared. "Your control orders you to obey!"

"I obey holder of contract only," the Caleban said. "You share no connectives with holder of contract."

"She ordered you to obey me!"

McKie held his breath, watching, waiting for his moment to act. It must be done with precision. The Caleban had been lucidly clear about that—for once. There could be little doubt of the communication. *"Abnethe gathers lines of her world into herself."* That was what Fanny Mae had said, and the meaning seemed clear. When Fanny Mae summoned Abnethe . . . a sacrifice must be made. Abnethe had to die, and her world would die with her.

"Your contract!" Cheo insisted.

"Contract declines of intensity," the Caleban said. "On this new track you must address me as Thyone. Name of love I receive from McKie: Thyone."

"McKie, what have you done?" Cheo demanded. He poised his fingers over the S'eye controls. "Why doesn't she respond to the whipping?"

"She never really did respond to the whippings," McKie said. "She responded to the violence and hate that went with them. The whip served only as a peculiar kind of focusing instrument. It put all the violence and hate into a single vulnerable . . . "

" . . . node," the Caleban said. "Vulnerable node."

"And that robbed her of energy," McKie said. "She manufactures emotion with her energy, you know. That requires a lot of eating. She's almost pure emotion, pure creation, and that's how the universe goes, Cheo."

Where was Abnethe? McKie wondered.

Cheo motioned to the Palenki, hesitated as McKie said, "It's no use, Cheo. We're feeding her faster than you can drain her."

"Feeding her?" Cheo bent his scarred head forward to peer at McKie.

"We've opened a giant jumpdoor in space," McKie said. "It's gathering free hydrogen and feeding it directly into Thyone."

"What is this . . . Thyone?" Cheo demanded.

"The star that is a Caleban," McKie said.

"What are you talking about?"

"Haven't you guessed?" McKie asked. He gave a subtle hand signal to the enforcers. Abnethe still hadn't shown up. Perhaps Cheo had confined her someplace. That changed things to the contingency plan. They were going to have to try getting a sentient through the jumpdoor.

The enforcers, responding to his signal, began moving closer to the opening. Each held a raygen ready.

"Guessed what?" Cheo asked.

I have to keep him distracted, McKie thought.

"Calebans manifest themselves in our universe several ways," he said. "They're stars, suns—which may really be feeding orifices. They've created these Beach-balls—which are probably intended as much to protect us as they are to house the *speaking* manifestation. Even with the Beachball's damping force, they can't hold back all the radiant energy of their speech. That's why it gets so hot in here."

McKie glanced at his ring of enforcers. They were moving closer and closer to the jumpdoor. Thank all the gods of space that Cheo had made the opening so large!

"Stars?" Cheo asked.

"This particular Caleban has been identified," McKie said. "She's Thyone in the Pleiades."

"But . . . the S'eye effect . . . "

"Star-eyes," McKie said. "At least, that's how I interpret it. I'm probably only partly right, but Thyone here admits she and her kind suspected the truth during their first attempts at communication."

Cheo moved his head slowly from side to side. "The jumpdoors . . . "

"Star-powered," McKie said. "We've known from the first they required stellar energies to breach space that way. The Taprisiots gave us a clue when they spoke of *embedments* and crossing Caleban *connectives* to . . . "

"You talk nonsense," Cheo growled.

"Undoubtedly," McKie agreed. "But it's a nonsense that moves reality in our universe."

"You think you distract me while your companions prepare to attack," Cheo said. "I will now show you another reality in your universe!" He twisted the jumpdoor controls.

"Thyone!" McKie shouted.

The jumpdoor's opening began moving toward McKie.

"I reply to McKie," the Caleban said.

"Stop Cheo," McKie said. "Confine him."

"Cheo confines himself," the Caleban said. "Cheo discontinues connectives."

The jumpdoor continued moving toward McKie, but he saw that Cheo appeared to be having trouble with the controls. McKie moved aside as the opening passed through the space where he had been.

"Stop him!" McKie called.

"Cheo stops himself," the Caleban said.

McKie sensed a definite wave of compassion with the words.

The jumpdoor opening turned on its axis, advanced once more on McKie. It moved a bit faster this time.

McKie dodged aside, scattering enforcers. Why weren't the damned fools trying to get through the opening? Afraid of being cut up? He steeled himself to dive through the opening on the next pass. Cheo had been conditioned to the thought of fear now. He wouldn't expect attack from someone who feared him. McKie swallowed in a dry throat. He knew what would happen to him. The molasses delay in the vortal tube would give Cheo just enough time. McKie would lose both legs—at the very least. He'd get through with a raygen, though, and Cheo would die. Given any luck, Abnethe could be found—and she'd die, too.

Again the jumpdoor plunged toward McKie.

He leaped, collided with an enforcer who had chosen the same instant to attack. They sprawled on hands and knees as the vortal tube slipped over them.

McKie saw Cheo's gloating face, the hand jerking at the controls. He saw a control arm snap over, heard a distant crackling as the jumpdoor ceased to exist.

Someone screamed.

McKie felt himself considerably surprised to be still on hands and knees in the purple gloom of the Beachball's interior. He held his position, allowed his memory to replay that last glimpse of Cheo. It had been a ghostly vision, a smoky substance visible through the Pan Spechi's body—and the visible substance had been that of the Beachball's interior.

"Discontinuity dissolves contract," the Caleban said.

McKie climbed slowly to his feet. "What's that mean, Thyone?"

"Statement of fact with meaning intensity-truth only for Cheo and companions," the Caleban said. "Self cannot give meaning to McKie for substance of another."

McKie nodded.

"That universe of Abnethe's was her own creation," he murmured. "A figment of her imagination."

"Explain figment," the Caleban said.

Cheo experienced the instant of Abnethe's death as a gradual dissolution of substance around and within him. Walls, floor, S'eye controls, ceiling, world—everything faded into nonbeing. He felt all the haste of his existence swollen into one sterile instant. And he found himself for a transitory moment sharing with the shadows of the nearby Palenki and other more distant islands of movement a place of existence which the mystics of his own species had never contemplated. It was, however, a place which an ancient Hindu or a Buddhist might have recognized—a place of Maya, illusion, a formless void possessed of no qualities.

The moment passed abruptly, and Cheo ceased to exist. Or it could be said that he discontinued in becoming one with the void-illusion. One cannot, after all, breathe an illusion or a void.

THE DOSADI EXPERIMENT

In memory of Babe
because she knew
how to enjoy life.

When the Calebans first sent us one of their giant metal "beachballs," communicating through this device to offer the use of jumpdoors for interstellar travel, many in the ConSentiency covertly began to exploit this gift of the stars for their own questionable purposes. Both the "Shadow Government" and some among the Gowachin people saw what is obvious today: that instantaneous travel across unlimited space involved powers which might isolate subject populations in gross numbers.

This observation at the beginning of the Dosadi Experiment came long before Saboteur Extraordinary Jorj X. McKie discovered that visible stars of our universe were either Calebans or the manifestations of Calebans in ConSentient space. (See *Whipping Star*, an account of McKie's discovery thinly disguised as fiction.)

What remains pertinent here is that McKie, acting for his Bureau of Sabotage, identified the Caleban called "Fannie Mae" as the visible star Thyone. This discovery of the Thyone-Fannie Mae identity ignited new interest in the Caleban Question and thus contributed to the exposure of the Dosadi Experiment—which many still believe was the most disgusting use of Sentients by Sentients in ConSentient history. Certainly, it remains the most gross psychological test of Sentient Beings ever performed, and the issue of informed consent has never been settled to everyone's satisfaction.

—From the first public account, *the Trial of Trials*

*Justice belongs to those who claim it, but let the claimant beware
lest he create new injustice by his claim and thus set the bloody
pendulum of revenge into its inexorable motion.*

—GOWACHIN APHORISM

"WHY ARE you so cold and mechanical in your Human relationships?"

Jorj X. McKie was to reflect on that Caleban question later. Had she been trying to alert him to the Dosadi Experiment and to what his investigation of that experiment might do to him? He hadn't even known about Dosadi at the time and the pressures of the Caleban communications trance, the accusatory tone she took, had precluded other considerations.

Still, it rankled. He didn't like the feeling that he might be a subject of her research into Humans. He'd always thought of that particular Caleban as his friend—if one could consider being friendly with a creature whose visible manifestation in this universe was a fourth-magnitude yellow sun visible from Central Central where the Bureau of Sabotage maintained its headquarters. And there was inevitable discomfort in Caleban communication. You sank into a trembling, jerking trance while they made their words appear in your consciousness.

But his uncertainty remained: had she tried to tell him something beyond the plain content of her words?

When the weather makers kept the evening rain period short, McKie liked to go outdoors immediately afterward and stroll in the park enclosure which BuSab provided for its employees on Central Central. As a Saboteur Extraordinary, McKie had free run of the enclosure and he liked the fresh smells of the place after a rain.

The park covered about thirty hectares, deep in a well of Bureau buildings. It was a scrambling hodgepodge of plantings cut by wide paths which circled and twisted through specimens from every inhabited planet of the known universe. No care had been taken to provide a particular area for any sentient species. If there was any plan to park it was a maintenance plan with plants requiring similar conditions and care held in their own sectors. Giant Spear Pines from Sasak occupied a knoll near one corner surrounded by mounds of Flame Briar from Rudiria. There were bold stretches of lawn and hidden scraps of lawn, and some flat stretches of greenery which were not lawns at all but mobile sheets of predatory leaf imprisoned behind thin moats of caustic water.

Rain-jeweled flowers often held McKie's attention to the exclusion of all else. There was a single planting of Lilium Grossa, its red blossoms twice his height casting long shadows over a wriggling carpet of blue Syringa, each miniature bloom opening and closing at random like tiny mouths gasping for air.

Sometimes, floral perfumes stopped his progress and held him in a momentary olfactory thralldom while his eyes searched out the source. As often as not, the plant would be a dangerous one—a flesh eater or poison-sweat variety. Warning signs in flashing Galach guarded such plantings. Sonabarriers, moats, and force

122

fields edged the winding paths in many areas.

McKie had a favorite spot in the park, a bench with its back to a fountain where he could sit and watch the shadows collect across fat yellow bushes from the floating islands of Tandaloor. The yellow bushes thrived because their roots were washed in running water hidden beneath the soil and renewed by the fountain. Beneath the yellow bushes there were faint gleams of phosphorescent silver enclosed by a force field and identified by a low sign:

"Sangeet Mobilus, a blood-sucking perennial from Bisaj. Extreme danger to all sentient species. Do not intrude any portion of your body beyond the force field."

As he sat on the bench, McKie thought about that sign. The universe often mixed the beautiful and the dangerous. This was a deliberate mixture in the park. The yellow bushes, the fragrant and benign Golden Iridens, had been mingled with Sangeet Mobilus. The two supported each other and both thrived. The Con-Sentient government which McKie served often made such mixtures . . . sometimes by accident.

Sometimes by design.

He listened to the plashing of the fountain while the shadows thickened and the tiny border lights came on along the paths. The tops of the buildings beyond the park became a palette where the sunset laid out its final display of the day.

In that instant, the Caleban contact caught him and he felt his body slip into the helpless communications trance. The mental tendrils were immediately identified—Fannie Mae. And he thought, as he often had, what an improbable name that was for a star entity. He heard no sounds, but his hearing centers responded as to spoken words, and the inward glow was unmistakable. It was Fannie Mae, her syntax far more sophisticated than during their earliest encounters.

"You admire one of us," she said, indicating his attention on the sun which had just set beyond the buildings.

"I try not to think of any star as a Caleban," he responded. "It interferes with my awareness of the natural beauty."

"Natural? McKie, you don't understand your own awareness, nor even how you employ it!"

That was her beginning—accusatory, attacking, unlike any previous contact with this Caleban he'd thought of as friend. And she employed her verb forms with new deftness, almost as though showing off, parading her understanding of his language.

"What do you want, Fannie Mae?"

"I consider your relationships with females of your species. You have entered marriage relationships which number more than fifty. Not so?"

"That's right. Yes. Why do you . . ."

"I am your friend, McKie. What is your feeling toward me?"

He thought about that. There was a demanding intensity in her question. He owed his life to this Caleban with an improbable name. For that matter, she owed her life to him. Together, they'd resolved the Whipping Star threat. Now, many Calebans provided the jumpdoors by which other beings moved in a single step from planet to planet, but once Fannie Mae had held all of those jumpdoor threads, her life threatened through the odd honor code by which Calebans maintained their contractual obligations. And McKie had saved her life. He had but to think about their past interdependence and a warm sense of camaraderie suffused him.

Fannie Mae sensed this.

"Yes, McKie, that is friendship, is love. Do you possess this feeling toward Human female companions?"

Her question angered him. Why was she prying? His private sexual relationships were no concern of hers!

"Your love turns easily to anger," she chided.

"There are limits to how deeply a Saboteur Extraordinary can allow himself to be involved with anyone."

"Which came first, McKie—the Saboteur Extraordinary or these limits?"

Her response carried obvious derision. Had he chosen the Bureau because he was incapable of warm relationships? But he really cared for Fannie Mae! He admired her . . . and she could hurt him because he admired her and felt . . . felt *this way*.

He spoke out of his anger and hurt.

"Without the Bureau there'd be no ConSentiency and no need for Calebans."

"Yes, indeed. People have but to look at a dread agent from BuSab and know fear."

It was intolerable, but he couldn't escape the underlying warmth he felt toward this strange Caleban entity, this being who could creep unguarded into his mind and talk to him as no other being dared. If only he had found a woman to share that kind of intimacy . . .

And this was the part of their conversation which came back to haunt him. After months with no contact between them, why had she chosen that moment—just three days before the Dosadi crisis burst upon the Bureau? She'd pulled out his ego, his deepest sense of identity. She'd shaken that ego and then she'd skewered him with her barbed question:

"Why are you so cold and mechanical in your Human relationships?"

Her irony could not be evaded. She'd made him appear ridiculous in his own eyes. He could feel warmth, yes . . . even love, for a Caleban but not for a Human female. This unguarded feeling he held for Fannie Mae had never been directed at any of his marital companions. Fannie Mae had aroused his anger, to verbal breast-beating, and finally to silent hurt. Still, the love remained.

Why?

Human females were bed partners. They were bodies which used him and which he used. That was out of the question with this Caleban. She was a star burning with atomic fires, her seat of consciousness unimaginable to other sentients. Yet, she could extract love from him. He gave this love freely and she knew it. There was no hiding an emotion from a Caleban when she sent her mental tendrils into your awareness.

She'd certainly known he would see the irony. That had to be part of her motive in such an attack. But Calebans seldom acted from a single motive—which was part of their charm and the essence of their most irritant exchanges with other sentient beings.

"McKie?" Softly in his mind.

"Yes." Angry.

"I show you now a fractional bit of my feeling toward your node."

Like a balloon being inflated by a swift surge of gas, he felt himself suffused by a projected sense of concern, of caring. He was drowning in it . . . wanted to drown in it. His entire body radiated this white-hot sense of protective attention. For a whole minute after it was withdrawn, he still glowed with it.

A fractional bit?

"McKie?" Concerned.

"Yes." Awed.

"Have I hurt you?"

He felt alone, emptied.

"No."

"The full extent of my nodal involvement would destroy you. Some Humans have suspected this about love."

Nodal involvement?

She was confusing him as she'd done in their first encounters. How could the Calebans describe love as . . . nodal involvement?

"Labels depend on viewpoint," she said. "You look at the universe through too narrow an opening. We despair of you sometimes."

There she was again, attacking.

He fell back on a childhood platitude.

"I am what I am and that's all I am."

"You may soon learn, friend McKie, that you're more than you thought."

With that, she'd broken the contact. He'd awakened in damp, chilly darkness, the sound of the fountain loud in his ears. Nothing he did would bring her back into communication, not even when he'd spent some of his own credits on a Taprisiot in vain attempt to call her.

His Caleban friend had shut him out.

We have created a monster—enormously valuable and even useful yet extremely dangerous. Our monster is both beautiful and terrifying. We do not dare use this monster to its full potential, but we cannot release our grasp upon it.

> —GOWACHIN ASSESSMENT
> OF THE DOSADI EXPERIMENT

A BULLET went *spang!* against the window behind Keila Jedrik's desk, ricocheted and screamed off into the canyon street far below her office. Jedrik prided herself that she had not even flinched. The Elector's patrols would take care of the sniper. The patrols which swept the streets of Chu every morning would home on the sound of the shot. She held the casual hope that the sniper would escape back to the Rim Rabble, but she recognized this hope as a weakness and dismissed it. There were concerns this morning far more important than an infiltrator from the Rim.

Jedrik reached one hand into the corner of early sunlight which illuminated the contact plates of her terminal in the Master Accountancy computer. Those flying fingers—she could almost diassociate herself from them. They darted like insects at the waiting keys. The terminal was a functional instrument, symbol of her status as a Senior Liaitor. It sat all alone in its desk slot—grey, green, gold, black, white and deadly. Its grey screen was almost precisely the tone of her desk top.

With careful precision, her fingers played their rhythms on the keys. The screen produced yellow numbers, all weighted and averaged at her command—a thin strip of destiny with violence hidden in its golden shapes.

Every angel carries a sword, she thought.

But she did not really consider herself an angel or her weapon a sword. Her real weapon was an intellect hardened and sharpened by the terrible decisions her planet required. Emotions were a force to be diverted within the self or to be used against anyone who had failed to learn what Dosadi taught. She knew her own weakness and hid it carefully: she'd been taught by loving parents (who'd concealed their love behind exquisite cruelty) that Dosadi's decisions were indeed terrible.

Jedrik studied the numbers on her computer display, cleared the screen and made a new entry. As she did this, she knew she took sustenance from fifty of her planet's Human inhabitants. Many of those fifty would not long survive this callous jape. In truth, her fingers were weapons of death for those who failed this test. She felt no guilt about those she slew. The imminent arrival of one Jorj X. McKie dictated her actions, precipitated them.

When she thought about McKie, her basic feeling was one of satisfaction. She'd waited for McKie like a predator beside a burrow in the earth. His name and identifying keys had been given to her by her chauffeur, Havvy, hoping to increase his value to her. She'd taken the information and made her usual investigation. Jedrik doubted that any other person on Dosadi could have come up with the result her sources produced: Jorj X. McKie was an adult human who could not possibly exist. No record of him could be found on all of Dosadi—not on the poisonous Rim, not in Chu's Warrens, not in any niche of the existing power structure. McKie did not exist, but he was due to arrive in Chu momentarily, smuggled into the city by a Gowachin temporarily under her control.

McKie was the precision element for which she had waited. He wasn't merely a possible key to the God Wall (not a bent and damaged key like Havvy) but clean and certain. She'd never thought to attack this lock with poor instruments. There'd be one chance and only one; it required the best.

Thus fifty Dosadi Humans took their faceless places behind the numbers in her computer. Bait, expendable. Those who died by this act wouldn't die immediately. Forty-nine might never know they'd been deliberately submitted to early death by her deliberate choice. Some would be pushed back to the Rim's desperate and short existence. Some would die in the violent battles she was precipitating. Others would waste away in the Warrens. For most, the deadly process would extend across sufficient time to conceal her hand in it. But they'd been slain in her computer and she knew it. She cursed her parents (and the others before them) for this unwanted sensitivity to the blood and sinew behind these computer numbers. Those loving parents had taught her well. She might never see the slain bodies, need give not another thought to all but one of the fifty; still she sensed them behind her computer display . . . warm and pulsing.

Jedrik sighed. The fifty were bleating animals staked out to lure a special beast onto Dosadi's poisonous soil. Her fifty would create a fractional surplus which would vanish, swallowed before anyone realized their purpose.

Dosadi is sick, she thought. And not for the first time, she wondered: *Is this really Hell?*

Many believed it.

We're being punished.

But no one knew what they'd done to deserve punishment.

Jedrik leaned back, looked across her doorless office to the sound barrier and milky light of the hall. A strange Gowachin shambled past her doorway. He was a frog figure on some official errand, a packet of brown paper clutched in his knobby hands. His green skin shimmered as though he'd recently come from water.

The Gowachin reminded her of Bahrank, he who was bringing McKie into her net, Bahrank who did her bidding because she controlled the substance to which he was addicted. More fool he to let himself become an addict to anything, even to living. One day soon Bahrank would sell what he knew about her to the Elector's spies; by then it would be too late and the Elector would learn only what she wanted him to learn when she wanted him to learn it. She'd chosen Bahrank with the same care she'd used at her computer terminal, the same care which had made her wait for someone precisely like McKie. And Bahrank was Gowachin. Once committed to a project, the frog people were notorious for carrying out their orders in a precise way. They possessed an inbred sense of order but understood the limits of law.

As her gaze traversed the office, the sparse and functional efficiency of the space filled her with quiet amusement. The office presented an image of her which she had constructed with meticulous care. It pleased her that she would be leaving here soon never to return, like an insect shedding its skin. The office was four paces wide, eight long. Twelve black metal rotofiles lined the wall on her left, dark sentinels of her methodical ways. She had reset their locking codes and armed them to destroy their contents when the Elector's toads pried into them. The Elector's people would attribute this to outrage, a last angry sabotage. It would be some time before accumulating doubts would lead them to reassessment and to frustrated questions. Even then they might not suspect her hand in the elimination of fifty Humans. She, after all, was one of the fifty.

This thought inflicted her with a momentary sense of unfocused loss. How pervasive were the seductions of Dosadi's power structure! How subtle! What she'd just done here introduced a flaw into the computer system which ruled the distribution of non-poisonous food in Dosadi's only city. Food—here was the real base of Dosadi's social pyramid, solid and ugly. The flaw removed her from a puissant niche in that pyramid. She had worn the persona of Keila Jedrik-Liaitor for many years. Long enough to learn enjoyment of the power system. Losing one valuable counter in Dosadi's endless survival game, she must now live and act only with the persona of Keila Jedrik-Warlord. This was an all-or-nothing move, a gambler's plunge. She felt the nakedness of it. But this gamble had begun long ago, far back in Dosadi's contrived history, when her ancestors had recognized the nature of this planet and had begun breeding and training for the individual who would take this plunge.

I am that individual, she told herself. *This is our moment.*

But had they truly assessed the problem correctly?

Jedrik's glance fell on the single window which looked out into the canyon street. Her own reflection stared back: a face too narrow, thin nose, eyes and mouth too large. Her hair could be an interesting black velvet helmet if she let it grow, but she kept it cropped short as a reminder that she was not a magnetic sex partner, that she must rely on her wits. That was the way she'd been bred and trained. Dosadi had taught her its cruelest lessons early. She'd grown tall while still in her teens, carrying more height in her body than in her legs so that she appeared even taller when seated. She looked down on most Gowachin and Human males in more ways than one. That was another gift (and lesson) from her *loving* parents and from their ancestors. There was no escaping this Dosadi lesson.

What you love or value will be used against you.

She leaned forward to hide her disquieting reflection, peered far down into the
street. There, that was better. Her fellow Dosadis no longer were warm and
pulsing people. They were reduced to distant movements, as impersonal as the
dancing figures in her computer.

Traffic was light, she noted. Very few armored vehicles moved, no pedestrians.
There'd been only that one shot at her window. She still entertained a faint hope
that the sniper had escaped. More likely a patrol had caught the fool. The Rim
Rabble persisted in testing Chu's defenses despite the boringly repetitive results. It
was desperation. Snipers seldom waited until the day was deep and still and the
patrols were scattered, those hours when even some among the most powerful
ventured out.

Symptoms, all symptoms.

Rim sorties represented only one among many Dosadi symptoms which she'd
taught herself to read in that precarious climb whose early stage came to climax in
this room. It was not just a thought, but more a sense of familiar awareness to
which she returned at oddly reflexive moments in her life.

*We have a disturbed relationship with our past which religion cannot explain.
We are primitive in unexplainable ways, our lives woven of the familiar and the
strange, the reasonable and the insane.*

It made some insane choices magnificently attractive.

Have I made an insane choice?

No!

The data lay clearly in her mind, facts which she could not obliterate by turning
away from them. Dosadi had been designed from a cosmic grab bag: "Give them
one of these and one of these and one of these . . ."

It made for incompatible pairings.

The DemoPol with which Dosadi juggled its computer-monitored society didn't
fit a world which used energy transmitted from a satellite in geosynchronous orbit.
The DemoPol reeked of primitive ignorance, something from a society which had
wandered too far down the path of legalisms—a law for everything and everything
managed by law. The canyon in which to build a city insulated from this poisonous
planet, and that only some twenty or so generations earlier, remained indigestible.
And that energy satellite which hovered beneath the God Wall's barrier—that
stank of a long and sophisticated evolution during which something as obviously
flawed as the DemoPol would have been discarded.

It was a cosmic grab bag designed for a specific purpose which her ancestors had
recognized.

We did not evolve on this planet.

The place was out of phase with both Gowachin and Human. Dosadi employed
computer memories and physical files side by side for identical purposes. And the
number of addictive substances to be found on Dosadi was outrageous. Yet this
was played off against a religion so contrived, so gross in its demands for "simple
faith" that the two conditions remained at constant war. The mystics died for their
"new insights" while the holders of "simple faith" used control of the addictive
substances to gain more and more power. The only real faith on Dosadi was that
you survived by power and that you gained power by controlling what others
required for survival. Their society understood the medicine of bacteria, virus and
brain control, but these could not stamp out the Rim and Warren Underground
where *jabua* faith healers cured their patients with the smoke of burning weeds.

And they could not stamp out (not yet) Keila Jedrik because she had seen what she had seen. Two by two the incompatible things ebbed and flowed around her, in the city of Chu and the surrounding Rim. It was the same in every case: a society which made use of one of these things could not naturally be a society which used the other.

Not naturally.

All around her, Jedrik sensed Chu with its indigestible polarities. They had only two species: Human and Gowachin. Why two? Were there no other species in this universe? Subtle hints in some of Dosadi's artifacts suggested an evolution for appendages other than the flexible fingers of Gowachin and Human.

Why only one city on all of Dosadi?

Dogma failed to answer.

The Rim hordes cuddled close, always seeking a way into Chu's insulated purity. But they had a whole planet behind them. Granted it was a poisonous planet, but it had other rivers, other places of potential sanctuary. The survival of both species argues for the building of more sanctuaries, many more than that pitiful hole which Gar and Tria thought they masterminded. No . . . Chu stood alone—almost twenty kilometers wide and forty long, built on hills and silted islands where the river slowed in its deep canyon. At last count, some eighty-nine million people lived here and three times that number eked a short life on the Rim—pressing, always pressing for a place in the poison-free city.

Give us your precious bodies, you stupid Rimmers!

They heard the message, knew its import and defied it. What had the people of Dosadi done to be imprisoned here? What had their ancestors done? It was right to build a religion upon hate for such ancestors . . . provided such ancestors were guilty.

Jedrik leaned toward the window, peered upward at the God Wall, that milky translucence which imprisoned Dosadi, yet through which those such as this Jorj X. McKie could come at will. She hungered to see McKie in person, to confirm that had not been contaminated as Havvy had been contaminated.

It was a McKie she required now. The transparently contrived nature of Dosadi told her that there must be a McKie. She saw herself as the huntress, McKie her natural prey. The false identity she'd built in this room was part of her bait. Now, in the season of McKie, the underlying religious cant by which Dosadi's powerful maintained their private illusions would crumble. She could already see the beginnings of that dissolution; soon, everyone would see it.

She took a deep breath. There was a purity in what was about to happen, a simplification. She was about to divest herself of one of her two lives, taking all of her awareness into the persona of that other Keila Jedrik which all of Dosadi would soon know. Her people had kept her secret well, hiding a fat and sleazy blonde person from their fellow Dosadis, exposing just enough of that one to "X" that the powers beyond the God Wall might react in the proper design. She felt cleansed by the fact that the disguise of that other life had begun to lose its importance. The whole of her could begin to surface in that other place. And McKie had precipitated this metamorphosis. Jedrik's thoughts were clear and direct now:

Come into my trap, McKie. You will take me higher than the palace apartments of the Council Hills.

Or into a deeper hell than any nightmare has imagined.

*How to start a war? Nurture your own latent hungers for power.
Forget that only madmen pursue power for its own sake. Let such
madmen gain power—even you. Let such madmen act behind their
conventional masks of sanity. Whether their masks be fashioned
from the delusions of defense or the theological aura of law, war
will come.*

—GOWACHIN APHORISM

THE ODALARM awoke Jorj X. McKie with a whiff of lemon. For just an instant his mind played tricks on him. He thought he was on Tutalsee's gentle planetary ocean floating softly on his garlanded island. There were lemons on his floating island, banks of Hibiscus and carpets of spicy Alyssum. His bowered cottage lay in the path of perfumed breezes and the lemon . . .

Awareness came. He was not on Tutalsee with a loving companion; he was on a trained bedog in the armored efficiency of his Central Central apartment; he was back in the heart of the Bureau of Sabotage; he was back at work.

McKie shuddered.

A planet full of people could die today . . . or tomorrow.

It would happen unless someone solved this Dosadi mystery. Knowing the Gowachin as he did, McKie was convinced of it. The Gowachin were capable of cruel decisions, especially where their species pride was at stake, or for reasons which other species might not understand. Bildoon, his Bureau chief, assessed this crisis the same way. Not since the Caleban problem had such enormity crossed the ConSentient horizon.

But where was this endangered planet, this Dosadi?

After a night of sleep suppression, the briefings about Dosadi came back vividly as though part of his mind had remained at work sharpening the images. Two operatives, one Wreave and one Laclac, had made the report. The two were reliable and resourceful. Their sources were excellent, although the information was sparse. The two also were bucking for promotion at a time when Wreaves and Laclacs were hinting at discrimination against their species. The report required special scrutiny. No BuSab agent, regardless of species, was above some internal testing, a deception designed to weaken the Bureau and gain coup merits upon which to ride into the director's office.

However, BuSab was still directed by Bildoon, a PanSpechi in Human form, the fourth member of his creche to carry that name. It had been obvious from Bildoon's first words that he believed the report.

"McKie, this thing could set Human and Gowachin at each others' throats."

It was an understandable idiom, although in point of fact you would go for the Gowachin abdomen to carry out the same threat. McKie already had acquainted himself with the report and, from internal evidence to which his long association with the Gowachin made him sensitive, he shared Bildoon's assessment. Seating himself in a grey chairdog across the desk from the director in the rather small, windowless office Bildoon had lately preferred, McKie shifted the report from one hand to the other. Presently, recognizing his own nervous mannerism, he put the report on the desk. It was on coded memowire which played to trained senses when passed through the fingers or across other sensitive appendages.

"Why couldn't they pinpoint this Dosadi's location?" McKie asked.

"It's known only to a Caleban."

130

"Well, they'll . . ."

"The Calebans refuse to respond."

McKie stared across the desk at Bildoon. The polished surface reflected a second image of the BuSab director, an inverted image to match the upright one. McKie studied the reflection. Until you focused on Bildoon's faceted eyes (how like an insect's eyes they were), this PanSpechi appeared much like a Human male with dark hair and pleasant round face. Perhaps he'd put on more than the form when his flesh had been molded to Human shape. Bildoon's face displayed emotions which McKie read in Human terms. The director appeared angry.

McKie was troubled.

"Refused?"

"The Calebans don't deny that Dosadi exists or that it's threatened. They refuse to discuss it."

"Then we're dealing with a Caleban contract and they're obeying the terms of that contract."

Recalling that conversation with Bildoon as he awakened in his apartment, McKie lay quietly thinking. Was Dosadi some new extension of the Caleban Question?

It's right to fear what we don't understand.

The Caleban mystery had eluded ConSentient investigators for too long. He thought of his recent conversation with Fannie Mae. When you thought you had something pinned down, it slipped out of your grasp. Before the Calebans' gift of jumpdoors, the ConSentiency had been a relatively slow and understandable federation of the known sentient species. The universe had contained itself in a shared space of recognizable dimensions. The ConSentiency of those days had grown in a way likened to expanding bubbles. It had been linear.

Caleban jumpdoors had changed that with an explosive acceleration of every aspect of life. Jumpdoors had been an immediately disruptive tool of power. They implied infinite usable dimensions. They implied many other things only faintly understood. Through a jumpdoor you stepped from a room on Tutalsee into a hallway here on Central Central. You walked through a jumpdoor here and found yourself in a garden on Paginui. The intervening "normal space" might be measured in light years or parsecs, but the passage from one place to the other ignored such old concepts. And to this day, ConSentient investigators did not understand how the jumpdoors worked. Concepts such as "relative space" didn't explain the phenomenon; they only added to the mystery.

McKie ground his teeth in frustration. Calebans inevitably did that to him. What good did it do to think of the Calebans as visible stars in the space his body occupied? He could look up from any planet where a jumpdoor deposited him and examine the night sky. Visible stars: ah, yes. Those are Calebans. What did that tell him?

There was a strongly defended theory that Calebans were but a more sophisticated aspect of the equally mysterious Taprisiots. The ConSentiency had accepted and employed Taprisiots for thousands of standard years. A Taprisiot presented sentient form and size. They appeared to be short lengths of tree trunk cut off at top and bottom and with oddly protruding stub limbs. When you touched them they were warm and resilient. They were fellow beings of the ConSentiency. But just as the Calebans took your flesh across the parsecs, Taprisiots took your awareness across those same parsecs to merge you with another mind.

Taprisiots were a communications device.

But current theory said Taprisiots had been introduced to prepare the ConSentiency for Calebans.

It was dangerous to think of Taprisiots as merely a convenient means of communication. Equally dangerous to think of Calebans as "transportation facilitators." Look at the socially disruptive effect of jumpdoors! And when you employed a Taprisiot, you had a constant reminder of danger: the communications trance which reduced you to a twitching zombie while you made your call. No . . . neither Calebans nor Taprisiots should be accepted without question.

With the possible exception of the PanSpechi, no other species knew the first thing about Caleban and Taprisiot phenomena beyond their economic and personal value. They were, indeed, valuable, a fact reflected in the prices often paid for jumpdoor and long-call services. The PanSpechi denied that they could explain these things, but the PanSpechi were notoriously secretive. They were a species where each *individual* consisted of five bodies and only one dominant ego. The four reserves lay somewhere in a hidden creche. Bildoon had come from such a creche, accepting the communal ego from a creche-mate whose subsequent fate could only be imagined. PanSpechi refused to discuss internal creche matters except to admit what was obvious on the surface: that they could grow a simulacrum body to mimic most of the known species in the ConSentiency.

McKie felt himself overcome by a momentary pang of xenophobia.

We accept too damned many things on the explanations of people who could have good reasons for lying.

Keeping his eyes closed, McKie sat up. His bedog rippled gently against his buttocks.

Blast and damn the Calebans! Damn Fannie Mae!

He'd already called Fannie Mae, asking about Dosadi. The result had left him wondering if he really knew what Calebans meant by friendship.

"Information not permitted."

What kind of an answer was that? Especially when it was the only response he could get.

Not permitted?

The basic irritant was an old one: BuSab had no real way of applying its "gentle ministrations" to the Calebans.

But Calebans had never been known to lie. They appeared painfully, explicitly honest . . . as far as they could be understood. But they obviously withheld information. Not permitted! Was it possible they'd let themselves be accessories to the destruction of a planet and that planet's entire population?

McKie had to admit it was possible.

They might do it out of ignorance or from some stricture of Caleban morality which the rest of the ConSentiency did not share or understand. Or for some other reason which defied translation. They said they looked upon all life as "precious nodes of existence." But hints at peculiar exceptions remained. What was it Fannie Mae had once said?

"Dissolved well this node."

How could you look at an individual life as a "node?"

If association with Calebans had taught him anything, it was that understanding between species was tenuous at best and trying to understand a Caleban could drive you insane. In what medium did a node dissolve?

McKie sighed.

For now, this Dosadi report from the Wreave and Laclac agents had to be accepted on its own limited terms. Powerful people in the Gowachin Confederacy had sequestered Humans and Gowachin on an unlisted planet. Dosadi—location unknown, but the scene of unspecified experiments and tests on an imprisoned population. This much the agents insisted was true. If confirmed, it was a shameful act. The frog people would know that, surely. Rather than let their shame be exposed, they could carry out the threat which the two agents reported: blast the captive planet out of existence, the population and all of the incriminating evidence with it.

McKie shuddered.

Dosadi, a planet of thinking creatures—*sentients*. If the Gowachin carried out their violent threat, a living world would be reduced to blazing gases and the hot plasma of atomic particles. Somewhere, perhaps beyond the reach of other eyes, something would strike fire against the void. The tragedy would require less than a standard second. The most concise thought about such a catastrophe would require a longer time than the actual event.

But if it happened and the other ConSentient species received absolute proof that it had happened . . . ahhh, then the ConSentiency might well be shattered. Who would use a jumpdoor, suspecting that he might be shunted into some hideous experiment? Who would trust a neighbor, if that neighbor's habits, language, and body were different from his own? Yes . . . there would be more than Humans and Gowachin *at each other's throats*. These were things all the species feared. Bildoon realized this. The threat to this mysterious Dosadi was a threat to all.

McKie could not shake the terrible image from his mind: an explosion, a bright blink stretching toward its own darkness. And if the ConSentiency learned of it . . . in that instant before their universe crumbled like a cliff dislodged in a lightning bolt, what excuses would be offered for the failure of reason to prevent such a thing?

Reason?

McKie shook his head, opened his eyes. It was useless to dwell on the worst prospects. He allowed the apartment's sleep gloom to invade his senses, absorbed the familiar presence of his surroundings.

I'm a Saboteur Extraordinary and I've a job to do.

It helped to think of Dosadi that way. Solutions to problems often depended upon the will to succeed, upon sharpened skills and multiple resources. BuSab owned those resources and those skills.

McKie stretched his arms high over his head, twisted his blocky torso. The bedog rippled with pleasure at his movements. He whistled softly and suffered the kindling of morning light as the apartment's window controls responded. A yawn stretched his mouth. He slid from the bedog and padded across to the window. The view stretched away beneath a sky like stained blue paper. He stared out across the spires and rooftops of Central Central. Here lay the heart of the domine planet from which the Bureau of Sabotage spread its multifarious tentacles.

He blinked at the brightness, took a deep breath.

The Bureau. The omnipresent, omniscient, omnivorous Bureau. The one source of unmonitored governmental violence remaining in the ConSentiency. Here lay the norm against which sanity measured itself. Each choice made here demanded utmost delicacy. Their common enemy was that never-ending sentient yearning for absolutes. And each hour of every waking workday, BuSab in all of its parts asked itself:

"What are we if we succumb to unbridled violence?"

The answer was there in deepest awareness:

"Then we are useless."

ConSentient government worked because, no matter how they defined it, the participants believed in a common justice personally achievable. The *Government* worked because BuSab sat at its core like a terrible watchdog able to attack itself or any seat of power with a delicately balanced immunity. Government worked because there were places where it could not act without being chopped off. An appeal to BuSab made the individual as powerful as the ConSentiency. It all came down to the cynical, self-effacing behavior of the carefully chosen BuSab tentacles.

I don't feel much like a BuSab tentacle this morning, McKie thought.

In his advancing years, he'd often experienced such mornings. He had a personal way of dealing with this mood: he buried himself in work.

McKie turned, crossed to the baffle into his bath where he turned his body over to the programmed ministrations of his morning toilet. The psyche-mirror on the bath's far wall reflected his body while it examined and adjusted to his internal conditions. His eyes told him he was still a squat, dark-skinned gnome of a Human with red hair, features so large they suggested an impossible kinship with the frog people of the Gowachin. The mirror did not reflect his mind, considered by many to be the sharpest legal device in the ConSentiency.

The Daily Schedule began playing to McKie as he emerged from the bath. The DS suited its tone to his movements and the combined analysis of his psycho-physical condition.

"Good morning, ser," it fluted.

McKie, who could interpret the analysis of his mood from the DS tone, put down a flash of resentment. Of course he felt angry and concerned. Who wouldn't under these circumstances?

"Good morning, you dumb inanimate object," he growled. He slipped into a supple armored pullover, dull green and with the outward appearance of cloth.

The DS waited for his head to emerge.

"You wanted to be reminded, ser, that there is a full conference of the Bureau Directorate at nine local this morning, but the . . ."

"Of all the stupid . . ." McKie's interruption stopped the DS. He'd been meaning for some time to reprogram the damned thing. No matter how carefully you set them, they always got out of phase. He didn't bother to bridle his mood, merely spoke the key words in full emotional spate: "Now you hear me, machine: don't you ever again choose that buddy-buddy conversational pattern when I'm in this mood! I want nothing *less* than a reminder of that conference. When you list such a reminder, don't even suggest remotely that it's my wish. Understood?"

"Your admonition recorded and new program instituted, ser." The DS adopted a brisk, matter of fact tone as it continued: "There is a new reason for alluding to the conference."

"Well, get on with it."

McKie pulled on a pair of green shorts and matching kilt of armored material identical to that of the pullover.

The DS continued:

"The conference was alluded to, ser, as introduction to a new datum: you have been asked not to attend."

McKie, bending to fit his feet into self-powered racing boots, hesitated, then:

"But they're still going to have a showdown meeting with all the Gowachin in the Bureau?"

"No mention of that, ser. The message was that you are to depart immediately this morning on the field assignment which was discussed with you. Code Geevee was invoked. An unspecified Gowachin Phylum has asked that you proceed at once to their home planet. That would be Tandaloor. You are to consult there on a problem of a legal nature."

McKie finished fitting the boots, straightened. He could feel all of his accumulated years as though there'd been no geriatric intervention. Geevee invoked a billion kinds of hell. It put him on his own with but one shopside backup facility: a Taprisiot monitor. He'd have his own Taprisiot link sitting safely here on CC while he went out and risked his vulnerable flesh. The Taprisiot served only one function: to note his death and record every aspect of his final moments—every thought, every memory. This would be part of the next agent's briefing. And the next agent would get his own Taprisiot monitor etcetera, etcetera, etcetera . . . BuSab was notorious for gnawing away at its problems. The Bureau never gave up. But the astronomical cost of such a Taprisiot monitor left the operative so gifted with only one conclusion: odds were not in his favor. There'd be no accolades, no cemetery rites for a dead hero . . . probably not even a physical substance of a hero for private grieving.

McKie felt less and less heroic by the minute.

Heroism was for fools and BuSab agents were not employed for their foolishness. He saw the reasoning, though. He was the best qualified non-Gowachin for dealing with the Gowachin. He looked at the nearest DS voder.

"Was it suggested that someone doesn't want me at that conference?"

"There was no such speculation."

"Who gave you this message?"

"Bildoon. Verified voiceprint. He asked that your sleep not be interrupted, that the message be given to you on awakening."

"Did he say he'd call back or ask me to call him?"

"No."

"Did Bilddon mention Dosadi?"

"He said the Dosadi problem is unchanged. Dosadi is not in my banks, ser. Did you wish me to seek more info . . ."

"No! I'm to leave immediately?"

"Bildoon said your orders have been cut. In relationship to Dosadi, he said, and these are his exact words: 'The worst is probable. They have all the motivation required.'"

McKie ruminated aloud: "All the motivation . . . selfish interest or fear . . ."

"Ser, are you inquiring of . . ."

"No, you stupid machine! I'm thinking out loud. People do that. We have to sort things out in our heads, put a proper evaluation on available data."

"You do it with extreme inefficiency."

This startled McKie into a flash of anger. "But this job takes a sentient, a *person*, not a machine! Only a person can make the responsible decision. And I'm the only agent who understands them sufficiently."

"Why not set a Gowachin agent to ferret out their . . ."

"So you've worked it out?"

"It was not difficult, even for a machine. Sufficient clues were provided. And since you'll get a Taprisiot monitor, the project involves danger to your person.

While I do not have specifics about Dosadi, the clear inference is that the
Gowachin have engaged in questionable activity. Let me remind McKie that the
Gowachin do not admit guilt easily. Very few non-Gowachin are considered by
them to be worthy of their company and confidence. They do not like to feel
dependent upon non-Gowachin. In fact, no Gowachin enjoys any dependent
condition, not even when dependent upon another Gowachin. This is at the root of
their law.''

This was a more emotionally loaded conversation than McKie had ever before
heard from his DS. Perhaps his constant refusal to accept the thing on a personal
anthropomorphic basis had forced it into this adaptation. He suddenly felt almost
shy with the DS. What it had said was pertinent, and more than that, vitally
important in a particular way: chosen to help him to the extent the DS was capable.
In McKie's thoughts, the DS was suddenly transformed into a valued confidante.

As though it knew his thoughts, the DS said:

"I'm still a machine. You are inefficient, but as you have correctly stated you
have ways of arriving at accuracy which machines do not understand. We can
only . . . guess, and we are not really programmed to guess unless specifically
ordered to do so on a given occasion. Trust yourself.''

"But you'd rather I were not killed?''

"That is my program.''

"Do you have any more helpful suggestions?''

"You would be advised to waste as little time as possible here. There was a tone
of urgency in Bildoon's voice.''

McKie stared at the nearest voder. Urgency in Bildoon's voice? Even under the
most urgent necessity, Bilddon had never sounded urgent to McKie. Certainly,
Dosadi could be an urgent matter, but . . . Why should that sound a sour note?

"Are you sure he sounded urgent?''

"He spoke rapidly and with obvious tensions.''

"Truthful?''

"The tone-spikes lead to that conclusion.''

McKie shook his head. Something about Bildoon's behavior in this matter
didn't ring true, but whatever it was it escaped the sophisticated reading circuits of
the DS.

And my circuits, too.

Still troubled, McKie ordered the DS to assemble a full travel kit and to read out
the rest of the schedule. He moved to the tool cupboard beside his bath baffle as the
DS began reeling off the schedule.

His day was to start with the Taprisiot appointment. He listened with only part of
his attention, taking care to check the toolkit as the DS assembled it. There were
plastipiks. He handled them gently as they deserved. A selection of stims followed. He rejected these, counting on the implanted sense/muscle amplifiers
which increased the capabilities of senior BuSab agents. Explosives in various
denominations went into the kit—raygens, pentrates. Very careful with these
dangerous items. He accepted multilenses, a wad of uniflesh with matching
mediskin, solvos, miniputer. The DS extruded a life-monitor bead for the Taprisiot
linkage. He swallowed it to give the bead time to anchor in his stomach before the
Taprisiot appointment. A holoscan and matching blanks were accepted, as were
ruptors and comparators. He rejected the adapter for simulation of target identities.
It was doubtful he'd have time or facilities for such sophisticated refinements.
Better to trust his own instincts.

Presently, he sealed the kit in its wallet, concealed the wallet in a pocket. The DS had gone rambling on:

". . . and you'll arrive on Tandaloor at a place called Holy Running. The time there will be early afternoon."

Holy Running!

McKie riveted his attention to this datum. A Gowachin saying skittered through his mind: *The Law is a blind guide, a pot of bitter water. The Law is a deadly contest which can change as waves change.*

No doubt of what had led his thoughts into that path. Holy Running was the place of Gowachin myth. Here, so their stories said, lived Mrreg, the monster who had set the immutable pattern of Gowachin character.

And now, McKie suspected he knew which Gowachin Phylum had summoned him. It could be any one of five Phyla at Holy Running, but he felt certain it'd be the worst of those five—the most unpredictable, the most powerful, the most feared. Where else could a thing such as Dosadi originate?

McKie addressed his DS:

"Send in my breakfast. Please record that the condemned person ate a hearty breakfast."

The DS, programmed to recognize rhetoric for which there was no competent response, remained silent while complying.

> *All sentient beings are created unequal. The best society provides*
> *each with equal opportunity to float at his own level.*
>
> —THE GOWACHIN PRIMARY

BY MID-AFTERNOON, Jedrik saw that her gambit had been accepted. A surplus of fifty Humans was just the right size to be taken by a greedy underling. Whoever it was would see the possibilities of continuing—ten here, thirty there—and because of the way she'd untroduced this *flaw*, the next people discarded would be mostly Humans, but with just enough Gowachin to smack of retaliation.

It'd been difficult carrying out her daily routine knowing what she'd set in motion. It was all very well to accept the fact that you were *going* into danger. When the actual moment arrived, it always had a different character. As the subtle and not so subtle evidence of success accumulated, she felt the crazy force of it rolling over her. Now was the time to think about her true power base, the troops who would obey her slightest hint, the tight communications linkage with the Rim, the carefully selected and trained lieutenants. Now was the time to think about McKie slipping so smoothly into her trap. She concealed elation behind a facade of anger. They'd expect her to be angry.

The evidence began with a slowed response at her computer terminal. Someone was monitoring. Whoever had taken her bait wanted to be certain she was expendable. Wouldn't want to eliminate someone and then discover that the eliminated someone was essential to the power structure. She'd made damned sure to cut a wide swath into a religion which could be made non-essential.

The microsecond delay from the monitoring triggered a disconnect on her telltale circuit, removing the evidence of her preparations before anyone could find it. She didn't think there'd be that much caution in anyone who'd accept this gambit, but unnecessary chances weren't part of her plan. She removed the telltale timer and locked it away in one of the filing cabinets, there to be destroyed with the other evidence when the Elector's toads came prying. The lonely blue flash would be confined by metal walls which would heat to a nice blood red before lapsing into slag and ashes.

In the next stage, people averted their faces as they walked past her office doorway.

Ahhh, the accuracy of the rumor-trail.

The avoidance came so naturally: a glance at a companion on the other side, concentration on material in one's hands, a brisk stride with gaze fixed on the corridor's ends. Important business up there. No time to stop and chat with Keila Jedrik today.

By the Veil of Heaven! They were so transparent!

A Gowachin walked by examining the corridor's blank opposite wall. She knew that Gowachin: one of the Elector's spies. What would he tell Elector Broey today? Jedrik glared at the Gowachin in secret glee. By nightfall, Broey would know who'd picked up her gambit, but it was too small a bite to arouse his avarice. He'd merely log the information for possible future use. It was too early for him to suspect a sacrifice move.

A Human male followed the Gowachin. He was intent on the adjustment of his neckline and that, of course, precluded a glance at a Senior Liaitor in her office. His name was Drayjo. Only yesterday, Drayjo had made courting gestures, bending toward her over this very desk to reveal the muscles under his light grey coveralls. What did it matter that Drayjo no longer saw her as a useful conquest. His face was a wooden door, closed, locked, hiding nothing.

Avert your face, you clog!

When the red light glowed on her terminal screen, it came as anticlimax. Confirmation that her gambit had been accepted by someone who would shortly regret it. Communication flowed across the screen:

"Opp SD22240268523ZX."

Bad news always developed its own coded idiom. She read what followed, anticipating every nuance:

"The Mandate of God having been consulted, the following supernumerary functions are hereby reduced. If your position screen carries your job title with an underline, you are included in the reduction.

"Senior Liaitor."

Jedrik clenched her fists in simulated anger while she glared at the underlined words. It was done, Opp-Out, the good old Double-O. Through its pliable arm, the DemoPol, the Sacred Congregation of the Heavenly Veil had struck again.

None of her elation showed through her Dosadi controls. Someone able to see beyond immediate gain would note presently that only Humans had received this particular good old Double-O. Not one Gowachin there. Whoever made that observation would come sniffing down the trail she'd deliberately left. Evidence would accumulate. She thought she knew who would read that accumulated evidence for Broey. It would be Tria. It was not yet time for Tria to entertain doubts. Broey would hear what Jedrik wanted him to hear. The Dosadi power game would be played by Jedrik's rules then, and by the time others learned the rules it'd be too late.

She counted on the factor which Broey labeled "instability of the masses." Religious twaddle! Dosadi's masses were unstable only in particular ways. Fit a conscious justification to their innermost unconscious demands and they became a predictable system which would leap into predictable actions—especially with a psychotic populace whose innermost demands could never be faced consciously by the individuals. Such a populace remained highly useful to the initiates. That was why they maintained the DemoPol with its mandate-of-God sample. The tools of government were not difficult to understand. All you needed was a pathway into the system, a place where what *you* did touched a new reality.

Broey would think himself the target of her action. More fool he.

Jedrik pushed back her chair, stood and strode to the window hardly daring to think about where her actions would truly be felt. She saw that the sniper's bullet hadn't even left a mark on the glass. These new windows were far superior to the old ones which had taken on dull streaks and scratches after only a few years.

She stared down at the light on the river, carefully preserving this moment, prolonging it.

I won't look up yet, not yet.

Whoever had accepted her gambit would be watching her now. Too late! Too late!

A streak of orange-yellow meandered in the river current: contaminants from the Warren factories . . . poisons. Presently, not looking too high yet, she lifted her gaze to the silvered layers of the Council Hills, to the fluting inverted-stalagmites of the high apartments to which the denizens of Chu aspired in their futile dreams. Sunlight gleamed from the power bulbs which adorned the apartments on the hills. The great crushing wheel of government had its hub on those hills, but the impetus for that wheel had originated elsewhere.

Now, having prolonged the moment while anticipation enriched it, Jedrik lifted her gaze to that region above the Council Hills, to the sparkling streamers and grey glowing of the barrier veil, to the God Wall which englobed her planet in its impenetrable shell. The Veil of Heaven looked the way it always looked in this light. There was no apparent change. But she *knew* what she had done.

Jedrik was aware of subtle instruments which revealed other suns and galaxies beyond the God Wall, places where other planets must exist, but her people had only this one planet. That barrier up there and whoever had created it insured this isolation. Her eyes blurred with quick tears which she wiped away with real anger at herself. Let Broey and his toads believe themselves the only objects of her anger. She would carve a way beyond them through that deadly veil. No one on Dosadi would ever again cower beneath the hidden powers who lived in the sky!

She lowered her gaze to the carpet of factories and Warrens. Some of the defensive walls were faintly visible in the layers of smoke which blanketed the teeming scramble of life upon which the city fed. The smoke erased fine details to separate the apartment hills from the earth. Above the smoke, the fluted buildings became more a part of sky than of ground. Even the ledged, set-back walls of the canyon within which Chu created its sanctuary were no longer attached to the ground, but floated separate from this place where people could survive to a riper maturity on Dosadi. The smoke dulled the greens of ledges and Rim where the Rabble waged a losing battle for suvival. Twenty years was old out there. In that pressure, they fought for a chance to enter Chu's protective confines by any means available, even welcoming the opportunity to eat garbage from which the poisons of this planet had been removed. The worst of Chu was better than their best, which only proved that the conditions of hell were relative.

I seek escape through the God Wall for the same reasons the Rabble seeks entrance to Chu.

In Jedrik's mind lay a graph with an undulant line. It combined many influences: Chu's precious food cycle and economics, Rim incursions, spots which flowed across their veiled sun, subtle planetary movements, atmospheric electricity, gravitational flows, magnetronic fluctuations, the dance of numbers in the Liaitor banks, the seemingly random play of cosmic rays, the shifting colors in the God Wall . . . and mysterious jolts to the entire system which commanded her most concentrated attention. There could be only one source for such jolts: a manipulative intelligence outside the planetary influence of Dosadi. She called that force "X," but she had broken "X" into components. One component was a simulation model of Elector Broey which she carried firmly in her head, not needing any of the mechanical devices for reading such things. "X" and all of its components were as real as anything else on the chart in her mind. By their interplay she read them.

Jedrik addressed herself silently to "X":

By your actions I know you and you are vulnerable.

Despite all of the Sacred Congregation's prattle, Jedrik and her people knew the God Wall had been put there for a specific purpose. It was the purpose which pressed living flesh into Chu from the rim. It was the purpose which jammed too many people into too little space while it frustrated all attempts to spread into any other potential sanctuary. It was the purpose which created people who possessed that terrifying mental template which could trade flesh for flesh . . . Gowachin or Human. Many clues revealed themselves around her and came through that radiance in the sky, but she refused as yet to make a coherent whole out of that purpose. Not yet.

I need this McKie!

With a Jedrik-maintained tenacity, her people knew that the regions beyond the barrier veil were not heaven or hell. Dosadi was hell, but it was a *created* hell. *We will know soon . . . soon.*

This moment had been almost nine Dosadi generations in preparation: the careful breeding of a specific individual who carried in one body the talents required for this assault on "X," the exquisitely detailed education of that weapon-in-fleshly-form . . . and there'd been all the rest of it—whispers, unremarked observations in clandestine leaflets, help for people who held particular ideas and elimination of others whose concepts obstructed, the building of a Rim-Warren communications network, the slow and secret assembly of a military force to match the others which balanced themselves at the peaks of Dosadi power . . . All of these things and much more had prepared the way for those numbers introduced into her computer terminal. The ones who appeared to rule Dosadi like puppets—those ones could be read in many ways and this time the rulers, both visible and hidden, had made one calculation while Jedrik had made another calculation.

Again, she looked up at the God Wall.

You out there! Keila Jedrik knows you're there. And you can be baited, you can be trapped. You are slow and stupid. And you think I don't know how to use your McKie. Ahh, sky demons, McKie will open your veil for me. My life's a wrath and you're the objects of my wrath. I dare what you would not.

Nothing of this revealed itself on her face nor in any movement of her body.

Arm yourself when the Frog God smiles.

—GOWACHIN ADMONITION

MCKIE BEGAN speaking as he entered the Phylum sanctus:

"I'm Jorj X. McKie of the Bureau of Sabotage."

Name and primary allegiance, that was the drill. If he'd been a Gowachin, he'd have named his Phylum or would've favored the room with a long blink to reveal the identifying Phylum tattoo on his eyelids. As a non-Gowachin, he didn't need a tattoo.

He held his right hand extended in the Gowachin peace sign, palm down and fingers wide to show that he held no weapon there and had not extended his claws. Even as he entered, he smiled, knowing the effect this would have on any Gowachin here. In a rare mood of candor, one of his old Gowachin teachers had once explained the effect of a smiling McKie.

"We feel our bones age. It is a very uncomfortable experience."

McKie understood the reason for this. He possessed a thick, muscular body—a swimmer's body with light mahogany skin. He walked with a swimmer's rolling gait. There were Polynesians in his Old Terran ancestry, this much was known in the Family Annals. Wide lips and a flat nose dominated his face; the eyes were large and placidly brown. There was a final genetic ornamentation to confound the Gowachin: red hair. He was the Human equivalent of the greenstone sculpture found in every Phylum house here on Tandaloor. McKie possessed the face and body of the Frog God, the Giver of Law.

As his old teacher had explained, no Gowachin ever fully escaped feelings of awe in McKie's presence, especially when McKie smiled. They were forced to hide a response which went back to the admonition which every Gowachin learned while still clinging to his mother's back.

Arm yourselves! McKie thought.

Still smiling, he stopped after the prescribed eight paces, glanced once around the room, then narrowed his attention. Green crystal walls confined the sanctus. It was not a large space, a gentle oval of perhaps twenty meters in its longest dimension. A single oval window admitted warm afternoon light from Tandaloor's golden sun. The glowing yellow created a contrived *spiritual ring* directly ahead of McKie. The light focused on an aged Gowachin seated in a brown chairdog which had spread itself wide to support his elbows and webbed fingers. At the Gowachin's right hand stood an exquisitely wrought wooden swingdesk on a scroll-work stand. The desk held one object: a metal box of dull blue about fifteen centimeters long, ten wide, and six deep. Standing behind the blue box in the servant-guard position was a red-robed Wreave, her fighting mandibles tucked neatly into the lower folds of her facial slit.

This Phylum was initiating a Wreave!

The realization filled McKie with disquiet. Bildoon had not warned him about Wreaves on Tandaloor. The Wreave indicated a sad shift among the Gowachin toward a particular kind of violence. Wreaves never danced for joy, only for death. And this was the most dangerous of Wreaves, a *female*, recognizable as such by the jaw pouches behind her mandibles. There'd be two males somewhere nearby to form the breeding triad. Wreaves never ventured from their home soil otherwise.

McKie realized he no longer was smiling. These damnable Gowachin! They'd known the effect a Wreave female would have on him. Except in the Bureau, where a special dispensation prevailed, dealing with Wreaves required the most delicate care to avoid giving offense. And because they periodically exchanged triad members, they developed extended families of gigantic proportions wherein offending one member was to offend them all.

These reflections did not sit well with the chill he'd experienced at sight of the blue box on the swingdesk. He still did not know the identity of this Phylum, but he knew what that blue box had to be. He could smell the peculiar scent of antiquity about it. His choices had been narrowed.

"I know you, McKie," the ancient Gowachin said.

He spoke the ritual in standard Galach with a pronounced burr, a fact which revealed he'd seldom been off this planet. His left hand moved to indicate a white chairdog positioned at an angle to his right beyond the swingdesk, yet well within striking range of the silent Wreave.

"Please seat yourself, McKie."

The Gowachin glanced at the Wreave, at the blue box, returned his attention to McKie. It was a deliberate movement of the pale yellow eyes which were moist with age beneath bleached green brows. He wore only a green apron with white shoulder straps which outlined crusted white chest ventricles. The face was flat and sloping with pale, puckered nostrils below a faint nose crest. He blinked and revealed the tattoos on his eyelids. McKie saw there the dark, swimming circle of the Running Phylum, that which legend said had been the first to accept Gowachin Law from the Frog God.

His worst fears confirmed, McKie seated himself and felt the white chairdog adjust to his body. He cast an uneasy glance at the Wreave, who towered behind the swingdesk like a red-robed executioner. The flexing bifurcation which served as Wreave legs moved in the folds of the robe, but without tension. This Wreave was not yet ready to dance. McKie reminded himself that Wreaves were careful in all matters. This had prompted the ConSentient expression, "a Wreave bet." Wreaves were noted for waiting for a sure thing.

"You see the blue box," the old Gowachin said.

It was a statement of mutual understanding, no answer required, but McKie took advantage of the opening.

"However, I do not know your companion."

"This is Ceylang, Servant of the Box."

Ceylang nodded acknowledgment.

A fellow BuSab agent had once told McKie how to count the number of triad exchanges in which a Wreave female had participated.

"A tiny bit of skin is nipped from one of her jaw pouches by the departing companion. It looks like a little pockmark."

Both of Ceylang's pouches were peppered with exchange pocks. McKie nodded to her, formal and correct, no offense intended, none given. He glanced at the box which she served.

McKie had been a Servant of the Box once. This was where you began to learn the limits of legal ritual. The Gowachin words for this novitiate translated as "The Heart of Disrespect." It was the first stage on the road to Legum. The old Gowachin here was not mistaken: Mckie as once of the few non-Gowachin ever admitted to Legum status, to the practice of law in this planetary federation, would *see* that blue box and know what it contained. There would be a small brown book printed on pages of ageless metal, a knife with the blood of many sentient beings dried on its black surface, and lastly a grey rock, chipped and scratched over the millennia in which it'd been used to pound on wood and call Gowachin courts into session. The box and its contents symbolized all that was mysterious and yet practical about Gowachin Law. The book was ageless, yet not to be read and reread; it was sealed in a box where it could be thought upon as a thing which marked a beginning. The knife carried the bloody residue of many endings. And the rock—that came from the natural earth where things only changed, never beginning or ending. The entire assemblage, box and contents, represented a window into the soul of the Frog God's minions. And now they were educating a Wreave as Servant of the Box.

McKie wondered why the Gowachin had chosen a deadly Wreave, but dared not enquire. The blue box, however, was another matter. It said with certainty that a planet called Dosadi would be named openly here. The thing which BuSab had uncovered was about to become an issue in Gowachin Law. That the Gowachin had anticipated Bureau action spoke well of their information sources. A sense of careful choosing radiated from this room. McKie assumed a mask of relaxation and remained silent.

The old Gowachin did not appear pleased by this. He said:

"You once afforded me much amusement, McKie."

That might be a compliment, probably not. Hard to tell. Even if it were a compliment, coming from a Gowachin it would contain signal reservations, especially in legal matters. McKie held his silence. This Gowachin was big power and no mistake. Whoever misjudged him would hear the Courtarena's final trumpet.

"I watched you argue your first case in our courts," the Gowachin said. "Betting was nine-point-three to three-point-eight that we'd see your blood. But when you concluded by demonstrating that eternal sloppiness was the price of liberty . . . ahhh, that was a master stroke. It filled many a Legum with envy. Your words clawed through the skin of Gowachin law to get at the meat. And at the same time you amused us. That was the supreme touch."

Until this moment, McKie had not even suspected that there'd been amusement for anyone in that first case. Present circumstances argued for truthfulness from the old Gowachin, however. Recalling that first case, McKie tried to reassess it in the light of this revelation. He remembered the case well. The Gowachin had charged a Low Magister named Klodik with breaking his most sacred vows in an issue of justice. Klodik's crime was the release of thirty-one fellow Gowachin from their primary allegiance to Gowachin Law and the purpose of that was to qualify the thirty-one for service in BuSab. The hapless prosecutor, a much-admired Legum named Pirgutud, had aspired to Klodik's position and had made the mistake of trying for a direct conviction. McKie had thought at the time that the wiser choice would've been to attempt discrediting the legal structure under which Klodik had been arraigned. This would have thrown judgment into the area of popular choice, and there'd been no doubt that Klodik's early demise would've been popular. Seeing this opening, McKie had attacked the prosecutor as a legalist, a stickler, one who preferred Old Law. Victory had been relatively easy.

When it had come to the knife, however, McKie had found himself profoundly reluctant. There'd been no question of selling Pirgutud back to his own Phylum. BuSab had needed a non-Gowachin Legum . . . the whole non-Gowachin universe had needed this. The few other non-Gowachin who'd attained Legum status were all dead, every last one of them in the Courtarena. A current of animosity toward the Gowachin worlds had been growing. Suspicion fed on suspicion.

Pirgutud had to die in the traditional, the formal, way. He'd known it perhaps better than McKie. Pirgutud, as required, had bared the heart area beside his stomach and clasped his hands behind his head. This extruded the stomach circle, providing a point of reference.

The purely academic anatomy lessons and the practice sessions on lifelike dummies had come to deadly focus.

"Just to the left of the stomach circle imagine a small triangle with an apex at the center of the stomach circle extended horizontally and the base even with the bottom of the stomach circle. Strike into the lower outside corner of this triangle and slightly upward toward the midline."

About the only satisfaction Mckie had found in the event was that Pirgutud had died cleanly and quickly with one stroke. McKie had not entered Gowachin Law as a "hacker."

What had there been in that case and its bloody ending to amuse the Gowachin? The answer filled McKie with a profound sense of peril.

The Gowachin were amused at themselves because they had so misjudged me! But I'd planned all along for them to misjudge me. That was what amused them!

Having provided McKie with a polite period for reflection, the old Gowachin continued:

"I'd bet against you, McKie. The odds, you understand? You delighted me nonetheless. You instructed us while winning your case in a classic manner which would've done credit to the best of us. That is one of the Law's purposes, of course: to test the qualities of those who choose to employ it. Now what did you expect to find when you answered our latest summons to Tandaloor?"

The question's abrupt shift almost caught McKie by surprise.

I've been too long away from the Gowachin, he thought. *I can't relax even for an instant.*

It was almost a palpable thing: if he missed a single beat of the rhythms in this room, he and an entire planet could fall before Gowachin judgment. For a civilization which based its law on the Courtarena where any participant could be sacrificed, anything was possible. McKie chose his next words with life-and-death care.

"You summoned me, that is true, but I came on official business of my Bureau. It's the Bureau's expectations which concern me."

"Then you are in a difficult position because you're also a Legum of the Gowachin Bar subject to our demands. Do you know me?"

This was a Magister, a *Foremost-Speaker* from the "Phylum of Phylums," no doubt of it. He was a survivor in one of the most cruel traditions known to the sentient universe. His abilities and resources were formidable and he was on his home ground. McKie chose the cautious response.

"On my arrival I was told to come to this place at this time. That is what I know."

The least thing that is known shall govern your acts. This was the course of evidence for the Gowachin. McKie's response put a legal burden on his questioner.

The old Gowachin's hands clutched with pleasure at the level of artistry to which this contest had risen. There was a momentary silence during which Ceylang gathered her robe tightly and moved even closer to the swingdesk. Now, there was tension in her movements. The Magister stirred, said:

"I have the disgusting honor to be High Magister of the Running Phylum, Aritch by name."

As he spoke, his right hand thrust out, took the blue box, and dropped it into McKie's lap. "I place the binding oath upon you in the name of the book!"

As McKie had expected, it was done swiftly. He had the box in his hands while the final words of the ancient legal challenge were ringing in his ears. No matter the ConSentient modifications of Gowachin Law which might apply in this situation, he was caught in a convoluted legal maneuvering. The metal of the box felt cold against his fingers. They'd confronted him with *the* High Magister. The Gowachin were dispensing with many preliminaries. This spoke of time pressures and a particular assessment of their own predicament. McKie reminded himself that he was dealing with people who found pleasure in their own failures, could be amused by death in the Courtarena, whose most consummate pleasure came when the currents of their own Law were changed artistically.

McKie spoke with the careful formality which ritual required if he were to emerge alive from this room.

"Two wrongs may cancel each other. Therefore, let those who do wrong do it together. That is the true purpose of Law."

Gently, McKie released the simple swing catch on the box, lifted the lid to verify the contents. This must be done with precise attention to formal details. A bitter, musty odor touched his nostrils as the lid lifted. The box held what he'd expected: the book, the knife, the rock. It occurred to McKie then that he was holding the original of all such boxes. It was a thing of enormous antiquity—thousands upon thousands of standard years. Gowachin professed the belief that the Frog God had created this box, this *very* box, and it contents as a model, the symbol of "the only workable Law."

Careful to do it with his right hand, McKie touched each item of the box in its turn, closed the lid and latched it. As he did his, he felt that he stepped into a ghostly parade of Legums, names imbedded in the minstrel chronology of Gowachin history.

Bishkar who concealed her eggs . . .

Kondush the Diver . . .

Dritaik who sprang from the march and laughed at Mrreg . . .

Tonkeel of the hidden knife . . .

McKie wondered then how they would sing about him. Would it be *McKie the blunderer?* His thoughts raced through review of the necessities. The primary necessity was Aritch. Little was known about this High Magister outside the Gowachin Federation, but it was said that he'd once won a case by finding a popular bias which allowed him to kill a judge. The commentary on this coup said Aritch "embraced the Law in the same way that salt dissolves in water." To the initiates, this meant Aritch personified the basic Gowachin attitude toward their Law: "respectful disrespect." It was a peculiar form of sanctity. Every movement of your body was as important as your words. The Gowachin made it an aphorism.

"You hold your life in your mouth when you enter the Courtarena."

They provided legal ways to kill any participant—judges, Legums, clients . . . But it must be done with exquisite legal finesse, with its justifications apparent to all observers, and with the most delicate timing. Above all, one could kill in the arena only when no other choice offered the same worshipful disrespect for Gowachin Law. Even while changing the Law, you were required to revere its sanctity.

When you entered the Courtarena, you had to feel that peculiar sanctity in every fiber. The forms . . . the forms . . . the forms . . . With that blue box in his hands, the deadly forms of Gowachin Law dominated every movement, every word. Knowing McKie was not Gowachin-born, Aritch was putting time pressures on him, hoping for an immediate flaw. They didn't want this Dosadi matter in the arena. That was the immediate contest. And if it did get to the arena . . . well, the crucial matter would be selection of the judges. Judges were chosen with great care. Both sides maneuvered in this, being cautious not to intrude a professional legalist onto the bench. Judges could represent those whom the Law had offended. They could be private citizens in any number satisfactory to the opposing forces. Judges could be (and often were) chosen for their special knowledge of a case at hand. But here you were forced to weigh the subtleties of prejudgement. Gowachin Law made a special distinction between prejudgment and bias.

McKie considered this.

The interpretation of bias was: "If I can rule for a particular side I will do so."

For prejudgment: "No matter what happens in the arena I will rule for a particular side."

Bias was permitted, but not prejudgment.

Aritch was the first problem, his possible prejudgments, his bias, his inborn and most deeply conditioned attitudes. In his deepest feelings, he would look down on all non-Gowachin legal systems as "devices to weaken personal character through appeals to illogic, irrationality, and to ego-centered selfishness in the name of high purpose."

If Dosadi came to the area, it would be tried under modified Gowachin Law. The modifications were a thorn in the Gowachin skin. They represented concessions made for entrance into the ConSentiency. Periodically, the Gowachin tried to make their Law the basis for all ConSentient Law.

McKie recalled that a Gowachin had once said of ConSentient Law:

"It fosters greed, discontent, and competitiveness not based on excellence but on appeals to prejudice and materialism."

Abruptly, McKie remembered that this was a quoatation attributed to Aritch, High Magister of the Running Phylum. Were there even more deeply hidden motives in what the Gowachin did here?

Showing signs of impatience, Aritch inhaled deeply through his chest ventricles, said:

"You are now my Legum. To be convicted is to go free because this marks you as enemy of all government. I know you to be such an enemy, McKie."

"You know me," McKie agreed.

It was more than ritual response and obedience to forms, it was truth. But it required great effort for McKie to speak it calmly. In the almost fifty years since he'd been admitted to the Gowachin Bar, he'd served that ancient legal structure four times in the Courtarena, a minor record among the ordinary Legums. Each time, his personal survival had been in the balance. In all of its stages, this contest was a deadly battle. The loser's life belonged to the winner and could be taken at the winner's discretion. On rare occasions, the loser might be sold back to his own Phylum as a menial. Even the losers disliked this choice.

Better clean death than dirty life.

The blood-encrusted knife in the blue box testified to the more popular outcome. It was a practice which made for rare litigation and memorable court performances.

Aritch, speaking with eyes closed and the Running Phylum tattoos formally displayed, brought their encounter to its testing point.

"Now McKie, you will tell me what official matters of the Bureau of Sabotage bring you to the Gowachin Federation."

Law must retain useful ways to break with traditional forms because nothing is more certain than that the forms of Law remain when all justice is gone.

—GOWACHIN APHORISM

HE WAS tall for a Dosadi Gowachin, but fat and ungroomed. His feet shuffled when he walked and there was a permanent stoop to his shoulders. A flexing wheezing overcame his chest ventricles when he became excited. He knew this and was aware that those around him knew it. He often used this characteristic as a warning, reminding people that no Dosadi held more power than he, and that power was deadly. All Dosadi knew his name: Broey. And very few misinterpreted the fact that he'd come up through the Sacred Congregations of the Heavenly Veil to his post as chief steward of Control: The Elector. His private army was Dosadi's largest, most efficient, and best armed. Broey's intelligence corps was a thing to invoke fear and admiration. He maintained a fortified suite atop his headquarters building, a structure of stone and plasteel which fronted the main arm of the river in the heart of Chu. Around this core, the twisting walled fortification of the city stepped outward in concentric rings. The only entrance to Broey's citadel was through a guarded Tube Gate in a subbasement, designated TG One. TG One admitted the select of the select and no others.

In the forenoon, the ledges outside Broey's windows were a roosting place for carrion birds, who occupied a special niche on Dosadi. Since the Lords of the Veil forbade the eating of sentient flesh by sentient, this task devolved upon the birds. Flesh from the people of Chu and even from the Rim carried fewer of the planet's heavy metals. The carrion birds prospered. A flock of them strutted along Broey's ledge, coughing, squawking, defecating, brushing against each other with avian insolence while they watched the outlying streets for signs of food. They also watched the Rim, but it had been temporarily denied to them by a sonabarrier. Bird sounds came through a voder into one of the suite's eight rooms. This was a yellow-green space about ten meters long and six wide occupied by Broey and two Humans.

Broey uttered a mild expletive at the bird noise. The confounded creatures interfered with clear thinking. He shuffled to the window and silenced the voder. In the sudden quiet he looked out at the city's perimeter and the lower ledges of the enclosing cliffs. Another Rim foray had been repulsed out there in the night. Broey had made a personal inspection in a convoy of armored vehicles earlier. The troops liked it that he occasionally shared their dangers. The carrion birds already had cleaned up most of the mess by the time the armored column swept through. The flat back structure of Gowachin, who had no front rib cage, had been easily distinguishable from the white framework which had housed Human organs. Only a few rags of red and green flesh had marked where the birds had abandoned their feast when the sonabarriers herded them away.

When he considered the sonabarriers, Broey's thoughts grew hard and clear. The sonabarriers were one of Gar's damned affectations! *Let the birds finish it.*

But Gar insisted a few bodies be left around to make the point for the Rim survivors that their attacks were hopeless.

The bones by themselves would be just as effective.

Gar was bloody minded.

Broey turned and glanced across the room past his two Human companions. Two of the walls were taken up by charts bearing undulant squiggles in many colors. On a table at the room's center lay another chart with a single red line. The line curved and dipped, ending almost in the middle of the chart. Near this terminus lay a white card and beside it stood a Human male statuette with an enormous erection which was labeled "Rabble." It was a subversive, forbidden artifact of Rim origin. The people of the Rim knew where their main strength lay: breed, breed, breed . . .

The Humans sat facing each other across the chart. They fitted into the space around them through a special absorption. It was as though they'd been initiated into the secrets of Broey's citadel through an esoteric ritual both forbidding and dangerous.

Broey returned to his chair at the head of the table, sat down, and quietly continued to study his companions. He experienced amusement to feel his fighting claws twitch beneath their finger shields as he looked at the two. Yes—trust them no more than they trusted him. They had their own troops, their own spies—they posed real threat to Broey but often their help was useful. Just as often they were a nuisance.

Quilliam Gar, the Human male who sat with his back to the windows, looked up as Broey resumed his seat. Gar snorted, somehow conveying that he'd been about to silence the voder himself.

Damned carrion birds! But they were useful . . . useful.

The Rim-born were always ambivalent about the birds.

Gar rode his chair as though talking down to ranks of the uninformed. He'd come up through the educational services in the Convocation before joining Broey. Gar was thin with an inner emaciation so common that few on Dosadi gave it any special notice. He had the hunter's face and eyes, carried his eighty-eight years as though they were twice that. Hairline wrinkles crawled down his cheeks. The bas-relief of veins along the backs of his hands and the grey hair betrayed his Rim origins, as did a tendency to short temper. The Labor Pool green of his clothing fooled very few, his face was that well known.

Across from Gar sat his eldest daughter and chief lieutenant, Tria. She'd placed herself there to watch the windows and the cliffs. She'd also been observing the carrion birds, rather enjoying their sounds. It was well to be reminded here of what lay beyond the city's outer gates.

Tria's face held too much brittle sharpness to be considered beautiful by any except an occasional Gowachin looking for an exotic experience or a Warren laborer hoping to use her as a step out of peonage. She often disconcerted her companions by a wide-eyed, cynical stare. She did this with an aristocratic sureness which commanded attention. Tria had developed the gesture for just this purpose. Today, she wore the orange with black trim of Special Services, but without a brassard to indicate the branch. She knew that this led many to believe her Broey's personal toy, which was true but not in the way the cynical supposed.

Tria understood her special value: she possessed a remarkable ability to interpret the vagaries of the DemoPol.

Indicating the red line on the chart in front of her, Tria said, "She has to be the one. How can you doubt it?" And she wondered why Broey continued to worry at the obvious.

"Keila Jedrik," Broey said. And again: "Keila Jedrik."

Gar squinted at his daughter.

"Why would she include herself among the fifty who . . ."

"She sends us a message," Broey said. "I hear it clearly now." He seemed pleased by his own thoughts.

Gar read something else in the Gowachin's manner.

"I hope you're not having her killed."

"I'm not as quick to anger as are you Humans," Broey said.

"The usual surveillance?" Gar asked.

"I haven't decided. You know, don't you, that she lives a rather celibate life? Is it that she doesn't enjoy the males of your species?"

"More likely they don't enjoy her," Tria said.

"Interesting. Your breeding habits are so peculiar."

Tria shot a measuring stare at Broey. She wondered why the Gowachin had chosen to wear black today. It was a robe-like garment cut at a sharp angle from shoulders to waist, clearing his ventricles. The ventricles revolted her and Broey knew this. The very thought of them pressing against her . . . She cleared her throat. Broey seldom wore black; it was the happy color of priestly celebrants. He wore it, though, with a remoteness which suggested that thoughts passed through his mind which no other person could experience.

The exchange between Broey and Tria worried Gar. He could not help but feel the oddity that each of them tried to present a threatening view of events by withholding some data and coloring other data.

"What if she runs out to the Rim?" Gar asked.

Broey shook his head.

"Let her go. She's not one to stay on the Rim."

"Perhaps we should have her picked up," Gar said.

Broey stared at him, then:

"I've gained the distinct impression that you've some private plan in mind. Are you prepared to share it?"

"I've no idea what you . . ."

"Enough!" Broey shouted. His ventricles wheezed as he inhaled.

Gar held himself very quiet.

Broey leaned toward him, noting that this exchange amused Tria.

"It's too soon to make decisions we cannot change! This is a time for ambiguity."

Irritated by his own display of anger, Broey arose and hurried into his adjoining office, where he locked the door. It was obvious that those two had no more idea than he where Jedrik had gone to ground. But it was still his game. She couldn't hide forever. Seated once more in his office, he called Security.

"Has Bahrank returned?"

A senior Gowachin officer hurried into the screen's view, looked up.

"Not yet."

"What precautions to learn where he delivers his cargo?"

"We know his entry gate. It'll be simple to track him."

"I don't want Gar's people to know what you're doing."

"Understood."

"That other matter?"

"Pcharky may have been the last one. He could be dead, too. The killers were thorough."

"Keep searching."

Broey put down a sense of disquiet. Some very un-Dosadi things were happening in Chu . . . and on the Rim. He felt that things occurred which his spies could not uncover. Presently, he returned to the more pressing matter.

"Bahrank is not to be interfered with until afterward."

"Understood."

"Pick him up well clear of his delivery point and bring him to your section. I will interview him personally."

"Sir, his addiction to . . ."

"I know the hold she has on him. I'm counting on it."

"We've not yet secured any of that substance, sir, although we're still trying."

"I want success, not excuses. Who's in charge of that?"

"Kidge, sir. He's very efficient in this . . ."

"Is Kidge available?"

"One moment, sir. I'll put him on."

Kidge had a phlegmatic Gowachin face and rumbling voice.

"Do you want a status report, sir?"

"Yes."

"My Rim contacts believe the addictive substance is derived from a plant called 'tibac.' We have no prior record of such a plant, but the outer Rabble has been cultivating it lately. According to my contacts, it's extremely addictive to Humans, even more so to us."

"No record? What's its origin? Do they say?"

"I talked personally to a Human who'd recently returned from upriver where the outer Rabble reportedly has extensive plantations of this 'tibac.' I promised my informant a place in the Warrens if he provides me with a complete report on the stuff and a kilo packet of it. This informant says the cultivators believe tibac has religious significance. I didn't see any point in exploring that."

"When do you expect him to deliver?"

"By nightfall at the latest."

Broey held his silence for a moment. *Religious significance.* More than likely the plant came from beyond the God Wall then, as Kidge implied. But why? What were *they* doing?

"Do you have new instructions?" Kidge asked.

"Get that substance up to me as soon as you can."

Kidge fidgeted. He obviously had another question, but was unwilling to ask it. Broey glared at him.

"Yes? What is it?"

"Don't you want the substance tested first?"

It was a baffling question. Had Kidge withheld vital information about the dangers of this tibac? One never knew from what quarter an attack might come. But Kidge was held in his own special bondage. He knew what could happen to him if he failed Broey. And Jedrik had handled this stuff. But why had Kidge asked this question? Faced with such unknowns, Broey tended to withdraw into himself, eyes veiled by the nictating membrane while he weighed the possibilities. Presently, he stirred, looked at Kidge in the screen.

"If there's enough of it, feed some to volunteers—both Human and Gowachin. Get the rest of it up to me immediately, even while you're testing, but in a sealed container."

"Sir, there are rumors about this stuff. It'll be difficult getting real volunteers."

"You'll think of something."

Broey broke the connection, returned to the outer room to make his political peace with Gar and Tria. He was not ready to blunt that pair . . . not yet.

They were sitting just as he'd left them. Tria was speaking:

". . . the hightest probability and I have to go on that."

Gar merely nodded.

Broey seated himself, nodded to Tria, who continued as though there'd been no hiatus.

"Clearly, Jedrik's a genius. And her Loyalty Index! That has to be false, contrived. And look at her decisions: one questionable decision in four years. One!"

Gar moved a finger along the red line on the chart. It was a curiously sensuous gesture, as though he were stroking flesh.

Broey gave him a verbal prod.

"Yes, Gar, what is it?"

"I was just wondering if Jedrik could be another . . ."

His glance darted ceilingward, back to the chart. They all understood his allusion to intruders from beyond the God Wall.

Broey looked at Gar as though awakening from an interrupted thought. What'd that fool Gar mean by raising such a question at this juncture? The required responses were so obvious.

"I agree with Tria's analysis," Broey said. "As to your question . . ." He gave a Human shrug. "Jedrik reveals some of the classic requirements, but . . ." Again, that shrug. "This is still the world God gave us."

Colored as they were by his years in the Sacred Congregation, Broey's words took on an unctuous overtone, but in this room the message was strictly secular.

"The others have been such disappointments," Gar said. "Especially Havvy." He moved the statuette to a more central position on the chart.

"We failed because we were too eager," Tria said, her voice snappish. "Poor timing."

Gar scratched his chin with his thumb. Tria sometimes disturbed him by that accusatory tone she took toward their failures. He said:

"But . . . if she turns out to be one of *them* and we haven't allowed for it . . ."

"We'll look through that gate when we come to it," Broey said. "*If* we come to it. Even another failure could have its uses. The food factories will give us a substantial increase at the next harvest. That means we can postpone the more troublesome political decisions which have been bothering us."

Broey let this thought hang between them while he set himself to identifying the lines of activity revealed by what had happened in this room today. Yes, the Humans betrayed unmistakable signs that they behaved according to a secret plan. Things were going well, then: they'd attempt to supersede him soon . . . and fail.

A door behind Tria opened. A fat Human female entered. Her body bulbed in green coveralls and her round face appeared to float in a halo of yellow hair. Her cheeks betrayed the telltale lividity of *dacon* addiction. She spoke subserviently to Gar.

"You told me to interrupt if . . ."

"Yes, yes."

Gar waved to indicate she could speak freely. The gesture's significance did not escape Broey. Another part of their set piece.

"We've located Havvy but Jedrik's not with him."

Gar nodded, addressed Broey:

"Whether Jedrik's an agent or another puppet, this whole thing smells of something *they* have set in motion."

Once more, his gaze darted ceilingward.

"I will act on that assumption," Tria said. She pushed her chair back, arose, "I'm going into the Warrens."

Broey looked up at her. Again, he felt his talons twitch beneath their sheaths. He said:

"Don't interfere with them."

Gar forced his gaze away from the Gowachin while his mind raced. Often, the Gowachin were difficult to read, but Broey had been obvious just then: he was confident that he could locate Jedrik and he didn't care who knew it. That could be very dangerous.

Tria had seen it, too, of course, but she made no comment, merely turned and followed the fat woman out of the room.

Gar arose like a folding ruler being opened to its limit. "I'd best be getting along. There are many matters requiring my personal attention."

"We depend on you for a great deal," Broey said.

He was not yet ready to release Gar, however. Let Tria get well on her way. Best to keep those two apart for a spell. He said:

"Before you go, Gar. Several things still bother me. Why was Jedrik so precipitate? And why destroy her records? What was it that we were not supposed to see?"

"Perhaps it was an attempt to confuse us," Gar said, quoting Tria. "One thing's for sure: it wasn't just an angry gesture."

"There must be a clue somewhere," Broey said.

"Would you have us risk an interrogation of Havvy?"

"Of course not!"

Gar showed no sign that he recognized Broey's anger. He said:

"Despite what you and Tria say, I don't think we can afford another mistake at this time. Havvy was . . . well . . ."

"If you recall," Broey said, "Havvy was not one of Tria's mistakes. She went along with us under protest. I wish now we'd listened to her." He waved a hand idly in dismissal. "Go see to your important affairs." He watched Gar leave.

Yes, on the basis of the Human's behavior it was reasonable to assume he knew nothing as yet about this *infiltrator* Bahrank was bringing through the gates. Gar would've concealed such valuable information, would not have dared raise the issue of a God Wall intrusion . . . Or would he? Broey nodded to himself. This must be handled with great delicacy.

*We will now explore the particular imprint which various govern-
ments make upon the individual. First, be sure you recognize the
primary governing force. For example, take a careful look at
Human history. Humans have been known to submit to many
constraints: to rule by Autarchs, by Plutarchs, by the power seek-
ers of the many Republics, by Oligarchs, by tyrant Majorities and
Minorities, by the hidden suasions of Polls, by profound instincts
and shallow juvenilities. And always, the governing force as we
wish you now to understand this concept was whatever the individual believed had control over his immediate survival. Survival
sets the pattern of imprint. During much of Human history (and the
pattern is similar with most sentient species) Corporation presi-
dents held more survival in their casual remarks than did the
figurehead officials. We of the ConSentiency cannot forget this as
we keep watch on the Multiworld Corporations. We dare not even
forget it of ourselves. Where you work for you own survival, this
dominates your imprint, this dominates what you believe.*

—INSTRUCTION MANUAL
BUREAU OF SABOTAGE

NEVER DO what your enemy wants you to do, McKie reminded himself

In this moment, Aritch was the enemy, having placed the binding oath of Legum
upon an agent of BuSab, having demanded information to which he had no right.
The old Gowachin's behavior was consistent with the demands of his own legal
system, but it immediately magnified the area of conflict by an enormous factor.
McKie chose a minimal response.

"I'm here because Tandaloor is the heart of the Gowachin Federation."

Aritch, who'd been sitting with his eyes closed to emphasize the formal
client-Legum relationship, opened his eyes to glare at McKie.

"I remind you *once* that I am your client."

Signs indicating a dangerous new tension in the Wreave servant were increasing, but McKie was forced to concentrate his attention on Aritch.

"You name your *self* client. Very well. The client must answer truthfully such
questions as the Legum asks when the legal issues demand it."

Aritch continued to glare at McKie, latent fire in the yellow eyes. Now, the
battle was truly joined.

McKie sensed how fragile was the relationship upon which his survival depended. The Gowachin, signatories to the great ConSentiency Pact binding the
species of the known universe, were legally subject to certain BuSab intrusions.
But Aritch had placed them on another footing. If the Gowachin Federation
disagreed with McKie/Agent, they could take him into the Courtarena as a Legum
who had wronged a client. With the entire Gowachin Bar arrayed against him,
McKie did not doubt which Legum would *taste the knife.* His one hope lay in
avoiding immediate litigation. That was, after all, the real basis of Gowachin Law.

Moving a step loser to specifics, McKie said:

"My Bureau has uncovered a matter of embarrassment to the Gowachin
Federation."

Aritch blinked twice.

"As we suspected."

McKie shook his head. They didn't *suspect,* they knew. He counted on this: that the Gowachin understood why he'd answered their summons. If any Sentiency under the Pact could understand his position, it had to be the Gowachin. BuSab reflected Gowachin philosophy. Centuries had passed since the great convulsion out of which BuSab had originated, but the ConSentiency had never been allowed to forget that birth. It was taught to the young of every species

"Once, long ago, a tyrannical majority captured the government. They said they would make all individuals equal. They meant they would not let any individual be better than another at doing anything. Excellence was to be suppressed or concealed. The tyrants made their government act with great speed 'in the name of the people.' They removed delays and red tape wherever found. There was little deliberation. Unaware that they acted out of an unconscious compulsion to prevent all change, the tyrants tried to enforce a grey sameness upon every population.

"Thus the powerful governmental machine blundered along at increasingly reckless speed. It took commerce and all the important elements of society with it. Laws were thought of and passed within hours. Every society came to be twisted into a suicidal pattern. People became unprepared for those changes which the universe demands. They were unable to change.

"It was the time of *brittle money,* 'appropriated in the morning and gone by nightfall,' as you learned earlier. In their passion for sameness, the tyrants made themselves more and more powerful. All others grew correspondingly weaker and weaker. New bureaus and directorates, odd ministries, leaped into existence for the most improbable purposes. These became the citadels of a new aristocracy, rulers who kept the giant wheel of government careening along, spreading destruction, violence, and chaos wherever they touched.

"In those desperate times, a handful of people (the Five Ears, their makeup and species never revealed) created the Sabotage Corps to slow that runaway wheel of government. The original corps was bloody, violent, and cruel. Gradually, the original efforts were replaced by more subtle methods. The governmental wheel slowed, became more manageable. Deliberation returned.

"Over the generations, that original Corps became a Bureau, the Bureau of Sabotage, with its present Ministerial powers, preferring diversion to violence, but ready for violence when the need arises."

They were words from McKie's own teens, generators of a concept modified by his experiences in the Bureau. Now, he was aware that his directorate composed of all the known sentient species was headed into its own entropic corridors. Someday, the Bureau would dissolve or be dissolved, but the universe still needed them. The old imprints remained, the old futile seeking after absolutes of sameness. It was the ancient conflict between what the individual saw as personal needs for immediate survival and what the totality required if *any* were to survive. And now it was the Gowachin versus the ConSentiency, and Aritch was the champion of his people.

McKie studied the High Magister carefully, sensitive to the unrelieved tensions in Wreave attendant. Would there be violence in this room? It was a question which remained unanswered as McKie spoke.

"You have observed that I am in a difficult position. I do not enjoy the embarrassment of revered teachers and friends nor of their compatriots. Yet, evidence has been seen . . ."

He let his voice trail off. Gowachin disliked dangling implications.

Aritch's claws slid from the sheaths of his webbed fingers.

"Your client wishes to hear of this evidence."

Before speaking, McKie rested his hand on the latch of the box in his lap.

"Many people from two species have disappeared. Two species: Gowachin and Human. Singly, these were small matters, but these disappearances have been going on for a long time—perhaps twelve or fifteen generations by the old Human reckoning. Taken together, these disappearances are massive. We've learned that there's a planet called Dosadi where these people were taken. Such evidence as we have has been examined carefully. It all leads to the Gowachin Federation."

Aritch's fingers splayed, a sign of acute embarrassment. Whether assumed or real, McKie could not tell.

"Does your Bureau accuse the Gowachin?"

"You know the function of my Bureau. We do not yet know the location of Dosadi, but we'll find it."

Aritch remained silent. He knew BuSab had never given up on a problem.

McKie raised the blue box.

"Having thrust this upon me, you've made me guardian of your fate, client. You've no rights to inquire as to my methods. I will not follow *old* law."

Aritch nodded.

"It was my argument that you'd react thus."

He raised his right hand.

The rhythmic "death flexion" swept over the Wreave and her fighting mandibles darted from her facial slit.

At the first movement from her, McKie whipped open the blue box, snatched out book and knife. He spoke with a firmness his body did not feel:

"If she makes the slightest move toward me, my blood will defile this book." He placed the knife against his own wrist. "Does your Servant of the Box know the consequences? The history of the Running Phylum would end. Another Phylum would be presumed to've accepted the Law from its Giver. The name of the Phylum's *last* High Magister would be erased from living thought. Gowachin would eat their own eggs at the merest hint that they had Running Phylum blood in their veins."

Aritch remained frozen, right hand raised. Then:

"McKie, you are revealed as a sneak. Only by spying on our most sacred rituals could you know this."

"Did you think me some fearful, pliable dolt, client? I am a true Legum. A Legum does not have to sneak to learn the Law. When you admitted me to your Bar you opened every door."

Slowly, muscles quivering, Aritch turned and spoke to the Wreave:

"Ceylang?"

She had difficulty speaking while her poison-tipped fighting mandibles remained extruded.

"Your command?"

"Observe this Human well. Study him. You will meet again."

"I obey."

"You may go, but remember my words."

"I remember."

McKie, knowing the death dance could not remain uncompleted, stopped her.

"Ceylang!"

Slowly, reluctantly, she looked at him.

"*Do* observe me well, Ceylang. I am what you hope to be. And I warn you: unless you shed your Wreave skin you will never be a Legum." He nodded in dismissal. "Now, you may go."

In a fluid swish of robes she obeyed, but her fighting mandibles remained out, their poison tips glittering. Somewhere in her triad's quarters, McKie knew, there'd be a small feathered pet which would die presently with poison from its mistress burning through its veins. Then the death dance would be ended and she could retract her mandibles. But the hate would remain.

When the door had closed behind the red robe, McKie restored book and knife to the box, returned his attention to Aritch. Now, when McKie spoke, it was really Legum to client without any sophistry, and they both knew it.

"What would tempt the High Magister of the renowned Running Phylum to bring down the Arch of Civilization?"

McKie's tone was conversational, between equals.

Aritch had trouble adjusting to the new status. His thoughts were obvious. If McKie had witnessed a Cleansing Ritual, McKie had to be accepted as a Gowachin. But McKie was *not* Gowachin. Yet he'd been accepted before the Gowachin Bar . . . and if he'd seen that most sacred ritual . . .

Presently, Aritch spoke.

"Where did you see the ritual?"

"It was performed by the Phylum which sheltered me on Tandaloor."

"The Dry Heads?"

"Yes."

"Did they know you witnessed?"

"They invited me."

"How did you shed your skin?"

"They scraped me raw and preserved the scrapings."

Aritch took some time digesting this. The Dry Heads had played their own secret game of Gowachin politics and now the secret was out. He had to consider the implications. What had they hoped to gain? He said:

"You wear no tattoo."

"I've never made formal application for Dry Heads membership."

"Why?"

"My primary allegiance is to BuSab."

"The Dry Heads know this?"

"They encourage it."

"But what motivated them to . . ."

McKie smiled.

Aritch glanced at a veiled alcove at the far end of the sanctum, back to McKie. A likeness to the Frog God?

"It'd take more than that."

McKie shrugged.

Aritch mused aloud:

"The Dry Heads supported Klodik in his crime when you . . ."

"Not crime."

"I stand corrected. You won Klodik's freedom. And after your victory the Dry Heads invited you to the Cleansing Ritual."

"A Gowachin in BuSab cannot have divided allegiance."

"But a Legum serves only the Law!"

"BuSab and Gowachin Law are not in conflict."

"So the Dry Heads would have us believe."

"Many Gowachin believe it."

"But Klodik's case was not a true test."

Realization swept through McKie: Aritch regretted more than a lost bet. He'd put his money with his hopes. It was time then to redirect this conversation.

"I am your Legum."

Aritch spoke with resignation.

"You are."

"Your Legum wishes to hear of the Dosadi problem."

"A thing is not a problem until it arouses sufficient concern." Aritch glanced at the box in McKie's lap. "We're dealing with differences in value, changes in values."

McKie did not believe for an instant this was the tenor of Gowachin defense, but Aritch's words gave him pause. The Gowachin combined such an odd mixture of respect and disrespect for their Law and all government. At the root lay their unchanging rituals, but above that everything remained as fluid as the seas in which they'd evolved. Constant fluidity was the purpose behind their rituals. You never entered any exchange with Gowachin on a sure-footed basis. They did something different every time . . . religiously. It was their nature. *All ground is temporary. Law is made to be changed.* That was their catechism. *To be a Legum is to learn where to place your feet.*

"The Dry Heads did something different," McKie said.

This plunged Aritch into gloom. His chest ventricles wheezed, indicating he'd speak *from the stomach.*

"The people of the ConSentiency come in so many different forms: Wreaves (a flickering glance doorward), Sobarips, Laclacs, Calebans, PanSpechi, Palenki, Chithers, Taprisiots, Humans, we of the Gowachin . . . so many. The unknowns between us defy counting."

"As well count the drops of water in a sea."

Aritch grunted, then:

"Some diseases cross the barriers between species."

McKie stared at him. Was Dosadi a medical experiment station? Impossible! There would be no reason for secrecy then. Secrecy defeated the efforts to study a common problem and the Gowachin knew it.

"You are not studying Gowachin-Human diseases."

"Some diseases attack the psyche and cannot be traced to any physical agent."

McKie absorbed this. Although Gowachin definitions were difficult to understand, they permitted no aberrant behavior. Different behavior, yes; aberrant behavior, no. You could challenge the Law, not the ritual. They were compulsive in this regard. They slew the ritual deviant out of hand. It required enormous restraint on their part to deal with another species.

Aritch continued:

"Terrifying psychological abrasions occur when divergent species confront each other and are forced to adapt to new ways. We seek new knowledge in this arena of behavior."

McKie nodded.

One of his Dry Head teachers had said it: "No matter how painful, life must adapt or die."

It was a profound revelation about how Gowachin applied their insight to themselves. Law changed, but it changed on a foundation which could not be permitted the slightest change. "Else, how do we know where we are or where we have been?" But encounters with other species changed the foundation. Life adapted . . . willingly or by force.

McKie spoke with care.

"Psychological experiments with people who've not given their informed consent are still illegal . . . even among the Gowachin."

Aritch would not accept this argument.

"The ConSentiency in all of its parts has accumulated a long history of scientific studies into behavioral and biomedical questions where people are the final test site."

McKie said:

"And the first issue when you propose such an experiment is 'How great is the known risk to the subjects?'"

"But, my dear Legum, *informed consent* implies that the experimenter knows all the risks and can describe them to his test subjects. I ask you: how can that be when the experiment goes beyond what you already know? How can you describe risks which you cannot anticipate?"

"You submit a proposal to many recognized experts in the field," McKie said. "They weigh the proposed experiment against whatever value the new knowledge is expected to uncover."

"Ahhh, yes. We submit our proposal to fellow researchers, to people whose *mission*, whose very view of their own personal identity is controlled by the belief that they can improve the lot of all sentient beings. Tell me, Legum: do review boards composed of such people reject many experimental proposals?"

McKie saw the direction of the argument. He spoke with care.

"They don't reject many proposals, that's true. Still, you didn't submit your Dosadi protocol to any outside review. Was that to keep it secret from your own people or from others?"

"We feared the fate of our proposal should it run the gauntlet of other species."

"Did a Gowachin majority approve your project?"

"No. But we both know that having a majority set the experimental guidelines gives no guarantee against dangerous projects."

"Dosadi has proved dangerous?"

Aritch remained silent for several deep breaths, then:

"It has proved dangerous."

"To whom?"

"Everyone."

It was an unexpected answer, adding a new dimension to Aritch's behavior. McKie decided to back up and test the revelation. "This Dosadi project was approved by a minority willing to accept a dangerous risk-benefit ratio."

"You have a way of putting these matters, McKie, which presupposes a particular kind of guilt."

"But a majority in the ConSentiency might agree with my description?"

"Should they ever learn of it."

"I see. Then, in accepting a dangerous risk, what were the future benefits you expected?"

Aritch emitted a deep grunt.

"Legum, I assure you that we worked only with volunteers and they were limited to Humans and Gowachin."

"You evade my question."

"I merely defer an answer."

"Then tell me, did you explain to your volunteers that they had a choice, that they could say 'no'? Did you tell them they might be in danger?"

"We did not try to frighten them . . . no."

"Was any one of you concerned about the free destiny of your *volunteers*?"

"Be careful how you judge us, McKie. There is a fundamental tension between science and freedom—no matter how science is viewed by its practitioners nor how freedom is sensed by those who believe they have it."

McKie was reminded of a cynical Gowachin aphorism: *To believe that you are free is more important than being free.* He said:

"Your volunteers were lured into this project."

"Some would see it that way."

McKie reflected on this. He still did not know precisely what the Gowachin had done on Dosadi, but he was beginning to suspect it'd be something repulsive. He could not keep this fear from his voice.

"We return to the question of expected benefits."

"Legum, we have long admired your species. You gave us one of our most trusted maxims: *No species is to be trusted farther than it is bound by its own interests.*"

"That's no longer sufficient justification for . . ."

"We derive another rule from your maxim: *It is wise to guide your actions in such a way that the interests of other species coincide with the interests of your species.*"

McKie stared at the High Magister. Did this crafty old Gowachin seek a Human-Gowachin conspiracy to suppress evidence of what had been done on Dosadi? Would he dare such a gambit? Just how bad was this Dosadi fiasco?

To test the issue, McKie asked:

"What benefits did you expect? I insist."

Aritch slumped. His chairdog accommodated to the new position. The High Magister favored McKie with a heavy-lidded stare for a long interval, then:

"You play this game better than we'd ever hoped."

"With you, Law and Government are always a game. I come from another arena."

"Your Bureau."

"And I was trained as a Legum."

"Are you *my* Legum?"

"The binding oath is binding on me. Have you no faith in . . ."

McKie broke off, overwhelmed by a sudden insight. Of course! The Gowachin had known for a long time that Dosadi would become a legal issue.

"Faith in what?" Aritch asked.

"Enough of these evasions!" McKie said. "You had your Dosadi problem in mind when you trained me. Now, you act as though you distrust your own plan.'

Aritch's lips rippled.

"How strange. You're more Gowachin than a Gowachin."

"What benefits did you expect when you took this risk?"

Aritch's fingers splayed, stretching the webs.

"We hoped for a quick conclusion and benefits to offset the natural animosities we knew would arise. But it's now more than twenty of your generations, not twelve or fifteen, that we've grasped the firebrand. Benefits? Yes, there are some, but we dare not use them or free Dosadi from bondage lest we raise questions which we cannot answer without revealing our . . . source.''

"The benefits!" McKie said. "Your *Legum* insists.''

Aritch exhaled a shuddering breath through his ventricles.

"Only the Caleban who guards Dosadi knows its location and she is charged to give access without revealing that place. Dosadi is peopled by Humans and Gowachin. They live in a single city they call Chu. Some ninety million people live there, almost equally divided between the two species. Perhaps three times that number live outside Chu, on the Rim, but they're outside the experiment. Chu is approximately eight hundred square kilometers.''

The population density shocked McKie. Millions per kilometer. He had difficulty visualizing it. Even allowing for a city's vertical dimension . . . and burrowing . . . There'd be some, of course, whose power bought them space, but the others . . . Gods! Such a city would be crawling with people, no escaping the pressure of your fellows anywhere except on that unexplained Rim. McKie said as much to Aritch.

The High Magister confirmed this.

"The population density is very great in some areas. The people of Dosadi call these areas 'Warrens' for good reason.''

"But why? With an entire planet to live on . . .''

"Dosadi is poisonous to our forms of life. All of their food comes from carefully managed hydroponics factories in the heart of Chu. Food factories and the distribution are managed by warlords. Everything is under a quasi-military form of management. But life expectancy in the city is four times that outside.''

"You said the population outside the city was much larger than . . .''

"They breed like mad animals.''

"What possible benefits could you have expected from . . .''

"Under pressure, life reveals its basic elements.''

McKie considered what the High Magister had revealed. The picture of Dosadi was that of a seething mass. Warlords . . . He visualized walls, some people living and working in comparative richness of space while others . . . Gods! It was madness in a universe where some highly habitable planets held no more than a few thousand people. His voice brittle, McKie addressed himself to the High Magister.

"These basic elements, the *benefits* you sought . . . I wish to hear about them.''

Aritch hitched himself forward.

"We have discovered new ways of association, new devices of motivation, unsuspected drives which can impose themselves upon an entire population.''

"I require specific and explicit enumeration of these discoveries.''

"Presently, Legum . . . presently.''

Why did Aritch delay? Were the so-called benefits insignificant beside the repulsive horror of such an experiment? McKie ventured another tack.

"You say this planet is poisonous. Why not remove the inhabitants a few at a time, subject them to memory erasure if you must, and feed them out into the ConSentiency as new . . .''

"We dare not! First, the inhabitants have developed an immunity to erasure, a by-product of those poisons which do get into their diet. Second, given what they have become on Dosadi . . . How can I explain this to you?''

"Why don't the people just leave Dosadi? I presume you deny them jumpdoors, but rockets and other mechanical . . .''

"We will not permit them to leave. Our Caleban encloses Dosadi in what she calls a 'tempokinetic barrier' which our test subjects cannot penetrate."

"Why?"

"We will destroy the entire planet and everything on it rather than loose this population upon the ConSentiency."

"What are the people of Dosadi that you'd even contemplate such a thing?"

Aritch shuddered.

"We have created a monster."

Every government is run by liars and nothing they say should be believed.

—ATTRIBUTED TO AN ANCIENT
HUMAN JOURNALIST

AS SHE hurried across the roof of the adjoining parking spire at midafternoon of her final day as a Liaitor, Jedrik couldn't clear her mind of the awareness that she was about to shed another mark of rank. Stacked in the building beneath her, each one suspended by its roof grapples on the conveyor track, were the vehicles of the power merchants and their minions. The machines varied from the giant *jaigers* heavy with armor and weapons and redundant engine systems, of the ruling few, down to the tiny black skitters assigned to such as herself. Ex-minion Jedrik knew she was about to take a final ride in the machine which had released her from the morning and evening crush on the underground walkways.

She had timed her departure with care. The ones who rode in the *jaigers* would not have reassigned her *skitter* and its driver. That driver, Havvy, required her special attentions in this last ride, this narrow time slot which she had set aside for dealing with him.

Jedrik sensed events rushing at their own terrible pace now. Just that morning she had loosed death against fifty Humans. Now, the avalanche gathered power.

The parking spire's roof pavement had been poorly repaired after the recent explosive destruction of three Rim guerrillas. Her feet adjusted to the rough paving as she huuried across the open area to the drop chute. At the chute, she paused and glanced westward through Chu's enclosing cliffs. The sun, already nearing its late afternoon line on the cliffs, was a golden glow beyond the God Wall's milky barrier. To her newly sensitized fears, that was not a sun but a malignant eye which peered down at her.

By now, the rotofiles in her office would've been ignited by the clumsy intrustion of the LP toads. There'd be a delay while they reported this, while it was bucked up through the hierarchy to a level where somebody dared make an important decision.

Jedrik fought against letting her thoughts fall into trembling shadows. After the rotofiles, other data would accumulate. The Elector's people would grow increasingly suspicious. But that was part of her plan, a layer with many layers.

Abruptly, she stepped into the chute, dropped to her parking level, stared across the catwalks at her *skitter* dangling among the others. Havvy sat on the sloping hood, his shoulders in their characteristic slouch. Good. He behaved as expected.

A certain finesse was called for now, but she expected no real trouble from anyone as shallow and transparent as Havvy. Still, she kept her right hand in the pocket where she'd secreted a small but adequate weapon. Nothing could be allowed to stop her now. She had selected and trained lieutenants, but none of them quite matched her capabilities. The military force which had been prepared for this moment needed Jedrik for that extra edge which could pluck victory from the days ahead of them.

For now, I must float like a leaf above the hurricane.

Havvy was reading a book, one of those pseudodeep things he regularly affected, a book which she knew he would not understand. As he read, he pulled at his lower lip with thumb and forefinger, the very picture of a deep intellectual involvement with important ideas. But it was only a picture. He gave no sign that he heard Jedrik hurrying toward him. A light breeze flicked the pages and he held them with one finger. She could not yet see the title, but assumed this book would be on the contraband list as was much of his reading. That was about the peak of Havvy's risk taking, not great but imbued with a certain false glamor. Another picture.

She could see him quite distinctly now in readable detail. He should have looked up by now but still sat absorbed in his book. Havvy possessed large brown eyes which he obviously believed he employed with deceptive innocence. The real innocence went far beyond his shallow attempts at deception. Jedrik's imagination easily played the scene should one of Broey's people confront Havvy in this pose.

"*A contraband book?*" Havvy would ask, playing his brown eyes for all their worthless innocence. "*I didn't think there were any more of those around. Thought you'd burned them all. Fellow handed it to me on the street when I asked what he was reading.*"

And the Elector's spy would conceal a sneer while asking, "*Didn't you question such a gift?*"

Should it come to that, things would grow progressively stickier for Havvy along the paths he could not anticipate. His *innocent* brown eyes would deceive one of the Elector's people no more than they deceived her. In view of this, she read other messages in the fact that Havvy had produced her key to the God Wall—this Jorj X. McKie. Havvy had come to her with his heavy-handed conspiratorial manner:

"The Rim wants to send in a new agent. We thought you might . . ."

And every datum he'd divulged about this oddity, every question he'd answered with his transparent candor, had increased her tension, surprise, and elation.

Jedrik thought upon these matters as she approached Havvy.

He sensed her presence, looked up. Recognition and something unexpected—a watchfulness half-shielded—came over him. He closed his book.

"You're early."

"As I said I'd be."

This new manner in Havvy set her nerves on edge, raised old doubts. No course remained for her except attack.

"Only toads don't break routine," she said.

Havvy's gaze darted left, right, returned to her face. He hadn't expected this. It was a bit more open risk than Havvy relished. The Elector had spy devices everywhere. Havvy's reaction told her what she wanted to know, however. She gestured to the *skitter*.

"Let's go."

He pocketed his book, slid down, and opened her door. His actions were a bit too brisk. The button tab on one of his green-striped sleeves caught a door handle.

He freed himself with an embarrassed flurry.

Jedrik slipped into the passenger harness. Havvy slammed the door a touch too hard. Nervous. Good. He took his place at the power bar to her left, kept his profile to her when he spoke.

"Where?"

"Head for the apartment."

A slight hesitation, then he activated the grapple tracks. The skitter jerked into motion, danced sideways, and slid smoothly down the diveway to the street.

As they emerged from the parking sprire's enclosing shadows, even before the grapple released and Havvy activated the skitter's own power, Jedrik firmed her decision not to look back. The Liaitor building had become part of her past, a pile of grey-green stones hemmed by other tall structures with, here and there, gaps to the cliffs and the river's arms. That part of her life she now excised. Best it were done cleanly. Her mind must be clear for what came next. What came next was war.

It wasn't often that a warrior force lifted itself out of Dosadi's masses to seek its place in the power structure. And the force she had groomed would strike fear into millions. It was the fears of only a few people that concerned her now, though, and the first of these was Havvy.

He drove with his usual competence, not overly proficient but adequate. His knuckles were white on the steering arms, however. It was still the Havvy she knew moving those muscles, not one of the evil identities who could play their tricks in Dosadi flesh. That was Havvy's usefulness to her and his failure. He was Dosadi-flawed, corrupted. That could not be permitted with McKie.

Havvy appeared to have enough good sense to fear her. Jedrik allowed this emotion to ferment in him while she studied the passing scene. There was little traffic and all of that was armored. The occasional tube access with its sense of weapons in the shadows and eyes behind the guard slits—all seemed normal. It was too soon for the hue and cry after an errant Senior Liaitor.

They went through the first walled checkpoint without delay. The guards were efficiently casual, a glance at the skitter and the identification brassards of the occupants. It was all routine.

The danger with routines, she told herself, was that they very soon became boring. Boredom dulled the senses. That was a boredom which she and her aides constantly guarded against among their warriors. This new force on Dosadi would create many shocks.

As Havvy took them up the normal ring route through the walls, the streets became wide, more open. There were garden plantings in the open here, poisonous but beautiful. Leaves were purple in the shadows. Barren dirt beneath the bushes glittered with corrosive droplets, one of Dosadi's little ways of protecting territory. Dosadi taught many things to those willing to learn.

Jedrik turned, studied Havvy, the way he appeared to concentrate on his driving with an air of stored-up energy. That was about as far as Havvy's learning went. He seemed to know some of his own deficiencies, must realize that many wondered how he held a driver's job, even for the middle echelons, when the Warrens were jammed with people violently avaricious for any step upward. Obviously, Havvy carried valuable secrets which he sold on a hidden market. She had to nudge that hidden market now. Her act must appear faintly clumsy, as though events of this day had confused her.

"Can we be overheard?" she asked.

That made no difference to her plans, but it was the kind of clumsiness which Havvy would misinterpret in precisely the way she now required.

"I've disarmed the transceiver the way I did before," he said. "It'll look like a simple breakdown if anyone checks."

To no one but you, she thought.

But it was the level of infantile response she'd come to expect from Havvy. She picked up his gambit, probing with real curiosity.

"You expected that we'd require privacy today?"

He almost shot a startled look at her, caught himself, then:

"Oh, no! It was a precaution. I have more information to sell you."

"But you *gave* me the information about McKie."

"That was to demonstrate my value."

Oh, Havvy! Why do you try?

"You have unexpected qualities," she said, and marked that he did not even detect the first level of her irony. "What's this information you wish to sell?"

"It concerns this McKie."

"Indeed?"

"What's it worth to you?"

"Am I your only market Havvy?"

His shoulder muscles bunched as his grip grew even tighter on the steering arms. The tensions in his voice were remarkably easy to read.

"Sold in the right place my information could guarantee maybe five years of easy living—no worries about food or good housing or anything."

"Why aren't you selling it in such a place?"

"I didn't say I *could* sell it. There are buyers and then there are buyers."

"And then there are the ones who just take?"

There was no need for him to answer and it was just as well. A barrier dropped in front of the skitter, forcing Havvy to a quick stop. For just an instant, fear gripped her and she felt her reflexes prevent any bodily betrayal of the emotion. Then she saw that it was a routine stop while repair supplies were trundled across the roadway ahead of them.

Jedrik peered out the window on her right. The interminable repair and strengthening of the city's fortifications was going on at the next lower level. Memory told her this was the eighth layer of city protection on the southwest. The noise of pounding rock hammers filled the street. Grey dust lay everywhere, clouds of it drifting. She smelled burnt flint and that bitter metallic undertone which you never quite escaped anywhere in Chu, the smell of the poison death which Dosadi ladled out to its inhabitants. She closed her mouth and took shallow breaths, noted absently that the labor crew was all Warren, all Human, and about a third of them women. None of the women appeared older than fifteen. They already had that hard alertness about the eyes which the Warren-born never lost.

A young male strawboss went by trailing a male assistant, an older man with bent shoulders and straggly grey hair. The older man walked with slow deliberation and the young strawboss seemed impatient with him, waving the assistant to keep up. The important subtleties of the relationship thus revealed were entirely lost on Havvy, she noted. The strawboss, as he passed one of the female laborers, looked her up and down with interest. The worker noted his attention and exerted herself with the hammer. The strawboss said something to his assistant, who went over and spoke to the young female. She smiled and glanced at the strawboss, nodded. The strawboss and assistant walked on without looking back. The obvious arrangement for later assignation would have gone without Jedrik's conscious notice except that the young female strongly resembled a woman she'd once known . . . dead now as were so many of her early companions.

A bell began to ring and the barrier lifted.

Havvy drove on, glancing once at the strawboss as they passed him. The glance was not returned, telling Jedrik that the strawboss had assessed the skitter's occupants much earlier.

Jedrick picked up the conversation with Havvy where they'd left it.

"What makes you think you could get more from me than from someone else?"

"Not more . . . It's just that there's less risk with you."

The truth was in his voice, that innocent instrument which told so much about Havvy. She shook her head.

"You want me to take the risk of selling higher up?"

After a long pause, Havvy said:

"You know a safer way for me to operate?"

"I'd have to use you somewhere along the line for verification."

"But I'd be under your protection then."

"Why should I protect you when you're no longer of value?"

"What makes you think this is all the information I can get?"

Jedrik allowed herself a sigh, wondered why she continued this empty game.

"We might both run into a taker, Havvy."

Havvy didn't respond. Surely, he'd considered this in his foolish game plan.

They passed a squat brown building on the left. Their street curved upward around the building and passed through a teeming square at the next higher level. Between two taller buildings on the right, she glimpsed a stretch of a river channel, then it was more buildings which enclosed them like the cliffs of Chu, growing taller as the skitter climbed.

As she'd known, Havvy couldn't endure her silence.

"What're you going to do?" he asked.

"I'll pay one year of such protection as I can offer."

"But this is . . ."

"Take it or leave it."

He heard the finality but, being Havvy, couldn't give up. It was his one redeeming feature.

"Couldn't we even discuss a . . ."

"We won't discuss anything! If you won't sell at my price, then perhaps I should become a taker."

"That's not like you!"

"How little you know. I can buy informants of your caliber far cheaper."

"You're a hard person."

Out of compassion, she ventured a tiny lesson. "That's how to survive. But I think we should forget this now. Your information is probably something I already know, or something useless."

"It's worth a lot more than you offered."

"So you say, but I know you, Havvy. You're not one to take big risks. Little risks sometimes, big risks never. Your information couldn't be of any great value to me."

"If you only knew."

"I'm no longer interested, Havvy."

"Oh, that's great! You bargain with me and then pull out after I've . . ."

"I was *not* bargaining!" Wasn't the fool capable of anything?

"But you . . ."

"Havvy! Hear me with care. You're a little tad who's stumbled onto something you believe is important. It's actually nothing of great importance, but it's big enough to frighten you. You can't think of a way to sell this information without putting your neck in peril. That's why you came to me. You presume to have me act as your agent. You presume too much."

Anger closed his mind to any value in her words.

"I take risks!"

She didn't even try to keep amusement from her voice. "Yes, Havvy, but never where you think. So here's a risk for you right out in the open. Tell me your valuable information. No strings. Let me judge. If I think it's worth more than I've already offered I'll pay more. If I already have this information or it's otherwise useless, you get nothing."

"The advantage is all on your side!"

"Where it belongs."

Jedrik studied Havvy's shoulders, the set of his head, the rippling of muscles under stretched fabric as he drove. He was supposed to be pure Labor Pool and didn't even know that silence was the guardian of the LP: *Learning silence, you learn what to hear*. The LP seldom volunteered anything. And here was Havvy, so far from that and other LP traditions that he might never have experienced the Warren. *Had* never experienced it until he was too old to learn. Yet he talked of friends on the Rim, acted as though he had his own conspiratorial cell. He held a job for which he was barely competent. And everything he did revealed his belief that all of these things would not tell someone of Jedrik's caliber the essential facts about him.

Unless his were a marvelously practiced act.

She did not believe such a marvel, but there was a cautionary element in recognizing the remote possibility. This and the obvious flaws in Havvy had kept her from using him as a key to the God Wall.

They were passing the Elector's headquarters now. She turned and glanced at the stone escarpment. Her thoughts were a thorn thicket. Every assumption she made about Havvy required a peculiar protective reflex. A non-Dosadi reflex. She noted workers streaming down the steps toward the tube entrance of the Elector's building. Her problem with Havvy carried an odd similarity to the problem she knew Broey would encounter when it came to deciding about an ex-Liaitor named Keila Jedrik. She had studied Broey's decisions with a concentrated precision which had tested the limits of her abilities. Doing this, she had changed basic things about herself, had become oddly non-Dosadi. They would no longer find Keila Jedrik in the DemoPol. No more than they'd find Havvy or this McKie there. But if she could do this . . .

Pedestrian traffic in this region of extreme caution had slowed Havvy to a crawl. More of the Elector's workers were coming up from the Tube Gate One exit, a throng of them as though released on urgent business. She wondered if any of her fifty flowed in the throng.

I must not allow my thoughts to wander.

To float like an *aware* leaf was one thing, but she dared not let herself enter the hurricane . . . not yet. She focused once more on the silent, angry Havvy.

"Tell me, Havvy, did you ever kill a person?"

His shoulders stiffened.

"Why do you ask such a question?"

She stared at his profile for an adequate time, obviously reflecting on this same question.

"I presumed you'd answer. I understand now that you will not answer. This is not the first time I've made that mistake."

Again, Havvy missed the lesson.

"Do you ask many people that question?"

"That doesn't concern you now."

She concealed a profound sadness.

Havvy hadn't the wit to read even the most blatant of the surface indicators. He compounded the useless.

"You can't justify such an intrusion into my . . ."

"Be still, little man! Have you learned nothing? Death is often the only means of evoking an appropriate answer."

Havvy saw this only as an utterly unscrupulous response as she'd known he would. When he shot a probing stare at her, she lifted an eyebrow in a cynical shrug. Havvy continued to divide his attention between the street and her face, apprehensive, fearful. His driving degenerated, became actively dangerous.

"Watch what you're doing, you fool!"

He turned more of his attention to the street, presuming this the great danger.

The next time he glanced at her, she smiled, knowing Havvy would be unable to detect any lethal change in this gesture. He already wondered if she would attack, but guessed she wouldn't do it while he was driving. He doubted, though, and his doubts made him even more transparent. Havvy was no marvel. One thing certain about him: he came from beyond the God Wall, from the lands of "X," from the place of McKie. Whether he worked for the Elector was immaterial. In fact, it grew increasingly doubtful that Broey would employ such a dangerous, a *flawed* tool. No pretense at foolhardy ignorance of Dosadi's basic survival lessons could be this perfect. The pretender would not survive. Only the truly ignorant could have survived to Havvy's age, allowed to go on living as a curiosity, a possible source of interesting data . . . *interesting* data, not necessarily useful.

Having left resolution of the Havvy Problem to the ultimate moment, wringing every last bit of usefulness from him, she knew her course clearly. Whoever protected Havvy, her questions placed the precisely modulated pressure upon them and left her options open.

"What is your valued information?" she asked.

Sensing now that he bought life with every response, Havvy pulled the skitter to the curb at a windowless building wall, stopped, and stared at her.

She waited.

"McKie . . ." He swallowed. "McKie comes from beyond the God Wall."

She allowed laughter to convulse her and it went deeper than she'd anticipated. For an instant, she was helpless with it and this sobered her. Not even Havvy could be permitted such an advantage.

Havvy was angry.

"What's funny?"

"You are. Did you imagine for even a second that I wouldn't reconigze someone alien to Dosadi? Little man, how *have* you survived?"

This time, he read her correctly. It threw him back on his only remaining resource and it even answered her question.

"Don't underestimate my value."

Yes, of course: the unknown value of "X." And there was a latent threat in his tone which she'd never heard there before. Could Havvy call on protectors from beyond the God Wall? That didn't seem possible, given his circumstances, but it had to be considered. It wouldn't do to approach her larger problem from a narrow viewpoint. People who could enclose an entire planet in an impenetrable barrier would have other capabilities she had not even imagined. Some of these creatures came and went at will, as though Dosadi were merely a casual stopping point. And the travelers from "X" could change their bodies; that was the single terrible fact which must never be forgotten; that was what had led her ancestors to breed for a Keila Jedrik.

Such considerations always left her feeling almost helpless, shaken by the ultimate unknowns which lay in her path. Was Havvy still Havvy? Her trusted senses answered: yes. Havvy was a spy, a diversion, an amusement. And he was something else which she could not fathom. It was maddening. She could read every nuance of his reactions, yet questions remained. How could you ever understand these creatures from beyond the Veil of Heaven? They were transparent to Dosadi eyes, but that transparency itself confused one.

On the other hand, how could the people of "X" hope to understand (and thus anticipate) a Keila Jedrik? Every evidence of her senses told her that Havvy saw only a surface Jedrik which she wanted him to see. His spying eyes reported what she wanted them to report. But the enormous interests at stake here dictated a brand of caution beyond anything she'd ever before attempted. The fact that she saw this arena of explosive repercussions, however, armed her with grim satisfaction. The idea that a Dosadi *puppet* might rebel against "X" and fully understand the nature of such rebellion, surely that idea lay beyond their capabilities. They were overconfident while she was filled with wariness. She saw no way of hiding her movements from the people beyond the God Wall as she his from her fellow Dosadis. "X" had ways of spying that no one completely evaded. They would know about the two Keila Jedriks. She counted on only one thing: that they could not see her deepest thoughts, that they'd read only that surface which she revealed to them.

Jedrik maintained a steady gaze at Havvy while these considerations flowed through her mind. Not by the slightest act did she betray what went on in her mind. That, after all, was Dosadi's greatest gift to its survivors.

"Your information is valueless," she said.

He was accusatory. "You already knew!"

What did he hope to catch with such a gambit? Not for the first time, she asked herself whether Havvy might represent the best that "X" might produce? Would they knowingly send their dolts here? It hardly seemed possible. But how could Havvy's childish incompetence command such tools of power as the God Wall implied? Were the people of "X" the decadent descendants of greater beings?

Even though his own survival demanded it, Havvy would not remain silent.

"If you didn't already know about McKie . . . then you . . . you don't believe me!"

This was too much. Even for Havvy it was too much and she told herself: *despite the unknown powers of "X," he will have to die. He muddies the water. Such incompetence cannot be permitted to breed.*

It would have to be done without passion, not like a Gowachin male weeding his own tads, but with a kind of clinical decisiveness which "X" could not misunderstand.

For now, she had arranged that Havvy take her to a particular place. He still had a role to perform. Later, with discreet attention to the necessary misdirections, she would do what had to be done. Then the next part of her plan could be assayed.

> *All persons act from beliefs they are conditioned not to question, from a set of deeply seated prejudices. Therefore, whoever presumes to judge must be asked: "How are you affronted?" And this judge must begin there to question inwardly as well as outwardly.*
>
> —"THE QUESTION"
> FROM RITUAL OF THE COURTARENA
> GUIDE TO SERVANTS OF THE BOX

"ONE MIGHT suspect you of trying to speak under water," McKie accused.

He still sat opposite Aritch in the High Magister's sanctus, and this near-insult was only one indicator marking the changed atmosphere between them. The sun had dropped closer to the horizon and its *spiritual ring* no longer outlined Aritch's head. The two of them were being more direct now, if not more candid, having explored individual capacities and found where profitable discourse might be directed.

The High Magister flexed his thigh tendons.

Knowing these people from long and close observation, McKie realized the old Gowachin was in pain from prolonged inactivity. That was an advantage to be exploited. McKie held up his left hand, enumerated on his fingers:

"You say the original volunteers on Dosadi submitted to memory erasure. The present population knows nothing about our ConSentient Universe."

"As far as the present Dosadi population comprehends, they are the only people on the only inhabited planet in existence."

McKie found this hard to believe. He held up a third finger.

Aritch stared with distaste at the displayed hand. *There were no webs between the alien fingers!*

McKie said, "And you tell me that a DemoPol backed up by certain religious injunctions is the primary tool of government there?"

"An original condition of our experiment," Aritch said.

It was not a comprehensive answer, McKie observed. Original conditions invariably changed. McKie decided to come back to this after the High Magister had submitted to more muscle pain.

"Do the Dosadi know the nature of the Caleban barrier which encloses them?"

"They've tried rocket probes, primitive electromagnetic projections. They understand that those energies they can produce will not penetrate their 'God Wall.'"

"Is that what they call the barrier?"

"That or 'The Heavenly Veil.' To some degree, these labels measure their attitude toward the barrier."

"The DemoPol can serve many government forms," McKie said. "What's the basic form of their government.?"

Aritch considered this, then:

"The form varies. They've employed some eighty different governmental forms."

Another nonresponsive answer. Aritch did not like to face the fact that their experiment had assumed warlord trappings. McKie thought about the DemoPol. In the hands of adepts and with a population responsive to the software probes by which the computer data was assembled, the DemoPol represented an ultimate tool for manipulation of a populace. The ConSentiency outlawed its use as an assault on individual rights and freedoms. The Gowachin had broken this prohibition, yes, but a more interesting datum was surfacing: Dosadi had employed some eighty different governmental forms without rejecting the DemoPol. That implied frequent changes.

"How often have they changed their form of government?"

"You can divide the numbers as easily as I," Aritch said. His tone was petulant.

McKie nodded. One thing had become quite clear.

"Dosadi's masses know about the DemoPol, but you won't let them remove it!"

Aritch had not expected this insight. He responded with revealing sharpness which was amplified by his muscle pains.

"How did you learn that?"

"You told me."

"I?"

"Quite plainly. Such frequent change is responsive to an irritant—the Demo-Pol. They change the forms of government, but leave the irritant. Obviously, they cannot remove the irritant. That was clearly part of your experiment—to raise a population resistant to the DemoPol."

"A resistant population, yes," Aritch said. He shuddered.

"You've fractured ConSentient Law in many places," McKie said.

"Does my Legum presume to judge me?"

"No. But if I speak with a certain bitterness, please recall that I am a Human. I embrace a profound sympathy for the Gowachin, but I remain Human."

"Ahhhh, yes. We must not forget the long Human association with Demo-Pols."

"We survive by selecting the best decision makers," McKie said.

"And a DemoPol elevates mediocrity."

"Has that happened on Dosadi?"

"No."

"But you wanted them to try many different governmental forms?"

The High Magister shrugged, remained silent.

"We Humans found that the DemoPol does profound damage to social relationships. It destroys preselected portions of a society."

"And what could we hope to learn by *damaging* our Dosadi society?"

"Have we arrived back at the question of expected benefits?"

Aritch stretched his aching muscles.

"You are persistent, McKie. I will say that."

McKie shook his head sadly.

"The DemoPol was always held up to us as the ultimate equalizer, a source of decision-making miracles. It was supposed to produce a growing body of knowledge about what a society really needed. It was thought to produce justice in all cases despite any odds."

Aritch was irritated. He leaned forward, wincing at the pain of his old muscles.

"One might make the same accusations about the *Law* as practiced everywhere except on Gowachin worlds!"

McKie suppressed a sharp response. Gowachin training had forced him to question assumptions about the uses of law in the ConSentiency, about the inherent rightness of any aristocracy, any power bloc whether majority or minority. It was a BuSab axiom that all power blocs tended toward aristocratic forms, that the descendants of decision makers dominated the power niches. BuSab never employed offspring of their agents.

Aritch repeated himself, a thing Gowachin seldom did.

"Law is delusion and fakery, McKie, everywhere except on the Gowachin worlds! You give your law a theological aura. You ignore the ways it injures your societies. Just as with the DemoPol, you hold up your law as the unvarying source of justice. When you . . ."

"BuSab has . . ."

"No! If something's wrong in your societies, what do you do? You create new law. You never think to remove law or disarm the law. You make more law! You create more legal professionals. We Gowachin sneer at you! We always strive to reduce the number of laws, the number of Legums. A Legums's first duty is to avoid litigation. When we create new Legums, we always have specific problems in mind. We anticipate the ways that laws damage our society."

It was the opening McKie wanted.

"Why are you training a Wreave?"

Belatedly, Aritch realized he had been goaded into revealing more than he had wanted.

"You are good, McKie. Very good."

"Why?" McKie persisted "Why a Wreave?"

"You will learn why in time."

McKie saw that Aritch would not expand on this answer, but there were other matters to consider now. It was clear that the Gowachin had trained him for a specific problem: Dosadi. To train a Wreave as Legum, they'd have an equally important problem in mind . . . perhaps the same problem. A basic difference in the approach to law, species differentiated, had surfaced, however, and this could not be ignored. McKie well understood that Gowachin disdain for all legal systems, including their own. They were educated from infancy to distrust any community of professionals, especially legal professionals. A Legum could only tread their religious path when he completely shared that distrust.

Do I share that distrust?

He thought he did. It came naturally to a BuSab agent. But most of the ConSentiency still held its professional communities in high esteem, ignoring the nature of the intense competition for new achievements which invariably overcame such communities: *new* achievements, *new* recognition. But the *new* could be illusion in such communities because they always maintained a peer review system nicely balanced with peer pressures for ego rewards.

"Professional always means power," the Gowachin said.

The Gowachin distrusted power in all of its forms. They gave with one hand and took with the other. Legums faced death whenever they used the Law. To make *new* law in the Gowachin Courtarena was to bring about the elegant dissolution of old law with a concomitant application of justice.

Not for the first time, McKie wondered about the unknown problems a High Magister must face. It would have to be a delicate existence indeed. McKie almost formed a question about this, thought better of it. He shifted instead to the unknowns about Dosadi. *God Wall? Heavenly Veil?*

"Does Dosadi often accept a religious oligarchy?"

"As an outward form, yes. They currently are presided over by a supreme Elector, a Gowachin by the name of Broey."

"Have Humans ever held power equal to Broey's?"

"Frequently."

It was one of the most responsive exchanges that McKie had achieved with Artich. Although he knew he was following the High Magister's purpose, McKie decided to explore this.

"Tell me about Dosadi's *social* forms."

"They are the forms of a military organization under constant attack or threat of attack. They form certain cabals, certain power enclaves whose influences shift."

"Is there much violence?"

"It is a world of constant violence."

McKie absorbed this. Warlords. Military society. He knew he had just lifted a corner of the real issue which had brought the Gowachin to the point of obliterating Dosadi. It was an area to be approached with extreme caution. McKie chose a flanking approach.

"Aside from the military forms, what are the dominant occupations? How do they perceive guilt and innocence? What are their forms of punishment, of absolution? How do they . . ."

"You do not confuse me, McKie. Consider, Legum: there are better ways to answer such questions."

Brought up short by the Magister's chiding tone, McKie fell into silence. He glanced out the oval window, realizing he'd been thrown onto the defensive with exquisite ease. McKie felt the nerves tingling along his spine. Danger! Tanda-loor's golden sun had moved perceptibly closer to the horizon. That horizon was a blue-green line made hazy by kilometer after kilometer of hair trees whose slender female fronds waved and hunted in the air. Presently, McKie turned back to Aritch.

Better ways to answer such questions.

It was obvious where the High Magister's thoughts trended. The experimenters would, of course, have ways of watching their experiment. They could also influence their experiment, but it was obvious there were limits to this influence. A population resistant to outside influences? The implied complications of this Dosadi problem daunted McKie. Oh, the circular dance the Gowachin always performed!

Better ways.

Aritch cleared his ventricle passages with a harsh exhalation, then:

"Anticipating the possibility that others would censure us, we gave our test subjects the Primary."

Devils incarnate! The Gowachin set such store on their damned Primary! Of course all people were created unequal and had to find their own level!

McKie knew he had no choice but to plunge into the maelstrom.

"Did you also anticipate that you'd be charged with violating sentient rights on a massive scale?"

Aritch shocked him by a brief puffing of jowls, the Gowachin shrug.

McKie allowed himself a warning smile.

"I remind the High Magister that *he* raised the issue of the Primary."

"Truth is truth."

McKie shook his head sharply, not caring what this revealed. The High Magister couldn't possibly have that low an estimation of his Legum's reasoning abilities. *Truth indeed!*

"I'll give you truth: the ConSentiency has laws on this subject to which the Gowachin are signatories!"

Even as the words fell from his lips, McKie realized this was precisely where Aritch had wanted him to go. *They've learned something from Dosadi! Something crucial!*

Aritch massaged the painful muscles of his thighs, said, "I remind *you*, Legum, that we peopled Dosadi with volunteers."

"Their descendants volunteered for nothing!"

"Ancestors always volunteer their descendants—for better or for worse. Sentient rights? Informed consent? The ConSentiency has been so busy building law upon law, creating its great illusion of rights, that you've almost lost sight of the Primary's guiding principle: to develop our capacities. People who are never challenged never develop *survival* strengths!"

Despite the perils, McKie knew he had to press for the answer to his original question: *benefits*.

"What've you learned from your monster?"

"You'll soon have a complete answer to that question."

Again, the implication that he could actually watch Dosadi. But first it'd be well to disabuse Aritch of any suspicion that McKie was unaware of the root implication. The issue had to be met head on.

"You're not going to implicate me."

"Implicate you?" There was no mistaking Aritch's surprise.

"No matter how you use what you've learned from Dosadi, you'll be suspected of evil intent. Whatever anyone learns from . . ."

"Oh, that. New data gives one power."

"And *you* do not confuse *me*, Aritch. In the history of every species there are many examples of places where new data has been gravely abused."

Aritch accepted this without question. They both knew the background. The Gowachin distrusted power in all of its forms, yet they used power with consummate skill. The trend of McKie's thoughts lay heavily in this room now. To destroy Dosadi would be to hide whatever the Gowachin had learned there. McKie, a non-Gowachin, therefore, would learn these things, would share the mantle of suspicion should it be cast. The historical abuses of new data occurred between the time that a few people learned the important thing and the time when that important thing became general knowledge. To the Gowachin and to BuSab it was the "Data Gap," a source of constant danger.

"We would not try to hide *what* we've learned," Aritch said, "only how we learned it."

"And it's just an academic question whether you destroy an entire planet and every person on it!"

"Ahh, yes: academic. What you don't know, McKie, is that one of our test subjects on Dosadi has initiated, all on her own, a course of events which will destroy Dosdai very quickly whether we act or not. You'll learn all about this very soon when, like the good Legum we know you to be, you go there to experience this monster with your own flesh."

In the name of all that we together hold holy I promise three things to the sacred congregation of people who are subject to my rule. In the first place, that the holy religion which we mutually espouse shall always preserve their freedom under my auspices; secondly, that I will temper every form of rapacity and inequity which may inflict itself upon us all; and thirdly, that I will command swift mercy in all judgments, that to me and to you the gracious Lord may extend His Recognition.

—THE OATH OF POWER,
DOSADI SACRED CONGREGATION PAPERS

BROEY AROSE from prayer, groped behind him for the chair, and sank into it. Enclosed darkness surrounded him. The room was a shielded bubble attached to the bottom of his Graluz. Around the room's thick walls was the warm water which protected his females and their eggs. Access to the bubble was through a floor hatch and a twisting flooded passage from the Graluz. Pressure in the bubble excluded the water, but the space around Broey smelled reassuringly of the Graluz. This helped reinforce the mood he now required.

Presently, the God spoke to him. Elation filled Broey. God spoke to him, only to him. Words hissed within his head. Scenes impinged themselves upon his vision centers.

Yes! Yes! I keep the DemoPol!

God was reassured and reflected that reassurance.

Today, God showed him a ritual Broey had never seen before. The ritual was only for Gowachin. The ritual was called Laupuk. Broey saw the ritual in all of its gory details, felt the *rightness* of it as though his very cells accepted it.

Responsibility, expiation—these were the lessons of Laupuk. God approved when Broey expressed understanding.

They communicated by words which Broey expressed silently in his thoughts, but there were other thoughts which God could not perceive. Just as God no doubt held thoughts which were not communicated to Broey. God used people, people used God. Divine intervention with cynical overtones. Broey had learned the Elector's role through a long and painful apprenticeship.

I am your servant, God.

As God admonished, Broey kept the secret of his private communion. It suited his purpose to obey, as it obviously suited God's purpose. There were times, though, when Broey wanted to shout it:

"You fools! I speak with the voice of God!"

Other Electors had made that mistake. They'd soon fallen from the seat of power. Broey, drawing on several lifetimes of assembled experiences, knew he must keep this power if he ever were to escape from Dosadi.

Anyway, the fools did his bidding (and therefore God's) without divine admonition. All was well. One presented a selection of thoughts to God . . . being careful always where and when one reviewed private thoughts. There were times when Broey felt God within him when there'd been no prayer, no preparations here in the blackness of this bubble room. God might peer out of Broey's eyes at any time—softly, quietly—examining His world and its works through mortal senses.

"I guard My servant well."

The warmth of reassurance which flowed through Broey then was like the

174

warmth of the Graluz when he'd still been a tad clinging to his mother's back. It was a warmth and sense of safety which Broey tempered with a deep awareness of that other Graluz time: a giant grey-green adult male Gowachin ravening through the water, devouring those tads not swift enough, alert enough to escape.

I was one of the swift.

Memory of that plunging, frantic flight in the Graluz had taught Broey how to behave with God.

In his bubble room's darkness, Broey shuddered. Yes, the ways of God were cruel. Thus armed a servant of God could be equally cruel, could surmount the fact that he knew what it was to be both Human and Gowachin. He need only be the pure servant of God. This thought he shared.

Beware, McKie. God has told me whence you come. I know your intentions. Hold fast to the narrow path, McKie. You risk my displeasure.

> *Behavioral engineering in all of its manifestations always degenerates into merciless manipulation. It reduces all (manipulators and manipulated alike) to a deadly "mass effect." The central assumption, that manipulation of individual personalities can achieve uniform behavioral responses, has been exposed as a lie by many species but never with more telling effect than by the Gowachin on Dosadi. Here, they showed us the "Walden Fallacy" in ultimate foolishness, explaining: "Given any species which reproduces by genetic mingling such that every individual is a unique specimen, all attempts to impose a decision matrix based on assumed uniform behavior will prove lethal."*
>
> —THE DOSADI PAPERS
> BUSAB REFERENCE

MCKIE WALKED through the jumpdoor and, as Aritch's aides had said, found himself on sand at just past Dosadi's midmorning. He looked up, seeking his first real-time view of the God Wall, wanting to share the Dosadi feeling of that enclosure. All he saw was a thin haze, faintly silver, disappointing. The sun circle was more defined than he'd expected and he knew from the holographic reproductions he'd seen that a few of the third-magnitude stars would be filtered out at night. What else he'd expected, McKie could not say, but somehow this milky veil was not it. Too thin perhaps. It appeared insubstantial, too weak for the power it represented.

The visible sun disk reminded him of another urgent necessity, but he postponed that necessity while he examined his surroundings.

A tall white rock? Yes, there it was on his left.

They'd warned him to wait beside that rock, that he'd be relatively safe there. Under no circumstances was he to wander from this contact point.

"We can tell you about the dangers of Dosadi, but words are not enough. Besides, the place is always developing new threats."

Things he'd learned in the briefing sessions over the past weeks reinforced the warning. The rock, twice as tall as a Human, stood only a few paces away, massive and forbidding. he went over and leaned against it. Sand grated beneath his feet. He smelled unfamiliar perfumes and acridities. The sun-warmed surface of the rock gave its energy to his flesh through the thin green coveralls they'd insisted he wear.

McKie longed for his armored clothing and its devices to amplify muscles, but such things were not permitted. Only a reduced version of his toolkit had been allowed and that reluctantly, a compromise. McKie had explained that the contents would be destroyed if anyone other than himself tried to pry into the kit's secrets. Still, they'd warned him never to open the kit in the presence of a Dosadi native.

"The most dangerous thing you can do is to underestimate any of the Dosadi."

McKie, staring around him, saw no Dosadi.

Far off across a dusty landscape dotted with yellow bushes and brown rocks, he identified the hazy spires of Chu rising out of its river canyon. Heat waves dizzied the air above the low scrub, giving the city a magical appearance.

McKie found it difficult to think about Chu in the context of what he'd learned during the crash course the Gowachin had given him. Those magical fluting spires reached heavenward from a muck where "you can buy anything . . . anything at all."

Aritch's aids had sewn a large sum in Dosadi currency into the seams of his clothing but, at the same time, had forced him to digest hair-rising admonitions about "any show of unprotected wealth."

The jumpdoor attendants had recapitulated many of the most urgent warnings, adding:

"You may have a wait of several hours. We're not sure. Just stay close to that rock where you'll be relatively safe. We've made protective arrangements which should work. Don't eat or drink anything until you get into the city. You'll be faintly sick with the diet change for a few days, but your body should adjust."

"*Should* adjust?"

"Give it time."

He'd asked about specific dangers to which he should be most alert.

"Stay clear of any Dosadi natives except your contacts. Above all, don't even appear to threaten anyone."

"What if I get drowsy and take a nap?"

They'd considered this, then:

"You know, that might be the safest thing to do. Anyone who'd dare to nap out there would have to be damned well protected. There'd be some risk, of course, but there always is on Dosadi. But they'd be awfully leery of anyone casual enough to nap out there."

Again, McKie glanced around.

Sharp whistlings and a low rasp like sand across wood came from behind the tall rock. Quietly, McKie worked his way around to where he could see the sources of these noises. The whistling was a yellow lizard almost the color of the bushes beneath which it crouched. The rasp came from a direction which commanded the lizard's attention. Its source appeared to be a small hole beneath another bush. McKie thought he detected in the lizard only a faint curiosity about himself. Something about the hole and the noise issuing from it demanded a great deal of concentrated attention.

Something stirred in the hole's blackness.

The lizard crouched, continued to whistle.

An ebony creature about the size of McKie's fist emerged from the hole, darted forward, saw the lizard. Wings shot from the newcomer's sides and it leaped upward, but it was too late. With a swiftness which astonished McKie, the lizard shot forward, balled itself around its prey. A slit opened in the lizard's stomach, surrounded the ebony creature. With a final rasping, the black thing vanished into the lizard.

All this time, the lizard continued to whistle. Still whistling it crawled into the hole from which its prey had come.

"Things are seldom what they seem to be on Dosadi," McKie's teachers had said.

He wondered now what he had just seen.

The whistling had stopped.

The lizard and its prey reminded McKie that, as he'd been warned, there had not been time to prepare him for every new detail on Dosadi. He crouched now and, once more, studied his immediate surroundings.

Tiny jumping things like insects inhabited the narrow line of shade at the base of the white rock. Green (blossoms?) opened and closed on the stems to the yellow bushes. The ground all around appeared to be a basic sand and clay, but when he peered at it closely he saw veins of blue and red discoloration. He turned his back on the distant city, saw far away mountains: a purple graph line against silver sky. Rain had cut an arroyo in that direction. He saw touches of darker green reaching from the depths. The air tasted bitter.

Once again, McKie made a sweeping study of his surroundings, seeking any sign of threat. Nothing he could identify. He palmed an instrument from his toolkit, stood casually and stretched while he turned toward Chu. When he stole a glance at the instrument, it revealed a sonabarrier at the city. Absently scratching himself to conceal the motion, he returned the instrument to his kit. Birds floated in the silver sky above the sonabarrier.

Why a sonabarrier? he wondered.

It would stop wild creatures, but not people. His teachers had said the sonabarrier excluded pests, vermin. The explanation did not satisfy McKie.

Things are seldom what they seem.

Despite the God Wall, that sun was hot. McKie sought the shady side of the rock. Seated there, he glanced at the small white disk affixed to the green lapel at his left breast: OP40331-D404. It was standard Galach script, the lingua franca of the ConSentiency.

"They speak only Galach on Dosadi. They may detect an accent in your speech, but they won't question it."

Aritch's people had explained that this badge identified McKie as an open-contract worker, one with slightly above average skills in a particular field, but still part of the Labor Pool and subject to assignment outside his skill.

"This puts you three hierarchical steps from the Rim," they'd said.

It'd been his own choice. The bottom of the social system always had its own communications channels flowing with information based on accurate data, instinct, dream stuff, and what was fed from the top with deliberate intent. Whatever happened here on Dosadi, its nature would be revealed in the unconscious processes of the Labor Pool. In the Labor Pool, he could tap that revealing flow.

"I'll be a weaver," he'd said, explaining that it was a hobby he'd enjoyed for many years.

The choice had amused his teachers. McKie had been unable to penetrate the reason for their amusement.

"It is of no importance right now. One choice is as good as another."

They'd insisted he concentrate on what he'd been doing at the time, learning the signal mannerisms of Dosadi. Indeed, it'd been a hectic period on Tandaloor after Aritch's insistence (with the most reasonable of arguments) that the best way for his Legum to proceed was to go personally to Dosadi. In retrospect, the arguments remained persuasive, but McKie had been suprised. For some reason which he could not now identify, he had expected a less involved *overview* of the experiment, watching through instruments and the spying abilities of the Caleban who guarded the place.

McKie was still not certain how they expected him to pull this hot palip from the cooker, but it was clear they expected it. Aritch had been mysteriously explicit:

"You are Dosadi's best chance for survival and our own best chance for . . . understanding."

They expected their Legum to save Dosadi while exonerating the Gowachin. It was a Legum's task to win for his client, but these had to be the strangest circumstances, with the client retaining the absolute power of destruction over the threatened planet.

On Tandaloor, McKie had been allowed just time for short naps. Even then, his sleep had been restless, part of his mind infernally aware of where he lay: the bedog strange and not quite attuned to his needs, the odd noises beyond the walls—water gurgling somewhere, always water.

When he'd trained there as a Legum, that had been one of his first adjustments: the uncertain rhythms of disturbed water. Gowachin never strayed far from water. The Graluz—that central pool and sanctuary for females, the place where Gowachin raised those tads which survived the ravenous *weeding* by the male parent—the Graluz always remained a central fixation for the Gowachin. As the saying put it:

"If you do not understand the Graluz, you do not understand the Gowachin."

As such sayings went, it was accurate only up to a point.

But there was always the water, contained water, the nervous slapping of wavelets against walls. The sound conveyed no fixed rhythms, but it was a profound clue to the Gowachin: contained, yet always different.

For all short distances, swimming tubes connected Gowachin facilities. They traversed along distances by jumpdoor or in hissing jetcars which moved on magnetic cushions. The comings and goings of such cars had disturbed McKie's sleep during the period of the crash course on Dosadi. Sometimes, desperately tired, his body demanding rest, he would find himself awakened by voices. And the subtle interference of the other sounds—the cars, the waves—made eavesdropping difficult. Awake in the night, McKie would strain for meaning. He felt like a spy listening for vital clues, seeking every nuance in the casual conversations of people beyond his walls. Frustrated, always frustrated, he had retreated into sleep. And when, as happened occasionally, all sound ceased, this brought him to full alert, heart pounding, wondering what had gone wrong.

And the odors! What memories they brought back to him. Graluz musk, the bitter pressing of exotic seeds, permeated every breath. Fern tree pollen intruded with its undertones of citrus. And the caraeli, tiny, froglike pets, invaded your sleep at every dawning with their exquisite belling arias.

During those earlier days of training on Tandaloor, McKie had felt more than a little lost, hemmed in by threatening strangers, constantly aware of the important matters which rode on his success. But things were different after the interview with Aritch. McKie was now a trained, tested, and proven Legum, not to mention a renowned agent of BuSab. Yet there were times when the mood of those earlier days intruded. Such intrusions annoyed him with their implication that he was being maneuvered into peril against his will, that the Gowachin secretly laughed as they prepared him for some ultimate humiliation. They were not above such a jest. Common assessment of Gowachin by non-Gowachin said the Frog God's people were so ultimately civilized they had come full circle into a form of primitive savagery. Look at the way Gowachin males slaughtered their own newborn tads!

Once, during one of the rare naps Aritch's people permitted him, McKie had awakened to sit up and try to shake off that depressing mood of doom. He told himself true things: that the Gowachin flattered him now, deferred to him, treated him with that quasireligious respect which they paid to all Legums. But there was no evading another truth: the Gowachin had groomed him for their Dosadi problem over a long period of time, and they were being less than candid with him about that long process and its intentions.

There were always unfathomed mysteries when dealing with Gowachin.

When he'd tried returning to sleep that time, it was to encounter disturbing dreams of massed sentient flesh (both pink and green) all naked and quite defenseless before the onslaughts of gigantic Gowachin males.

The dream's message was clear. The Gowachin might very well destroy Dosadi in the way (and for similar reasons) that they winnowed their own tads—searching, endlessly searching, for the strongest and most resilient survivors.

The problem they'd dumped in his lap daunted McKie. If the slightest inkling of Dosadi leaked into common awareness without a concurrent justification, the Gowachin Federation would be hounded unmercifully. The Gowachin had clear and sufficient reason to destroy the evidence—or let the evidence destroy itself.

Justification.

Where was that to be found? In the elusive benefits which had moved the Gowachin to mount this experiment?

Even if he found that justification, Dosadi would be an upheaval in the ConSentiency. It'd be the subject of high drama. More than twenty generations of Humans and Gowachin surfacing without warning! Their lonely history would titillate countless beings. The limits of language would be explored to wring the last drop of emotive essence from this revelation.

No matter how explained, Gowachin motives would come in for uncounted explorations and suspicions.

Why did they *really* do it? What happened to their original volunteers?

People would look backward into their own ancestry—Human and Gowachin alike. "Is that what happened to Uncle Elfred?" Gowachin phylum records would be explored. "Yes! Here are two—gone without record!"

Aritch's people admitted that "a very small minority" had mounted this project and kept the lid on it. Were they completely sane, this Gowachin cabal?

McKie's short naps were always disturbed by an obsequious Gowachin bowing over his bedog, begging him to return at once to the briefing sessions which prepared him for survival on Dosadi.

Those briefing sessions! The implied prejudices hidden in every one raised more questions than were answered. McKie tried to retain a reasoned attitude, but irritants constantly assailed him.

Why had the Gowachin of Dosadi taken on Human emotional characteristics? Why were Dosadi's Humans aping Gowachin social compacts? Were the Dosadi truly aware of why they changed governmental forms so often?

The bland answer to these frequent questions enraged McKie.

"All will be made clear when you experience Dosadi for yourself."

He'd finally fallen into a counterirritant patter:

"You don't really know the answer, do you? You're hoping I'll find out for you!"

Some of the data recital bored McKie. While listening to a Gowachin explain what was known about Rim relationships, he would find himself distracted by people passing in the multisentient access way outside the briefing area.

Once, Ceylang entered and sat at the side of the room, watching him with a hungry silence which rubbed McKie's sensibilities to angry rawness. He'd longed for the blue metal box then, but once the solemn investment had pulled the mantel of Legumic protection around him, the box had been removed to its sacred niche. He'd not see it again unless this issue entered the Courtarena. Ceylang remained an unanswered question among many. Why did that dangerous Wreave female haunt this room without contributing one thing? He suspected they allowed Ceylang to watch him through remote spy devices. Why did she choose that once to come in person? To let him know he was being observed? It had something to do with whatever had prompted the Gowachin to train a Wreave. They had some future problem which only a Wreave could solve. They were grooming this Wreave as they'd groomed him. Why? What Wreave capabilities attracted the Gowachin? How did this Wreave female differ from other Wreaves? Where were her loyalties? What was the 'Wreave Bet'?

This led McKie into another avenue never sufficiently explored: what Human capabilities had led the Gowachin to him? Dogged persistence? A background in Human law? The essential individualism of the Human?

There were no sure answers to these questions, no more than there were about the Wreave. Her presence continued to fascinate him, however. McKie knew many things about Wreave society not in common awareness outside the Wreave worlds. They were, after all, integral and valued partners in BuSab. In shared tasks, a camaraderie developed which often prompted intimate exchanges of information. Beyond the fact that Wreaves required a breeding triad for reproduction, he knew that Wreaves had never discovered a way to determine in advance which of the triad would be capable of nursing the offspring. This formed an essential building stone in Wreave society. Periodically, this person from the triad would be exchanged for a like person from another triad. This insured their form of genetic dispersion and, of equal importance, built countless linkages throughout their civilization. With each such linkage went requirements for unquestioning support in times of trouble.

A Wreave in the Bureau had tried to explain this:

"Take, for example, the situation where a Wreave is murdered or, even worse, deprived of essential vanity. The guilty party would be answerable *personally* to millions upon millions of us. Wherever the triad exchange has linked us, we are required to respond intimately to the insult. The closest thing you have to this, as I understand it, is familial responsibility. We have this familial responsibility for vendetta where such affronts occur. You have no idea how difficult it was to release those of us in BuSab from this . . . this bondage, this network of responsibility."

The Gowachin would know this about the Wreaves, McKie thought. Had this characteristic attracted the Gowachin or had they chosen in spite of it, making their decision because of some other Wreave aspect? Would a Wreave Legum continue to share that network of familial responsibility? How could that be? Wreave society could only offend a basic sensibility of the Gowachin. The Frog God's people were even more . . . more *exclusive* and individual than Humans. To the Gowachin, family remained a private thing, walled off from strangers in an isolation which was abandoned only when you entered your chosen phylum.

As he waited beside the white rock on Dosadi, McKie reflected on these matters, biding his time, listening. The alien heat, the smells and unfamiliar noises, disturbed him. He'd been told to listen for the sound of an internal combustion engine. Internal combustion! But the Dosadi used such devices outside the city because they were more powerful (although much larger) than the beamed impulse drivers which they used within Chu's walls.

"The fuel is alcohol. Most of the raw materials come from the Rim. It doesn't matter how much poison there is in such fuel. They ferment bushes, trees, ferns . . . anything the Rim supplies."

A sleepy quiet surrounded McKie now. For a long time he'd been girding himself to risk the thing he knew he would have to do once he were alone on Dosadi. He might never again be this alone here, probably not once he was into Chu's Warrens. He knew the futility of trying to contact his Taprisiot monitor. Aritch, telling him the Gowachin knew BuSab had bought "Taprisiot insurance," had said:

"Not even a Taprisiot call can penetrate the God Wall."

In the event of Dosadi's destruction, the Caleban contract ended. McKie's Taprisiot might even have an instant to complete the death record of McKie's memories. Might. That was academic to McKie in his present circumstances. The Calebans owed him a debt. The Whipping Star threat had been as deadly to Calebans as to any other species which had ever used jumpdoors. The threat had been real and specific. Users of jumpdoors and the Caleban who controlled those jumpdoors had been doomed. "Fannie Mae" had expressed the debt to McKie in her own peculiar way:

"The owing of me to thee connects to no ending."

Aritch could have alerted his Dosadi guardian against any attempt by McKie to contact another Caleban. McKie doubted this. Aritch had specified a ban against Taprisiot calls. But all Calebans shared an awareness at some level. If Aritch and company had been lulled into a mistaken assumption about the security of their barrier around Dosadi . . .

Carefully, McKie cleared his mind of any thoughts about Taprisiots. This wasn't easy. It required a Sufi concentration upon a particular *void*. There could be no accidental thrust of his mind at the Taprisiot waiting in the safety of Central Central with its endless patience. Everything must be blanked from awareness except a clear projection toward Fannie Mae.

McKie visualized her: the star Thyone. He recalled their long hours of mental give and take. He projected the warmth of emotional attachment, recalling her recent demonstration of "nodal involvement."

Presently, he closed his eyes, amplified that internal image which now suffused his mind. He felt his muscles relax. The warm rock against his back, the sand beneath him, faded from awareness. Only the glowing presence of a Caleban remained in his mind.

"Who calls?"

The words touched his auditory centers, but not his ears.

"It's McKie, friend of Fannie Mae. Are you the Caleban of the God Wall?"

"I am the God Wall. Have you come to worship?"

McKie felt his thoughts stumble. Worship? The projection from this Caleban was echoing and portentous, not at all like the probing curiosity he always sensed in Fannie Mae. He fought to regain that first clear image. The inner glow of a Caleban contact returned. He supposed there might be something worshipful in this experience. You were never absolutely certain of a Caleban's meaning.

"It's McKie, friend of Fannie Mae," he repeated.

The glow within McKie dimmed, then: "But you occupy a point upon Dosadi's wave."

That was a familiar kind of communication, one to which McKie could apply previous experience in the hope of a small understanding, an approximation.

"Does the God Wall permit me to contact Fannie Mae?"

Words echoed in his head:

"One Caleban, all Caleban."

"I wish converse with Fannie Mae."

"You are not satisfied with your present body?"

McKie felt his body then, the trembling flesh, the zombie-like trance state which went with Caleban or Taprisiot contact. The question had no meaning to him, but the body contact was real and it threatened to break off communication. Slowly, McKie fought back to that tenuous mind-presence.

"I am Jorj X. McKie. Calebans are in my debt."

"All Calebans know this debt."

"Then honor your debt."

He waited, trying not to grow tense.

The glow within his head was replaced by a new presence. It insinuated itself into McKie's awareness with penetrating familiarity—not full mental contact, but rather a playing upon those regions of his brain where sight and sound were interpreted. McKie recognized this new presence.

"Fannie Mae!"

"What does McKie require?"

For a Caleban, it was quite a direct communication. McKie, noting this, responded more directly:

"I require your help."

"Explain."

"I may be killed here . . . ahh, have an end to my node here on Dosadi."

"Dosadi's wave," she corrected him.

"Yes. And if that happens, if I die here, I have friends on Central Central . . . on Central Central's wave . . . friends there who must learn everything that's in my mind when I die."

"Only Taprisiot can do this. Dosadi contract forbids Taprisiots."

"But if Dosadi is destroyed . . ."

"Contract promise passes no ending, McKie."

"You cannot help me?"

"You wish advice from Fannie Mae?"

"Yes."

"Fannie Mae able to maintain contact with McKie while he occupies Dosadi's wave."

Constant trance? McKie was shocked.

She caught this.

"No trance. McKie's nexus known to Fannie Mae."

"I think not. I can't have any distractions here."

"Bad choice."

She was petulant.

"Could you provide me with a personal jumpdoor to . . ."

"Not with node ending close to ending for Dosadi wave."

"Fannie Mae, do you know what the Gowachin are doing here on Dosadi? This . . ."

"Caleban contract, McKie."

Her displeasure was clear. You didn't question the honor of a Caleban's word-writ. The Dosadi contract undoubtedly contained specific prohibitions against any revelations of what went on here. McKie was dismayed. He was tempted to leave Dosadi immediately.

Fannie Mae got this message, too.

"McKie can leave now. Soon, McKie cannot leave in his own body/node."

"Body/node?"

"Answer not permitted."

Not permitted!

"I thought you were my friend, Fannie Mae!"

Warmth suffused him.

"Fannie Mae possess friendship for McKie."

"Then why won't you help me?"

"You wish to leave Dosadi's wave in this instant?"

"No!"

"Then Fannie Mae cannot help."

Angry, McKie began to break the contact.

Fannie Mae projected sensations of frustrations and hurt. "Why does McKie refuse advice? Fannie Mae wishes . . ."

"I must go. You know I'm in a trance while we're in contact. That's dangerous here. We'll speak another time. I appreciate your wish to help and your new clarity, but . . ."

"Not clarity! Very small hole in understanding but Human keeps no more dimension!"

Obvious unhappiness accompanied this response, but she broke the contact. McKie felt himself awakening, his fingers and toes trembling with cold. Caleban contact had slowed his metabolism to a dangerous low. He opened his eyes.

A strange Gowachin clad in the yellow of an armored vehicle driver stood over him. A tracked machine rumbled and puffed in the background. Blue smoke enveloped it. McKie stared upward in shock.

The Gowachin nodded companionably.

"You are ill?"

We of the Sabotage Bureau remain legalists of a special category. We know that too much law injures a society; it is the same with too little law. One seeks a balance. We are like the balancing force among the Gowachin: without hope of achieving heaven in the society of mortals, we seek the unattainable. Each agent knows his own conscience and why he serves such a master. That is the key to us. We serve a mortal conscience for immortal reasons. We do it without hope of praise or the sureness of success.

—THE EARLY WRITINGS OF BILDOON,
PANSPECHI CHIEF OF BUSAB

THEY MOVED out onto the streets as soon as the afternoon shadows gloomed the depths of the city, Tria and six carefully chosen companions, all of them young Human males. She'd musked herself to key them up and she led them down dim byways where Broey's spies had been eliminated. All of her troop was armored and armed in the fashion of an ordinary sortie team.

There'd been rioting nearby an hour earlier, not sufficiently disruptive to attract large military attention, but a small Gowachin salient had been eliminated from a Human enclave. A sortie team was the kind of thing this Warren could expect after such a specific species adjustment. Tria and her six companions were not likely to suffer attack. None of the rioters wanted a large-scale mopping up in the area.

A kind of hushed, suspenseful waiting pervaded the streets.

They crossed a wet intersection, green and red ichor in the gutters. The smell of the dampness told her that a Graluz had been broached and its waters freed to wash through the streets.

That would attract retaliation. Some Human children were certain to be killed in the days ahead. An old pattern.

The troop crossed the riot area presently, noting the places where bodies had fallen, estimating casualties. All bodies had been removed. Not a scrap remained for the birds.

They emerged from the Warrens soon afterward, passing through a Gowachin-guarded gate, Broey's people. A few blocks along they went through another gate, Human guards, all in Gar's pay. Broey would learn of her presence here soon, Tria knew, but she'd said she was going into the Warrens. She came presently to an alleyway across from a Second Rank building. The windowless grey of the building's lower floors presented a blank face broken only by the lattice armor of the entrance gate. Behind the gate lay a dimly lighted passage. Its deceptively plain walls concealed spy devices and automatic weapons.

Holding back her companions with a hand motion, Tria waited in the dark while she studied the building entrance across from her. The gate was on a simple latch. There was one doorguard in an alcove on the left near the door which was dimly visible beyond the armorwork of the gate. A building defense force stood ready to come at the doorguard's summons or at the summons of those who watched through the spy devices.

Tria's informants said this was Jedrik's bolt hole. Not in the deep Warrens after all. Clever. But Tria had maintained an agent in this building for years, as she kept agents in many buildings. A conventional precaution. Everything depended on timing now. Her agent in the building was poised to eliminate the inner guards at the spy device station. Only the doorguard would remain. Tria waited for the agreed upon moment.

The street around her smelled of sewage: an open reclamation line. Accident? Riot damage? Tria didn't like the feeling of this place. What was Jedrik's game? Were there unknown surprises built into this guarded building? Jedrik must know by now that she was suspected of inciting the riot—and of other matters. But would she feel safe there in her own enclave? People tended to feel safe among their own people. She couldn't have a very large force around her, though. Still, some private plot worked itself through the devious pathways of Jedrik's mind, and Tria had not yet fathomed all of that plot. There were surface indicators enough to risk a confrontation, a parley. It was possible that Jedrik flaunted herself here to attract Tria. The potential in that possibility filled Tria with excitement.

Together, we'd be unbeatable!

Yes, Jedrik fitted the image of a superb agent. With the proper organization around her . . .

Once more, Tria glanced left and right. The streets were appropriately empty. She checked the time. Her moment had come. With hand motions, she sent flankers out left and right and another young male probing straight across the street to the gate. When they were in place, she slipped across with her three remaining companions in a triangular shield ahead.

The doorguard was a Human with grey hair and a pale face which glistened yellow in the dim light of the passage. His lids were heavy with a recent dose of his personal drug, which Tria's agent had supplied.

Tria opened the gate, saw that the guard carried a round dead-man switch in his right hand as expected. His grin was gap toothed as he held the switch toward her. She knew he'd recognized her. Much depended now on her agent's accuracy.

"Do you want to die for the frogs?" Tria asked.

He knew about the rioting, the trouble in the streets. And he was Human, with Human loyalties, but he knew she worked for Broey, a Gowachin. The question was precisely calculated to fill him with indecision. Was she a turncoat? He had his Human loyalties and a fanatic's dependence upon this guard post which kept him out of the depths. And there was his personal addiction. All doorguards were addicted to something, but this one took a drug which dulled his senses and made it difficult for him to correlate several lines of thought. He wasn't supposed to use his drug on duty and this troubled him now. There were so many matters to be judged, and Tria had asked the right question. He didn't want to die for the frogs.

She pointed to the dead-man's switch, a question.

"It's only a signal relay," he said. "No bomb in this one."

She remained silent, forcing him to focus on his doubts.

The guard swallowed, "What do you . . ."

"Join us or die."

He peered past her at the others. Things such as this happened frequently in the Warrens, not very often here on the slopes which led up to the heights. The guard was not a one trusted with full knowledge of whom he guarded. He had explicit instructions and a dead-man relay to warn of intruders. Others were charged with making the more subtle distinctions, the real decisions. That was this building's weak point.

"Join who?" he asked.

There was a false belligerency in his voice, and she knew she had him then.

"Your own kind."

This locked his drug-dulled mind onto its primary fears. He knew what he was supposed to do: open his hand. That released the alarm device in the dead-man switch. He could do this of his own volition and it was supposed to deter attackers from killing him. A dead man's hand opened anyway. But he'd been fed with suspicions to increase his doubts. The device in his hand might not be a simple signal transmitter. What if it actually were a bomb? He'd had many long hours to wonder about that.

"We'll treat you well," Tria said.

She put a companionable arm around his shoulder, letting him get the full effect of her musk while she held out her other hand to show that it carried no weapon. "Demonstrate to my companion here how you pass that to your relief."

One of the young males stepped forward.

The guard showed how it was done, explaining slowly as he passed the device. "It's easy once you get the trick to it."

When her companion had the thing firmly in hand, she raised her arm from the guard's shoulder, touched his carotid artery with a poisoned needle concealed in a fingernail. The guard had only time to draw one gasping breath, his eyes gaping, before he sank from her embrace.

"I treated him well," she said.

Her companions grinned. It was the kind of thing you learned to expect from Tria. They dragged the body out of sight into the guard alcove, and the young male with the signal device took his place at the door. The others protected Tria with their bodies as they swept into the building. The whole operation had taken less than two minutes. Everything was working smoothly, as Tria's operations were expected to work.

The lobby and its radiating hallways were empty.

Good.

Her agent in this building deserved a promotion.

They took a stairway rather than trust an elevator. It was only three short flights. The upper hallway also was empty. Tria led the way to the designated door, used the key her agent had supplied. The door opened without a sound and they surged into the room.

Inside, the shades had been pulled, and there was no artificial illumination. Her companions took up their places at the closed door and along both flanking walls. This was the most dangerous moment, something only Tria could handle.

Light came from thin strips where shades did not quite seal a south window. Tria discerned dim shapes of furniture, a bed with an indeterminate blob of darkness in it.

"Jedrik?" A whisper.

Tria's feet touched soft fabric, a sandal.

"Jedrik?"

Her shin touched the bed. She held a weapon ready while she felt for the dark blob. It was only a mound of bedding. She turned.

The bathroom door was closed, but she could make out a thin slot of light at the bottom of the door. She skirted the clothing and sandal on the floor, stood at one side, and motioned a companion to the other side. Thus far they had operated with a minimum of sound.

Gently, she turned the knob, thrust open the door. There was water in the tub and a body face down, one arm hanging flaccidly over the edge, fingers dangling. A dark purple welt was visible behind and beneath the left ear. Tria lifted the head by the hair, stared at the face, lowered it gently to avoid splashing. It was her agent, the one she'd trusted for the intelligence to set up this operation. And the death was characteristic of a Gowachin ritual slaying: that welt under the ear. A Gowachin talon driven in there to silence the victim before drowning? Or had it just been made to appear like a Gowachin slaying?

Tria felt the whole operation falling apart around her, sensed the uneasiness of her companions. She considered calling Gar from where she stood, but a feeling of fear and revulsion came over her. She stepped out into the bedroom before opening her communicator and thumbing the emergency signal.

"Central." The voice was tense in her ear.

She kept her own voice flat. "Our agent's dead."

Silence. She could imagine them centering the locator on her transmission, then: "There?"

"Yes. She's been murdered."

Gar's voice came on: "That can't be. I talked to her less than an hour ago. She . . ."

"Drowned in a tub of water," Tria said. "She was knocked out first—something sharp driven in under an ear."

There was silence again while Gar absorbed this data. He would have the same uncertainties as Tria.

She glanced at her companions. They had taken up guard positions facing the doorway to the hall. Yes, if attack came, it would come from there.

The channel to Gar remained open, and now Tria heard a babble of terse orders with only a few words intelligible: ". . . team . . . don't let . . . time . . ." Then, quite clearly: "They'll pay for this!"

Who will pay? Tria wondered.

She was beginning to make a new assessment of Jedrik.

Gar came back on: "Are you in immediate danger?"

"I don't know." It was a reluctant admission.

"Stay right where you are. We'll send help. I've notified Broey."

So that was the way Gar saw it. Yes. That was most likely the proper way to handle this new development. Jedrik had eluded them. There was no sense in proceeding alone. It would have to be done Broey's way now.

Tria shuddered as she issued the necessary orders to her companions. They prepared to sell themselves dearly if an attack came, but Tria was beginning to doubt there'd be an immediate attack. This was another message from Jedrik. The trouble came when you tried to interpret the message.

The military mentality is a bandit and raider mentality. Thus, all military represents a form of organized banditry where the conventional mores do not prevail. The military is a way of rationalizing murder, rape, looting, and other forms of theft which are always accepted as part of warfare. When denied an outside target, the military mentality always turns against its own civilian population, using identical rationalizations for bandit behavior.

—BUSAB MANUAL, CHAPTER FIVE:
"THE WARLORD SYNDROME"

MCKIE, AWAKENING from the communications trance, realized how he must've appeared to this strange Gowachin towering over him. Of course a Dosadi Gowachin would think him ill. He'd been shivering and mumbling in the trance, perspiration rolling from him. McKie took a deep breath.

"No, I'm not ill."

"Then it's an addiction?"

Recalling the many substances to which the Dosadi could be addicted, McKie almost used this excuse but thought better of it. This Gowachin might demand some of the addictive substance.

"Not an addiction," McKie said. He lifted himself to his feet, glanced around. The sun had moved perceptibly toward the horizon behind its streaming veil.

And something new had been added to the landscape—that gigantic tracked vehicle, which stood throbbing and puffing smoke from a vertical stack behind the Gowachin intruder. The Gowachin maintained a steady, intense concentration on McKie, disconcerting in its unwavering directness. McKie had to ask himself: was this some threat, or his Dosadi contact? Aritch's people had said a vehicle would be sent to the contact point, but . . .

"Not ill, not an addiction," the Gowachin said. "Is it some strange condition which only Humans have?"

"I *was* ill," McKie said. "But I'm recovered. The condition has passed."

"Do you often have such attacks?"

"I can go years without a recurrence."

"Years? What causes this . . . condition?"

"I don't know."

"I . . . ahhhh." The Gowachin nodded, gestured upward with his chin. "An affliction of the Gods, perhaps."

"Perhaps."

"You were completely vulnerable."

McKie shrugged. Let the Gowachin make of that what he could.

"You were not vulnerable?" Somehow, this amused the Gowachin, who added: "I am Bahrank. Perhaps that's the luckiest thing which has ever happened to you."

Bahrank was the name Aritch's aides had given as McKie's first contact.

"I am McKie."

"You fit the description, McKie, except for your, ahhh, condition. Do you wish to say more?"

McKie wondered what Bahrank expected. This was supposed to be a simple contact handing him on to more important people. Aritch was certain to have knowledgeable observers on Dosadi, but Bahrank was not supposed to be one of them. The warning about this Gowachin had been specific.

"Bahrank doesn't know about us. Be extremely careful what you reveal to him. It'd be very dangerous to you if he were to learn that you came from beyond the God Veil."

The jumpdoor aides had reinforced the warning.

"If the Dosadi penetrate your cover, you'll have to return to your pickup point on your own. We very much doubt that you could make it. Understand that we can give you little help once we've put you on Dosadi."

Bahrank visibly came to a decision, nodding to himself.

"Jedrik expects you."

That was the other name Aritch's people had provided. "Your cell leader. She's been told that you're a new infiltrator from the Rim. Jedrik doesn't know your true origin."

"Who does know?"

"We cannot tell you. If you don't know, then that information cannot be wrested from you. We assure you, though, that Jedrik isn't one of our people."

McKie didn't like the sound of that warning. ". . . wrested from you." As usual, BuSab sent you into the tiger's mouth without a full briefing on the length of the tiger's fangs.

Bahrank gestured toward his tracked vehicle. "Shall we go?"

McKie glanced at the machine. It was an obvious war device, heavily armored with slits in its metal cab, projectile weapons protruding at odd angles. It looked squat and deadly. Aritch's people had mentioned such things.

"We saw to it that they got only primitive armored vehicles, projectile weapons and relatively unimportant explosives, that sort of thing. They've been quite resourceful in their adaptations of such weaponry, however."

Once more, Bahrank gestured toward his vehicle, obviously anxious to leave.

McKie was forced to suppress an abrupt feeling of profound anxiety. What had he gotten himself into? He felt that he had awakened to find himself on a terrifying slide into peril, unable to control the least threat. The sensation passed, but it left him shaken. He delayed while he continued to stare at the vehicle. It was about six meters long with heavy tracks, plus other wheels faintly visible within the shadows behind the tracks. It sported a conventional antenna at the rear for tapping the power transmitter in orbit beneath the barrier veil, but there was a secondary system which burned a stinking fuel. The smoke of that fuel filled the air around them with acridity.

"For what do we wait?" Bahrank demanded. He glared at McKie with obvious fear and suspicion.

'We can go now," McKie said.

Bahrank turned and led the way swiftly, clambering up over the tracks and into a shadowed cab. McKie followed, found the interior a tightly cluttered place full of a bitter, oily smell. There were two hard metal seats with curved backs higher than the head of a seated Human or Gowachin. Bahrank already occupied the seat on the left, working switches and dials. McKie dropped into the other seat. Folding arms locked across his chest and waist to hold him in place; a brace fitted itself to the back of his head. Bahrank threw a switch. The door through which they'd entered closed with a grinding of servomotors and the solid clank of locks.

An ambivalent mood swept over McKie. He had always felt faint agoraphobia in open places such as the area around the rock. But the dim interior of this war machine, with its savage reminders of primitive times, touched an atavistic chord in his psyche and he fought an urge to claw his way outside. This was a trap!

An odd observation helped him overcome the sensation. There was glass over the slits which gave them their view of the outside. Glass. He felt it. Yes, glass. It was common stuff in the ConSentiency—strong yet fragile. He could see that this glass wasn't very thick. The fierce appearance of this machine had to be more show than actuality, then.

Bahrank gave one swift, sweeping glance to their surroundings, moved levers which set the vehicle into lurching motion. It emitted a grinding rumble with an overriding whine.

A track of sorts led from the white rock toward the distant city. It showed the marks of this machine's recent passage, a roadway to follow. Glittering reflections danced from bright rocks along the track. Bahrank appeared very busy with whatever he was doing to guide them toward Chu.

McKie found his own thoughts returning to the briefings he'd received on Tandaloor.

"Once you enter Jedrik's cell you're on your own."

Yes . . . he felt very much alone, his mind a clutter of data which had little relationship to any previous experience. And this planet could die unless he made sense out of that data plus whatever else he might learn here.

Alone, alone . . . If Dosadi died there'd be few sentient watchers. The Caleban's tempokinetic barrier would contain most of that final destructive flare. The Caleban would, in fact, feed upon the released energy. That was one of the things he'd learned from Fannie Mae. One consuming blast, a *meal* for a Caleban, and BuSab would be forced to start anew and without the most important piece of physical evidence—Dosadi.

The machine beneath McKie thundered, rocked, and skidded, but always returned to the track which led toward Chu's distant spires.

McKie studied the driver covertly. Bahrank showed uncharacteristic behavior for Gowachin: more direct, more Human. That was it! His Gowachin instincts had been contaminated by contact with Humans. Aritch was sure to despise that, fear it. Bahrank drove with a casual expertise using a complex control system. McKie counted eight different levers and arms which the Gowachin employed. Some were actuated by knees, others by his head. His hands reached out while an elbow deflected a lever. The war machine responded.

Bahrank spoke presently without taking his attention from driving.

"We may come under fire on the second ledge. There was quite a police action down there earlier."

McKie stared at him.

"I thought we had safe passage through."

"You Rimmers are always pressing."

McKie peered out the slits: bushes, barren ground, that lonely track they followed.

Bahrank spoke.

"You're older than any Rimmer I ever saw before."

Aritch's people had warned McKie about this as a basic flaw in his cover, the need to conceal the subtle signs of age.

They'd provided him with some geriatric assistance and an answer to give when challenged. He used that answer now.

"It ages you in a hurry out here."

"It must."

McKie felt that something in Bahrank's response eluded him, but dared not pursue this. It was an unproductive exchange. And there was that reference to a "police action." McKie knew that the Rim Rabble, excluded from Chu, tried periodic raids, most often fruitless. Barbaric!

"What excuse did you use to come out here?" McKie asked.

Bahrank shot a probing glance at him, raised one webbed hand from the controls to indicate a handle in the roof over his head. The handle's purpose was unknown to McKie, and he feared he had already betrayed too much ignorance. But Bahrank was speaking.

"Officially, I'm scouting this area for any hidden surprises the Rimmers may have stored out here. I often do that. Unofficially, everyone thinks I've a secret pond out here full of fertile females."

A pond . . . not a Graluz. Again, it was a relatively fruitless exchange with hidden undertones.

McKie stared silently ahead through a slit. Their dusty track made a slow and wide sweep left, abruptly angled down onto a narrow ledge cut from red rock walls. Bahrank put them through a series of swift changes in speed: slow, fast, slow, fast. The red rock walls raced past. McKie peered out and downward on his side. Far below lay jungle verdure and, in the distance, the smoke and spires of Chu—fluted buildings ranked high over dim background cliffs.

The speed changes appeared purposeless to McKie. And the dizzy drop off the cliff on his side filled him with awe. Their narrow ledge hugged the cliff, turning as the cliff turned—now into shadows and now into light. The machine roared and groaned around him. The smell of oil made his stomach heave. And the faraway city seemed little closer than it had from the cliff top, except that it was taller, more mysterious in its smoky obscurity.

"Don't expect any real trouble until we reach the first ledge," Bahrank said.

McKie glanced at him. First ledge? Yes, that'd be the first elevation outside the city's walls. The gorge within which Chu had been raised came down to river level in broad steps, each one numbered. Chu had been anchored to island hills and flats where the river slowed and split into many arms. And the hills which had resisted the river were almost solid iron ore, as were many of the flanking ledges.

"Glad to get off there," Bahrank said.

Their narrow ledge had turned at right angles away from the cliff onto a broad ramp which descended into grey-green jungle. The growth enclosed them in abrupt green shadows. McKie, looking out to the side, identified hair fronds and broad leaf ficus, giant spikes of barbed red which he had never before seen. Their track, like the jungle floor, was grey mud. McKie looked from side to side; the growth appeared an almost equal mixture of Terran and Tandaloor, interspersed with many strange plants.

Sunlight made him blink as they raced out of the overhanging plants onto a plain of tall grass which had ben trampled, blasted, and burned by recent violence. He saw a pile of wrecked vehicles off to the left, twisted shards of metal with, here and there, a section of track or a wheel aimed at the sky. Some of the wrecks looked similar to the machine in which he now rode.

Bahrank skirted a blast hole at an angle which gave McKie a view into the hole's depths. Torn bodies lay there. Bahrank made no comment, seemed hardly to notice.

Abruptly, McKie saw signs of movement in the jungle, the flitting presence of both Humans and Gowachin. Some carried what appeared to be small weapons—the glint of a metal tube, bandoliers of bulbous white objects around their necks. McKie had not tried to memorize all of Dosadi's weaponry; it was, after all, primitive, but he reminded himself now that primitive weapons had created these scenes of destruction.

Their track plunged again into overhanging growth, leaving the battlefield behind. Deep green shadows enclosed the lurching, rumbling machine. McKie, shaken from side to side against the restraints, carried an odor memory with him: deep, bloody musks and the beginnings of rot. Their shaded avenue made a sharp right turn, emerged onto another ledge slashed by a plunging cut into which Bahrank took them, turning onto another cliff-hugging ledge.

McKie stared across Bahrank through the slits. The city was nearer now. Their rocking descent swept his gaze up and down Chu's towers, which lifted like silvery organ pipes out of the Council Hills. The far cliff was a series of misted steps fading into purple grey. Chu's Warrens lay smokey and hazed all around the fluted towers. And he could make out part of the city's enclosing outer wall. Squat forts dotted the wall's top, offset for enfilading fire. The city within the wall seemed so tall. McKie had not expected it to appear so tall—but that spoke of the population pressures in a way that could not be misunderstood.

Their ledge ended at another battlefield plain strewn with bodies of metal and flesh, the death stink an inescapable vapor. Bahrank spun his vehicle left, right, dodged piles of torn equipment, avoided craters where mounds of flesh lay beneath insect blankets. Ferns and other low growth were beginning to spring upright after the monstrous trampling. Grey and yellow flying creatures sported in the ferntops, uncaring of all that death. Aritch's aides had warned McKie that Dosadi's life existed amidst brutal excesses, but the actuality sickened him. He identified both Gowachin and Human forms among the sprawled corpses. The sleek green skin of a young Gowachin female, orange fertility marks prominent along her arms, especially revolted him. McKie turned sharply away, found Bahrank studying him with tawny mockery in the shining Gowachin eyes. Bahrank spoke as he drove.

"There're informers everywhere, of course, and after this . . ." His head nodded left and right. ". . . you'll have to move with more caution than you might've anticipated.

A brittle explosion punctuated his words. Something struck the vehicle's armor on McKie's side. Again they were a target. And again. The clanging of metal against metal came thickly, striking all around them, even on the glass over the view slits.

McKie suppressed his shock. That thin glass did not shatter. He knew about thick shields of tempered glass, but this put a new dimension on what he'd been told about the Dosadi. Quite resourceful, indeed!

Bahrank drove with apparent unconcern.

More explosive attacks came from directly in front of them, flashes of orange in the jungle beyond the plain.

"They're testing," Bahrank said. He pointed to one of the slits.

"See? They don't even leave a mark on that new glass."

McKie spoke from the depths of his bitterness.

"Sometimes you wonder what all this proves except that our world runs on distrust."

"Who trusts?"

Bahrank's words had the sound of a catechism.

McKie said:

"I hope our friends know when to stop testing."

"They were told we couldn't take more'n eighty millimeter."

"Didn't they agree to pass us through?"

"Even so, they're expected to try a few shots if just to keep me in good graces with my superiors."

Once more, Bahrank put them through a series of dazzling speed changes and turns for no apparent reason. McKie lurched against the restraints, felt bruising pain as an elbow hit the side of the cab. An explosion directly behind rocked them up onto the left track. As they bounced, Bahrank spun them left, avoided another blast which would've landed directly on them along their previous path. McKie, his ears ringing from the explosions, felt the machine bounce to a stop, reverse as more explosions erupted ahead. Bahrank spun them to the right, then left, once more charged full speed ahead right into an unbroken wall of jungle. With explosions all around, they crashed through greenery, turned to the right along another shadowed muddy track. McKie had lost all sense of direction, but the attack had ceased.

Bahrank slowed them, took a deep breath through his ventricles.

"I knew they'd try that."

He sounded both relieved and amused.

McKie, shaken by the brush with death, couldn't find his voice.

Their shadowy track snaked through the jungle for a space, giving McKie time to recover. By then, he didn't know what to say. He couldn't understand Bahrank's amusement, the lack of enduring concern over such violent threat.

Presently, they emerged onto an untouched, sloping plain as smooth and green as a park lawn. It dipped gently downward into a thin screen of growth through which McKie would see a silver-green tracery of river. What caught McKie's attention, however, was a windowless, pock-walled grey fortress which lifted from the plain in the middle distance. It towered over the growth screening the river. Buttressed arms reached toward them to enclose a black metal barrier.

"That's our gate," Bahrank said.

Bahrank turned them left, lined up with the center of the buttressed arms. "Gate Nine and we're home through the tube," he said.

McKie nodded. Walls, tubes, and gates: those were the keys to Chu's defenses. They had "barrier and fortress minds" on Dosadi. This tube would run beneath the river. He tried to place it on the map which Aritch's people had planted in his mind. He was supposed to know the geography of this place, its geology, religions, social patterns, the intimate layout of each island's walled defenses, but he found it hard to locate himself now on that mental map. He leaned forward to the slit, peered upward as the machine began to gather speed, saw the great central spire with its horizontal clock. All the hours of map briefing snicked into place.

"Yes, Gate Nine."

Bahrank, too busy driving, did not reply.

McKie dropped his gaze to the fortress, stifled a gasp.

The rumbling machine was plunging downslope at a frightening pace, aimed directly toward that black metal barrier. At the last instant, when it seemed they would crash into it, the barrier leaped upward. They shot through into a dimly illuminated tube. The gate thundered closed behind them. Their machine made a racketing sound on metal grating beneath the tracks.

Bahrank slowed them, shifted a lever beside him. The machine lifted onto wheels with an aburpt reduction in noise which made McKie feel that he'd been deafened. The feeling was heightened by the realization that Bahrank had said the same thing to him several times.

"Jedrik says you come from beyond the far mountains. Is that true?"

"Jedrik says it." He tried to make it sound wry, but it came out almost questioning.

Bahrank was concentrating on a line of thought, however, as he drove them straight down the grating floor of the dim tube.

"There's a rumor that you Rimmers have started a secret settlement back there, that you're trying to build your own city.

"An interesting rumor."

"Isn't it, though?"

The single line of overhead lights in the tube left the cab's interior darker than it'd been outside, illuminated by only the faint reflections from instruments and dials. But McKie had the odd sensation that Bahrank saw him clearly, was studying every expression. Despite the impossibility of this, the thought persisted. What was behind Bahrank's probing?

Why do I feel that he sees right through me?

These disquieting conjectures ended as they emerged from the tube onto a Warren street. Bahrank spun them to the right along a narrow alleyway in deep grey shadows.

Although he'd seen many representations of these streets the actuality deepened McKie's feelings of misgiving. So dirty . . . oppressive . . . so many people. They were everywhere!

Bahrank drove slowly now on the silent wheels, the tracks raised off the paving. The big machine eased its way through narrow little streets, some paved with stone, some with great slabs of gleaming black. All the streets were shaded by overhanging upper stories whose height McKie could not judge through the slits. He saw shops barred and guarded. An occasional stairway, also guarded, led up or down into repellent darkness. Only Humans occupied these streets, and no casual, pedestrian expressions on any of them. Jaws were set on grim mouths. Hard, questioning eyes peered at the passing vehicle. Both men and women wore the universal dark, one-piece clothing of the Labor Pool.

Noting McKie's interest, Bahrank spoke.

"This is a Human enclave and you have a Gowachin driver."

"Can they see us in here?"

"They know. And there's trouble coming."

"Trouble?"

"Gowachin against Human."

This appalled McKie, and he wondered if this were the source of those forebodings which Aritch and aides would not explain: destruction of Dosadi from within. But Bahrank continued:

"There's a growing separation between Humans and Gowachin, worse than it's ever been. You may be the last Human to ride with me."

Aritch and company had prepared McKie for Dosadi's violence, hunger, and distrust, but they'd said nothing about species against species . . . only that someone they refused to name could destroy the place from within. What was Bahrank trying to say? McKie dared not expose his ignorance by probing, and this inability dismayed him.

Bahrank, meanwhile, nosed their machine out of a narrow passage onto a wider street which was crowded by carts, each piled with greenery. The carts moved aside slowly as the armored vehicle approached, hatred plain in the eyes of the Humans who moved with the carts. The press of people astonished McKie: for every cart (and he lost count of them within a block) there were at least a hundred people crowding around, lifting arms high, shouting at the ring of people who stood shoulder to shoulder around each cart, their backs to the piled contents and obviously guarding those contents.

McKie, staring at the carts, realized with a shocked sense of recognition that he was staring at carts piled with garbage. The crowds of people were buying garbage.

Again, Bahrank acted the part of tour guide.

"This is called the Street of the Hungry. That's very select garbage, the best."

McKie recalled one of Aritch's aides saying there were restaurants in Chu which specialized in garbage from particular areas of the city, that no poison-free food was wasted.

The passing scene compelled McKie's attention: hard faces, furtive movements, the hate and thinly suppressed violence, all of this immersed in a *normal* commercial operation based on garbage. And the numbers of people! They were everywhere around: in doorways, guarding and pushing the carts, skipping out of Bahrank's path. New smells assaulted McKie's nostrils, a fetid acridity, a stink such as he had never before experienced. Another thing surprised him: the appearance of antiquity in this Warren. He wondered if all city populations crowded by threats from outside took on this ancient appearance. By ConSentient standards, the population of Chu had lived here only a few generations, but the city looked older than any he'd ever seen.

With an abrupt rocking motion, Bahrank turned their machine down a narrow street, brought them to a stop. McKie, looking out the slit on his right, saw an arched entry in a grimy building, a stairway leading downward into gloom.

"Down there's where you meet Jedrik," Bahrank said. "Down those stairs, second door on your left. It's a restaurant."

"How'll I know her?"

"Didn't they tell you?"

"I . . ." McKie broke off. He'd seen pictures of Jedrik during the Tandaloor briefings, realized now that he was trying to delay leaving Bahrank's armored cocoon.

Bahrank appeared to sense this.

"Have no fear, McKie. Jedrik will know you. And McKie . . ."

McKie turned to face the Gowachin.

". . . go directly to the restaurant, take a seat, wait for Jedrik. You'll not survive long here without her protection. Your skin's dark and some Humans prefer even the green to the dark in this quarter. They remember Pylash Gate here. Fifteen years isn't long enough to erase that from their minds."

Nothing about a Pylash Gate had been included in McKie's briefings and now he dared not ask.

Bahrank moved the switch which opened McKie's door. Immediately, the stink of the street was amplified to almost overpowering proportions. Bahrank, seeing him hesitate, spoke sharply.

"Go quickly!"

McKie descended in a kind of olfactory daze, found himself standing on the side of the street, the object of suspicious stares from all around. The sight of Bahrank driving away was the cutting of his last link to the ConSentiency and all the familiar things which might protect him. Never in his long life had McKie felt this much alone.

No legal system can maintain justice unless every participant— magisters, prosecutors, Legums, defendants, witnesses, all—risks life itself in whatever dispute comes before the bar. Everything must be risked in the Courtarena. If any element remains outside the contest and without personal risk, justice inevitably fails.

—GOWACHIN LAW

NEAR SUNSET there was a fine rain which lasted well into darkness, then departed on the gorge wind which cleared Dosadi's skies. It left the air crystalline, cornices dripping puddles in the streets. Even the omnipresent Warren stink was diluted and Chu's inhabitants showed a predatory lightness as they moved along the streets.

Returning to headquarters in an armored troop carrier which carried only his most trusted Gowachin, Broey noted the clear air even while he wondered at the reports which had brought him racing from the Council Hills. When he entered the conference room, Broey saw that Gar already was there standing with his back to the dark window which looked out on the eastern cliffs. Broey wondered how long Gar had been there. No sign of recognition passed between Gowachin and Human, but this only emphasized the growing separation of the species. They'd both seen the reports which contained that most disturbing datum: the killing of a Human double agent under circumstances which pointed at Broey himself.

Broey crossed to the head of the conference table, flipped the toggle which activated his communicator, addressed the screen which only he could see.

"Assemble the Council and link for conference."

The response came as a distorted buzz filtered through scramblers and suppressed by a privacy cone. Gar, standing across the room, could make no sense out of the noises coming from the communicator.

While he waited for the Council members to come on the conference link Broey seated himself at the communicator, summoned a Gowachin aide to the screen, and spoke in a low voice masked by the privacy cone.

"Start a security check on all Humans in positions where they might threaten us. Use Plan D."

Broey glanced up at Gar. The Human's mouth worked silently. He was annoyed by the privacy cone and his inability to tell exactly what Broey was doing. Broey continued speaking to his aide.

"I'll want the special force deployed as I told you earlier . . . Yes . . ."

Gar pointedly turned his back on this conversation, stared out at the night.

Broey continued to address his aide in the screen.

"No! We must include even the Humans in this conference. Yes, that's the report Gar made to me. Yes, I also received that information. Other Humans can be expected to riot and drive out their Gowachin neighbors, and there'll be retaliations. Yes, that was my thought when I saw the report."

Broey turned off the privacy cone and scrambler. Tria had just come onto his screen with an override, interrupting the conversation with his security aide. She spoke in a low, hurried voice with only a few words intelligible to Gar across the room. But Broey's suspicions were becoming obvious. He heard Tria out, then:

"Yes . . . it would be logical to suppose that such a killing was made to look like Gowachin work for . . . I see. But the scattered incidents which . . . Indeed? Well under the circumstances . . ."

He left the thought incomplete, but his words drew a line between Human and Gowachin, even at the highest levels of his Advisory Council.

"Tria, I must make my own decisions on this."

While Broey was speaking, Gar brought up a chair and placed it near the communicator, then sat down. Broey had finished his conversation with Tria and restored the privacy circuits, however, and even though he sat nearby Gar could not penetrate their protective screen. He was close enough now, though, to hear the buzzing of the privacy system and the sound annoyed Gar. He did not try to conceal his annoyance.

Broey saw Gar, but gave no indication that he approved or disapproved Gar's nearness.

"So I understand," Broey said. "Yes . . . I'll issue those orders as soon as I've finished here. No . . . Agreed. That would be best." He closed the circuit. The annoying buzz stopped.

"Jedrik means to set Gowachin against Human, Human against Gowachin," Gar said.

"If so, it's been a long time in secret preparation," Broey said.

His words implied many things: that there was conspiracy in high places, that the situation had achieved dangerous momentum without being detected, that all of the inertial forces could not now be anticipated.

"You expect it to get worse," Gar said.

"Hopefully."

Gar stared at him for a long period, then:

"Yes."

It was clear that Broey wanted a well-defined condition to develop, one which would provide clear predictions of the major consequences. He was prepared for this. When Broey understood the situation to his own satisfaction, he'd use his own undeniable powers to gain as much as possible during a period of upset.

Gar broke the silence.

"But if we've misunderstood Jedrik's intent—"

"It helps us when the innocent suffer," Broey said, paraphrasing part of an old axiom which every Dosadi knew.

Gar completed the thought for thim.

"But who's innocent?"

Before Broey could respond, his screen came alight with the assembled faces of his Council, each face in its own little square. Broey conducted the conference quickly, allowing few interruptions. There were no house arrests, no direct accusations, but his words and manner divided them by species. When he was through, Gar imagined the scrambling which must be going on right then in Chu while the powerful assembled their defenses.

Without knowing how he sensed this, Gar felt that this was exactly what Jedrik had wanted, and that it'd been a mistake for Broey to increase the tensions.

After turning off the communicator, Broey sat back and addressed himself to Gar with great care.

"Tria tells me that Jedrik cannot be found."

"Didn't we expect that?"

"Perhaps." Broey puffed his jowls. "What I don't understand is how a simple Liaitor could elude my people *and* Tria."

"I think we've underestimated this Jedrik. What if she comes from . . ." His chin jerked ceilingward.

Broey considered this. He'd been supervising the interrogation of Bahrank at a secure post deep in the Council Hills when the summons to headquarters had interrupted. The accumulating reports indicated a kind of trouble Chu had known at various times, but never at this magnitude. And Bahrank's information had been disappointing. He'd delivered this Rim infiltrator named McKie to such and such an address. (Security had been unable to check this in time because of the riot.) Bahrank's beliefs were obvious. And perhaps the Rimmers *were* trying to build their own city beyond the mountains. Broey thought this unlikely. His sources in the Rim had proved generally trustworthy and his special source was always trustworthy. Besides, such a venture would require gigantic stocks of food, all of it subject to exposure in the regular accounting. That, after all, was the Liaitor function, why he had . . . No, that was not probable. The Rim subsisted on the lowest of Chu's leavings and whatever could be wrested from Dosadi's poisonous soil. No . . . Bahrank was wrong. This McKie was peculiar, but in quite another way. And Jedrik must've known this before anyone else—except himself. The paramount question remained: who'd helped her?

Broey sighed.

"We have a long association, Gar. A person of your powers who has worked his way from the Rim through the Warrens . . ."

Gar understood. He was being told that Broey looked upon him with active suspicion. There'd never been any real trust between them, but this was something else: nothing openly spoken, nothing direct or specific, but the meaning clear. It was not even sly; it was merely Dosadi.

For a moment, Gar didn't know which way to turn. There'd always been this possibility in his relationship with Broey, but long acceptance had lulled Gar into a dangerous dependency. Tria had been his most valuable counter. He needed her now, but she had other, much more demanding, duties at this juncture.

Gar realized now that he would have to precipitate his own plans, calling in all of the debts and dependencies which were his due. He was distracted by the sound of many people hurrying past in the outer hall. Presumably, things were coming to a head faster than expected.

Gar stood up, stared vaguely out the windows at those dark shadows in the night which were the Rim cliffs. While waiting for Broey, Gar had watched darkness settle there, watched the spots of orange appear which were the Rim's cookfires. Gar knew those cookfires, knew the taste of the food which came from them, knew the flesh-dragging dullness which dominated existence out there. Did Broey expect him to flee back to that? Broey would be astonished at the alternatives left to Gar.

"I will leave you now," Broey said. He arose and waddled from the room. What he meant was: "Don't be here when I return."

Gar continued to stare out the windows. He seemed lost in angry reverie. Why hadn't Tria reported yet? One of Broey's Gowachin aides came in, fussed over papers on a corner table.

It was actually no more than five minutes that Gar remained standing thus. He shook himself presently, turned, and let himself out of the room.

Scarcely had he set foot in the outer passage than a troop of Broey's Gowachin shouldered their way past him into the conference room. They'd been waiting for him to leave.

Angry with himself for what he knew he must do, Gar turned left, strode down the hall to the room where he knew he'd find Broey. Three Gowachin wearing Security brassards followed him, but did not interfere. Two more Gowachin guarded Broey's door, but they hesitated to stop him. Gar's power had been felt here too long. And Broey, not expecting Gar to follow, had failed to issue specific orders. Gar counted on this.

Broey, instructing a group of Gowachin aides, stood over a table cluttered with charts. Yellow light from fixtures directly overhead played shifting shadows on the charts as the aides bent over the table and made notes. Broey broke off at the intrusion, his surprise obvious.

Gar spoke before Broey could order him removed.

"You still need me to keep you from making the worst mistake of your life."

Broey straightened, did not speak, but the invitation for Gar to continue was there.

"Jedrik's playing you like a fine instrument. You're doing precisely what she wants you to do."

Broey's cheeks puffed. The shrug angered Gar.

"When I first came here, Broey, I took certain precautions to insure my continued health should you ever consider violence against me."

Again, Broey gave that maddening Gowachin shrug. This was all so mundane. Why else did this fool Human continue alive and at liberty?

"You've never been able to discover what I did to insure myself against you," Gar said. "I have no addictions. I'm a prudent person and, naturally, have means of dying before your experts on pain could overcome my reason. I've done all of the things you might expect of me . . . and something more, something you now need *desperately* to know."

"I have my own precautions, Gar."

"Of course, and I admit I don't know what they are.'

"So what do you propose?"

Gar gave a little laugh, not quite gloating.

"You know my terms."

Broey shook his head from side to side, an exquisitely Human gesture.

"Share the rule? I'm astonished at you, Gar."

"Your astonishment hasn't reached its limits. You don't know what I've really done."

"Which is?"

"Shall we retire to a more private place and discuss it?"

Broey looked around at his aides, waved for them to leave.

"We will talk here."

Gar waited until he heard the door close behind him on the last of the departing aides.

"You probably know about the death fanatics we've groomed in the Human enclaves."

"We are prepared to deal with them."

"Properly motivated, fanatics can keep great secrets, Broey."

"No doubt. Are you now going to reveal such a secret?"

"For years now, my fanatics have lived on reduced rations, preserving and exporting their surplus rations to the Rim. We have enough, megatons of food out there. With a whole planet in which to hide it, you'll never find it. City food, every bit of it and we will . . ."

"Another city!"

"More than that. Every weapon the city of Chu has, we have."

Broey's ventricle lips went almost green with anger.

"So you never really left the Rim?"

"The Rim-born cannot forget."

"After all that Chu has done for you . . ."

"I'm glad you didn't mention blasphemy."

"But the Gods of the Veil gave us a mandate!"

"Divide and rule, subdivide and rule even more powerfully, fragment and rule absolutely."

"That's not what I meant." Broey breathed deeply several times to restore his calm. "One city and only one city. That is our mandate."

"But the other city will be built."

"Will it?"

"We've dug in the factories to provide our own weapons and food. If you move against our people inside Chu, we'll come at you from the outside, shatter your walls and . . ."

"What do you propose?"

"Open cooperation for a separation of the species, one city for Gowachin, one for Human. What you do in Chu will be your own business then, but I'll tell you that we of the new city will rid ourselves of the DemoPol and its aristocracy."

"You'd create another aristocracy?"

"Perhaps. But my people will die for the vision of freedom we share. We no longer provide our bodies for Chu!"

"So that's why your fanatics are all Rim-born."

"I see that you don't yet understand Broey. My people are not merely Rim-born; they are willing, even *eager*, to die for their vision."

Broey considered this. It was a difficult concept for a Gowachin, whose Graluz guilt was always transformed into a profound respect for the survival drive. But he saw where Gar's words must lead, and he built an image in his mind of fleshly Human waves throwing themselves onto all opposition without inhibitions about pain, death, or survival in any respect. They might very well capture Chu. The idea that countless Rim immigrants lived within Chu's walls in readiness for such sacrifice filled him with deep disquiet. It required strong self-control to conceal this reaction. He did not for an instant doubt Gar's story. It was just the kind of thing this dry-fleshed Rimmer would do. But why was Gar revealing this now?

"Did Jedrik order you to prepare me for . . ."

"Jedrik isn't part of our plan. She complicates matters for us, but the kind of upset she's igniting is just the sort of thing we can exploit better than you."

Broey weighed this with what he knew about Gar, found it valid as far as it went, but it still did not answer the basic question.

"Why?"

"I'm not ready to sacrifice my people," Gar said.

That had the ring of partial truth. Gar had shown many times that he could make hard decisions. But numbered among his fanatic hordes there doubtless were certain skills he'd prefer not losing—not yet. Yes, that was the way Gar's mind worked. And Gar would know the profound respect for life which matured in a Gowachin breast after the weeding frenzy. Gowachin, too, could make bloody decisions, but the guilt . . . oh, the guilt . . . Gar counted on the guilt. Perhaps he counted too much.

"Surely, you don't expect me to take an open and active part in your Rim city project?"

"If not open, then passive."

"And you insist on sharing the rule of Chu?"

"For the interim."

"Impossible!"

"In substance if not in name."

"You have been my advisor."

"Will you precipitate violence between us with Jedrik standing there to pick up whatever she can gain from us?"

"Ahhhhhh . . ." Broey nodded.

So that was it! Gar was not part of this Jedrik thing. Gar was afraid of Jedrik, more afraid of her than he was of Broey. This gave Broey cause for caution. Gar was not easily made fearful. What did he know of this Jedrik that Broey did not know? But now there was a sufficient reason for compromise. The unanswered questions could be answered later.

"You will continue as my chief advisor," Broey said.

It was acceptable. Gar signified his consent by a curt nod.

The compromise left an empty feeling in Broey's digestive nodes, though. Gar knew he'd been manipulated to reveal his fear of Jedrik. Gar could be certain that Broey would try to neutralize the Rim city project. But the magnitude of Gar's plotting went far beyond expectations, leaving too many unknowns. One could not make accurate decisions with unsufficient data. Gar had given away information without receiving an equal exchange. That was not like Gar. Or was that a correct interpretation of what'd happened here? Broey knew he had to explore this, risking one piece of accurate information as bait.

"There's been a recent increase of mystical experiences by Gowachin in the Warrens."

"You know better than to try that religious nonsense on me!"

Gar was actually angry.

Broey concealed his amusement. Gar did not know then (or did not accept) that the God of the Veil sometimes created illusions in his flock, that God spoke truly to his anointed and would even answer some questions.

Much had been revealed here, more than Gar suspected. Bahrank had been right. And Jedrik would know about Gar's Rim city. It was possible that Jedrik wanted Broey to know and had maneuvered Gar into revealing the plot. If Gar saw this, that would be enough to make him fearful.

Why didn't the God reveal this to me? Broey wondered. *Am I being tested?*

Yes, that had to be the answer, because there was one thing certain now:

This time, I'll do what the God advises.

People always devise their own justifications. Fixed and immovable Law merely provides a convenient structure within which to hang your justifications and the prejudices behind them. The only universally acceptable law for mortals would be one which fitted every justification. What obvious nonsense. Law must expose prejudice and question justification. Thus, Law must be flexible, must change to fit new demands. Otherwise, it becomes merely the justification of the powerful.

—GOWACHIN LAW
(THE BUSAB TRANSLATION)

IT REQUIRED a moment after Bahrank drove away for McKie to recover his sense of purpose. The buildings rose tall and massive over him, but through a quirk of this Warren's growth, an opening to the west allowed a spike of the silvery afternoon sunlight to slant into the narrow street. The light threw hard shadows on every object, accented the pressure of Human movement. McKie did not like the way people looked at him: as though everyone measured him for some private gain.

Slowly, McKie pressed through the passing throng to the arched entry, observing all he could without seeming to do so. After all those years in BuSab, all of the training and experience which had qualified him for such a delicately powerful agency, he possessed superb knowledge of the ConSentiency's species. He drew on that knowledge now, sensing the powerful secrecy which governed these people. Unfortunately, his experience also was replete with knowledge of what species could do to species, not to mention what a species could do to itself. The Humans around him reminded him of nothing more than a mob about to explode.

Moving with a constant readiness to defend himself, he went down a short flight of stairs into cool shadows where the foot traffic was lighter but the smells of rot and mold were more pronounced.

Second door on the left.

He went to the doorway to which Bahrank had directed him, peered into the opening: another stairway down. Somehow, this dismayed him. The picture of Chu growing in his mind was not at all what Aritch's people had drawn. Had they deliberately misled him? If so, why? Was it possible they really didn't understand their monster? The array of answers to his questions chilled him. What if a few of the observers sent here by Aritch's people had chosen to capitalize on whatever power Dosadi provided?

In all of his career, McKie had never before come across a world so completely cut off from the rest of the universe. This planet was *alone*, without many of the amenities which graced the other ConSentient worlds: no common access to jumpdoors, no concourse of the known species, none of the refined pleasures nor the sophisticated traps which occupied the denizens of other worlds. Dosadi had developed its own ways. And the instructors on Tandaloor had returned time and again to that constant note of warning—that these lonely *primitives* would take over the ConSentiency if released upon the universe.

"Nothing restrains them. Nothing."

That was, perhaps, an overstatement. Some things did restrain the Dosadi physically. But they were not held back by the conventions or mores of the ConSentiency. Anything could be purchased here, any forbidden depravity which the imagination might conceive. This idea haunted McKie. He thought of this and of the countless substances to which many Dosadi were addicted. The power leverage such things gave to the unprincipled few was terrifying.

He dared not pause here wrestling with his indecisions, though. McKie stepped into the stairwell with a boldness which he did not feel, following Bahrank's directions because he had no choice. The bottom landing was a wider space in deep shadows, one dim light on a black door. Two Humans dozed in chairs beside the door while a third squatted beside them with what appeared to be a crude projectile weapon in his hands.

"Jedrik summoned me," McKie said.

The guard with the weapon nodded for him to proceed.

McKie made his way past them, glanced at the weapon: a length of pipe with a metal box at the back and a flat trigger atop the box held by the guard's thumb. McKie almost missed a step. The weapon was a dead-man bomb! Had to be. If that guard's thumb relaxed for any reason, the thing no doubt would explode and kill everyone in the stairwell. McKie glanced at the two sleepers. How could they sleep in such circumstances?

The black door with its one dim light commanded his attention now. A strong smell of highly seasoned cooking dominated the other stinks here. McKie saw that it was a heavy door with a glittering spyeye at face level. The door opened at his approach. He stepped through into a large low room crowded—*jammed!*—with people seated on benches at trestle tables. There was barely room for passage between the benches. And everywhere that McKie looked he saw people spooning food into their mouths from small bowls. Waiters and waitresses hurried through the narrow spaces slapping down bowls and removing empties.

The whole scene was presided over by a fat woman seated at a small desk on a platform at his left. She was positioned in such a way that she commanded the entry door, the entire room, and swinging doors at the side through which the serving people flowed back and forth. She was a monstrous woman and she sat her perch as though she had never been anywhere else. Indeed, it was easy for McKie to imagine that she could not move from her position. Her arms were bloated where they squeezed from the confines of short-sleeved green coveralls. Her ankles hung over her shoe tops in folds.

Take a seat and wait.

Bahrank had been explicit and the warning clear.

McKie looked for an opening on the benches. Before he could move, the fat woman spoke in a squeaky voice.

"Your name?"

McKie's gaze darted toward those beady eyes in their folds of fat.

"McKie."

"Thought so."

She raised a dimpled finger. From somewhere in the crush a young boy came hurrying. He could not have been over nine years old but his eyes were cold with adult wisdom. He looked up to the fat woman for instructions.

"This is the one. Guide him."

The boy turned and, without looking to see if McKie followed, hurried down the narrow pathway where the doors swung back and forth to permit the passage of the servitors. Twice, McKie was almost run down by waiters. His guide was able to anticipate the opening of every door and skipped aside.

At the end of this passage, there was another solid black door with spyeye. The door opened onto a short passage with closed doors on both sides, a blank wall at the end. The blank wall slid aside for them and they descended into a narrow, rock-lined way lighted by widely spaced bulbs overhead. The walls were damp and evil smelling. Occasionally, there were wide places with guards. They passed through several guarded doors, climbed up and went down. McKie lost track of the turns, the doors, and guard posts. After a time, they climbed to another short hallway with doors along its sides. The boy opened the second door on the right, waited for McKie to enter, closed the door. It was all done without words. McKie heard the boy's footsteps recede.

The room was small and dimly lighted by windows high in the wall opposite the door. A trestle table about two meters long with benches down both sides and a chair at each end almost filled the space. The walls were grey stone and unadorned. McKie worked his way around to the chair at the far end, sat down. He remained seated there silently for several minutes, absorbing this place. It was cold in the room: Gowachin temperature. One of the high windows behind him was open a crack and he could hear street noises: a heavy vehicle passing, voices arguing, many feet. The sense of the Warren pressing in upon this room was very strong. Nearer at hand from beyond the single door, he heard crockery banging and an occasional hiss as of steam.

Presently, the door opened and a tall, slender woman entered, slipping through the door at minimal opening. For a moment as she turned, the light from the windows concentrated on her face, then she sat down at the end of the right-hand bench, dropping into shadows.

McKie had never before seen such hard features on a woman. She was brittle rock with ice crystal eyes of palest blue. Her black hair was closely cropped into a stiff bristle. He repressed a shudder. The rigidity of her body amplified the hard expression on her face. It was not the hardness of suffering, not that alone, but something far more determined, something anchored in a kind of agony which might explode at the slightest touch. On a ConSentient world where the geriatric arts were available, she could have been any age between thirty-five and one hundred and thirty-five. The dim light into which she had seated herself complicated his scrutiny, but he suspected she was younger than thirty-five.

"So *you* are McKie."

He nodded.

"You're fortunate Adril's people got my message. Broey's already searching for you. I wasn't warned that you were so dark."

He shrugged.

"Bahrank sent word that you could get us all killed if we're not careful with you. He says you don't have even rudimentary survival training."

This surprised McKie, but he held his silence.

She sighed. "At least you have the good sense not to protest. Well . . .welcome to Dosadi, McKie. Perhaps I'll be able to keep you alive long enough for you to be of some use to us."

Welcome to Dosadi!

"I'm Jedrik as you doubtless already know."

"I recognize you."

This was only partly true. None of the representations he'd seen had conveyed the ruthless brutality which radiated from her.

A hard smile flickered on her lips, was gone.

"You don't respond when I welcome you to our planet."

McKie shook his head. Aritch's people had been specific in their injunction:

"She doesn't know your origin. Under no circumstances may you reveal to her that you come from beyond the God Wall. It could be immediately fatal."

McKie continue to stare silently at her.

A colder look came over Jedrik's features, something in the muscles at the corners of the mouth and eyes.

"We shall see. Now: Bahrank says you carry a wallet of some kind and that you have currency sewn into your clothing. First, hand me the wallet."

My toolkit?

She reached an open hand toward him.

"I'll warn you once, McKie. If I get up and walk out of here you'll not live more than two minutes."

Every muscle quivering protest, he slipped the toolkit from its pocket, extended it.

"And I'll warn you, Jedrik: I'm the only person who can open this without being killed and the contents destroyed."

She accepted the toolkit, turned its flat substance over in her hands.

"Really?"

McKie had begun to interest her in a new way. He was less than she'd expected, yet more. Naive, of course, incredibly naive. But she'd already known that of the people from beyond the God Wall. It was the most suitable explanation. Something was profoundly wrong in the Dosadi situation. The people beyond the Veil would have to send their best here. This McKie was their best? Astonishing.

She arose, went to the door, rapped once.

McKie watched her pass the toolkit to someone outside, heard a low-voice conversation, neither half of it intelligible. In a flashing moment of indecision, he'd considered trying for some of the toolkit's protective contents. Something in Jedrik's manner and the accumulation of unknowns all around had stopped him.

Jedrik returned to her seat empty-handed. She stared at him a moment, head cocked to one side, then:

"I'll say several things to you. In a way, this is a test. If you fail, I guarantee you'll not survive long on Dosadi. Understood?"

When McKie failed to respond, she pounded a fist on the table.

"Understood?"

"Say what you have to say."

"Very well. It's obvious to me that those who instructed you about Dosadi warned you not to reveal your true origin. Yet, most of those who've talked to you for more than a few seconds suspect you're not one of us—not from Chu, not from the Rim, not from anywhere on Dosadi." Her voice took on a new harshness. "But I know it. Let me tell you, McKie, that there's not even a child among us who's failed to realize that the people imprisoned on Dosadi did not originate here!"

McKie stared at her, shocked.

Imprisoned.

As she spoke, he knew she was telling him the truth. Why hadn't Aritch or the others warned him? Why hadn't he seen this for himself? Since Dosadi was poison to both Human and Gowachin, rejected them, of course they'd know they hadn't originated here.

She gave him time to absorb this before continuing. "There are others among us from your realm, perhaps some we've not identified, better trained. But I was taught to act only on certainty. Of you I'm certain. You do not originate on Dosadi.

I've put it to the question and I've the present confirmation of my own senses. You come from beyond the God Wall. Your actions with Bahrank, with Adril, with me . . .'' She shook her head sadly.

Aritch set me up for this!

This thought brought back a recurrent question which continued to nag McKie; BuSab's discovery of the Dosadi experiment. Were the Gowachin that clumsy? Would they make such slips? The original plan to conceal this project must have been extensive. Yet, key facts had leaked to BuSab agents. McKie felt overwrought from asking himself the same questions over and over without satisfaction. And now, Jedrik's pressures compounded the burden. The only suitable answer was that Aritch's people had done everything with the intent of putting him in this position. They'd deliberately leaked information about Dosadi. And McKie was their target.

To what purpose?

"Can we be overheard?" he asked.

"Not by my enemies on Dosadi."

He considered this. She'd left open the question of whether anyone from beyond the God Wall might eavesdrop. McKie pursed his lips with indecision. She'd taken his toolkit with such ridiculous ease . . . yet, what choice had he? They wouldn't get anything from the kit and someone out there, one of Jedrik's underlings, would die. That could have a useful effect on Jedrik. He decided to play for time.

"There're many things I could tell you. So many things. I hardly know where to begin."

"Begin by telling me how you came through the God Wall."

Yes, he might be able to confuse her with a loose description of Calebans and jumpdoors. Nothing in her Dosadi experience could've prepared Jedrik for such phenomena. McKie took a deep breath. Before he could speak there was a rap on the door.

Jedrik raised a hand for silence, leaned over, and opened the door. A skinny young man with large eyes beneath a high forehead and thin blond hair slipped through, placed McKie's toolkit on the table in front of Jedrik.

"It wasn't very difficult," he said.

McKie stared at the kit in shock. It lay open with all of its contents displayed in perfect order.

Jedrik gestured the youth to the seat opposite her. She reached for a raygen.

McKie could no longer contain himself.

"Careful! That's dangerous!"

"Be still, McKie. You know nothing of danger."

She removed the raygen, examined it, replaced it neatly, looked at the young man.

"All right, Stiggy. Tell me."

The youth began removing the items from the toolkit one by one, handling each with a knowledgeable correctness, speaking rapidly.

McKie tried hard to follow the conversation, but it was in a code he could not understand. The expressions on their faces were eloquent enough, however. They were elated. Whatever Stiggy was saying about the dangerous toys in McKie's toolkit, his revelations profited both of them.

The uncertainties which had begun during McKie's ride with Bahrank reached a new intensity. The feeling had built up in him like a sickness: disquiet stomach, pains in his chest, and, lastly, an ache across his forehead. He'd wondered for a time if he might be the victim of some new disease native to Dosadi. It could not be the planet's food because he'd eaten nothing yet. The realization came over him as he watched Jedrik and Stiggy that his reactions were his own reasoning system trying to reject something, some assumption or set of assumptions which he'd accepted without question. He tried to empty his mind, not asking any questions in particular. Let come into his awareness what may. It would all have a fresh appraisal.

Dosadi requires you to be coldly brutal in all of your decisions. No exceptions.

Well . . . he'd let go of the toolkit in the belief that someone would die trying to open it. But he'd issued a warning. That warning could've helped them. Probably did.

I must become exactly like them or I cannot survive—let alone succeed.

At last, McKie felt Aritch's fear of Dosadi, understood the Gowachin desperation. What a terrible training ground for the recognition and use of power!

Jedrik and Stiggy finished their conversation over the toolkit. Stiggy closed the kit, arose with it in one hand, speaking at last in words McKie understood.

"Yes, we must lose no time."

Stiggy left with the kit.

Jedrik faced McKie. The toolkit and its contents had helped answer the most obvious question about McKie and his kind. The people beyond the God Wall were the degenerate descendants of those who'd invented such devices. It was the only workable explanation. She felt almost sorry for this poor fool. But that was not a permissible emotion. He must be made to understand that he had no choice but to obey her.

"Now, McKie, you will answer all of my questions."

"Yes."

It was utter submission and she knew it.

"When you've satisfied me in all matters," she said, "then we'll eat and I'll take you to a place where you'll be reasonably safe."

The Family/Clan/Factions of the Rim are still responding to their defeat in the mass attempt on our defenses of last Decamo. They appear severely chastened. Small police actions are all that we need anticipate over the next planning period. Further, our operatives in the Rim find no current difficulties in steering the F/C/F toward a natural and acceptable cultural rejection of economic developments which might lead them to improved food production.

—FROM A DOSADI BUREAU OF
CONTROL DOCUMENT

AN ANGRY Broey, full out and uninhibited anger, was something to see and quite a number of his Gowachin aides had seen this emotional display during the night. It was now barely dawn. Broey had not slept in two days; but the fourth group of his aides stood before him in the sanctum to receive the full spate of his displeasure. The word had already gone out through their ranks and they, like the others, did not try to hide their fear or their anxious eagerness to restore themselves in Broey's good graces.

Broey stood near the end of the long table where, earlier, he had met with Gar and Tria. The only visible sign of his long sleepless hours was a slight pitting of the fatty nodes between his ventricles. His eyes were as sharp as ever and his voice had lost none of its bite.

"What I'd like explained is how this could happen without a word of warning. And it's not just that we failed to detect this, but that we continued to grind out complacent reports, reports which went exactly contrary to what actually was happening."

The aides massed at the other end of the table, all standing, all fidgeting, were not assuaged by Broey's use of "we." They heard him clearly. He was saying: "You! You! You!"

"I will be satisfied by nothing less than an informant," Broey said. "I want a Human informant, either from Chu or from the Rim. I don't care how you get this informant. We must find that store of city food. We must find where they have started their blasphemous Rim city."

One of his aides, a slender young Gowachin in the front rank, ventured a cautious question which had been repeated several times by other chastened aides during the night.

"If we move too strongly against Humans in the Warrens, won't that feed the unrest that . . ."

"We'll have more riots, more turning of Gowachin against Human and Human against Gowachin," Broey agreed. "That's a consequence we are prepared to accept."

This time they understood that Broey used the royal "we." Broey would accept the consequences. Some of his aides, however, were not ready to accept a war between the species within the city's walls. One of the aides further back in the ranks raised an arm.

"Perhaps we should use only Human troops in the Warrens. If we . . ."

"Who would that fool?" Broey demanded. "We have taken the proper steps to maintain our hold on Chu. You have one task and one task only: find that store of food and those hidden factories. Unless we find them we're finished. Now, get out of here. I don't want to see any of you until you can report success!"

They filed out silently.

Broey stood looking down at the blank screen of his communicator. Alone at last, he allowed his shoulders to slump, breathed heavily through both mouth and ventricles.

What a mess! What a terrible mess.

He knew in his node of nodes that he was behaving precisely as Jedrik wanted him to behave. She had left him no alternatives. He could only admire her handling of the situation while he waited for the opening which he knew must come. But what a magnificent intellect operated in that Human head. And a female at that! Gowachin females never developed such qualities. Only on the Rim were Gowachin females used as other than breeders. Human females, on the other hand, never ceased to amaze him. This Jedrik possessed real leadership qualities. Whether she was the one to take over the Electorship remained to be seen.

Broey found himself recalling those first moments of terrible awareness in the Graluz. Yes, this was the way of the world. If one chose the survivors by other than a terrible testing process, all would die. It would be the end of both species. At least, it would be the end of them on Dosadi, and only Dosadi mattered.

He felt bereft, though. He felt betrayed by his God. Why had God failed to warn him? And when questioned, how could God respond that only evil could penetrate the mind of a fanatic? Wasn't God omnipotent? Could any awareness be closed to God? How could God be *God* then?

I am your God!

He could never forget that voiceless voice reverberating in his head.

Was that a lie?

The idea that they were puppets of a false god was not a new one. But if this were the case, then the other uses of those like Pcharky eluded him. What was the purpose of being a Gowachin in Human form or vice versa if not to elude the God of the Veil? Quite obviously, Jedrik operated on such a premise. What other motive could she have than to prolong her own life? As the City was to the Rim, so was the power to elude the God (false God or true) to those of the City. No other assumption fitted a Dosadi justification.

We are plagued by a corrupt polity which promotes unlawful and/or immoral behavior. Public interest has no practical significance in everyday behavior among the ruling factions. The real problems of our world are not being confronted by those in power. In the guise of public service, they use whatever comes to hand for personal gain. They are insane with and for power.

—FROM A CLANDESTINE DOCUMENT
CIRCULATED ON DOSADI

IT WAS dark when a disguised Jedrik and undisguised McKie emerged onto the streets. She led them down narrow passages, her mind full of things McKie had revealed. Jedrik wore a blonde wig and puff-out disguise which made her appear heavy and hunched.

As they passed an open courtyard, McKie heard music. He almost stumbled. The music came from a small orchestra—delicate tympany, soft strings, and a rich chorus of wind instruments. He did not recognize the melody, but it moved him more deeply than any other music of his experience. It was as though the music were played only for him. Aritch and company had said nothing about such magnificent music here.

People still thronged the streets in numbers which astonished him. But now they appeared to pay him little notice.

Jedrik kept part of her attention on McKie, noting the fools with their musical dalliance, noting how few people there were on the streets—little more than her own patrols in this quarter. She'd expected that, but the actuality held an eerie mood in the dim and scattered illumination from lighted corners.

She had debated providing McKie with a crude disguise, but he obviously didn't have the cunning to carry off the double deception she required. She'd begun to sense a real intelligence in him, though. McKie was an enigma. Why had he never encountered the opportunities to sharpen that intelligence? Sensing the sharpness in him, she could not put off the thought that she had missed something vital in his accounts of that social entity which he called the ConSentiency. Whether this failure came from actual concealment by McKie or through his inadequacies, she was not yet willing to judge. The enigma set her on edge. And the mood in the streets did nothing to ease her emotions. She was glad when they crossed the line into the area completely controlled by her own personal cell.

The bait having been trailed through the streets by one who would appear a tame underling, Jedrik allowed herself a slight relaxation. Broey would have learned by this time about the killing of Tria's double agent. He would react to that and to the new bait. It was almost time for phase two of her design for Broey.

McKie followed her without question, acutely aware of every strange glance cast their way. He was emptied of all resistance, knowing he could not survive if he failed to follow Jedrik through the smelly, repellent darkness of her streets.

The food from the restuarant sat heavily in his stomach. It had been tasty: a stew of odd shapes full of shredded greenery, and steaming hot. But he could not shake the realization that his stew had been compounded of someone's garbage.

Jedrik had left him very little. She hadn't learned of the Taprisiot, or the bead in his stomach which probably would not link him to the powers of the ConSentiency if he died. She had not learned of the standard BuSab implantation devices which amplified his senses. And, oddly, she had not explored many of his revelations about BuSab. She'd seemed much more interested in the money hidden about his person and had taken possession of all of it. She'd examined the currency carefully.

"This is real."

He wasn't sure, but he thought she'd been surprised.

"This was given to you *before* you were sent to Dosadi?"

"Yes."

She was a while absorbing the implications, but appeared satisfied. She'd given him a few small currency tokens from her own pockets.

"Nobody'll bother you for these. If you need anything, ask. We may be able to gratify some of your needs."

It was still dark, lighted only by illumination at corners, when they came to the address Jedrik sought. Grey light suffused the street. A young Human male of about ten squatted with his back against the stone wall at the building's corner. As Jedrik and McKie approached, he sprang up, alert. He nodded once to Jedrik.

She did not acknowledge, but by some hidden signal the boy knew she had received his message. He relaxed once more against the wall.

When McKie looked back a few paces beyond where the boy had signaled, he was gone. No sound, no sign—just gone.

Jedrik stopped at a shadowed entryway. It was barred by an openwork metal gate flanked by two armed guards. The guards opened the gate without words. Beyond the gate there was a large, covered courtyard illuminated by glowing tubes on right and left. Three of its sides were piled to the courtyard cover with boxes of various sizes—some taller than a Human and narrow, others short and fat. Set into the stacks as though part of the courtyard's walls was one narrow passage leading to a metal door opposite the gateway.

McKie touched Jedrik's arm.

"What's in the boxes?"

"Weapons." She spoke as though to a cretin.

The metal door was opened from within. Jedrik led McKie into a large room at least two stories tall. The door clanged shut behind them. McKie sensed several Humans along the courtyard wall on both sides of him, but his attention had been captured by something else.

Dominating the room was a gigantic cage suspended from the ceiling. Its bars sparkled and shimmered with hidden energies. A single Gowachin male sat cross-legged in a hammock at the cage's center. McKie had seldom seen a ConSentient Gowachin that aged. His nose crest was fringed by flaking yellow crusts. Heavy wrinkles wormed their way beneath watery eyes beginning to glaze with the degeneration which often blinded Gowachin who lived too long away from water. His body had a slack appearance, with loose muscles and pitted indentations along the nodes between his ventricles. The hammock suspended him off the cage floor and that floor shimmered with volatile energies.

Jedrik paused, divided her attention between McKie and the old Gowachin. She seemed to expect a particular reaction from McKie, but he wasn't certain she found what she sought.

McKie stood a moment in silent examination of the Gowachin. Prisoner? What was the significance of that cage and its shimmering energies? Presently, he glanced around the room, recording the space. Six armed Human males flanked the door through which he and Jedrik had entered. A remarkable assortment of objects crammed the room's walls, some with purpose unknown to him but many recognizable as weapons: spears and swords, flame-throwers, garish armor, bombs, pellet projectors . . .

Jedrik moved a pace closer to the cage. The occupant stared back at her with faint interest. She cleared her throat.

"Greetings, Pcharky. I have found my key to the God Wall."

The old Gowachin remained silent, but McKie thought he saw a sparkle of interest in the glazed eyes.

Jedrik shook her head slowly from side to side, then: "I have a new datum, Pcharky. The Veil of Heaven was created by creatures called Calebans. They appear to us as suns."

Pcharky's glance flickered to McKie, back to Jedrik. The Gowachin knew the source of her new datum.

McKie renewed his speculations about the old Gowachin. That cage must be a prison, its walls enforced by dangerous energies. Bahrank had spoken of conflict between the species. Humans controlled this room. Why did they imprison a Gowachin? Or . . . was this caged Gowachin, this Pcharky, another agent from Tandaloor? With a tightening of his throat, McKie wondered if his own fate might be to live out his days in such a cage.

Pcharky grunted, then:

"The God Wall is like this cage but more powerful."

His voice was a husky croaking, the words clear Galach with an obvious Tandaloor accent. McKie, his fears reinforced, glanced at Jedrik, found her studying him. She spoke.

"Pcharky has been with us for a long time, very long. There's no telling how many people he has helped to escape from Dosadi. Soon, I may persuade him to be of service to me."

McKie found himself shocked to silence by the possibilities glimpsed through her words. Was Dosadi in fact an investigation of the Caleban mystery? Was that the secret Aritch's people concealed here? McKie stared at the shimmering bars of Pcharky's cage. Like the God Wall? But the God Wall was enforced by a Caleban.

Once more, Jedrik looked at the caged Gowachin.

"A sun confines enormous energies, Pcharky. Are your energies inadequate?

"But Pcharky's attention was on McKie. The old voice croaked.

"Human, tell me: Did you come here willingly?"

"Don't answer him," Jedrik snapped.

Pcharky closed his eyes. Interview ended.

Jedrik, accepting this, whirled and strode to the left around the cage.

"Come along, McKie." She didn't look back, but continued speaking. "Does it interest you that Pcharky designed his own cage?"

"He designed it? Is it a prison?"

"Yes."

"If he designed it . . . how does it hold him?"

"He knew he'd have to serve my purposes if he were to remain alive."

She had come to another door which opened onto a narrow stairway. It climbed to the left around the cage room. They emerged into a long hallway lined with narrow doors dimly lighted by tiny overhead bulbs. Jedrik opened one of these doors and led the way into a carpeted room about four meters wide and six long. Dark wood panels reached from floor to waist level, shelves loaded with books above. McKie peered closely: books . . . actual paper books. He tried to recall where he'd ever before seen such a collection of primitive . . . But of course, these were not primitive. These were one of Dosadi's strange recapitulations.

Jedrik had removed her wig, stopped midway in the room to turn and face McKie.

"This is my room. Toilet there." She pointed to an opening between shelves. "That window . . ." Again, she pointed, this time to an opening opposite the toilet door. ". . . is one-way to admit light, and it's our best. As Dosadi measures such things, this is a relatively secure place"

He swept his gaze around the room.

Her room?

McKie was struck by the amount of living space, a mark of power on Dosadi; the absence of people in the hall. By the standards of this planet, Jedrik's room, this building, represented a citadel of power.

Jedrik spoke, an odd note of nervousness in voice and manner.

"Until recently, I also had other quarters: a prestigious apartment on the slopes of the Council Hills. I was considered a climber with excellent prospects, my own skitter and driver. I had access to all but the highest codes in the master banks, and that's a powerful tool for those who can use it. Now . . ." She gestured. ". . . this is what I have chosen. I must eat swill with the lowest. No males of rank will pay the slightest attention to me. Broey thinks I'm cowering somewhere, a pallet in the Warrens. But I have this . . ." Again, that sweeping gesture. ". . . and this." One finger tapped her head. "I need nothing more to bring those Council Hills crashing down."

She stared into McKie's eyes.

He found himself believing her.

She was not through speaking.

"You're definitely male Human, McKie."

He didn't know what to make of that, but her air of braggadocio fascinated him.

"How did you lose that other . . ."

"I didn't lose it. I threw it away. I no longer needed it. I've made things move faster than our precious Elector, or even your people, can anticipate. Broey thinks to wait for an opening against me?'' She shook her head.

Captivated, McKie watched her cross to the window, open a ventilator above it. She kicked a wooden knob below the adjoining bookshelves, pulled out a section of paneling which trailed a double bed. Standing across the bed from McKie, she began to undress. She dropped the wig to the floor, slipped off the coverall, peeled the bulging inner disguise from her flesh. Her skin was pale cream.

''McKie, I am your teacher.''

He remained silent. She was long waisted, slim, and graceful. The creamy skin was marked by two faint scars to the left of the pubic wedge.

''Take off your clothes,'' she said.

He swallowed.

She shook her head.

''McKie, McKie, to survive here you must become Dosadi. You don't have much time. Get your clothes off.''

Not knowing what to expect, McKie obeyed.

She watched him carefully.

''Your skin is lighter than I expected where the sun has not darkened you. We will bleach the skin of your face and hands tomorrow.''

McKie looked at his hands, at the sharp line where his cuffs had protected his arms. Dark skin. He recalled Bahrank talking of dark skin and a place called Pylash Gate. To mask the unusual shyness he felt, he looked at Jedrik, asked about Pylash Gate.

''So Bahrank mentioned that? Well, it was a stupid mistake. The Rim sent in shock troops and foolish orders were given for the gate's defenses. Only one troop survived there, all dark-skinned like you. The suspicion of treachery was natural.''

''Oh.''

He found his attention compelled toward the bed. A dark maroon spread covered it.

Jedrik approached him around the foot of the bed. She stopped less than a hand's width away from him . . . creamy flesh, full breasts. He looked up into her eyes. She stood half a head over him, an expression of cold amusement on her face.

McKie found the musky smell of her erotically stimulating. She looked down, saw this, laughed, and abruptly hurled him onto the bed. She landed with him and her body was all over him, hot and hard and demanding.

It was the strangest sexual experience of McKie's life. Not lovemaking, but violent attack. She groaned, bit at him, clawed. And when he tried to caress her, she became even more violent, frenzied. Through it all, she was oddly careful of his pleasure, watching his reactions, reading him. When it was over, he lay back, spent. Jedrik sat up on the edge of the bed. The blankets were a twisted mess. She grabbed a blanket, threw it across the room, stood up, whirled back to look down at him.

''You are very sly and tricky, McKie.''

He drew in a trembling breath, remained silent.

''You tried to catch me with softness,'' she accused. ''Better than you have tried that with me. It will not work.''

McKie marshalled the energy to sit up and restore some order to the bed. His shoulder pained him where she'd scratched. He felt the ache of a bite on his neck. He crawled into the bed, pulled the blankets up to his chin. She was a madwoman, absolutely mad. Insane.

Presently, Jedrik stopped looking at him. She recovered the blanket from across the room, spread it on the bed, joined him. He was acutely conscious of her staring at him with an openly puzzled frown.

"Tell me about the relationships between men and women on your worlds."

He recounted a few of the love stories he knew, fighting all the while to stay awake. It was difficult to stifle the gaping yawns. She kept punching his shoulder.

"I don't believe it. You're making this up."

"No . . . no. It's true."

"You have women of your own there?"

"Women of my . . .Well, it's not like that, not ownership . . . ahhh, not possession."

"What about children?"

"What about them?"

"How're they treated, educated?"

He sighed, sketched in some details from his own childhood.

After a while she let him go to sleep. He awakened several times during the night, conscious of the strange room and bed, of Jedrik breathing softly beside him. Once, he thought he felt her shoulders shaking with repressed sobs.

Shortly before dawn, there was a scream in the next block, a terrifying sound of agony loud enough to waken all but the most hardened or the most fatigued. McKie, awake and thinking, felt Jedrik's breathing change. He lay tense and watchful, awaiting a repetition or another sound which might explain that eerie scream. A threatening silence gripped the night. McKie built an image in his mind of what could be happening in the buildings around them: some people starting from sleep not knowing (perhaps not caring) what had awakened them; lighter sleepers grumbling and sinking back into restless slumber.

Finally, McKie sat up, peered into the room's shadows. His disquiet communicated itself to Jedrik. She rolled over, looked up at him in the pale dawn light now creeping into the shadows.

"There are many noises in the Warrens that you learn to ignore," she said.

Coming from her, it was almost conciliatory, almost a gesture of apology, of friendship.

"Someone screamed," he said.

"I knew it must be something like that."

"How can you sleep through such a sound?"

"I didn't."

"But how can you ignore it?"

"The sounds you ignore are those which aren't immediately threatening to you, those which you can do nothing about."

"Someone was hurt."

"Very likely. But you must not burden your soul with things you cannot change."

"Don't you want to change . . . that?"

"I am changing it."

Her tone, her attitude were those of a lecturer in a schoolroom, and now there was no doubt that she was being deliberately helpful. Well, she'd said she was his teacher. And he must become completely Dosadi to survive.

"How're you changing things?"

"You're not capable of understanding yet. I want you to take it one step at a time, one lesson at a time."

He couldn't help asking himself then:
What does she want from me now?
He hoped it was not more sex.
"Today," she said, "I want you to meet the parents of three children who work in our cell."

If you think of yourselves as helpless and ineffectual, it is certain that you will create a despotic government to be your master. The wise despot, therefore, maintains among his subjects a popular sense that they are helpless and ineffectual.

—THE DOSADI LESSON:
A GOWACHIN ASSESSMENT

ARITCH STUDIED Ceylang carefully in the soft light of his green-walled relaxation room. She had come down immediately after the evening meal, responsive to his summons. They both knew the reason for that summons: to discuss the most recent report concerning McKie's behavior on Dosadi.

The old Gowachin waited for Ceylang to seat herself, observing how she pulled the red robe neatly about her lower extremities. Her features appeared composed, the fighting mandibles relaxed in their folds. She seemed altogether a figure of secure competence, a Wreave of the ruling classes—not that Wreaves recognized such classes. It disturbed Aritch that Wreaves tested for survival only through a complex understanding of sentient behavior, rigid performance standards based on ancient ritual, whose actual origins could only be guessed; there was no written record.

But that's why we chose her.

Aritch grunted, then:

"What can you say about the report?"

"McKie learns rapidly."

Her spoken Galach had a faint sibilance.

Aritch nodded.

"I would say rather that he *adapts* rapidly. It's why we chose him."

"I've heard you say he's more Gowachin than the Gowachin."

"I expect him soon to be more Dosadi than the Dosadi."

"If he survives."

"There's that, yes. Do you still hate him?"

"I have never hated him. You do not understand the spectrum of Wreave emotions."

"Enlighten me."

"He has violated my essential pride of self. This requires a specific reaction in kind. Hate would only dull my abilities."

"But *I* was the one who gave you the orders which had to be countermanded."

"My oath of service to the Gowachin contains a specific injunction, that I cannot hold any one of my teachers responsible for either understanding or obeying the Wreave protocols of courtesy. It is the same injunction which frees us to serve McKie's Bureau."

"You do not consider McKie one of your teachers?"

She studied him for a moment, then:

"Not only do I exclude him, but I know him to be one who has learned much about our protocols."

"What if I were to say he is one of your teachers?"

Again, she stared at him.

"I would revise my estimations of him—and of you."

Aritch took a deep breath.

"Yet, you must learn McKie as though you lived in his skin. Otherwise, you will fail us."

"I will not fail you. I know the reasons you chose me. Even McKie will know in time. He dares not spill my blood in the Courtarena, or even subject me to public shame. Were he to do either of these things, half the Wreave universe would go hunting him with death in their mandibles."

Aritch shook his head slowly from side to side.

"Ceylang! Didn't you hear him warn you that you must shed your Wreave skin?"

She was a long time responding and he noted the subtle characterstics which he'd been told were the Wreave adjustments to anger: a twitching of the jowls, tension in the pedal bifurcations . . .

Presently, she said:

"Tell me what that means, Teacher."

"You will be charged with peforming under *Gowachin* Law, performing as though you were another McKie. He adapts! Haven't you observed this? He is capable of defeating you—and us—in such a way, *in such a way* that your Wreave universe would shower him with adulation for his victory. That cannot be permitted. Too much is at stake."

Ceylang trembled and showed other signs of distress.

"But I am Wreave!"

"If it comes to the Courtarena, you no longer can be Wreave."

She inhaled several shallow breaths, composed herself.

"If I become too much McKie, aren't you afraid I might hesitate to slay him?"

"McKie would not hesitate."

She considered this.

"Then there's only one reason you chose me for this task."

He waited for her to say it.

"Because we Wreaves are the best in the universe at learning the behavior of others—both overt and covert."

"And you dare not rely on any supposed inhibitions he may or may not have!"

After a long pause, she said:

"You are a better teacher than I'd suspected. Perhaps you're even better than *you* suspected."

"Their law! It is a dangerous foundation for nonauthentic traditions. It is no more than a device to justify false ethics!"

—GOWACHIN COMMENT ON CONSENTIENT LAW

WHILE THEY dressed in the dim dawn light coming through the single window, McKie began testing what Jedrik meant by being his teacher.

"Will you answer any question I ask about Dosadi?"

"No."

Then what areas would she withhold from him? He saw it at once: those areas where she gained and held personal power.

"Will anyone resent it that we . . . had sex together?"

"Resent? Why should anyone resent that?"

"I don't . . ."

"Answer my question!"

"Why do I have to answer your every question?"

"To stay alive."

"You already know everything I . . ."

She brushed this aside.

"So the people of your ConSentiency sometimes resent the sexual relationships of others. They are not sure, then, how they use sex to hold power over others."

He blinked. Her quick, slashing analysis was devastating.

She peered at him.

"McKie, what can you do here without me? Don't you know yet that the ones who sent you intended you to die here?"

"Or survive in my own peculiar way."

She considered this. It was another idea about McKie which she had put aside for later evaluation. Indeed, he might well have hidden talents which her questions had not yet exposed. What annoyed her now was the sense that she didn't know enough about the ConSentiency to explore this. Could not take the time right now to explore it. His response disturbed her. It was as though everything she could possibly do had already been decided for her by powers of which she knew next to nothing. They were leading her by the nose, perhaps, just as she led Broey . . . just as those mysterious Gowachin of the ConSentiency obviously had led McKie . . . poor McKie. She cut this short as unprofitable speculation. Obviously, she had to begin at once to search out McKie's talent. Whatever she discovered would reveal a great deal about his ConSentiency.

"McKie, I hold a great deal of power among the Humans and even among some Gowachin in the Warrens—and elsewhere. To do this, I must maintain certain fighting forces, including those who fight with physical weapons."

He nodded. Her tone was that of lecturing to a child, but he accepted this, recognizing the care she took with him.

"We will go first," she said, "to a nearby training area where we maintain the necessary edge on one of my forces."

Turning, she led him out into the hall and down a stairway which avoided the room of the cage. McKie was reminded of Pcharky, though, thinking about that gigantic expenditure of space with its strange occupant.

"Why do you keep Pcharky caged?" he asked, addressing Jedrik's back.

"So I can escape."

She refused to elaborate on this odd answer.

217

Presently, they emerged into a courtyard nestled into the solid walls of towering buildings. Only a small square of sky was visible directly overhead and far away. Artificial lighting from tubes along the walls provided an adequate illumination. It revealed two squads facing each other in the center of the courtyard. They were Humans, both male and female; all carried weapons: a tube of some sort with a wandlike protrusion from the end near their bodies. Several other Humans stood at observation positions around the two squads. There was a guard station with a desk at the door through which McKie and Jedrik had emerged.

"That's an assault force," Jedrik said, indicating the squads in the courtyard. She turned and consulted with the two young men at the guard station.

McKie made a rough count of the squads: about two hundred. It was obvious that everything had stopped because of Jedrik's presence. He thought the force was composed of striplings barely blooded in Dosadi's cruel necessities. This forced him to a reevaluation of his own capabilities.

From Jedrik's manner with the two men, McKie guessed she knew them well. They paid close attention to everything she said. They, too, struck him as too young for responsibility.

The training area was another matter. It bore a depressing similarity to other such facilities he'd seen in the backwaters of the ConSentiency. War games were a constant lure among several species, a lure which BuSab had managed thus far to channel into such diversions as weapons fetishes.

Through the omnipresent stink, McKie smelled the faint aroma of cooking. He sniffed.

Turning to him, Jedrik spoke:

"The trainees have just been fed. That's part of their pay."

It was as though she'd read his mind, and now she watched him for some reaction.

McKie glanced around the training area. They'd just been fed here? There wasn't a scrap or crumb on the ground. He thought back to the restaurant, belatedly aware of a fastidious care with food that he'd seen and passed right over.

Again, Jedrik demonstrated the ease with which she read his reactions, his very thoughts.

"Nothing wasted," she said.

She turned away.

McKie looked where her attention went. Four women stood at the far side of the courtyard, weapons in their hands. Abruptly, McKie focused on the woman to the left, a competent-looking female of middle years. She was carrying a . . . it couldn't be, but . . .

Jedrik headed across the courtyard toward the woman. McKie followed, peered closely at the woman's weapon. It was an enlarged version of the pentrate from his kit! Jedrik spoke briefly to the woman.

"Is that the new one?"

"Yes. Stiggy brought it up this morning."

"Useful?"

"We think so. It focuses the explosion with somewhat more concentration than our equipment."

"Good. Carry on."

There were more training cadre near the wall behind the women. One, an older man with one arm, tried to catch Jedrik's attention as she led McKie toward a nearby door.

"Could you tell us when we . . ."

"Not now."

In the passage beyond the door, Jedrik turned and confronted McKie.

"Your impressions of our training? Quick!"

"Not sufficiently versatile."

She'd obviously probed for his most instinctive reaction, demanding the gut response unmonitored by reason. The answer brought a glowering expression to her face, an emotional candor which he was not to appreciate until much later. Presently, she nodded.

"They are a commando. More functions of a commando should be interchangeable. Wait here."

She returned to the training area. McKie, watching through the open door, saw her speak to the woman with the pentrate. When Jedrik returned, she nodded to McKie with an expression of approval.

"Anything else?"

"They're awfully damned young. You should have a few seasoned officers among them to put a rein on dangerous impetuosity."

"Yes, I've already set that in motion. Hereafter, McKie, I want you to come out with me every morning for about an hour. Watch the training, but don't interfere. Report your reactions to me."

He nodded. Cearly, she considered him useful and that was a step in the right direction. But it was an idiotic assignment. These violent infants possessed weapons which could make Dosadi uninhabitable. There was an atavistic excitement in the situation, though. He couldn't deny that. Something in the Human psyche responded to mass violence—really, to violence of any sort. It was related to Human sexuality, an ancient stirring from the most primitive times.

Jedrik was moving on, however.

"Stay close."

They were climbing an inside stairway now and McKie, hurrying to keep up, found his thoughts locked on that pentrate in the hands of one of Jedrik's people. The speed with which they'd copied and enlarged it dazzled him. It was another demonstration of why Aritch feared Dosadi.

At the top of the stairs, Jedrik rapped briefly at a door. A male voice said, "Come in."

The door swung open, and McKie found himself presently in a small, unoccupied room with an open portal at the far wall into what appeared to be a larger, well-lighted area. Voices speaking so softly as to be unintelligible came from there. A low table and five cramped chairs occupied the small room. There were no windows, but a frosted overhead fixture provided shadowless illumination. A large sheet of paper with colored graph lines on it covered the low table.

A swish of fabric brought McKie's attention to the open portal. A short, slender woman in a white smock, grey hair, and the dark, penetrating stare of someone accustomed to command entered, followed by a slightly taller man in the same white. He looked older than the woman, except his hair remained a lustrous black. His eyes, too, held that air of command. The woman spoke.

"Excuse the delay, Jedrik. We've been changing the summation. There's now no point where Broey can anticipate and change the transition from riots to full-scale warfare."

McKie was surprised by the abject deference in her voice. This woman considered herself to be far below Jedrik. The man took the same tone, gesturing to chairs.

"Sit down, please. This chart is our summation."

As the woman turned toward him, McKie caught a strong whiff of something pungent on her breath, a not unfamiliar smell. He'd caught traces of it several times in their passage through the Warrens. She went on speaking as Jedrik and McKie slipped into chairs.

"This is not unexpected." She indicated the design on the paper.

The man intruded.

"We've been telling you for some time now that Tria is ready to come over."

"She's trouble," Jedrik said.

"But Gar . . ."

It was the woman, arguing, but Jedrik cut her off.

"I know: Gar does whatever she tells him to do. The daughter runs the father. He thinks she's the most wonderful thing that ever happened, able to . . ."

"Her abilities are not the issue," the man said.

The woman spoke eagerly.

"Yes, it's her influence on Gar that . . ."

"Neither of them anticipated my moves," Jedrik said, "but I anticipated their moves."

The man leaned across the table, his face close to Jedrik's. He appeared suddenly to McKie like a large, dangerous animal—dangerous because his actions could never be fully predicted. His hands twitched when he spoke.

"We've told you every detail of our findings, every source, every conclusion. Now, are you saying you don't share our assessment of . . ."

"You don't understand," Jedrik said.

The woman had drawn back. Now, she nodded.

Jedrik said:

"It isn't the first time I've had to reassess your conclusions. Hear me: Tria will leave Broey when she's ready, not when he's ready. It's the same for anyone she serves, even Gar."

They spoke in unison:

"Leave Gar?"

"Leave anyone. Tria serves only Tria. Never forget that. Especially don't forget it if she comes over to us."

The man and woman were silent.

McKie thought about what Jedrik had said. Her words were another indication that someone on Dosadi might have other than personal aims. Jedrik's tone was unmistakable: she censured and distrusted Tria because Tria served *only* selfish ambition. Therefore, Jedrik (and this other pair by inference) served some unstated mutual purpose. Was it a form of patriotism they served, species-oriented? BuSab agents were always alert for this dangerous form of tribal madness, not necessarily to suppress it, but to make certain it did not explode into a violence deadly to the ConSentiency.

The white-smocked woman, after mulling her own thoughts, spoke:

"If Tria can't be enlisted for . . . what I mean is, we can use her own self-serving to hold her." She corrected herself. "Unless you believe we cannot convince her we'll overcome Broey." She chewed at her lip, a fearful expression in her eyes.

A shrewd look came over Jedrik's face.

"What is it you suspect?"

The woman pointed to the chart on the table.

"Gar still shares in the major decisions. That shouldn't be, but it is. If he . . ."

The man spoke with subservient eagerness.

"He has some hold on Broey!"

The woman shook her head.

"Or Broey plays a game other than the one we anticipated."

Jedrik looked at the woman, the man, at McKie. She spoke as though to McKie, but McKie realized she was addressing the air.

"It's a specific thing. Gar has revealed something to Broey. I know what he's revealed. Nothing else could force Broey to behave this way." She nodded at the chart. "We *have* them!"

The woman ventured a question.

"Have we done well?"

"Better than you know."

The man smiled, then:

"Perhaps this is the time to ask if we could have larger rooms. The damn' children are always moving the furniture. We bump . . ."

"Not now!"

Jedrik arose. McKie followed her example.

"Let me see the children," Jedrik said.

The man turned to the open portal.

"Get out here, you! Jedrik wants you!"

Three children came scurrying from the other room. The woman didn't even look at them. The man favored them with an angry glare. He spoke to Jedrik.

"They've brought no food into this house in almost a week."

McKie studied the children carefully as he saw Jedrik was doing. They stood in a row just inside the room and, from their expressions, it was impossible to tell their reactions to the summons. They were two girls and a boy. The one on the right, a girl, was perhaps nine; on the left, another girl, was five or six. The boy was somewhat older, perhaps twelve or thirteen. He favored McKie with a glance. It was the glance of a predator who recognizes ready prey, but who already has eaten. All three bore more resemblance to the woman than to the man, but the parentage was obvious: the eyes, the set of the ear, nose . . .

Jedrik had completed her study. She gestured to the boy.

"Start sending him to the second training team."

"About time," the woman said. "We'll be glad to get him out of here."

"Come along, McKie."

In the hall, Jedrik said:

"To answer your question, they're pretty typical."

McKie, who had only wondered silently, swallowed in a dry throat. The petty goals of these people: to get a bigger room where they could live without bumping into furniture. He'd sensed no affection for each other in that couple. They were companions of convenience. There had been not the smallest hint of emotion for each other when they spoke. McKie found it difficult to imagine them making love, but apparently they did. They had produced three children.

Realization came like an explosion in his head. Of course they showed no emotion! What other protection did they have? On Dosadi, anything cared for was a club to beat you into somebody else's line. And there was another thing.

McKie spoke to Jedrik's back as they went down the stairs.

"That couple—they're addicted to something."

Surprisingly, Jedrik stopped, looked back up at him.

"How else do you think I hold such a pair? The substance is called *dis*. It's very rare. It comes from the far mountains, far beyond the . . . far beyond. The Rim sends parties of children as bearers to obtain *dis* for me. In a party of fifty, thirty can expect to die on such a trek. Do you get the measure of it, McKie?"

Once more, they headed down the stairs.

McKie, realizing she'd taken the time to teach him another lesson about Dosadi, could only follow, stunned, while she led him into a room where technicians bleached the sun-darkened areas of his skin.

When they emerged, he no longer carried the stigma of Pylash Gate.

> *When the means of great violence are widespread, nothing is more dangerous to the powerful than that they create outrage and injustice, for outrage and injustice will certainly ignite retaliation in kind.*
>
> —BuSab Manual

"It is no longer classifiable as rioting," the aide said.

He was a short Gowachin with pinched features, and he looked across the room to where Broey sat facing a dead communicator. There was a map on the wall behind the aide, its colors made brilliant by harsh morning light coming in the east windows. Below the map, a computer terminal jutted from the wall. Occasionally it clicked.

Gar came into the room from the hall, peered around as though looking for someone, left.

Broey noted the intrustion, glanced at the map.

"Still no sign of where she's gone to ground?"

"Nothing certain."

"The one who paraded McKie through the streets . . ."

"Clearly an expendable underling."

"Where did they go?"

The aide indicated a place on the map, a group of buildings in the Warrens to the northwest.

Broey stared at the blank face of his communications screen. He'd been tricked again. He knew it. That damnable Human female! Violence in the city teetered on the edge of full-scale war: Gowachin against Human. And still nothing, not even a hint at the location of Gar's Rim stores. the blasphemous factories. It was an unstable condition which could not continue much longer.

His communications screen came alive with a report: violent fighting near Gate Twenty-One. Broey glanced at the map. That made it more than one hundred clearly defined battles between the species along an unresolved perimeter. The report spoke of new weapons and unsuccessful attempts to capture specimens.

Gate Twenty-One?

That wasn't far from the place where McKie had been paraded through . . .

Several things slipped into a new relationship in Broey's mind. He looked at his aide, who stood waiting obediently at the map.

"Where's Gar?"

Aides were summoned, sent running. Gar was not to be found.

"Tria?"

She, too, was unavailable.

Gar's fanatics remained neutral, but more of Jedrik's pattern was emerging. Everything pointed to an exquisite understanding of the weakness implicit in the behavior of Gar and Tria.

And I thought I was the only one who saw that!

Broey hesitated.

Why would the God not speak to him other than to say "I am watched."

Broey felt tricked and betrayed in his innermost being. This had a cleansing effect on his reason. He could only depend on himself. And he began to sense a larger pattern in Jedrik's behavior. Was it possible that Jedrik shared *his* goals? The possibility excited him.

He looked at the aides who'd come running with the negative information about Gar and Tria, began to snap orders.

"Get our people out of all those Warrens, except that corridor to the northeast. Reinforce that area. Everyone else fall back to the secondary walls. Let no Humans inside that perimeter. Block all gates. Get moving!"

This last was shouted as his aides hesitated.

Perhaps it already was too late. He realized now that he'd allowed Jedrik to bait and distract him. It was clear that she'd created in her mind an almost perfect simulation model of Broey. And she'd done it from a Liaitor position! Incredible. He could almost feel sorry for Gar and Tria. They were like puppets dancing to Jedrik's strings.

I was no better.

It came over him that Jedrik's simulation probably encompassed this very moment of realization. Admiration for her permeated him.

Superb!

Quietly, he issued orders for the sequestering of Gowachin females within the inner Graluz bastions which he'd had the foresight to prepare. His people would thank him for that.

Those who survived the next few hours.

The attack by those who want to die—this is the attack against which you cannot prepare a perfect defense.

—HUMAN APHORISM

BY THE third morning, McKie felt that he might have lived all of his life on Dosadi. The place demanded every element of attention he could muster.

He stood alone in Jedrik's room, staring absently at the unmade bed. She expected him to put the place in order before her return. He knew that. She'd told him to wait here and had gone away on urgent business. He could only obey.

Concerns other than an unmade bed distracted him, though. He felt now that he understood the roots of Aritch's fears. The Gowachin of Tandaloor might very well destroy this place, even if they knew that by doing so they blasted open that bloody region where every sentient hid his most secret fears. He could see this clearly now. How the Running Phylum expected him to avoid that monstrous decision was a more elusive matter.

There were secrets here.

McKie sensed Dosadi like a malignant organism beneath his feet, jealously keeping those secrets from him. This place was the enemy of the ConSentiency, but he found himself emotionally siding with Dosadi. It was betrayal of BuSab, of his Legum oath, everything. But he could not prevent that feeling or recognition of it. In the course of only a few generations, Dosadi had become a particular thing. Monstrous? Only if you held to your own precious myths. Dosadi might be the greatest cleansing force the ConSentiency had ever experienced.

The whole prospect of the ConSentiency had begun to sicken him. And Aritch's Gowachin. Gowachin Law? Stuff Gowachin Law!

It was quiet in Jedrik's room. Painfully quiet.

He knew that out on the streets of Chu there was violent warfare between Gowachin and Human. Wounded had been rushed through the training courtyard while he was there with Jedrik. Afterward, she'd taken him to her command post, a room across the hall and above Pcharky's cage. He'd stood nearby, watched her performance as though she were a star on an entertainment circuit and he a member of the audience. It was fascinating. Broey will do this. Broey will give that order. And each time, the reports revealed how precisely she had anticipated her opponent.

Occasionally, she mentioned Gar or Tria. He was able to detect the subtle difference in her treatment of that pair.

On their second night together, Jedrik had aroused his sexual appetites softly, deftly. She had treated him to a murmurous compliance, and afterward had leaned over him on an elbow to smile coldly.

"You see, McKie: I can play your game."

Shockingly, this had opened an area of awareness within him which he'd not even suspected. It was as though she'd held up his entire previous life to devastating observation.

And *he* was the observer!

Other beings formed lasting relationships and operated from a secure emotional base. But he was a product of BuSab, the Gowachin . . . and much that had gone before. It had become increasingly obvious to him why the Gowachin had chosen him to groom for this particular role.

I was damaged and they could rebuild me the way they wanted!

Well, the Gowachin could still be surprised by what they produced. Dosadi was evidence of that. They might not even suspect what they'd actually produced in McKie.

He was bitter with a bitterness he knew must've been fermenting in him for years. The loneliness of his own life with its central dedication to BuSab had been brought to a head by the loneliness of this imprisoned planet. An incredible jumble of emotions had sorted themselves out, and he felt new purpose burning within him.

Power!

Ahhhh . . . that was how it felt to be Dosadi!

He'd turned away from Jedrik's cold smile, pulled the blankets around his shoulder.

Thank you, loving teacher.

Such thoughts roamed through his mind as he stood alone in the room the following day and began to make the bed. After her revelation, Jedrik had resumed her interest in his memories, napping only to awaken him with more questions.

In spite of his sour outlook, he still felt it his duty to examine her behavior in every possible light his imagination could produce. Nothing about Dosadi was too absurd. He had to build a better picture of this society and its driving forces.

Before returning to Jedrik's room, he'd made another tour of the training courtyard with her. There'd been more new weapons adapted from his kit, and he'd realized the courtyard was merely Jedrik's testing ground, that there must be many more training areas for her followers.

McKie had not yet revealed to her that Aritch's people might terminate Dosadi's people with violence. She'd been centering on this at dawn. Even while they shared the tiny toilet cubicle off her room she'd pressed for answers.

For a time, McKie had diverted her with questions about Pcharky. What were the powers in that cage? At one point, he'd startled her.

"Pcharky knows something valuable he hopes to trade for his freedom."

"How'd you know?"

"It's obvious. I'll tell you something else: he came here of his own free will . . . for whatever purpose."

"You learn quickly, McKie."

She was laughing at him and he glared at her.

"All right! I don't know that purpose, but it may be that you only think you know it."

For the briefest flicker, something dangerous glared from her eyes, then:

"Your *jumpdoors* have brought us many fools, but Pcharky is one of the biggest fools. I know why he came. There've been many like him. Now . . . there is only one. Broey, for all of his power, cannot search out his own Pcharky. And Keila Jedrik is the one who frustrates him."

Too late, she realized that McKie had goaded her into this performance. How had he done that? He'd almost found out too much too soon. It was dangerous to underestimate this naive intruder from beyond the God Wall.

Once more, she'd begun probing for things he had not yet revealed. Time had protected him. Aides had come urging an early inspection of the new weapons. They were needed.

Afterward, they'd gone to the command post and then to breakfast in a Warren dining room. All through breakfast, he'd plied her with questions about the fighting. How extensive was it? Could he see some of the prisoners? Were they using the weapons built from the patterns in his kit? Were they winning?

Sometimes she merely ignored his questions. Most of her answers were short, distracted. Yes. No. No. Yes. McKie realized she was answering in monosyllables to fend him off. He was a distraction. Something important had been communicated to her and he'd missed it. Although this angered him, he tried to mask the emotion, striving to penetrate her wall of concern. Oddly, she responded when he changed his line of questioning to the parents of the three children and the conversation there.

"You started to designate a particular place: 'Beyond the . . .' Beyond what?"

"It's something Gar thinks I don't know. He thinks only his death fanatics have that kind of rapport with the Rim."

He stared at her, caught by a sudden thought. By now, he knew much about Gar

and Tria. She answered his questions about them with candor, often using him
openly to clarify her own thoughts. But—death fanatics?

"Are these fanatics homosexual?"

She pounced.

"How'd you know?"

"A guess."

"What difference would it make?"

"Are they?"

"Yes."

McKie shuddered.

She was peremptory.

"Explain!"

"When Humans for any reason go terminal where survival of their species is
concerned, it's relatively easy to push them the short step further into *wanting* to
die."

"You speak from historical evidence?"

"Yes."

"Example."

"With rare exceptions, primitive Humans of the tribal eras reserved their
homosexuals as the ultimate shock troops of desperation. They were the troops of
last resort, sent into battle as berserkers who expected, who *wanted*, to die."

She had to have the term *berserkers* explained, then showed by her manner that
she believed him. She considered this, then:

"What does your ConSentiency do about this susceptibility?"

"We take sophisticated care to guide all natural sexual variants into constructive, survival activities. We protect them from the kinds of pressures which might
tip them over into behavior destructive of the species."

Only later had McKie realized she had not answered his question: *beyond what?*
She'd rushed him off to a conference room where more than twenty Humans were
assembled, including the two parents who'd made the chart about Tria and Gar.
McKie realized he didn't even know their names.

It put him at a disadvantage not knowing as many of these people by sight and
name as he should. They, of course, had ready memories of everyone important
around them and, when they used a name, often did it with such blurred movement
into new subjects that he was seldom sure who had been named. He saw the key to
it, thought. Their memories were anchored in explicit references to relative
abilities of those around them, relative dangers. And it wasn't so much that they
concealed their emotions as that they *managed* their emotions. Nowhere in their
memories could there be any emotive clouding such as thoughts of love or
friendship. Such things weakened you. Everything operated on the strict basis of
quid pro quo, and you'd better have the cash ready—whatever that cash might be.
McKie, pressed all around by questions from the people in the conference room,
knew he had only one real asset: he was a key they might use to open the God Wall.
Very important asset, but unfortunately owned by an idiot.

Now, they wanted his information about death fanatics. They milked him dry,
then sent him away like a child who has performed for his elders but is sent to his
room when important matters are brought up for discussion.

The more control, the more that requires control. This is the road to chaos.

—PANSPECHI APHORISM

BY THE fourth morning of the battle for Chu, Tria was in a vile humor. Her forces had established lines holding about one-eighth of the total Warren territory, mostly low buildings, except along Broey's corridor to the Rim. She did not like the idea that Jedrik's people held an unobstructed view down onto most of the death fanatics' territory. And most of those leaders who'd thrown in their lot with Tria were beginning to have second thoughts, especially since they'd come to realize that this enclave had insufficient food production facilities to maintain itself. The population density she'd been forced to accept was frightening: almost triple the Warren norm.

Thus far, neither Broey nor Jedrik had moved in force against her. Tria had finally been brought to the inescapable conclusion that she and Gar were precisely where Jedrik wanted them. They'd been cut out of Broey's control as neatly and cleanly as though by a knife. There was no going back. Broey would never accept Human help under present circumstances. That, too, spoke of the exquisite care with which Jedrik had executed her plan.

Tria had moved her command post during the night to a high building which faced the canyon walls to the north. Only the river, with a single gate under it, separated her from the Rim. She'd slept badly, her mind full of worries. Chief among her worries was the fact that none of the contact parties she'd sent out to the Rim had returned. There'd been no fires on the Rim ledges during the night. No word from *any* of her people out there.

Why?

Once more, she contemplated her position, seeking some advantage, any advantage. One of her lines was anchored on Broey's corridor to the Rim, one line on the river wall with its single gate, and the rest of her perimeter meandered through a series of dangerous salients from the fifth wall to the river.

She could hear sounds of battle along the far side of Broey's corridor. Jedrik's people used weapons which made a great deal of noise. Occasionally, an explosive projectile landed in Tria's enclave. These were rare, but she'd taken casualties and the effect on morale was destructive. That was a major problem with fanatics: they demanded to be used, to be wasted.

Tria stared down at the river, aware of the bodies drifting on its poison currents—both Human and Gowachin bodies, but more Gowachin than Human. Presently, she turned away from the scene, padded into the next room, and roused Gar.

"We must contact Jedrik," she said.

He rubbed sleep from his eyes.

"No! We must wait until we make contact with our people on the Rim. Then we can . . ."

"Faaaaa!"

She'd seldom showed that much disgust with him.

"We're not going to make contact with our people on the Rim. Jedrik and Broey have seen to that. It wouldn't surprise me if they were cooperating to isolate us."

"But we've . . ."

"Shut up, Father!" She held up her hands, stared at them. "I was never really

227

good enough to be one of Broey's chief advisors. I always suspected that. I always pressed too hard. Last night, I reviewed as many of my decisions as I could. Jedrik deliberately made me look good. She did it oh so beautifully!''

"But our forces on the Rim . . .''

"May not be ours! They may be Jedrik's.''

"Even the Gowachin?''

"Even the Gowachin.''

Gar could hear a ringing in his ears. Contact Jedrik? Throw away all of their power?

"I'm good enough to recognize the weakness of a force such as ours,'' Tria said. "We can be goaded into spending ourselves uselessly. Even Broey didn't see that, but Jedrik obviously did. Look at the salients along her perimeter!''

"What have salients . . .

"They can be pinched off and obliterated! Even *you* must see that.''

"Then pull back, and . . .''

"Reduce our territory?'' She stared at him, aghast. "If I even intimate I'm going to do that, our auxiliaries will desert wholesale. Right now they're . . .''

"Then attack!''

"To gain what?''

Gar nodded. Jedrik would fall back across mined areas, blast the fanatics out of existence. She held enough territory that she could afford such destruction. Clearly, she'd planned on it.

"Then we must pinch off Broey's corridor.''

"That's what Jedrik wants us to do. It's the only negotiable counter we have left. That's why we must contact Jedrik.''

Gar shook his head in despair.

Tria was not finished, though.

"Jedrik might restore us to a share of power in the Rim city if we bargain for it now. Broey would never do that. Do you understand now the mistake you made with Broey?''

"But Broey was going to . . .''

"You failed to follow my orders, Father. You must see now why I always tried to keep you from making independent decisions.''

Gar fell into abashed silence. This was his daughter, but he could sense his peril.

Tria spoke.

"I will issue orders presently to all of our commanders. They will be told to hold at all costs. They will be told that you and I will try to contact Jedrik. They will be told why.''

"But how can . . .''

"We will permit ourselves to be captured.''

MANY THINGS conspired to frustrate McKie. Few people other than Jedrik answered his questions. Most responded as though to a cretin. Jedrik treated him as though he were a child of unknown potential. At times, he knew he amused her. Other times, she punished him with an angry glance, by ignoring him, or just by going away—or worse, sending him away.

It was now late afternoon of the fifth day in the battle for Chu, and Broey's forces still held out in the heart of the city with their slim corridor to the Rim. He knew this from reports he'd overheard. He stood in a small room off Jedrik's command post, a room containing four cots where, apparently she and/or her commanders snatched occasional rest. One tall, narrow window looked out to the south Rim. McKie found it difficult to realize that he'd come across that Rim just six days previously.

Clouds had begun to gather over the Rim's terraced escarpments, a sure sign of a dramatic change in the weather. He knew that much, at least, from his Tandaloor briefings. Dosadi had no such thing as weather control. Awareness of this left him feeling oddly vulnerable. Nature could be so damnably capricious and dangerous when you had no grip on her vagaries.

McKie blinked, held his breath for a moment.

Vagaries of nature.

The vagaries of sentient nature had moved the Gowachin to set up this experiment. Did they really hope to control that vast, seething conglomerate of motives? Or had they some other reason for Dosadi, a reason which he had not yet penetrated? Was this, after all, a test of Caleban mysteries? He thought not.

He knew the way Aritch and aides *said* they'd set up this experiment. Observations here bore out their explanations. None of that data was consistent with an attempt to understand the Calebans. Only that brief encounter with Pcharky, a thing which Jedrik no longer was willing to discuss.

No matter how he tried, McKie couldn't evade the feeling that something essential lay hidden in the way this planet had been set upon its experimental course; something the Gowachin hadn't revealed, something they perhaps didn't even understand themselves. What'd they done at the beginning? They had this place, Dosadi, the subjects, the Primary . . . yes, the Primary. The inherent inequality of individuals dominated Gowachin minds. And there was that damnable DemoPol. How had they mandated it? Better yet: how did they maintain that mandate?

Aritch's people had hoped to expose the inner workings of sentient social systems. So they said. But McKie was beginning to look at that explanation with Dosadi eyes, with Dosadi scepticism. What had Fannie Mae meant about not being able to leave here in his own body/node? How could he be Jedrik's *key* to the God Wall? McKie knew he needed more information than he could hope to get from Jedrik. Did Broey have this information? McKie wondered if he might in the end have to climb the heights to the Council Hills for his answers. Was that even possible now?

When he'd asked for it, Jedrik had given him almost the run of this building, warning:

"Don't interfere."

Interfere with what?

When he'd asked, she'd just stared at him.

She had, however, taken him around to familiarize everyone with his status. He was never quite sure what that status might be, except that it was somewhere between guest and prisoner.

Jedrik had required minimal conversation with her people. Often, she'd use only hand waves to convey the necessary signals of passage. The whole traverse was a lesson for McKie, beginning with the doorguards.

"McKie." Pointing at him.

The guards nodded.

Jedrik had other concerns.

"Team Nine?"

"Back at noon."

"Send word."

Everyone subjected McKie to a hard scrutiny which he felt certain would let them identify him with minimal interruption.

There were two elevators: one an express from a heavily guarded street entrance on the side of the building, the other starting above the fourth level at the ceiling of Pcharky's cage. They took this one, went up, pausing at each floor for guards to see him.

When they returned to the cage room, McKie saw that a desk had been installed just inside the street door. The father of those three wild children sat there watching Pcharky, making occasional notations in a notebook. McKie had a name for him now, Ardir.

Jedrik paused at the desk.

"McKie can come and go with the usual precautions."

McKie, addressing himself finally to Jedrik, had said:

"Thanks for taking this time with me."

"No need to be sarcastic, McKie."

He had not intended sarcasm and reminded himself once more that the usual amenities of the ConSentiency suffered a different interpretation here.

Jedrik glanced through Ardir's notes, looked up at Pcharky, back to McKie. Her expression did not change.

"We will meet for dinner."

She left him then.

For his part, McKie had approached Pcharky's cage, noting the tension this brought to the room's guards and observers. The old Gowachin sat in his hammock with an indifferent expression on his face. The bars of the cage emitted an almost indiscernible hissing as they shimmered and glowed.

"What happens if you touch the bars?" McKie asked.

The Gowachin jowls puffed in a faint shrug.

McKie pointed.

"There's energy in those bars. What is that energy? How is it maintained?"

Pcharky responded in a hoarse croaking.

"How is the universe maintained? When you first see a thing, is that when it was created?"

"Is it a Caleban thing?"

Shrug.

McKie walked around the cage, studying it. There were glistening bulbs wherever the bars crossed each other. The rods upon which the hammock was suspended came from the ceiling. They penetrated the cage top without touching it. The hammock itself appeared to be fabric. It was faintly blue. He returned to his position facing Pcharky.

"Do they feed you?"

No answer.

Ardir spoke from behind him.

"His food is lowered from the ceiling. His excreta are hosed into the reclamation lines."

McKie spoke over his shoulder.

"I see no door into the cage. How'd he get in there?"

"It was built around him according to his own instructions."

"What are the bulbs where the bars cross?"

"They came into existence when he activated the cage."

"How'd he do that?"

"We don't know. Do you?"

McKie shook his head from side to side.

"How does Pcharky explain this?"

"He doesn't."

McKie had turned away to face Ardir, probing, moving the focus of questions from Pcharky to the planetary society itself. Ardir's answers, especially on matters of religion and history, were banal.

Later, as he stood in the room off the command post reviewing the experience, McKie found his thoughts touching on a matter which had not even come into question.

Jedrik and her people had known for a long time that Dosadi was a Gowachin creation. They'd known it long before McKie had appeared on the scene. It was apparent in the way they focused on Pcharky, in the way they reacted to Broey. McKie had added one significant datum: that Dosadi was a Gowachin *experiment*. But Jedrik's people were not using him in the ways he might expect. She said he was the key to the God Wall, but how was he that key?

The answer was not to be found in Ardir. That one had not tried to evade McKie's questions, but the answers betrayed a severely limited scope to Ardir's knowledge and imagination.

McKie felt deeply disturbed by this insight. It was not so much what the man said as what he did not say when the reasons for speaking openly in detail were most demanding. Ardir was no dolt. This was a Human who'd risen high in Jedrik's hierarchy. Many speculations would've crossed his mind. Yet he made no mention of even the more obvious speculations. He raised no questions about the way Dosadi history ran to a single cutoff point in the past without any trace of evolutionary beginnings. He did not appear to be a religious person and even if he were, Dosadi would not permit the more blatant religious inhibitions. Yet Ardir refused to explore the most obvious discrepancies in those overt religious attitudes McKie had been told to expect. Ardir played out the right attitudes, but there was no basis for them underneath. It was all surface.

McKie suddenly despaired of ever getting a deep answer from any of these people—even from Jedrik.

An increase in the noise level out in the command post caught McKie's attention. He opened the door, stood in the doorway to study the other room.

A new map had been posted on the far wall. There was a position board, transparent and covered with yellow, red, and blue dots, over the map. Five women and a man—all wearing earphones—worked the board, moving the colored markers. Jedrik stood with her back to McKie, talking to several commanders who'd just come in from the streets. They still carried their weapons and packs. It was their conversation which had attracted McKie. He scanned the room, noted two communications screens at the left wall, both inactive. They were new since his last view of the room and he wondered at their pupose.

An aide leaned in from the hallway, called out:

"Gate Twenty-One just reported. Everything has quieted there. They want to know if they should keep their reserves on the alert."

"Have them stand down," Jedrik said.

"The two prisoners are being brought here," the aide added.

"I see it," Jedrik said.

She nodded toward the position board.

McKie, following the direction of her gaze, saw two yellow markers being moved with eight blue companions. Without knowing how he understood this, he saw that this must be the prisoners and their escort. There were tensions in the command post which told him this was an important event. Who were those prisoners?

One of Jedrik's commanders spoke.

"I saw the monitor at . . ."

She was not listening to him and he broke off. Two people on the position board exchanged places, trading earphones. The messenger who'd called out the information about the gate and the prisoners had gone. Another messenger came in presently, conferred in a soft voice with people near the door.

In a few moments, eight young Human males entered carrying Gar and Tria securely trussed with what appeared to be shining wire. McKie recognized the pair from Aritch's briefings. The escort carried their prisoners like so much meat, one at each leg and each arm.

"Over here," Jedrik said, indicating two chairs facing her.

McKie found himself suddenly aware, in an extremely Dosadi way, of many of the nuances here. It filled him with elation.

The escort crossed the room, not bothering to steer clear of all furniture. The messenger from the hallway delayed his departure, reluctant to leave. He'd recognized the prisoners and knew something important was to happen.

Gar and Tria were dumped into the two chairs.

"Release their bindings," Jedrik said.

The escort obeyed.

Jedrik waited, staring across at the position board. The two yellow and eight blue markers had been removed. She continued to stare at the board, though. Something there was more important than these two prisoners. She pointed to a cluster of red markers in an upper corner.

"See to that."

One of her commanders left the room.

McKie took a deep breath. He'd spotted the flicker of her movement toward the commander who'd obeyed. So that was how she did it! McKie moved farther into the room to put Jedrik in profile to him. She made no response to his movement, but he knew she was aware of him. He stepped closer to what he saw as the limit of her tolerance, noted a faint smile as she turned toward the prisoners.

There was an abrupt silence, one of those uncomfortable moments when people realize there are things they must do, but everyone is reluctant to start. The messenger still stood by the door to the hall, obviously wanting to see what would happen here. The escort who'd brought the prisoners remained standing in a group at one side. They were almost huddled, as though seeking protection in their own numbers.

Jedrik glanced across at the messenger.

"You may go."

She nodded to the escort.

"And you."

McKie held his cautious distance, waiting, but Jedrik took no notice of him. He saw that he not only would be allowed to stay, but that he was expected to use his wits, his off-world knowledge. Jedrik had read things in his presence: a normal distrust, caution, patience. And the fears, of course.

Jedrik took her time with the prisoners. She leaned forward, examined first Tria, then Gar. From the way she looked at them, it was clear to McKie she weighed many possibilities on how to deal with this pair. She was also building the tensions and this had its effect. Gar broke.

"Broey has a way of describing people such as you," Gar said. "He calls you 'rockets,' which is to say you are like a display which shoots up into the sky—and falls back."

Jedrik grinned.

McKie understood. Gar was not managing his emotions very well. It was a weakness.

"Many rockets in this universe must die unseen," Jedrik said.

Gar glared at her. He didn't like this response, glanced at Tria, saw from her expression that he had blundered.

Tria spoke now, smiling faintly.

"You've taken a personal interest in us, Jedrik."

To McKie, it was as though he'd suddenly crossed a threshold into the understanding of another language. Tria's was a Dosadi statement, carrying many messages. She'd said that Jedrik saw an opportunity for personal gain here and that Tria knew this. The faint smile had been the beginning of the statement. McKie felt a new awe at the special genius of the Dosadi awareness. He moved a step closer. There was something else about Tria . . . something odd.

"What is that one to you?"

Tria spoke to Jedrik, but a flicker of the eyes indicated McKie.

"He has a certain utility," Jedrik said.

"Is that the reason you keep him near you?"

"There's no single reason."

"There've been certain rumors . . ."

"One uses what's available," Jedrik said.

"Did you plan to have children by him?"

Jedrik shook with silent mirth. McKie understood that Tria probed for weaknesses, found none.

"The breeding period is so incapacitating for a female," Tria said.

The tone was deliberately goading, and McKie waited for a response.

Jedrik nodded.

"Offspring produce many repercussions down through the generations. Never a casual decision for those of us who understand."

Jedrik looked at Gar, forcing McKie to shift his attention.

Gar's face went suddenly bland, which McKie interpreted as shock and anger.

The man had himself under control quickly, however. He stared at McKie, directed a question to Jedrik.

"Would his death profit us?"

Jedrik glanced at McKie.

Shocked by the directness of the question, McKie was at least as intrigued by the assumptions in Gar's question. *"Us!"* Gar assumed that he and Jedrik had common cause. Jedrik was weighing that assumption and McKie, filled with elation, understood. He also recognized something else and realized he could now repay all of Jedrik's patient teaching.

Tria!

Something about Tria's way of holding her head, the inflections in her spoken Galach, struck a chord in McKie's memory. Tria was a Human who'd been trained by a PanSpechi—that way of moving the eyes before the head moved, the peculiar emphasis in her speech mannerisms. But there were no PanSpechi on Dosadi. Or were there?

None of this showed on McKie's face. He continued to radiate distrust, caution, patience. But he began to ask himself if there might be another loose thread in this Dosadi mystery. He saw Jedrik looking at him and, without thinking about it, gave her a purely Dosadi eye signal to follow him, returned to the adjoining room. It was a measure of how she read him that she came without question.

"Yes?"

He told her what he suspected.

"These PanSpechi, they are the ones who can grow a body to simulate that of another species?"

"Except for the eyes. They have faceted eyes. Any PanSpechi who could act freely and simulate another species would be only the surface manifestation. The freely moving one is only one of five bodies; it's the holder of the ego, the identity. This passes periodically to another of the five. It's a PanSpechi crime to prevent that transfer by surgically fixing the ego in only one of the bodies."

Jedrik glanced out the doorway. "You're sure about her?"

"The pattern's there."

"The faceted eyes, can that be disguised?"

"There are ways: contact lenses or a rather delicate operation. I've been trained to detect such things, however, and I can tell you that the one who trained her is not Gar."

She looked at him.

"Broey?"

"A Graluz would be a great place to conceal a creche but . . ." He shook his head. ". . . I don't think so. From what you tell me about Broey . . ."

"Gowachin," she agreed. "Then who?"

"Someone who influenced her when she was quite young."

"Do you wish to interrogate the prisoners?"

"Yes, but I don't know their potential value."

She stared him in open wonder. His had been an exquisitely penetrating Dosadi-style statement. It was as though a McKie she thought she knew had been transformed suddenly right in front of her eyes. He was not yet sufficiently Dosadi to trust completely, but she'd never expected him to come this far this quickly. He did deserve a more detailed assessment of the military situation and the relative abilities of Tria and Gar. She delivered this assessment in the Dosadi way: barebones words, swift, clipped to an essential spareness which assumed a necessary broad understanding by the listener.

Absorbing this, McKie sensed where she limited her recital, tailoring it for his abilities. In a way, it was similar to a response by his Daily Schedule back on Central Central. He could see himself in her attitudes, read her assessment of him. She was favoring him with a limited, grudging respect tempered by a certain fondness as by a parent toward a child. And he knew that once they returned to the other room, the fondness would be locked under a mask of perfect concealment. It was there, though. It was there. And he dared not betray her trust by counting on that fondness, else it would be locked away forever.

"I'm ready," he said.

They returned to the command post, McKie with a clearer picture of how to operate here. There was no such thing as mutual, unquestioning trust. You always questioned. You always managed. A sort of grudging respsect was the nearest they'd reveal openly. They worked together to survive, or when it was overwhelmingly plain that there was personal advantage in mutual action. Even when they united, they remained ultimate individualists. They suspected any gift because no one gave away anything freely. The safest relationships were those in which the niches of the hierarchy were clear and solidly held—minimum threat from above and from below. The whole thing reminded McKie of stories told about behavior in human bureaucracies of the classical period before deep space travel. And many years before he had encountered a multispecies corporation which had behaved similarly until the ministrations of BuSab had shown them the error of their ways. They'd used every dirty trick available: bribing, spying and other forms of covert and overt espionage, fomenting dissent in the opposition, assassination, blackmail, and kidnapping. Few in the ConSentiency had not heard of InterRealm Supply, now defunct.

McKie stopped three paces from the prisoners.

Tria spoke first.

"Have you decided what to do with us?"

"There's useful potential in both of you," McKie said, "but we have other questions."

The "we" did not escape Tria or Gar. They both looked at Jedrik, who stood impassively at McKie's shoulder.

McKie addressed himself to Gar.

"Is Tria really your daughter, your natural child?"

Tria appeared surprised and, with his new understanding, McKie realized she was telling him she didn't care if he saw this reaction, that it suited her for him to see this. Gar, however, had betrayed a flicker of shock. By Dosadi standards, he was dumbfounded. Then Tria was not his natural daughter, but until this moment, Tria had never questioned their relationship.

"Tell us," McKie said.

The Dosadi spareness of the words struck Gar like a blow. He looked at Jedrik. She gave every indication of willingness to wait forever for him to obey, which was to say that she made no response either to McKie's words or Gar's behavior.

Visibly defeated, Gar returned his attention to McKie.

"I went with two females, only the three of us, across the far mountains. We tried to set up our own production of pure food there. Many on the Rim tried that in those days. They seldom came back. Something always happens: the plants die for no reason, the water source runs dry, something steals what you grow. The Gods are jealous. That's what we always said."

He looked at Tria, who studied him without expression.

"One of the two women died the first year. The other was sick by the following harvest season, but survived through the next spring. It was during that harvest . . . we went to the garden . . . ha! The garden! This child was there. We had no idea of where she'd come from. She appeared to be seven or eight years old, but her reactions were those of an infant. That happens often enough on the Rim—the mind retreats from something too terrible to bear. We took her in. Sometimes you can train such a child back to usefulness. When the woman died and the crop failed, I took Tria and we headed back to the Rim. That was a very bad time. When we returned . . . I was sick. Tria helped me then. We've been together ever since."

McKie found himself deeply touched by this recital and hard put to conceal his reaction. He was not positive that he did conceal it. With his new Dosadi awareness, he read an entire saga into that sparse account of events which probably were quite ordinary by Rim standards. He found himself enraged by the other data which could be read into Gar's words.

PanSpechi trained!

That was the key. Aritch's people had wanted to maintain the purity of their experiment: only two species permitted. But it would be informative to examine PanSpechi applications. Simple. Take a Human female child. Put her exclusively under PanSpechi influence for seven or eight years. Subject that child to selective memory erasure. Hand her over to convenient surrogate parents on Dosadi.

And there was more: Aritch lied when he said he knew little about the Rim, that the Rim was outside the experiment.

As these thoughts went through his head, McKie returned to the small adjoining room. Jedrik followed. She waited while he assembled his thoughts.

Presently, McKie looked at her, laid out his deductions. When he finished, he glanced at the doorway.

"I need to learn as much as I can about the Rim."

"Those two are a good source."

"But don't you require them for your other plans, the attack on Broey's corridor?"

"Two things can go forward simultaneously. You will return to their enclave with them as my lieutenant. That'll confuse them. They won't know what to make of that. They will answer your questions. And in their confusion they'll reveal much that they might otherwise conceal from you."

McKie absorbed this. Yes . . . Jedrik did not hesitate to put him into peril. It was an ultimate message to everyone. McKie would be totally at the mercy of Gar and Tria. Jedrik was saying, "See! You cannot influence me by any threat to McKie." In a way, this protected him. In an extremely devious Dosadi way, this removed many possible threats to McKie, and it told him much about what her true feelings toward him could be. He spoke to this.

"I detest a cold bed."

Her eyes sparkled briefly, the barest touch of moisture, then, arming him:

"No matter what happens to me, McKie—free us!"

*Given the proper leverage at the proper point, any sentient aware-
ness may be exploded into astonishing self-understanding.*

—FROM AN ANCIENT HUMAN MYSTIC

"UNLESS SHE makes a mistake, or we find some unexpected advantage, it's only a
matter of time until she overruns us," Broey said.

He sat in his aerie command post at the hightest point of the dominant building
on the Council Hills. The room was an armored oval with a single window about
fifteen meters away directly in front of Broey looking out on sunset through the
river's canyon walls. A small table with a communicator stood just to his left. Four
of his commanders waited near the table. Maps, position boards, and the other
appurtenances of command, with their attendants, occupied most of the room's
remaining space.

Broey's intelligence service had just brought him the report that Jedrik had taken
Gar and Tria captive.

One of his commanders, slender for a Gowachin and with other deprivation
marks left from birth on the Rim, glanced at his three companions, cleared his
throat.

"Is it time to capitulate?"

Broey shook his head in a Human gesture of negation.

It's time I told them, he thought.

He felt emptied. God refused to speak to him. Nothing in his world obeyed the
old mandates.

We've been tricked.

The Powers of the God Wall had tricked him, had tricked his world and all of its
inhabitants. They'd . . .

"This McKie," the commander said.

Broey swallowed, then:

"I doubt if McKie has even the faintest understanding of how she uses him."

He glanced at the reports on his communicator table, a stack of reports about
McKie. Broey's intelligence service had been active.

"If we captured or killed him . . ." the commander ventured.

"Too late for that," Broey said.

"Is there a chance we won't have to capitulate?"

"There's always that chance."

None of the four commanders liked this answer. Another of them, fat and silky
green, spoke up:

"If we have to capitulate, how will we know the . . ."

"We must never capitulate, and we must make certain she knows this," Broey
said. "She means to exterminate us."

There! He'd told them.

They were shocked but beginning to understand where his reasoning had led
him. He saw the signs of understanding come over their faces.

"The corridor . . ." one of them ventured.

Broey merely stared at him. The fool must know they couldn't get more than a
fraction of their forces onto the Rim before Jedrik and Tria closed off that avenue.
And even if they could escape to the Rim, what could they do? They hadn't the
faintest idea of where the damned factories and food stores were buried.

"If we could rescue Tria," the slim commander said.

Broey snorted. He'd prayed for Tria to contact him, to open negotiations. There'd been not a word, even after she'd fallen back into that impossible enclave. Therefore, Tria had lost control of her people outside the city. All othe other evidence supported this conclusion. There was no contact with the Rim. Jedrik's people had taken over out there. Tria would've sent word to him the minute she recognized the impossibility of her position. Any valuable piece of information, any counter in this game would've leaped into Tria's awareness, and she'd have recognized who the highest bidder must be.

Who was the highest bidder? Tria, after all, was Human.

Broey sighed.

And McKie—an idiot savant from beyond the God Wall, a *weapons* expert. Jedrik must've known. But how? Did the Gods talk to her? Broey doubted this. Jedrik gave every evidence of being too clever to be sucked in by trickster Gods.

More clever, more wary, more Dosadi than I.

She deserved the victory.

Broey arose and went to the window. His commanders exchanged worried glances behind him. Could Broey *think* them out of this mess?

A corner of his slim corridor to the Rim was visible to Broey. He could not hear the battle, but explosive orange blossoms told him the fighting continued. He knew the gamble Jedrik took. Those Gowachin beyond the God Wall, the ones who'd created this hellish place, were slow—terrifyingly slow. But eventually they would be unable to misunderstand Jedrik's intentions. Would they step in, those mentally retarded Gowachin out there, and try to stop Jedrik? She obviously thought they would. Everything she did told Broey of the care with which Jedrik had prepared for the stupids from Outside. Broey almost wished her success, but he could not bear the price he and his people would have to pay.

Jedrik had the time-edge on him. She had McKie. She had played McKie like a superb instrument. And what would McKie do when he realized the final use Jedrik intended to make of him? Yes . . . McKie was a perfect tool for Jedrik. She'd obviously waited for that perfect instrument, had known when it arrived.

Gods! She was superb!

Broey scratched at the nodes between his ventricles. Well, there were still things a trapped people could do. He returned to his commanders.

"Abandon the corridor. Do it quietly, but swiftly. Fall back to the prepared inner walls."

As his commanders started to turn away, Broey stopped them.

"I also want some carefully selected volunteers. The fix we're in must be explained to them in such a way that there's no misunderstanding. They will be asked to sacrifice themselves in a way no Gowachin has ever before contemplated."

"How?"

It was the slender one.

Broey addressed himself to this one. A Gowachin born on the Rim should be the first to understand.

"We must increase the price Jedrik's paying. Hundreds of their people for every *one* of ours."

"Suicide missions," the slender one said.

Broey nodded, continued:

"One more thing. I want Havvy brought up here and I want orders issued to increase the food allotment to those Humans we've held in special reserve."

Two of his commanders spoke in unison:

"They won't sacri . . ."

"I have something else in mind for them."

Broey nodded to himself. Yes indeed. Some of those Humans could still serve his purposes. It wasn't likely they could serve him as McKie served Jedrik, but there was still a chance . . . yes, a chance. Jedrik might not be certain of what Broey could do with his Humans. Havvy, for example. Jedrik had certainly considered and discarded Havvy. In itself, that might be useful. Broey waved for his commanders to leave and execute his orders. They'd seen the new determination in him. They'd pass that along to the ones beneath them. That, too, would serve his purposes. It would delay the moment when his people might suspect that he was making a desperate gamble.

He returned to his communicator, called his search people, urged them to new efforts. They might still achieve what Jedrik obviously had achieved with Pcharky . . . if they could find a Pcharky.

Knowledge is the province of the Legum, just as knowledge is a source of crime.

—GOWACHIN LAW

MCKIE TOLD himself that he might've known an assignment from Jedrik could not be simple. There had to be Dosadi complications.

"There can be no question in their minds that you're really my lieutenant."

"Then I must be your lieutenant."

This pleased her, and she gave him the bare outline of her plan, warning him that the upcoming encounter could not be an act. He must respond as one who was fully aware of this planet's demands.

Night fell over Chu while she prepared him and, when they returned to the command post where Gar and Tria waited, the occasion presented itself as Jedrik had told him it would. It was a sortie by Broey's people against Gate Eighteen. Jedrik snapped the orders at him, sent him running.

"Find the purpose of that!"

McKie paused only to pick up four waiting guards at the command post door, noting the unconcealed surprise in Gar and Tria. They'd formed a particular opinion of McKie's position and now had to seek a new assessment. Tria would be most upset by this, confused by self-doubts. McKie knew Jedrik would immediately amplify those doubts, telling Gar and Tria that McKie would go with them when he returned from Gate Eighteen.

"You must consider his orders as my orders."

Gate Eighteen turned out to be more than a minor problem. Broey had taken the gate itself and two buildings. One of the attackers, diving from an upper window into one of Jedrik's best units, had blown himself up with a nasty lot of casualties.

"More than a hundred dead," a breathless courier told him.

McKie didn't like the implications of a suicide attack, but couldn't pause to assess it. They had to eliminate this threat. He gave orders for two feints while a third force blasted down one of the captured buildings, smothering the gate in rubble. That left the other captive building isolated. The swiftness of this success dazzled Jedrik's forces, and the commanders snapped to obedience when McKie issued orders for them to take cpatives and bring those captives to him for interrogation.

At McKie's command, one of this original four guards brought a map of the area, tacked it to a wall. Less than an hour had passed since he'd left Jedrik, but McKie felt that he'd entered another world, one even more primitive than that surrounding the incredible woman who'd set all of this in motion. It was the difference between second- and third-hand reports of action and the physical feeling of that action all around him. Explosions and the hissing of flamers down on the street jarred his awareness.

Staring at the map, McKie said, "This has all the marks of a trap. Get all but a holding force out of the area. Tell Jedrik."

People scurried to obey.

One of the guards and two sub-commanders remained. The guard spoke.

"What about this place?"

McKie glanced around him. It was a square room with brown walls. Two windows looked out on the street away from the battle for the isolated building near the gate. He'd hardly looked at the room when they'd brought him here to set up his command post. Four streets with isolated holdouts cushioned him from the main battle. They could shoot a cable bridge to another building if things became hot here. And it'd help morale if he remained in the danger area.

He spoke to one of the sub-commanders:

"Go down to the entry. Call all the elevators down there and disable all but one. Stand by that one with a holding force and put guards in the stairway. Stand by yourself to bring up captives. Comment?"

"I'll send up two cable teams and make sure the adjoining buildings are secure."

Of course! McKie nodded.

Gods! How these people reacted in emergencies. They were as direct and cutting as knives.

"Do it," McKie said.

He had less than a ten-minute wait before two of Jedrik's special security troops brought up the first captive, a young Gowachin whose eyelids bore curious scars—scroll-like and pale against the green skin.

The two security people stopped just inside the doorway. They held the Gowachin firmly, although he did not appear to be struggling. The sub-commander who'd brought them up closed the door as he left.

One of the captors, an older man with narrow features, nodded as he caught McKie's attention.

"What'll we do with him?"

"Tie him in a chair," McKie instructed.

He studied the Gowachin as they complied.

"Where was he captured?"

"He was trying to escape from that building through a perimeter sewage line."

"Alone?"

"I don't know. He's the first of a group of prisoners. The others are waiting outside."

They had finished binding the young Gowachin, now took up position directly behind him.

McKie studied the captive. He wore black coveralls with characteristic deep vee to clear the ventricles. The garment had been cut and torn in several places. He'd obviously been searched with swift and brutal thoroughness. McKie put down a twinge of pity. The scar lines on the prisoner's eyelids precluded anything but the most direct Dosadi necessities.

"They did a poor job removing your Phylum tattoos," McKie said. He'd already recognized the scar lines: Deep Swimmers. It was a relatively unimportant Phylum, small in numbers and sensitive about their status.

The young Gowachin blinked. McKie's opening remark had been so conversational, even-toned, that the shock of his words came after. Shock was obvious now in the set of the captive's mouth.

"What is your name, please?" McKie asked, still in that even, conversational way.

"Grinik."

It was forced out of him.

McKie asked one of the guards for a notebook and stylus, wrote the Gowachin's name in it, adding the Phylum identification.

"Grinik of the Deep Swimmers," he said. "How long have you been on Dosadi?"

The Gowachin took a deep, ventricular breath, remained silent. The security men appeared puzzled. This interrogation wasn't going as they'd expected. McKie himself did not know what to expect. He still felt himself recovering from the surprise at recognition of the badly erased Phylum tattoos.

"This is a very small planet," McKie said. "The universe from which we both come is very big and can be very cruel. I'm sure you didn't come here expecting to die."

If this Grinik didn't know the deadly plans of his superiors, that would emerge shortly. McKie's words could be construed as a personal threat beyond any larger threat to Dosadi as a whole. It remained to see how Grinik reacted.

Still, the young Gowachin hesitated.

When in doubt, remain silent.

"You appear to've been adequately trained for this project," McKie said. "But I doubt if you were told everything you should know. I even doubt if you were told things essential to you in your present position."

"Who are you?" Grinik demanded. "How dare you speak here of matters which . . ." He broke off, glanced at the two guards standing at his shoulders.

"They know all about us," McKie lied.

He could smell the sweet perfume of Gowachin fear now, a floral scent which he'd noted only on a few previous occasions. The two guards also sensed this and showed faint smiles to betray that they knew its imports.

"Your masters sent you here to die," McKie said. "They may very well pay heavily for this. You ask who I am? I am Jorj X. McKie, Legum of the Gowachin Bar, Saboteur Extraordinary, senior lieutenant of Jedrik who will shortly rule all of Dosadi. I make formal imposition upon you. Answer my questions for the Law is at stake."

On the Gowachin worlds, that was a most powerful motivator. Grinik was shaken by it.

"What do you wish to know?"

He barely managed the words.

"Your mission on Dosadi. The precise instructions you were given and who gave them to you."

"There are twenty of us. We were sent by Mrreg."

That name! The implications in Gowachin lore stunned McKie. He waited, then:

"Continue."

"Two more of our twenty are out there."

Grinik motioned to the doorway, clearly pleading for his captive associates.

"Your instructions?"

"To get our people out of this terrible place."

"How long?"

"Just . . . sixty hours remain."

McKie exhaled slowly. So Aritch and company had given up on him. They were going to eliminate Dosadi.

"Where are the other members of your party?"

"I don't know."

"You were, of course, a reserve team trained and held in readiness for this mission. Do you realize how poorly you were trained?"

Grinik remained silent.

McKie put down a feeling of despair, glanced at the two guards. He understood that they'd brought him this particular captive because this was one of three who were not Dosadi. Jedrik had instructed them, of course. Many things became clearer to him in his new awareness. Jedrik had put sufficient pressure on the Gowachin beyond the God Wall. She still had not imagined the extremes to which those Gowachin might go in stopping her. It was time Jedrik learned what sort of fuse she'd lighted. And Broey must be told. Especially Broey—before he sent many more suicide missions.

The outer door opened and the sub-commander leaned in to speak.

"You were right about the trap. We mined the area before pulling back. Caught them nicely. The gate's secure now, and we've cleared out that last building."

McKie pursed his lips, then:

"Take the prisoners to Jedrik. Tell her we're coming in."

A flicker of suprise touched the sub-commander's eyes.

"She knows."

Still the man hesitated.

"Yes?"

"There's one Human prisoner out here you should question before leaving."

McKie waited. Jedrik knew he was coming in, knew what had gone on here, knew about the Human prisoner out there. She wanted him to question this person. Yes . . . of course. She left nothing to chance . . . by her standards. Well, her standards were about to change, but she might even know that.

"Name?"

"Havvy. Broey holds him, but he once served Jedrik. She says to tell you Havvy is a reject, that he was contaminated."

"Bring him in."

Havvy surprised him. The surface was that of a bland-faced nonentity, braggadocio clearly evident under a mask of secret knowledge. He wore a green uniform with a driver's brassard. The uniform was wrinkled, but there were no visible rips or cuts. He'd been treated with more care than the Gowachin who was being led out of the room. Havvy replaced the Gowachin in the chair.

McKie waved away the bindings.

Unfocused questions created turmoil in McKie's mind. He found it difficult to delay. Sixty hours! But he felt that he could almost touch the solution to the Dosadi mystery, that in only a few minutes he would know names and real motives for the ones who'd created this monster. Havvy? He'd served Jedrik. In what way? Why rejected? Contaminated?

Unfocused questions, yes.

Havvy sat in watchful tension, casting an occasional glance around the room, at the windows. There were no more explosions out there.

As McKie studied him more carefully, certain observations emerged. Havvy was small but solid, one of those Humans of lesser stature who concealed heavy musculature which could surprise you if you suddenly bumped into them. It was difficult to guess his age, but he was not Dosadi. A member of Grinik's team? Doubtful. Clearly not Dosadi, though. He didn't examine those around him with an automatic status assessment. His reactions were slow. Too much that should remain under shutters flowed from within him directly to the surface. Yes, that was the ultimate revelation. It bothered McKie that so much went unseen beneath the surface here, so much for which Aritch and company had not prepared him. It would take a lifetime to learn all the nuances of this place, and he had less than sixty hours remaining to him.

All of this flowed through McKie's mind in an eyeblink. He reached his decision, motioned the guards and others to leave.

One of the security people started to protest, but McKie silenced him with a glance, pulled up a chair, and sat down facing the captive.

The door closed behind the last of the guards.

"You were sent here deliberately to seek me out," McKie said.

It was not the opening Havvy had expected. He stared into McKie's eyes. A door slammed outside. There was the sound of several doors opening and shutting, the shuffling of feet. An amplified voice called out:

"Move these prisoners out!"

Havvy chewed at his upper lip. He didn't protest. A deep sigh shook him, then: "You're Jorj X. McKie of BuSab?"

McKie blew out through pursed lips. Did Havvy doubt the evidence of his own senses? Surprising. McKie shook his head, continued to study the captive.

"You can't be McKie!" Havvy said.

"Ahhhhhh . . ." It was pressed out of McKie.

Something about Havvy: the body moved, the voice spoke, but the eyes did not agree.

McKie thought about what the Caleban, Fannie Mae, had said. *A light touch.* He was overtaken by an abrupt certainty: someone other than Havvy looked out through the man's eyes. Yessss. Artich's people controlled the Caleban who maintained the barrier around Dosadi. The Caleban could contact selected people here. She'd have a constant updating on everything such people learned. There must be many such spies on Dosadi, all trained not to betray the Caleban contact—no twitching, no lapses into trance. No telling how many agents Aritch possessed here.

Would all the other people on Dosadi remain unaware of such a thing, though? That was a matter to question.

"But you must be McKie." Havvy said. "Jedrik's still working out of . . ." He broke off.

"You must've provided her with some amusement by your bumbling," McKie said. "I assure you, however, that BuSab is *not* amused."

A gloating look came over Havvy's face.

"No, she hasn't made the transfer yet."

"Transfer?"

"Haven't you figured out yet how Pcharky's supposed to buy his freedom?"

McKie felt off balance at this odd turn.

"Explain."

"He's supposed to transfer your identity into Jedrik's body and her identity into your body. I think she was going to try that with me once, but . . ."

Havvy shrugged.

It was like an explosion in McKie's newly sensitized awareness. Rejected! Contaminated! Body exchange! McKie was accusatory!

"Broey sent you!"

"Of course." Offensive.

McKie contained his anger. The Dosadi complexities no longer baffled him as once they had. It was like peeling back layer upon layer of concealment. With each new layer you expected to find *the* answer. But that was a trap the whole universe set for the unwary. It was the ultimate mystery and he hated mystery. There were those who said this was a necessary ingredient for BuSab agents. You eliminated that which you hated. But everything he'd uncovered about this planet showed him how little he'd known previously about any mystery. Now, he understood something new about Jedrik. There was little doubt that Broey's Human messenger told the truth.

Pcharky had penetrated the intricacies of PanSpechi ego transfer. He'd done it without a PanSpechi as his subject, unless . . .yes . . . that expanded the implications in Tria's history. Their PanSpechi experiment had assumed even more grotesque proportions.

"I will speak directly to your Caleban monitor," McKie said.

"My what?"

It was such obvious dissimulation that McKie only snorted. He leaned forward.

"I will speak directly to Aritch. See that he gets this message without any mistakes."

Havvy's eyes became glassy. He shuddered.

McKie felt the inner tendrils of an attempted Caleban contact in his own awareness, thrust them aside.

"No! I will speak openly through your agent. Pay close attention, Aritch. Those who created this Dosadi horror cannot run far enough, fast enough, or long enough to escape. If you wish to make every Gowachin in the universe a target for violence, you are proceeding correctly. Others, including BuSab, can employ mass violence if you force it upon them. Not a pleasant thought. But unless you adhere to your own Law, to the honored relationship between Legum and Client, your shame will be exposed. Innocent Gowachin as well as you others whose legal status has yet to be determined—all will pay the bloody price."

Havvy's brows drew down in puzzlement.

"Shame?"

"They plan to blast Dosadi out of existence."

Havvy pressed back into the chair, glared at McKie.

"You're lying."

"Even you, Havvy, are capable of recognizing a truth. I'm going to release you, pass you back through the lines to Broey. Tell him what you learned from me.''

"It's a lie! They're not going to . . .''

"Ask Aritch for yourself.''

Havvy didn't ask "Aritch who?'' He lifted himself from the chair.

"I will.''

"Tell Broey we've less than sixty hours. None of us who can resist mind erasure will be permitted to escape.''

"Us?''

McKie nodded, thinking: *Yes, I am Dosadi now*. He said:

"Get out of here.''

It afforded him a measure of amusement that the door was opened by the sub-commander just as Havvy reached it.

"See to him yourself,'' McKie said, indicating Havvy. "I'll be ready to go in a moment.''

Without any concern about whether the sub-commander understood the nature of the assignment, McKie closed his eyes in thought. There remained the matter of Mrreg, who'd sent twenty Gowachin from Tandaloor to get *his people* off the planet. Mrreg. That was the name of the mythical monster who'd tested the first primitive Gowachin people almost to extinction, setting the pattern of their deepest instincts.

Mrreg?

Was it code, or did some Gowachin acutally use that name? Or was it a role that some Gowachin filled?

> *Does a populace have informed consent when a ruling minority acts in secret to ignite a war, doing this to justify the existence of the minority's forces? History already has answered that question. Every society in the ConSentiency today reflects the historical judgment that failure to provide full information for informed consent on such an issue represents an ultimate crime.*
>
> —FROM THE TRIAL OF TRIALS

LESS THAN an hour after closing down at Gate Eighteen, McKie and his escort arrived back at Jedrik's headquarters building. He led them to the heavily guarded side entrance with its express elevator, not wanting to pass Pcharky at this moment. Pcharky was an unnecessary distraction. He left the escort in the hallway with instructions to get food and rest, signaled for the elevator. The elevator door was opened by a small Human female of about fifteen years who nodded him into the dim interior.

McKie, his natural distrust of even the young on this planet well masked, nevertheless kept her under observation as he accepted the invitation. She was a gamin child with dirty face and hands, a torn grey single garment cut off at the knees. Her very existence as a Dosadi survivor said she'd undoubtedly sold her body many times for scraps of food. He realized how much Dosadi had influenced him when he found that he couldn't raise even the slightest feeling of censure at this knowledge. You did what the conditions around you demanded when those conditions were overwhelming. It was an ultimate question: this or death? And certainly some of them chose death.

"Jedrik," he said.

She worked her controls and he found himself presently in an unfamiliar hallway. Two familiar guards stood at a doorway down the hall, however. They betrayed not the slightest interest in him as he opened the door between them swiftly and strode through.

It was a tiny anteroom, empty, but another door directly in front of him. He opened this with more confidence than he felt, entered a larger space full of projection-room gloom with shadowed figures seated facing a holographic focus on his left. McKie identified Jedrik by her profile, slipped into a seat beside her.

She kept her attention on the h-focus where a projection of Broey stood looking out at something over their shoulders. McKie recognized the subtle slippage of computer simulation. That was not a flesh-and-blood Broey in the focus.

Someone on the far side of the room stood up and crossed to sit beside another figure in the gloom. McKie recognized Gar as the man moved through one of the projection beams.

McKie whispered to Jedrik, "Why simulation?"

"He's beginning to do things I didn't anticipate."

The suicide missions. McKie looked at the simulation, wondered why there was no sync-sound. Ahhh, yes. They were lip reading, and it was silent to reduce distractions, to amplify concentration. Yes, Jedrik was reworking the simulation model of Broey which she carried in her head. She would also carry another model, even more accurate than the one of Broey, which would give her a certain lead time on the reactions of one Jorj X. McKie.

"Would you really have done it?" he asked.

"Why do you distract me with such nonsense?"

He considered. Yes, it was a good question. He already knew the answer. She would have done it: traded bodies with him and escaped outside the God Wall as McKie. She might still do it, unless he could anticipate the mechanics of the transfer.

By now, she knew about the sixty-hour limit and would suspect its significance. Less than sixty hours. And the Dosadi could make extremely complex projections from limited data. Witness this Broey simulation.

The figure in the focus was talking to a fat Human female who held a tube which McKie recognized as a communicator for field use.

Jedrik spoke across the room to Gar.

"She still with him?"

"Addicted."

A two-sentence exchange, and it condensed an entire conversation about possible uses of that woman. McKie did not ask addicted to what. There were too many such substances on Dosadi, each with peculiar characteristics, often involving odd monopolies with which everyone seemed familiar. This was a telltale gap in Aritch's briefings: the monopolies and their uses.

As McKie absorbed the action in the focus, the reasons behind this session became more apparent. Broey was refusing to believe the report from Havvy.

And there was Havvy in the focus.

Jedrik favored McKie with one flickering glance as Havvy-simulation appeared. Certainly. She factored McKie into her computations.

McKie compressed his lips. She knew Havvy would contaminate me. They couldn't say "I love you" on this damned planet. Oh, no. They had to create a special Dosadi production number.

"Most of the data for this originated before the breakup," McKie said. "It's useless. Rather than ask the computer to play pretty pictures for us, why don't we examine our own memories? Surely, somewhere in the combined experiences with Broey . . ."

A chuckle somewhere to the left stopped him.

Too late, McKie saw that every seat in the room had an arm keyed to the simulations. They were doing precisely what he's suggested, but in a more sophisticated way. The figures at the focus were being adjusted to the combined memories. There was such a keyed arm at McKie's right hand. He suddenly realized how tactless and lecturing he still must appear to these people. They didn't waste energy on unnecessary words. Anyone who did must be subnormal, poorly trained or . . . or not from Dosadi.

"Does he always state the obvious?" Gar asked.

McKie wondered if he'd blown his lieutenancy, lost the opportunity to explore the mystery of the Rim, but . . . no, there wasn't time for that now. He'd have to penetrate the Rim another way.

"He's new," Jedrik said. "New is not necessarily naive, as you should know."

"He has you doing it now," Gar said.

"Guess again."

McKie put a hand to the simulation controls under his right hand, tested the keys. He had it in a moment. They were similar to such devices in the ConSentiency, an adaptation from the DemoPol inputs, no doubt. Slowly, he changed the Broey at the focus, heavier, the sagging jowls and node wattles of a breeding male Gowachin. McKie froze the image.

"Tentative?" Gar asked.

Jedrik answered for him.

"It's knowledge he brought here with him." She did something to her controls, stopped the projection, and raised the room lights.

McKie noted that Tria was nowhere in the room.

"The Gowachin have sequestered their females somewhere," McKie said. "That somewhere should not be difficult to locate. Send word to Tria that she must not mount her attack on Broey's corridor just yet."

"Why delay?" Gar demanded.

"Broey will have all but evacuated the corridor by now," McKie said.

Gar was angry and showing it.

"Not a single one of them has gone through that Rim gate."

"Not to the Rim," Jedrik said.

It was clear to her now. McKie had supplied the leverage she needed. It was time now to employ him as she'd always intended. She glanced at McKie.

"We have unfinished business. Are you ready?"

He held his silence. How could he answer such a Dosadi-weighted question? There were so many things left unspoken on this planet, only the native-born could understand them all. McKie felt once more that he was a dull outsider, a child of dubious potential among normal adults.

Jedrik arose, looked across at Gar.

"Send word to Tria to hold herself in readiness for another assignment. Tell Broey. Call him on an open line. We now have an excellent use for your fanatics. If only a few of your people fight through to that Graluz complex, it'll be enough and Broey will know it.''

McKie noted that she spoke to Gar with a familiar teaching emphasis. It was the curiously weighted manner she'd once used with McKie, but no longer found necessary. His recognition of this amused her.

"Come along, McKie. We haven't much time.''

Does a population have informed consent when that population is not taught the inner workings of its monetary system, and then is drawn, all unknowing, into economic adventures?.

—FROM THE TRIAL OF TRIALS

FOR ALMOST an hour after the morning meal, Aritch observed Ceylang as she worked with the McKie simulator. She was pushing herself hard, believing Wreave honor at stake, and had almost reached the pitch Aritch desired.

Ceylang had set up her own simulator situation: McKie interviewing five of Broey's Gowachin. She had the Gowachin come to McKie in surrender, hands extended, the webbed fingers exposed to show that the talons were withdrawn.

Simulator-McKie merely probed for military advantages.

"Why does Broey attack in this fashion?''

Or he'd turn to some places outside the h-focus of the simulator.

"Send reinforcements into that area.''

Nothing about the Rim.

Earlier, Ceylang had tried the issue with a prisoner simulation where the five Gowachin tried to confuse McKie by presenting a scenario in which Broey massed his forces at the corridor. The makings of a breakout to the Rim appeared obvious.

Simulator-McKie asked the prisoners why they had lied.

Ceylang cleared the simulator and sat back. She saw Aritch at the observation window, opened a channel to him.

"Something has to be wrong in the simulation. McKie cannot be led into questioning the purposes of the Rim.''

"I assure you that simulation is remarkable in its accuracy. Remarkable.''

"Then why . . .''

"Perhaps he already knows the answer. Why don't you try him with Jedrik? Here . . .'' Aritch operated the controls at the observer station. "This might help. This is a record of McKie in recent action on Dosadi.''

The simulator presented a view down a covered passage through a building. Artificial light. Darkness at the far end of the passage. McKie, two blocky guards in tow, approached the viewers.

Ceylang recognized the scene. She'd watched this action at Gate Eighteen from several angles, had seen this passage empty before the battle, acquainting herself with the available views. As she'd watched it then, the passage had filled with Human defenders. There was a minor gate behind the viewer and she knew the viewer itself to be only a bright spot, a fleck of glittering impurity in an otherwise drab brick over the gate's archway.

Now, the long passage seemed strange to Ceylang without its throng of defenders. There were only a few workmen along its length as McKie passed. The workmen repaired service pipes in the ceiling. A cleanup crew washed down patches of blood at the far end of the passage, the high-water mark of the Gowachin attack. An officer leaned against a wall near the viewer, a bored expression on his face which did not mislead Ceylang. He was there to watch McKie. Three soldiers squatted nearby rolling hexi-bones for coins which lay in piles before each man. Every now and then, one of the gamblers would pass a coin to the watching officer. A repair supervisor stood with his back to the viewer, notebook in hand, writing a list of supplies to complete the job. McKie and his guards were forced to step around these people. As they passed, the officer turned, looked directly into the viewer, smiled.

"That officer," Ceylang said. "One of your people?"

"No."

The viewpoint shifted, looking down on the gate itself, McKie in profile. The gatekeeper was a teenager with a scar down his right cheek and a broken nose. McKie showed no signs of recognition, but the youth knew McKie.

"You go through on request."

"When did she call?"

"Ten."

"Let us through."

The gate was opened. McKie and his guards went through, passed beyond the viewer's focus.

The youthful gatekeeper stood up, smashed the viewer. The h-focus went blank. Aritch looked down from his observation booth for a moment before speaking.

"Who called?"

"Jedrik?" Ceylang spoke without thinking.

"What does that conversation tell you? Quickly!"

"That Jedrik anticipated his movements, was observing him all the time."

"What else?"

"That McKie . . . knows this, knows she can anticipate him."

"She carries a better simulation of him in her head than we have . . . there." Aritch pointed at the h-focus area.

"But they left so much unspoken!" Ceylang said.

Aritch remained silent.

Ceylang closed her eyes. It was like mind reading. It confused her.

Aritch interrupted her musings.

"What about that officer and the gatekeeper?"

She shook her head.

"You're wise to use living observers there. They all seem to know when they're being watched. And how it's done."

"Even McKie."

"He didn't look at the viewers."

"Because he assumed from the first that we'd have him under almost constant observation. He's not concerned about the mechanical intrusions. He has built a simulation McKie of his own who acts on the surface of the real McKie."

"That's your assumption?"

"We arrived at this from observation of Jedrik in her dealings with McKie. She peels away the simulation layers one at a time, coming closer and closer to the actuality at the core."

Another observation bothered Ceylang.

"Why'd the gatekeeper shut down that viewer just then?"

"Obviously because Jedrik told him to do that."

Ceylang shuddered.

"Sometimes I think those Dosadi play us like a fine instrument."

"But of course! That's why we sent them our McKie."

> *The music of a civilization has far-reaching consequences on consciousness and, thus, influences the basic nature of a society. Music and its rhythms divert and compel the awareness, describing the limits within which a consciousness, thus fascinated, may operate. Control the music, then, and you own a powerful tool with which to shape the society.*
>
> —THE DOSADI ANALYSIS, BUSAB DOCUMENTS

IT WAS a half-hour before Jedrik and McKie found themselves in the hallway leading to her quarters. McKie, aware of the effort she was expending to conceal a deep weariness, watched her carefully. She concentrated on presenting a show of vitality, her attention glued on the prospect ahead. There was no way of telling what went on in her mind. McKie did not attempt to break the silence. He had his own worries.

Which was the real Jedrik? How was she going to employ Pcharky? Could he resist her?

He knew he was close to a solution of the Dosadi mystery, but the prospect of the twin gambles he was about to take filled him with doubts.

On coming from the projection room, they'd found themselves in a strange delaying situation, as though it were something planned for their frustration. Everything had been prepared for their movement—guards warned, elevator waiting, doors opened. But every time they thought the way clear, they met interference. Except for the obvious importance of the matters which delayed them, it was easy to imagine a conspiracy.

A party of Gowachin at Gate Seventy wanted to surrender, but they demanded a parley first. One of Jedrik's aides didn't like the situation. Something about the assessment of the offer bothered her, and she wanted to discuss it with Jedrik. She stopped them halfway down the first hall outside the projection room.

The aide was an older woman who reminded McKie vaguely of a Wreave lab worker at BuSab, one who'd always been suspicious of computers, even antagonistic toward them. This Wreave had read every bit of history he could find about the evolution of such instruments and liked to remind his listeners of the misuses of the DemoPol. Human history had provided him with abundant ammunition, what with its periodic revolts against "enslavement by machines." Once, he'd cornered McKie.

"Look here! See this sign: 'Gigo.' That's a very old sign that was hung above one of your ancient computers. It's an acronym: 'Garbage In, Garbage Out.' You see! They knew."

Yes. Jedrik's female aide reminded him of that Wreave.

McKie listened to her worries. She roamed all around a central disquiet, never settling on a particular thing. Aware of Aritch's deadline and Jedrik's fatigue, McKie felt the pressures bearing down upon him. The aide's data was accurate. Others had checked it. Finally, he could hold his impatience no longer.

"Who fed this data into your computer?"

The aide was startled at the interruption, but Jedrik turned to him, waiting.

"I think it was Holjance," the aide said. "Why?"

"Get him in here."

"Her."

"Her, then! Make sure she's actually the one who fed in that data."

Holjance was a pinch-faced woman with deep wrinkles around very bright eyes. Her hair was dark and wiry, skin almost the color of McKie's. Yes, she was the one who'd fed the data into the computer because it had arrived on her shift, and she'd thought it too important to delegate.

"What is it you want?" she demanded.

He saw no rudeness in this. It was Dosadi directness. Important things were happening all around. *Don't waste time.*

"You saw this assessment of the surrender offer?" he asked.

"Yes."

"Are you satisfied with it?"

"The data went in correctly."

"That's not my question."

"Of course I'm satisfied!"

She stood ready to defend herself against any charge that she'd slighted the job.

"Tell me, Holjance," he said, "if you wanted the Gowachin computers to produce inaccurate assessments, what would you do?"

She thought about this a moment, blinked, glanced almost furtively at Jedrik who appeared lost in thought. "Well, sir, we have a regular filtering procedure for preventing . . ."

"That's it," Jedrik said. "If I were a Gowachin, I would not be doing that right now."

Jedrik turned, barked orders to the guards behind her.

"That's another trap! Take care of it."

As they emerged from the elevator on Jedrik's floor, there was another delay, one of the escort who'd been with McKie at Gate Eighteen. His name was Todu Pellas and McKie addressed him by name, noting the faint betrayal of pleasure this elicited. Pellas, too, had doubts about carrying out a particular order.

"We're supposed to back up Tria's move by attacking across the upper parkway, but there are some trees and other growth knocked down up there that haven't been moved for two days."

"Who knocked down those trees?" McKie asked.

"We did."

McKie understood. You feinted. The Gowachin were supposed to believe this would provide cover for an attack, but there'd been no attack for two days.

"They must be under pretty heavy strain," Jedrik said.

McKie nodded. That, too, made sense. The alternative Gowachin assumption was that the Humans were trying to fake them into an attack at that point. But the cover had not been removed by either side for two days.

Jedrik took a deep breath.

"We have superior firepower and when Tria . . . well, you should be able to cut right through there to . . ."

McKie interrupted.

"Call off that attack."

"But . . ."

"Call it off!"

She saw the direction of his reasoning. Broey had learned much from the force which Gar and Tria had trained. And Jedrik herself had provided the final emphasis in the lesson. She saw there was no need to change her orders to Pellas.

Pellas had taken it upon himself to obey McKie, not waiting for Jedrik's response, although she was his commander. He already had a communicator off his belt and was speaking rapidly into it.

"Yes! Dig in for a holding action."

He spoke in an aside to Jedrik.

"I can handle it from here."

In a few steps, Jedrik and McKie found themselves in her room. Jedrik leaned with her back against the door, no longer trying to conceal her fatigue.

"McKie, you're becoming very Dosadi."

He crossed to the concealing panels, pulled out the bed.

"You need rest."

"No time."

Yes, she knew all about the sixty-hour deadline—less than fifty-five hours now. Dosadi's destruction was a reaction she hadn't expected from "X," and she blamed herself.

He turned, studied her, saw that she'd passed some previously defined limit of personal endurance. She possessed no amplifiers of muscles or senses, none of the sophisticated aids McKie could call upon in emergencies. She had nothing but her own magnificent mind and body. And she'd almost run them out. Still, she pressed on. This told him a great deal about her motivation.

McKie found himself deeply touched by the fact that she'd not once berated him for hiding that ultimate threat which Aritch held over Dosadi. She'd accepted it that someone in Aritch's position could erase an entire planet, that McKie had been properly maneuvered into concealing this.

The alternative she offered filled McKie with misgivings.

Exchange bodies?

He understood now that this was Pcharky's function, the price the old Gowachin paid for survival. Jedrik had explained.

"He will perform this service one more time. In exchange, we release him from Dosadi."

"If he's one of the original . . . I mean, why doesn't he just leave?"

"We haven't provided him with a body he can use."

McKie had suppressed a feeling of horror. But the history of Dosadi which Jedrik unfolded made it clear that a deliberate loophole had been left in the Caleban contract which imprisoned this planet. Fannie Mae had even said it. He could leave in another body. That was the basic purpose behind this experiment.

New bodies for old!

Aritch had expected this to be the ultimate enticement, luring McKie into the Gowachin plot, enlisting McKie's supreme abilities and his powerful position in BuSab.

A new body for his old one.

All he'd have to do would be to cooperate in the destruction of a planet, conceal the real purpose of this project, and help set up another body-trade planet better concealed.

But Aritch had not anticipated what might be created by Jedrik plus McKie. They now shared a particular hate and motivation.

Jedrik still stood at the door waiting for him to decide.

"Tell me what to do," he said.

"You're sure that you're willing to . . ."

"Jedrik!"

He thought he saw the beginning of tears. It wasn't that she hid them, but that they reached a suppression level barely visible and she defied them. She found her voice, pointed.

"That panel beside the bed. Pressure latch."

The panel swung wide to reveal two shimmering rods about two centimeters in diameter. The rods danced with the energies of Pcharky's cage. They emerged from the floor, bent at right angles about waist height and, as the panel opened, they rotated to extend into the room—two glowing handles about a meter apart.

McKie stared at them. He felt a tightness in his breast. What if he'd misread Jedrik? Could he be sure of any Dosadi? This room felt as familiar to him now as his quarters on CC. It was here that Jedrik had taught him some of the most essential Dosadi lessons. Yet . . . he knew the old pattern of what she proposed. The discarded body with its donor ego had always been killed immediately. Why?

"You'll have your answer to that question when we've done this thing."

A Dosadi response, ambiguous, heavy with alternatives.

He glanced around the room, found it hard to believe that he'd known this place only these few days. His attention returned to the shimmering rods. Another trap?

He knew he was wasting precious time, that he'd have to go through with this. But what would it be like to find himself in Jedrik's flesh, wearing her body as he now wore his own? PanSpechi transferred an ego from body to body. But something unspeakable which they would not reveal happened to the donor.

McKie took a trembling breath.

It had to be done. He and Jedrik shared a common purpose. She'd had many opportunities to use Pcharky simply to escape or to extend her life . . . the way, he realized now, that Broey had used the Dosadi secret. The fact that she'd waited for a McKie forced him to believe her. Jedrik's followers trusted her—and they were Dosadi. And if he and Jedrik escaped, Aritch would find himself facing a far different McKie from the one who'd come so innocently across the Rim. They might yet stay Aritch's hand.

The enticement had been real, though. No doubting that. Shed an old body, get a new one. And the Rim had been the major source of *raw material:* strong, resilient bodies. Survivors.

"What do I do?" he asked.

He felt a hand on his shoulder, and she spoke from beside him.

"You are very Dosadi, McKie. Astonishing."

He glanced at her, saw what it had cost her to move here from the door. He slipped a hand around her waist, eased her to a sitting position on the bed and within reach of the rods.

"Tell me what to do."

She stared at the rods, and McKie realized it was rage driving her, rage against Aritch, the embodiment of "X," the embodiment of a contrived fate. He understood this. The solution of the Dosadi mystery had left him feeling empty, but on the edges there was such a rage as he'd never before experienced. He was still BuSab, though. He wanted no more bloodshed because of Dosadi, no more Gowachin justifications.

Jedrik's voice interrupted his thoughts and he saw that she also shared some of his misgivings.

"I come from a long line of heretics. None of us doubted that Dosadi was a crime, that somewhere there was a justice to punish the criminals."

McKie almost sighed. Not the old Messiah dream! Not that! He would not fill that role, even for Dosadi.

It was as though Jedrik read his mind. Perhaps, with that simulation model of him she carried in her head, this was exactly what she did.

"We didn't expect a hero to come and save us. We knew that whoever came would suffer from the same deficiencies as the other non-Dosadi we saw here. You were so . . . slow. Tell me, McKie, what drives a Dosadi?"

He almost said, "Power."

She saw his hesitation, waited.

"The power to change your condition," he said.

"You make me very proud, McKie."

"But how did you know I was . . ."

"McKie!"

He swallowed, then: "Yes, I guess that was the easiest part for you."

"It was much more difficult finding your abilities and shaping you into a Dosadi."

"But I might've been . . ."

"Tell me how I did it, McKie."

It was a test. He saw that. How had she known absolutely that he was the one she needed?

"I was sent here in a way that evaded Broey."

"And that's not easy." Her glance flickered ceilingward. "They tried to bait us from time to time. Havvy . . ."

"Compromised, contaminated . . ."

"Useless. Sometimes, a stranger looks out of Havvy's eyes."

"My eyes are my own."

"The first thing Bahrank reported about you."

"But even before that . . ."

"Yes?"

"They used Havvy to tell you I was coming . . . and he told you that you could use my body. He had to be truthful with you up to a point. You could read Havvy! How clever they thought they were being! I had to be vulnerable . . . really vulnerable."

"The first thing . . ."

". . . you found out about me." He nodded. "Suspicions confirmed. All of that money on my person. Bait. I was someone to be eliminated. I was a powerful enemy of your enemies."

"And you were angered by the right things."

"You saw that?"

"McKie, you people are so easy to read. So *easy*!"

"And the weapons I carried. You were supposed to use those to destroy yourselves. The implications . . ."

"I would've seen that if I'd had first-hand experience of Aritch. You *knew* what he intended for us. My mistake was to read your fears as purely personal. In time . . .''

''We're wasting time.''

''You fear we'll be too late?''

Once more, he looked at the shimmering rods. What was it Pcharky did? McKie felt events rushing over him, engulfing him. What bargain had Jedrik really driven with Pcharky? She saw the question on his face.

''My people knew all along that Pcharky was just a tool of the God who held us prisoner. We forced a bargain on that God—that Caleban. Did you think we would not recognize the identity between the powers of that cage and the powers of our God Wall? No more delays, McKie. It's time to test our bargain.''

> *Geriatric or other life extension for the powerful poses a similar threat to a sentient species as that found historically in the dominance of a self-perpetuating bureaucracy. Both assume prerogatives of immortality, collecting more and more power with each passing moment. This is power which draws a theological aura about itself: the unassailable Law, the God-given mandate of the leader, manifest destiny. Power held too long within a narrow framework moves farther and farther away from the adaptive demands of changed conditions. The leadership grows ever more paranoid, suspicious of inventive adaptations to change, fearfully protective of personal power and, in the terrified avoidance of what it sees as risk, blindly leads its people into destruction.*
>
> —BUSAB MANUAL

''VERY WELL, I'll tell you what bothers me,'' Ceylang said. ''There are too many things about this problem that I fail to understand.''

From her seated position, she looked across a small, round room at Aritch, who floated gently in a tiny blue pool. His head at the pool's lip was almost on a level with Ceylang's. Again, they had worked late into the night. She understood the reasons for this, the time pressures were quite apparent, but the peculiar Gowachin flavor of her training kept her in an almost constant state of angry questioning.

This whole thing was so un-Wreave!

Ceylang smoothed the robe over her long body. The robe was blue now, one step away from Legum black. Appropriately, there was blue all around her: the walls, the floor, the ceiling, Aritch's pool.

The High Magister rested his chin on the pool's edge to speak.

''I require specific questions before I can even hope to penetrate your puzzlement.''

''Will McKie defend or prosecute? The simulator . . .''

''Damn the simulator! Odds are that he'll make the mistake of prosecuting. Your own reasoning powers should . . .''

''But if he doesn't?''

''Then selection of the judicial panel becomes vital.''

Ceylang twisted her body to one side, feeling the chairdog adjust for her comfort. As usual, Aritch's answer only deepened her sense of uncertainty. She voiced that now.

"I continue to have this odd feeling that you intend me to play some role which I'm not supposed to discover until the very last instant."

Aritch breathed noisily through his mouth, splashed water onto his head.

"This all may be moot. By this time day after tomorrow, Dosadi *and* McKie may no longer exist."

"Then I will not advance to Legum?"

"Oh, I'm fairly certain you'll be a Legum."

She studied him, sensing irony, then:

"What a delicate line you walk, High Magister."

"Hardly. My way is wide and clear. You know the things I cannot countenance. I cannot betray the Law or my people."

"I have similar inhibitions. But this Dosadi thing—so tempting."

"So dangerous! Would a Wreave don Human flesh to learn the Human condition? Would you permit a Human to penetrate Wreave society in this . . ."

"There are some who might conspire in this! There are even Gowachin who . . ."

"The opportunities for misuse are countless."

"Yet you say that McKie already is more Gowachin than a Gowachin."

Aritch's webbed hands folded over the pool's edge, the claws extended.

"We risked much in training him for this task."

"More than you risk with me?"

Aritch withdrew his hands, stared at her, unblinking.

"So that's what bothers you."

"Precisely."

"Think, Ceylang, how near the core of Wreavedom you would permit me to come. Thus far and no farther will we permit you."

"And McKie?"

"May already have gone too far for us to permit his continued existence."

"I heed your warning, Aritch. But I remain puzzled as to why the Calebans couldn't prevent . . ."

"They profess not to understand the ego transfer. But who can understand a Caleban, let alone control one in a matter so delicate? Even this one who created the God Wall . . ."

"It's rumored that McKie understands Calebans."

"He denies it."

She rubbed her pocked left jowl with a prehensile mandible, felt the many scars of her passage through the Wreave triads. Family to family to family until it was a single gigantic family. Yet, all were Wreave. This Dosadi thing threatened a monstrous parody of Wreavedom. Still . . .

"So fascinating," she murmured.

"That's its threat."

"We should pray for the death of Dosadi."

"Perhaps."

She was startled.

"What . . ."

'This might not die with Dosadi. Our sacred bond assures that you will leave here with this knowledge. Many Gowachin know of this thing."

"And McKie."

"Infections have a way of spreading," Aritch said. "Remember *that* if this comes to the Courtarena."

There are some forms of insanity which, driven to an ultimate expression, can become the new models of sanity.

—BuSab Manual

"McKie?"

It was the familiar Caleban presence in his awareness, as though he heard and felt someone (or some*thing*) which he knew was not there.

The preparation had been deceptively simple. He and Jedrik clasped hands, his right hand and her left, and each grasped one of the shimmering rods with the other hand.

McKie did not have a ready identity for this Caleban and wondered at the questioning in her *voice*. He agreed, however, that he was indeed McKie, shaping the thought as subvocalized conversation. As he spoke, McKie was acutely aware of Jedrik beside him. She was more than just another person now. He carried a tentative simulation model of her, sometimes anticipating her responses.

"You make mutual agreement?" the Caleban asked.

McKie sensed Pcharky then: a distant presence, the monitor for this experience. It was as though Pcharky had been reduced to a schematic which the Caleban followed, a set of complex rules, many of which could not be translated into words. Some part of McKie responded to this as though a monster awakened within him, a sleeping monster who sat up full of anger at being aroused thus, demanding:

"Who is it that dares awaken me?"

McKie felt his body trembling, felt Jedrik trembling beside him. The Caleban/Taprisiot-trembling, the sweaty response to trance! He saw these phenomena now in different light. When you walked at the edge of this abyss . . .

While these thoughts passed through his mind, he felt a slight shift, no more than the blurred reflection of something which was not quite movement. Now, while he still felt his own flesh around him, he also felt himself possessed of an inner contact with Jedrik's body and knew she shared this experience.

Such a panic as he had not thought possible threatened to overwhelm him. He felt Jedrik trying to break the contact, to stop this hideous sharing, but they were powerless in the grip of a force which would not be stopped.

No time sense attached itself to this experience, but a fatalistic calm overcame them almost simultaneously. McKie felt awareness of Jedrik/flesh deepen. Curiousity dominated him now.

So this is woman!

This is man?

They shared the thoughts across an indistinct bridge.

Fascination gripped McKie. He probed deeper.

He/She could feel himself/herself breathing. And the differences! It was not the genitalia, the presence or lack of breasts. She felt bereft of breasts. He felt acutely distressed by their presence, self-consciously aware of profound implications. The sense of difference went back beyond gamete McKie/Jedrik.

McKie sensed her thoughts, her reactions.

Jedrik: "You cast your sperm upon the stream of time."

McKie: "You enclose and nurture . . ."

"I cast/I nurture."

It was as though they looked at an object from opposite sides, aware belatedly that they both examined the same thing.

"We cast/we nurture."

Obscuring layers folded away, and McKie found himself in Jedrik's mind, she in his. Their thoughts were one entity.

The separate Dosadi and ConSentient experiences melted into a single relationship.

"Aritch . . . ah, yes. You see? And your PanSpechi friend, Bildoon. Note that. You suspected, but now you know . . ."

Each set of experiences fed on the other, expanding, refining . . . condensing, discarding, creating . . .

So that's the training of a Legum.

Loving parents? Ahhh, yes, loving parents.

"I/we will apply pressure there . . . and there . . . They must be maneuvered into choosing that one as judge. Yes, that will give us the required leverage. Let them break their own code."

And the awakened monster stirred within them. It had no dimension, no place, only existence. They felt its power.

"I do what I do!"

The power enveloped them. No other awareness was permitted. They sensed a primal current, unswerving purpose, a force which could override any other thing in their universe. It was not God, not Life, not any particular species. It was something so far beyond such articulations that Jedrik/McKie could not even contemplate it without a sense that the next instant would bring obliteration. They felt a question hurled at their united, fearful awareness. The question was framed squarely in anger, astonishment, cold amusement, and threat.

"For *this* you awaken *me*?"

Now, they understood why the old body and donor-ego had always been slain immediately. This terrible sharing made a . . . made a noise. It awakened a questioner.

They understood the question without words, knowing they could never grasp the full meaning and emotive thrust, that it would burn them out even to try. Anger . . . astonishment . . . cold amusement . . . threat. The question as their own united mind(s) interpreted it represented a limit. It was all that Jedrik/McKie could accept.

The instrusive questioner receded.

They were never quite sure afterward whether they'd been expelled or whether they'd fled in terror, but the parting words were burned into their combined awareness.

"Let the sleeper sleep."

They walked softly in their minds then. They understood the warning, but knew it could never be translated in its fullest threat for any other sentient being.

Concurrent: McKie/Jedrik felt a projection of terror from the God Wall Caleban, unfocused, unexplained. It was a new experience in the male-female collective memory. Caleban Fannie Mae had not even projected this upon original McKie when she'd thought herself doomed.

Concurrent: McKie/Jedrik felt a burntout fading from Pcharky. Something in that terrible contact had plunged Pcharky into his death spiral. Even as McKie/Jedrik realized this, the old Gowachin died. It was a slammed door. But this came after a blazing realization by McKie/Jedrik that Pcharky had shared the original decision to set up the Dosadi experiment.

McKie found himself clothed in living, breathing flesh which routed its messages through his awareness. He wasn't sure which of their two bodies he possessed, but it was distinct, separate. It wrapped him in Human senses: the taste of salt, the smell of perspiration, and the omnipresent Warren stink. One hand held cold metal, the other clasped the hand of a fellow Human. Perspiration drenched this body, made the clasped hands slippery. He felt that knowing which hand held another hand was of utmost importance, but he wasn't ready to face that knowledge. Awareness of self, this new self, and a whole lifetime of new memories, demanded all of the attention he could muster.

Focus: A Rim city, never outside Jedrik's control because she had fed the signals through to Gar and Tria with exquisite care, and because those who gave the orders on the Rim had shared in the generations of selective breeding which had produced Jedrik. She was a biological weapon whose sole target was the God Wall.

Focus: Loving parents can thrust their child into deadly peril when they know everything possible has been done to prepare that child for survival.

The oddity to McKie was that he felt such things as personal memories.

"I did that."

Jedrik suffered the throes of similar experiences.

Which body?

So that was the training of a BuSab agent. Clever . . . almost adequate. Complex and full of much that she found to be new, but why did it always stop short of a full development?

She reviewed the sessions with Aritch and Ceylang. A matched pair. The choice of Ceylang and the role chosen for her appeared obvious. How innocent! Jedrik felt herself free to pity Ceylang. When allowed to run its course, this was an interesting emotion. She had never before felt pity in uncolored purity.

Focus: McKie actually loved her. She savored this emotion in its ConSentient complexity. The straight flow of selected emotions fascinated her. They did not have to be bridled!

In and out of this creative exchange there wove an intimacy, a pure sexuality without inhibitions.

McKie, savoring the amusement Jedrik had felt when Tria had suggested a McKie/Jedrik breeding, found himself caught by demanding male eroticism and knew by the sensation that he retained his old body.

Jedrik, understanding McKie's long search for a female to complete him, found her amusement converted to the desire to demonstrate that completion. As she turned toward him, releasing the dull rod which had once shimmered in contact with Pcharky, she found herself in McKie's flesh looking into her own eyes.

McKie gasped in the mirror experience.

Just as abruptly, driven by shock, they shifted back into familiar flesh: McKie male, Jedrik female. Instantly, it became a thing to explore—back—and forth. Eroticism was forgotten in this new game.

"We can be either sex/body at will!"

It was something beyond Taprisiots and Calebans, far more subtle than the crawling progression of a PanSpechi ego through the bodies from its creche.

The knew the source of this odd gift even as they sank back on the bed, content to be familiar male and female for a time.

The sleeping monster.

This was a gift with barbs in it, something *loving parents* might give their child in the knowledge that it was time for this lesson. Yet they felt revitalized, knowing they had for an instant tapped an energy source without limits.

A pounding on the door interrupted this shared reverie.

"Jedrik! Jedrik!"

"What is it?"

"It's Broey. He wished to talk to McKie."

They were off the bed in an instant.

Jedrik glanced at McKie, knowing she had not one secret from him, that they shared a reasoning base. Out of the mutual understanding in this base, she spoke for both of them.

"Does he say why?"

"Jedrik . . ."

They both recognized the voice of a trusted aide and heard the fear in it.

". . .it's midmorning and there is no sun. God has turned off the sun!"

"Sealed us in . . ."

". . . to conceal the final blast."

Jedrik opened the door, confronted the frightened aide.

"Where is Broey?"

"Here—in your command post. He came alone without escort."

She glanced at McKie. "You will speak for us."

Broey waited near the position board in the command post. Watchful Humans stood within striking distance. He turned as McKie and Jedrik entered. McKie noted that the Gowachin's body was, indeed, heavy with breeding juices as anticipated. Unsettling for a Gowachin.

"What are your terms, McKie?"

Broey's voice was guttural, full of heavy breathing.

McKie's features remained Dosadi-bland, but he thought: *Broey thinks I'm responsible for the darkness. He's terrified.*

McKie glanced at the threatening black of the windows before speaking. He knew this Gowachin from Jedrik's painstaking study. Broey was a sophisticate, a collector of sophistication who surrounded himself with people of the same stripe. He was a professional sophisticate who read everything through that peculiar Dosadi screen. No one could come into his circle who didn't share this pose. All else remained outside and inferior. He was an ultimate Dosadi, a distillation, almost as Human as Gowachin because he'd obviously once worn a Human body. He was Gowachin at his origins, though—no doubt of it.

"You followed my scent," McKie said."

"Excellent!"

Broey brightened. He had not expected a Dosadi exchange, pared to the nonemotional essentials..

"Unfortunately," McKie said, "you have no position from which to negotiate. Certain things will be done. You will comply willingly, your compliance will be forced, or we will act without you."

It was a deliberate goading on McKie's part, a choice of non-Dosadi forms to abbreviate this confrontation. It said more than anything else that McKie came from beyond the God Wall, that the darkness which held back the daylight was the least of his resources.

Broey hesitated, then:

"So?"

The single word fell on the air with countless implications: an entire exchange discarded, hopes dashed, a hint of sadness at lost powers, and still with that sophisticated reserve which was Broey's signature. It was more subtle than a shrug, more powerful in its Dosadi overtones that an entire negotiating session.

"Questions?" McKie asked.

Broey glanced at Jedrik, obviously surprised by this. It was as though he appealed to her: they were both Dosadi, were they not? This outsider came here with his gross manners, his lack of Dosadi understanding. How could one speak to such one? He addressed Jedrik.

"Have I not already stated my submission? I came alone, I . . ."

Jedrik picked up McKie's cue.

"There are certain . . . peculiarities to our situation."

"Peculiarities?"

Broey's nictating membrane blinked once.

Jedrik allowed her manner to convey a slight embarrassment.

"Certain delicacies of the Dosadi condition must be overlooked. We are now, all of us, abject supplicants . . . and we are dealing with people who do not speak as we speak, act as we act . . ."

"Yes." He pointed upward. "The mentally retarded ones. We are in danger then."

It was not a question. Broey peered upward, as though trying to see through the ceiling and intervening floors. He drew in a deep breath.

"Yes."

Again, it was compressed communication. Anyone who could put the God Wall there could crush an entire planet. Therefore, Dosadi and all of its inhabitants had been brought to a common subjection. Only a Dosadi could have accepted it this quickly without more questions, and Broey was an ultimate Dosadi.

McKie turned to Jedrik. When he spoke, she anticipated every word, but she waited him out.

"Tell your people to stop all attacks."

He faced Broey.

"And your people."

Broey looked from Jedrik to McKie, back to Jedrik with a puzzled expression openly on his face, but he obeyed.

"Which communicator?"

Where pain predominates, agony can be a valued teacher.

—DOSADI APHORISM

MCKIE AND Jedrik had no need to discuss the decision. It was a choice which they shared and knew they shared through a memory-selection process now common to both of them. There was a loophole in the God Wall and even though that wall now blanketed Dosadi in darkness, a Caleban contract was still a Caleban contract. The vital question was whether the Caleban of the God Wall would respond.

Jedrik in McKie's body stood guard outside her own room while a Jedrik-fleshed McKie went alone into the room to make the attempt. Who should he try to contact? Fannie Mae? The absolute darkness which enclosed Dosadi hinted at an absolute withdrawal of the guardian Caleban. And there was so little time.

McKie sat cross-legged on the floor of the room and tried to clear his mind. The constant strange discoveries in the female body he now wore interfered with concentration. The moment of exchange left an aftershock which he doubted would ever diminish. They had but to share the desire for the change now and it occurred. But this different body—ahh, the multiplicity of differences created its own confusions. These went far beyond the adjustments to different height and weight. The muscles of his/her arms and hips felt wrongly attached. The bodily senses were routed through different unconscious processes. Anatomy created its own patterns, its own instinctual behavior. For one thing, he found it necessary to develop consciously monitored movements which protected his/her breasts. The movements were reminiscent of those male adjustments by which he prevented injury to testes. These were movements which a male learned early and relegated to an automatic behavior pattern. The problem in the female body was the he had to *think* about such behavior. And it went far beyond the breast-testes interlock.

As he tried to clear his mind for the Caleban contact, these webbed clusters of memory intruded. It was maddening. He needed to clear away bodily distractions, but this female body demanded his attention. In desperation, he hyperventilated and burned his awareness into a pineal focus whose dangers he knew only too well. This was the way to permanent identity loss if the experience were prolonged. It produced a sufficient clarity, however, that he could fill his awareness with memories of Fannie Mae.

Silence.

He sensed time's passage as though each heartbeat were a blow.

Fear hovered at the edges of the silence.

It came to him that something had put a terrible fear into the God Wall Caleban.

McKie felt anger.

"Caleban! You owe me!"

"McKie?"

The response was so faint that he wondered whether it might be his hopes playing tricks on him.

"Fannie Mae?"

"Are you McKie?"

That was stronger, and he recognized the familiar Caleban presence in his awareness.

"I am McKie and you owe me a debt."

"If you are truly McKie . . . why are you so . . . strange . . . changed?"

"I wear another body."

McKie was never sure, but he thought he sensed consternation. Fannie Mae responded more strongly then.

"I remove McKie from Dosadi now? Contract permits."

"I will share Dosadi's fate."

"McKie!"

"Don't argue with me, Fannie Mae. I will share Dosadi's fate unless you remove another node/person with me."

He projected Jedrik's patterns then, an easy process since he shared all of her memories.

"She wears McKie's body?"

It was accusatory.

"She wears *another* body," McKie said. He knew the Caleban saw his new relationship with Jedrik. Everything depended now on the interpretation of the Caleban contract.

"Jedrik is Dosadi," the Caleban protested.

"So am I Dosadi . . . now."

"But you are McKie!"

"And Jedrik is also McKie. Contact her if you don't believe me."

He broke the contact with an angry abruptness, found himself sprawled on the floor, still twitching. Perspiration bathed the female body which he still wore. The head ached.

Would Fannie Mae do as he'd told her? He knew Jedrik was as capable of projecting his awareness as he was of projecting hers. How would Fannie Mae interpret the Dosadi contract?

Gods! The ache in this head was a burning thing. He felt alien in Jedrik's body, misused. The pain persisted and he wondered if he'd done irreparable harm to Jedrik's brain through that intense pineal focus.

Slowly, he pushed himself upright, got to his feet. The Jedrik legs felt weak beneath him. He though of Jedrik outside that door, trembling in the zombielike trance required for this mind-to-mind contact. What was taking so long? Had the Calebans withdrawn?

Have we lost?

He started for the door but before he'd taken the second step, light blazed around him. For a fractional hearbeat he thought it was the final fire to consume Dosadi, but the light held steady. He glanced around, found himself in the open air. It was a place he recognized immediately: the courtyard of the Dry Head compound on Tandaloor. He saw the familiar phylum designs on the surrounding walls: green Gowachin script on yellow bricks. There was the sound of water splashing in the corner pool. A group of Gowachin stood in an arched entry directly ahead of him and he recognized one of his old teachers. Yes—this was a Dry Head sanctum. These people had protected him, trained him, introduced him to their most sacred secrets.

The Gowachin in the shadowed entry were moving excitedly into the courtyard, their attention centered on a figure sprawled near them. The figure stirred, sat up.

McKie recognized his own body there.

Jedrik!

It was an intense mutual need. The body exchange required less than an eyeblink. McKie found himself in his own familiar body, seated on cool tiles. The approaching Gowachin bombarded him with questions.

"McKie, what is this?"

"You fell through a jumpdoor?"

"Are you hurt?"

He waved the questions away, crossed his legs, and fell into the long-call trance focused on that bead in his stomach. That bead Bildoon had never expected him to use!

As it was paid to do, the Taprisiot waiting on CC enfolded his awareness. McKie rejected contact with Bildoon, made six calls through the responsive Taprisiot. The calls went to key agents in BuSab, all of them ambitious and resourceful, all of them completely loyal to the agency's mandate. He transmitted his Dosadi information in full bursts, using the technique derived from his exchanges with Jedrik—mind-to-mind.

There were few questions and those easily answered.

"The Caleban who holds Dosadi imprisoned plays God. It's the letter of the contract."

"Do the Calebans approve of this?"

That questions came from a particularly astute Wreave agent sensitive to the complications implicit in the fact that the Gowachin were training Ceylang, a Wreave female, as a Legum.

"The concepts of approval or disapproval are not applicable. The role was necessary for that Caleban to carry out the contract."

"It was a game?"

The Wreave agent was outraged.

"Perhaps. There's one thing certain: the Calebans don't understand harmful behavior and ethics as we understand them."

"We've always known that."

"But now we've really learned it."

When he'd made the six calls, McKie sent his Taprisiot questing for Aritch, found the High Magister in the Running Phylum's conference pool.

"Greetings, Client."

McKie projected wry amusement. He sensed the Gowachin's shock.

"There are certain things which your Legum instructs you to do under the holy seal of our relationship," McKie said.

"You will take us into the Courtarena, then?"

The High Magister was perceptive and he was a beneficiary of Dosadi's peculiar gifts, but he was not a Dosadi. McKie found it relatively easy to manipulate Aritch now, enlisting the High Magister's deepest motivations. When Aritch protested against cancelling the God Wall contract, McKie revealed only the first layer of stubborn determination.

"You will not add to your Legum's difficulties."

"But what will keep them on Dosadi?"

"Nothing."

"Then you will defend rather than prosecute?"

"Ask your pet Wreave," McKie said. "Ask Ceylang."

He broke the contact then, knowing Aritch could only obey him. The High Magister had few choices, most of them bad ones. And Gowachin Law prevented him from disregarding his Legum's orders once the patter of the contest was set.

McKie awoke from the call to find his Dry Head friends clustered around Jedrik. She was explaining their predicament. Yes . . . There were advantages to having two bodies with one purpose. McKie got to his feet. She saw him, spoke.

"My head feels better."

"It was a near thing." And he added:
"It still is. But Dosadi is free."

In the classical times of several species, it was the custom of the powerful to nudge the powercounters (money or other economic tabulators, status points, etc.) into occasional violent perturbations from which the knowledgeable few profited. Human accounts of this experience reveal edifying examples of this behavior (for which, see Appendix G). Only the PanSpechi appear to have avoided this phenomenon, possibly because of creche slavery.

—COMPARATIVE HISTORY, THE BUSAB TEXT

MCKIE MADE his next series of calls from the room the Dry Heads set aside for him. It was a relatively large room reserved for Human guests and contained well-trained chairdogs and a wide bedog which Jedrik eyed with suspicion despite her McKie memories of such things. She knew the things had only a rudimentary brain, but still they were . . . *alive.*

She stood by the single window which looked out on the courtyard pool, turning when she heard McKie awaken from his Taprisiot calls.

"Suspicions confirmed," he said.

"Will our agent friends leave Bildoon for us?" she asked.

"Yes."

She turned back to the window.

"I keep thinking how the Dosadi sky must look now . . . without a God Wall. As bright as this." She nodded toward the courtyard seen through the window. "And when we get jumpdoors . . ."

She broke off. McKie, of course, shared such thoughts. This new intimacy required considerable adjustment.

"I've been thinking about your training as a Legum," she said.

McKie knew where her thoughts had gone.

The Gowachin chosen to train him had all appeared open in their relationship. He had been told that his teachers were a select group chosen for excellence, the best available for the task: making a Gowachin Legum out of a non-Gowachin.

A silk purse from a sow's ear!

His teachers had appeared to lead conventional Gowachin lives, keeping the usual numbers of fertile females in family tanks, weeding the Graluz tads with necessary Gowachin abandon. On the surface of it, the whole thing had assumed a sense of the ordinary. They had introduced him to intimate aspects of their lives when he'd inquired, answered his questions with disarming frankness.

McKie's Jedrik-amplified awareness saw this in a different light now. The contests between Gowachin phylums stood out sharply. And McKie knew now that he had not asked the right questions, that his teachers had been selected by different rules than those revealed to him at the time, that their private instructions from their Gowachin superiors contained nuances of vital importance which had been hidden from their student.

Poor Ceylang.

These were unsettling reflections. They changed his understanding of Go-wachin honor, called into question all of those inadvertent comparisons he'd made between Gowachin forms and the mandate of his own BuSab. His BuSab training came in for the same questioning examination.

Why . . . why . . . why . . . why . . .

Law? Gowachin Law?

The value in having a BuSab agent as a Legum of the Gowachin had gained a dimension. McKie saw these matters now as Jedrik had once seen through the God Wall. There existed other forces only dimly visible behind the visible screen. An unseen power structure lay out there—people who seldom appeared in public, decision makers whose lightest whim carried terrible import for countless worlds. Many places, many worlds would be held in various degrees of bondage. Dosadi had merely been an extreme case for a special purpose.

New bodies for old. Immortality. And a training ground for people who made terrible decisions.

But none of them would be as completely Dosadi as this Jedrik-amplified McKie.

He wondered where the Dosadi decision had been made. Aritch had not shared in it; that was obvious. There were others behind Aritch—Gowachin and non-Gowachin. A shadowy power group existed. It could have its seat on any world of the ConSentiency. The power merchants would have to meet occasionally, but not necessarily face to face. And never in the public eye. Their first rule was secrecy. They would employ many people who lived at the exposed fringes of their power, people to carry out shadowy commands—people such as Aritch.

And Bildoon.

What had the PanSpechi hoped to gain? A permanent hold on his creche's ego? Of course. That . . . plus new bodies—Human bodies, undoubtedly, and un-marked by the stigmata of his PanSpechi origins.

Bildoon's behavior—and Aritch's—appeared so transparent now. And there'd be Mrreg nearby creating the currents in which Aritch swam. Puppet leads to Puppet Master.

Mrreg.

That poor fool, Grinik, had revealed more than he thought.

And Bildoon.

"We have two points of entry," McKie said.

She agreed.

"Bildoon and Mrreg. The latter is the more dangerous."

A crease beside McKie's nose began to itch. He scratched at it absently, grew conscious that something had changed. He stared around, found himself standing at the window and clothed in a female body.

Damn! It happened so easily.

Jedrik stared up at him with his own eyes. She spoke with his voice, but the overtones were pure Jedrik. They both found this amusing.

"The powers of your BuSab."

He understood.

"Yes, the watchdogs of justice."

"Where were the watchdogs when my ancestors were lured into this Dosadi trap?"

"Watchdogs of justice, very dangerous role," he agreed.

"You know our feelings of outrage," she said.

"And I know what it is to have loving parents."

"Remember that when you talk to Bildoon."

Once more, McKie found himself on the bed, his old familiar body around him.

Presently, he felt the mental tendrils of a Taprisiot call, sensed Bildoon's awareness in contact with him. McKie wasted no time. The shadow forces were taking the bait.

"I have located Dosadi. The issue will come to the Courtarena. No doubt of that. I want you to make the preliminary arrangements. Inform the High Magister Aritch that I make the formal imposition of the Legum. One member of the judicial panel must be a Gowachin from Dosadi. I have a particular Gowachin in mind. His name is Broey."

"Where are you?"

"On Tandaloor."

"Is that possible?"

McKie masked his sadness. *Ahhh, Bildoon, how easily you are read.*

"Dosadi is temporarily out of danger. I have taken certain retaliatory precautions."

McKie broke the contact.

Jedrik spoke in a musing voice.

"Ohh, the perturbations we spread."

McKie had no time for such reflections.

"Broey will need help, a support team, an extremely reliable troop which I want you to select for him."

"Yes, and what of Gar and Tria?"

"Let them run free. Broey will pick them up later."

Communal/managed economics have always been more destructive of their societies than those driven by greed. This is what Dosadi says: Greed sets its own limits, is self-regulating.

—THE DOSADI ANALYSIS/BUSAB TEXT

MCKIE LOOKED around the Legum office they'd assigned him. Afternoon smells from Tandaloor's fern jungles came in an open window. A low barrier separated him from the Courtarena with its ranks of seats all around. His office and adjoining quarters were small but fitted with all requisite linkages to libraries and the infrastructure to summon witnesses and experts. It was a green-walled space so deceptively ordinary that its like had beguiled more than one non-Gowachin into believing he knew how to perform here. But these quarters represented a deceptive surface riding on Gowachin currents. No matter that the ConSentient Pact modified what the Gowachin might do here, this was Tandaloor, and the forms of the frog people dominated.

Seating himself at the single table in the office space, McKie felt the chairdog adjust itself beneath him. It was good to have a chairdog again after Dosadi's unrelenting furniture. He flipped a toggle and addressed the Gowachin face which appeared on the screen inset into his table.

"I require testimony from those who made the actual decision to set up the Dosadi experiment. Are you prepared to meet this request?"

"Do you have the names of these people?"

Did this fool think he was going to blurt out: "Mrreg"?

"If you force me to it," McKie warned, "I will bind Aritch to the Law and extract the names from him."

This had no apparent effect on the Gowachin. He addressed McKie by name and title, adding:

"I leave the formalities to you. Any witness I summon must have a name."

McKie suppressed a smile. Suspicions confirmed. This was a fact which the watchful Gowachin in the screen was late recognizing. Someone else had read the interchange correctly, however. Another, older, Gowachin face replaced the first one on the screen.

"What're you doing, McKie?"

"Determining how I will proceed with this case."

"You will proceed as a Legum of the Gowachin Bar."

"Precisely."

McKie waited.

The Gowachin peered narrowly at him from the screen.

"Jedrik?"

"You are speaking to Jorj X. McKie, a Legum of the Gowachin Bar."

Belatedly, the older Gowachin saw something of the way the Dosadi experience had changed McKie.

"Do you wish me to place you in contact with Aritch?"

McKie shook his head. They were so damned obvious, these underlings.

"Aritch didn't make the Dosadi decision. Aritch was chosen to take the blow if it came to that. I will accept nothing less than the one who made that ultimate decision which launched the Dosadi experiment."

The Gowachin stared at him coldly, then:

"One moment. I will see what I can do."

The screen went blank, but the audio remained. McKie heard the voices.

"Hello . . . Yes, I'm sorry to interrupt at this time."

"What is it?"

That was a deep and arrogant Gowachin voice, full of annoyance at the interruption. It was also an accent which Dosadi could recognize in spite of the carefully overlaid masking tones. Here was one who'd used Dosadi.

The voice of the older Gowachin from McKie's screen continued:

"The Legum bound to Aritch has come up with a sensitive line of questioning. He wishes to speak to you."

"To me? But I am preparing for Laupuk."

McKie had no idea what Laupuk might be, but it opened a new window on the Gowachin for him. Here was a glimpse of the rarified strata which had been concealed from him all of those years. This tiny glimpse confirmed him in the course he'd chosen.

"He is listening to us at this time."

"Listening . . . why?"

The tone carried threats, but the Gowachin who'd intercepted McKie's demands went on, unwavering:

"To save explanations. It's clear that he'll accept nothing less than speaking to you. This caller is McKie, but . . ."

"Yes?"

"You will understand."

"I presume you have interpreted things correctly. Very well. Put him on."

McKie's screen flickered, revealed a wide view of a Gowachin room such as he'd never before seen. A far wall held spears and cutting weapons, streamers of colorful pennants, glistening rocks, ornate carvings in a shiny black substance. All this was backdrop for a semireclining chairdog occupied by an aged Gowachin who sat spraddle-legged being anointed by two younger Gowachin males. The attendants poured a thick, golden substance onto the aged Gowachin from green crystal flasks. The flasks were of a spiral design. The contents were gently massaged into the Gowachin's skin. The old Gowachin glistened with the stuff and when he blinked—no Phylum tattoos.

"As you can see," he said, "I'm being prepared for . . ."

He broke off, recognizing that he spoke to a non-Gowachin. Certainly, he'd known his. It was a slow reaction for a Dosadi.

"This is a mistake," he said.

"Indeed." McKie nodded pleasantly. "Your name?"

The old Gowachin scowled at this gaucherie, then chuckled.

"I am called Mrreg."

As McKie had suspected. And why would a Tandaloor Gowachin assume the name, no, the *title* of the mythical monster who'd imbued the frog people with a drive toward savage testing? The implications went far beyond this planet, colored Dosadi.

"You made the decision for the Dosadi experiment?"

"Someone had to make it."

That was not a substantive answer, and McKie decided to take it to issue. "You are not doing me any favors! I now know what it means to be a Legum of the Gowachin Bar and I intend to employ my powers to their limits."

It was as though McKie had worked some odd magic which froze the scene on his screen. The two attendants stopped pouring unguent, but did not look toward the pickup viewer which was recording their actions for McKie. As for Mrreg, he sat utterly still, his eyes fixed unblinking upon McKie.

McKie waited.

Presently, Mrreg turned to the attendant on his left.

"Please continue. There is little time."

McKie took this as though spoken to himself.

"You're my client. Why did you send a proxy?"

Mrreg continued to study McKie.

"I see what Ekris meant." Then, more briskly: "Well, McKie, I followed your career with interest. It now appears I did not follow you closely enough. Perhaps if we had not . . ."

He left the thought incomplete.

McKie picked up on this.

"It was inevitable that I escape from Dosadi."

"Perhaps."

The attendants finished their work, departed, taking the oddly shaped crystal flasks with them.

"Answer my question," McKie said.

"I am not required to answer your question."

"Then I withdraw from this case."

Mrreg hunched forward in sudden alarm. "You cannot! Aritch isn't . . ."

"I have no dealings with Aritch. My client is that Gowachin who made the Dosadi decision."

"You are engaging in strange behavior for a Legum. Yes, bring it." This last was addressed to someone offscreen. Another attendant appeared, carrying a white garment shaped somewhat like a long apron with sleeves. The attendant proceeded to put this onto Mrreg, who ignored him, concentrating on McKie.

"Do you have any idea what you're doing, McKie?"

"Preparing to act for my client."

"I see. Who told you about me?"

McKie shook his head.

"Did you really believe me unable to detect your presence or interpret the implications of what my own senses tell me?"

McKie saw that the Gowachin failed to see beneath the surface taunting. Mrreg turned to the attendant who was tying a green ribbon at the back of the apron. The old Gowachin had to lean forward for this. "A little tighter," he said.

The attendant retied the ribbon.

Addressing McKie, Mrreg said, "Please forgive the distraction. This must proceed at its own pace."

McKie absorbed this, assessed it Dosadi fashion. He could see the makings of an important Gowachin ritual here, but it was a new one to him. No matter. That could wait. He continued speaking, probing this Mrreg.

"When you found your own peculiar uses for Dosadi . . ."

"Peculiar? It's a universal motivation, McKie, that one tries to reduce the competition."

"Did you assess the price correctly, the price you might be asked to pay?"

"Oh, yes. I knew what I might have to pay."

There was a clear tone of resignation in the Gowachin's voice, a rare tone for his species. McKie hesitated. The attendant who'd brought the apron left the room, never once glancing in McKie's direction, although there had to be a screen to show whatever Mrreg saw of his caller.

"You wonder why I sent a proxy to hire the Legum?" Mrreg asked.

"Why Aritch?"

"Because he's a candidate for . . . greater responsibilities. You know, McKie, you astonish me. Undoubtedly you know what I could have done to you for this impertinence, yet that doesn't deter you."

This revealed more than Mrreg might have intended, but he remained unaware (or uncaring) of what McKie saw. For his part, McKie maintained a bland exterior, as blank as that of any Dosadi.

"I have a single purpose," McKie said. "Not even my client will sway me from it."

"The function of a Legum," Mrreg said.

The attendant of the white apron returned with an unsheathed blade. McKie glimpsed a jeweled handle and glittering sweep of cutting edge about twenty centimeters long. The blade curved back upon itself in a tight arc at the tip. The attendant, his back to McKie, stood facing Mrreg. The blade no longer visible.

Mrreg, his left side partly obscured from McKie by the attendant, leaned to the right and peered up at the screen through which he watched McKie.

"You've never been appraised of the ceremony we call Laupuk. It's very important and we've been remiss in leaving this out of your education. Laupuk was essential before such a . . . project as Dosadi could be set in motion. Try to understand this ritual. It will help you prepare your case."

"What is your Phylum?" McKie asked.

"That's no longer important but . . . very well. It was Great Awakening. I was High Magister for two decades before we made the Dosadi decision."

"How many Rim bodies have you used up?"

"My final one. That, too, is no longer important. Tell me, McKie when did you suspect Aritch was only a proxy?"

"When I realized that not all Gowachin were born Gowachin."

"But Aritch . . ."

"Ahh, yes: Aritch aspires to greater responsibilities."

"Yes . . . of course. I see. The Dosadi decision had to go far beyond a few phylums or a single species. There had to be a . . . I believe you Humans call it a 'High Command.' Yes, that would've become obvious to one as alert as you now appear. Your many marriages deceived us, I think. Was that deliberate?"

Secure behind his Dosadi mask, McKie decided to lie.

"Yes."

"Ahhhhhhhhh."

Mrreg seemed to shrivel into himself, but rallied.

"I see. We were made to believe you some kind of dilettante with perverted emotions. It'd be judged a flaw which we could exploit. Then there's another High Command and we never suspected."

It all came out swiftly, revealing the wheels within wheels which ruled Mrreg's view of the ConSentient universe. McKie marveled at how much more was said than the bare words. This one had been a long time away from Dosadi and had not been born there, but there were pressures on Mrreg now forcing him to the limits of what he'd learned on Dosadi.

McKie did not interrupt.

"We didn't expect you to penetrate Aritch's role, but that was not our intent, as you know. I presume . . ."

Whatever Mrreg presumed, he decided not to say it, musing aloud instead.

"One might almost believe you were born on Dosadi."

McKie remained silent, allowing fear in that conjecture to fill Mrreg's consciousness.

Presently, Mrreg asked, "Do you blame all Gowachin?"

Still, McKie remained silent.

Mrreg became agitated.

"We are a government of sorts, my High Command. People can be induced not to question a government."

McKie decided to press this nerve.

"Governments always commit their entire populations when the demands grow heavy enough. By their passive acceptance, these populations become accessories to whatever is done in their name."

"You've provided free use of jumpdoors for the Dosadi?"

McKie nodded. "The Calebans are aware of their obligation. Jedrik has been busy instructing her compatriots."

"You think to loose the Dosadi upon the ConSentiency and hunt down my High Command? Have a care, McKie. I warn you not to abandon your duties as a Legum, or to turn your back on Aritch."

McKie continued silent.

"Don't make that error, McKie. Aritch is your client. Through him you represent all Gowachin."

"A Legum requires a responsible client," McKie said. "Not a proxy, but a client whose acts are brought into question by the case being tried."

Mrreg revealed Gowachin signs of deep concern.

"Hear me, McKie. I haven't much time."

In a sudden rush of apprehension, McKie focused on the attendant with the blade who stood there partly obscuring the seated Gowachin. Mrreg spoke in a swift spill of words.

"By our standards, McKie, you are not yet very well educated in Gowachin necessities. That was our error. And now your . . . impetuosity has put you into a position which is about to become untenable."

The attendant shifted slightly, arms moving up. McKie glimpsed the blade tip at the attendant's right shoulder.

"Gowachin don't have families as do Humans or even Wreaves," Mrreg said. "We have graduated advancement into groups which hold more and more responsibility for those beneath them. This was the pattern adopted by our High Command. What you see as a Gowachin family is only a breeding group with its own limited rules. With each step up in responsibility goes a requirement that we pay an increasing price for failure. You ask if I know the price? Ahhh, McKie. The breeding male Gowachin makes sure that only the swiftest, most alert of his tads survive. A Magister upholds the forms of the Law. The High Command answers to a . . . Mrreg. You see? And a Mrreg must make only the best decisions. No failures. Thus . . . Laupuk."

As he spoke the final word, the blade in the attendant's hands flashed out and around in a shimmering arc. It caught the seated Gowachin at the neck. Mrreg's head, neatly severed, was caught in the loop at the blade's tip, lifted high, then lowered onto the white apron which now was splashed with green gore.

The scene blanked out, was replaced by the Gowachin who had connected McKie with Mrreg.

"Aritch wishes to consult his Legum," the Gowachin said.

In a changing universe, only a changing species can hope to be immortal and then *only if its eggs are nurtured in widely scattered environments. This predicts a wealth of unique individuals.*

—INSIGHTS (A GLIMPSE OF EARLY HUMAN PHILOSOPHY),
BUSAB TEXT

JEDRIK MADE made contact with McKie while he waited for the arrival of Aritch and Ceylang. He had been staring absently at the ceiling, evaluating in a profoundly Dosadi way how to gain personal advantage from the upcoming encounter, when he felt the touch of her mind on his.

McKie locked himself in his body.

"No transfer."

"Of course not."

It was a tiny thing, a subtle shading in the contact which could have been overlooked by anyone with a less accurate simulation model of Jedrik.

"You're angry with me," McKie said.

He projected irony, knew she'd read this correctly.

When she responded, her anger had been reduced to irritation. The point was not the shading of emotion, it was that she allowed such emotion to reveal itself.

"You remind me of one of my early lovers," she said.

McKie thought of where Jedrik was at this moment: safely rocked in the flower-perfumed air of his floating island on the planetary sea of Tutalsee. How strange such an environment must be for a Dosadi—no threats, fruit which could be picked and eaten without a thought of poisons. The memories she'd taken from him would coat the island with familiarity, but her flesh would continue to find that a strange experience. His memories—yes. The island would remind her of all those wives he'd taken to the honeymoon bowers of that place.

McKie spoke from this awareness.

"No doubt that early lover failed to show sufficient appreciation of your abilities, outside the bedroom, that is. Which one was it . . ."

And he named several accurate possibilities, lifting them from the memories he'd taken from Jedrik.

Now, she laughed. He sensed the untainted response, real humor and unchecked.

McKie was reminded in his turn of one of his early wives, and this made him think of the breeding situation from which Jedrik had come—no confusions between a choice for breeding mate and a lover taken for the available enjoyment of sex. One might even actively dislike the breeding mate.

Lovers . . . wives . . . What was the difference, except for the socially imprinted conventions out of which the roles arose? But Jedrik did remind him of that one particular woman, and he explored this memory, wondering if it might help him now in his relationship with Jedrik. He'd been in his midthirties and assigned to one of his first personal BuSab cases, sent out with no oldtimer to monitor and instruct him. The youngest Human agent in the Bureau's history ever to be released on his own, so it was rumored. The planet had been one of the Ylir group, very much unlike anything in McKie's previous experience: an ingrown place with deep entryways in all of the houses and an oppressive silence all around. No animals, no birds, no insects—just that awesome silence within which a fanatic religion was reported forming. All conversations were low voiced and full of subtle intonations which suggested an inner communication peculiar to Ylir and somehow making sport with all outsiders not privy to their private code. Very like Dosadi in this.

His wife of the moment, safely ensconced on Tutalsee, had been quite the opposite: gregarious, sportive, noisy.

Something about that Ylir case had sent McKie back to this wife with a sharpened awareness of her needs. The marriage had gone well for a long time, longer than any of the others. And he saw now why Jedrik reminded him of that one: they both protected themselves with a tough armor of femininity, but were extremely vulnerable behind that facade. When the armor collapsed, it collapsed totally. This realization puzzled McKie because he read his own reaction clearly: he was frightened.

In the eyeblink this evaluation took, Jedrik read him:

"We have not left Dosadi. We've taken it with us."

So that was why she'd made this contact, to be certain he mixed this datum into his evaluations. McKie looked out the open window. It would be dusk soon here on Tandaloor. The Gowachin home planet was a place which had defied change for thousands of standard years. In some respects, it was a backwater.

The ConSentiency will never be the same.

The tiny trickle of Dosadi which Aritch's people had hoped to cut off was now a roaring cataract. The people of Dosadi would insinuate themselves into niche after niche of ConSentient civilization. What could resist even the lowliest Dosadi? Laws would change. Relationships would assume profound and subtle differences. Everything from the most casual friendship to the most complex business relationship would take on some Dosadi character.

McKie recalled Aritch's parting question as Aritch had sent McKie to the jumpdoor which would put him on Dosadi.

"Ask yourself if there might be a price too high to pay for the Dosadi lesson."

That had been McKie's first clue to Aritch's actual motives and the word *lesson* had bothered him, but he'd missed the implications. With some embarrassment, McKie recalled his glib answer to Aritch's question:

"It depends on the lesson."

True, but how blind he'd been to things any Dosadi would have seen. How ignorant. Now, he indicated to Jedrik that he understood why she'd called such things to his attention.

"Aritch didn't look much beyond the uses of outrage and injustice . . . ."

"And how to turn such things to personal advantage."

She was right, of course. McKie stared out at the gathering dusk. Yes, the species tried to make everything its own. If the species failed, then forces beyond it moved in, and so on, *ad infinitum.*

I do what I do.

He recalled those words of the sleeping monster with a shudder, felt Jedrik recoil. But she was proof even against this.

"What powers your ConSentiency had."

Past tense, right. And not *our* ConSentiency because that already was a thing of the past. Besides . . . she was Dosadi.

"And the illusions of power," she said.

He saw at last what she was emphasizing, and her own shared memories in his mind made the lesson doubly impressive. She'd known precisely what McKie's personal ego-focus might overlook. Yet, this was one of the glues which held the ConSentiency together.

"Who can imagine himself immune from any retaliation?" he quoted.

It was right out of the BuSab Manual.

Jedrik made no response.

McKie needed no more emphasis from her now. The lesson of history was clear. Violence bred violence. If this violence got out of hand, it ran a course depressing in its repetitive pattern. More often than not, that course was deadly to the innocent, the so-called "enlistment phase." The ex-innocents ignited more violence and more violence until either reason prevailed or all were destroyed. There were a sufficient number of cinder blocks which once had been planets to make the lesson clear. Dosadi had come within a hair of joining that uninhabited, uninhabitable list.

Before breaking contact, Jedrik had another point to make.

"You recall that in those final days, Broey increased the rations for his Human auxiliaries, his way of saying to them: 'You'll be turned out onto the Rim soon to fend for yourselves.'"

"A *Dosadi* way of saying that."

"Correct. We always held that thought in reserve: that we should breed in such numbers that some would survive no matter what happened. We would thus begin producing species which could survive there without the city of Chu . . . or any other city designed solely to produce nonpoisonous foods."

"But there's always a bigger force waiting in the wings."

"Make sure Aritch understands that."

> *Choose containable violence when violence cannot be avoided.*
> *Better this than epidemic violence.*
>
> —LESSONS OF CHOICE, THE BUSAB MANUAL

THE SENIOR attendant of the Courtarena, a squat and dignified Gowachin of the Assumptive Phylum, confronted McKie at the arena door with a confession:

"I have delayed informing you that some of your witnesses have been excluded by Prosecution challenge."

The attendant, whose name was Darak, gave a Gowachin shrug, waited.

McKie glanced beyond the attendant at the truncated oval of the arena entrance which framed a lower section of the audience seats. The seats were filled. He had expected some such challenge for this first morning session of the trial, saw Darak's words as a vital revelation. They were accepting his gambit. Darak had signaled a risky line of attack by those who guided Ceylang's performance. They expected McKie to protest. He glanced back at Aritch, who stood quietly submissive three steps behind his Legum. Aritch gave every appearance of having resigned himself to the arena's conditions.

"The forms must be obeyed."

Beneath that appearance lay the hoary traditions of Gowachin Law—*The guilty are innocent. Governments always do evil. Legalists put their own interests first. Defense and prosecution are brother and sister. Suspect everything.*

Aritch's Legum controlled the initial posture and McKie had chosen defense. It hadn't surprised him to be told that Ceylang would prosecute. McKie had countered by insisting that Broey sit on a judicial panel which would be limited to three members. This had caused a delay during which Bildoon had called McKie, probing for any betrayal. Bildoon's approach had been so obvious that McKie had at first suspected a feint within a feint.

"McKie, the Gowachin fear that you have a Caleban at your command. That's a force which they . . ."

"The more they fear the better."

McKie had stared back at the screen-framed face of Bildoon, observing the signs of strain. Jedrik was right: the non-Dosadi were very easy to read.

"But I'm told you left this Dosadi in spite of a Caleban contract which prohibited . . ."

"Let them worry. Good for them."

McKie watched Bildoon intently without betraying a single emotion. No doubt there were others monitoring this exchange. Let them begin to see what they faced. Puppet Bildoon was not about to uncover what those shadowy forces wanted. They had Bildoon here on Tandaloor, though, and this told McKie an essential fact. The PanSpechi chief of BuSab was being offered as bait. This was precisely the response McKie sought.

Bildoon had ended the call without achieving his purpose. McKie had nibbled only enough to insure that Bildoon would be offered again as bait. And the puppet masters still feared that McKie had a Caleban at his beck and call.

No doubt the puppet masters had tried to question their God Wall Caleban. McKie hid a smile, thinking how that conversation must have gone. The Caleban had only to quote the letter of the contract, and if the questioners became accusatory the Caleban would respond with anger, ending the exchange. And the Caleban's words would be so filled with terms subject to ambiguous translation that the puppet masters would never be certain of what they heard.

As he stared at the patiently waiting Darak, McKie saw that they had a problem, those shadowy figures behind Artich. Laupuk had removed Mrreg from their councils and his advice would have been valuable now. McKie had deduced that the correct reference was "The Mrreg" and that Aritch headed the list of possible successors. Aritch might be Dosadi-trained but he was not Dosadi-born. There was a lesson in this that the entire ConSentiency would soon learn.

And Broey as a judge in this case remained an unchangeable fact. Broey was Dosadi-born. The Caleban contract had kept Broey on his poison planet, but it had not limited him to a Gowachin body. Broey knew what it was to be both Human and Gowachin. Broey knew about the Pcharkys and their use by those who'd held Dosadi in bondage. And Broey was now Gowachin. The forces opposing McKie dared not name another Gowachin judge. They must choose from the other species. They had an interesting quandary. And without a Caleban assistant, there were no more Pcharkys to be had on Dosadi. The most valuable *coin* the puppet masters had to offer was lost to them. They'd be desperate. Some of the older ones would be very desperate.

Footsteps sounded around the turn of the corridor behind Aritch. McKie glanced back, saw Ceylang come into view with her attendants. McKie counted no less than twenty leading Legums around her. They were out in force. Not only Gowachin pride and integrity, but their sacred view of Law stood at issue. And the desperate ones stood behind them, goading. McKie could almost see those shadowy figures in the shape of this entourage.

Ceylang, he saw, wore the black robes and white-striped hood of Legum Prosecutor, but she'd thrown back the hood to free her mandibles. McKie detected tension in her movements. She gave no sign of recognition, but McKie saw her through Dosadi eyes.

I frighten her. And she's right.

Turning to address the waiting attendant and speaking loudly to make sure that the approaching group hear, McKie said:

"Every law must be tested. I accept that you have given me formal announcement of a limit on my defense."

Darak, expecting outraged protest and a demand for a list of the excluded witnesses, showed obvious confusion.

"Formal announcement?"

Ceylang and entourage came to a stop behind Aritch.

McKie went on in the same loud voice:

"We stand here within the sphere of the Courtarena. All matters concerning a dispute in the arena are formal in this place."

The attendant glanced at Ceylang, seeking help. This response threatened him. Darak, hoping someday to be a High Magister, should now be recognizing his inadequacies. He would never make it in the politics of the Gowachin Phyla, especially not in the coming Dosadi age.

McKie explained as though to a neophyte:

"Information to be verified by my witnesses is known to me in its entirety. I will present the evidence myself."

Ceylang, having stooped to hear a low-voiced comment from one of her Gowachin advisors, showed surprise at this. She raised one of her ropey tendrils, called, "I protest. The Defense Legum cannot give . . ."

"How can you protest?" McKie interrupted. "We stand here before no judicial panel empowered to rule on any protest."

"I make *formal* protest!" Ceylang insisted, ignoring an advisor on her right who was tugging at her sleeve.

McKie permitted himself a cold smile.

"Very well. Then we must call Darak into the arena as witness, he being the only party present who is outside our dispute."

The edges of Aritch's jaws came down in a Gowachin grimace.

"At the end, I warned them not to go with the Wreave," he said. "They cannot say they came here unwarned."

Too late, Ceylang saw what had happened. McKie would be able to question Darak on the challenges to the witnesses. Some of those challenges were certain to be overturned. At the very least, McKie would know who the Prosecution feared. He would know it in time to act upon it. There would be no delays valuable to Prosecution. Tension, fear, and pride had made Ceylang act precipitately. Aritch had been right to warn them, but they counted on McKie's fear of the interlocked Wreave triads. Let them count. Let them blunt their awareness on that and on a useless concern over the excluded witnesses.

McKie motioned Darak through the doorway into the arena, heard him utter an oath. The reason became apparent as McKie pressed through in the crowded surge of the Prosecutor's party. The instruments of Truth-by-Pain had been arrayed on their ancient rack below the judges. Seldom brought out of their wrappings even for display to visiting dignitaries these days, the instruments had not been employed in the arena within the memory of a living witness. McKie had expected this display. It was obvious that Darak and Ceylang had not. It was interesting to note the members of Ceylang's entourage who were watching for McKie's response.

He gave them a grin of satisfaction.

McKie turned his attention to the judicial panel. They had given him Broey. The ConSentiency, acting through BuSab, held the right of one appointment. Their choice delighted McKie. Bait, indeed! Bildoon occupied the seat on Broey's right. The PanSpechi chief of bureau sat there all bland and reserved in his unfamiliar Gowachin robes of water green. Bildoon's faceted eyes glittered in the harsh arena lighting. The third judge had to be the Gowachin choice and undoubtedly maneuvered (as Bildoon had been) by the puppet masters. It was a Human and McKie, recognizing him, missed a step, recovered his balance with a visible effort.

What were they doing?

The third judge was named Mordes Parando, a noted challenger of BuSab actions. He wanted BuSab eliminated—either outright or by removing some of the bureau's key powers. He came from the planet Lirat, which provided McKie with no surprises. Lirat was a natural cover for the shadowy forces. It was a place of enormous wealth and great private estates guarded by their own security forces. Parando was a man of somewhat superficial manners which might conceal a genuine sophisticate, knowledgeable and erudite, or a completely ruthless autocrat of Broey's stamp. He was certainly Dosadi-trained. And his features bore the look of the Dosadi Rim.

There was one more fact about Parando which no one outside Lirat was supposed to know. McKie had come upon it quite by chance while investigating a Palenki who'd been an estate guard on Lirat. The turtlelike Palenki were notoriously dull, employed chiefly as muscle. This one had been uncommonly observant.

"Parando makes advice on Gowachin Law."

This had been responsive to a question about Parando's relationship with the estate guard being investigated. McKie, not seeing a connection between question and answer, had not pursued the matter, but had tucked this datum away for future investigation. He had been mildly interested at the time because of the rumored existence of a legalist enclave on Lirat and such enclaves had been known to test the limits of legality.

The people behind Aritch would expect McKie to recognize Parando. Would they expect Parando to be recognized as a legalist? They were certain to know the danger of putting Parando on a Gowachin bench. Professional legalists were absolutely prohibited from Gowachin judicial service.

"Let the people judge."

Why would they need a legalist here? Or were they expecting McKie to recognize the Rim origins of Parando's body? Were they warning McKie not to raise *that* issue here? Body exchange and the implications of immortality represented a box of snakes no one wanted to open. And the possibility of one species spying on another . . . There was fragmentation of the ConSentiency latent in this case. More ways than one.

If I challenge Parando, his replacement may be more dangerous. If I expose him as a legalist after the trial starts . . . Could they expect me to do that? Let us explore it.

Knowing he was watched by countless eyes, McKie swept his gaze around the arena. Above the soft green absorbent oval where he stood were rank on rank of benches, every seat occupied. Muted morning light from the domed translucent ceiling illuminated rows of Humans, Gowachin, Palenki, Sobarips . . . McKie identified a cluster of ferret Wreaves just above the arena, limber thin with a sinuous flexing in every movement. They would bear watching. But every species and faction in the ConSentiency would be represented here. Those who could not come in person would watch these proceedings via the glittering transmitter eyes which looked down from the ceiling's edges.

Now, McKie looked to the right at the witness pen set into the wall beneath the ranked benches. He identified every witness he'd called, even the challenged ones. The forms were being obeyed. While the ConSentient Covenant required certain modifications here, this arena was still dominated by Gowachin Law. To accent that, the blue metal box from the Running Phylum occupied the honor place on the bench in front of the judicial panel.

Who will taste the knife here?

Protocol demanded that Prosecutor and Defense approach to a point beneath the judges, abase themselves, and call out acceptance of the arena's conditions. The Prosecutor's party, however, was in disarray. Two of Ceylang's advisors were whispering excited advice to her.

The members of the Judicial panel conferred, glancing at the scene below them. They could not act formally until the obeisance.

McKie passed a glance across the panel, absorbed Broey's posture. The Dosadi Gowachin's enlightened greed was like an anchor point. It was like Gowachin Law, changeable only on the surface. And Broey was but the tip of the Dosadi advisory group which Jedrik had approved.

Holding his arms extended to the sides, McKie marched forward, abased himself face down on the floor, stood and called out.

"I accept this arena as my friend. The conditions here are my conditions but Prosecution has defiled the sacred traditions of this place. Does the court give me leave to slay her outright?"

There was an exclamation behind him, the sound of running, the sudden flopping of a body onto the arena's matted floor. Ceylang could not address the court before this obeisance and she knew it. She and the others now also knew something else just as important—that McKie was ready to slay her despite the threat of Wreave vendetta.

In a breathless voice, Ceylang called out her acceptance of the arena's conditions, then:

"I protest this trick by Defense Legum!"

McKie saw the stirring of Gowachin in the audience. A trick? Didn't Ceylang know yet how the Gowachin dearly loved legal tricks?

The members of the judicial panel had been thoroughly briefed on the surface demands of the Gowachin forms, though it was doubtful that Bildoon understood sufficiently what went on beneath those forms. The PanSpechi confirmed this now by leaning forward to speak.

"Why does the senior attendant of this court enter ahead of the Legums?"

McKie detected a fleeting smile on Broey's face, glanced back to see Darak standing apart from the prosecution throng, alone and trembling.

McKie took one step forward.

"Will the court direct Darak to the witness pen? He is here because of a formal demand by the Prosecutor."

"This is the senior attendant of your court," Ceylang argued. "He guards the door to . . ."

"Prosecution made formal protest to a matter which occurred in the presence of this attendant," McKie said. "As an attendant, Darak stands outside the conflicting interests. He is the only reliable witness."

Broey stirred, looked at Ceylang, and McKie realized how strange the Wreave must appear to a Dosadi. This did not deter Broey, however.

"Did you protest?"

It was a direct question from the bench. Ceylang was required to answer. She looked to Bildoon for help but he remained silent. Parando also refused to help her. She glanced at Darak. The terrified attendant could not take his attention from the instruments of pain. Perhaps he knew something specific about their presence in the arena.

Ceylang tried to explain.

"When Defense Legum suggested an illegal . . ."

"Did you protest?"

"But the . . ."

"This court decides on all matters of legality. Did you protest?"

"I did."

It was forced out of her. A fit of trembling passed over the slender Wreave form.

Broey waved Darak to the witness pen, had to add a vocal order when the frightened attendant failed to understand. Darak almost ran to the shelter of the pen.

Silence pervaded the arena. The silence of the audience was an explosive thing. They sat poised in the watching ovals, all of those species and factions with their special fears. By now, they'd heard many stories and rumors. Jumpdoors had spread the Dosadi emigres all across the ConSentiency. Media representatives had been excluded from Dosadi and this court on the Gowachin argument that they were "prey to uninformed subjective reactions," but they would be watching here through the transmitter eyes at the ceiling.

McKie looked at nothing in particular but taking in every detail. There were more than three judges in this arena and Ceylang certainly must realize that. Gowachin Law turned upon itself, existing "only to be changed." But that watching multitude was quite another matter. Ceylang must be made to understand that she was a sacrifice of the arena. ConSentient opinion stood over her like a heavy sledge ready to smash down.

It was Parando's turn.

"Will opposing Legums make their opening arguments now?"

"We can't process while a formal protest is undecided," McKie said.

Parando understood. He glanced at the audience, at the ceiling. His actions were a direct signal: Parando knew which *judges* really decided here. To emphasize it, he ran a hand from the front of his neck down his chest, the unique Rim Raider's salute from Dosadi signifying "Death before surrender." Subtle hints in the movement gave McKie another datum: Parando was a Gowachin in a Human body. They'd dared put two Gowachin on that panel!

With Dosadi insight, McKie saw why they did this. They were prepared to produce the Caleban contract here. They were telling McKie that *they* would expose the body-exchange secret if he forced them to it. All would see that loophole in the Caleban contract which confined the Dosadi-born, but released outsiders in Dosadi flesh.

They think I'm really Jedrik in this flesh!

Parando revealed even more. His people intended to find the Jedrik body and kill it, leaving this *McKie* flesh forever in doubt. He could protest his McKie identity all he wanted. They had but to demand that he prove it. Without the other person . . . What had their God Wall Caleban told them?

"He is McKie, she is McKie. He is Jedrik, she is Jedrik."

His mind in turmoil, McKie wondered if he dared risk an immediate mind contact with Jedrik. Together, they'd already recognized this danger. Jedrik had hidden herself on McKie's hideaway, a floating island on Tutalsee. She was there with a special Taprisiot contract prohibiting unwanted calls which might inadvertently reveal her location.

The judges, led by Parando, were acting, however, moving for an immediate examination of Darak. McKie forced himself to perform as a Legum.

His career in ruins, the attendant answered like an automaton. In the end, McKie restored most of his witnesses. There were two notable exceptions: Grinik (that flawed thread which might have led to The Mrreg) and Stiggy. McKie was not certain why they wanted to exclude the Dosadi weapons genius who'd transformed a BuSab wallet's contents into instruments of victory. Was it that Stiggy had broken an *unbreakable* code? That made sense only if Prosecution intended to play down the inherent Dosadi superiority.

Still uncertain, McKie prepared to retire and seek a way to avoid Parando's gambit, but Ceylang addressed the bench.

"The issue of witnesses having been introduced by Defense," she said, "Prosecution wishes to explore this issue. We note many witnesses from Dosadi called by Defense. There is a noteworthy omission whose name has not yet been introduced here. I refer to a Human by the name of Jedrik. Prosecution wishes to call Keila Jedrik as . . ."

"One moment!"

McKie searched his mind for the forms of an acceptable escape. He knew that his blurted protest had revealed more than he wanted. But they were moving faster than he'd expected. Prosecution did not really want Jedrik as a witness, not in a Gowachin Courtarena where the roles were never quite what they appeared to non-Gowachin. This was a plain message to McKie.

"We're going to find her and kill her."

With Bildoon and Parando concurring, a jumpdoor was summoned and Ceylang played her trump.

"Defense knows the whereabouts of witness Keila Jedrik."

They were forcing the question, aware of the emotional bond between McKie and Jedrik. He had a choice: argue that a personal relationship with the witness excluded her. But Prosecution and all the judges had to concur. They obviously would not do this—not yet. A harsh lock on his emotions, McKie gave the jumpdoor instructions.

Presently, Jedrik stepped onto the arena floor, faced the judges. She'd been into the wardrobe at his bower cottage and wore a yellow and orange sarong which emphasized her height and grace. Open brown sandals protected her feet. There was a flame red blossom at her left ear. She managed to look exotic and fragile.

Broey spoke for the judges.

"Do you have knowledge of the issues at trial here?"

"What issues are at trial?"

She asked it with a childlike innocence which did not even fool Bildoon. They were forced to explain, however, because of those other *judges* to whom every nuance here was vital. She heard them out in silence.

"An alleged experiment on a sentient population confined to a planet called Dosadi . . . lack of informed consent by subject population charged . . . accusations of conspiracy against certain Gowachin and others not yet named . . ."

Two fingers pressed to his eyes in the guise of intense listening, McKie made contact with Jedrik, suggesting, conferring. They had to find a way out of this trap! When he looked up, he saw the suspicions in Parando's face: *Which body, which ego? McKie? Jedrik?*

In the end, Ceylang hammered home the private message, demanding whether Jedrik had "any personal relationship with Defense Legum?"

Jedrik answered in a decidedly un-Dosadi fashion.

"Why . . . yes. We are lovers."

In itself, this was not enough to exclude her from the arena unless Prosecution and the entire judicial panel agreed. Ceylang proposed the exclusion. Bildoon and Parando were predictable in their agreement. McKie waited for Broey.

"Agreed."

Broey had a private compact with the shadow forces then. Jedrik and McKie had expected this, but had not anticipated the form the confirmation would take.

McKie asked for a recess until the following morning.

With the most benign face on it, this was granted. Broey announced the decision, smiling down at Jedrik. It was a measure of McKie's Dosadi conditioning that he could not find it in himself to blame Broey for wanting personal victory over the person who had beaten him on Dosadi.

Back in his quarters, Jedrik put a hand on McKie's chest, spoke with eyes lowered.

"Don't blame yourself, McKie. This was inevitable. Those judges, none of them, would've allowed any protest from you before seeing me in person on that arena floor."

"I know."

She looked up at him, smiling."

"Yes . . . of course. How like one person we are."

For a time after that, they reviewed the assessment of the aides chosen for Broey. Shared memories etched away at minutiae. Could any choice be improved? Not one person was changed—Human or Gowachin. All of those advisors and aides were Dosadi-born. They could be depended upon to be loyal to their origins, to their conditioning, to themselves individually. For the task assigned to them, they were the best available.

McKie brought it to a close.

"I can't leave the immediate area of the arena until the trial's over."

She knew that, but it needed saying.

There was a small cell adjoining his office, a bedog there, communications instruments, Human toilet facilities. They delayed going into the bedroom, turned to a low-key argument over the advisability of a body exchange. It was procrastination on both sides, outcome known in advance. Familiar flesh was familiar flesh, less distracting. It gave each of them an edge which they dared not sacrifice. McKie could play Jedrik and Jedrik could play McKie, but that would be dangerous play now.

When they retired, it was to make love, the most tender experience either had known. There was no submission, only a giving, sharing, an open exchange which tightened McKie's throat with joy and fear, sent Jedrik into a fit of un-Dosadi sobbing.

When she'd recovered, she turned to him on the bed, touched his right cheek with a finger.

"McKie."

"Yes?"

"I've never had to say this to another person, but . . ." She silenced his attempted interruption by punching his shoulder, leaning up on an elbow to look down at him. It reminded McKie of their first night together, and he saw that she had gone back into her Dosadi shell . . . but there was something else, a difference in the eyes.

"What is it?"

"Just that I love you. It's a very interesting feeling, especially when you admit it openly. How odd."

"Stay here with me."

"We both know I can't. There's no safe place here for either of us, but the one who . . ."

"Then let's . . ."

"We've already decided against an exchange."

"Where will you go?"

"Best you don't know."

"If . . ."

"No! I wouldn't be safe as a witness; I'm not even safe at your side. We both . . ."

Don't go back to Dosadi."

"Where is Dosadi? It's the only place where I could ever feel at home, but Dosadi no longer exists."

"I meant . . ."

"I know."

She sat up, hugged her knees, revealing the sinewy muscles of her shoulders and back. McKie studied her, trying to fathom what it was she hid in that Dosadi shell. Despite the intimacy of their shared memories, something about her eluded him. It was as though he didn't want to learn this thing. She would flee and hide, of course, but . . . He listened carefully as she began to speak in a faraway voice.

"It'd be interesting to go back to Dosadi someday. The differences . . ."

She looked over her shoulder at him.

"There are those who fear we'll make over the ConSentiency in Dosadi's image. We'll try, but the result won't be Dosadi. We'll take what we judge to be valuable, but that'll change Dosadi more than it changes you. Your masses are less alert, slower, less resourceful, but you're so numerous. In the end, the ConSentiency will win, but it'll no longer be the ConSentiency. I wonder what it'll be when . . ."

She laughed at her own musings, shook her head.

"And there's Broey. They'll have to deal with Broey and the team we've given him. Broey Plus! Your ConSentiency hasn't the faintest grasp of what we've loosed among them.

"The predator in the flock."

"To Broey, your people are like the Rim—a natural resource."

"But he has no Pcharkys."

"Not yet."

"I doubt if the Calebans ever again will participate in . . ."

"There may be other ways. Look how easy it is for us."

"But we were printed upon each other by . . ."

"Exactly! And they continue to suspect that you're in my body and I'm in yours. Their entire experience precludes the free shift back and forth, one body to another . . ."

"Or this other thing . . ."

He caressed her mind.

"Yes! Broey won't suspect until too late what's in store for him. They'll be a long time learning there's no way to sort you from . . . me!"

This last was an exultant shout as she turned and fell upon him. It was a wild replay of their first night together. McKie abandoned himself to it. There was no other choice, no time for the mind to dwell on depressing thoughts.

In the morning, he had to tap his implanted amplifiers to bring his awareness to the required pitch for the arena. The process took a few minutes while he dressed.

Jedrik moved softly with her own preparations, straightened the bedog and caressed its resilient surface. She summoned a jumpdoor then, held him with a lingering kiss. The jumpdoor opened behind her as she pushed away from him.

McKie smelled familiar flowers, glimpsed the bowers of his Tutalsee island before the door blinked out of existence, hiding Jedrik and the island from him. Tutalsee? The moment of shocked understanding delayed him. She'd counted on that! He recovered, sent his mind leaping after her.

I'll force an exchange! By the Gods . . .

His mind met pain, consuming, blinding pain. It was agony such as he'd not even imagined could exist.

Jedrik!

His mind held an unconscious Jedrik whose awareness had fled from pain. The contact was so delicate, like holding a newborn infant. The slightest relaxation and he knew he would lose her to . . . He felt that terrifying monster of the first exchange hovering in the background, but love and concern armed him against fear.

Frantic, McKie held that tenuous contact while he called a jumpdoor. There was a small delay and when the door opened, he saw through the portal the black, twisted wreckage which had been his bower island. A hot sun beat down on steaming cinders. And in the background, a warped metal object which might have been one of Tutalsee's little four-place flitters rolled over, gurgled, and sank. The visible wreckage said the destructive force had been something like a pentrate, swift and all-consuming. The water around the island still bubbled with it. Even while he watched, the island began breaking up, its cinders drifting apart on the long, low waves. A breeze flattened the steaming smoke. Soon, there'd be nothing to show that beauty had floated here. With a pentrate, there would be nothing to recover . . . not even bodies to . . .

He hesitated, still holding his fragile grasp on Jedrik's unconscious presence. The pain was only a memory now. Was it really Jedrik in his awareness, or only his remembered imprint of her? He tried to awaken the sleeping presence, failed. But small threads of memory emerged, and he saw that the destruction had been Jedrik's doing, response to attack. The attackers had wanted a live hostage. They hadn't anticipated that violent, unmistakable message.

"You won't hold *me* over McKie's head!"

But if there were no bodies . . .

Again, he tried to awaken that unconscious presence. Her memories were there, but she remained dormant. The effort strengthened his grip upon her presence, though. And he told himself it had to be Jedrik, or he wouldn't know what had happened on the bower island.

Once more, he searched the empty water. Nothing. A pentrate would've torn and battered everything around it. Shards of metal, flesh reduced to scattered cinders . . .

She's dead. She has to be dead. A pentrate . . .

But that familiar presence lay slumbering in his mind.

The door clacker interrupted his reverie. McKie released the jumpdoor, turned to look through the bedside viewer at the scene outside his Legum quarters. The expected deputation had arrived. Confident, the puppet masters were moving even before confirmation of their Tutalsee gambit. They could not possibly know yet what McKie knew. There could be no jumpdoor or any other thread permitted to connect this group to Tutalsee.

McKie studied them carefully, keeping a bridle on his rage. There were eight of them, so contained, so well schooled in Dosadi self-control. So transparent to a

Jedrik-amplified McKie. They were four Humans and four Gowachin. Overconfident. Jedrik had seen to that by leaving no survivors.

Again, McKie tried to awaken that unconscious presence. She would not respond.

Have I only built her out of my memories?

There was no time for such speculation. Jedrik had made her choice on Tutalsee. He had other choices to make here and now—for both of them. That ghostly presence locked in his mind would have to wait.

McKie punched the communicator which linked him to Broey, gave the agreed-upon signal.

"It's time."

He composed himself then, went to the door.

They'd sent no underlings. He gave them that. But they addressed him as Jedrik, made the anticipated demands, gloated over the hold they had upon him. It was only then that McKie saw fully how well Jedrik had measured these people; and how she had played upon her McKie in those last hours together like an exquisitely tuned instrument. Now, he understood why she'd made that violent choice.

As anticipated, the members of the delegation were extremely surprised when Broey's people fell upon them without warning.

For the Gowachin, to stand alone against all adversity is the most sacred moment of existence.

—THE GOWACHIN, A BUSAB ANALYSIS

THE EIGHT prisoners were dumped on the arena floor, bound and shackled. McKie stopped near them, waiting for Ceylang to arrive. It was not yet dawn. The ceiling above the arena remained dark. A few of the transmitter eyes around the upper perimeter glittered to reveal that they were activated. More were coming alive by the moment. Only a few of the witness seats were occupied, but people were streaming in as word was passed. The judicial bench remained empty.

The outer areaway was a din of Courtarena security forces coming and going, people shouting orders, the clank of weapons, a sense of complete confusion there which gradually resolved itself as Broey led his fellow judges up onto their bench. The witness pen was also filling, people punching sleep from their eyes, great gaping yawns from the Gowachin.

McKie looked to Broey's people, the ones who'd brought in the prisoners. He nodded for the captors to leave, giving them a Dosadi hand signal to remain available. They left.

Ceylang passed them as she entered, still fastening her robe. She hurried to McKie's side, waited for the judges to be seated before speaking.

"What is the meaning of this? My attendants . . ."

Broey signaled McKie.

McKie stepped forward to address the bench, pointed to the eight bound figures who were beginning to stir and push themselves upright.

"Here you see my client."

Parando started to speak, but Broey silenced him with a sharp word which McKie did not catch. It sounded like "frenzy."

Bildoon sat in fearful fascination, unable to wrest his attention from the bound figures, all of whom remained silent. Yes, Bildoon would recognize those eight prisoners. In his limited, ConSentient fashion, Bildoon was sharp enough to recognize that he was in personal danger. Parando, of course, knew this immediately and watched Broey with great care.

Again, Broey nodded to McKie.

"A fraud has been perpetrated upon this court," McKie said. "It is a fraud which was perpetrated against those great and gallant people, the Gowachin. Both Prosecution and Defense are its victims. The Law is its ultimate victim."

It had grown much quieter in the arena. The observer seats were jammed, all the transmitter eyes alive. The faintest of dawn glow touched the translucent ceiling. McKie wondered what time it was. He had forgotten to put on any timepiece.

There was a stir behind McKie. He glanced back, saw attendants belatedly bringing Aritch into the arena. Oh, yes—they would have risked any delay to confer with Aritch. Aritch was supposed to be the other McKie expert. Too bad that this Human who looked like McKie was no longer the McKie they thought they knew.

Ceylang could not hold her silence. She raised a tendril for attention.

"This Tribunal . . ."

McKie interrupted.

". . . is composed of three people. Only three."

He allowed them a moment to digest this reminder that Gowachin trial formalities still dominated this arena, and were like no other such formalities in the ConSentiency. It could've been fifty judges up there on that bench. McKie had witnessed Gowachin trials where people were picked at random off the streets to sit in judgment. Such jurists took their duties seriously, but their overt behavior could lead another sentient species to question this. The Gowachin chattered back and forth, arranged parties, exchanged jokes, asked each other rude questions. It was an ancient pattern. The jurists were required to become "a single organism." Gowachin had their own ways of rushing that process.

But this Tribunal was composed of just three judges, only one of them visibly Gowachin. They were separate entities, their actions heavy with mannerisms foreign to the Gowachin. Even Broey, tainted by Dosadi, would be unfamiliar to the Gowachin observers. No "single organism" here holding to the immutable forms beneath Gowachin Law. That had to be deeply disturbing to the Legums who advised Ceylang.

Broey leaned forward, addressed the arena.

"We'll dispense with the usual arguments while this new development is explored."

Again, Parando tried to interrupt. Broey silenced him with a glance.

"I call Aritch of the Running Phylum," McKie said.

He turned.

Ceylang stood in mute indecision. Her advisors remained at the back of the arena conferring among themselves. There seemed to be a difference of opinion among them.

Aritch shuffled to the death-focus of the arena, the place where every witness was required to stand. He glanced at the instruments of pain arrayed beneath the judicial bench, cast a wary look at McKie. The old High Magister appeared harried and undignified. That hurried conference to explore this development must've been a sore trial to the old Gowachin.

McKie crossed to the formal position beside Aritch, addressed the judges.

"Here we have Aritch, High Magister of the Running Phylum. We were told that if guilt were to be found in this arena, Aritch bore that guilt. He, so we were led to believe, was the one who made the decision to imprison Dosadi. But how can that be so? Aritch is old, but he isn't as old as Dosadi. Then perhaps his alleged guilt is to be found in concealing the imprisonment of Dosadi. But Aritch summoned an agent of BuSab and sent that agent openly to Dosadi."

A disturbance among the eight shackled prisoners interrupted McKie. Several of the prisoners were trying to get to their feet, but the links of the shackles were too short.

On the judicial bench, Parando started to lean forward, but Broey hauled him back.

Yes, Parando and others were recalling the verities of a Gowachin Courtarena, the constant reversals of concepts common throughout the rest of the ConSentiency.

To be guilty is to be innocent. Thus, to be innocent is to be guilty.

At a sharp command from Broey, the prisoners grew quiet.

McKie continued.

"Aritch, conscious of the sacred responsibilities which he carried upon his back as a mother carries her tads was deliberately named to receive the punishment blow lest that punishment be directed at all Gowachin everywhere. Who chose this innocent High Magister to suffer for all Gowachin?"

McKie pointed to the eight shackled prisoners.

"Who are these people?" Parando demanded.

McKie allowed the question to hang there for a long count. Parando knew who these eight were. Did he think he could divert the present course of events by such a blatant ploy?

Presently, McKie spoke.

"I will enlighten the court in due course. My duty, however, comes first. My client's *innocence* comes first."

"One moment."

Borey held up a webbed hand.

One of Ceylang's advisors hurried past McKie, asked and received permission to confer with Ceylang. A thwarted Parando sat like a condemned man watching this conversation as though he hoped to find reprieve there. Bildoon had hunched forward, head buried in his arms. Broey obviously controlled the Tribunal.

The advisor Legum was known to McKie, one Lagag of a middling reputation, an officer out of breeding. His words to Ceylang were low and intense, demanding.

The conference ended, Lagag hurried back to his companions. They now understood the tenor of McKie's *defense*. Aritch must have known all along that he could be sacrificed here. The ConSentient Covenant no longer permitted the ancient custom where the Gowachin audience had poured into the arena to kill with bare hands and claws the *innocent* defendant. But let Aritch walk from here with the brand of innocence upon him; he would not take ten paces outside the arena's precincts before being torn to pieces.

There'd been worried admiration in the glance Lagag had given McKie in passing. Yes . . . now they understood why McKie had maneuvered for a small and vulnerable judicial panel.

The eight prisoners began a new disturbance which Broey silenced with a shout. He signaled for McKie to continue.

"Aritch's design was that I expose Dosadi, return and defend him against the charge that he had permitted illegal psychological experiments upon an unsuspecting populace. He was prepared to sacrifice himself for others."

McKie sent a wry glance at Aritch. Let the High Magister try to fight in half-truths in that defense!

"Unfortunately, the Dosadi populace was *not* unsuspecting. In fact, forces under the command of Keila Jedrik had moved to take control of Dosadi. Judge Broey will affirm that she had succeeded in this."

Again, McKie pointed to the shackled prisoners.

"But these conspirators, these people who designed and profited from the Dosadi Experiment, ordered the death of Keila Jedrik! She was murdered this morning on Tutalsee to prevent my using her at the proper moment to prove Aritch's *innocence*. Judge Broey is witness to the truth of what I say. Keila Jedrik was brought into this arena yesterday only that she might be traced and killed!"

McKie raised both arms in an eloquent gesture of completion, lowered his arms.

Aritch looked stricken. He saw it. If the eight prisoners denied the charges, they faced Aritch's fate. And they must know by now that Broey wanted them *Gowachin-guilty*. They could bring in the Caleban contract and expose the body-exchange plot, but that risked having McKie defend or prosecute them because he'd already locked them to his actual *client*, Aritch. Broey would affirm this, too. They were at Broey's mercy. If they were *Gowachin-guilty*, they walked free only here on Tandaloor. *Innocent*, they died here.

As though they were one organism, the eight turned their heads and looked at Aritch. Indeed! What would Aritch do? If he agreed to sacrifice himself, the eight might live. Ceylang, too, focused on Aritch.

Around the entire arena there was a sense of collective held breath.

McKie watched Ceylang. How candid had Aritch's people been with their Wreave? Did she know the full Dosadi story?

She broke the silence, exposing her knowledge. She chose to aim her attack at McKie on the well-known dictum that, when all else failed, you tried to discredit the opposing Legum.

"McKie, is this how you defend these eight people whom only *you* name as client?" Ceylang demanded.

Now, it was delicate. Would Broey go along?

McKie countered her probe with a question of his own.

"Are you suggesting that you'd prosecute these people?"

"I didn't charge them! You did."

"To prove Aritch's innocence."

"But you call them client. Will you defend them?"

A collective gasp arose from the cluster of advisors behind her near the arena doorway. They'd seen the trap. If McKie accepted the challenge, the judges had no choice but to bring the eight into the arena under Gowachin forms. Ceylang had trapped herself into the posture of prosecutor against the eight. She'd said, in effect, that she affirmed their guilt. Doing so, she lost her case against Aritch and her life was immediately forfeit. She was caught.

Her eyes glittered with the unspoken question.

What would McKie do?

Not yet, McKie thought. *Not yet, my precious Wreave dupe.*

He turned his attention to Parando. Would they dare introduce the Caleban contract? The eight prisoners were only the exposed tip of the shadowy forces, a vulnerable tip. They could be sacrificed. It was clear that they saw this and didn't like it. No Gowachin Mrregs here with that iron submission to responsibility! They loved life and its power, especially the ones who wore Human flesh. How precious life must be for those who'd lived many lives! *Very* desperate, indeed.

To McKie's Dosadi-conditioned eyes, it was as though he read the prisoners' thoughts. They were safest if they remained silent. Trust Parando. Rely on Broey's enlightened greed. At the worst, they could live out what life was left to them here on Tandaloor, hoping for new bodies before the flesh they now wore ran out of vitality. As long as they still lived they could hope and scheme. Perhaps another Caleban could be hired, more Pcharkys found . . .

Aritch broke, unwilling to lose what had almost been his.

The High Magister's Tandaloor accent was hoarse with protest.

"But I did supervise the tests on Dosadi's population!"

"To what tests do you refer?"

"The Dosadi . . ."

Aritch fell silent, seeing the trap. More than a million Dosadi Gowachin already had left their planet. Would Aritch make targets of them? Anything he said could open the door to proof that the Dosadis were superior to non-Dosadis. Any Gowachin (or Human, for that matter) could well become a target in the next few minutes. One had only to denounce a selected Human or Gowachin as Dosadi. ConSentient fears would do the rest. And any of his arguments could be directed into exposure of Dosadi's real purpose. He obviously saw the peril in that, had seen it from the first.

The High Magister confirmed this analysis by glancing at the Ferret Wreaves in the audience. What consternation it would create among the secretive Wreaves to learn that another species could masquerade successfully as one of their own!

McKie could not leave matters where they stood, though. He threw a question at Aritch.

"Were the original transportees to Dosadi apprised of the nature of the project?"

"Only *they* could testify to that."

"And their memories were erased. We don't even have historical testimony on this matter."

Aritch remained silent. Eight of the original designers of the Dosadi project sat near him on the arena floor. Would he denounce them to save himself? McKie thought not. A person deemed capable of performing as The Mrreg could not possess such a flaw. Could he? Here was the real point of no return.

The High Magister confirmed McKie's judgment by turning his back on the Tribunal, the ages-old Gowachin gesture of submission. What a shock Aritch's performance must have been for those who'd seen him as a possible Mrreg. A poor choice except at the end, and that'd been as much recognition of total failure as anything else.

McKie waited, knowing what had to happen now. Here was Ceylang's moment of truth.

Broey addressed her.

"You have suggested that you would prosecute these eight prisoners. The matter is in the hands of Defense Legum."

Broey shifted his gaze.

"How say you, Legum McKie?"

The moment to test Broey had come. McKie countered with a question.

"Can this Courtarena suggest another disposition for these eight prisoners?"

Ceylang held her breath.

Broey was pleased. He had triumphed in the end over Jedrik. Broey was certain in his mind that Jedrik did not occupy this Legum body on the arena floor. Now, he could show the puppet masters what a Dosadi-born could do. And McKie saw that Broey intended to move fast, much faster than anyone had expected.

Anyone except Jedrik, and she was only a silent (memory?) in McKie's awareness.

Having given the appearance of deliberation, Broey spoke.

"I can order these eight bound over to ConSentient jurisdiction if McKie agrees."

The eight stirred, subsided.

"I agree," McKie said. He glanced at Ceylang. She made no protest, seeing the futility. Her only hope now lay in the possible deterrent presence of the Ferret Wreaves.

"Then I so order it," Broey said. He spared a triumphant glance for Parando. "Let a ConSentient jurisdiction decide if these eight are guilty of murder and other conspiracy."

He was well within the bounds of the Covenant between the ConSentiency and Gowachin, but the Gowachin members of his audience didn't like it. Their Law was best! Angry whistlings could be heard all around the arena.

Broey rose half-out of his seat, pointed at the instruments of pain arrayed beneath him. Gowachin in the audience fell silent. They, better than anyone, knew that no person here, not even a member of the audience, was outside the Tribunal's power. And many understood clearly now why those bloody tools had been displayed here. Thoughtful people had anticipated the problem of keeping order in this arena.

Responding to the silent acceptance of his authority, Broey sank back into his seat.

Parando was staring at Broey as though having just discovered the presence of a monster in this Gowachin form. Many people would be reassessing Broey now.

Aritch held his attitude of complete submission.

Ceylang's thoughts almost hummed in the air around her. Every way she turned, she saw only a tangle of unmanageable tendrils and a blocked passage.

McKie saw that it was time to bring matters to a head. He crossed to the foot of the judicial bench, lifted a short spear from the instruments there. He brandished the barbed, razor-edged weapon.

"Who sits on this Tribunal?"

Once, Aritch had issued such a challenge. McKie, repeating it, pointed with the spear, answered his own question.

"A Gowachin of my choice, one supposedly wronged by the Dosadi project. Were you wronged, Broey?"

"No."

McKie faced Parando.

"And here we have a human from Lirat. Is that not the case, Parando?"

"I am from Lirat, yes."

McKie nodded.

"I am prepared to bring a parade of witnesses into this arena to testify as to your occupation on Lirat. Would you care to state that occupation?''

"How dare you question this Tribunal?''

Parando glared down at McKie, face flushed.

"Answer his question.''

It was Broey.

Parando looked at Bildoon, who still sat with face concealed in his arms, face down on the bench. Something about the PanSpechi repelled Parando, but he knew he had to have Bildoon's vote to overrule Broey. Parando nudged the PanSpechi. Inert flesh rolled away from Parando's hand.

McKie understood.

Facing doom, Bildoon had retreated into the creche. Somewhere, an unprepared PanSpechi body was being rushed into acceptance of that crushed identity. The emergence of a new Bildoon would require considerable time. They did not have that time. When the creche finally brought forth a functioning persona, it would not be heir to Bildoon's old powers in BuSab.

Parando was alone, exposed. He stared at the spear in McKie's hand.

McKie favored the arena with a sweeping glance before speaking once more to Parando.

"I quote that renowned expert on Gowachin Law, High Magister Aritch: 'ConSentient Law always makes aristocrats of its practitioners. Gowachin Law stands beneath that pretension. Gowachin Law asks: Who knows the people? Only such a one is fit to judge in the Courtarena.' That is Gowachin Law according to High Magister Aritch. That is the law in this place.''

Again, McKie gave Parando a chance to speak, received only silence.

"Perhaps you are truly fit to judge here,'' McKie suggested. "Are you an artisan? A philospher? Perhaps you're a humorist? An artist? Ahhh, maybe you are that lowliest of workmen, he who tends an automatic machine?''

Parando remained silent, gaze locked on the spear.

"None of these?'' McKie asked. "Then I shall supply the answer. You are a professional legalist, one who gives legal advice, even to advice on Gowachin Law. You, a Human, not even a Legum, dare to speak of Gowachin Law!''

Without any muscular warning signal, McKie leaped forward, hurled the spear at Parando, saw it strike deeply into the man's chest.

One for Jedrik!

With bubbling gasp, Parando sagged out of sight behind the bench.

Broey, seeing the flash of anger in McKie's effort, touched the blue box in front of him.

Have no fear, Broey. Not yet. I still need you.

But now, more than Broey knew it was really McKie in this flesh. Not Jedrik. Those members of the shadow force watching this scene and able to plot would make the expected deduction because they did not know how freely and completely Jedrik and McKie had shared. To the shadow force, McKie would've known Parando's background. They'd trace out that mistake in short order. So this was McKie in the arena. But he'd left Dosadi. There could be only one conclusion in the plotters' minds.

McKie had Caleban help!

They had Calebans to fear.

And McKie thought: *You have only McKie to fear.*

He grew aware that grunts of Gowachin approval were sounding all around the arena. They accepted him as a Legum, thus they accepted his argument.

Such a judge deserved killing.

Aritch set the precedent. McKie improved on it.

Both had found an approved way to kill a flawed judge, but McKie's act had etched a Gowachin precedent into the ConSentient legal framework. The compromise which had brought Gowachin and ConSentient Law into the Covenant of shared responsibility for the case in this arena would be seen by the Gowachin as a first long step toward making their Law supreme over all other law.

Aritch had half-turned, looking toward the bench, a glittering appraisal in his eyes which said the Gowachin had salvaged something here after all.

McKie strode back to confront Ceylang. He faced her as the forms required while he called for judgment.

"Bildoon?"

Silence.

"Parando?"

Silence.

"Broey?"

"Judgment for Defense."

The Dosadi accent rang across the arena. The Gowachin Federation, only member of the ConSentiency which dared permit a victim to judge those accused of victimizing him, had received a wound to its pride. But they'd also received something they would consider of inestimable value—a foothold for their Law in the ConSentiency, plus a memorable court performance which was about to end in the drama they loved best.

McKie stepped to within striking distance of Ceylang, extended his right hand straight out to the side, palm up.

"The knife."

Attendants scurried. There came the sound of the blue box being opened. Presently, the knife handle was slapped firmly into McKie's palm. He closed his fingers around it, thinking as he did so of all those countless others who had faced this moment in a Gowachin Courtarena.

"Ceylang?"

"I submit to the ruling of this court."

McKie saw the Ferret Wreaves rise from their seats as one person. They stood ready to leap down into the arena and avenge Ceylang no matter the consequences. They could do nothing else but carry out the role which the Gowachin had designed for them. Few in the arena had misunderstood their presence here. No matter the measurement of the wound, the Gowachin did not suffer such things gladly.

An odd look of camaraderie passed between Ceylang and McKie then. Here they stood, the only two non-Gowachin in the ConSentient universe who had passed through that peculiar alchemy which transformed a person into a Legum. One of them was supposed to die immediately, and the other would not long survive that death. Yet, they understood each other the way siblings understand each other. Each had shed a particular *skin* to become something else.

Slowly, deliberately, McKie extended the tip of his blade toward Ceylang's left jowl, noting the myriad pocks of her triad exchanges there. She trembled but remained firm. Deftly, with the swiftest of flicking motions, McKie added another pock to those on her left jowl.

The Ferret Wreaves were the first to understand. They sank back into their seats.

Ceylang gasped, touched a tendril to the wound. Many times she had been set free by such a wound, moving on to new alliances which did not completely sunder the old.

For a moment, McKie thought she might not accept, but the increasing sounds of approval all around the arena overcame her doubts. The noise of that approval climbed to a near deafening crescendo before subsiding. Even the Gowachin joined this. How dearly they loved such legal nuances!

Pitching his voice for Ceylang alone, McKie spoke.

"You should apply for a position in BuSab. The new director would look with favor upon your application."

"You?"

"Make a Wreave bet on it."

She favored him with the grimace which passed for a smile among Wreaves, spoke the traditional words of triad farewell.

"We are well and truly wed."

So she, too, had seen the truth in their unique closeness.

McKie betrayed the extent of his esoteric knowledge by producing the correct response.

"By my mark I know you."

She showed no surprise. A good brain there, not up to Dosadi standards, but good.

Well and truly wed.

Keeping a firm lock on his emotions (the Dosadi in him helped), McKie crossed to confront Aritch.

"Client Aritch, you are innocent."

McKie displayed the fleck of Wreave blood on the knife tip.

"The forms have been obeyed and you are completely exonerated. I rejoice with all of those who love justice."

At this point in the old days, the jubilant audience would've fallen on the hapless client, would've fought for bloody scraps with which to parade through the city. No doubt Aritch would've preferred that. He was a traditionalist. He confirmed that now.

"I am glad to quit these times, McKie."

McKie mused aloud.

"Who will be the Mrreg now that you're . . . disqualified? Whoever it is, I doubt he'll be as good as the one he replaces. It will profit that next Mrreg to reflect upon the fragile and fugitive value to be gained from the manipulation of others."

Glowering, Aritch turned and shambled toward the doorway out of the arena.

Some of the Gowachin from the audience already were leaving, no doubt hoping to greet Aritch outside. McKie had no desire to witness that remnant of an ancient ritual. He had other concerns.

Well and truly wed.

Something burned in his eyes. And still he felt that soft and sleeping presence in his awareness.

Jedrik?

No response.

He glanced at Broey who, true to his duty as a judge, would be the last to leave the arena. Broey sat blandly contemplating this place where he'd displayed the first designs of his campaign for supremacy in the ConSentiency. He would accept nothing less short of his own death. Those shadowy puppet masters would be the first to feel his rule.

That fitted the plan McKie and Jedrik had forged between them. In a way, it was still the plan of those who'd bred and conditioned Jedrik for the tasks she'd performed so exquisitely.

It was McKie's thought that those nameless, faceless Dosadis who stood in ghostly ranks behind Jedrik had made a brave choice. Faced with the evidence of body exchange all around, they'd judged that to be a deadly choice—the conservatism of extinction. Instead, they'd trusted sperm and ova, always seeking the new and better, the changed, the adapted. And they'd launched their simultaneous campaign to eliminate the Pcharkys of their world, reserving only that one for their final gamble.

It was well that this explosive secret had been kept here. McKie felt grateful to Ceylang. She'd known, but even when it might've helped her, she'd remained silent. BuSab would now have time to forge ways of dealing with this problem. Ceylang would be valuable there. And perhaps more would be learned about PanSpechi, Calebans, and Taprisiots. If only Jedrik . . .

He felt a fumbling in his memories.

"If only Jedrik what?"

She spoke laughingly in his mind as she'd always spoken there.

McKie suppressed a fit of trembling, almost fell.

"Careful with our body," she said. "It's the only one we have now."

"Whose body?"

She caressed his mind.

"Ours, love."

Was it hallucination? He ached with longing to hold her in his arms, to feel her arms around him, her body pressed to him.

"That's lost to us forever, love, but see what we have in exchange."

When he didn't respond, she said:

"One can always be watching while the other acts . . . or sleeps."

"But where are you?"

"Where I've always been when we exchanged. See?"

He felt her parallel to him in the shared flesh and, as he voluntarily drew back, he came to rest in contact with her mutual memories, still looking from his own eyes but aware that someone else peered out there, too, that someone else turned this body to face Broey.

Fearful that he might be trapped here, McKie almost panicked, but Jedrik gave him back the control of their flesh.

"Do you doubt me, love?"

He felt shame. There was nothing she could hide from him. He knew how she felt, what she'd been willing to sacrifice for him.

"You'd have made their perfect Mrreg."

"Don't even suggest it."

She went pouring through his arena memories then and her joy delighted him.

"Oh, marvelous, McKie. Beautiful! I couldn't have done it better. And Broey still doesn't suspect."

Attendants were taking the eight prisoners out of the arena now, all of them still shackled. The audience benches were almost empty.

A sense of joy began filtering through McKie.

I lost something but I gained something.

"You didn't lose as much as Aritch."

"And I gained more."

McKie permitted himself to stare up at Broey then, studying the Gowachin judge with Dosadi eyes and two sets of awareness. Aritch and the eight accused of murder were things of the past. They and many others like them would be dead or powerless before another ten-day. Broey already had shown the speed with which he intended to act. Supported by his troop of Jedrick-chosen aides, Broey would occupy the seats of power, consolidating lines of control in that shadow government, eliminating every potential source of opposition he could touch. He believed Jedrik dead and, while McKie was clever, McKie and BuSab were not a primary concern. One struck at the real seats of power. Being Dosadi, Broey could not act otherwise. And he'd been almost the best his planet had ever produced. Almost.

Jedrik-within chuckled.

Yes, with juggernaut certainty, Broey would create a single target for BuSab. And Jedrik had refined the simulation pattern by which Broey could be anticipated. Borey would find McKie waiting for him at the proper moment.

Behind McKie would be a new BuSab, an agency directed by a person whose memories and abilities were amplified by the one person superior to Broey that Dosadi had ever produced.

Standing there in the now silent arena, McKie wondered:

When will Broey realize he does our work for us?

"When we show him that he failed to kill *me*!"

In the purest obedience to Gowachin forms, without any sign of the paired thoughts twining through his mind, McKie bowed toward the surviving jurist, turned, and left. And all the time, Jedrik-within was planning . . . plotting . . . planning . . .

THE SANTAROGA BARRIER

1

THE SUN went down as the five-year-old Ford camper-pickup truck ground over the pass and started down the long grade into Santaroga Valley. A crescent-shaped turnoff had been leveled beside the first highway curve. Gilbert Dasein pulled his truck onto the gravel, stopped at a white barrier fence and looked down into the valley whose secrets he had come to expose.

Two men already had died on this project, Dasein reminded himself. Accidents. *Natural* accidents. What was down there in that bowl of shadows inhabited by random lights? Was there an accident waiting for him?

Dasein's back ached after the long drive up from Berkeley. He shut off the motor, stretched. A burning odor of hot oil permeated the cab. The union of truckbed and camper emitted creakings and poppings.

The valley stretching out below him looked somehow different from what Dasein had expected. The sky around it was a ring of luminous blue full of sunset glow that spilled over into an upper belt of trees and rocks.

There was a sense of quiet about the place, of an island sheltered from storms. *What did I expect the place to be?* Dasein wondered.

He decided all the maps he'd studied, all the reports on Santaroga he'd read, had led him to believe he knew the valley. But maps were not the land. Reports weren't people.

Dasein glanced at his wristwatch: almost seven. He felt reluctant to continue.

Far off to the left across the valley, strips of green light glowed among trees. That was the area labeled "greenhouses" on the map. A castellated block of milky white on an outcropping down to his right he identified as the Jaspers Cheese Cooperative. The yellow gleam of windows and moving lights around it spoke of busy activity.

Dasein grew aware of insect sounds in the darkness around him, the swoop-humming of air through nighthawks' wings and, away in the distance, the mournful baying of hounds. The voice of the pack appeared to come from beyond the Co-op.

He swallowed, thinking that the yellow windows suddenly were like baleful eyes peering into the valley's darker depths.

Dasein shook his head, smiled. That was no way to think. Unprofessional. All the ominous nonsense muttered about Santaroga had to be put aside. A scientific investigation could not operate in that atmosphere. He turned on the cab's dome light, took his briefcase from the seat beside him. Gold lettering on the brown leather identified it: "Gilbert Dasein—Department of Psychology—University of California—Berkeley."

In a battered folder from the case he began writing: "Arrived Santaroga Valley approximately 6:45 p.m. Setting is that of a prosperous farm community . . . "

Presently, he put the case and folder aside.

Prosperous farm community, he thought. How could he know it was prosperous? No—prosperity wasn't what he saw. That was something he knew from the reports.

The real valley in front of him now conveyed a sense of waiting, of quietness punctuated by occasional tinklings of cowbells. He imagined husbands and wives down there after a day of work. What did they discuss now in their waiting darkness?

What did Jenny Sorge discuss with her husband—provided she had a husband? It seemed impossible she'd still be single—lovely, nubile Jenny. It was more than a year since they'd last seen each other at the University.

Dasein sighed. No escaping thoughts of Jenny—not here in Santaroga. Jenny contained part of Santaroga's mystery. She was an element of the Santaroga Barrier and a prime subject for his present investigation.

Again, Dasein sighed. He wasn't fooling himself. He knew why he'd accepted this project. It wasn't the munificent sum those chain stores were paying the university for this study, nor the generous salary provided for himself.

He had come because this was where Jenny lived.

Dasein told himself he'd smile and act normal, *perfectly normal*, when he met her. He was here on business, a psychologist detached from his usual teaching duties to make a market study in Santaroga Valley.

What was a perfectly normal way to act with Jenny, though? How did one achieve normalcy when encountering the paranormal?

Jenny was a Santarogan—and the normalcy of this valley defied normal explanations.

His mind went to the reports, "the known facts." All the folders of data, the collections of official pryings, the second-hand secrets which were the stock in a trade of the bureaucracy—all this really added up to a single "known fact" about Santaroga: There was something extraordinary at work here, something far more disturbing than any so-called market study had ever tackled before.

Meyer Davidson, the soft looking, pink fleshed little man who'd presented himself as the agent of the investment corporation, the holding company behind the chain stores paying for this project, had put it in an angry nutshell at the first orientation meeting: "The whole thing about Santaroga boils down to this—Why were we forced to close our branches there? Why won't even *one* Santarogan trade with an outsider? That's what we want to know. What's this Santaroga Barrier which keeps us from doing business there?"

Davidson wasn't as soft as he looked.

Dasein started the truck, turned on his headlights, resumed his course down the winding grade.

All the data was a single datum.

Outsiders found no houses for rent or sale in this valley.

Santaroga officials said they had no juvenile delinquency figures for the state's statistics.

Servicemen from Santaroga always returned when they were discharged. In fact, no Santarogan had ever been known to move out of the valley.

Why? Was it a two-way barrier?

And the curious anomalies: The data had included a medical journal article by Jenny's uncle, Dr. Lawrence Piaget, reputedly the valley's leading physician. The article: "The Poison Oak Syndrome in Santaroga." Its substance: Santarogans had a remarkable susceptibility to allergens when forced to live away from their valley for extended periods. This was the chief reason for service rejection of Santaroga's youths.

Data equaled datum.

Santaroga reported no cases of mental illness or mental deficiency to the State Department of Mental Hygiene. No Santarogan could be found in a state mental hospital. (The psychiatrist who headed Dasein's university department, Dr. Chami Selador, found this fact "alarming.")

Cigarette sales in Santaroga could be accounted for by transient purchasers.

Santarogans manifested an iron resistance to national advertising. (An un-American symptom, according to Meyer Davidson.)

No cheese, wines or beers made outside the valley could be marketed to Santarogans.

All the valley's businesses, including the bank, were locally owned. They flatly rejected outside investment money.

Santaroga had successfully resisted every "pork barrel" government project the politicians had offered. Their State Senator was from Porterville, ten miles behind Dasein and well outside the valley. Among the political figures Dasein had interviewed to lay the groundwork for his study, the State Senator was one of the few who didn't think Santarogans were "a pack of kooks, maybe religious nuts of some kind."

"Look, Dr. Dasein," he'd said, "all this mystery crap about Santaroga is just that—crap."

The Senator was a skinny, intense man with a shock of gray hair and red-veined eyes. Barstow was his name; one of the old California families.

Barstow's opinion: "Santaroga's a last outpost of American individualism. They're Yankees, Down Easters living in California. Nothing mysterious about 'em at all. They don't ask special favors and they don't fan my ears with stupid questions. I wish all my constituents were as straightforward and honest."

One man's opinion, Dasein thought.

An isolated opinion.

Dasein was down into the valley proper now. The two-lane road leveled into a passage through gigantic trees. This was the Avenue of the Giants winding between rows of *sequoia gigantea*.

There were homes set back in the trees. The datum-data said some of these homes had been here since the gold rush. The scroll work of carpenter gothic lined their eaves. Many were three stories high, yellow lights in their windows.

Dasein grew aware of an absence, a negative fact about the houses he saw: No television flicker, no cathode living rooms, no walls washed to skimmed-milk gray by the omnipresent tube.

The road forked ahead of him. An arrow pointed left to "City Center" and two arrows directed him to the right to "The Santaroga House" and "Jaspers Cheese Co-op."

Dasein turned right.

His road wound upward beneath an arch: "Santaroga, The Town That Cheese Built." Presently, it emerged from the redwoods into an oak flat. The Co-op loomed gray white, bustling with lights and activity behind a chain fence on his right. Across the road to his left stood Dasein's first goal here, a long three-story inn built in the rambling 1900 style with a porch its full length. Lines of multipaned windows (most dark) looked down onto a gravel parking area. The sign at the entrance read: "Santaroga House—Gold Rush Museum—Hours 9 a.m. to 5 p.m."

Most of the cars nosed to a stone border parallel to the porch were well-kept older models. A few shiny new machines were parked in a second row as though standing aloof.

Dasein parked beside a 1939 Chevrolet whose paint gleamed with a rich waxy gloss. Red-brown upholstery visible through the windows appeared to be hand-tailored leather.

Rich man's toy, Dasein thought.

He took his suitcase from the camper, turned to the inn. There was a smell of new mown lawn in the air and the sound of running water. It reminded Dasein of his childhood, his aunt's garden with the brook along the back. A strong sense of nostalgia gripped him.

Abruptly, a discordant note intruded. From the upper floors of the inn came the raucous sound of a man and woman arguing, the man's voice brusk, the woman's with a strident fishwife quality.

"I'm not staying in this godforsaken hole one more night," the woman screamed. "They don't want our money! They don't want us! You do what you want; I'm leaving!"

"Belle, stop it! You've . . . "

A window slammed. The argument dimmed to a muted screeching-mumbling.

Dasein took a deep breath. The argument restored his perspective. Here were two more people with their noses against the Santaroga Barrier.

Dasein strode along the gravel, up four steps to the porch and through swinging doors with windows frosted by scroll etching. He found himself in a high-ceilinged lobby, crystal chandeliers overhead. Dark wood paneling, heavily grained like ancient charts enclosed the space. A curved counter stretched across the corner to his right, an open door behind it from which came the sound of a switchboard. To the right of this counter was a wide opening through which he glimpsed a dining room—white tablecloths, crystal, silver. A western stagecoach was parked at his left behind brass posts supporting a maroon velvet rope with a "Do Not Touch" sign.

Dasein stopped to study the coach. It smelled of dust and mildew. A framed card on the boot gave its history: "Used on the San Francisco-Santaroga route from 1868 to 1871." Below this card was a slightly larger frame enclosing a yellowed sheet of paper with a brass legend beside it: "A note from Black Bart, the Po-8 Highwayman." In sprawling script on the yellow paper it read:

> *"So here I've stood while wind and rain*
> *Have set the trees a-sobbin'*
> *And risked my life for that damned stage*
> *That wasn't worth the robbin'."*

Dasein chuckled, shifted his briefcase to his left arm, crossed to the counter and rang the call bell.

A bald, wrinkled stick of a man in a black suit appeared in the open doorway, stared at Dasein like a hawk ready to pounce. "Yes?"

"I'd like a room," Dasein said.

"What's your business?"

Dasein stiffened at the abrupt challenge. "I'm tired," he said. "I want a night's sleep."

"Passing through, I hope," the man grumbled. He shuffled to the counter, pushed a black registry ledger toward Dasein.

Dasein took a pen from its holder beside the ledger, signed.

The clerk produced a brass key on a brass tag, said: "You get two fifty-one next to that dang' couple from L.A. Don't blame me if they keep y'awake arguing." He slapped the key onto the counter. "That'll be ten dollars . . . in advance."

"I'm hungry," Dasein said, producing his wallet and paying. "Is the dining room open?" He accepted a receipt.

"Closes at nine," the clerk said.

"Is there a bellboy?"

"You look strong enough to carry your own bag." He pointed beyond Dasein. "Room's up them stairs, second floor."

Dasein turned. There was an open area behind the stagecoach. Scattered through it were leather chairs, high wings and heavy arms, a few occupied by elderly men sitting, reading. Light came from heavy brass floor lamps with fringed shades. A carpeted stairway led upward beyond the chairs.

It was a scene Dasein was to think of many times later as his first clue to the real nature of Santaroga. The effect was that of holding time securely in a bygone age.

Vaguely troubled, Dasein said: "I'll check my room later. May I leave my bag here while I eat?"

"Leave it on the counter. No one'll bother it."

Dasein put the case on the counter, caught the clerk studying him with a fixed stare.

"Something wrong?" Dasein asked.

"Nope."

The clerk reached for the briefcase under Dasein's arm, but Dasein stepped back, removed it from the questing fingers, met an angry stare.

"Hmmmph!" the clerk snorted. There was no mistaking his frustration. He'd wanted a look inside the briefcase.

Inanely, Dasein said: "I . . . uh, want to look over some papers while I'm eating." And he thought: *Why do I need to explain?*

Feeling angry with himself, he turned, strode through the passage into the dining room. He found himself in a large square room, a single massive chandelier in the center, brass carriage lamps spaced around walls of dark wood paneling. The chairs at the round tables were heavy with substantial arms. A long teak bar stretched along the wall at his left, a wood-framed mirror behind it. Light glittered hypnotically from the central chandelier and glasses stacked beneath the mirror.

The room swallowed sounds. Dasein felt he had walked into a sudden hush with people turning to look at him. Actually, his entrance went almost unnoticed.

A white-coated bartender on duty for a scattering of customers at the bar glanced at him, went back to talking to a swarthy man hunched over a mug of beer.

Family groups occupied about a dozen of the tables. There was a card game at the table near the bar. Two tables held lone women busy with their forks.

There was a division of people in this room, Dasein felt. It was a matter of nervous tension contrasted with a calmness as substantial as the room itself. He decided he could pick out the transients—they appeared tired, more rumpled; their children were closer to rebellion.

As he moved farther into the room, Dasein glimpsed himself in the bar mirror—

fatigue lines on his slender face, the curly black hair mussed by the wind, brown eyes glazed with attention, still driving the car. A smudge of road dirt drew a dark line beside the cleft in his chin. Dasein rubbed at the smudge, thought: *Here's another transient.*

"You wish a table, sir?"

A Negro waiter had appeared at his elbow—white jacket, hawk nose, sharp Moorish features, a touch of gray at the temples. There was a look of command about him all out of agreement with the menial costume. Dasein thought immediately of Othello. The eyes were brown and wise.

"Yes, please: for one," Dasein said.

"This way, sir."

Dasein was guided to a table against the near wall. One of the carriage lamps bathed it in a warm yellow glow. As the heavy chair enveloped him, Dasein's attention went to the table near the bar—the card game . . . four men. He recognized one of the men from a picture Jenny had carried: Piaget, the doctor uncle, author of the medical journal article on allergens. Piaget was a large, gray-haired man, bland round face, a curious suggestion of the Oriental about him that was heightened by the fan of cards held close to his chest.

"You wish a menu, sir?"

"Yes. Just a moment . . . the men playing cards with Dr. Piaget over there."

"Sir?"

"Who are they?"

"You know Dr. Larry, sir?"

"I know his niece, Jenny Sorge. She carried a photo of Dr. Piaget."

The waiter glanced at the briefcase Dasein had placed in the center of the table. "Dasein," he said. A wide smile put a flash of white in the dark face. "You're Jenny's friend from the school."

The waiter's words carried so many implications that Dasein found himself staring, open-mouthed.

"Jenny's spoken of you, sir," the waiter said.

"Oh."

"The men playing cards with Dr. Larry—you want to know who they are." He turned toward the players. "Well, sir, that's Captain Al Marden of the Highway Patrol across from Dr. Larry. On the right there, that's George Nis. He manages the Jaspers Cheese Co-op. The fellow on the left is Mr. Sam Scheler. Mr. Sam runs our independent service station. I'll get you that menu, sir."

The waiter headed toward the bar.

Dasein's attention remained on the card players, wondering why they held his interest so firmly. Marden, sitting with his back partly turned toward Dasein, was in mufti, a dark blue suit. His hair was a startling mop of red. He turned his head to the right and Dasein glimpsed a narrow face, tight-lipped mouth with a cynical downtwist.

Scheler of the independent service station (Dasein wondered about this designation suddenly) was dark skinned, an angular Indian face with flat nose, heavy lips. Nis, across from him, was balding, sandy-haired, blue eyes with heavy lids, a wide mouth and deeply cleft chin.

"Your menu, sir."

The waiter placed a large red-covered folder in front of Dasein.

"Dr. Piaget and his friends appear to be enjoying their game," Dasein said.

"That game's an institution, sir. Every week about this hour, regular as sunset—dinner here and that game."

"What do they play?"

"It varies, sir. Sometimes it's bridge, sometimes pinochle. They play whist on occasion and even poker."

"What did you mean—*independent* service station?" Dasein asked. He looked up at the dark Moorish face.

"Well, sir, we here in the valley don't mess around with those companies fixin' their prices. Mr. Sam, he buys from whoever gives him the best offer. We pay about four cents less a gallon here."

Dasein made a mental note to investigate this aspect of the Santaroga Barrier. It was in character, not buying from the big companies, but where did they get their oil products?

"The roast beef is very good, sir," the waiter said, pointing to the menu.

"You recommend it, eh?"

"I do that, sir. Grain fattened right here in the valley. We have fresh corn on the cob, potatoes Jaspers—that's with cheese sauce, very good, and we have hothouse strawberries for dessert."

"Salad?" Dasein asked.

"Our salad greens aren't very good this week, sir. I'll bring you the soup. It's borscht with sour cream. And you'd like beer with that. I'll see if I can't get you some of our local product."

"With you around I don't need a menu," Dasein said. He returned the red-covered folder. "Bring it on before I start eating the tablecloth."

"Yes, sir!"

Dasein watched the retreating black—white coated, wide, confident. Othello, indeed.

The waiter returned presently with a steaming bowl of soup, a white island of sour cream floating in it, and a darkly amber mug of beer.

"I note you're the only Negro waiter here," Dasein said. "Isn't that kind of type casting?"

"You asking if I'm their *show* Negro, sir?" The waiter's voice was suddenly wary.

"I was wondering if Santaroga had any integration problems."

"Must be thirty, forty colored families in the valley, sir. We don't rightly emphasize the distinction of skin color here." The voice was hard, curt.

"I didn't mean to offend you," Dasein said.

"You didn't offend me." A smile touched the corners of his mouth, was gone. "I must admit a Negro waiter is a kind of institutional accent. Place like this . . ." He glanced around the solid, paneled room. " . . . must've had plenty of Negro waiters here in its day. Kind of like local color having me on the job." Again, that flashing smile. "It's a good job, and my kids are doing even better. Two of 'em work in the Co-op; other's going to be a lawyer."

"You have three children?"

"Two boys and a girl. If you'll excuse me, sir; I have other tables."

"Yes, of course."

Dasein lifted the mug of beer as the waiter left.

He held the beer a moment beneath his nose. There was a tangy odor about it with a suggestion of cellars and mushrooms. Dasein remembered suddenly that Jenny had praised the local Santaroga beer. He sipped it—soft on the tongue, smooth, clean aftertaste of malt. It was everything Jenny had said.

Jenny, he thought. *Jenny . . . Jenny . . .*

Why had she never invited him to Santaroga on her regular weekend trips home? She'd never missed a weekend, he recalled. Their dates had always been in midweek. He remembered what she'd told him about herself: orphaned, raised by the uncle, Piaget, and a maiden aunt . . . Sarah.

Dasein took another drink of the beer, sampled the soup. They did go well together. The sour cream had a flavor reminiscent of the beer, a strange new tang.

There'd never been any mistaking Jenny's affection for him, Dasein thought. They'd had a *thing*, chemical, exciting. But no *direct* invitation to meet her family, see the valley. A hesitant probing, yes—what would he think of setting up practice in Santaroga? Sometime, he must talk to Uncle Larry about some interesting cases.

What cases? Dasein wondered, remembering. The Santaroga information folders Dr. Selador had supplied were definite: ''No reported cases of mental illness.''

Jenny . . . Jenny . . .

Dasein's mind went back to the night he'd proposed. No hesitant probing on Jenny's part then— Could he live in Santaroga?

He could remember his own incredulous demand: ''Why do we have to live in Santaroga?''

''Because I can't live anywhere else.'' That was what she'd said. ''Because I can't live anywhere else.''

Love me, love my valley.

No amount of pleading could wring an explanation from her. She'd made that plain. In the end, he'd reacted with anger boiling out of injured manhood. Did she think he couldn't support her any place but in Santaroga?

''Come and see Santaroga,'' she'd begged.

''Not unless you'll consider living outside.''

Impasse.

Remembering the fight, Dasein felt his cheeks go warm. It'd been finals week. She'd refused to answer his telephone calls for two days . . . and he'd refused to call after that. He'd retreated into a hurt shell.

And Jenny had gone back to her precious valley. When he'd written, swallowed his pride, offered to come and see her—no answer. Her valley had swallowed her.

This valley.

Dasein sighed, looked around the dining room, remembering Jenny's intensity when she spoke about Santaroga. This paneled dining room, the Santarogans he could see, didn't fit the picture in his mind.

Why didn't she answer my letters? he asked himself. *Most likely she's married. That must be it.*

Dasein saw his waiter come around the end of the bar with a tray. The bartender signaled, called: ''Win.'' The waiter stopped, rested the tray on the bar. Their heads moved close together beside the tray. Dasein received the impression they were arguing. Presently, the waiter said something with a chopping motion of the head, grabbed up the tray, brought it to Dasein's table.

''Doggone busybody,'' he said as he put the tray down across from Dasein, began distributing the dishes from it. ''Try to tell me I can't give you Jaspers! Good friend of Jenny's and I can't give him Jaspers.''

The waiter's anger cooled; he shook his head, smiled, put a plate mounded with food before Dasein.

"Too doggone many busybodies in this world, y' ask me."

"The bartender," Dasein said. "I heard him call you 'Win.' "

"Winston Burdeaux, sir, at your service." He moved around the table closer to Dasein. "Wouldn't give me any Jaspers beer for you this time, sir." He took a frosted bottle from the tray, put it near the mug of beer he'd served earlier. "This isn't as good as what I brought before. The food's real Jaspers, though. Doggone busybody couldn't stop me from doing that."

"Jaspers," Dasein said. "I thought it was just the cheese."

Burdeaux pursed his lips, looked thoughtful. "Oh, no, sir. Jaspers, that's in all the products from the Co-op. Didn't Jenny ever tell you?" He frowned. "Haven't you ever been up here in the valley with her, sir?"

"No." Dasein shook his head from side to side.

"You *are* Dr. Dasein—Gilbert Dasein?"

"Yes."

"You're the fellow Jenny's sweet on, then." He grinned, said: "Eat up, sir. It's *good* food."

Before Dasein could collect his thoughts, Burdeaux turned, hurried away.

"*You're the fellow Jenny's sweet on,*" Dasein thought. Present tense . . . not past tense. He felt his heart hammering, cursed himself for an idiot. It was just Burdeaux's way of talking. That was all it could be.

Confused, he bent to his food.

The roast beef in his first bite lived up to Burdeaux's prediction—tender, juicy. The cheese sauce on the potatoes had a flowing tang reminiscent of the beer and the sour cream.

The fellow Jenny's sweet on.

Burdeaux's words gripped Dasein's mind as he ate, filled him with turmoil.

Dasein looked up from his food, seeking Burdeaux. The waiter was nowhere in sight. *Jaspers.* It was this rich tang, this new flavor. His attention went to the bottle of beer, the non-Jaspers beer. *Not as good?* He sampled it directly from the bottle, found it left a bitter metallic aftertaste. A sip of the first beer from the mug—smooth, soothing. Dasein felt it cleared his head as it cleared his tongue of the other flavor.

He put down the mug, looked across the room, caught the bartender staring at him, scowling. The man looked away.

They were small things—two beers, an argument between a waiter and a bartender, a watchful bartender—nothing but clock ticks in a lifetime, but Dasein sensed danger in them. He reminded himself that two investigators had met fatal accidents in the Santaroga Valley—*death by misadventure* . . . a car going too fast around a corner, off the road into a ravine . . . a fall from a rocky ledge into a river—drowned. *Natural* accidents, so certified by state investigation.

Thoughtful, Dasein returned to his food.

Presently, Burdeaux brought the strawberries, hovered as Dasein sampled them.

"Good, sir?"

"Very good. Better than that bottle of beer."

"My fault, sir. Perhaps another time." He coughed discreetly. "Does Jenny know you're here?"

Dasein put down his spoon, looked into his dish of strawberries as though trying to find his reflection there. His mind suddenly produced a memory picture of Jenny in a red dress, vital, laughing, bubbling with energy. "No . . . not yet," he said.

"You know Jenny's still a single girl, sir?"

Dasein glanced across to the card game. How leathery tan the players' skin looked. *Jenny not married?* Dr. Piaget looked up from the card game, said something to the man on his left. They laughed.

"Has . . . is she in the telephone directory, Mr. Burdeaux?" Dasein asked.

"She lives with Dr. Piaget, sir. And why don't you call me Win?"

Dasein looked up at Burdeaux's sharp Moorish face, wondering suddenly about the man. There was just a hint of southern accent in his voice. The probing friendliness, the volunteered information about Jenny—it was all faintly southern, intimate, kindly . . . but there were undertones of something else: a questing awareness, harsh and direct. The psychologist in Dasein was fully alert now.

"Have you lived very long here in the valley, Win?" Dasein asked.

" 'Bout twelve years, sir."

"How'd you come to settle here?"

Burdeaux shook his head. A rueful half-smile touched his lips. "Oh, you wouldn't like to hear about that, sir."

"But I would." Dasein stared up at Burdeaux, waiting. Somewhere there was a wedge that would open this valley's mysteries to him. *Jenny not married?* Perhaps Burdeaux was that wedge. There was an open shyness about his own manner, Dasein knew, that invited confidences. He relied upon this now.

"Well, if you really want to know, sir," Burdeaux said. "I was in the N'Orleans jailhouse for cuttin' up." (Dasein noted a sudden richening of the southern accent.) "We was doin' our numbers, usin' dirty language that'd make your neck hair walk. I suddenly heard myself doin' that, sir. It made me review my thinkin' and I saw it was kid stuff. Juvenile." Burdeaux mouthed the word, proud of it. "Juvenile, sir. Well, when I got out of that jailhouse, the high sheriff tellin' me never to come back, I went me home to my woman and I tol' Annie, I tol' her we was leavin'. That's when we left to come here, sir."

"Just like that, you left?"

"We hit the road on our feet, sir. It wasn't easy an' there was some places made us wish we'd never left. When we come here, though, we knew it was worth it."

"You just wandered until you came here?"

"It was like God was leadin' us, sir. This place, well, sir, it's hard to explain. But . . . well, they insist I go to school to better myself. That's one thing. I can speak good standard English when I want . . . when I think about it." (The accent began to fade.)

Dasein smiled encouragingly. "These must be very nice people here in the valley."

"I'm going to tell you something, sir." Burdeaux said. "Maybe you can understand if I tell you about something happened to me here. It's a thing would've hurt me pretty bad one time, but here . . . We were at a Jaspers party, sir. It was right after Willa, my girl, announced her engagement to Cal Nis. And George, Cal's daddy, came over and put his arm across my shoulder. 'Well there, Win, you old nigger bastard,' he said, 'we better have us a good drink and a talk together because our kids are going to make us related.' That was it, Mr. Dasein. He didn't mean a thing calling me nigger. It was just like . . . like the way we call a pale blond fellow here Whitey. It was like saying my skin's black for identification the way you might come into a room and ask for Al Marden and I'd say: 'He's that red-headed fellow over there playing cards.' As he was saying it I knew that's all he meant. It just came over me. It was being accepted for what I am. It was the friendliest thing George could do and that's why he did it.''

Dasein scowled trying to follow the train of Burdeaux's meaning. Friendly to call him nigger?

"I don't think you understand it," Burdeaux said. "Maybe you'd have to be black to understand. But . . . well, perhaps this'll make you see it. A few minutes later, George said to me: 'Hey, Win, I wonder what kind of grandchildren we're going to have—light, dark or in between?' It was just a kind of wonderment to him, that he might have black grandchildren. He didn't care, really. He was curious. He found it interesting. You know, when I told Annie about that afterward, I cried. I was so happy I cried."

It was a long colloquy. Dasein could see realization of this fact come over Burdeaux. The man shook his head, muttered: "I talk too much. Guess I'd better . . . ''

He broke off at a sudden eruption of shouting at the bar near the card players. A red-faced fat man had stepped back from the bar and was flailing it with a briefcase as he shouted at the bartender.

"You sons of bitches!" he screamed. "You think you're too goddamn' good to buy from me! My line isn't good enough for you! You can make better . . . ''

The bartender grabbed the briefcase.

"Leggo of that, you son of a bitch!" the fat man yelled. "You all think you're so goddamn' good like you're some foreign country! An *outsider* am I? Let me tell you, you pack of foreigners! This is America! This is a free . . . ''

The red-headed highway patrol captain, Al Marden, had risen at the first sign of trouble. Now, he put a large hand on the screamer's shoulder, shook the man once.

The screaming stopped. The angry man whirled, raised the briefcase to hit Marden. In one long, drawn-out second, the man focused on Marden's glaring eyes, the commanding face, hesitated.

"I'm Captain Marden of the Highway Patrol," Marden said. "And I'm telling you we won't have any more of this." His voice was calm, stern . . . and, Dasein thought, faintly amused.

The angry man lowered the briefcase, swallowed.

"You can go out and get in your car and leave Santaroga," Marden said. "Now. And don't come back. We'll be watching for you, and we'll run you in if we ever catch you in the valley again."

Anger drained from the fat man. His shoulders slumped. He swallowed, looked around at the room of staring eyes. "I'm glad to go," he muttered. "Nothing'd make me happier. It'll be a cold day in hell when I ever come back to your dirty little valley. You stink. All of you stink." He jerked his shoulder from Marden's grasp, stalked out through the passage to the lobby.

Marden returned to the card game shaking his head.

Slowly, the room returned to its previous sounds of eating and conversation. Dasein could feel a difference, though. The salesman's outburst had separated Santarogans and transients. An invisible wall had gone up. The transient families at their tables were hurrying their children, anxious to leave.

Dasein felt the same urgency. There was a pack feeling about the room now—hunters and hunted. He smelled his own perspiration. His palms were sweaty. He noted that Burdeaux had gone.

This is stupid! he thought. *Jenny not married?*

He reminded himself that he was a psychologist, an observer. But the observer had to observe himself.

Why am I reacting this way? he wondered. *Jenny not married?*

Two of the transient families already were leaving, herding their young ahead of them, voices brittle, talking about going "on to the next town."

Why can't they stay here? he asked himself. *The rates are reasonable.*

He pictured the area in his mind: Porterville was twenty-five miles away, ten miles outside the valley on the road he had taken. The other direction led over a winding, twisting mountain road some forty miles before connecting with Highway 395. The closest communities were to the south along 395, at least seventy miles. This was an area of National Forests, lakes, fire roads, moonscape ridges of lava rock—all of it sparsely inhabited except for the Santaroga Valley. Why would people want to travel through such an area at night rather than stay at this inn?

Dasein finished his meal, left the rest of the beer. He had to talk this place over with his department head, Dr. Chami Selador, before making another move. Burdeaux had left the check on a discreet brown tray—three dollars and eighty-six cents. Dasein put a five dollar bill on the tray, glanced once more around the room. The surface appeared so damn' normal! The card players were intent on their game. The bartender was hunched over, chatting with two customers. A child at a table off to the right was complaining that she didn't want to drink her milk.

It wasn't normal, though, and Dasein's senses screamed this fact at him. The brittle surface of this room was prepared to shatter once more and Dasein didn't think he would like what might be revealed. He wiped his lips on his napkin, took his briefcase and headed for the lobby.

His suitcase stood atop the desk beside the register. There was a buzzing and murmurous sound of a switchboard being operated in the room through the doors at the rear corner. He took the suitcase, fingered the brass room key in his pocket—two fifty-one. If there was no phone in the room, he decided he'd come down and place his call to Chami from a booth.

Feeling somewhat foolish and letdown after his reaction to the scene in the dining room, Dasein headed for the stairs. A few eyes peered at him over the tops of newspapers from the lobby chairs. The eyes looked alert, inquisitive.

The stairs led to a shadowy mezzanine—desks, patches of white paper. A fire door directly ahead bore the sign: "To Second Floor. Keep this door closed."

The next flight curved left, dim overhead light, wide panels of dark wood. It led through another fire door into a hall with an emergency exit sign off to the left. An illuminated board opposite the door indicated room two fifty-one down the hall to the right. Widely spaced overhead lights, the heavy pile of a maroon carpet underfoot, wide heavy doors with brass handles and holes for old-fashioned passkeys gave the place an aura of the Nineteenth Century. Dasein half expected to see a maid in ruffled cap, apron with a bow at the back, long skirt and black stockings, sensible shoes—or a portly banker type with tight vest and high collar, an expanse of gold chain at the waist. He felt out of place, out of style here.

The brass key worked smoothly in the door of two fifty-one; it let him into a room of high ceilings, one window looking down onto the parking area. Dasein turned on the light. The switch controlled a tasseled floor lamp beside a curve-fronted teak dresser. The amber light revealed a partly opened doorway into a tiled bathroom (the sound of water dripping there), a thick-legged desk-table with a single straight chair pushed against it. The bed was narrow and high with a heavily carved headboard.

Dasein pushed down on the surface of the bed. It felt soft. He dropped his suitcase onto the bed, stared at it. An edge of white fabric protruded from one end.

He opened the suitcase, studied the contents. Dasein knew himself for a prissy, meticulous packer. The case now betrayed a subtle disarray. Someone had opened it and searched it. Well, it hadn't been locked. He checked the contents—nothing missing.

Why are they curious about me? he wondered.

He looked around for a telephone, found it, a standard French handset, on a shelf beside the desk. As he moved, he caught sight of himself in the mirror above the dresser—eyes wide, mouth in a straight line. Grim. He shook his head, smiled. The smile felt out of place.

Dasein sat down in the straight chair, put the phone to his ear. There was a smell of disinfectant soap in the room—and something like garlic. After a moment, he jiggled the hook.

Presently, a woman's voice came on: "This is the desk."

"I'd like to place a call to Berkeley," Dasein said. He gave the number. There was a moment's silence, then: "Your room number, sir?"

"Two fifty-one."

"One moment, please."

He heard the sound of dialing, ringing. Another operator came on the line. Dasein listened with only half his attention as the call was placed. The smell of garlic was quite strong. He stared at the high old bed, his open suitcase. The bed appeared inviting, telling him how tired he was. His chest ached. He took a deep breath.

"Dr. Selador here."

Selador's India-*cum*-Oxford accent sounded familiar and close. Dasein bent to the telephone, identified himself, his mind caught suddenly by that feeling of intimate nearness linked to the knowledge of the actual distance, the humming wires reaching down almost half the length of the state.

"Gilbert, old fellow, you made it all right, I see." Selador's voice was full of cheer.

"I'm at the Santaroga House, Doctor."

"I hear it's quite comfortable."

"Look's that way." Through his buzzing tiredness, Dasein felt a sense of foolishness. Why had he made this call? Selador's sharp mind would probe for underlying meanings, motives.

"I presume you didn't call just to tell me you've arrived," Selador said.

"No . . . I . . . " Dasein realized he couldn't express his own vague uneasiness, that it wouldn't make sense, this feeling of estrangement, the separation of Santarogans and Outsiders, the pricklings of warning fear. "I'd like you to look into the oil company dealings with this area," Dasein said. "See if you can find out how they do business in the valley. There's apparently an independent service station here. I want to know who supplies the gas, oil, parts—that sort of thing."

"Good point, Gilbert. I'll put one of our . . . " There was a sudden crackling, bapping sound on the line. It stopped and there was dead silence.

"Dr. Selador?"

Silence.

Damn! Dasein thought. He jiggled the hook. "Operator. Operator!"

A masculine voice came on the line. Dasein recognized the desk clerk's twang. "Who's that creating all that commotion?" the clerk demanded.

"I was cut off on my call to Berkeley," Dasein said. "Could you . . . "

"Line's out," the clerk snapped.

"Could I come down to the lobby and place the call from a pay phone?" Dasein asked. As he asked it, the thought of walking that long distance down to the lobby repelled Dasein. The feeling of tiredness was a weight on his chest.

"There's no line out of the valley right now," the clerk said. "Call can't be placed."

Dasein passed a hand across his forehead. His skin felt clammy and he wondered if he'd picked up a germ. The room around him seemed to expand and contract. His mouth was dry and he had to swallow twice before asking: "When do they expect to have the line restored?"

"How the hell do I know?" the clerk demanded.

Dasein took the receiver away from his ear, stared at it. This was a very peculiar desk clerk . . . and a very peculiar room the way it wavered and slithered with its stench of garlic and its . . .

He grew aware of a faint hissing.

Dasein's gaze was drawn on a string of growing astonishment to an old-fashioned gaslight jet that jutted from the wall beside the hall door.

Stink of garlic? Gas!

A yapping, barking voice yammered on the telephone.

Dasein looked down at the instrument in his hand. How far away it seemed. Through the window beyond the phone he could see the Inn sign: *Gold Rush Museum*. Window equaled air. Dasein found muscles that obeyed, lurched across the desk, fell, smashing the telephone through the window.

The yapping voice grew fainter.

Dasein felt his body stretched across the desk. His head lay near the shattered window. He could see the telephone cord stretching out the window. There was cool air blowing on a distant forehead, a painful chill in his lungs.

They tried to kill me, he thought. It was a wondering thought, full of amazement. His mind focused on the two investigators who'd already died on this project—accidents. Simple, easily explained accidents . . . just like this one!

The air—how cold it felt on his exposed skin. His lungs burned with it. There was a hammering pulse at his temple where it pressed against the desk surface. The pulse went on and on and on . . .

A pounding on wood joined the pulse. For a space, they beat in an insane syncopation.

"You in there! Open up!" How commanding, that voice. *Open up*, Dasein thought. That meant getting to one's feet, crossing the room, turning a door handle . . .

I'm helpless, he thought. *They could still kill me.*

He heard metal rasp against metal. The air blew stronger across his face. Someone said: "Gas!"

Hands grabbed Dasein's shoulders. He was hauled back, half carried, half dragged out of the room. The face of Marden, the red-haired patrol captain, swung across his vision. He saw the clerk: pale, staring face, bald forehead glistening under yellow light. There was a brown ceiling directly in front of Dasein. He felt a rug, hard and rasping, beneath his back.

A twanging voice said: "Who's going to pay for that window?" Someone else said: "I'll get Dr. Piaget."

Dasein's attention centered on Marden's mouth, a blurred object seen through layers of distortion. There appeared to be anger lines at the corners of the mouth. It turned toward the hovering pale face of the desk clerk, said: "To hell with your window, Johnson! I've told you enough times to get those gas jets out of this place. How many rooms still have them?''

"Don't you take that tone with me, Al Marden. I've known you since . . .''

"I'm not interested in how long you've known me, Johnson. How many rooms still have those gas jets?''

The clerk's voice came with an angry tone of hurt: "Only this'n an' four upstairs. Nobody in the other rooms.''

"Get 'em out by tomorrow night,'' Marden said.

Hurrying footsteps interrupted the argument. Dr. Piaget's round face blotted out Dasein's view of the ceiling. The face wore a look of concern. Fingers reached down, spread Dasein's eyelids. Piaget said: "Let's get him on a bed.''

"Is he going to be all right?'' the clerk asked.

"It's about time you asked,'' Marden said.

"We got him in time,'' Piaget said. "Is that room across the hall empty?''

"He can have 260,'' the clerk said. "I'll open it.''

"You realize this is Jenny's fellow from the school you almost killed?'' Marden asked, his voice receding as he moved away beside the clerk.

"Jenny's fellow?'' There was the sound of a key in a lock. "But I thought. . . .''

"Never mind what you thought!''

Piaget's face moved close to Dasein. "Can you hear me, young fellow?'' he asked.

Dasein drew in a painful breath, croaked, "Yes.''

"You'll have quite a head, but you'll recover.''

Piaget's face went away. Hands picked Dasein up. The ceiling moved. There was another room around him: like the first one—tall ceiling, even the sound of dripping water. He felt a bed beneath his back, hands beginning to undress him. Sudden nausea gripped him. Dasein pushed the hands away.

Someone helped him to the bathroom where he was sick. He felt better afterward—weak, but with a clearer head, a better sense of control over his muscles. He saw it was Piaget who'd helped him.

"Feel like getting back to bed now?'' Piaget asked.

"Yes.''

"I'll give you a good shot of iron to counteract the gas effect on your blood,'' Piaget said. "You'll be all right.''

"How'd that gas jet get turned on?'' Dasein asked. His voice came out a hoarse whisper.

"Johnson got mixed up fooling with the valves in the kitchen,'' Piaget said. "Wouldn't have been any harm done if some idiot hadn't opened the jet in your room.''

"I coulda sworn I had 'em all turned off.'' That was the clerk's voice from somewhere beyond the bathroom door.

"They better be capped by tomorrow night,'' Marden said.

They sounded so reasonable, Dasein thought. Marden appeared genuinely angry. The look on Piaget's face could be nothing other than concern.

Could it have been a real accident? Dasein wondered.

He reminded himself then two men had died by accident in this valley while engaged in the investigation.

"All right,'' Piaget said. "Al, you and Pim and the others can clear out now. I'll get him to bed.''

"Okay, Larry. Clear out, all of you.'' That was Marden.

"I'll get his bags from the other room." That was a voice Dasein didn't recognize.

Presently, with Piaget's help, Dasein found himself in pajamas and in the bed. He felt clearheaded, wide awake and lonely even with Piaget still in the room.

Among strangers, Dasein thought.

"Here, take this," Piaget said. He pressed two pills into Dasein's mouth, forced a glass of water on him. Dasein gulped, felt the pills rasp down his throat in a wash of water.

"What was that?" Dasein asked as he pushed the glass away.

"The iron and a sedative."

"I don't want to sleep. The gas . . . "

"You didn't get enough gas to make that much difference. Now, you rest easy." Piaget patted his shoulder. "Bed rest and fresh air are the best therapy you can get. Someone'll look in on you from time to time tonight. I'll check back on you in the morning."

"Someone," Dasein said. "A nurse?"

"Yes," Piaget said, his voice brusk. "A nurse. You'll be as safe here as in a hospital."

Dasein looked at the night beyond the room's window. *Why the feeling of danger now, then?* he wondered. *Is it reaction?* He could feel the sedative blurring his senses, soothing him. The sense of danger persisted.

"Jenny will be happy to know you're here," Piaget said. He left the room, turning off the light, closing the door softly.

Dasein felt he had been smothered in darkness. He fought down panic, restored himself to a semblance of calm.

Jenny . . . Jenny . . .

Marden's odd conversation with the clerk, Johnson, returned to him. " . . . *Jenny's fellow from the school . . . "*

What had Johnson thought? What was the thing Marden had cut short?

Dasein fought the sedative. The drip-drip of water in the bathroom invaded his awareness. The room was an alien cell.

Was it just an accident?

He remembered the fragmented confusion of the instant when he'd focused on that hissing gas jet. Now, when the danger was past, he felt terror.

It couldn't have been an accident!

But why would Johnson want to kill him?

The disconnected telephone call haunted Dasein. Was the line really down? What would Selador do? Selador knew the dangers here.

Dasein felt the sedative pulling him down into sleep. He tried to focus on the investigation. It was such a fascinating project. He could hear Selador explaining the facets that made the Santaroga Project such a glittering gem—

"*Taken singly, no item in this collection of facts could be considered alarming or worthy of extended attention. You might find it interesting that no person from Cloverdale, California, could be found in a mental hospital. It might be of passing interest to learn that the people of Hope, Missouri, consumed very little tobacco. Would you be alarmed to discover that all the business of Enumclaw, Washington, were locally owned? Certainly not. But when you bring all of these and the other facts together into a single community, something disturbing emerges. There is a difference at work here.*"

The drip of water in the bathroom was a compelling distraction. *Dangerous difference*, Dasein thought. *Who'll look in on me?* he wondered.

It occurred to him to ask himself then who had sounded the alarm. The breaking window had alerted someone. The most likely person would be Johnson, the room clerk. Why would he bring help to the person he was trying to kill? The paranoia in his own thoughts began to impress itself on Dasein.

It was an accident, Dasein thought. *It was an accident in a place of dangerous difference.*

Dasein's morning began with a sensation of hunger. He awoke to cramping pains. Events of the night flooded into his memory. His head felt as though it had been kicked from the inside.

Gently, he pushed himself upright. There was a window directly ahead of him with the green branch of an oak tree across it. As though his muscles were controlled by some hidden force, Dasein found himself looking up at the door to see if there was a gas jet. Nothing met his questing gaze but a patch on the wallpaper to mark the place where a jet had been.

Holding his head as level as possible, Dasein eased himself out of bed and into the bathroom. A cold shower restored some of his sense of reality.

He kept telling himself: *It was an accident.*

A bluejay was sitting on the oak branch screeching when Dasein emerged from the bathroom. The sound sent little clappers of pain through Dasein's head. He dressed hurriedly, hunger urging him. The bluejay was joined by a companion. They screeched and darted at each other through the oak tree, their topknots twitching. Dasein gritted his teeth, faced the mirror to tie his tie. As he was finishing the knot, he saw reflected in the mirror the slow inward movement of the hall door. A corner of a wheeled tray appeared. Dishes clattered. The door swung wider.

Jenny appeared in the doorway pushing the tray. Dasein stared at her in the mirror, his hands frozen at the tie. She wore a red dress, her long black hair caught in a matching bandeaux. Her skin displayed a healthy tan. Blue eyes stared back at him in the mirror. Her oval face was set in a look of watchful waiting. Her mouth was as full as he remembered it, hesitating on the edge of a smile, a dimple flickering at her left cheek.

"Finish your tie," she said. "I've brought you some breakfast." Her voice had a well-remembered, throaty, soothing tone.

Dasein turned, moved toward her as though pulled by strings. Jenny abandoned the cart, met him half way. She came into his arms, lifting her lips to be kissed. Dasein, feeling the warmth of her kiss and the familiar pressure of her against him, experienced a sensation of coming home.

Jenny pulled away, studied his face. "Oh, Gil," she said, "I've missed you so much. Why didn't you even write?"

He stared at her, surprised to silence for a moment, then: "But I did write. You never answered."

She pushed away from him, her features contorted by a scowl. "Ohhh!" She stamped her foot.

"Well, I see you found him." It was Dr. Piaget in the doorway. He pushed the cart all the way into the room, closed the door.

Jenny whirled on him. "Uncle Larry! Did you keep Gil's letters from me?"

Piaget looked from her to Dasein. "Letters? What letters?"

"Gil wrote and I never got the letters!"

"Oh." Piaget nodded. "Well, you know how they are at the post office sometimes—valley girl, fellow from outside."

"Ohhh! I could scratch their eyes out!"

"Easy, girl." Piaget smiled at Dasein.

Jenny whirled back into Dasein's arms, surprised him with another kiss. He broke away slightly breathless.

"There," she said. "That's for being here. Those old biddies at the post office can't dump *that* in the trash basket."

"What old biddies?" Dasein asked. He felt he had missed part of the conversation. The warmth of Jenny's kisses, her open assumption nothing had changed between them, left him feeling defenseless, wary. A year had passed, after all. He'd managed to stay away from here for a year—leaning on his wounded masculine ego, true, fearful he'd find Jenny married . . . lost to him forever. But what had she leaned on? She could've come to Berkeley, if only for a visit.

And I could've come here.

Jenny grinned.

"Why're you grinning?" he demanded. "And you haven't explained this about the post office and the . . . "

"I'm grinning because I'm so happy," she said. "I'm grinning because I see the wheels going around in your head. Why didn't one of us go see the other before now? Well, *you're* here as I knew you would be. I just *knew* you would be." She hugged him impulsively, said: "About the post office . . . "

"I think Gilbert's breakfast is getting cold," Piaget said. "You don't mind if I call you Gilbert?"

"He doesn't mind," Jenny said. Her voice was bantering, but there was a sudden stiffness in her body. She pushed away from Dasein.

Piaget lifted a cover from one of the plates on the cart, said: "Jaspers omelette, I see. *Real* Jaspers."

Jenny spoke defensively with a curious lack of vitality: "I made it myself in Johnson's kitchen."

"I see," Piaget said. "Yes . . . well, perhaps that's best."

He indicated the plate. "Have at it, Gilbert."

The thought of food made Dasein's stomach knot with hunger. He wanted to sit down and bolt the omelette . . . but something made him hesitate. He couldn't evade the nagging sense of danger.

"What's this Jaspers business?" he asked.

"Oh, that," Jenny said, pulling the cart over to the chair by the desk. "That just means something made with a product from the Co-op. This is our cheddar in the omelette. Sit down and eat."

"You'll like it," Piaget said. He crossed the room, put a hand on Dasein's shoulder, eased him into the chair. "Just let me have a quick look at you." He pinched Dasein's left ear lobe, studied it, looked at his eyes. "You're looking pretty fit. How's the head?"

"It's better now. It was pretty fierce when I woke up."

"Okay. Eat your breakfast. Take it easy for a day or two. Let me know if you feel nauseated again or have any general symptoms of lethargy. I suggest you eat liver for dinner and I'll have Jenny bring you some more iron pills. You weren't in there long enough to cause you any permanent trouble."

"When I think of that Mr. Johnson's carelessness, I want to take one of his cleavers to him," Jenny said.

"We *are* bloodthirsty today, aren't we," Piaget said.

Dasein picked up his fork, sampled the omelette. Jenny watched him, waiting. The omelette was delicious—moist and with a faint bite of cheese. He swallowed, smiled at her.

Jenny grinned back. "You know," she said, "that's the first food I ever cooked for you."

"Don't rush him off his feet, girl," Piaget said. He patted her head, said: "I'll leave you two for now. Why don't you bring your young man along home for dinner? I'll have Sarah make what he needs." He glanced at Dasein. "That all right with you?"

Dasein swallowed another bite of the omelette. The cheese left a tangy aftertaste that reminded him of the unpasteurized beer Burdeaux had served. "I'd be honored, sir," he said.

"Honored, yet," Piaget said. "We'll expect you around seven." He glanced at his wristwatch. "It's almost eight-thirty, Jenny. Aren't you working today?"

"I called George and told him I'd be late."

"He didn't object?"

"He knows . . . I have a friend . . . visiting." She blushed.

"Like that, eh? Well, don't get into any trouble." Piaget turned, lumbered from the room with a head-down purposeful stride.

Jenny turned a shy, questioning smile on Dasein. "Don't mind Uncle Larry," she said. "He darts around like that—one subject then another. He's a very real, wonderful person."

"Where do you work?" Dasein asked.

"At the Co-op."

"The cheese factory?"

"Yes. I'm . . . I'm on the inspection line."

Dasein swallowed, reminded himself he was here to do a market study. He was a spy. And what would Jenny say when she discovered that? But Jenny posed a new puzzle. She had a superior talent for clinical psychology—even according to Dr. Selador whose standards were high. Yet . . . she worked in the cheese factory.

"Isn't there any work . . . in your line here?" he asked.

"It's a good job," she said. She sat down on the edge of the desk, swung her legs. "Finish your breakfast. I didn't make that coffee. It's out of the hotel urn. Don't drink it if it's too strong. There's orange juice in the metal pitcher. I remembered you take your coffee black and didn't bring any . . ."

"Whoa!" he said.

"I'm talking too much I know it," she said. She hugged herself. "Oh, Gil, I'm so happy you're here. Finish your breakfast and you can take me across to the Co-op. Maybe I can take you on the guided tour. It's a fascinating place. There are lots of dark corners back in the storage cave."

Dasein drained his coffee, shook his head. "Jenny, you are incorrigible."

"Gil, you're going to love it here. I know you are," she said.

Dasein wiped his lips on his napkin. She was still in love with him. He could see that in every look. And he . . . he felt the same way about her. It was still *love me love my valley*, though. Her words betrayed it. Dasein sighed. He could see the blank wall of an unresolvable difference looming ahead of them. If her love could stand the discovery of his true role here, could it also stand breaking away from the valley? Would she come away with him?

"Gil, are you all right?" she asked.

He pushed his chair back, got up. "Yes. I'm . . . "

The telephone rang.

Jenny reached behind her on the desk, brought the receiver to her ear. "Dr. Dasein's room." She grinned at Dasein. The grin turned to a scowl. "Oh, it's you, Mr. Pem Johnson, is it? Well, I'll tell you a thing or two, Mr. Johnson! I think you're a criminal the way you almost killed Dr. Dasein! If you'd . . . No! Don't you try to make excuses! Open gas jets in the rooms! I think Dr. Dasein ought to sue you for every cent you have!"

A tinny, rasping noise came from the phone. Dasein recognized only a few words. The grin returned to Jenny's face. "It's Jenny Sorge, that's who it is," she said. "Don't you . . . well, I'll tell you if you'll be quiet for a minute! I'm here bringing Dr. Dasein what the doctor ordered for him—a good breakfast. He doesn't dare eat anything you'd have prepared for him. It'd probably have poison in it!"

Dasein crossed to a trunk stand where his suitcase had been left, opened it. He spoke over his shoulder. "Jenny, what's he want, for heaven's sake?"

She waved him to silence.

Dasein rummaged in the suitcase looking for his briefcase. He tried to remember what had been done with it in the confusion of the previous night, looked around the room. No sign of it. Someone had gone to the other room for his things. Maybe whoever it was had missed the briefcase. Dasein thought of the case's contents, wet his lips with his tongue. Every step of his program to unravel the mystery of the Santaroga Barrier was outlined there. In the wrong hands, that information could cause him trouble, throw up new barriers.

"I'll tell him," Jenny said.

"Wait a minute," Dasein said. "I want to talk to him." He took the phone from her. "Johnson?"

"What do you want?" There was that twangy belligerency, but Dasein couldn't blame him after the treatment he'd received from Jenny.

"My briefcase," Dasein said. "It was in the other room. Would you send up someone with a key and . . . "

"Your damned briefcase isn't in that room, mister! I cleaned the place out and I ought to know."

"Then where is it?" Dasein asked.

"If it's the case you were so touchy about last night, I saw Captain Marden leave with something that looked like it last night after all the commotion you caused."

"I caused?" Outrage filled Dasein's voice. "See here, Johnson! You stop twisting the facts!"

After only a heartbeat of silence, Johnson said: "I was, wasn't I? Sorry."

Johnson's abrupt candor disarmed the psychologist in Dasein. In a way, it reminded him of Jenny. Santarogans, he found, displayed a lopsided reality that was both attractive and confusing. When he'd collected his thoughts, all Dasein could say was: "What would Marden be doing with my case?"

"That's for him to say and you to find out," Johnson said with all his old belligerence. There was a sharp click as he broke the connection.

Dasein shook his head, put the phone back on its hook.

"Al Marden wants you to have lunch with him at the Blue Ewe," Jenny said.

"Hmmm?" He looked up at her, bemused, her words taking a moment to register. "Marden . . . lunch?"

"Twelve noon. The Blue Ewe's on the Avenue of the Giants where it goes through town . . . on the right just past the first cross street."

"Marden? The Highway patrol captain?"

"Yes. Johnson just passed the message along." She slipped down off the desk, a flash of knees, a swirl of the red skirt. "Come along. Escort me to work."

Dasein picked up his suitcoat, allowed himself to be led from the room.

That damn' briefcase with all its forms and notes and letters, he thought. *The whole show!* But it gave him a perverse feeling of satisfaction to know that everything would be out in the open. *I wasn't cut out to be a cloak and dagger type.*

There was no escaping the realization, though, that revelation of his real purpose here would intensify Santaroga's conspiracy of silence. And how would Jenny react?

2

DASEIN'S FIRST impression of the Jasper Cheese Cooperative with the people at work in and around it was that the place was a hive. It loomed whitely behind its fence as Jenny led him from the Inn. He found it an odd companion for the Inn, just across the road, nestled against a steep hill, poking odd squares and rectangles up onto an outcropping. The previous night's brooding look had been replaced by this appearance of humming efficiency with electric carts buzzing across the yard, their platforms loaded with oblong packages. People walked with a leaning sense of purpose.

A hive, Dasein thought. There must be a queen inside and these were the workers, guarding, gathering food.

A uniformed guard, a police dog on a leash beside him, took Dasein's name as Jenny introduced him. The guard opened a gate in the chain-link fence. His dog grinned wolfishly at Dasein, whined.

Dasein remembered the baying he'd heard when he'd first looked down into the valley. That had been less than fourteen hours ago, Dasein realized. The time felt stretched out, longer. He asked himself why dogs guarded the Co-op. The question bothered him.

The yard they crossed was an immaculate concrete surface. Now that he was close to the factory, Dasein saw that it was a complex of structures that had been joined by filling the between areas with odd additions and covered walkways.

Jenny's mood changed markedly once they were well inside the grounds. Dasein saw her become more assertive, sure of herself. She introduced Dasein to four persons while crossing the yard—Willa Burdeaux among them. Willa turned out to be a small husky-voiced young woman with a face that was almost ugly in its tiny, concise sharpness. She had her father's deeps-of-darkness skin, a petite figure.

"I met your father last night," Dasein said.

"Daddy told me," she said. She turned a knowing look on Jenny, added: "Anything I can do, just tell me, honey."

"Maybe later," Jenny said. "We have to be running."

"You're going to like it here, Gilbert Dasein," Willa said. She turned away with a wave, hurried across the yard.

Disturbed by the undertones of the conversation, Dasein allowed himself to be led down a side bay, into a wide door that opened onto an aisle between stacked cartons of Jaspers Cheese. Somewhere beyond the stacks there was a multiplexity of sounds—hissings, stampings, gurgling water, a clank-clank-clank.

The aisle ended in a short flight of wide steps, up to a loading bay with hand trucks racked along its edge. Jenny led him through a door marked "Office."

It was such an ordinary place—clips of order forms racked along a wall, two desks with women seated at them typing, a long counter with a gate at one end, windows opening onto the yard and a view of the Inn, a door labeled "Manager" beyond the women.

The door opened as Dasein and Jenny stopped at the counter. Out stepped one of the card players from the Inn's dining room—the balding sandy hair, the deeply cleft chin and wide mouth—George Nis. The heavily lidded blue eyes swept past Dasein to Jenny.

"Problems in Bay Nine, Jenny," Nis said. "You're needed over there right away."

"Oh, darn!" Jenny said.

"I'll take care of your friend," Nis said. "We'll see if we can't let you off early for your dinner date."

Jenny squeezed Dasein's hand, said: "Darling, forgive me. Duty and all that." She blinked a smile at him, whirled and was back out the door, the red skirt swirling.

The women at their typewriters looked up, seemed to take in Dasein with one look, went back to their work. Nis came to the gate in the counter, opened it.

"Come on in, Dr. Dasein." He extended a hand.

The handshake was firm, casual.

Dasein followed the man into an oak-paneled office, unable to get his mind off the fact that Nis knew about the dinner date with Jenny. How could the man know? Piaget had extended the invitation only a few minutes before.

They sat down separated by a wide desk, its top empty of papers. The chairs were padded, comfortable with sloping arms. In large frames behind Nis hung an aerial photograph of the Co-op and what appeared to be a ground plan. Dasein recognized the layout of the yard and front of the building. The back became heavy dark lines that wandered off into the hill like the tributaries of a river. They were labeled with the initial *J* and numbers—*J–5 . . . J–14 . . .*

Nis saw the direction of Dasein's gaze, said: "Those are the storage caverns—constant temperature and humidity." He coughed discreetly behind a hand, said: "You catch us at an embarrassing moment, Dr. Dasein. I've nobody I can release to show you through the plant. Could Jenny bring you back another day?"

"At your convenience," Dasein said. He studied Nis, feeling oddly wary, on guard.

"Please don't wear any cologne or hair dressing or anything like that when you come," Nis said. "You'll notice that our women wear no makeup and we don't allow female visitors from outside to go into the cave or storage areas. It's quite easy to contaminate the culture, give an odd flavor to an entire batch."

Dasein was suddenly acutely aware of the aftershave lotion he'd used that morning.

"I'll be pure and clean," he said. He looked to the right out the windows, caught suddenly by motion there on the road between the Co-op and the Inn.

A peculiar high-wheeled vehicle went lurching past. Dasein counted eight pairs of wheels. They appeared to be at least fifteen feet in diameter, big ballooning doughnuts that hummed on the pavement. The wheels were slung on heavy arms like insect legs.

In an open cab, high up in front, four leashed hounds seated behind him, rode Al Marden. He appeared to be steering by using two vertical handles.

"What in the devil is that?" Dasein demanded. He jumped up, crossed to the window to get a better look at the machine as it sped down the road. "Isn't that Captain Marden driving it?"

"That's our game warden's bush buggy," Nis said. "Al acts as game warden sometimes when the regular man's sick or busy on something else. Must've been out patroling the south hills. Heard there were some deer hunters from outside messing around there this morning."

"You don't allow outsiders to hunt in the valley, is that it?" Dasein asked.

"*Nobody* hunts in the valley," Nis corrected him. "Too much chance of stray bullets hitting someone. Most of the people around this area know the law, but we occasionally get someone from down south who blunders in. There're very few places the buggy can't get to them, though. We set them straight in a hurry."

Dasein imagined that giant-wheeled monstrosity lurching over the brush, descending on some hapless hunter who'd blundered into the valley. He found his sympathies with the hunter.

"I've never seen a vehicle like that before," Dasein said. "Is it something new?"

"Sam, Sam Scheler, built the bush buggy ten, twelve years ago," Nis said. "We were getting some poachers from over by Porterville then. They don't bother us anymore."

"I imagine not," Dasein said.

"I hope you'll forgive me," Nis said. "I do have a great deal of work and we're short-handed today. Get Jenny to bring you back later in the week . . . after . . . well, later in the week."

After what? Dasein wondered. He found himself strangely alert. He'd never felt this clearheaded before. He wondered if it could be some odd after effect of the gas.

"I'll, ah, let myself out," he said, rising.

"The gate guard will be expecting you," Nis said. He remained seated, his gaze fixed on Dasein with an odd intensity until the door closed between them.

The women in the outer office glanced up as Dasein let himself through the counter gate, went back to their work. A gang of men was loading hand trucks on the ramp when Dasein emerged. He felt their eyes boring into him as he made his way down the dock above them. A sliding door off to the left opened suddenly. Dasein glimpsed a long table with a conveyor belt down its middle, a line of men and women working along it, sorting packages.

Something about the people in that line caught his attention. They were oddly dull-eyed, slow in their actions. Dasein saw their legs beneath the table. The legs appeared to be held in stocks.

The door closed.

Dasein continued out into the sunshine, disturbed by what he had seen. Those workers had appeared . . . mentally retarded. He crossed the yard wondering. Problems in Bay 9? Jenny was a competent psychologist. More than competent. What did she do here? What did she *really* do?

The gate guard nodded to him, said: "Come again, Dr. Dasein." The man went into his little house, lifted a telephone, spoke briefly into it.

'The gate guard will be expecting you,' Dasein thought.

He crossed to the Inn, ran lightly up the steps and into the lobby. A gray-haired

woman sat behind the desk working at an adding machine. She looked up at
Dasein.

"Could I get a line out to Berkeley?" he asked.

"All the lines are out," she said. "Some trouble with a brush fire."

"Thanks."

Dasein went outside, paused on the long porch, scanned the sky. Brush fire?
There wasn't a sign or smell of smoke.

Everything about Santaroga could appear so natural, he thought, if it weren't for
the underlying sense of strangeness and secrecy that made his neck hairs crawl.

Dasein took a deep breath, went down to his truck, nursed it to life.

This time, he took the turn to 'City Center.' The Avenue of the Giants widened
to four lanes presently with homes and business mixed at seeming random on both
sides. A park opened on the left—paved paths, central bandstand, flower borders.
Beyond the park, a stone church lifted an imposing spire into the sky. The sign on
its lawn read: "Church of All Faiths . . . Sermon: 'Intensity of God response as a
function of anxiety.' "

Intensity of God response? Dasein wondered. It was quite the oddest sermon
announcement he had ever seen. He made a mental note to try and catch that
sermon on Sunday.

The people on the streets began to catch Dasein's attention. Their alertness, the
brisk way they moved, was a contrast to the dullness of the line he'd seen in the
Co-op. Who were those dull creatures? For that matter, who were these swiftly
striding folk on the streets?

There was vitality and a happy freedom in the people he saw, Dasein realized.
He wondered if the mood could be infectious. He had never felt more vital himself.

Dasein noted a sign on his right just past the park: A gamboling sheep with the
letters "Blue Ewe" carved in a rolling script. It was a windowless front laced with
blue stone, an impersonal façade broken only by wide double doors containing
one round glass port each.

So Marden wanted to have lunch with him there. Why? It seemed obvious the
patrol captain had taken the briefcase. Was he going to pull the 'go-and-never-
darken-my-door' routine he'd used on the hapless salesman in the dining room of
the Inn? Or would it be something more subtle designed for 'Jenny's friend from
the school'?

At the far end of the town, the street widened once more to open a broad access
to a twelve-sided service station. Dasein slowed his truck to admire the structure. It
was the largest service station he had ever seen. A canopy structure jutted from
each of the twelve sides. Beneath each canopy were three rows of pumps, each row
designed to handle four vehicles. Just beyond it, separated from the giant wheel of
the station, stood a building containing rows of grease racks. Behind the station
was a football-field-sized parking area with a large building at the far end labeled
"Garage."

Dasein drove into the station, stopped at an outside row of pumps, got out to
study the layout. He counted twenty grease racks, six cars being serviced. Cars
were coming and going all around him. It was another hive. He wondered why
none of the datum-data mentioned this complex. The place swarmed with young
men in neat blue-gray uniforms.

One of the neat young men came trotting up to Dasein, said: "What grade, sir?"

"Grade?"

"What octane gas do you want?"

"What do you have?"

"Eighty, ninety and a hundred-plus."

"Fill it with ninety and check the oil."

Dasein left the young man to his labors, walked out toward the street to get a better perspective on the station. It covered at least four acres, he estimated. He returned to the truck as the young man emerged from beneath the hood holding the dipstick.

"Your oil's down a bit more than a quart," the young man said.

"Put in thirty-weight detergent," Dasein said.

"Excuse me," he said, "but I heard this clunker drive in. We carry an aircraft grade of forty weight. I'd recommend you use it. You won't burn quite as much."

"What's it cost?"

"Same as all the others—thirty-five cents a quart."

"Okay." Dasein shook his head. Aircraft grade at that price? Where did *Mr. Sam* buy it?

"How do you like Santaroga?" the young man asked, his voice bright with the invitation for a compliment.

"Fine," Dasein said. "Beautiful little town. You know, this is the biggest service station I've ever seen. It's a wonder there haven't been any newspaper or magazine articles about it."

"Old Sam doesn't cotton to publicity," the attendant said.

"Why's it so damn' big?" Dasein asked.

"Has to be big. It's the only one in the valley." The young man worked his way around the engine, checking the water in the radiator, the level in the battery. He grinned at Dasein. "Kinda surprises most outsiders. We find it handy. Some of the farmers have their own pumps and there's service at the airport, but they all get their supplies through Sam." He closed the hood.

"And where does Old Sam get *his* supplies?"

The attendant leveled a probing stare at Dasein. "I sure hope you haven't taken on a sideline with one of the big oil companies, sir," he said. "If you're thinking of selling to Sam, forget it."

"I'm just curious," Dasein said. The attendant's choice of words was puzzling. *Sideline?* Dasein chose to ignore it for the moment, intent on the larger question.

"Sam orders his supplies once a year on open bid," the attendant said. He topped off the truck's gas tank, returned the hose to its holder. "This year it's a little company in Oklahoma. They truck it up here on convoys."

"That so?"

"I wouldn't say it if it weren't so."

"I wasn't questioning your word," Dasein said. "I was registering surprise."

"Don't see much to get surprised about. Person ought to buy where he gets the most value for his money. That'll be three dollars and three cents."

Dasein counted out the change, said: "Is there a pay phone around here?"

"If you're making a local call, there's a phone inside you can use, Dr. Dasein," the attendant said. "The pay phones are over there beside the rack building, but no sense wasting your time if you're calling outside. Lines are down. There was a fire over on the ridge."

Dasein went to full alert, glared at the attendant. "How'd you know my name?" he demanded.

"Heck, mister, it's all over town. You're Jenny's fellow from the city. You're the reason she sends all the locals packing."

The grin that went with this statement should have been completely disarming, but it only made Dasein more wary.

"You're going to like it here," the attendant said. "Everybody does." The grin faded somewhat. "If you'll excuse me, sir. I've other cars to service."

Dasein found himself staring at a retreating back. *He suspected I might represent an oil company,* Dasein thought, *but he knows my name . . . and he knows about Jenny.* It was a curious disparity and Dasein felt it should tell him something. It could be the simple truth, though.

A long Green Chrysler Imperial pulled into the empty space on the other side of the pumps. The driver, a fat man smoking a cigarette in a holder, leaned out, asked: "Hey! This the road out to 395?"

"Straight ahead," Dasein said.

"Any gas stations along the way?"

"Not here in the valley," Dasein said. "Maybe something outside." He shrugged. "I've never been out that way."

"You damn' natives," the driver growled. The Imperial shot ahead in a surge of power, swerved out onto the avenue and was gone.

"Up yours," Dasein muttered. "Who the hell you calling a native?"

He climbed into his truck, turned back the way he had come. At the fork, he headed up the mountain toward Porterville. The road climbed up, up—winding its way out of the redwoods and into a belt of oaks. He came at last to the turn off where he'd taken his first long look at the valley. He pulled out and parked.

A light smokey haze obscured details, but the Co-op stood out plainly and the slash burner of a sawmill off to the left. The town itself was a patch of color in the trees—tile roofs—and there was a serpentine river line out of the hills straight across from him. Dasein glanced at his wristwatch—five minutes to ten. He debated going out to Porterville and placing his call to Selador there. That would crowd him on the date with Marden, though. He decided to post a letter to Selador, have the "burned out phone lines" story checked from that end.

Without his briefcase and notes, Dasein felt at a disadvantage. He rummaged in the glove compartment, found a small gas-record notebook and stub of pencil, began setting down his observations for later formal entry in his report.

"The township itself is small," he wrote, "but it appears to serve a large market area. There are a great many people about during the day. Note twelve double pumps in service station. Transients?

"Odd alertness about the natives. Sharpness of attitude toward each other and *outsiders.*

"Question local use of Jaspers products. Why won't the cheese travel? What's the reason for the decided local preference? It tastes different than what I bought outside. What about aftertaste? Subjective? What relationship to the beer?

"Investigate use of Jaspers as a label. Adjective?"

Something big was moving through the trees on the hill beyond the Co-op. The movement caught Dasein's attention. He studied it a moment. Too many trees intervened to permit a clear look

Dasein went around to the camper back, found his binoculars there. He focused them on the movement in the trees. The donut-wheeled bush buggy leaped into view. Marden was driving. It threaded its way through trees and buck brush. The thing appeared to be herding something . . . or someone. Dasein scanned ahead for a clearing, found one, waited. Three men in hunting clothes emerged, hands clasped over their heads. Two dogs flanked them, watchful, guarding. The hunters appeared angry, frightened.

The group angled down into a stand of redwoods, was lost to view. Dasein climbed back into the cab, made a note on what he had seen.

It was all of a pattern, he thought. These were things that could be resolved by natural, logical explanations. A law enforcement officer had picked up three illegal hunters. That was what law enforcement officers were supposed to do. But the incident carried what Dasein was coming to recognize as a Santaroga twist. There was something about it out of phase with the way the rest of the world operated.

He headed his truck back into the valley, determined to question Marden about the captive hunters.

3

THE BLUE Ewe's interior was a low-key grotto, its walls painted in varying intensities of pastel blue. Rather ordinary banquette booths with tables flanked an open area of tables and chairs. A long bar with a mirror decorated by dancing sheep occupied the back wall.

Marden awaited him in one of the booths. A tall iced drink stood in front of him. The patrol captain appeared relaxed, his red hair neatly combed. The collar tabs of his uniform shirt carried the double bars of a captain. He wore no coat. His eyes followed Dasein's approach with an alert directness.

"Care for a drink?" he asked as Dasein sat down.

"What's that you're having?" Dasein nodded at the iced drink.

"Kind of an orange beer with Jaspers."

"I'll try it," Dasein said.

Marden raised a hand toward the bar, called: "Another ade, Jim." He returned his attention to Dasein. "How's your head today?"

"I'm fine," Dasein said. He found himself feeling edgy, wondering how Marden would bring up the subject of the briefcase. The drink was put in front of him. Dasein welcomed it as a distraction, sipped it. His tongue encountered a sharp orange flavor with the tangy, biting overtone of Jaspers.

"Oh, about your briefcase," Marden said.

Dasein put down his drink with careful deliberation, met Marden's level, measuring stare. "Yes?"

"Hope it hasn't inconvenienced you, my taking it."

"Not too much."

"I was curious about technique mostly," Marden said. "I already knew why you were here, of course."

"Oh?" Dasein studied Marden carefully for a clue to the man's mood. How could he know about the project?

Marden took a long swallow of the orange beer, wiped his mouth. "Great stuff, this."

"Very tasty," Dasein agreed.

"You've laid out a pretty routine approach, really," Marden said. He stared at Dasein. "You know, I've the funny feeling you don't realize how you're being used."

There was amusement in Marden's narrow face. It touched off abrupt anger in Dasein, and he struggled to hide his reaction. "What's that supposed to mean?" he asked.

"Would it interest you to know you've been a subject of discussion before our Town Council?" Marden asked.

"Me?"

"You. Several times. We knew they'd get to you sooner or later. Took 'em longer than we expected." Marden shook his head. "We circulated a photograph of you to key people—waiters, waitresses, bartenders, clerks . . . "

"Service station attendants," Dasein said. The pattern was becoming clear. He made no attempt to conceal his anger. How dared they?

Marden was sweet reasonableness. "They were bound to get wind of the fact that one of our girls was sweet on you," he said. "That's an edge, you understand. You use any edge you can find."

"Who's this *they* you keep referring to?" Dasein demanded.

"Hmmmm," Marden said.

Dasein took three deep breaths to calm himself. He had never really expected to hide his purpose here indefinitely, but he had hoped for more time before exposure. What the devil was this crazy patrol captain talking about?

"You pose quite a problem," Marden said.

"Well, don't try tossing me out of the valley the way you did that stupid salesman last night or those hunters you got today," Dasein said. "I'm obeying the law."

"Toss you out? Wouldn't think of it. Say, what would you like to eat? We did come here for lunch."

Dasein found himself psychologically off balance, his anger diverted by this sudden change of subject, his whole attitude hampered by feelings of guilt.

"I'm not hungry," he growled.

"You will be by the time the food gets here. I'll order for both of us." Marden signaled the waiter, said: "Two salads Jaspers on the special lunch."

"I'm not hungry," Dasein insisted.

"You will be." Marden smiled. "Hear a big two-fisted outsider in a Chrysler Imperial called you a native today. Did that tick you off?"

"News certainly gets around here," Dasein said.

"It certainly does, Doc. Of course, what that fellow's *mistake* says to me is that you're just a natural Santarogan. Jenny didn't make any mistake about *you*."

"Jenny has nothing to do with this."

"She has everything to do with it. Let's understand each other, Doc. Larry needs another psychologist and Jenny says you're one of the best. We can make a good place here in the valley for a fellow like you."

"How big a place?" Dasein asked, his mind on the two investigators who'd died here. "About six feet long and six feet deep?"

"Why don't you stop running away from yourself, Dasein?"

"I learned early," Dasein said, "that a good run was better than a bad stand."

"Huh?" Marden turned a puzzled frown on him.

"I'm not running away from myself," Dasein said. "That's what I mean. But I'm not going to stand still while you order my life for me the way you ordered those salads."

"You don't like the food you don't have to eat it," Marden said. "Am I to understand you won't consider the job Larry's offering?"

Dasein looked down at the table, absorbing the implications of the offer. The smart thing would be to play along, he knew. This was his opportunity to get behind the Santaroga Barrier, to find out what really went on in the valley. But he couldn't escape the thought of the Town Council at its meetings, questioning Jenny about him, no doubt, discussing *preparations* for the Dasein invasion! The anger wouldn't stay down.

"You and Jenny and the rest, you have it all figured out, eh?" he asked. "Throw the poor sucker a bone. Buy him off with a . . . "

"Slack off, Doc," Marden said. The voice was level and still with that tone of amusement. "I'm appealing to your intelligence, not to your greed. Jenny says you're a very sharp fellow. That's what we're counting on."

Dasein gripped his hands into fists beneath the table, brought himself under control. So they thought he was a poor innocent jerk to be maneuvered by a pretty female and money!

"You think I'm being used," he said.

"We *know* you're being used."

"You haven't said by whom."

"Who's behind it? A group of financiers, Doc, who don't like what Santaroga represents. They want in and they can't get in."

"The Santaroga Barrier," Dasein said.

"That's what they call it."

"Who are *they*?"

"You want names? Maybe we'll give them to you if that suits our purposes."

"You want to use me, too, is that it?"

"That isn't the way Santaroga runs, Dasein."

The salads came. Dasein looked down into an inviting array of greens, diced chicken and a creamy golden dressing. A pang of hunger gripped him. He sampled a bite of chicken with the dressing, tasted the now familiar tang of a Jaspers cheese in it. The damned stuff was ubiquitous, he thought. But he had to admit it was delicious. Perhaps there was something in the claim that it wouldn't travel.

"Pretty good, isn't it?" Marden asked.

"Yes, it is." He studied the patrol captain a moment. "How does Santaroga run, Captain?"

"Council government with Town Meeting veto, annual elections. Every resident above age eighteen has one vote."

"Basic Democracy," Dasein said. "Very nice when you have a community this size, but . . . "

"We had three thousand voters and fifty-eight hundred proxies at the last Town Meeting," Marden said. "It can be done if people are interested in governing themselves. We're interested, Dasein. That's how Santaroga's run."

Dasein gulped the bite of salad in his mouth, put down his fork. Almost nine thousand people over age eighteen in the valley! That was twice as many as he'd estimated. What did they all do? A place like this couldn't exist by taking in each others' wash.

"You want me to marry Jenny, settle here—another voter," Dasein said. "Is that it?"

"That's what Jenny appears to want. We tried to discourage her, but . . . " He shrugged.

"Discourage her—like interfering with the mails?"

"What?"

Dasein saw Marden's obvious puzzlement, told him about the lost letters.

"Those damn' biddies," Marden said. "I guess I'll have to go down there and read them the riot act. But that doesn't change things, really."

"No?"

"No. You love Jenny, don't you?"

"Of course I love her!"

It was out before Dasein could consider his answer. He heard his own voice, realized how basic this emotion was. Of course he loved Jenny. He'd been sick with longing for her. It was a wonder he'd managed to stay away this long— testimony to wounded masculine pride and the notion he'd been rejected.

Stupid pride!

"Well, fine," Marden said. "Finish your lunch, go look around the valley, and tonight you talk things over with Jenny."

He can't really believe it's that simple, Dasein thought.

"Here," Marden said. He brought Dasein's briefcase from the seat, put it on the table between them. "Make your market study. They already know everything you can find out. That's not really how they want to use you."

"How *do* they want to use me?"

"Find out for yourself, Doc. That's the only way you'll believe it."

Marden returned to his salad, eating with gusto.

Dasein put down his fork, asked: "What happened to those hunters you picked up today?"

"We cut off their heads and pickled them," Marden said. "What'd you think? They were fined and sent packing. You want to see the court records?"

"What good would that do?"

"You know, Doc," Marden said, pointing a fork at Dasein, "you're taking this much the same way Win did—Win Burdeaux."

Taking what? Dasein wondered. But he asked: "*How* did Win take it?"

"He fought it. That's according to pattern, naturally. He caved in rather quickly, though, as I remember. Win was tired of running even before he got to Santaroga."

"You amateur psychologists," Dasein sneered.

"That's right, Doc. We could use another good professional."

Dasein felt baffled by Marden's unassailable good nature.

"Eat your salad," Marden said. "It's good for what ails you."

Dasein took another bite of the chicken drenched in Jaspers sauce. He had to admit the food was making him feel better. His head felt clear, mind alert. Hunger crept up on one at times, he knew. Food took off the pressures, allowed the mind to function.

Marden finished eating, sat back.

"You'll come around," he said. "You're confused now, but if you're as sharp as Jenny says, you'll see the truth for yourself. I think you'll like it here."

Marden slid out of the booth, stood up.

"I'm just supposed to take your word for it that I'm being used," Dasein said.

"I'm not running you out of the valley, am I?" Marden asked.

"Are the phone lines still burned out?" Dasein asked.

"Darned if I know," Marden said. He glanced at his watch. "Look, I have work to do. Call me after you've talked to Jenny."

With that, he left.

The waiter came up, started collecting dishes.

Dasein looked up into the man's round face, took in the gray hair, the bent shoulders. "Why do you live here?" he asked.

"Huh?" The voice was a gravelly baritone.

"Why do you live in Santaroga?" Dasein asked.

"You nuts? This is my home."

"But why this place rather than San Francisco, say, or Los Angeles?"

"You are nuts! What could I get there I can't get here?" He left with the dishes.

Dasein stared at his briefcase on the table. Market study. On the seat beyond it, he could see the corner of a newspaper. He reached across the table, captured the paper. The masthead read: "Santaroga Press."

The left-hand column carried an international news summary whose brevity and language startled Dasein. It was composed of paragraph items, one item per story.

Item: "Those nuts are still slowly killing each other in Southeast Asia."

It slowly dawned on Dasein that this was the Vietnam news.

Item: "The dollar continues to slip on the international money market, although this fact is being played down or suppressed in the national news. The crash is going to make Black Friday look like a picnic."

Item: "The Geneva disarmament talks are disarming nobody except the arrogant and the complacent. We recall that the envoys were still talking the last time the bombs began to fall."

Item: "The United States Government is still expanding that big hidey hole under the mountain by Denver. Wonder how many military bigshots, government officials and their families have tickets into there for when the blowup comes?"

Item: "France thumbed its nose at the U.S. again this week, said to keep U.S. military airplanes off French airbases. Do they know something we don't know?"

Item: "Automation nipped another .4 percent off the U.S. job market last month. The bites are getting bigger. Does anyone have a guess as to what's going to happen to the excess population?"

Dasein lowered the paper, stared at it without seeing it. The damned thing was subversive! Was it written by a pack of Communists? Was that the secret of Santaroga?

He looked up to see the waiter standing beside him.

"That your newspaper?" the man asked.

"Yes."

"Oh. I guess Al must've given it to you." He started to turn away.

"Where does this restaurant buy its food?" Dasein asked.

"From all over the valley, Dr. Dasein. Our beef comes from Ray Allison's ranch up at the head of the valley. Our chickens come from Mrs. Larson's place out west of here. The vegetables and things we get at the greenhouses."

"Oh. Thanks." Dasein returned to the newspaper.

"You want anything else, Dr. Dasein? Al said to give you anything you want. It's on his bill."

"No, thank you."

The waiter left Dasein to the paper.

Dasein began scanning through it. There were eight pages, only a few advertisements at the beginning, and half the back page turned over to classified. The display ads were rather flat announcements: "Brenner and Sons have a new consignment of bedroom furniture at reasonable prices. First come, first served. These are all first quality local.

"Four new freezer lockers (16 cubic feet) are available at the Lewis Market.

Call for rates.'' The illustration was a smiling fat man holding open the door of a freezer locker.

The classified advertisements were mostly for trades: ''Have thirty yards of hand-loomed wool (54 inches wide)—need a good chain saw. Call Ed Jankey at Number One Mill.

''That '56 Ford one-ton truck I bought two years ago is still running. Sam Scheler says its worth about $50 or a good heifer. William McCoy, River Junction.''

Dasein began thumbing back through the paper. There was a garden column: ''It's time to turn the toads loose in your garden to keep down the snails.''

And one of the inside pages had a full column of meeting notices. Reading the column, Dasein was caught by a repetitive phrase: ''Jaspers will be served.''

Jaspers will be served, he thought. *Jaspers . . . Jaspers . . .* It was everywhere. Did they really consume that much of the stuff? He sensed a hidden significance in the word. It was a unifying thing, something peculiarly Santarogan.

Dasein turned back to the newspaper. A reference in a classified ad caught his eye: ''I will trade two years' use of one half of my Jaspers Locker (20 cubic feet in level five of the Old Section) for six months of carpenter work. Leo Merriot, 1018 River Road.''

What the devil was a Jaspers Locker? Whatever it was, ten cubic feet of it for two years was worth six months' carpentry—no small item, perhaps four thousand dollars.

A splash of sunlight brought his head up in time to see a young couple enter the restaurant. The girl was dark haired with deeply set brown eyes and beautiful, winged eyebrows, her young man fair, blue-eyed, a chisled Norman face. They took the booth behind Dasein. He watched them in the tilted bar mirror. The young man glanced over his shoulder at Dasein, said someting to the girl. She smiled.

The waiter served them two cold drinks.

Presently, the girl said: ''After the Jaspers, we sat there and listened to the sunset, a rope and a bird.''

''Sometime you should feel the fur on the water,'' her companion said. ''It's the red upness of the wind.''

Dasein came to full alert. That haunting, elusive quality of almost-meaning—it was schizophrenic or like the product of a psychedelic. He strained to hear more, but they had their heads together, whispering, laughing.

Abrupty, Dasein's memory darted back more than three years to his department's foray into LSD experiments and he recalled that Jenny Sorge, the graduate student from Santaroga, had demonstrated an apparent immunity to the drug. The experiments, abandoned in the glare of sensational LSD publicity, had never confirmed this finding and Jenny had refused to discuss it. The memory of that one report returned to plague Dasein now.

Why should I recall that? he wondered.

The young couple finished whatever they'd ordered, got up and left the restaurant.

Dasein folded the newspaper, started to put it into his briefcase. A hand touched his arm. He looked up to find Marden staring down at him.

''I believe that's my paper,'' he said. He took it from Dasein's hand. ''I was halfway to the forks before I remembered it. See you later.'' He hurried out, the paper tucked under his arm.

The casual bruskness, the speed with which he'd been relieved of that interesting publication, left Dasein feeling angry. He grabbed up his briefcase, ran for the door, was in time to see Marden pulling away from the curb in a patrol car.

To hell with you! he thought. *I'll get another one.*

The drugstore on the corner had no newspaper racks and the skinny clerk informed him coldly that the local newspaper could be obtained "by subscription only." He professed not to know where it was published. The clerk in the hardware store down the street gave him the same answer as did the cashier in the grocery store across from where he'd parked his truck.

Dasein climbed into the cab, opened his briefcase and made notes on as many of the paper's items as he could recall. When his memory ran dry, he started up the truck, began cruising up and down the town's streets looking for the paper's sign or a job printing shop. He found nothing indicating the *Santaroga Press* was printed in the town, but the signs in a used car lot brought him to an abrupt stop across the street. He sat there staring at the signs.

A four-year-old Buick bore the notice in its window: "This one's an oil burner but a good buy at $100."

On a year-old Rover: "Cracked block, but you can afford to put a new motor in it at this price: $500."

On a ten-year-old Chevrolet: "This car owned and maintained by Jersey Hofstedder. His widow only wants $650 for it."

His curiosity fully aroused, Dasein got out and crossed to Jersey Hofstedder's Chevrolet, looked in at the dash. The odometer recorded sixty-one thousand miles. The upholstery was leather, exquisitely fitted and tailored. Dasein couldn't see a scratch on the finish and the tires appeared to be almost new.

"You want to test drive it, Dr. Dasein?"

It was a woman's voice and Dasein turned to find himself face to face with a handsome gray-haired matron in a floral blouse and blue jeans. She had a big, open face, smooth tanned skin.

"I'm Clara Scheler, Sam's mother," she said. "I guess you've heard of my Sam by now."

"And you know me, of course," Dasein said, barely concealing his anger. "I'm Jenny's fellow from the city."

"Saw you this morning with Jenny," she said. "That's one fine girl there, Dr. Dasein. Now, if you're interested in Jersey's car, I can tell you about it."

"Please do," Dasein said.

"Folks around here know how Jersey was," she said. "He was a goldanged perfectionist, that's what. He had every moving part of this car out on his bench. He balanced and adjusted and fitted until it's just about the sweetest running thing you ever heard. Got disc brakes now, too. You can see what he did to the upholstery."

"Who was Jersey Hofstedder?" Dasein asked.

"Who . . . oh, that's right, you're new. Jersey was Sam's chief mechanic until he died about a month ago. His widow kept the Cord touring car Jersey was so proud of, but she says a body can only drive one car at a time. She asked me to sell the Chevvy. Here, listen to it."

She slipped behind the wheel, started the motor.

Dasein bent close to the hood. He could barely hear the engine running.

"Got dual ignition," Clara Scheler said. "Jersey bragged he could get thirty miles to the gallon with her and I wouldn't be a bit surprised."

"Neither would I," Dasein said.

"You want to pay cash or credit?" Clara Scheler asked.

"I . . . haven't decided to buy it," Dasein said.

"You and Jenny couldn't do better than starting out with Jersey's old car," she said. "You're going to have to get rid of that clunker you drove up in. I heard it. That one isn't long for this world unless you do something about those bearings."

"I . . . if I decide to buy it, I'll come back with Jenny," Dasein said. "Thank you for showing it to me." He turned, ran back to his truck with a feeling of escape. He had been strongly tempted to buy Jersey Hofstedder's car and found this astonishing. The woman must be a master salesman.

He drove back to the Inn, his mind in a turmoil over the strange personality which Santaroga presented. The bizarre candor of those used car signs, the ads in the *Santaroga Press*—they were all of the same pattern.

Casual honesty, Dasein thought. *That could be brutal at the wrong time.*

He went up to his room, lay down on the bed to try to think things through, make some sense out of the day. Marden's conversation over lunch sounded even more strange in review. A job with Piaget's clinic? The hauntingly obscure conversation of the young couple in the restaurant plagued him. Drugged? And the newspaper which didn't exist—except by subscription. Jersey Hofstedder's car—Dasein was tempted to go back and buy it, drive it out to have it examined by an *outside* mechanic.

A persistent murmuring of voices began to intrude on Dasein's awareness. He got up, looked around the room, but couldn't locate the source. The edge of sky visible through his window was beginning to gray. He walked over, looked out. Clouds were moving in from the northwest.

The murmur of voices continued.

Dasein made a circuit of the room, stopped under a tiny ventilator in the corner above the dresser. The desk chair gave him a step up onto the dresser and he put his ear to the ventilator. Faint but distinct, a familiar television jingle advertising chewing gum came from the opening.

Smiling at himself, Dasein stepped down off the dresser. It was just somebody watching TV. He frowned. This was the first evidence he'd found that they even had TV in the valley. He considered the geography of the area—a basin. To receive TV in here would require an antenna on one of the surrounding hills, amplifiers, a long stretch of cable.

Back onto the dresser he went, ear to the ventilator. He found he could separate the TV show (a daytime serial) from a background conversation between three or four women. One of the women appeared to be instructing another in knitting. Several times he heard the word "Jaspers" and once, very distinctly, "A vision, that's all; just a vision."

Dasein climbed down from the dresser, went into the hall. Between his door and the window at the end with its "Exit" sign there were no doors. Across the hall, yes, but not on this side. He stepped back into his room, studied the ventilator. It appeared to go straight through the wall, but appearances could be deceiving. It might come from another floor. What was in this whole rear corner of the building, though? Dasein was curious enough now to investigate.

Downstairs he trotted, through the empty lobby, outside and around to the back. There was the oak tree, a rough-barked patriarch, one big branch curving across a second-floor window. That window must be his, Dasein decided. It was in the right place and the branch confirmed it. A low porch roof over a kitchen service area angled outward beneath the window. Dasein swept his gaze toward the corner, counted three other windows in that area where no doors opened into a room. All three windows were blank with drawn shades.

No doors, but three windows, Dasein thought.

He set a slower pace back up to his room. The lobby was still empty, but there were sounds of voices and the switchboard from the office behind the desk.

Once more in his room, Dasein stood at the window, looked down on the porch roof. The slope was shallow, shingles dry. He eased open the window, stepped out onto the roof. By leaning against the wall, he found he could work his way sideways along the roof.

At the first window, he took a firm grip on the ledge, looked for a gap in the curtain. There was no opening, but the sound of the TV was plain when he pressed his ear against the glass. He heard part of a soap commercial and one of the women in the room saying: "That's enough of this channel, switch to NBC."

Dasein drew back, crept to the next window. There was a half-inch gap at the bottom of the shade. He almost lost his balance bending to peer in it, caught himself, took a firm grip on the ledge and crouched to put his eyes to the gap.

The swimming wash of cathode gray in a shadowy room met his gaze. He could just make out a bank of eight TV receivers against the wall at his right. Five women sat in comfortable arm chairs at a good viewing distance from the screens. One of the women he noted with some satisfaction was knitting. Another appeared to be making notes on a shorthand pad. Yet another was operating some sort of recorder.

There was a businesslike women-at-work look about the group. They appeared to be past middle age, but when they moved it was with the grace of people who remained active. A blonde woman with a good figure stood up on the right, racked a clip-board across the face of the top right-hand screen, turned off the set. She flopped back into her chair with an exaggerated fatigue, spoke loudly:

"My God! Imagine letting that stuff pour uncensored into your brain day after day after day after . . . "

"Save it for the report, Suzie!" That was the woman with the recorder.

Report? Dasein asked himself. *What report?*

He swept his gaze around the room. A row of filing cabinets stood against the far wall. He could just see the edge of a couch directly under the window. A pull-down stairway of the type used for access to attics occupied the corner at the left. There were two typewriters on wheeled stands behind the women.

Dasein decided it was one of the most peculiar rooms he had ever seen. Here were all the fixtures of normalcy, but with that odd Santaroga twist to them. Why the secrecy? Why eight TV receivers? What was in the filing cabinets? What report?

From time to time, the women made notes, used the recorder, switched channels. All the time, they carried on casual conversations only parts of which were audible to Dasein. None of it made much sense—small talk: "I decided against putting in pleats; they're so much trouble." "If Fred can't pick me up after work, I'll need a ride to town."

His exposed position on the roof began to bother Dasein. He told himself there was nothing else to be learned from a vigil at the window. What explanation could he give if he were caught here?

Carefully, he worked his way back to his room, climbed in, closed the window. Again, he checked the hall. There just was no door into that strange room at this level. He walked down to the exit sign, opened a narrow door onto a back landing. An open stairway with doweled railing wound up and down from the landing.

Dasein peered over the railing, looked down two stories to a basement level. He looked up. The stairwell was open to a skylight above the third floor.

Moving quietly, he climbed to the next level, opened the landing door onto another hall. He stepped in, looked at the wall above the secret room. Two steps from the landing there was another door labeled "Linen Supplies." Dasein tried the handle—locked.

Frustrated, he turned back to the landing. As he stepped from the hall, his right foot caught on a loose edge of carpeting. In one terrifying instant, Dasein saw the railing and the open stairwell flash toward him. His right shoulder hit the rail with a splintering crash, slowing his fall but not stopping it. He clutched at the broken rail with his left hand, felt it bend out, knew then that he was going over—three stories down to the basement. The broken rail in his hand made a screeching sound as it bent outward. It all seemed to be happening in a terrible slow motion. He could see the edges of the descending stairway where they had been painted and the paint had run in little yellow lines. He saw a cobweb beneath one of the risers, a ball of maroon lint caught in it.

The broken rail came free in one last splintering crack and Dasein went over. In this deadly instant, as he saw in his mind his own body splattered on the concrete three floors down, strong hands grabbed his ankles. Not quite realizing what had happened, Dasein swung head down, released the broken rail and saw it turn and twist downward.

He felt himself being pulled upward like a doll, dragged against the broken edges of the railing, turned over onto his back on the landing.

Dasein found himself looking up into the scowling black face of Win Burdeaux.

"That was a mighty close one, sir," Burdeaux said.

Dasein was gasping so hard he couldn't answer. His right shoulder felt like a giant ball of pain. The fingers of his left hand were bent inward with an agonizing cramp from the strength with which he had gripped the rail.

"I heard someone try the supply closet door," Burdeaux said. "I was in there, sir, and I came out. There you were going through the railing, sir. How did that happen?"

"Carpet," Dasein gasped. "Tripped."

Burdeaux bent to examine the area at the landing door. He straightened, said: "I'll be blessed if that carpet isn't torn there, sir. That's a very dangerous situation."

Dasein managed to straighten his cramped fingers. He took a deep breath, tried to sit up. Burdeaux helped him. Dasein noted that his shirt was torn. There was a long red scratch on his stomach and chest from being dragged across the broken rail.

"You best take it easy for a few minutes, sir," Burdeaux said. "You want for me to call the doctor?"

"No . . . no, thank you."

"It wouldn't take but a minute, sir."

"I'll . . . be all right."

Dasein looked at the torn carpet, a jagged edge of maroon fabric. He remembered the piece of railing as it had tumbled away into the stairwell and found it strange that he had no recollection of hearing the thing hit the bottom. There was another picture in his mind, equally disturbing: the fatal accidents of the two previous investigators. Dasein pictured himself dead at the bottom of that stairwell, the investigation—all very natural, regrettable, but natural. Such things happened.

But were they accidents?

His shoulder was beginning to throb.

"I'd better get down to my room . . . and change," Dasein said. The pain in his shoulder, intense now, told him he had to have medical attention. He could feel some instinct in himself fighting the idea, though, even as he struggled upright.

Burdeaux reached out to help him to his feet, but Dasein pulled away, knowing the irrationality of the act as he did it.

"Sir, I mean you no harm," Burdeaux said. There was a gentle chiding in the tone.

Was my fear of him that obvious? Dasein asked himself.

He remembered then the strong hands grabbing his ankles, the lifesaving catch at the brink of the stairwell. A feeling of apology overcame Dasein.

"I . . . know you don't," he said. "You saved my life. There aren't words to thank you for that. I . . . was thinking about the broken rail. Shouldn't you see about fixing that?"

Using the wall as a support, Dasein gained his feet. He stood there panting. The shoulder was a massive agony.

"I will lock this door here, sir," Burdeaux said, his voice gentle, but firm. "I am going to call the doctor, sir. You are favoring your shoulder. I suspect there is much pain in it. Best the doctor see you, sir."

Dasein turned away, wondering at his own ambivalence. A doctor had to see the shoulder—yes. But did it have to be Piaget? Hugging the wall for support, Dasein moved down the steps. Piaget . . . Piaget . . . Piaget. Had Piaget been called on the two fatal *accidents?* Movement sent fiery pain through the shoulder. Piaget . . . Piaget . . . How could this incident on the stairs have been anything except an accident? Who could have predicted he'd be in that particular place at that particular moment?

There came the sound of the door being closed and latched above him. Burdeaux's heavy footsteps sounded on the stairs. The vibration sent more pain through the aching shoulder. Dasein clutched the shoulder, paused on the second floor landing.

"Sir?"

Dasein turned, looked up at the dark Moorish face, noting the expression of concern.

"It will be best, sir," Burdeaux said, "if you do not go out on the roof again. You may be subject to falls, sir. A fall from that roof would be very dangerous."

4

THE RAIN storm hit the valley just before dark. Dasein was settled into a heavy old-fashioned chair in the Piaget house by then, his shoulder immobilized by a firm bandage, Jenny sitting across from him on a hassock, an accusing look on her face.

A gentle, unswerving Burdeaux had driven him to the clinic adjoining Piaget's house and had seen him into the antiseptic atmosphere of a tiled emergency room before leaving.

Dasein didn't know what he'd expected—certainly not the cold professional detachment with which Piaget had set about treating the shoulder.

"Torn ligaments and a slight dislocation," Piaget had said. "What were you trying to do—commit suicide?"

Dasein winced as a bandage was drawn tightly into place. "Where's Jenny?"

"Helping with dinner. We'll tell her about your damn' foolishness after we have you repaired." Piaget secured the end of a bandage. "You haven't told me what you were up to."

"I was snooping!" Dasein growled.

"Were you now?" He adjusted a sling around Dasein's neck, set it to immobilize the arm. "There, that should hold you for awhile. Don't move that arm any more than you have to. I guess I don't have to tell you that. Leave your coat off. There's a covered walkway to the house—right through that door. Go on in and I'll send Jenny to entertain you until dinner."

The covered walkway had glass sides and was lined with potted geraniums. The storm struck as Dasein was making his way between the pots and he paused a moment to look at a new-mown lawn, rows of standard roses, a lowering blue-gray sky. The wind whipped rain down a street beyond the roses, bending the branches of a line of white birches. There were people hurrying along the sidewalk beside the birches. The damp hems of their coats lashed their legs in each gust.

Dasein felt a bit light-headed, chilled in spite of the walkway's protection. *What am I doing here?* he asked himself. He swallowed in a dry throat, hurried on to the door of the house and into a paneled living room full of big furniture. There was the faint smell of a coal fire in the room. His shoulder was a place of dull throbbing. He made his way across the room, past a sideboard full of massive cut-glass pieces, lowered himself carefully into a deep, soft chair of corded green upholstery.

The lack of movement and its temporary easing of pain filled him with a momentary sense of relief. Then the shoulder began throbbing again.

A door slammed—hurrying feet.

Jenny burst upon him through a wide archway to the left. Her face was flushed. A damp wisp of hair strayed at her temple. She was wearing a simple orange dress, a shocking splash of color in the dull tones of the big room. With an odd sense of detachment, Dasein remembered telling her once that orange was his favorite color. The memory filled him with an unexplainable wariness.

"Gil, for heavens sake!" she said, stopping in front of him, hands on hips.

Dasein swallowed.

Jenny looked at his open shirt, the edge of bandages, the sling. Abruptly, she dropped to her knees, put her head in his lap, clutching at him, and he saw she was crying—silent tears that spread shiny dampness across her cheeks.

"Hey!" Dasein said. "Jenny . . . " The tears, the lack of contortion in her face—he found it embarrassing. She filled him with a sense of guilt, as though he'd betrayed her in some way. The feeling overrode his pain and fatigue.

Jenny took his left hand, pressed her cheek against it. "Gil," she whispered. "Let's get married—right away."

Why not? he wondered. But the guilt remained . . . and the unanswered questions. Was Jenny bait in a trap that had been set for him? Would she even know it if she were? Did the worm know it was impaled on the hook to lure the trout?

A soft cough sounded from the archway to Dasein's left.

Jenny pulled back, but still held his hand.

Dasein looked up to find Piaget there. The man had changed to a blue smoking jacket that made him look even more the mandarin. The big head was tipped slightly to the right with an air of amusement, but the dark eyes stared out speculatively.

Behind Piaget, amber wall sconces had been turned on in a dining room. Dasein could see a large oval table set with three places on white linen, the gleam of silver and crystal.

"Jenny?" Piaget said.

She sighed, released Dasein's hand, retreated to the green ottoman, sat down with her legs curled under her.

Dasein grew aware of the smell of roasting meat savory with garlic. It made him acutely aware of hunger. In the heightening of his senses, he detected an enticing tang, recognized the *Jaspers* odor.

"I think we should discuss your susceptibility to accidents," Piaget said. "Do you mind, Gilbert?"

"By all means," Dasein said. He sat watching the doctor carefully. There was an edge of caution in Piaget's voice, a hesitancy that went beyond a host's reluctance to engage in an embarrassing conversation.

"Have you had many painful accidents?" Piaget asked. He strode across the room as he spoke, crossing to a quilted leather chair behind Jenny. When he sat, he was looking across Jenny's shoulder at Dasein and Dasein had the abrupt suspicion that this position had been chosen with care. It aligned Piaget and Jenny against him.

"Well?" Piaget asked.

"Why don't we trade answers?" Dasein countered. "You answer a question for me and I answer a question for you."

"Oh?" Piaget's face relaxed into the bemused smile of a private joke.

Jenny looked worried.

"What's your question?" Piaget asked.

"A bargain's a bargain," Dasein said. "First, an answer. You ask if I've been involved in many accidents. No, I have not. That is, not before coming here. I can recall one other—a fall from an apple tree when I was eight."

"So," Piaget said. "Now, you have a question for me."

Jenny frowned, looked away.

Dasein felt a sudden dryness in his throat, found his voice rasping when he spoke: "Tell me, Doctor—how did the two investigators die—the ones who came before me?"

Jenny's head snapped around. "Gil!" There was outrage in her voice.

"Easy, Jenny," Piaget said. A nerve began ticking on the broad plane of his left cheek. "You're on the wrong track, young man," he growled. "We're not savages here. There's no need. If we want someone to leave, he leaves."

"And you don't want me to leave?"

"Jenny doesn't want you to leave. And that's two questions from you. You owe me an answer."

Dasein nodded. He stared across Jenny at Piaget, reluctant to look at her.

"Do you love Jenny?" Piaget asked.

Dasein swallowed, lowered his gaze to meet a pleading stare in Jenny's eyes. Piaget knew the answer to that question! Why did he ask it now?

"You know I do," Dasein said.

Jenny smiled, but two bright tears beaded her eyelashes.

"Then why did you wait a year to come up here and tell her so?" Piaget asked. There was an angry, accusatory bite in his voice that made Dasein stiffen.

Jenny turned, stared at her uncle. Her shoulders trembled.

"Because I'm a damn' stubborn fool," Dasein said. "I don't want the woman I love to tell me where I have to live."

"So you don't like our valley," Piaget said. "Maybe we can change your opinion about that. You willing to let us try?"

No! Dasein thought. *I'm not willing!* But he knew this answer, visceral and instinctive, would come out petulant, childish. "Do your damnedest," he muttered.

And Dasein wondered at himself. What were his instincts telling him? What was wrong with this valley that put him on guard at every turn?

"Dinner's ready."

It was a woman's voice from the archway.

Dasein turned to find a gaunt gray female in a gray dress standing there. She was a Grant Woods early American come to life, long-nosed, wary of eye, disapproval in every line of her face.

"Thank you, Sarah," Piaget said. "This is Dr. Dasein, Jenny's young man."

Her eyes weighed Dasein, found him wanting. "The food's getting cold," she said.

Piaget lifted himself out of his chair. "Sarah's my cousin," he said. "She comes from the old Yankee side of the family and abolutely refuses to dine with us if we eat at a fashionable hour."

"Damn' foolishness, the hours you keep," she muttered. "My father was always in bed by this time."

"And up at dawn," Piaget said.

"Don't you try to make fun of me, Larry Piaget," she said. She turned away. "Come to table. I'll bring the roast."

Jenny crossed to Dasein, helped him to his feet. She leaned close, kissed his cheek, whispered: "She really likes you. She told me so in the kitchen."

"What're you two whispering?" Piaget demanded.

"I was telling Gil what Sarah said about him."

"Oh, what'd Sarah say?"

"She said: 'Larry isn't going to browbeat that young man. He has eyes like Grandpa Sather.' "

Piaget turned to study Dasein. "By George, he has. I hadn't noticed." He turned away with an abrupt cutting-off motion, led the way into the dining room. "Come along, or Sarah will change her good opinion. We can't have that."

To Dasein, it was one of the strangest dinners of his life. There was the pain of his injured shoulder, a steady throb that impelled him to an alertness that made every word and motion stand out in sharp relief. There was Jenny—she had never looked more warmly feminine and desirable. There was Piaget, who declared a conversational truce for the meal and plied Dasein with questions about his courses at the University, the professors, fellow students, his ambitions. There was Sarah, hovering with the food—a muttering specter who had soft looks only for Jenny.

With Sarah, it's what Jenny wants, Jenny gets, Dasein thought.

Finally, there was the food: a rib roast cooked to a medium rare perfection, the Jaspers sauce over peas and potato pancakes, the local beer with its palate-cleansing tang, and fresh peaches with honey for dessert.

Beer with dinner struck Dasein as strange at first until he experienced the play of tastes, a subtle mingling of flavor esters that made individual savors stand out on his tongue even as they were combining to produce entirely new sensations. It was a crossing of senses, he realized—smells tasted, colors amplifying the aromas.

At the first serving of beer, Piaget had tasted it, nodded. "Fresh," he said.

"Within the hour just like you ordered," Sarah snapped. And she'd cast a strange probing stare at Dasein.

It was shortly after 9:30 when Dasein left.

"I had your truck brought around," Piaget said. "Think you can drive it, or shall I have Jenny take you back to the hotel?"

"I'll be all right," Dasein said.

"Don't take those pain pills I gave you until you're safely in your room," Piaget said. "Don't want you running off the road."

They stood on the broad verandah at the front of the house then, street lights casting wet shadows of the birches onto the lawn. The rain had stopped, but there was a chilled feeling of dampness in the night air.

Jenny had thrown his coat around his shoulders. She stood beside him, a worried frown on her face. "Are you *sure* you'll be all right?"

"You ought to know I can steer with one hand," he said. He grinned at her.

"Sometimes I think you're a terrible man," she said. "I don't know why I put up with you."

"It's chemistry," he said.

Piaget cleared his throat. "Tell me, Gilbert," he said. "What *were* you doing on the hotel roof?"

Dasein felt an abrupt pang of fear, a sense of incongruity in the timing of that question.

What the hell! he thought. *Let's see what a straight answer does.*

"I was trying to find out why you're so all-fired secret about your TV," he said.

"Secret?" Piaget shook his head. "That's just a pet project of mine. They're analyzing the silly infantilisms of TV, producing data for a book I have in mind."

"Then why so secret?" Dasein felt Jenny clutching his arm, ignored the fear he sensed in her reaction.

"It's consideration for the sensibilities of others, not secrecy," Piaget said. "Most TV drives our people wild. We monitor the news, of course, but even that is mostly pap, sugar-coated and spoon-fed."

There was a ring of partial truth in Piaget's explanation, Dasein felt, but he wondered what was being left out. What else were those women *researching* in that room.

"I see," Dasein said.

"You owe me an answer now," Piaget said.

"Fire away."

"Another time," Piaget said. "I'll leave you two to say good night, now."

He went inside, closed the door.

Presently, Dasein was headed down the street in his truck, the tingling sensation of Jenny's kiss still warm on his lips.

He arrived at the wye intersection to the hotel shortly before ten, hesitated, then bore to the right on the road out of the valley to Porterville. There was an odd feeling of self-preservation in the decision, but he told himself it was just because he wanted to drive for awhile . . . and think.

What is happening to me? he wondered. His mind felt abnormally clear, but he was enveloped by such a feeling of disquiet that his stomach was knotted with it. There was an odd broadening to his sense of being. It made him realize that he had forced himself inward with his concentration on psychology, that he had narrowed his world. Something was pushing at his self-imposed barriers now, and he sensed things lurking *beyond*, things which he feared to confront.

Why am I here? he asked himself.

He could trace a chain of cause and effect back to the university, to Jenny . . . but again he felt the interference of things outside this chain and he feared these things.

The night sped past his truck and he realized he was fleeing up the mountain, trying to escape the valley.

He thought of Jenny as she'd appeared this night: an elf in orange dress and orange shoes, lovely Jenny dressed to please him, her sincerity and love all transparent on her face.

Bits and pieces of the dinner conversation began coming back to him. *Jaspers.* "This is the old Jaspers—deep." That had been Jenny tasting the sauce. "Almost time to put down a new section of Jaspers in number five." That had been Sarah bringing in the dessert. And Piaget: "I'll talk to the boys about it tomorrow."

Now, recalling this, Dasein realized there'd been a faint, familiar tang even in the honey. He wondered then about the way *Jaspers* figured so often in their conversations. They never strayed far from it, seemed to find nothing unusual in the constancy of it. They talked Jaspers . . . and at the oddest moments.

He was at the pass out of the valley now, trembling with an ambivalent feeling of escape . . . and of loss.

There'd been a fire across the slopes through which Dasein was now descending. He smelled damp ashes on the wind that whipped through the ventilators, recalled the reported trouble with telephone lines. Clouds had begun to clear away here outside the valley. Dead trees stood out on the burned slopes like Chinese characters brushstroked on the moonlighted hills.

Abruptly, his mind clamped on a logical reason for coming out of the valley: *The telephone! I have to call Selador and confer. There are no lines out of the valley, but I can call from Porterville . . . before I go back.*

He drove steadily then, his being suspended, static, held in a curious lack of emotion—nothing on his mind. Even the pain of his shoulder receded.

Porterville loomed out of the night, the highway becoming a wide main street with a blue and white "Bus Depot" sign on the left over an all-night cafe—two big truck-trailer rigs there beside a little convertible and a green and white Sheriff's car. An orange glow across the street was "Frenchy's Mother Lode Saloon," The cars at the curb conveyed a general decrepit look, depressingly alike in their battered oldness.

Dasein drove past, found a lonely phone booth beneath a street light at the corner of a darkened Shell station. He turned in, stopped beside the booth. The truck's engine was hot and tried to go on running with a clunking, jerking motion after he shut off the ignition. He stopped the motion with the clutch, sat for a moment looking at the booth. Presently, he got out. The truck creaked with distress at his movement.

The Sheriff's car drove past, its headlights casting enormous shadows on a white fence behind the phone booth.

Dasein sighed, went into the booth. He felt strangely reluctant to make the call, had to force himself.

Presently, Selador's precise accent came on the line: "Gilbert? Is that you, Gilbert? Have they repaired the deuced telephone lines?"

"I'm calling from Porterville, just outside the valley."

"Is something wrong, Gilbert?"

Dasein swallowed. Even at long distance, Selador managed to remain perceptive. *Something wrong?* Dasein delivered a brief recital of his accidents.

After a prolonged silence, Selador said: "That's very odd, Gilbert, but I fail to see how you can construe these incidents as other than accidents. With the gas, for example, they put out a great effort to save you. And your tumble—how could anyone possibly have known you'd be the one to pass that way?"

"I just wanted you to know about them," Dasein said. "Piaget thinks I'm accident prone."

"Piaget? Oh, yes—the local doctor. Well, Gilbert, one should always discount pronouncements that go outside one's specialty. I doubt Piaget's qualified to diagnose an accident prone, even if there were such a syndrome—which I sincerely disbelieve." Selador cleared his throat. "You don't seriously think these people have malignant designs against you?"

Selador's sane, level tones had a soothing effect on Dasein. He was right, of course. Here, removed from the valley, the events of the past twenty-four hours took on a different shade of meaning.

"Of course not," Dasein said.

"Good! You've always struck me as a very level head, Gilbert. Let me caution you now that you may have intruded upon a situation where people are being genuinely careless. Under those circumstances, the Inn might be an extremely dangerous place, and you should leave."

"To go where?" Dasein asked.

"There must be other accommodations."

Carelessness at the Inn? Dasein wondered. Then why were no others injured? A dangerous place, yes—but only because it was part of the valley. He felt a strong reluctance to agree with Selador. It was as though his own reluctance were based on data unavailable to Selador.

Abruptly, Dasein saw how the loose carpet could have been aimed at him. He thought of a baited trap. The bait? That was the TV room, of course—an odd place certain to arouse his curiosity. Around the bait would be several traps, all avenues covered. He wondered what trap he had missed on the roof. As he thought about it, Dasein recalled how the stair rail had broken.

"Are you there, Gilbert?"

Selador's voice sounded thin and distant.

"Yes—I'm here."

Dasein nodded to himself. It was so beautifully simple. It answered all the vague uneasiness that had plagued him about the accidents. So simple—like a child's drawing on a steamy window: no excess lines or unnecessary data. Bait and traps.

Even as he saw it, Dasein realized Selador wouldn't accept this solution. It smacked of paranoia. If the theory were wrong, it would be paranoic. It implied organization, the involvement of many people, many officials.

"Is there something else you wanted, Gilbert? We're paying for some rather costly silence."

Dasein came to himself suddenly. "Yes, sir. You recall Piaget's article about Santarogans and allergens?"

"Quite." Selador cleared his throat.

"I want you to query the public health officials and the department of agriculture. Find out if they have chemical analyses of the valley's farm products—including the cheese."

"Public health . . . agriculture . . . cheese," Selador said. Dasein could almost see him making notes. "Anything more?"

"Perhaps. Could you get to the attorneys for the real estate board and the chain store people? I'm sure they must've explored possibilities of legal recourse on the leased land they . . . "

"What're you driving at, Gilbert?"

"The chain stores leased the property and built their expensive installations before discovering the Santarogans wouldn't trade with them. Is this a pattern? Do Santaroga realtors trap unwary outsiders?"

"Conspiracy to defraud," Selador said. "I see. I'm rather inclined to believe, Gilbert, that this avenue already has been exhausted."

Hearing him, Dasein thought Selador's usual acuteness had been blunted. Perhaps he was tired.

"Most likely," Dasein said. "It wouldn't hurt, though, for me to see what the legal eagles were thinking. I might get some new clues on the scene."

"Very well. And, Gilbert, when are you going to send me copies of your notes?"

"I'll mail some carbons tonight from Porterville."

"Tomorrow will be all right. It's getting late and . . . "

"No, sir. I don't trust the Santaroga post office."

"Why?"

Dasein recounted Jenny's anger at the women in the post office. Selador chuckled.

"They sound like a veritable band of harpies," Selador said. "Aren't there laws against tampering with the mails? But, of course, determined people and all that. I hope you found Miss Sorge in good health."

"As beautiful as ever," Dasein said, keeping his voice light. He wondered suddenly about Selador. *Miss* Sorge. No hesitation, no question at all about her being unmarried.

"We're exploring the source of their petrol supply," Selador said. "Nothing on that yet. Take care of yourself, Gilbert. I shouldn't want anything to happen to you."

"That makes two of us," Dasin said.

"Good-bye, then," Selador said. His voice sounded hesitant. A click signaled the breaking of the connection.

Dasein hung up, turned at a sound behind him. A Sheriff's car was pulling into the station. It stopped facing the booth. A spotlight flashed in Dasein's eyes. He heard a door open, footsteps.

"Turn that damn' light out of my eyes!" Dasein said.

The light was lowered. He discerned a bulky shape in uniform standing outside the booth, the gleam of a badge.

"Anything wrong?" It was an oddly squeaky voice to come from that bulk.

Dasein stepped out of the booth, still angry at the way they had flashed the light in his eyes. "Should there be?"

"You damn' Santarogans," the deputy muttered. "Must be important for one of you to come over to make a phone call."

Dasein started to protest he wasn't a Santarogan, remained silent as his mind was caught by a flow of questions. What made outsiders assume he was a Santarogan? The fat man in the Chrysler and now this deputy. Dasein recalled Marden's words. What was the identifying tag?

"If you're through, you best be getting home," the deputy said. "Can't park here all night."

Dasein saw an abrupt mental image of his gas gauge—it was faulty and registered almost empty even when the tank was full. Would they believe he had to wait for the station to open in the morning? What if they roused an attendant and found his tank took only a few gallons?

Why am I debating petty deceptions? Dasein wondered.

It occurred to him that he was reluctant to return to Santaroga. Why? Was living in the valley turning him into a Santarogan?

"That's a real artistic bandage you're wearing," the deputy said. "Been in an accident?"

"Nothing important," Dasein said. "Strained some ligaments."

"Good night, then," the deputy said. "Take it easy on that road." He returned to his car, said someting in a low voice to his companion. They chuckled. The car pulled slowly out of the station.

They mistook me for a Santarogan, Dasein thought, and he considered the reaction which had accompanied that mistake. They'd resented his presence here, but with an odd kind of diffidence . . . as though they were afraid of him. They hadn't hesitated to leave him alone here, though—no question of his being a criminal.

Disturbed by the incident and unable to explain his disturbance, Dasein climbed back into his truck, headed for Santaroga.

Why had they assumed he was a Santarogan? The question kept gnawing at him.

A bump in the road made him acutely conscious of his shoulder. The pain had settled into a dull ache. His mind felt clear and alert, though, poised on a knife-edge peak of observation. He began to wonder about this sensation as he drove.

The road flowed beneath him, climbing . . . climbing . . .

As though part of the road's pattern, disconnected images began flowing through his mind. They came with words and phrases, madly jumbled, no thought of order. Meaning eluded him. Feeling suddenly light-headed, he tried to grapple with the sensations—

Cave . . . limping man . . . fire . . .

What cave? he wondered. *Where have I seen a limping man? What fire? Is it the fire that destroyed the telephone lines?*

He had the sudden impression that he was the limping man. Fire and cave eluded him.

Dasein felt he wasn't reasoning, but was pawing through old thoughts. Images—labels summoned objects before his mind's eye: *Car.* He saw Jersey Hofstedder's polished old machine. *Fence.* He saw the chain-link fence around the Co-op. *Shadows.* He saw bodiless shadows.

What's happening to me?

He felt trembly with hunger . . . sweaty. Perspiration rolled off his forehead and cheeks. He tasted it on his lips. Dasein opened his window, allowed the cold wind to whip around him.

At the turn-off where he'd stopped the first evening, Dasein pulled onto the gravel, shut off engine and lights. The clouds were gone and an oblate silver moon rode low on the horizon. He stared down into the valley—widely spaced lights, blue-green from the greenhouses far to his left, the bustle and stir from the Co-op off to the right.

Up here, Dasein felt removed from all that, isolated. The darkness enclosed him.

Cave? he wondered.

Jaspers?

It was difficult to think with his body behaving in this oddly erratic fashion. His shoulder throbbed. There was a nodule of aching in his left lung. He was aware of a tendon in his left ankle—not pain, but knowledge of a weakness there. He could trace in his mind the fiery line of scratches down his chest where Burdeaux had dragged him across the broken bannisters.

A picture of the map on George Nis's wall flashed into his mind, was gone.

He felt *possessed*. Something had taken over his body. It was an ancient, frightening thought. Mad. He gripped the steering wheel, imagined that it writhed, jerked his hands away.

His throat was dry.

Dasein took his own pulse, staring at the luminous dial on his wristwatch. The second hand jumped oddly. It was either that or his pulse was rapid and erratic. Something was distorting his time sense.

Have I been poisoned? he wondered. *Was there something in Piaget's dinner? Ptomaine?*

The black bowl of the valley was a forbidding hand that could reach up and grab him.

Jaspers, he thought. *Jaspers.*

What did it really mean?

He sensed a oneness, a collective solitude focusing on the cooperative. He imagined something lurking outside there in the darkness, hovering at the edge of awareness.

Dasein put a hand to the seat. His fingers groped across the briefcase with its notes and documents, all the things that said he was a scientist. He tried to cling to this idea.

I'm a scientist. This uneasiness is what Aunt Nora would've called "the vapors."

What the scientist had to do was very clear in Dasein's mind. He had to insinuate himself into the Santaroga world, find his place in their oneness, live their life for a time, think as they thought. It was the one sure way to plumb the valley's mystery. There was a Santaroga state of mind. He had to put it on like a suit of clothes, fit it to his understanding.

This thought brought the sensation that something intruded on his inner awareness. He felt that an ancient being had risen there and examined him. It filled his whole subconscious, peering, urgent, restless—sensed only by reflection, indistinct, blurred . . . but real. It moved within him, something heavy and blundering.

The sensation passed.

When it was gone, there was an emptiness in Dasein such that it explained the whole concept of being empty. He felt himself to be a floating chip lost on an endless sea, fearful of every current and eddy that moved him.

He knew he was projecting. He was afraid to go back down into the valley, afraid to run away.

Jaspers.

There was another thing he had to do, Dasein knew. Again, he pictured the map on George Nis's wall, the black tributary lines, the ganglia pattern.

Cave.

He shivered, stared toward the distant bustling that was the Co-op. What lay hidden there behind the chain fence, the guards, the dogs and the prowling bush buggy?

There could be a way to find out.

Dasein stepped from the truck, locked the cab. The only weapon he could find in the camper was a rusty hunting knife with a mildewed sheath. He slipped the sheath onto his belt, working clumsily one-handed, feeling more than a little foolish, but aware also of that inner sense of danger. There was a penlight, too. He pocketed it.

The movement set his shoulder throbbing. Dasein ignored the pain, telling himself it would be too easy to find a physical excuse for not doing what he knew he had to do.

A narrow game trail led down the hill from the upper end of the guard fence. Dasein picked his way down the trail, marking the path in the moonlight until it descended into brush-choked shadows.

Branches pulled at his clothing. He bulled his way through, guiding himself by the moon and the bustle of the Co-op, which was visible whenever he topped a ridge. Whatever the Santaroga mystery, Dasein knew, the answer lay there behind that chain fence.

Once, he stumbled and slid down a hillside into a dry creekbed. Following the creekbed brought him out onto a tiny alluvial plain that opened onto a panoramic view of the Co-op and the valley beyond bathed in moonlight. Twice, he startled deer, which went bounding and leaping off into the night. There were frequent scampering sounds in the brush as small creatures fled his blundering approach.

Holding to a narrow game trail, he came at last to a rock ledge about a thousand yards from the Co-op's fence and five hundred feet above it. Dasein sat down on a rock to catch his breath and, in the sudden silence, heard a powerful engine laboring somewhere to his right. A light swept the sky. He crept back into a low copse of buck brush, crouched there.

The sound of the engine grew louder, louder. A set of giant wheels climbed out against the stars to occupy a hill above him. From somewhere above the wheels, a light flashed on, swept across the brush, probing, pausing, darting back and forth.

Dasein recognized the bush buggy, a monster vehicle some two hundred feet away. He felt exposed, naked with only a shield of thin brush between him and that nightmare creation. The light washed over the leaves above him.

Here it comes, he thought. *It'll come right down the hill onto me.*

The sound of the engine had grown muter while the bush buggy paused to search its surroundings. It was so near Dasein heard a dog whining on it, remembered the dogs that had accompanied Marden.

The dogs will smell me, he thought.

He tried to draw himself into as tight a ball as possible.

The engine sounds grew suddenly louder.

Dasein moved a branch, ventured a look through the brush, preparing himself to leap up and run. But the big machine turned up the ridge upon which it had emerged. It passed across the hills above Dasein, the noise and light receding.

When it was gone, he took a moment to calm himself, crept out to the lip of the rock ledge. Dasein saw then why the buggy had not come down upon him. This was a dead end, no trail down from here. He would have to climb up where the machine had emerged upon the hill, backtrack on it to find a way down.

He started to turn away, paused at sight of a black gash in the floor of the ledge off to his right. Dasein crossed to the break in the rock, looked down into darkness. The break in the rock wasn't more than three feet across, opening out to the face of the ledge, narrowing to a point about twenty feet to his right. Dasein knelt, risked a brief flash of his penlight. The light revealed a smooth-walled rock chimney leading down to another ledge. What was more important, he could see a game trail down there in the moonlight.

Dasein slid his feet over the edge of the chimney, sat down there with his legs hanging into the darkness, considered the problem. The injured shoulder made him hesitate. Without that, he'd have gone right over, worked his way down, back against one side, feet against the other. Dangerous, yes—but a thing he had done many times in mountains rougher than these. The other ledge was no more than fifty feet down there.

He looked around him, wondering if he dared risk it. In this instant, his mind offered up the datum that he had forgotten to mail off the carbons of his note to Selador. It was like a cold dash of water in the face. He felt that his own body had betrayed him, that he had conspired against himself.

How could I have forgotten? he wondered. There was anger in the thought, and fear. Perspiration bathed his palms. He glanced at the luminous dial of his wristwatch: almost midnight. There came over him then the almost overpowering desire to retrace his way back to the road and the camper.

He was suddenly more afraid of what his own body might do to him than he was of any danger which could come out of the night or of the climb down this simple rock chimney. Dasein sat there trembling, recalling his feeling that he was *possessed*.

This was madness!

He shook his head angrily.

There was no turning back; he had to go down there, find a way into that Co-op, expose its secrets. While the strength of anger was upon him, Dasein probed across the chimney with his feet, found the other side, slid off his perch and began working his way down. At each movement of his back, his shoulder stabbed him with pain. He gritted his teeth, felt his way down through the darkness. Rock scraped across his back. Once, his right foot slipped and he strained with the left for purchase.

The floor of the chimney when he found it was almost an anticlimax, a slope of loose rock which slid from beneath his feet and cascaded him out onto the game trail he had seen from above.

Dasein lay there a moment regaining his breath, allowing the fire in his shoulder to subside to a dull throb.

Presently, he struggled to his feet, marked where the moonlighted trail led down to his right. He picked his way down through a screen of brush onto a sloping meadow dotted with the dark shapes of oaks. Moonlight gleamed on the fence beyond the meadow. There it was, the boundary of the Co-op. He wondered if he could climb that fence one-handed. It would be galling to come this far only to be stopped by a fence.

As he stood there examining the meadow and the fence, a deep humming sound impressed itself on him. It came from off to his right. He searched for the source of the sound, eyes hunting through shadows. Was that a gleam of metal down there, something round emerging from the meadow? He crouched low in the dry grass. There was a heavy odor of mushrooms all around. He recognized it abruptly—the smell of *Jaspers*. It came over Dasein that he was staring at a ventilator.

Ventilator!

He lifted himself to his feet, trotted across the meadow toward the sound. There was no mistaking that sound nor the wash of Jaspers-saturated air that enveloped him. There was a big fan at work down there under the earth.

Dasein stopped beside the ventilator outlet. It was about four feet across, stood approximately the same distance above the meadow topped by a cone-shaped rain hood. He was about to examine the fastenings of the hood when he heard a snuffling sound and crackling of brush from the direction of the fence. He ducked behind the ventilator as two uniformed guards emerged from the brush beyond the fence, dogs sniffling hungrily ahead of them, straining at their leashes.

If they get my scent, Dasein thought.

He crouched behind the ventilator breathing softly through his mouth. There was a tickling sensation on the back of his tongue. He wanted to cough, clear his throat, fought down the impulse. Dogs and guards had stopped directly below him.

A glaring light washed across the ventilator, swept the ground on both sides. One of the dogs whined eagerly. There was a rattling sound, a sharp command from one of the guards.

Dasein held his breath.

Again, something rattled. The sounds of guards and dogs moved along the fence. Dasein ventured a quick glance around the ventilator. They were flashing a light along the base of the fence, looking for tracks. One of the guards laughed. Dasein felt the touch of a light breeze on his cheeks, realized he was downwind from the dogs, allowed himself to relax slightly. The rattling sound came once more. Dasein saw it was one of the guards dragging a stick along the fence.

The casual mood of the guards caused him to relax even more. He took a deep breath. They were going over a low hill now, down the other side. The night swallowed them.

Dasein waited until he no longer could hear them before straightening. His left knee was trembling and it took a moment for this to subside.

Guards, dogs, that big bush buggy—all spoke of something important here. Dasein nodded to himself, began examining the ventilator. There was a heavy screen beneath the rain cap. He ventured a flash of the penlight, saw hood and screen were a welded unit held to the ventilator by heavy sheet metal screws.

Dasein brought out his hunting knife, tried one of the screws. Metal screeched against metal as he turned it. He stopped, listened. His ears detected only the sounds of the night. There was an owl somewhere in the brush above him. Its mournful call floated across the night. Dasein returned to the screw. It came out in his hand and he pocketed it, moved on to the next one. There were four in all.

When the last screw was out, he tried the screen. It and the hood lifted with a rasping metallic protest. He flashed his penlight inside, saw smooth metal walls going straight down about fifteen feet before curving back toward the hills.

Dasein returned the screen and hood to their normal position, went searching under the oaks until he found a fallen branch about six feet long. He used this to prop the hood and screen, peered once more down the ventilator with the penlight.

It was going to take two hands getting in there, he realized. No other way. Gritting his teeth, he removed the sling, stuffed it into a pocket. Even without the sling, he knew the arm wasn't going to be much use . . . except perhaps in an emergency. He felt the rim of the ventilator—sharp, rough metal. *The sling*, he thought. He brought it out, rolled it into a pad for his hands. Using this pad, he hauled himself across the lip of the ventilator. The pad slipped and he felt metal bite his stomach. He grabbed the edge, swung himself inward. Metal ripped buttons off his shirt. He heard them clatter somewhere below. His good hand found a purchase over a bit of the sling; he dropped down, pain screaming in his injured shoulder, swung his feet to the opposite side, turned and braced himself. Feet and back held. He slipped the hunting knife out of its sheath, reached up, knocked the limb prop aside.

Screen and hood came down with a clang he felt must have been heard for a mile. He waited, listening.

Silence.

Slowly, he began inching his way down.

Presently, his feet encountered the curve. He straightened, used the penlight. The ventilator slanted back under the hill at a gentle slope of about twenty degrees. There was something soft under his left foot. The light revealed the sling. He picked it up. The front of his shirt was sticking to his skin. He turned the light on it, saw red wetness, a section of skin scraped off by the lip of the ventilator. The pain was as a minor scratch compared to his shoulder.

I'm a mess, he thought. *What the hell am I doing here?*

The answer was there in his mind, clear and disturbing. He was here because he had been maneuvered into a one-way passage as direct and confining as this ventilator tube. Selador and friends formed one side of the passage; Jenny and fellow Santarogans formed the other side.

And here he was.

Dasein lifted the sling. It was torn but still serviceable. He gripped one end in his teeth, managed to restore it to a semblance of its former position.

There was only one way to go now. He dropped to his knees, crawled backward down the ventilator, using his light occasionally to probe the darkness.

The Jaspers odor filled the confined space. It was a tangy essence of mushrooms here. He received the distinct impression it cleared his head.

The tube went on and on and on . . . He took it one step at a time. It curved slowly toward what he felt was south and the slope steepened. Once, he slipped, slid downward for twenty feet, cutting his left hand on a rivet. He wasn't positive, but he thought the sound of the fan motor grew louder.

Again, the tube turned—and again. Dasein lost all sense of direction in the confining darkness. Why had they constructed this ventilator with so many turns? he wondered. Had they followed a natural fault in the rock? It seemed likely.

His left foot encountered an edge of emptiness.

Dasein stopped, used the penlight. Its feeble glow illuminated a flat metal wall about six feet away and a square of shadows beneath it. He turned the light downward, exposed a box-like opening about five feet deep with a heavy screen for one side. The sound of the fan motor came from somewhere behind the screen and it definitely was louder here.

Bracing himself with a hand in the screen, Dasein lowered himself into the box. He stood there a moment examining his surroundings. The wall opposite the screen appeared different from the others. There were six roundhead bolts in it held by flanged metal keepers as though they'd been designed to stay in that position while nuts were tightened from the outside.

Dasein pried up one of the flanges with his knife, turned the bolt. It moved easily, too easily. He pulled back on it, turned it once more. That took more effort and he was rewarded by having the bolt work backward into his hand. The nut dropped outside with a sound of falling on wood.

He waited, listening for a response to that sound.

Nothing.

Dasein put his eye to the bolt hole, peered out into an eerie red gloom. As his eye grew accustomed to it, he made out a section of heavy screen across from him, packages piled behind the screen.

He drew back. Well, Nis had said this was a storage cave.

Dasein applied himself to the other bolts. He left the bolt in the upper right corner, bent the metal out and swung it aside. There was a wooden catwalk immediately below him with three wing nuts on it. He slipped out to the catwalk, scooped up the wing nuts. The other nuts obviously had dropped through the space between the boards of the walk. He looked around, studying what he saw with care, absorbing the implications of this place.

It was a troglodyte cave illuminated by dim red light. The light came from globes beneath the catwalk and above it, casting enormous shadows on a rock wall behind the ventilator panel and over stacked tiers of cage-walled compartments. The cages were stuffed with packages and reminded Dasein of nothing more than a public freezer locker.

The richly moist odor of Jaspers was all around him.

A sign to his right down the catwalk labeled this area as "Bay 21—D–1 to J–5."

Dasein returned his attention to the ventilator, restored three of the bolts, forcing the cover plate back into position. A crease remained in the metal where he had bent it, but he thought it would pass casual inspection.

He looked up and down the catwalk.

Where would he find one of these compartments he could open to examine the contents? He crossed to the one opposite the ventilator plate, looked for a door. Could he find a compartment left unlocked by a careless Santarogan . . . provided he could find the door? There apparently was no door on the first compartment he inspected. The lack of a door filled Dasein with unease. There had to be a door!

He stepped back, studied the line of compartments, gasped as he saw the answer. The fronts of the compartments slid aside in wooden channels . . . and there were no locks. Simple peg latches held them.

Dasein opened the front of a compartment, pulled out a small cardboard box. Its label read: "Auntie Beren's spiced crab apples. Ex. April '55." He replaced the box, extracted a salami-shaped package. Its label read: "Limburger exposed early 1929." Dasein replaced the limburger, closed the compartment.

Exposed?

Methodically, Dasein worked his way down the line in Bay 21, examining one or two packages in each compartment. Most of the time it was written "Ex" with a date. The older packages spelled it out.

Exposed.

Dasein sensed his mind racing. *Exposed. Exposed to what? How?*

The sound of footsteps on the lower catwalk behind him brought Dasein whirling around, muscles tense. He heard a compartment door slide open. Papers rustled.

Softly, Dasein worked his way along the catwalk away from the sound. He passed steps, one set leading up, one down, hesitated. He couldn't be certain whether he was going deeper into the cave complex or out of it. There was another catwalk above him, a rock ceiling dimly visible above that. There appeared to be at least three tiers of catwalks below him.

He chose the steps going up, lifted his head slowly above the floor level of the next walk, glanced both ways.

Empty.

This level was like the one below except for the rock ceiling. The rock appeared to be a form of granite, but with oily brown veins.

Moving as silently as he could, Dasein climbed out onto the walk, moved back in the direction of the ventilator listening for the person he had heard on the lower level.

Someone was whistling down there, an idiot tune repeated endlessly. Dasein pressed his back against a cage, peered down through the openings in the walk. There came a scraping of wood against wood. The whistling went away to his left, receded into silence.

That probably was the way out, then.

He had heard the person down there but hadn't been able to see him—a fact which could work both ways.

Placing his feet carefully, Dasein moved along the walk. He came to a cross way, peered around it. Empty both ways. The gloom appeared a little thicker to the left.

It occurred to Dasein that up to this point he hadn't felt the need to worry about how he was going to get out of the cave complex. He had been too intent on solving the mystery. But the mystery remained . . . and here he was.

I can't just go marching out, he thought. *Or can't I? What could they do to me?*

His throbbing shoulder, memory of the gas jet, the knowledge that two previous investigators had died in this valley—these were sufficient answer to the question, he thought.

Wood slammed against wood off to the front and below. Footsteps pounded along a catwalk—at least two pair of feet, possibly more. The running stopped almost directly beneath him. There came a low-voiced conversation, mostly unintelligible and sounding like instructions. Dasein recognized only three words—" . . . back . . . " " . . . away . . . " and a third word which set him in motion runing softly down the dim side passage to his left.

" . . . ventilator . . . "

A man beneath him had said "ventilator" sharply and distinctly.

The pounding of feet resumed down there spreading out through the catwalks.

Dasein searched frantically ahead for a place to hide. There was a sound of machinery humming somewhere down there. The catwalk turned left at about a fifteen degree angle, and he saw the cave walls were converging here—fewer tiers below and smaller compartments on each side. The walk angled more sharply to the right and there was only his walk and the one below, single compartments on each side.

He had put himself into a dead-end side passage, Dasein realized. Still, there was the sound of machinery ahead.

His catwalk ended in a set of wooden stairs going down. There was no choice; he could hear someone running behind him.

Dasein went down.

The stairs turned left into a rock passage—no compartments, just the cave. There was a louvered door on the right, loud sound of an electric motor in there. His pursuer was at the head of the steps above.

Dasein opened the door, slipped through, closed the door. He found himself in a rectangular chamber about fifty feet long, twenty feet wide and some fifteen feet to the ceiling. A row of large electric motors lined the left wall, all of them extending into round metal throats with fanblades blurring the air there. The far wall was one giant metal screen and he could feel air rushing out of it toward the fans.

The right wall was piled high with cardboard cartons, sacks and wood boxes. There was a space between the pile and the ceiling and it appeared darker up there. Dasein scrambled up the pile, crawled along it, almost fell into a space hollowed out of boxes and sacks near the far end. He slid into the hole, found himself on what felt like blankets. His hand encountered something metallic, which groping fingers identified as a flashlight.

The louvered door slammed open. Feet pounded into the room. Someone scrambled up the far end of the pile. A woman's voice said: "Nothing up here."

There came the sound of someone dropping lightly to the floor.

There'd been something familiar about the woman's voice. Dasein was willing to swear he'd heard it before.

A man said: "Why'd you run this way? Did you hear something?"

"I thought so, but I wasn't sure," the woman said.

"You sure there's nothing on top of the stores?"

"Look for yourself."

"Doggone, I wish we could use real lights in here."

"Now, don't you go doing something foolish."

"Don't worry about me. Doggone that Jenny anyway, getting herself mixed up with an outsider!"

"Don't pick on Jenny. She knows what she's doing."

"I guess so, but it sure makes a lot of stupid extra work, and you know what's liable to happen if we don't find him pretty soon."

"So let's hurry it up."

They went out, closed the door.

Dasein lay quietly absorbing the import of what they'd said. Jenny knew what she was doing, did she? What would happen if they didn't find him?

If felt good to stretch out on the blankets. His shoulder was a steady aching throb. He brought up the flashlight he'd found here, pressed its switch. The thing produced a dull red glow. The light revealed a tight little nest—blankets, a pillow, a canteen half full of water. He drank some of it thirstily, found it heavy with Jaspers.

He supposed nothing in the cave could escape that flavor.

A fit of shivering took over his muscles. The canteen's cap rattled as he replaced it. When the trembling passed, he sat staring at the canteen in the dim red light.

Nothing in the cave could escape the Jaspers flavor!

That was it!

Exposed!

Something that could exist in this cave—a mould or a fungus, something related to mushrooms and dark places, something that wouldn't travel . . . a *Jaspers* something invaded anything exposed to this environment.

But why was it so important to keep this fact secret? Why the dogs and the guards?

He heard the louvered door open, close, turned off the red flashlight. Someone ran lightly across the rock floor to a point just below him.

"Gilbert Dasein!" a voice hissed at him.

Dasein stiffened.

"It's Willa Burdeaux," the voice hissed. "It's Willa, Jenny's friend. I know you're in there, in the place Cal made for us. Now, you listen. Arnulf will be right back from the upper end and I have to be out of here before that. You don't have much time. There's too much Jaspers in here for someone who's not used to it. You're breathing it and it's going in your pores and everything.''

What the hell? Dasein thought.

He crawled up out of the nest, leaned out and looked down at Willa Burdeaux's dark, harshly-beautiful face.

''Why can't I take too much of it?'' he asked.

''Hasn't that Jenny explained anything to you?'' she whispered. ''Well, no time now. You have to get out of here. Do you have a watch?''

''Yes, but . . . ''

''There's no time to explain; just listen. Give me fifteen minutes to get Arnulf out of the way. He's such a prig. In fifteen minutes you come out of this room. Turn left the way you came in, but go down instead of up. Take the second crossway to your left and after that keep to your left. It's easy to remember. Left turns only. You want the ramp out of Bay 2–G. I've left the ramp's door unlocked. Lock it after you. It'll be about twenty steps straight in front of that door to an emergency gate. The gate's unlocked. Go out and lock it after you. The Inn's right across the road. You ought to be able to make that on your own.''

''Apparently, you've been rather busy.''

''I was in the office when they sounded the alarm. Now, get down out of sight and do just what I told you.''

Dasein ducked back into the nest.

Presently, he heard the door open and close. He looked at his wristwatch: five minutes to three a.m. Where had the time gone?

Could he believe Willa Burdeaux? he wondered.

There'd been something about that black pixie face, an intensity . . . Dasein thought of compartments loaded with valuable food, all unlocked. Why should this evidence of a basic honesty alarm him? Perhaps it wasn't honesty. Fear could control behavior, too.

Could he believe Willa? Did he have a choice?

So this was a trysting place Cal Nis had made for the two of them. Why not? People in love usually wanted to be alone together.

Jenny knew what she was doing.

What did she know?

His mind felt clear and oiled, working at a furious pace. What was the danger in exposure to Jaspers? He thought of that dull-eyed line he'd glimpsed up there in the Co-op.

Was that what happened?

Dasein fought down a seige of trembling.

Ten minutes after three, the moment of decision, came more quickly than he wanted. He had no choice and knew it. His shoulder had gone stiff and there was a painful burning along his scraped chest and stomach. Favoring his shoulder, Dasein eased himself down off the storage pile.

The ramp door was unlocked as Willa had promised. He let himself out into a darkened side yard, hesitated. The stars overhead looked cold and close. It *was* cold. He felt goose pimples along his arms. There was no sign of a guard out here, but he glimpsed lights and motion far up on the hillside.

Lock the ramp door, she'd said.

Dasein locked the door, darted across the yard. It was a narrow gate in the chain fence. The hinges creaked and he thought the latch unnaturally loud. There was a hasp and padlock. He closed the lock.

A narrow path led along the fence to the road. There was the Inn across the way—dark, but inviting. A dim yellow light glowed through the double doors. Using the light as a beacon, Dasein limped down the path and across to the Inn.

The lobby was empty, most of its lights turned off. There was the sound of snoring from the switchboard room behind the desk.

Dasein slipped quietly across the lobby, up the stairs and down the hall to his room.

The key—had he turned it in or left it in the truck? No . . . here it was in his pocket. He opened the door softly, stepped into the darkness of his room. He'd spent only one night in this room but it suddenly was a haven.

The truck! It was still up there on the road to Porterville. The hell with it. He'd hire a ride up tomorrow and drive it down.

That Willa Burdeaux! Why had she done this?

Dasein began slipping out of his clothes. He wanted nothing more than a hot shower and bed. It was slow work undressing in the dark, but he knew a light might tell someone what time he'd returned.

What difference does that make? he asked himself. His clothing, torn, smeared with dirt, still stinking of the cave, was evidence enough of where he'd been and what he'd done.

Abruptly, he felt he no longer could sneak around.

Angry at himself, he turned on the light.

Directly ahead of him on the bedstand was a bottle of beer with a note attached to it. Dasein lifted the note, read it: "This isn't much, but it's all I could get. You'll need it in the morning. I'll call Jenny and tell her you're all right. —Willa."

Dasein picked up the bottle, looked at the label. There was a blue stamp on it: "Exposed January 1959."

5

A STEADY, loud pounding invaded Dasein's dream.

He felt he was trapped inside a giant drum. Reverberations beat through his brain. Each drumbeat became a stab of pain along his temples, through his shoulders, across his stomach.

He was the drum! That was it!

His lips were dry. Thirst spread a scabby dustiness over his throat. His tongue was thick, fuzzy.

My God! Would the pounding never stop?

He awoke feeling he'd been caught in a caricature of a hangover. The blankets were twisted around his body, immobilizing his injured shoulder. The shoulder felt better, and that was a relief, but something had to be done about his head and that insane pounding.

His free arm was asleep. It tingled painfully when he tried to move it. Sunlight filtered through a tear in the curtain on the room's single window. One thin ray outlined in dust motes stabbed across the room. It dazzled him, hurt his eyes.

That damned pounding!

"Hey! Open up in there!"

It was a masculine voice from outside.

Dasein felt he knew that voice. Marden, the CHP captain? What was he doing here at this hour. Dasein lifted his wristwatch, stared at it—ten twenty-five.

The pounding resumed.

"Just a minute!" Dasein shouted. His own voice sent waves of pain through his head.

Blessedly, the pounding stopped.

Dasein gasped with relief, twisted himself out of the blankets, sat up. The room's walls began going around and around in a mad circle.

For the love of heaven! he thought. *I've heard of hangovers, but nothing like this.*

"Open the door, Dasein.

That definitely was Marden.

"Right with you," Dasein rasped.

What's wrong with me? he wondered. He knew he'd had no more than the beers with dinner. They couldn't possibly explain his present malaise. Could it be delayed reaction to the gas?

Beer.

There was something about beer.

Slowly so as not to dislocate his neck, Dasein turned his head toward the bedstand. Yes, there was a beer. Willa had thoughtfully provided an opener. He levered the cap off the bottle, drank hungrily.

Waves of soothing relief spread out from his stomach. He put down the empty bottle, stood up. *Hair of the dog*, he thought. *Hair of the Jaspers dog.* The bottle was redolent with the mushroom tang.

"Are you all right in there, Dasein?"

To hell with you, mister, Dasein thought. He tried to take a step, was rewarded with instant nausea and a wave of dizziness. He leaned against the wall breathing slowly, deeply.

I'm sick, he thought. *I've caught something.*

The beer felt as though it had begun to boil in his stomach.

"Open this door, Dasein! Now!"

All right—all right, Dasein thought. He stumbled to the door, unlocked it, stepped back.

The door was flung open to reveal Al Marden in uniform, the captain's bars glistening at his neck. His visored cap was pushed back to reveal a sweaty band of red hair.

"Well," he said. "Haven't we been the busy one?"

He stepped into the room, closed the door. He carried something round and chromed in his left hand—a thermos. What the devil was he doing here at this hour with a thermos? Dasein wondered.

One hand against the wall to steady himself, Dasein made his way back to the bed, sat on the edge.

Marden followed.

"I hope you're worth all this trouble," he said.

Dasein looked up at the narrow, cynical face, remembering the glimpse he'd had of the high-wheeled bush buggy wheeling down the road out there with

Marden steering, and the dogs beside him. That had been a proper setting for this man. There was an elevated look about him, a peering-down-at-the-world's-stupidity. What was it about him? Was it the Santaroga look? But what had the Porterville deputies seen, then? What had the man in the Chrysler seen.

Do I look that way? Dasein wondered.

"I brought you some coffee," Marden said. "You look like you could use it." He opened the thermos, poured steaming amber liquid into the cup-top.

A rich smell of Jaspers rode on the steam from the cup. The smell set Dasein trembling, sent a pulsing, throbbing ache through his head. The ache seemed timed to a wavering reflection on the surface of the coffee as Marden presented it.

Dasein took the cup in both hands, tipped his head back and drank with a gulping eagerness. The coffee produced the same sensation of soothing as the beer.

Marden refilled the cup.

Dasein sipped the coffee. He could feel it settling his stomach, his mind coming alert. Marden no longer appeared superior—only amused.

Why was a hangover amusing?

"The Jaspers, that's what gave me the screaming fantods, isn't it?" Dasein asked. He returned the cup.

Marden concentrated on restoring the cap to the thermos.

"A person can get too much of it, eh?" Dasein persisted, recalling what Willa Burdeaux had said.

"Overexposure too soon can cause a hangover," Marden admitted. "You'll be all right when you get used to it."

"So you came up to play the good Samaritan," Dasein said. He could feel the beginnings of anger.

"We found your truck up on the Porterville road and got worried about you," Marden said. "You can't abandon a vehicle like that."

"I didn't abandon it."

"Oh? What'd you do?"

"I went for a walk."

"And caused one helluva lot of trouble," Marden said. "If you wanted a tour of the Co-op and the storage caves, all you had to do was ask."

"And I'd have had a nice safe guided tour."

"Any kind of tour you wanted."

"So you came up to arrest me."

"Arrest you? Don't talk stupid."

"How'd you know where I was?"

Marden looked at the ceiling, shook his head. "You're all alike, you young folks," he said. "That Willa's too damn' romantic, but she doesn't lie worth git all. None of us do, I guess." He turned his glance full of cynical amusement on Dasein. "You're feeling better?"

"Yes!"

"Aren't we the intense one." He pursed his lips. "By the way, we broke into your truck and hot-wired it to drive it down. It's parked out front."

"Gee, thanks."

Dasein looked down at his hands. Anger and frustration twisted through him. He knew Marden wasn't a fit object for this anger . . . nor Jenny . . . nor Piaget . . . No person or thing presented itself to him as an object for anger—yet the emotion remained. He trembled with it.

"You sure you're all right?" Marden asked.

"Yes, I'm all right!"

"Okay, okay," Marden murmured. He turned away, but not before Dasein saw the smile forming on his lips.

The smile, not the man, brought Dasein's anger to focus. That smile! It embodied Santaroga—self-satisfied, superior, secretive. He jumped to his feet, strode to the window, whipped up the curtain.

Blazing sunshine on a flower garden, a small stream, and beyond that the flat with its broken edge dropping down into the redwoods. It was a day of brassy heat with the oaks sitting motionless, sun-drenched on the hillsides. He counted three plumes of smoke hanging on the still air, glimpsed a serpentine track of blue-green river in the distance.

This vale of pastoral beauty that was Santaroga, this was a fitting object for his anger, Dasein decided: Santaroga, this island of people in the wilderness. He pictured the valley as a swarming place behind a façade like a pyramid: solid, faceless, enduring. In there, behind the façade, Santaroga did something to its people. They lost personal identity and became masks for something that was the same in all of them.

He sensed a one-pointedness here such that every Santarogan became an extension of every other Santarogan. They were like rays spreading out from a pinhole in a black curtain.

What lay behind the black curtain?

There, he knew, was the real substance against which his anger was directed. The valley existed within an evil enchantment. The Santarogans had been trapped by a black sorcery, transmuted into the faceless pyramid.

With this thought, Dasein's anger faded. He realized he, too, had a place in this pyramid. It was like an ecological pyramid planted in the wilderness except for this gnome-change. The base of the pyramid had been firmly imbedded in the earth, extending roots deep into a moist, dank cave.

He could see the shape of this problem.

One thing set this valley apart—Jaspers. It brought Santarogans back as though they were addicted. He thought of his own craving reaction. It was the substance of the cave, the thing the pores drank and the lungs inhaled.

Marden stirred in the room behind him.

Dasein turned, looked at the man.

Santarogans became extensions of that cave and its substance. There was a drug-effect at work in this valley. It was a material in a way similar to lysergic acid diethylamide—LSD.

How did it work? he wondered.

Did it shift the serotonin balance?

Dasein felt his mind working with remarkable clarity, sorting out possibilities, setting up avenues of investigation.

"If you're feeling all right now, I'll be running along," Marden said. "Before you get any more harebrained ideas for night excursions, let us know, huh?"

"Well, naturally," Dasein said.

For some reason, this provoked a fit of laughter in Marden. He was still laughing as he let himself out.

"To hell with you, wise-guy Santarogan," Dasein muttered.

He turned back to the window.

Objectivity was going to be a problem, he saw. He had no guinea pig except himself. What was the Jaspers effect on himself? An impression of heightened awareness? Could it be an actual heightened awareness in the pattern of LSD? This would require careful evaluation. What was the source of the morning-after symptoms? Withdrawal?

He began to focus on the Santaroga personality pattern, their alertness, their abrupt mannerisms, their apparent honesty. If awareness actually were heightened, would that explain the honest advertising? Could you be anything but bluntly honest with a wide-awake human being?

Avenues of attack opened all around. Barriers collapsed like sand walls before the waves of his new awareness, but the exposed vistas continued their own mysteries.

Jenny.

Again, Dasein recalled how she'd been dropped from the university's attempt to evaluate LSD. *No apparent reaction.* The ones running the tests had wanted to explore this phenomenon, but Jenny had refused. Why? She'd been written off, of course—"a curious anomaly." The evaluation had gone on to its natural end in the publicity fiasco.

Jenny.

Dasein went into the shower, humming to himself, his mind busy. His shoulder felt remarkably improved in spite of the way he'd mistreated it during the night . . . or perhaps because of that—the exercise.

I'll call Jenny, he thought, as he dressed. *Maybe we can meet for lunch.*

The prospect of seeing Jenny filled him with a wondering delight. He sensed his own protectiveness toward her, the mutual emotional dependence. Love, that was what it was. It was a sensation that wouldn't submit to analysis. It could only be experienced.

Dasein sobered.

His love for Jenny required that he save her from the Santaroga enchantment. She'd have to help him whether she knew it or not, whether she wanted it or not.

A brisk double knock sounded on his door.

"Come in," he called.

Jenny slipped in, closed the door.

She wore a white dress, red scarf, red handbag and shoes. The outfit made her skin appear dark and exotic. She paused a moment at the door, her hand resting lightly on the knob, eyes wide and probing.

"Jen!" he said.

All in one swift dash, she was across the room into his arms, hugging him. Her lips were warm and soft on his. There was a clean spicy smell about her.

She pulled back, looked up at him. "Oh, darling, I was so frightened. I kept imagining you driving off a cliff somewhere, your car wrecked, you in the wreckage. Then Willa called. Why would you do such a thing?"

He put a finger on the tip of her nose, pressed gently. "I'm perfectly capable of taking care of myself."

"I don't know about that. Do you feel all right now? I met Al in the lobby. He said he brought you some Jaspers coffee."

"I've had my hair of the dog."

"Your hair of . . . Oh. But why would you . . . "

"But me no buts. I'm sorry I worried you, but I have a job to do."

"Oh, that!"

"I'm going to do the job I'm being paid to do."

"You gave your word, I suppose?"

"That's only part of it."

"Then they'll have to get something from you."

"More than *something*, Jenny, m'love."

She grinned. "I like it when you call me your love."

"Stop changing the subject."

"But it's such a nice subject."

"Agreed. Another time, though, eh?"

"How about tonight?"

"You're a forward wench, aren't you."

"I know what I want."

Dasein found himself studying her there in his arms. What had Willa said? *"Jenny knows what she's doing."* Whatever it was, he couldn't doubt her love for him. It was there in her eyes and her voice, a radiance and vivacity that couldn't be mistaken.

Still, there was the certainty two men had died on this investigation—accidents! The fading pain in his shoulder and its implications couldn't be doubted either.

"You're so quiet suddenly," Jenny said, looking up at him.

He took a deep breath. "Can you get me some Jaspers?"

"I almost forgot," she said. She pulled away, rummaged in her handbag. "I brought you a square of cheese and some wheat crackers for your lunch today. They're from Uncle Larry's locker. I knew you'd need it because . . ." She broke off, produced a sack from the bag. "Here they are." She proffered a brown paper sack, stared at him. "Gil! You said *Jaspers*." There was a wary look in her eyes.

"Why not?" He took the bag. She was reluctant to part with it, her fingers trailing across the paper as he pulled it away.

"I don't want to trick you, darling," she said.

"Trick me? How?"

She swallowed and her eyes glistened with unshed tears. "We gave you an awfully strong dose last night, and then you went down into that stupid cave. Was it bad this morning?"

"I had quite a hangover, if that's what you mean."

"I can just barely remember how it was when I was a chid," she said. "When you're growing up, your body changing, there are some severe metabolic adjustments. At the school, when I took part in that crazy LSD test, I had a hangover the next morning." She ran a finger along his forehead. "Poor dear. I'd have been here this morning, but Uncle Larry needed me in the clinic. Anyway, he said you weren't in any danger; Willa got you out in time."

"What would've happened if she hadn't got me out?"

Her eyes clouded as though with pain.

"What?" he insisted.

"You mustn't think about that."

"About what?"

"It can't happen to you anyway. Uncle Larry says you're the wrong type."

"Wrong type for what—turning into a zombie like those I saw in the Co-op?"

"Zombies? What're you talking about?"

He described what he'd glimpsed through the wide door.

"Oh . . . them." She looked away from him, her manner suddenly distant. "Gilbert, are you going to put them in your report?"

"Maybe."

"You mustn't."

"Why not? Who are they? *What* are they?"

"We take care of our own," she said. "They're useful members of the community."

"But not quite all there."

"That's right." She looked up at him with a fierce intensity. "If the state takes them over, they'll be moved out of the valley—most of them. That can be very bad for Santarogans, Gilbert. Believe me."

"I believe you."

"I knew you would."

"They're the failures, eh? The ones Jaspers ruined."

"Gilbert!" she said. Then—"It's not what you think. Jaspers is . . . something wonderful. We call it a "Consciousness Fuel.' It opens your eyes and your ears, it turns on your mind, it . . . " She broke off, smiled at him. "But you already know."

"I know what it appears to be," he said. He glanced at the bag in his hand. What did he hold here? Was it a paradisical gift for all mankind or something out of hell? Was it the evil enchantment he'd pictured, or an ultimate freedom?

"It's wonderful and you know it by now," Jenny said.

"Then why aren't you all shouting it from the rooftops?" he demanded.

"Gil!" She stared at him accusingly.

Abruptly, Dasein thought of what Meyer Davidson's reaction would be . . . Davidson and his cohorts, the eager young executives and the hard-eyed older men.

What he held here in his hand was their enemy.

To those men in their oddly similar dark suits, their cold eyes weighing and dismissing everything, the people of this valley were a foe to be defeated. As he thought of it, Dasein realized all customers were "The Enemy" to these men. Davidson and his kind were pitted against each other, yes, competitive, but among themselves they betrayed that they were pitted more against the masses who existed beyond that inner ring of knowledgable financial operation.

The alignment was apparent in everything they did, in their words as well as their actions. They spoke of "package grab-level" and "container flash time"— of "puff limit" and "acceptance threshold." It was an "in" language of military-like maneuvering and combat. They knew which height on a shelf was most apt to make a customer grab an item. They knew the "flash time"—the shelf width needed for certain containers. They knew how much empty air could be "puffed" into a package to make it appear a greater bargain. They knew how much price and package manipulation the customer would accept without jarring him into a "rejection pattern."

And we're their spies, Dasein thought. *The psychiatrists and psychologists—all the "social scientists"—we're the espionage arm.*

He sensed the vast maneuvering of these armies, the conspiracy to maintain "The Enemy" in a sleepy state of unawareness—malleable. Whatever the leaders of these armies did among themselves to each other, they maintained their inner code. No one betrayed the *real* war.

Dasein never before viewed the market-study world in quite this way. He thought of the brutal honesty in Santaroga's advertising, crumpled the neck of the paper bag in his hand.

What was this stuff doing to him? He turned away from Jenny to hide a surge of anger. It was making him imagine crazy things! Armies!

There was no way to avoid Jaspers here in Santaroga. The investigation required that he *not* avoid it.

I must insinuate myself into their minds, he reminded himself. *I must live their life, think as they think.*

He saw the situation then as Jenny and her fellow Santarogans must see it. They were involved in a form of guerrilla warfare. They had achieved a way of life which wouldn't be tolerated by the *outside*. Santaroga offered too much of a threat to the oligarchs of the money-industry world. The only hope for Santaroga lay in isolation and secrecy.

Shout it from the rooftops, indeed. No wonder she'd snapped at him in surprise.

Dasein turned, looked at Jenny standing there patiently waiting for him to think his way through the maze. She smiled encouraging at him and he suddenly saw all Santarogans through her. They were the buffalo Indians, people who needed to get away by themselves, to live and hunt in the way their instincts told them. The trouble was, they lived in a world which couldn't be culturally neutral. That world out there would keep trying to make people—all people—be everywhere alike.

Straddling both worlds, thinking with the drug and thinking with his memories of the *outside*, he felt a deep sadness for Jenny. Santaroga would be destroyed—no doubt of that.

"I'm sure you see it," Jenny said.

"Jaspers would be equated with LSD, with narcotics," he said. "It'd be legislated against as the Santaroga hashish. You'd be sneered out of existence, destroyed."

"I never doubted you'd understand once you were exposed," she said. She moved into his arms, leaned against him, hugging him fiercely. "I trusted you, Gil. I knew I couldn't be wrong about you."

He couldn't find words to answer her. A profound sadness held him. *Exposed.*

"You'll still have to do your report, of course," she said. "It wouldn't solve anything if you failed. They'd just find somebody else. We're getting kind of tired of it."

"Yes—I'll have to do a report," he said.

"We understand."

Her voice sent a shudder through Dasein. "*We understand.*" That was the *We* which had searched his bag, had almost killed him . . . had actually killed two men.

"Why are you shivering?" Jenny asked.

"Just a chill," he said.

He thought then of the *thing* he had sensed lurking just beyond his awareness, that restless, urgently peering ancient being which had risen within his consciousness like the neck of a dinosaur. It was still there, studying, waiting to judge.

"I only work half a day today," Jenny said. "Some of my friends have arranged a picnic at the lake. They want to meet you." She leaned back, peered up at him. "I want to show you off, too."

"I . . . don't think I can go swimming," he said.

"Your poor shoulder," she said. "I know. But the lake's beautiful this time of year. We'll have a bonfire tonight."

Which We *is that?* he asked himself.

"It sounds wonderful," he said

And he wondered as he spoke why his stomach knotted with a congestion of fear. He told himself it wasn't Jenny he feared—not this warm and beautiful woman. It might be goddess-Jenny he feared, though . . . this was a thought that rose in his mind to leer at him.

Dasein sneered at himself then, thinking that he read too much into every nuance of this valley and its people. That was the psychoanalyst's disease, of course—seeing everything through a haze of reasoning.

"Get some rest and meet me downstairs at noon," Jenny said.

She pulled away, went to the door, turned there to stare at him. "You're acting very odd, Gil," she said. "Is something bothering you?"

Her voice carried a weighted probing that brought Dasein to sudden alertness. This wasn't the spontaneous Jenny worried about the man she loved. This was an . . . an *observer* probing for something personally dangerous.

"Nothing food and rest won't cure," he said. He tried to sound bantering, knew he'd failed.

"I'll see you in a little while," she said, still in that distant tone.

Dasein watched the door close behind her. He had the feeling he'd been playing to a special kind of camera, one that pursued irrelevancies. An untethered thought wove through his mind: . . . *the exposure of personality, method and character.*

Who wants to expose my personality, method and character? Dasein asked himself. He felt this was a dangerous question, full of charge and countercharge.

The sack of food felt heavy in his hand. Dasein stared down at it, aware of his hunger, equally aware of the threat in this package. Did the Jaspers create irreversible change?

He tossed the sack onto his bed, went to the door, peered out into the hall. Empty. He stepped out, looked down the expanse of wall that concealed the TV room. It took a moment for him to realize something was wrong with that wall. It was like a dislocation of reality—a door occupied a space in that wall where no door had been.

As though pulled by strings, Dasein went to the door, stared at it. The door was framed in the same worn, polished wood that framed the other doors. Well-preserved age, that was the effect. This was a door that had always been here, that's what it said. The number plate carried a slight dent and a touch of tarnish at the edges where the maids' polishing rags had missed. There was a patina of long wear about the handle.

Dasein shook his head. He was tempted to try the door, resisted. He found himself frightened by what might lie beyond. Normalcy—a bed, a bath, desk and chairs—that would be the worst thing of all. The number plate—262—fascinated him. He toyed with the eerie sensation that he'd seen it before . . . right here. The door was too ordinary.

Abruptly, Dasein whirled back and into his room, threw open his window. A look through the windows from the porch roof would solve the mystery. He started to climb out, stopped. A man stood on a rose-bordered walk beyond the giant oak tree.

Dasein recognized Winston Burdeaux. He was pumping a hand sprayer that sent dust over the roses. As Dasein stared, Burdeaux looked up, waved.

Later, Dasein told himself. *I'll look later.*

He nodded to Burdeaux, withdrew, pulled the curtain.

So they'd cut a door through that wall, had they? What were they trying to do? Destroy his sense of reality?

The sack on the bed caught Dasein's attention. It drew him across the room. He saw it as an ultimate temptaton. It was more than food. There was a hunger in him only the Jaspers could fulfill. Dasein felt abruptly that he was like Tennyson's Ulysses, his aim "to strive, to seek, to find and not to yield." Still, the thought of the Jaspers in that sack drew his hand. He felt the paper tear beneath his fingers.

Jaspers cheese. That tantalizing aroma lifted from it. With a feeling of spiritual helplessness, he found a bite of the cheese in his mouth. The food radiated a sensation of warmth as it went down his throat. He continued eating, hypnotized by his own actions.

Slowly, he sank back onto the bed, leaned against the pillow, gazed up at the ceiling. The wood grain in a beam wavered like the lifting and falling of the sea. It filled him with awe, undiluted and terrifying. He felt his own consciousness stood as a barrier opposing the external world, and that external world was a stupid mechanism without feeling or compassion.

His own identity became a narrowing beam of light, and he sensed a massive, streaming unconsciousness growing larger, larger . . . larger . . . building up an intolerable weight.

It's a psychedelic, he told himself. *Don't let go.*

But there was no stopping the movement now. His awareness, exploding up and out, riding a geyser of sense revelation, lifted him into a state of floating consciousness.

There was no inwardness now, only a timeless sense of being that existed without anxiety. Dasein found himself reveling in the sensation. His mind quested.

Where are the children? he asked himself.

It was a shocking sense of revelation for him to realize he'd seen no children or schools in the valley.

Where are the children? Why haven't any of the other investigators remarked on this?

The other investigators are dead, he reminded himself.

Death—that was an oddly nonfrightening thought. He felt he had risen through a consciousness decompression into a zone beyond all power struggles. The valley, the Jaspers, had become a condition of his being. The room full of probing sunlight, the leaves of the oak outside his window—all was beauty, innocent, uncluttered. The external universe had become translated into a part of himself, wise, compassionate.

Dasein marveled at the feeling. The universe *out there*—it was as though he had just created that universe. *Nama-Rupa* he thought. *I am Nama-Rupa—name and form, creator of the universe in which I live.*

The pain of his injured shoulder occupied his drifting attention momentarily. Pain, a brief crisis, something against which to project memories of pleasure. The pain faded.

There came the sound of tires on gravel. He heard a bird singing. The sounds were a moire playing against his awareness. They danced and scintillated.

He remembered Jenny's probing stare.

This was an ugly, shocking memory that jerked him up short, compressed him. He found difficulty breathing. There was a sensation that he had been caught up in history, but it was a kind of history he'd never experienced, peopled by goddesses and creatures of terrifying powers. It was a history moving at an astonishing speed, defying all preconceived notions of slowness. It was like a series of events that he couldn't separate or distinguish. They flashed across his consciousness, leaving him irrevocably changed.

The Jaspers, he thought. *I cannot return . . . to . . . what . . . I was . . . before.*

Tears rolled down his cheeks.

He thought of the way his bag had been searched. A sob shook him. What did they want?

Dasein found himself believing there were demons around him, cunning, seeking his blood and being, hungry for his soul. They gibbered beyond the charmed circle of his lonely awareness. The sensation, primitive as a witch dance, refused to leave. They were robots, automata with grimacing malleable faces and headlight eyes.

He began to tremble, knew he was perspiring heavily, but it was a distant sensation, something happening to a foreign person.

Head whirling, Dasein heaved himself off the bed, lurched to his feet, stumbled across the room. At the wall, he turned, stumbled back—forth and back . . . back and forth. No hiding place existed for him. Sunlight streaming in the window took on grotesque forms—lizards with human faces, silvery gnomes, insects with clock-face wings . . .

He slumped to the floor, clawed at the rug. A red braided pattern extruded claws that reached for him. He retreated to the bed, fell across it. The ceiling undulated with inverted waves.

Somewhere, someone played a piano—Chopin.

Dasein felt abruptly that he was the piano. The sounds struck a crystal brilliance through him, plucking out his anguish. Glaring white clarity began to seep over him. He grew aware his clothes were soaked with perspiration. His palms were slippery. He sensed he had come a long distance through a dangerous passage. The journey had leeched all strength from him.

But he saw the room now with an uncluttered innocence. The ceiling beams were objects to be understood, their grain receding back into trees . . . to seedlings . . . to seeds . . . to trees. Every artifact that met his vision extended into past and future for him. Nothing remained static.

All was motion and he was a part of that motion.

Waves of sleep began creeping from the back of his mind—higher . . . higher . . . higher.

Sleep enveloped him.

In the darkness of his sleep, something laughed and laughed and laughed and laughed . . .

Dasein awoke with a feeling he'd been asleep for a long time—perhaps a lifetime. A chuckle lifted from his throat. He heard the noise coming from himself as from a stranger and it frightened him. A glance at his wristwatch told him he'd been asleep more than two hours.

Again, the stranger-chuckle teased his throat.

He pushed himself off the bed, wondering at his weakness. His shoulder felt better, though, the pain diminishing to a dull ache.

A rap sounded on his door.

"Yes?" Dasein called.

"It's Win Burdeaux, sir. Miss Jenny asked me to remind you she'll be here for you in about a half hour."

"Oh . . . thank you."

"That's all right, sir. Hope you had a nice nap."

Dasein stood staring at the door for a moment. *How did Burdeaux know I was asleep?*

Perhaps I snored.

No further sound came from the hall, but Dasein knew Burdeaux had gone away.

Thoughtful, Dasein stripped out of his wrinkled clothes, showered and changed. He felt angry, frustrated. They were watching him every minute. It would be so easy, he knew, to let his anger become rage. This was no time for rage, though.

He wondered then if there was a season for rage.

A sensation of wetness drew his attention to his right hand. He was surprised to find himself still holding a washrag. Innocent thing with a green and white braided edge. He threw it into the bathroom where it landed with a wet slap.

Another rap sounded on his door and he knew it was Jenny.

Decision gripped Dasein.

He stroke across the room, threw open the door. She stood there in an orange jumper dress with white blouse, a smile deepening the dimple on her left cheek.

"I'm glad you're ready," she said. "Hurry up or we'll be late."

As he allowed her to lead him out and down the stairs, Dasein wondered if imagination had played a trick on him, or had there been a brief moment of worry before she smiled?

Jenny carried on a continuing babble of unanswerable conversation as they went down the stairs, through the lobby onto the porch.

"You'll love the lake this time of year. I wish I could spend more time there. You're not favoring your shoulder as much as you did. I'll bet it's better. Uncle Larry wants you to stop by later for him to check you. All the gang are anxious to meet you. Here they are now."

The gang occupied a stake truck.

Dasein recognized Willa Burdeaux's pixie face in the cab. She sat beside a blonde, rather craggy-faced youth with large innocent blue eyes. As he looked at her, she winked slowly, deliberately. At least a dozen couples stood in the back of the truck . . . and there were odd singles: a tall, brown-haired man with fierce dark eyes—Walter Somebody; Dasein failed to catch the last name . . . a set of twin young women, plump with long sandy hair, round faces—Rachel and Mariella.

Jenny performed the introductions too fast for Dasein to catch all the names, but he did focus on the fact that the young man with Willa Burdeaux was her fiancé, Cal Nis.

Reaching hands helped him into the back of the truck, pulled Jenny up beside him. There were boxes around the edge for seats. Dasein found himself crowded into a box with Jenny snuggled beside him. He began to absorb the carnival air of the people around him—uninhibited laughter, bantering private jokes.

The truck rumbled into motion. Wind whipped them. Dasein had an impression of passing trees, patches of sky, lurching movement . . . and the omnipresent laughter.

It grew on him that he and Jenny were being excluded from the laughter.

Was it a sense of delicacy in the group? Were they allowing the stranger time to acclimate himself?

He tried to see the situation as a psychologist, but his own involvement kept intruding. There was no way to focus his analytical eye on details without finding his own shadow across the scene. To cap it, his injured shoulder began to ache where Jenny pressed against it. Jenny's wind-tossed hair brushed his face. Each lurch of the truck sent a twinge through his shoulder.

The situation began to take on a nightmare quality.

Jenny stretched up, spoke into his ear: "Oh, Gil—I've dreamed of this day . . . when you'd be here, one of us."

One of us, Dasein thought. *Am I really one of them?*

Walter Somebody obviously had mistaken Jenny's move toward Dasein's ear. He waved and shouted from across the truck: "Hey! No smooching before dark!"

This brought a short burst of laughter from the group, but no general shift in their attention. They continued to look and speak around Dasein and Jenny.

Smooching.

The word sent Dasein's mind into high gear. It was a word no longer in common use *outside*, a word out of its time and place. On this Walter's lips, though, it had carried the inflection of familiarity. It was a word they used here in the valley.

Dasein began to see Santaroga in a new light. They were conservatives here in the true sense of the word. They were clinging to the past, resisting change. He modified this thought: They resisted *some* change. They were people who had made a judgment that some things from the past should be maintained. This was what made them foreign. The world *outside* was moving away from them. The valley had become a preserve for conditions of another time.

The truck turned off onto another track through an avenue of overhanging sycamores. Great patches of maple-shaped leaves cast a green-gold aura over their world.

A jolting bump made Dasein wince with pain as Jenny lurched against his shoulder.

The truck emerged from the sycamores, passed through a stand of bull pine onto a grassy flat that merged into beach sand edging a cerulean lake.

Dasein stared out the open rear of the truck, hardly aware of the cascade of people leaping down to the grass, ignoring Jenny's urgings that they leave. Something about this lake—some sense of familiarity—had struck him with a feeling of beauty and menace.

A narrow floating walkway reached out from the beach to a float and diving platform—the wood all dark silver-gray from the sun. There were rowboats tied along one side of the diving float.

Beauty and menace.

The sensation passed and he wondered at himself. He was seeing phantoms, focusing too much inward.

"Is it your shoulder?" Jenny asked.

"It'll be all right," Dasein said.

He followed her down off the truck, wishing he could let himself go, become a laughing part of this group. They were having fun here—carrying boxes to tables set under the trees, preparing fires in rock pits. Some wandered off into the trees, returned in bathings suits.

Jenny had attached herself to a group laying out picnic lunches on the tables. Presently, she joined the scampering movement toward the water, shedding her dress to reveal an orange one-piece bathing suit beneath. She was a naiad, limbs flashing brown and lithe in the sun.

She waved to him from the float, shouted: "See you in a minute, darling!"

Dasein watched her dive into the lake with a feeling she was suddenly lost to him. He experienced an intense jealousy, imagining himself a decrepit old man surrounded by playing children, unable to join them in their happiness.

He looked around at lake and verging woods. There was a breeze across the water. The breeze had summer in it, fragrant with grass and evergreen needles. He wished suddenly for some drink with which to salute this breeze and day, some potion that would make him a part of the scene.

Slowly, Dasein walked down to the floating walk and out onto the boards. There were fleece clouds in the sky, and as he stared down at the water, he saw those clouds floating on the lake bottom. Waves shattered the illusion. Jenny swam up, leaned her elbows on the boards. Her face all dripping water, smiling, had never seemed more lovely.

"Darling, why don't you come out to the float and sun yourself while we swim?" she asked.

"All right," he said. "Maybe I can scull around in one of those boats."

"You go easy on that shoulder or I'll tell Uncle Larry," she said. She kicked away from the walk, swam lazily out toward the float.

Dasein followed, making his way through dripping swimmers running up and down the walk. It struck him as odd how this crowd saw him but didn't see him. They made way for him, but never looked at him. They shouted across him, but not to him.

He moved to the first boat in the line, untied its painter and prepared to get into it. Jenny was swimming some fifty feet out, a slow, smooth crawl that took her diagonally away from the float.

Dasein stood up, moved to step into the boat. As he stepped, something pushed him in the middle of the back. His foot kicked the gunwale, thrusting the boat out into the water. He saw he was going to fall into the lake, thought: *Oh, damn! I'll get my clothes all wet*. The stern of the boat was turning toward him and he thought of trying to reach for it, but his left foot on the dock slipped in a patch of wet wood. Dasein found himself turning sideways without any control over his motion.

The edge of the boat, seen out of the corner of an eye, rushed toward him. He tried to reach up, but that was the side of his bad shoulder. His arm wouldn't move fast enough.

There was an explosion of blackness in his head. Dasein felt himself sinking into an enveloping cold, soundless, all dark and inviting.

A part of his mind screamed: *Beauty! Menace!*

He thought that an odd combination.

There was a distant ache in his lungs and it was cold—terrifyingly cold. He felt pressure . . . and the cold . . . all distant and unimportant.

I'm drowning, he thought.

It was an unexciting thought—something that concerned another person.

They won't see me . . . and I'll drown.

The cold grew more immediate—wet.

Something turned him violently.

Still, everything remained remote—all happening to that *other* being which he knew to be himself, but which could not concern him.

Jenny's voice broke on him like a thunderclap: "Help me! Please! Someone help me! Oh, God! Won't someone help me? I love him! Please help me!"

He grew aware suddenly of other hands, other voices.

"All right, Jen. We've got him."

"Please save him!" Her voice carried a sobbing intensity.

Dasein felt himself draped across something hard that pressed into his abdomen. Warmth gushed from his mouth. There was a blinding, terrible pain in his chest.

Abruptly, he began to cough—gasping, the pain tearing at his throat and bronchia.

"He swallowed a lot of water." It was a man's voice, almost vacant of emotion.

Jenny's voice came pleading beside Dasein's ear: "Is he breathing? Please don't let anything happen to him." Dasein felt wetness on his neck, and still Jenny's voice pleading there beside him: "I love him. Please save him."

That same unemotional male voice answered: "We understand, Jenny."

And another voice, husky, feminine: "There's only one thing to do, of course."

"We're doing it!" Jenny screamed. "Don't you understand?"

Even as hands picked Dasein up, began carrying him, Dasein wondered: *Doing what?*

His coughing had subsided, but the pain in his chest remained. It hurt when he breathed.

Presently, there was grass under his back. Something warm and confining was wrapped around him. It was an oddly womblike sensation.

Dasein opened his eyes, found himself staring up at Jenny, her dark hair framed by blue sky. She managed a trembling smile.

"Oh, thank God," she whispered.

Hands lifted his shoulders. Jenny's face went away. A cup full of steaming brown liquid was pressed against his lips. Dasein experienced the almost overpowering smell of Jaspers, felt hot coffee burn down his throat.

Immediately, a sense of warmth and well-being began to seep outward through his body. The cup was pulled away, returned when he moved his mouth toward it.

Someone laughed, said something that Dasein couldn't quite catch. It sounded like, "Take a full load." But that didn't make sense and he rejected it.

The hands eased him gently back to the grass. That vacant masculine voice said: "Keep him warm and quiet for awhile. He's okay."

Jenny's face returned. Her hand stroked his head.

"Oh, darling," she said. "I looked at the dock and you were gone. I didn't see you fall, but I knew. And no one was paying any attention. It took me so long to get there. Oh, your poor head. Such a bruise."

Dasein felt the throbbing then as though her words had turned it on—a pulsing ache at the temple and across his ear. *A blow like that—shouldn't I have X-rays?* he wondered. *How do they know I haven't a fractured skull . . . or concussion?*

"Cal says the boat must've been tipping away from you as you hit it," Jenny said. "I don't think you've broken anything."

Pain shot through him as she touched the bruise.

"It's just a bad bruise."

Just a bad bruise! he thought. He was filled with abrupt anger at her. How could they be so casual?

Still, that feeling of warmth spread out through him, and he thought: *Of course I'm all right. I'm young, healthy. I'll heal. And I have Jenny to protect me. She loves me.*

Something about this train of thought struck him as profoundly wrong then. He blinked. As though that were the creative mechanism, his vision blurred, resolved into flashes of gemlike light, red, orange, yellow, brown, green, violet, blue light with offshooting crystal shards.

The light resolved into a membranous inward sensation, a perception of perception that reached out through his mind. He *saw* then strong pulses of his own heart, the tender brain sheathing that rose and fell with the pulse, the damaged area—just a bruise, skull intact.

Dasein grew aware then why the Santarogans showed so little concern for his injury. They *knew* the injury through him. If he were like them, he would tell them when he needed help.

Then why didn't they try to rescue me until Jenny came? Dasein asked himself. And the answer lay there to wonder at: *Because I didn't cry out for help in my thoughts!*

"You shouldn't sleep now, I don't think," Jenny said.

She found his left hand, gripped it. "Isn't there something about not sleeping after a head injury?"

Dasein stared up at her, seeing the dark wings of her hair disarrayed from rescuing him, the way her eyes seemed to touch him, so intense was her concentration. There was dampness on her lashes and he felt that he might look behind her eyes and find the way to a magic land.

"I love you," he whispered.

She pressed a finger against his lips. "I know."

I am a Santarogan now, Dasein thought.

He lay there rolling the thought in his mind, filled by this odd awareness that let him reach out to Jenny even when she released his hand and left him alone there on the grass. There was nothing of telepathy in this awareness. It was more knowledge of mood in those around him. It was a lake in which they all swam. When one disturbed the water, the others knew it.

My God! What this Jaspers could do for the world! Dasein thought.

But this thought sent roiling waves through the lake of mutual awareness. There was storm in this thought. It was dangerous. Dasein recoiled from it.

He remembered then why he had come here and saw the conflict from a new perspective. The people who'd sent him—what did they want?

Proof, he thought.

He found he couldn't focus on what *they* wanted to prove. It was all tied up with Jersey Hofstedder's car and the blunt Yankee insularity of these people.

Jenny's friends were noticing him now, Dasein saw. They looked at him— directly at him. They spoke to him. And when he felt he wanted to get up and go to the big fire they'd built against the evening chill, strong hands came without bidding and helped him.

Night fell.

Dasein found himself seated on a blanket beside Jenny. Someone was playing a guitar in the darkness. Moon colored half the lake, leaving a great black stone of night against one side. Wind-wrinkled water lapped at the stone and he felt that if the blackness could only be moved it would blaze in light to reveal fairyland.

Jenny snuggled against him, murmured: "You're feeling better. I know it."

He agreed with her silently.

Torches flamed down by the lake—people securing the boats. Someone handed him a sandwich redolent with Jaspers. He ate, his attention on the torches and the fire—the trees around them gleaming red, grotesque shadows lurching, dove wings of smoke against the moon. Abruptly, Dasein secreted part of his sandwich in a pocket.

For no reason he could explain, Dasein remembered a time shortly after Jenny had left the school. It had rained. He remembered reaching out his window to feel the rain, seeing the wet sparkle of the lawn beneath a window, like a broken necklace scattered there.

Abruptly, the wind across the lake shifted, stung his eyes with smoke. He swallowed a mouthful of the smoke and it brought him to an intense awareness of the here and now, Jenny beside him . . . waiting.

As he thought about her, she reached up, pulled his lips down on hers. It was a long kiss, full of guitar music, remembered rain and the taste of smoke.

How can I ever explain this? Dasein wondered. *Selador would think me mad.*

Jenny stirred against him at this thought, stroked his neck.

"Let's get married soon," she whispered.

Why not? Dasein asked himself. *I'm a Santarogan now.*

But this thought brought a surge of fear that tightened his chest and made Jenny shiver. She pulled away, stared at him with worry in her eyes.

"Everything will be all right," she whispered. "You'll see."

The worry remained in her voice, though. And Dasein sensed menace in the night. The guitarist struck a sour note, fell silent.

Dasein saw that moonlight had moved into the black area of the lake . . . and it revealed no fairyland—only more lake, more trees.

The night was definitely cold now.

Once more, Jenny pressed her lips to his.

Dasein knew he still loved her. It was a real thing to which he could cling. But there was no more magic in this night. He felt that he had skirted madness and the thing had left its taint on him.

When she pulled away, he whispered: "I want to marry you, Jenny. I love you . . . but . . . I need time. I need . . . "

"I know, darling," she said. She stroked his cheek. "Take all the time you need."

Her voice carried a withdrawing note compounded as she pulled back. Dasein felt the night's coldness then, the stillness of their companions.

Abruptly, there was a stirring in the people around them. They began moving toward the truck.

"It's time to go back," Jenny said.

Back where? Dasein asked himself.

Jenny stood up, helped him to his feet. He stumbled in a brief spasm of dizziness. Jenny steadied him.

"Do you want Uncle Larry to look at your head tonight?" she asked.

Piaget, Dasein thought. That was the *back* at which he was aimed. Piaget. They would continue their trade of truths. The Jaspers change was forcing it.

"I'll see him in the morning," Dasein said.

"Not tonight?"

In my own sweet time, Dasein thought. And he said: "Not tonight."

The answer seemed to trouble Jenny. She sat barely touching him on the ride back to town.

6

WHEN THEY were gone, leaving Dasein standing alone behind his truck in the Inn yard, he stared up at the darkness of the sky, lost in thought. Jenny's good-night kiss—strained, trembling—still tingled on his lips. There was a smell of exhaust gases and oil in the air. From somewhere inside the building came the faint sound of music—a radio. The gravel of the driveway felt hard and immediate under his feet.

Slowly, Dasein brought his right hand from his pocket, opened it to stare at the small ball of matter there—an object indistinctly seen in the light from the Inn sign. Now, there was a strong smell of Jaspers around him.

Dasein studied the object in his hand—a compressed ball of bread, cheese and ham, a bit of one of the sandwiches from the picnic.

Did they know I secreted this? he wondered.

He debated going inside and changing his clothes. The pants and shirt he'd worn on the picnic, garments that had been soaked and allowed to dry on him, felt wrinkled and twisted against his body.

Dasein felt that his mind wandered around this decision: to change or not to change, that was the question. The object in his hand was more immediate, though. Selador. Yes, Selador had to get this and examine it.

I'm not thinking clearly, Dasein told himself.

He felt torn between extremes, between decisions of enormous moment. *The head injury?* he wondered. But he trusted the Jaspers-induced insight that told him the injury wasn't serious. Still . . . decisions . . .

With intense concentration, Dasein forced himself to get into his truck. He leaned against the steering wheel, put the compressed ball of the Jaspers sandwich on the seat beside him. There was warm wetness at his seat and he pulled his wallet from his hip pocket, felt the water trapped in it. The wallet went beside the bit of sandwich.

Now, Dasein told himself. *Now, I will go.*

But it was several minutes before he could muster the strength of decision to start the motor and pull out of the parking area and onto the road toward Porterville. He drove slowly, conscious of the blocking dullness inhibiting his motions.

The headlights picked out a wedge of flowing roadway and bordering trees—yellow center line, guard rails, driveways. Dasein opened his window, leaned out into the wind trying to clear his head. Now, he was on the winding road up out of the valley and the slowness of his mind grew like a deadly weight.

Headlights came toward him, passed.

Dark mass of rock beside the road—yellow center lines, twisting scars of repair lines on the paving . . . stars overhead . . . He came at last to the notch that led out through the black skeletons of burned trees.

Dasein felt something was drawing him back, ordering him to turn around and return to Santaroga. He fought it. Selador had to get that bit of food and analyze it. Duty. Promises. Had to get out to Porterville.

Somewhere in his mind, Dasein sensed a looming black shape, anonymous, terrifying. It studied him.

With an inner snapping sensation, Dasein felt his mind clear. The thing was so abrupt he almost lost control of the wheel, swerved across the center line and back, tires squealing.

The road, the night, the steering wheel, his foot on the accelerator—all slammed against his senses with a confused immediacy. Dasein hit the brakes, slowed almost to a crawl. Every nerve end yammered at him. His head whirled. Dasein clung to the wheel, concentrated on steering. Slowly, his senses sorted themselves out. He took a deep, trembling breath.

Drug reaction, he told himself. *Have to tell Selador.*

Porterville was the same dull street he had remembered—cars parked at the tavern, the single light beating down on the darkened gas station.

Dasein pulled to a stop beside the telephone booth, remembering the deputies who'd questioned him there, mistaking him for a Santarogan. Had they been premature? he wondered.

He gave the operator Selador's number, waited impatiently, tapping his finger against the wall. A faint and reedy woman's voice came on the line—"Selador residence."

Dasein leaned into the phone. "This is Gilbert Dasein. Let me speak to Dr. Selador."

"I'm sorry. The Seladors are out for the evening. Is there a message?"

"Damn!" Dasein stared at the phone. He felt an irrational anger at Selador. It took a conscious effort of logic for Dasein to tell himself Selador had no real reason to hang around the telephone. Life went on its normal way back in Berkeley.

Is there a message, sir?" the reedy voice repeated.

"Tell him Gilbert Dasein called," Dasein said. "Tell him I'm sending him a package for chemical analysis."

"A package for chemical analysis. Yes sir. Is that all?"

"That's all."

Dasein replaced the receiver on its hook with a feeling of reluctance. He felt abandoned suddenly—alone up here with no one outside really caring whether he lived or died.

Why not chuck them all? he asked himself. *Why not marry Jenny, tell the rest of the world to go to hell?*

It was an intensely inviting prospect. He could feel himself sinking into quiet security back in the valley. Santaroga beckoned to him with that security. It was *safe* there.

That very sense of safety, though, was edged with danger. Dasein sensed it . . . a lurking something in the outer darkness. He shook his head, annoyed at the tricks his mind was playing. The *vapors*, again!

He returned to the truck, found a jar in the back where he'd kept a store of matches. He dumped out the matches, put in the remains of the sandwich, sealed the jar, packaged it with the remnants of a cardboard grocery box and a scrap of wrapping paper, tied the whole thing with a length of fishline and addressed it to Selador. When it was done, he wrote a covering letter on a page from his notebook, listed his reactions there painstakingly—the drug effect, the *accident* at the lake and his own impressions of the group . . . the wall they threw up to keep him at a distance . . . Jenny's terror . . .

It all went into the letter.

The effort of recalling the incidents made his head ache where he'd hit the edge of the boat. He found an envelope in his case, addressed the letter and sealed it.

With a sense of satisfaction, Dasein started up the truck, found a dark side street and parked. He locked the cab, climbed into the back and lay down to wait for morning when the Porterville post office would open.

They won't control the mail over here, he told himself. *Let Selador get the sample of Jaspers . . . we'll soon know what it is.*

He closed his eyes and his lids became like a movie screen for a fantasy—Jenny cringing, crying out, pleading with him. Selador laughing. A gigantic Dasein figure stood bound like Prometheus, the eyes glazed . . . panting with exertion . . .

Dasein's eyes popped open.

Waking fantasy!

He was over the hill—around the bend!

Hesitantly, he closed his eyes. Only darkness . . . but there was sound in this darkness—Selador laughing.

Dasein pressed his hands over his ears. The sound changed to tolling bells, slow cadence . . . mournful. He opened his eyes. The sound stopped.

He sat up, pushed himself back into a corner, eyes open. It was cold in the camper and there was a musty smell. He found his sleeping bag, wrapped it around him, sat there with his eyes open. There were cricket sounds outside, faint creakings in the truck's metal.

Slowly, sleep crept up on him. His eyelids drooped, popped open.

How long would it take for the Jaspers effect to wear off? he wondered. Surely, this was drug effect.

His eyes closed.

Somewhere in an echoing box, Jenny whispered: "Oh, Gil—I love you. Gil, I love you . . . ''

He went to sleep with her voice whispering to him.

7

DAYLIGHT FOUND Dasein staring up at the camper's metal ceiling with a sense of disorientation. He recognized the ceiling, but couldn't locate it in space. His head and shoulder throbbed. Ceiling . . . familiar ceiling.

A car horn honked. It brought him to the present and awareness. He threw off the twisted folds of his sleeping bag, climbed out into a gray, overcast day. His chin felt rough and stubbly. There was a sour taste in his mouth.

Two passing schoolboys stared at him, whispering.

I must look a sight, Dasein thought. He looked down at his clothes. They were twisted and wrinkled as though he had gone swimming in them and then slept in them until they dried. Dasein smiled to himself, thinking that was exactly what had happened.

He climbed into the cab, turned around and found the main street, drove down it until he saw the Post Office sign over the porch of a general store.

The postmaster had to finish selling candy to a girl before he could come around behind his caged counter to weigh Dasein's package and letter. The man was tall, pale with thinning black hair, darting, wary blue eyes. He sniffed once at Dasein, said: "That'll be eighty-four for the package and five for the letter."

Dasein pushed a dollar bill under the cage.

The man made change, looked once more at the package. "What's in the package, mister?''

"Specimens for analysis at our laboratory," Dasein said.

"Oh."

The man didn't appear curious about specimens of what. "Any return address?" he asked.

"Dr. Gilbert Dasein, general delivery, Santaroga," he said.

"Dasein," the man said with sudden interest. "Dasein . . . seems I got a package for a Dasein. Just a minute."

He disappeared into the back, returned in a moment with a box about a foot square wrapped neatly and tied with a heavy twine. Even from a distance, Dasein recognized Selador's precise script on the address.

Selador writing me here? Dasein wondered.

The air of conspiracy in this gave Dasein the abrupt sensation of being completely transparent to Selador. The man could send a package here and *know* it would be picked up. Immediately, Dasein told himself this was the simplest thing to figure—given the Santaroga Post Office situation as he'd described it to Selador.

There remained, though, the feeling he was a pawn and his every move was known to the masters of the game.

"Let's see your identification," the postmaster said.

Dasein showed it.

"Sign here," the man said.

Dasein signed, took the package. It felt heavy.

"Funny thing you Santarogans using my Post Office," the postmaster said. "Something wrong with your own?"

Santarogans . . . plural, Dasein thought. He said: "Is some other . . . Santarogan using your Post Office?"

"Well—used to be," the man said. "Negro fellow over there . . . Burdeaux, as I recollect. He used to send some mail from here. Got a package here once from Louisiana. Long time ago that was."

"Oh, yes," Dasein said, not knowing how else to acknowledge this information.

"Haven't seen Burdeaux in quite a spell," the postmaster mused. "Nice fellow. Hope he's all right."

"Quite all right," Dasein said. "Well—thank you." He took his package, went out to the truck.

With a feeling of caution he couldn't explain, Dasein left the package unopened on the seat beside him while he drove east on the road to Santaroga until he found a shady spot in which to pull off.

The box contained a .32 caliber automatic pistol with an extra clip and a box of cartridges. Wired to the trigger guard was a note from Selador: "Gilbert—This has been gathering dust in my bureau drawer for many years and I'm probably an old woman for sending it to you, but here it is. I think I'm sending it in the hope you won't have to use it. The situation you describe, however, has filled me with the oddest sensations of disquiet that I can remember. I hope you're being extremely cautious."

On the reverse side of the note was a scrawled postscript: "No news yet on the investigations you requested. These things move slowly. You give me hope, though, that we'll get the goods on these people." It was signed: "S."

Dasein hefted the automatic, fought down an impulse to heave it out the window. The thing embodied ultimate menace. What had he said to prompt Selador to send it? Or was this part of some obscure motivational gambit Selador was setting up?

Could it be a reminder of duty? His bruised head ached with thought.

A line in Selador's note came back to him and he reread it: " . . . *get the goods on these people.*"

Is that what I'm supposed to do? Dasein wondered. *Am I to set them up for prosecution?*

He remembered Marden alluding to the reasons an investigator had been sent.

Dasein swallowed. Selador's line, read once more, looked like a slip. Had the good doctor tipped his hand? Sending a gun wasn't like the man. In fact, Dasein realized if he'd been asked, he would've said Selador wasn't even the type to *own* a gun.

What to do with the damn' thing now that he had it?

Dasein checked it, found the clip full, no cartridge in the chamber. He resisted the impulse to shove it in the glove compartment and forget it. If the truck were searched . . .

Damn Selador!

Feeling foolish as he did it, Dasein slipped the gun into a hip pocket, pulled his coat over it. He'd settle with Selador later. Right now there was Piaget . . . and Piaget had some answers to give.

8

PIAGET WAS in his office with a patient when Dasein arrived. The gaunt, gray Sarah opened the door, allowed he could wait in the living room. With a grudging show of hospitality, she added that she would bring him some coffee if he wanted it.

With a stomach-gripping pang, Dasein realized he was ravenous with hunger. He wondered if he could mention this fact.

As though she'd read his mind, Sarah said. "I'll bet you haven't eaten breakfast." She looked him up and down. "You look like you'd slept in those clothes. You doctors are all alike. Never care how you look."

"As a matter of fact, I haven't eaten," Dasein said.

"You're going to lead Jenny some life," she said. But she softened her words with a smile.

Dasein stared in wonder at a double, whiteboned row of false teeth in the wrinkled face.

"Got a leftover apple roll and some Jaspers cream," Sarah said. "Bet you'd like that."

She turned away, went out through the dining room into a glistening white kitchen, which Dasein glimpsed once through a swinging door. The door went slap-slap behind her.

Dasein thought about that smile, recalled Jenny saying Sarah liked him. On impulse, he followed her into the kitchen.

"Bet you don't like feeding people in the living room," he said.

"Feed people wherever they have to be fed," she said.

She put a dish on an oval table beside windows looking onto a flower garden brilliant in the morning sun. "Sit here, young man," she said. She poured a thick flow of cream from a pitcher onto the golden mound of crust in the dish.

Dasein inhaled a strong smell of Jaspers. His hand trembled as he picked up the spoon Sarah placed within his reach. The trembling stopped at his first swallow of the food.

The pastry was sweet and soothing, rich with apples.

With a detached feeling of shock, Dasein watched his hand guide the spoon into the pastry for another bite, saw the food conveyed to his mouth, felt himself swallow it.

Soothing.

I'm addicted to the stuff, he thought.

"Something wrong?" Sarah asked.

"I . . . . " He put down his spoon. "You've trapped me, haven't you?" he asked.

"What're you talking about?" Sarah asked.

"What's it . . . " He nodded toward the pastry. " . . . doing to me?"

"You feel strange?" Sarah asked. "Got a fluttery feeling behind your eyes?"

"I'm . . . " He shook his head. Her words sounded insane. *Fluttery feeling behind his eyes!*

"I'll bring Doctor Larry," Sarah said. She darted out a connecting door at the back of the kitchen and he saw her running along the covered walkway to the clinic.

Presently, she reappeared with Piaget in tow. The doctor's face wore a worried frown.

"What's this Sarah's telling me?" Piaget asked. He put a hand under Dasein's chin, stared into Dasein's eyes.

"What's she telling you what?" Dasein asked. The words sounded foolish as they spilled from his lips. He brushed Piaget's hand aside. The doctor's frown, the squinting eyes—he looked like an angry Buddha.

"You seem to be all right," Piaget said. "Any strange symptoms of . . . "

"You've trapped me," Dasein said. "That's what I told her. You've trapped me." He gestured at the plate in front of him. "With this."

"Ohhh," Piaget said.

"Is he just fighting it?" Sarah asked.

"Probably," Piaget said.

"Don't make sense," Sarah said.

"It happens," Piaget said.

"I know, but . . . "

"Will you two stop talking about me like I was a blob of something on a slide!" Dasein raged. He pushed away from the table, jumped to his feet. The motion sent his bowl of food sliding off the table with a crash.

"Now look what you've done!" Sarah said.

"I'm a human being," Dasein said, "not some sort of . . . "

"Easy, lad, easy," Piaget said.

Dasein whirled away, brushed past Piaget. He had to get away from this pair or be consumed by rage. Dasein's mind kept focusing on the weapon in his hip pocket.

Damn Selador!

"Here, now—wait a minute!" Piaget said.

"Don't try to stop me," Dasein growled. The gun felt large and cold against his hip.

Piaget fell silent—a stillness that Dasein imagined came up from the toes to stare out of measuring eyes. It was as though the man receded to become a figure seen through a reversed telescope—remote, secretive.

"Very well," Piaget said. His voice came from that far away.

Deliberately, Dasein turned, went out the door, through the living room—out of the house. He felt his feet hitting the concrete of the front walk, the grass parking strip. His truck's door handle was cold under his hand. He started the motor, wondering at his own sensations—dreamlike.

A street flowed past, receded—signposts . . . pavement crawling beneath his vision . . . the Inn. He parked facing the long porch, an old green car on his left, make indeterminate, unimportant.

As though awakening, Dasein found his right hand on the Inn's front door—tugging, tugging. The door resisted. A sign on the center panel stared back at him.

"Closed."

Dasein peered at the sign. *Closed?*

"Your luggage is right here by the steps, Dr. Dasein."

The voice Dasein recognized immediately—the infuriating Al Marden: *Authority . . . Secrecy . . . Conspiracy.*

Dasein turned, feeling himself bundled into a tight ball of consciousness. There was Marden standing halfway down the porch: red-haired, the narrow face, the green eyes, the tight-lipped mouth drawn into a straight line that could have signified any emotion from anger to amusement.

"So you're turning me out," Dasein said.

"Hotel's closed," Marden said. "Health department."

"The Inn, the restaurant, too?" Dasein asked.

"All closed." It was a flat square of voice brooking no appeal.

"I can just go back where I came from, eh?" Dasein asked.

"Suit yourself."

"You have other hotels," Dasein said.

"Do we?"

"You must."

"Must we?"

Dasein stared at the patrol captain, experiencing the same sensation he'd had with Piaget. The man receded.

"You can leave or go back to Dr. Piaget's," Marden said. "He'll likely put you up." So far away, that voice.

"Back to Piaget's," Dasein said. "How'd you know I just came from there?"

Marden remained silent, eyes withdrawn . . . distant.

"You move fast around here," Dasein said.

"When we have to."

Back to Piaget's? Dasein asked himself. He smiled, husbanding his tight ball of consciousness. *No!* They hadn't thought of everything. They hadn't thought of *quite* everything.

Still smiling, Dasein scooped up his suitcase from beside the steps, strode down to the truck, threw the bag into the cab, climbed behind the wheel.

"Best let people help you who know how," Marden called.

There was just a faint trace of worry in his voice now. It broadened Dasein's smile, stayed with him as a satisfying memory as he drove back toward the town.

In the rear-view mirror, Dasein saw the patrol car following him. They wouldn't let him park in town, Dasein knew, but he remembered the map posted on a window of Scheler's service station. The map had shown a state park on the road west—Sand Hills State Park.

Down the main street he drove, Marden's patrol car right behind. There was the giant service station directly ahead. Dasein saw the telephone kiosk beside the parking area, swerved in so suddenly that Marden went past, screeched to a stop, backed up. Dasein already was out of the truck and at the kiosk.

Marden stopped the patrol car on the street, waited, staring at Dasein. The patrol car's motor seemed to rumble disapprovingly. Dasein turned, looked back at the service station—such a strange normality to the activity there: cars pulling in, out . . . no one paying the slightest attention to Marden or to the object of his attention.

Dasein shrugged, went into the booth, closed the door.

He put a dime in the slot, dialed the operator, asked for the Cooperative's number.

"If you want Jenny, Dr. Dasein, she's already gone home." Dasein stared at the telephone mouthpiece in front of him, letting the import of that supercilious female voice sink home. Not only did they know who was calling, they knew what he wanted before he could say it!

Dasein stared out at Marden, attention focused on the green eyes, the cynical green eyes.

Anger boiled in Dasein. He put it down. Damn them! Yes, he wanted to talk to Jenny. He'd talk to her in spite of them.

"I don't have Dr. Piaget's number."

A distinctly audible sigh came over the line.

Dasein looked at the telephone directory chained to the kiosk wall, felt a wave of guilt, unreasonable, damning, instantly repressed. He heard the operator dialing, the ring.

Jenny's voice answered.

"Jenny!"

"Oh, hello, Gilbert."

Dasein experienced a cold sensation in his stomach. Her voice was so casual.

"You know they're trying to run me out of the valley, Jenny?" he asked.

Silence.

"Jenny?"

"I heard you." Still that casual . . . distance in her tone.

"Is that all you have to say?" His voice betrayed hurt anger.

"Gilbert . . . " There was a long pause, then: " . . . maybe it'd be . . . better . . . if you . . . just for a while, just for a while, went . . . well . . . outside."

He sensed strain beneath the casual tone now.

"Jenny, I'm driving out to the Sand Hills Park and live in my camper. They're not running me out."

"Gilbert, don't!"

"You . . . want me to leave?"

"I . . . Gilbert, please come back and talk to Uncle Larry."

"I talked to Uncle Larry."

"Please. For me."

"If you want to see me, come out to the park."

"I . . . don't dare."

"You don't dare?" He was outraged. What pressure had they applied to her?

"Please don't ask me to explain."

He hesitated, then: "Jenny, I'm setting up camp in the park. To make my point. I'll be back after I make my point."

"For the love of heaven, Gilbert—please be careful."

"Careful of what?"

"Just . . . careful."

Dasein felt the gun in his pocket, a heavy weight that brought his mind to bear on the nameless threats of this valley. That was the thing—the threats were nameless. They lacked form. What use was a gun against a formless target?

"I'll be back, Jenny," he said. "I love you."

She began crying. He heard the sobs distinctly before she broke the connection.

His muscles stiff with anger, Dasein marched back to his truck, pulled it around the police car and headed out the east road, Marden right behind.

Let the son-of-a-bitch follow, Dasein told himself. He could feel the reckless inanity of his actions, but there remained a driving current underneath that told him he had to do this. This was asking for a showdown. That was the thing. A showdown. Perhaps a showdown was needed to provide answers.

He crossed the river on a concrete bridge, glimpsed rows of greenhouses off to the left through the trees. The road climbed up through the trees, emerged into scrub country—madrone and mesquite. It twisted down through the scrub and again the land changed. In the distance there were tree-covered heights, but in between stretched low mounds of hills topped by gnarled bushes, scattered weedy growths with bare gray dirt and pools of black water, miasmic water untouched by growing things, in the low spots.

A smell of sulfur, dank and suffocating, hung over the land.

With almost a sense of recognition, Dasein realized these must be the sand hills. A broken sign came into view on the right. It dangled from one post. Another post leaned at a crazy angle.

Sand Hills State Park. Public camp ground.

Twin ruts led off through the sand to the right toward a fenced area with a doorless outhouse at one end and crumbling stone fireplaces spaced around the edge.

Dasein turned into the ruts. The truck lurched and growled its way to the parking area. He stopped beside one of the stone fireplaces, stared around. The place was outrageously drab.

A sound of wheels and laboring car engine brought Dasein's attention to the left. Marden pulled the patrol car to a stop beside him, leaned across to the open window.

"What're you stopping here for, Dasein?" There was just a touch of petulance in Marden's tone.

"This is a state park isn't it?" Dasein asked. "Any law says I can't camp here?"

"Don't get smart with me, Dasein!"

"Unless you have a legal objection, I'm going to camp here," Dasein said.

"Here?" Marden gestured at the desolation of the place.

"I find it relatively friendly after Santaroga," Dasein said.

"What're you trying to prove, Dasein?"

Dasein answered him with a silent stare.

Marden pulled back into the patrol car. Dasein could see the man's knuckles white on the steering wheel. Presently, the patrol captain leaned back, glared up at Dasein. "Okay, mister. It's your funeral."

The patrol car leaped ahead, made a sand-spewing turn around the parking area, roared out to the highway and headed back toward town.

Dasein waited for the dust to settle before getting out. He climbed into the camper, checked his emergency larder—beans, powdered milk and powdered eggs, canned frankfurters, two bottles of ketchup, a can of syrup and a half empty box of prepared pancake mix . . . coffee, sugar . . . He sighed, sat down on the bunk.

The window opposite framed a view of the sand hills and the doorless outhouse. Dasein rubbed his forehead. There was an ache behind his eyes. The bruise on his head throbbed. The pitiless light beating down on the drab hills filled him with a sense of self-accusation.

For the first time since pointing his truck down into the valley, Dasein began to question his own actions. He felt there was an air of insanity around everything he had done. It was a mad pavane—Jenny . . . Marden . . . Burdeaux, Piaget, Willa, Scheler, Nis . . . It was mad, yet with its own kind of sense. His brushes with disaster became a part of the stately nonsense.

And there was Jersey Hofstedder's car—somehow the most significant thing of all.

He felt he had been down once more beneath the lake, rising now into a brutal honesty with himself. Jenny's *"We"* lost some of its terrors. That was the *We* of the cave and the Jaspers, the *We* that waited patiently for him to make his decision.

The decision was his, he saw. No matter what the substance out of that dim red cave did to the psyche, the decision was his. It had to be his decision or the mad pavane lost all meaning.

I'm still fighting it, he thought. *I'm still afraid I'll wind up "fluttery behind the eyes" and standing on a wrapping line at the Co-op.*

Restlessly, he climbed down out of the camper, stood on the sand absorbing the mid-afternoon heat. A single crow flew overhead so close he heard the rushing harp sound of wind through its plumage.

Dasein gazed after the bird thinking how strange to see only one crow. They were not a solitary bird. But here was this one—alone as he was alone.

What was I before that I cannot return to? he wondered. And he thought if he made the decision against Santaroga he'd be like that solitary crow, a creature without its own kind anywhere.

The problem, he knew, lay in a compulsion somewhere within him to make an honest report to those who'd hired him. The Jaspers clarity-of-being urged it. His own remembered sense of duty urged it. To do anything less would be a form of dishonesty, an erosion of selfdom. He felt a jealous possessiveness about this self. No smallest part of it was cheap enough to discard.

This self of his, old but newly seen, precious beyond anything he'd ever imagined, placed a terrifying burden on him, Dasein saw. He remembered the wildness of the Jaspers revelation, the gamut he'd run to come though to this peak.

The *had-I-but-known* quality of his immediate past settled on him then like a fog that chilled him in spite of the afternoon's heat. Dasein shivered. How pleasant it would be, he thought, to have no decisions. How tempting to allow that restlessly stirring *something* within his consciousness lift up its ancient snake's head and devour the disturbing parts of his awareness.

His view of the valley's people took on an Olympian cast. They stood beside him for a moment in ghostly ranks, godlike, masters of the primitive.

Are they testing me? he wondered.

Then why would Jenny say she dared not come here to him?

And where are the children?

A coldly rational part of his mind weighed his thinking and found the balance uncertain. *How much of what's in my mind is the drug thinking?* he asked himself.

At the fulcrum of any decision, that was the essential question. Where could he find solid ground upon which to stand and say, ''The things I'm to decide about are there . . . and there . . . and there . . . ?''

No one could help him find this ground, he knew. It must be a lonely search. If he made an honest report to Meyer Davidson's crew, that would doom Santaroga. But to make a false report would be to plant a cancer within himself.

He had separated himself from Santaroga in a definite way, like a knife stroke, Dasein realized. The Jaspers package he'd sent for analysis to Selador loomed in his mind. The cutting off had begun there.

It had been a gesture, nothing more. Symbolic. Some part of him had known even as he mailed it that the package would arrive with whatever Jaspers it had contained completely dissipated. He'd been sending a gesture of defiance to the Santaroga part of himself, Dasein realized.

Had Burdeaux done that? he wondered. What packages had Burdeaux exchanged with Louisiana?

The package to Selador—it had been like a thrown rock that could not reach its mark. He remembered as a child throwing a rock at a cat too far away to hit. Gray cat. He remembered the sudden bird silence in his aunt's garden, the gray cat slinking into view . . . the rock landing short.

Piaget was the gray cat.

The cat in the garden had looked up, momentarily surprised by the sound, weighed the situation, and returned to its hunting with an insulting disdain for distant boys with distant rocks.

What had Piaget done?

Dasein experienced a sudden *deitgrasp*, an act of self-discovery in which the sky appeared to shimmer. He realized in this instant why he felt so terrifyingly lonely.

He had no group, no place in a hive of fellow-activity, nothing to shield him from personal decisions that might overwhelm him. Whatever decision he made, no matter the consequences, that was *his* decision. Selador might face the shame of his agent's failure. The school might lose its munificent grant. The unique *thing* that was Santaroga might be dissipated.

All because of a decision, a gesture really, by a lone man standing in a patch of barren sand hills, his mind caught up in fantasies about a solitary crow and a gray cat.

It was a moment for positive action, and all he could think to do was re-enter the camper and eat.

As he moved in the confining space preparing himself a powdered-egg mess in the frying pan, the truck emitted protesting creaks. Hunger gnawed at him, but he didn't want this food. He knew what he wanted—what he had fled here to escape, what his body craved until it was an ache at the core of him—

Jaspers.

9

AT FULL dark, Dasein switched on the camper's wall light, retreated into his notes. He felt he had to keep his mind occupied, but the fetid smell of the campground intruded. The camper was a tiny world with sharp boundaries, but it couldn't hold off the universe out there. Dasein peered out a window at stars: bright holes punched in blackness. They amplified his sense of loneliness. He jerked his gaze away.

The notes . . .

Always the same items floated to the surface:

Where were the children?

What failure of the Jaspers change produced zombies?

How could a whole community be ignited with the unconscious desire to kill a person?

What was the Jaspers essence? What was it? What did it do to the body's chemistry?

Dasein sensed the danger in putting his hand to these questions. They were questions and at the same time an answer. This probing—this was what ignited the community.

He had to do it. Like a child poking at a sore, he had to do it. But once he had done it, would he turn then and tell the whole story to Meyer Davidson's crowd?

Even if he did find the answers and decided to make a full and honest report, would Santaroga permit it?

There were forces at work out there, Dasein realized, against which he was but a candle flickering in a gale.

He grew aware of footsteps crunching on the sand, turned off the light, opened the door and peered out.

A ghostly blur of a figure in the starlight, a woman in a light dress or a small man in a coat, was approaching along the tracks from the highway.

"Who's there?" Dasein called.

"Gil!"

"Jenny!"

He jumped down, strode to meet her. "I thought you couldn't come out here. You told me . . . "

"Please don't come any closer," she said. She stopped about ten paces from him. Such an oddly brittle quality to her voice—Dasein hesitated.

"Gil, if you won't come back to Uncle Larry's you must leave the valley," she said.

"You want me to leave?"

"You must."

"Why?"

"I . . . they want you to go."

"What have I done?"

"You're dangerous to us. We all know it. We can feel it. You're dangerous."

"Jen . . . do you think I'd hurt you?"

"I don't know! I just know you're dangerous."

"And you want me to leave?"

"I'm ordering you to leave."

"Ordering me?" He heard hysteria in her voice.

"Gil, please."

"I can't go, Jen. I can't."

"You must."

"I can't."

"Then come back to Uncle Larry's. We'll take care of you."

"Even if I turn into a zombie?"

"Don't say that!"

"It could happen, couldn't it?"

"Darling, we'll take care of you whatever happens!"

"You take care of your own."

"Of course we do."

"Jenny, do you know I love you?"

"I know," she whispered.

"Then why are you doing this to me?"

"We're not doing anything to you." She was crying, speaking through sobs. "It's you who're doing . . . whatever it is you're doing."

"I'm only doing what I have to do."

"You don't have to do anything."

"Would you have me be dishonest . . . lie?"

"Gil, I'm begging you. For my sake . . . for your own sake, leave."

"Or come back to Uncle Larry's?"

"Oh, please."

"What'll happen to me if I don't?"

"If you really love me . . . Oh, Gil, I couldn't stand it if . . . if . . ."

She broke off, crying too hard to speak.

He moved toward her. "Jen, don't."

The crying stopped abruptly and she began backing away, shaking her head at him. "Stay away from me!"

"Jenny, what's wrong with you?"

She retreated even faster.

"Jenny, stop it."

Suddenly, she whirled, began running down the track. He started to run after her, stopped. What was the use?

Her voice came back to him in a hysterical scream: "Stay away from me! I love you! Stay away!"

He stood in shocked silence until he heard a car door slam out there on the highway. Lights came on; a car raced back toward town.

He remembered the soft moon of her face in the starlight, two black holes for eyes. It had been like a mask. He trudged back to the camper, his mind in turmoil. *"I love you! Stay away!"*

What do I really know about Jenny? he asked himself.

Nothing . . . except that she loved him.

Stay away?

Could that have been Jenny demanding, begging, ordering?

This speared his mind with a touch of madness. It transcended the irrationality of people in love.

"You're dangerous. We all know it."

Indeed, they must.

In the Jaspers oneness he'd experienced at the lake, they must know him for a danger. If he could stay away from the stuff, kick it—would they know him then?

How could they help but know him then? His action would be the ultimate betrayal.

He thought of Santaroga then as a deceptive curtain of calmness over a pool of violence. Olympian-like, they'd surmounted the primitive—yes. But the primitive was still there, more explosive because it could not be recognized and because it had been held down like a coiled spring.

Jenny must sense it, he thought. Her love for him would give her a touch of clarity.

"Stay away from me!"

Her cry still rang in his ears.

And this was how the other investigators had died—releasing the explosion that was Santaroga.

Voices intruded on Dasein's reverie. They came from the other side of the camper away from the road. One voice definitely was that of a woman. He couldn't be sure about the other two. Dasein stepped around the camper, stared off toward the dank pools and sand hills. It was a shadowed starlit landscape with a suggestion of a glow in it.

A flashlight came into view across the hills. It wavered and darted. There were three black, lurching figures associated with the light. Dasein thought of Macbeth's witches. They walked and slid down a hill, skirted a pool and came on toward the campground.

Dasein wondered if he should call out. Perhaps they were lost. Why else would three people be out here in the night?

There was a burst of laughter from the group, vaguely childlike. The woman's voice came clearly out of the dark then: "Oh, Petey! It's so good to have you with us."

Dasein cleared his throat, said: "Hello." Then, louder: "Hello!"

The light stabbed toward him. The lilting woman's voice said: "Someone's in the campground."

There was a masculine grunt.

"Who is it?" she asked.

"Just a camper," Dasein said. "Are you lost?"

"We've just been out frogging." It sounded very like the voice of a young boy.

The trio came on toward him.

"Pretty poor place to camp," the woman said.

Dasein studied the approaching figures. That was a boy on the left—definitely a boy. He appeared to be carrying a bow and a quiver of arrows. The woman had a long gigging pole, a bulky bag of some kind on one shoulder. The man carried the flashlight and a string of bullfrogs. They stopped beside the camper and the woman leaned against it to remove a shoe and pour sand from it.

"Been out to the pond," she said.

"Hunh!" the man grunted.

"We got eight of them," the boy said. "Mom's gonna fry 'em for breakfast."

"Petey had his heart set on it," the woman said. "I couldn't say no, not on his first day home."

"I passed," the boy said. "Pop didn't pass, but I did."

"I see," Dasein said. He studied the man in the light reflected off the aluminum side of the camper. He was a tall man, slim, rather gawky. Wisps of blonde hair protruded from a stocking cap. His eyes were as vacant as two pieces of blue glass.

The woman had put the shoe back on, now had the other one off emptying it. She was wrapped in a heavy coat that gave her the appearance of having been molded in a corrugated barrel. She was short, wouldn't stand any taller than the man's shoulder, but there was a purposeful air about her that reminded Dasein of Clara Scheler at the used-car lot.

"Bill's the first one in his family in eight generations didn't make it," she said, restoring the shoe and straightening. "They think it was something in his mother's diet before he was born. We were engaged before . . . Why'm I telling you all this? I don't think I know you."

"Dasein . . . Gilbert Dasein," he said. And he thought: *So this is how they take care of their own.*

"Jenny's fellow!" the woman said. "Well, now."

Dasein looked at the boy. *Petey.* He appeared to be no more than twelve, almost as tall as the woman. His face when the flashlight beam brushed it was a carbon copy of the man's. No denying parenthood there.

"Turn the light over here, Bill," the woman said. She spoke carefully and distinctly as one might to a very young child. "Over here, hon."

"Over there, Pop." The boy directed the man's uncertain hand.

"That's it, love," the woman said. "I think I got the gigging hook caught in my coat." She fussed with a length of line at her side.

"Hunh," the man said.

Dasein stared at him with a cold feeling of horror. He could see himself there, Jenny "taking care" of him, their children helping.

"There," the woman said, pulling the line free and attaching it to the gigging pole. "Turn the light down toward the ground now, Bill. Toward the ground, hon."

"Down this way, Pop," the boy said, helping.

"That's a love," the woman said. She reached out, patted the man's cheek.

Dasein felt something obscene in the gesture, wanted to turn away, couldn't.

"He's real good, Bill is," the woman said.

The boy began playing with his bow, drawing it, releasing it.

"What you doing out here, Dr. Dasein?" the woman asked.

"I . . . wanted to be . . . alone for awhile." He forced himself to look at her.

"Well, this is a place to be alone all right," she said. "You feel all right? No . . . *flutters* . . . or anything?"

"Quite all right," Dasein said. He shuddered.

The boy had knocked an arrow into the bow, was waving it about.

"I'm Mabel Jorick," the woman said. "This is Bill, my husband; our son, Petey. Petey's been . . . you know, with Doc Piaget. Just got his bill of health."

"I passed," the boy said.

"Indeed you did, love." She looked at Dasein. "He's going outside to college next year."

"Isn't he kind of young?" Dasein asked.

"Fifteen," she said.

"Hunh," the man said.

The boy had drawn the bow to its full arc, Dasein saw. The arrow tip glittered in the light from the flash.

Up, down . . . right, left the arrow pointed.

Dasein moved uneasily as the tip traversed his chest—across, back. Sweat started on his forehead. He felt menace in the boy.

Instinctively, Dasein moved to put the man between himself and Petey, but Jorick moved back, stared off toward the highway.

"I think he hears the car," the woman said. "My brother, Jim, coming to pick us up." She shook her head wonderingly. "He has awful good hearing, Bill has."

Dasein felt a crisis rushing upon him, dropped to his hands and knees. As he fell, he heard the bow twang, felt the wind of an arrow brush the back of his neck, heard it slam into the side of the camper.

"Petey!" the woman shouted. She snatched the bow from him. "What're you doing?"

"It slipped, Ma."

Dasein climbed to his feet studying these people narrowly.

"Hunh," the man said.

The mother turned toward Dasein, the bow in her hand.

"He tried to kill me," Dasein whispered.

"It was just an accident!" the boy protested.

The man lifted the flashlight, a menacing gesture.

Without looking at him, the woman said: "Point it toward the ground, hon." She pushed the light down, stared at Dasein. "You don't think . . . ."

"It was an accident," the boy said.

Dasein looked at the arrow. It had penetrated halfway through the camper's wall on a level with his chest. He tried to swallow in a dry throat. If he hadn't ducked at just that instant . . . An accident. A regrettable accident. The boy was playing with a bow and arrow. It slipped.

Death by misadventure.

What warned me? Dasein wondered.

He knew the answer. It lay there in his mind, clearly readable. He had come to recognize the Santaroga pattern of menace. The means might differ, but the pattern carried a sameness—something lethal in an apparently innocent context.

"It was just an accident," the woman whispered. "Petey wouldn't harm a fly."

She didn't believe it, Dasein saw.

And that was another thing. He was still connected by a tenuous thread to the Jaspers oneness. The warning message along that line was unmistakable. She'd received it, too.

"Wouldn't he?" Dasein asked. He looked once more at the arrow protruding from the camper.

The woman turned, grabbed her son's shoulder in one hand, shook the bow at him. "You want to go back?" she demanded. "Is that it?"

"Hunh," the man said. He shuffled his feet uneasily.

"It was an accident," the boy said. He obviously was near tears.

The woman turned a pleading look on Dasein. "You wouldn't say anything to Doctor Larry, would you?"

"Say anything?" Dasein stared at her stupidly.

"He might . . . you know, misunderstand."

Dasein shook his head. What was she talking about?

"It's so hard," the woman said. "After Bill, I mean. You know how it is over there." She gestured vaguely with her head. "The way they keep such a close watch on you, picking at every little symptom. It's so hard having a son there . . . knowing, seeing him only at visiting hours and . . . and never really being sure until . . ."

"I'm all right, Mom," the boy said.

"Of course you are, love." She kept her eyes on Dasein.

"I wouldn't deliberately hurt anyone," Petey said.

"Of course you wouldn't, love."

Dasein sighed.

"I passed," the boy said. "I'm not like Pop,"

"Hunh," the man said.

Dasein felt like crying.

"You wouldn't say anything, would you?" the woman pleaded.

So Piaget had rewarding work for him here in the valley, Dasein thought. A clinic job . . . working with young people. And it was tied up with Jaspers, of course.

"Are they going to send me back?" Petey asked. There was fear in his voice.

"Dr. Dasein, please . . ." the woman begged.

"It was an accident," Dasein said. He knew it had not been an accident. The woman knew it. The arrow had been meant to kill. He said: "Perhaps you'd better take the bow and arrows away from him for awhile."

"Oh, don't you worry about that," she said. There was a deep sighing of relief in her tone.

A car pulled to a stop on the highway at the entrance to the campground.

"There's Jim now," the woman said. She turned away, her shoulder bag swinging toward Dasein. A rich aroma of Jaspers wafted across Dasein. It came from the bag.

Dasein stopped his right hand as it automatically reached toward the bag.

Mabel Jorick glanced back at him. "I want to thank you for being so understanding," she said. "If there's ever anything . . . " She broke off, noting Dasein's attention on the bag. "Bet you smelled the coffee," she said. "You want it?"

Dasein found himself unable to keep from nodding.

"Well, here." She swung the bag around in front of her. "Thermos is almost full. I just had one cup out at the pond. Spilled most of that. Petey, you run along, help your dad out to the car."

"All right, Mom. Good night, Dr. Dasein."

Dasein was unable to take his gaze from the woman's hands pulling a shiny metal thermos from the bag.

"Take the thermos," she said, holding it toward him. "You can return it when you come back to town. We're only half a block from the clinic on Salmon Way."

Dasein felt his fingers close around the currugated sides of the thermos. He began trembling.

"You sure you're all right?" the woman asked.

"I'm . . . it's the aftereffect . . . shock, I guess," he said.

"Sure. I'm so sorry." She moved behind Dasein to the camper, broke off the protruding arrow. "I'm going to give this to Petey as a reminder of how careful he should be."

Dasein tore his attention away from the thermos, looked along the sand track. Petey and his father were almost halfway to the highway. The car's lights carved out a funnel of brilliance there. A horn honked once.

"If you're sure you're all right," the woman said. "I better be going." She looked at the camper, glanced once more at Dasein. "If there's ever anything we can do . . . "

"I'll . . . bring your thermos back as soon as I can," Dasein said.

"Oh, no hurry; no hurry at all." She pulled her coat tightly around her, trudged off toward the highway. About twenty paces away, she paused, turned. "That was real sweet of you, Dr. Dasein. I won't forget it."

Dasein watched until the car turned back toward town. Before the car was out of sight, he was in the camper, the lid off the thermos, pouring himself a steaming cup of the coffee.

His hands trembled as he lifted the cup.

All the time and matter had been reduced to this moment, this cup, this Jaspers rich steam enveloping him. He drained the cup.

It was a sensation of rays spreading out from a pinhead spot in his stomach. Dasein groped his way to his bunk, wrapped the sleeping bag around him. He felt supremely detached, a transitory being. His awareness moved within a framework of glowing nets.

There was terror here. He tried to recoil, but the nets held him. *Where is the self that once I was?* he thought. He tried to hold onto a *self* that bore some familiarity, one he could identify. The very idea of a self eluded him. It became an ear-shaped symbol he interpreted as mind-in-action.

For a flickering instant he felt he had encountered the solid ground, a core of relative truth from which he could make his decisions and justify all his experiences. His eyes flew open. In the faint starlight reflected into the camper he saw something glittering on the wall, recognized the head of Petey's arrow.

There it was—the relative truth: an arrowhead. It had originated; it had ceased. *Everything with origin has cessation*, he told himself.

He sensed the stirring in his consciousness then, the ancient *thing* abiding there, the mind eater. *Sleep*, Dasein told himself. There was an *atman* of sleep within him. It resisted awakening. It was infinite, circular. He lay spread on its rim.

Dasein slept.

10

DAWN LIGHT awakened him.

The coffee in the thermos was cold and had lost its Jaspers savor. He sipped it anyway to ease the dryness in his throat.

There will be a place like a school, he thought. *A boarding school . . . with visiting hours. It will have the Santaroga difference. It will be something besides a school.*

He stared at the thermos. It was empty. The bitter taste of its contents remained on his tongue, a reminder of his weakness in the night. The Jaspers had immersed him in nightmares. He remembered dreaming of glass houses, a shattering of glass that tumbled about him . . . screaming.

House of glass, he thought. *Greenhouses*.

The sound of an approaching car intruded. Dasein stepped outside into chilly morning air. A green Chevrolet was bumping up the track toward him. It looked familiar. He decided the car either was Jersey Hofstedder's machine or its double.

Then he saw the beefy, gray-haired woman driving the car and he knew. It was Sam Scheler's mother—Clara, the car dealer.

She pulled to a stop beside Dasein, slid across the seat and got out his side.

"They told me you were here and by golly you are," she said. She stood facing Dasein, a covered dish in her hands.

Dasein looked at the car. "Did you drive clear out here to try to sell me that car again?" he asked.

"The car?" She looked around at the car as though it had appeared there by some form of magic. "Oh, Jersey's car. Plenty of time for that . . . later. I brought you some hair of the dog." She presented the dish.

Dasein hesitated. Why should she bring him anything?

"Petey's my grandson," she said. "Mabel, my daughter, told me how nice you were last night." She glanced at the stub of the arrow in the side of Dasein's camper, returned her attention to Dasein. "Occurred to me maybe your problem's you don't realize how much we want you to be one of us. So I brought you some of my sour cream stew—plenty of Jaspers."

She thrust the dish at him.

Dasein took it. Smooth, warm china under his hands. He fought down an unreasonable impulse to drop the dish and smash it. He was afraid suddenly. Perspiraton made his palms slippery against the dish.

"Go on, eat it," she said. "It'll set you up for the day."

I must not do it, Dasein told himself.

But that was irrational. The woman was just being kind, thoughtful . . . Petey's grandmother. Thought of the boy brought the incident of the night flooding back into his mind.

School . . . observation . . . Jaspers . . .

A whuffling noise from the green Chevrolet distracted him. A gray-muzzled old black-and-white border collie eased itself over onto the front seat, climbed down to the sand. It moved with the patient pain of old age, sniffed at Clara's heels.

She reached down, patted the dog's head. "I brought Jimbo," she said. "He doesn't get out in the country much anymore. Dang nigh thirty-five years old and I think he's going blind." She straightened, nodded to the dish in Dasein's hands. "Go ahead, eat it."

But Dasein was fascinated by the dog. Thirty-five? That was equivalent to more than two hundred years in a human. He put the dish on the camper's steps, bent to stare at the dog. *Jimbo*. Going blind, she said, but its eyes carried that same disturbing *Jaspers* directness he saw in all the humans.

"You like dogs?" Clara Scheler asked.

Dasein nodded. "Is he really thirty-five?"

"Thirty-six in the spring . . . if he lasts."

Jimbo ambled across to Dasein, aimed the gray muzzle at his face, sniffed. Apparently satisfied, he curled up at the foot of the camper's steps, sighed, stared off across the sand hills.

"You going to eat or aren't you?" Clara asked.

"Later," Dasein said. He was remembering how Jersey Hofstedder's car had figured in his thoughts—a key to Santaroga. Was it the car? he wondered. Or was the car just a symbol? Which was the important thing—the car or the symbol?

Seeing his attention on the car, Clara said: "It's still priced at $650 if you want it."

"I'd like to drive it," Dasein said.

"Right now?"

"Why not?"

She glanced at the dish on the camper's step, said: "That stew won't heat very well . . . and the Jaspers fades, you know."

"I had your daughter's coffee last night," Dasein said.

"No . . . aftereffects?"

It was a practical question. Dasein found himself probing his own bodily sensations—head injury fading, shoulder pain almost gone—a bit of latent anger over Petey's arrow, but nothing time wouldn't heal.

"I'm fine."

"Well! You're coming around," she said. "Jenny said you would. Okay." She gestured toward the green Chevrolet. "Let's take a spin up the highway and back. You drive." She climbed into the right-hand seat, closed the door.

The dog raised his head from his paws.

"You stay there, Jimbo," she said. "We'll be right back."

Dasein went around, climbed behind the wheel. The seat seemed to mould itself to his back.

"Comfortable, huh?" Clara asked.

Dasein nodded. He had an odd feeling of *déjà vu*, that he'd driven this car before. It felt right beneath his hands. The engine purred alive, settled into an almost noiseless motion. He backed the car around, eased it over the ruts and out the track to the highway, turned right away from town.

A touch on the throttle and the old Chevrolet leaped ahead—fifty . . . sixty . . . seventy. He eased back to sixty-five. It cornered like a sports car.

"Got torsion bars," Clara said. "Doesn't roll worth a sweet damn. Isn't she pretty?"

Dasein touched the brakes—no fading and the nose strayed not an inch. It was as though the car rode on tracks.

"This car's in better shape right now than the day it came off the assembly line," Clara said.

Dasein silently agreed with her. It was a pleasure to drive. He liked the leather smell of the interior. The hand-finished wood of the dash glistened with a dull luster. There was no distraction from it, just a tight cluster of instruments set up high to be read easily without taking his eyes too long from the road.

"Notice how he padded the dash on this side," Clara said. "Inch-and-a-half thick and a thin roll of metal underneath. He cut the steering wheel about a third of the way back, offset it on a U-joint. Hit anything with this car and you won't have that wheel sticking out your back. Jersey was making safe cars before Detroit even heard the word."

Dasein found a wide spot at a turn, pulled off, turned around and headed back to the campground. He knew he had to have this car. It was everything this woman said.

"Tell you what," Clara said. "I'll deliver the car over to the Doc's when I get back. We'll figure out the details later. You won't find me hard to deal with, though I can't give you much for that clunker of a truck."

"I . . . don't know how I can pay for it," Dasein said. "But . . . "

"Say no more. We'll figure out something."

The track into the campground came into view. Dasein slowed, turned off onto the ruts, shifted down to second.

"You really ought to use the seatbelt," Clara said. "I noticed you . . . " She broke off as Dasein stopped behind the camper. "Something's wrong with Jimbo!" she said, and she was out of the car and across to the dog.

Dasein turned off the ignition, jumped out and ran around to her side.

The dog lay almost over on its back, feet stretched out stiff, neck curved backward, its mouth open and tongue extended.

"He's dead," Clara said. "Jimbo's dead."

Dasein's attention went to the dish on the steps. Its cover had been pushed aside and the contents disturbed. There was a splash of gravy beside the lid. Again, he looked at the dog. The sand was scratched in a wide swirl around Jimbo.

Abruptly, Dasein bent to the dish of stew, sniffed it. Beneath the heavy odor of Jaspers there was a bitter aroma that curled his nostrils.

"Cyanide?" he asked. He stared accusingly at Clara Scheler.

She looked at the dish. "Cyanide?"

"You were trying to kill me!"

She picked up the dish, smelled it. Her face went pale. She turned, stared wide-eyed at Dasein.

"Oh, my God! The paint bleach," she said. She dropped the dish, whirled away, dashed to the car before Dasein could stop her. The Chevrolet leaped to life, turned in a whirl of sand and roared out the track to the highway. It made a skidding turn onto the highway, raced back toward town.

Dasein stared after her.

She tried to kill me, he thought. *Cyanide. Paint bleach.*

But he couldn't shake the memory of her pale, wide-eyed stare. She'd been surprised, as shocked as he was. *Paint bleach*. He stared down at the dead dog. Would she have left the dish there near her dog if she'd known it contained poison? Not likely. Then why had she run?

Paint bleach.

There was contaminated food at her house, Dasein realized. She was racing back to get it before it killed anyone.

I would've eaten the stew, Dasein thought.

An accident . . . another bloody accident.

He kicked the fallen dish aside, dragged the dog out of the way, got behind the wheel of his camper. The Ford's engine was a dismal, throbbing mess after Jersey's car. He maneuvered it gently out to the highway, turned toward town.

Accident, he thought.

A pattern was emerging, but he found it difficult to accept. There was a Holmesian flavor to his thought—" . . . *when you have eliminated the impossible, whatever remains, however improbable, must be the truth*."

Jenny had screamed: "Stay away from me. I love you."

That was consistent. She did love him. Therefore, he had to stay away from her.

For the time being.

The road forked and he turned right, following the direction by a sign labeled: "Greenhouses."

There was a bridge over the river—an old-fashioned bridge that crowned in the middle . . . heavy planks rattling under the wheels. The river foamed and bunched itself over the shell-backs of smooth stones under the bridge.

Dasein slowed the truck at the far side, taken suddenly by a warning sense of caution which he had learned to trust.

The road followed the river's right bank. He paced the current, glanced upstream toward the bridge, found it hidden by a stand of willows.

It came over Dasein that there was something sliding and treacherous about the river. He thought of a liquid snake, venomous, full of evil energy. It contained a concentration of malevolence as it slipped down the rapids beside the road. And the sound—it laughed at him.

Dasein drew a sigh of relief when the road turned away from the river, wound over two low hills and down into a shallow valley. He glimpsed the glass through trees. It was an expanse of glistening green and covered a much larger area than he'd expected.

The road ended at a paved parking lot in front of a long stone building. More stone buildings—tile roofs, curtained windows—stepped in ranks up the hill beside the greenhouses.

A great many cars waited in the parking lot, a fact Dasein found curious—at least a hundred cars.

And there were people—men walking between the greenhouses, white-coated figures behind the glass, briskly striding women coming and going.

Dasein drove down the line of cars looking for a place to park. He found a slot beyond the end of the long stone building, pulled in to a stop and stared around.

Chanting.

Dasein turned toward the sound; it came from the ranks of buildings beyond the greenhouses. A troop of children came marching into view down a path between the buildings. They carried baskets. Three adults accompanied them. They counted a marching cadence. The troop wound out of sight down into the greenhouse level.

A tight feeling gripped Dasein's chest.

Footsteps sounded on his left. Dasein turned to find Piaget striding down the line of cars toward him. The doctor's bulky figure was accented by a long white smock. He was hatless, his hair wind mussed.

Piaget turned into the slot beside Dasein, stopped to stand looking in the truck's open window.

"Well," he said. "Jenny said there'd be an arriving."

Dasein shook his head. There was almost meaning in Piaget's words, but the sense eluded him. He wet his lips with his tongue. "What?"

Piaget scowled. "Jenny knows rapport. She said you'd probably show up here." His voice sounded suddenly full of effort.

An arriving, Dasein thought.

It was a label for an event, a statement withholding judgment. He studied Piaget's wide, bland face.

"I saw children," Dasein said.

"What did you expect?"

Dasein shrugged. "Are you going to run me off?"

"Al Marden says the ones that run get the fever," Piaget said. "The ones that watch get the benefit."

"Count me among the watchers," Dasein said.

Piaget grinned, opened the truck door. "Come."

Dasein remembered the river, hesitated. He thought of the torn carpet in the Inn's hallway, the open gas jet, the lake, the arrow . . . the paint bleach. He thought of Jenny running away from him—*"Stay away from me! I love you."*

"Come along," Piaget said.

Still hesitating, Dasein said: "Why're the children kept here?"

"We must push back at the surface of childhood," Piaget said. "It's a brutal, animate thing. But there's food growing." He gestured at the expanse of greenhouses. "There's educating. There's useful energy. Waste not; want not."

Again, Dasein shook his head. *Almost-meaning.*

Push back at the surface of childhood?

It was like schizophrenic talk and he recalled the incident in the Blue Ewe, the haunting conversation of the young couple.

How could one hear a sunset?

"You . . . you're not speaking English," Dasein complained.

"I'm speaking," Piaget said.

"But . . ."

"Jenny says you'll be an understander." Piaget scratched his cheek, a pensive look on his face. "You have the training, Dasein." Again, his voice took on that leaden effort. "Where's your *Weltanschauung?* You do have a world view? The whole is greater than the sum of its parts. What is it?"

Piaget's arm swept out to include the greenhouse complex and the entire valley, the world and the universe beyond.

Dasein's mouth felt dry. The man was insane.

"You contain the Jaspers experience," Piaget said. "Digest it. Jenny says you can do it. Reality shoots through her words."

The tight sensation was a pain in Dasein's chest. Thoughts tumbled through his mind without order or sense.

In a heavy voice, Piaget said: "For approximately one in five hundred, the Jaspers cannot . . . " He spread his arms, palms up. "You are not one of those few. I stake a reputation on it. You will be an opening person."

Dasein looked at the stone building, the hurrying people. All that action and purpose. He sensed it all might be like the dance of bees—motions designed to show him a direction. The direction escaped him.

"I will try to put it in the words of *outside*," Piaget said. "Perhaps then . . . " He shrugged, leaned against the side of the door to bring his broad face close to Dasein. "We sift reality through screens composed of ideas. These idea systems are limited by language. That is to say: language cuts the grooves in which our thoughts must move. If we seek new validity forms, we must step outside the language."

"What's that have to do with the children?" Dasein nodded toward the greenhouses.

"Dasein! We have a common instinctive experience, you and I. What happens in the unformed psyche? As individuals, as cultures and societies, we humans reenact every aspect of the instinctive life that has accompanied our species for uncounted generations. With the Jaspers, we take off the binding element. Couple that with the brutality of childhood? No! We would have violence, chaos. We would have no society. It's simple, isn't it? We must superimpose a limiting order on the innate patterns of our nervous systems. We must have common interests."

Dasein found himself grappling with these ideas, trying to see through them to some sense in Piaget's earlier words. *Push back at the surface of childhood? World view?*

"We must meet the survival needs of individuals," Piaget said. "We know the civilization-culture-society outside is dying. They *do* die, you know. When this is about to happen, pieces break off from the parent body. Pieces cut themselves free, Dasein. Our scalpel—that was Jaspers. Think, man! You've lived out there. It's a Virgilian autumn . . . the dusk of civilization."

Piaget stepped back, studied Dasein.

For his part, Dasein found himself suddenly fascinated by the doctor. There was a timeless essence in the man, powerful, intrusive on everything about him. Framed in the white smock's collar was an Egyptian head, strong cheeks and jaws, a nose out of Moses' time, white even teeth behind thin lips.

Piaget smiled, a deaf smile of ultimate stubbornness, let a honeyed look flow across the landscape around them, the greenhouses, the people.

Dasein knew then why he'd been sent here. No mere market report had prompted this. Marden had nailed it. He was here to break this up, smash it.

The Santarogans were working their children here, training them. Child labor. Piaget seemed not to care how much he revealed.

"Come along," Piaget said. "I'll show you our school."

Dasein shook his head. What would it be in there? An accidental push against broken glass? A child with a knife?

"I'm . . . I have to think," Dasein said.

"Are you sure?" Piaget's words dropped on the air like a challenge.

Dasein thought of a fortress abbey in the Dark Ages, warrior monks. All this was contained in Piaget and his valley, in the confidence with which Santarogans defied the *outside*. Were they really confident? he wondered. Or were they actors hypnotized by their own performance?

"You've been a swimmer on the surface," Piaget said. "You haven't even seen the struggle. You haven't yet developed the innocent eye that sees the universe uncluttered by past assumptions. You were programmed and sent here to break us up."

Dasein paled.

"To be programmed is to be prejudiced," Piaget said. "Because prejudice is selecting and rejecting and that is programming." He sighed. "Such pains we take with you because of our Jenny."

"I came here with an open mind," Dasein said.

"Not prejudiced?" Piaget raised his eyebrows.

"So you're contending with . . . groups outside over what's the right way . . . "

"Contending is too soft a word, Dasein. There's a power struggle going on over control of the human consciousness. We are a cell of health surrounded by plague. It's not men's minds that are at stake, but their consciousness, their awareness. This isn't a struggle over a market area. Make no mistake about it. This is a struggle over what's to be judged valuable in our universe. Outside, they value whatever can be measured, counted or tabulated. Here, we go by different standards."

Dasein sensed threat in Piaget's voice. There was no longer a veneer of pretense here. The doctor was setting up the sides in a war and Dasein felt caught in the middle. He was, he knew, on more dangerous ground than he'd ever been before. Piaget and his friends controlled the valley. An ex-post-facto accident would be child's play for them.

"The ones who hired me," Dasein said, "they're men who believe . . . "

"Men!" Piaget sneered. "Out there . . . " He pointed beyond the hills which enclosed the valley. " . . . they're destroying their environment. In the process, they're becoming not-men! We are men." He touched his chest. "They are not. Nature is a unified field. A radical change in environment means the inhabitants must change to survive. The not-men out there are changing to survive."

Dasein gaped at Piaget. That was it, of course. The Santarogans were conservatives . . . unchanging. He'd seen this for himself. But there was a fanatic intensity to Piaget, a religious fervor, that repelled Dasein. So it was a struggle over men's minds . . .

"You are saying to yourself," Piaget said, "that these fool Santarogans have a pscheletic substance which makes them inhuman."

It was so close to his thoughts that Dasein grew still with fear. Could they read minds? Was that a by-product of the Jaspers substance?

"You're equating us with the unwashed, sandaled users of LSD," Piaget said. "Kooks, you would say. But you are like them—unaware. We are aware. We have truly released the mind. We have a power medicine—just as whiskey and gin and aspirin and tobacco . . . and yes, LSD, just as these are power medicines. But you must see the difference. Whiskey and the other depressants, these keep their subjects docile. Our medicine releases the animal that has never been tamed . . . up to now."

Dasein looked at the greenhouses.

"Yes," Piaget said. "Look here. That is where we domesticate the human animal."

With a shock of awareness, Dasein realized he had heard too much ever to be allowed out of the valley. They had passed a point of no return with him. In his present state of mind, there was only one answer for the Santarogans: they had to kill him. The only question remaining was: Did they know it? Was any of this conscious? Or did it truly operate at the level of instinct?

If he precipitated a crisis, Dasein knew he'd find out. Was there a way to avoid it? he wondered. As he hesitated, Piaget moved around the truck, climbed in beside him.

"You won't come with me," he said. "I'll go with you."

"You'll go with me?"

"To my house; to the clinic." He turned, studied Dasein. "I love my niece, you understand? I'll not have her hurt if I can prevent it."

"If I refuse?"

"Ahh, Gilbert, you would make the angels weep. We don't want weeping, do we? We don't want Jenny's tears. Aren't you concerned about her?"

"I've some anxiety about . . . "

"When anxiety enters, inquiry stops. You have a hard head, Gilbert. A hard head makes a sore back. Let us go to the clinic."

"What kind of death trap have you set up there?"

Piaget glared at him in outrage. "Death trap?"

Holding as reasonable a tone as he could manage, Dasein said: "You're trying to kill me. Don't deny it. I've . . . "

"I'm disgusted with you, Gilbert. When have we tried to kill you?"

Dasein took a deep breath, held up his right hand, enumerated the *accidents*, dropping a finger for each one until his hand was clenched into a fist. He had left out only the incident with Petey Jorick . . . and that because of a promise.

"Accidents!" Piaget said.

"As we both know," Dasein said, "there are very few real accidents in this world. Most of what we call accidents are unconscious violence. You say you've opened your mind. Use it."

"Pah! Your thoughts are like muddy water!"

"Let the muddy water stand and it becomes clear," Dasein said.

"You can't be serious." He glared at Dasein. "But I see that you are." He closed his eyes momentarily, opened them. "Well, would you believe Jenny?"

Stay away from me! I love you! Dasein thought.

"Let's go to your clinic," Dasein said. He started the truck, backed out of the parking lot and headed toward town.

"Trying to kill you," Piaget muttered. He stared out at the landscape rushing past them.

Dasein drove in silence . . . thinking, thinking, thinking. The instant he headed toward Jenny, the old fantasies gripped him. Jenny and her valley! The place had enveloped him in its aura—crazy, crazy, crazy! But the pattern was emerging. It was going together with its own Santaroga kind of logic.

"So not everyone can take your . . . power medicine?" Dasein asked. "What happens to the ones who fail?"

"We take care of our own," Piaget growled. "That's why I keep hoping you'll stay."

"Jenny's a trained psychologist. Why don't you use her?"

"She does her tour of duty."

"I'm going to ask Jenny to leave with me," Dasein said. "You know that, don't you?"

Piaget sniffed.

"She can break away from your . . . Jaspers," Dasein said. "Men go into the service from here. They must . . . "

"They always come home when it's over," Piaget said. "That's in your notes. Don't you realize how unhappy they are out there?" He turned toward Dasein. "Is that the choice you'd offer Jenny?"

"They can't be all that unhappy about leaving," Dasein said. "Otherwise you clever people would've found another solution."

"Hmmph!" Piaget snorted. "You didn't even do your homework for the people who hired you." He sighed. "I'll tell you, Gilbert. The draft rejects most of our young men—severe allergy reaction to a diet which doesn't include periodic administration of Jaspers. They can only get that here. The approximately six percent of our young people who go out do so as a duty to the valley. We don't want to call down the federal wrath on us. We have a political accommodation with the state, but we're not large enough to apply the same technique nationally."

They've already decided about me, Dasein thought. *They don't care what they tell me.*

The realization brought a tight sensation of fear in the pit of his stomach.

He rounded a corner and came parallel with the river. Ahead stood the clump of willows and the long, downsweeping curve to the bridge. Dasein recalled his projection of evil onto the river, stepped on the throttle to get this place behind him. The truck entered the curve. The road was banked nicely. The bridge came into view. There was a yellow truck parked off the road at the far side, men standing behind it drinking out of metal cups.

"Look out!" Piaget shouted.

In that instant, Dasein saw the reason for the truck—a gaping hole in the center of the bridge where the planks had been removed. That was a county work crew and they'd opened at least a ten foot hole in the bridge.

The truck sped some forty feet during the moment it took Dasein to realize his peril.

Now, he could see a two-by-four stretched across each end of the bridge, yellow warning flags tied at their centers.

Dasein gripped the steering wheel. His mind shifted into a speed of computation he had never before experienced. The effect was to slow the external passage of time. The truck seemed to come almost to a stop while he reviewed the possibilities—

Hit the brakes?

No. Brakes and tires were old. At this speed, the truck would skid onto the bridge and into the hole.

Swerve off the road?

No. The river waited on both sides—a deep cut in the earth to swallow them.

Aim for a bridge abutment to stop the truck?

Not at this speed and without seat belts.

Hit the throttle to increase speed?

That was a possibility. There was the temporary barrier to break through, but that was only a two-by-four. The bridge rose in a slight arc up and over the river. The hole had been opened in the center. Given enough speed, the truck could leap the hole.

Dasein jammed the throttle to the floorboards. The old truck leaped ahead. There came a sharp cracking sound as they smashed through the barrier. Planks clattered beneath the wheels. There came a breathless instant of flying, a spring-crushing lurch as they landed across the hole, the "crack" of the far barrier.

He hit the brakes, came to a screeching stop opposite the workmen. Time resumed its normal pace as Dasein stared out at the crew—five men, faces pale, mouths agape.

"For the love of heaven!" Piaget gasped. "Do you always take chances like that?"

"Was there any other way to get us out of that mess?" Dasein asked. He lifted his right hand, stared at it. The hand was trembling.

Piaget reflected a moment, then: "You took what was probably the only way out . . . but if you hadn't been driving so damn' fast on a blind . . . ''

"I will make you a bet," Dasein said. "I'll bet the work on that bridge wasn't necessary, that it was either a mistake or some sort of make-work."

Dasein reached for his door handle, had to grope twice to get it in his hand, then found it took a conscious surge of effort to open the door. He stepped out, found his knees rubbery. He stood a moment, took several deep breaths, then moved around to the front of the truck.

Both headlights were smashed and there was a deep dent stretching across both fenders and the grill.

Dasein turned his attention to the workmen. One, a stocky, dark-haired man in a plaid shirt and dungarees stood a step ahead of the others. Dasein focused on the man, said: "Why wasn't there a warning sign back there around the corner?"

"Good God, man!" the fellow said. His face reddened. "Nobody comes down that road this time of day."

Dasein walked down the road toward a pile of planks, dirt and oil on them testifying that they'd been taken from the bridge. They looked to be three-by-twelve redwood. He lifted the end of one, turned it over—no cracks or checks. It gave off the sharp sound of an unbroken board when he dropped it back to the pile.

He turned to see the workman he'd addressed approaching. Piaget was several paces behind the man.

"When did you get the order to do this work?" Dasein asked.

"Huh?" The man stopped, stared at Dasein with a puzzled frown.

"When did you get orders to repair this bridge?" Dasein asked.

"Well . . . we decided to come up here about an hour ago. What the hell difference does it make? You've smashed the . . . ''

"You decided?" Dasein asked. "Aren't you assigned to jobs?"

"I'm the road crew foreman in this valley, mister. I decide, not that it's any of your business."

Piaget came to a stop beside the man, said: "Dr. Dasein, this is Josh Marden, Captain Marden's nephew."

"Nepotism begins at home, I see," Dasein said, his tone elaborately polite. "Well, Mr. Marden, or may I call you Josh?"

"Now, you look here, Dr. Das . . . ''

"Josh, then," Dasein said, still in that tone of calm politeness. "I'm very curious, Josh. These appear to be perfectly sound planks. Why'd you decide to replace them?"

"What the hell diff . . . ''

"Tell him, Josh," Piaget said. "I confess to a certain curiosity of my own."

Marden looked at Piaget, back to Dasein. "Well . . . we inspected the bridge . . . We make regular inspections. We just decided to do a little preventive maintenance, put in new planks here and use the old ones on a bridge that doesn't get as much traffic. There's nothing unusual about . . . ''

"Is there any *urgent* road work in this valley?" Dasein asked. "Is there some job you put off to come to this . . . ''

"Now, look here, Mister!" Marden took a step toward Dasein. "You've no call to . . . ''

"What about the Old Mill Road?" Piaget asked. "Are those pot holes still on the curve by the ditch?"

"Now, look, Doc," Marden said, whirling toward Piaget. "Not you, too. We decided . . ."

"Easy does it, Josh," Piaget said. "I'm just curious. What about the Old Mill Road?"

"Aw, Doc. It was such a nice day and the . . ."

"So that work still has to be done," Piaget said.

"I win the bet," Dasein said. He headed back toward his truck.

Piaget fell into step beside him.

"Hey!" Marden shouted. "You've broken county property and those boards you landed on are probably . . ."

Dasein cut him off without turning. "You'd better get that bridge repaired before somebody else has trouble here."

He slid behind the wheel of his truck, slammed the door. Reaction was setting in now: his whole body felt tense with anger.

Piaget climbed in beside him. The truck rattled as he closed his door. "Will it still run?" he asked.

"Accident!" Dasein said.

Piaget remained silent.

Dasein put the truck in gear, eased it up to a steady thirty-five miles an hour. The rear-view mirror showed him the crew already at work on the bridge, one of their number with a warning flag trudging back around the blind corner.

"Now, they send out a flagman," Dasein said.

A corner cut off the view in the mirror. Dasein concentrated on driving. The truck had developed new rattles and a front-end shimmy.

"They *have* to be accidents," Piaget said. "There's no other explanation."

A stop sign came into view ahead. Dasein stopped for the main highway. It was empty of traffic. He turned right toward town. Piaget's protestations deserved no answer, he thought, and he gave no answer.

They entered the outskirts of town. There was Scheler's station on the left. Dasein pulled in behind the station, drove back to the large shed-roofed metal building labeled "Garage."

"What're you doing here?" Piaget asked. "This machine isn't worth . . ."

"I want it repaired sufficiently to get me out of Santaroga," Dasein said.

The garage doors were open. Dasein nosed the truck inside, stopped, climbed out. There was a steady sound of work all around—clanging of metal, machinery humming. Lines of cars had been angled toward benches down both sides of the garage. Lights glared down on the benches.

A stocky, dark-skinned man in stained white coveralls came from the back of the garage, stopped in front of the truck.

"What the devil did you hit?" he asked.

Dasein recognized one of the quartet from the card game at the Inn—Scheler himself.

"Doctor Piaget here will tell you all about it," Dasein said. "I want some headlights put on this thing and you might have a look at the steering."

"Why don't you junk it?" Scheler asked.

The truck door slammed and Piaget came up on the right. "Can you fix it, Sam?" he asked.

"Sure, but it isn't worth it."

"Do it anyway and put it on my bill. I don't want our friend here to think we're trying to trap him in the valley."

"If you say so, Doc."

Scheler turned around, shouted: "Bill! Take that Lincoln off the rack and put this truck on. I'll write up a ticket."

A young man in greasy blue coveralls came around from the left bench where he had been hidden by a Lincoln Continental lifted halfway up on a hoist. The young man had Scheler's build and dark skin, the same set of face and eyes: bright blue and alert.

"My son, Bill," Scheler said. "He'll take care of it for you."

Dasein felt a twinge of warning fear, backed against the side of his truck. The garage around him had taken on the same feeling of concentrated malevolence he had sensed in the river.

Scheler started through the space between the Lincoln and an old Studebaker truck, called over his shoulder: "If you'll sign the ticket over here, Dr. Dasein, we'll get right at it."

Dasein took two steps after him, hesitated. He felt the garage closing in around him.

"We can walk to the clinic from here," Piaget said. "Sam will call when your rig's ready."

Dasein took another step, stopped, glanced back. Young Bill Scheler was right behind him. The sense of menace was a pounding drumbeat in Dasein's head. He saw Bill reach out a friendly hand to guide him between the cars. There was no doubt of the innocent intention of that hand, the smiling face behind it, but Dasein saw the hand as the embodiment of danger. With an inarticulate cry, Dasein sprang aside.

The young mechanic, caught off balance with nothing ahead of his thrusting arm, lurched forward, stumbled, fell. As he fell, the hoist with the Lincoln on it came crashing down. It rocked twice, subsided. Bill Scheler lay halfway under it. One of his legs twitched, was still.

A pool of red began to flow beneath the car.

Piaget dashed past him shouting for Scheler to raise the hoist.

A compressor began thumping somewhere in the background. The Lincoln jerked, began to rise. It exposed a body, its head smashed beyond recognition by one of the hoist's arms.

Dasein whirled away, ran out of the garage and was sick. *That could've been me*, he thought. *That was meant for me*. He grew aware of a great bustle of activity, the sound of a siren in the distance.

Two mechanics emerged from the garage with a pale-faced, staggering Sam Scheler between them.

It was his son, Dasein thought. He felt that this was of the deepest significance, but his shocked mind gave no explanation for that feeling.

He heard one of the mechanics with Scheler say: "It was an accident, Sam. Nothing you could do."

They went into the station with him.

A siren began giving voice in the distance. Its wailing grew louder. Dasein backed off to the edge of the station's parking area, stood against a low fence.

His truck, nosed into the garage, lurched into motion, was swallowed by the building.

The ambulance droned its way into the parking area, turned, backed into the garage. Presently, it emerged, drove away with its siren silent.

Piaget came out of the garage.

He was an oddly subdued man, indecisive in his walk—short strides, soft of step. He saw Dasein, approached with an air of diffidence. There was a smear of blood down the right side of his white smock, black grease at the hem, grease on the left arm.

Blood and grease—they struck Dasein as an odd combination but things out of which an entire scene could be reconstructed. He shuddered.

"I . . . I need a cup of coffee," Piaget said. He closed his eyes briefly, opened them to stare pleadingly at Dasein. "There's a café around the corner. Would you . . ." He broke off to take a deep, trembling breath. "I brought that boy into the world." He shook his head. "Just when you think you're the complete doctor, immune to all personal involvement . . ."

Dasein experienced a surge of compassion for Piaget, stepped away from the fence to take the doctor's arm. "Where's this café? I could use something myself."

The café was a narrow brick building squeezed between a hardware store and a dark little shop labeled "Bootery." The screen door banged behind them. The place smelled of steam and the omnipresent Jaspers. One of Scheler's station attendants—dark green jacket and white hat—sat at a counter on the left staring into a cup of coffee. A man in a leather apron, horn-callused hands, gray hair, was eating a sandwich at the far end of the counter.

Dasein steered Piaget into a booth opposite the counter, sat down across from him.

The station attendant at the counter, turned, glanced at them. Dasein found himself confronted by a face he knew to be another Scheler—the same set to the blue eyes, the same blocky figure and dark skin. The man looked at Piaget, said: "Hi, Doc. There was a siren."

Piaget lifted his gaze from the tabletop, looked at the speaker. The glaze left Piaget's eyes. He took two shallow breaths, looked away, back to the man at the counter.

"Harry," Piaget said, and his voice was a hoarse croak. "I . . . couldn't . . ." He broke off.

The man slid off the counter stool. His face was a pale, frozen mask. "I've been sitting here . . . feeling . . ." He brushed a hand across his mouth. "It was . . . Bill!" He whirled, dashed out of the café. The door slammed behind him.

"That's Scheler's other son," Piaget said.

"He knew," Dasein said, and he recalled the experience at the lake, the feeling of rapport.

Life exists immersed in a sea of unconsciousness, he reminded himself. *In the drug, these people gain a view of that sea.*

Piaget studied Dasein a moment, then: "Of course he knew. Haven't you ever had a tooth pulled? Couldn't you feel the hole where it had been?"

A slender red-haired woman in a white apron, lines of worry on her face, came up to the booth, stood looking down at Piaget. "I'll bring your coffee," she said. She started to turn away, hesitated. "I . . . felt it . . . and Jim next door came to the back to tell me. I didn't know how to tell Harry. He just kept sitting there . . . getting lower and lower . . . knowing really but refusing to face it. I . . ." She shrugged. "Anything besides coffee?"

Piaget shook his head. Dasein realized with a sense of shock the man was near tears.

The waitress left, returned with two mugs of coffee, went back to the kitchen—all without speaking. She, too, had sensed Piaget's emotions.

Dasein sighed, lifted his coffee, started to put the mug to his lips, hesitated. There was an odd bitter odor beneath the omnipresent Jaspers tang in the coffee. Dasein put his nose to the mug, sniffed. Bitter. A plume of steam rising from the dark liquid assumed for Dasein the shape of a hooded cobra lifting its fanged head to strike him.

Shakily, he returned the mug to the table, looked up to meet Piaget's questioning gaze.

"There's poison in that coffee," Dasein rasped.

Piaget looked at his own coffee.

Dasein took the mug from him, sniffed at it. The bitter odor was missing. He touched his tongue to it—heat, the soothing flow of Jaspers . . . coffee . . .

"Is something wrong?"

Dasein looked up to find the waitress standing over him. "There's poison in my coffee," he said.

"Nonsense." She took the mug from Dasein's hand, started to drink.

Piaget stopped her with a hand on her arm. "No, Vina—this one." He handed her the other mug.

She stared at it, smelled it, put it down, dashed for the kitchen. Presently, she returned carrying a small yellow box. Her face was porcelain white, freckles standing out across her cheeks and nose like the marks of some disease.

"Roach powder," she whispered. "I . . . the box was spilled on the shelf over the counter. I . . . " She shook her head.

Dasein looked at Piaget, but the doctor refused to meet his gaze.

"Another accident," Dasein said, holding his voice even. "Eh, doctor?"

Piaget wet his lips with his tongue.

Dasein slid out of the booth, pushing the waitress aside. He took the mug of poisoned coffee, poured it deliberately on the floor. "Accidents will happen, won't they . . . Vina?"

"Please," she said. "I . . . didn't . . . "

"Of course you didn't," Dasein said.

"You don't understand," Piaget said.

"But I *do* understand," Dasein said. "What'll it be next time? A gun accident? How about something heavy dropped from a roof? Accidentally, of course." He turned, strode out of the cafe, stood on the sidewalk to study his surroundings.

It was such a *normal* town. The trees on the parking strip were so normal. The young couple walking down the sidewalk across from him—they were so normal. The sounds—a truck out on the avenue to his right, the cars there, a pair of jays arguing in the treetops, two women talking on the steps of a house down the street to his left—such an air of normalcy about it all.

The screen door slapped behind him. Piaget came up to stand at Dasein's side. "I know what you're thinking," he said.

"Do you, really?"

"I know how all this must look to you."

"Is that so?"

"Believe me," Piaget said, "all this is just a terrible series of coincidences that . . . "

"Coincidence!" Dasein whirled on him, glaring. "How far can you stretch credulity, doctor? How long can you rationalize before you have to admit . . . "

"Gilbert, I'd cut off my right arm rather than let anything happen to you. It'd break Jenny's heart to . . . ."

"You actually don't see it, do you?" Dasein asked, his voice filled with awe. "You don't see it. You refuse to see it."

"Dr. Dasein?"

The voice came from his right. Dasein turned to find Harry—"Scheler's other son"—standing there, hat in hand. He looked younger than he had in the café—no more than nineteen. There was a sad hesitancy in his manner.

"I wanted to . . ." He broke off. "My father said to tell you . . . We know it wasn't your fault that . . ." He looked into Dasein's eyes, a look that pleaded for help.

Dasein felt a pang of rapport for the young man. There was a basic decency at work here. In the midst of their own grief, the Schelers had taken time to try to ease Dasein's feelings.

They expected me to feel guilt about this, Dasein thought. The fact that he'd experienced no such feeling filled Dasein now with an odd questing sensation of remorse.

If I hadn't . . . He aborted the thought. *If I hadn't what? That accident was meant for me.*

"It's all right, Harry," Piaget said. "We understand."

"Thanks, Doc." He looked at Piaget with relief. "Dad said to tell you . . . the car, Dr. Dasein's truck . . . The new headlights are in it. That's all we can do. The steering . . . You'll just have to drive slow unless you replace the whole front end."

"Already?" Dasein asked.

"It doesn't take long to put in headlights, sir."

Dasein looked from the youth to Piaget. The doctor returned his stare with an expression that said as clearly as words: *"They want your truck out of there. It's a reminder . . . ."*

Dasein nodded. Yes. The truck would remind them of the tragedy. This was logical. Without a word, he set off for the garage.

Piaget sped up, matched his pace to Dasein's.

"Gilbert," he said, "I must insist you come over to the house. Jenny can . . . ."

"Insist?"

"You're being very pig-headed, Gilbert."

Dasein put down a surge of anger, said: "I don't want to hurt Jenny any more than you do. That's why I'm going to direct my own steps. I don't really want you to know what I'm going to do next. I don't want any of you waiting there in my path with one of your . . . accidents."

"Gilbert, you *must* put that idea out of your mind! None of us want to hurt you."

They were on the parking area between the station and the garage now. Dasein stared at the gaping door to the garage, overcome suddenly by the sensation that the door was a mouth with deadly teeth ready to clamp down on him. The door yawned there to swallow him.

Dasein hesitated, slowed, stopped.

"What is it now?" Piaget asked.

"Your truck's just inside," Harry Scheler said. "You can drive it and . . . ."

"What about the bill?" Dasein asked, stalling for time.

"I'll take care of that," Piaget said. "Go get your truck while I'm settling up. Then we'll go to . . . ."

"I want the truck driven out here for me," Dasein said. He moved to one side, out of the path of anything that might come spewing from that mouth-door.

"I can understand your reluctance to go back in there," Piaget said, "but really . . ."

"You drive it out for me, Harry," Dasein said.

The youth stared at Dasein with an oddly trapped look. "Well, I have some . . . "

"Drive the damn' car out for him!" Piaget ordered. "This is nonsense!"

"Sir?" Harry looked at Piaget.

"I said drive the damn' car out here for him!" Piaget repeated. "I've had as much of this as I can stomach!"

Hesitantly, the youth turned toward the garage door. His feet moved with a dragging slowness.

"See here, Gilbert," Piaget said, "you can't really believe we . . . "

"I believe what I see," Dasein said.

Piaget threw up his hands, turned away in exasperation.

Dasein listened to the sounds from the garage. They were subdued in there—voices, only a few mechanical noises, the whirring buzz of some machine.

A door slammed. It sounded like the door to the truck. Dasein recognized the grinding of his starter. The engine caught with its characteristic banging, as drowned immediately in a roaring explosion that sent a blast of flame shooting out the garage door.

Piaget leaped back with an oath.

Dasein ran diagonally past him to look into the garage. He glimpsed figures rushing out a door at the far end. His truck stood in the central traffic aisle at the core of a red-orange ball of flame. As he stared at the truck, a burning something emerged from the flames, staggered, fell.

Behind Dasein, someone screamed: "Harry!"

Without consciously willing it, Dasein found himself dashing through the garage door to grab into the flames and drag the youth to safety. There were sensations of heat, pain. A roaring-crackling sound of fire filled the air around him. The smell of gasoline and char invaded Dasein's nostrils. He saw a river of fire reach toward him along the floor. A blazing beam crashed down where the youth had lain. There were shouts, a great scrambling confusion.

Something white was thrown over the figure he was dragging, engulfed the flames. Hands eased him aside. Dasin realized he was out of the garage, that Piaget was using his white smock to smother the fire on Harry.

Someone appeared to be doing something similar to both Dasein's arms and the front of his jacket, using a coat and a car robe. The coat and robe were pulled away. Dasein stared down at his own arms—black and red flesh, blisters forming. The sleeves of his shirt and jacket ended at the elbows in jagged edgings of char.

The pain began—a throbbing agony along the backs of both arms and hands. Through a world hazed by the pain, Dasein saw a station-wagon screech to a rocking stop beside him, saw men carry the smock-shrouded figure of Harry into the back of the wagon. More hands eased Dasein into the seat beside the driver.

There were voices: "Easy there." "Get 'em to the clinic, Ed, and don't loiter." "Give us a hand here." "Here! Over here!"

There was a sound of sirens, the pounding throb of heavy truck engines.

Dasein heard Piaget's voice from the rear of the station-wagon: "Okay, Ed. Let's get going."

The wagon slipped into motion, dipped onto the street, turned, gathered speed.

Dasein looked at the driver, recognized one of the station attendants, turned to peer into the back.

Piaget crouched there working over the injured youth.

"How bad is he?" Dasein asked.

"He was wearing long johns," Piaget said. "They helped. He seems to've protected his face by burying it in his cap, but his back is bad. So're his legs and arms and his hands."

Dasein stared at the injured youth.

"Will he . . . "

"I think we got to him in time," Piaget said. "I gave him a shot to put him out." He looked at Dasein's arms. "Do you want a needle?"

Dasein shook his head from side to side. "No."

What made me rush in there to save him? Dasein asked himself. It had been an instinctive reaction. Saving Harry had precipitated him into a semihelpless situation, needing medical attention himself, caught in a car with two Santarogans. Dasein probed at his embryo *Jaspers awareness*, the sixth sense which had warned him of danger. He found nothing. The threat appeared to have been withdrawn. *Is that why I acted to save Harry?* Dasein wondered. *Did I hope to propitiate Santaroga by saving one of their own even while they were trying to kill me?*

"Another accident," Piaget said, and his voice carried a questioning tone of self-doubt.

Dasein met the doctor's probing gaze, nodded.

The station-wagon turned onto a tree-lined street, and Dasein recognized the broad, brown-shingled front of Piaget's house. They drove past it and onto a graveled driveway that curved around to the rear through a tall board fence and under a portico jutting from a two-storey brick building.

In spite of his pain, Dasein realized this building lay concealed from the street by the fence and a border planting of evergreens, that it must be part of the complex which included Piaget's house. It all seemed hazily significant.

White-coated attendants rushed a gurney out of the building, eased the burned youth from the rear of the station-wagon. Piaget opened Dasein's door, said: "Can you get out under your own power, Gilbert?"

"I . . . think so."

Dasein held his arms out in front of him, slid from the car. The pain and the motion required all his attention. There was a beginning ache along his forehead now and down the right side of his face. The brick building, a pair of swinging glass doors, hands gently guiding him—all seemed rather distant and receding.

I'm blacking out, he thought. He felt it might be extremely dangerous to sink into unconsciousness. With a start, he realized he had been eased into a wheelchair, that it was speeding down a green-walled hallway. The surge of awareness sent his senses crashing into the pain. He felt himself recoiling toward the blessed relief of unconsciousness. It was an almost physical thing, as though his body was bouncing between limiting walls—unconsciousness or pain.

Bright lights!

The light was all around him. He heard scissors snipping, looked down to see hands working the scissors. They were cutting the sleeves of his jacket and shirt, lifting the fabric away from seared flesh.

That's my flesh, Dasein thought. He tore his gaze away from it.

Dasein felt something cool at his left shoulder, a pricking sensation, a pulling. A hand holding a hypodermic moved across his plane of vision. The important thing to Dasein in this moment was that his vision was limited to a plane. There was light, a foggy glittering out of which hands moved and faces appeared. He felt himself being undressed. Something cool, soothing, sliding was being applied to his hands and arms, to his face.

They've given me a shot to put me out, he thought. He tried to think about the danger then, about being totally helpless here. Consciousness refused to respond. He couldn't push his awareness through the glittering fog.

There were voices. He concentrated on the voices. Someone said: "For the love of heaven! He was carrying a gun." Another voice: "Put that down!"

For some reason, this amused Dasein, but his body refused to laugh.

He thought then of his camper as he'd last seen it—a ball of orange flame. All his records had been in there, Dasein realized. Every bit of evidence he'd accumulated about Santaroga had gone up in that fire. *Evidence?* he thought. *Notes . . . speculations . . .* It was all still in his mind, subject to recall.

But memory is lost at death! he thought.

Fear galvanized a miniscule core of selfdom in him. He tried to shout. No sound came. He tried to move. Muscles refused to obey.

When the darkness came, it was like a hand that reached up and seized him.

11

DASEIN AWOKE remembering a dream—a conversation with faceless gods.

"Dunghills rise and castles fall." In the dream, something with an echo-box voice had said that. *"Dunghills rise and castles fall."*

Dasein felt it important to remember all the dream. Yes. "I'm the man who woke up." That was what he'd tried to tell the faceless gods. "I'm the man who woke up."

The dream was a flowing pattern in his memory, a *process* that couldn't be separated from himself. It was full of pure deeds and anguish. There was a chronic frustration in it. He had tried to do something that was inherently impossible. What had he tried to do? It eluded him.

Dasein remembered the hand of darkness that had preceded the dream. He caught his breath and his eyes popped open. Daylight. He was in a bed in a green-walled room. Out a window at his left he could see a twisted red branch of madrone, oily green leaves, blue sky. He felt his body then: bandages and pain along his arms, bandages across his forehead and his right cheek. His throat felt dry and there was a sourness on his tongue.

Still, the dream clung to him. It was a disembodied *thing*. Disembodied. Death! That was a clue. He knew it. Dasein recalled Piaget speaking of "a common instinctive experience." What did instinct have to do with the dream? Instinct. Instinct. What was instinct? An innate pattern impressed on the nervous system. Death. Instinct.

"Look inward, look inward, oh Man, oh thyself," the faceless gods of the dream had said. He recalled that now and felt like sneering.

It was the old know-thyself syndrome, the psychologist's disease. Inward, ever inward. The death instinct was in there with all the other instincts. Know thyself?

Dasein sensed then he couldn't know himself without dying. Death was the background against which life could know itself.

A throat was cleared to Dasein's right.

He tensed, turned his head to look toward the sound.

Winston Burdeaux sat in a chair beside the door. The brown eyes staring out of Burdeaux's Moorish face held a quizzical expression.

Why Burdeaux? Dasein wondered.

"I'm happy to see you're awake, sir," Burdeaux said.

There was a soothing sense of companionship in the man's rumbling voice. Was that why Burdeaux had been brought in? Dasein wondered. Had Burdeaux been picked to soothe and lull the victim?

But I'm still alive, Dasein thought.

If they'd wanted to harm him, what better opportunity had presented itself? He'd been helpless, unconscious . . .

"What time is it?" Dasein asked. The movement of speaking hurt his burned cheek.

"It's almost ten o'clock of a beautiful morning," Burdeaux said. He smiled, a flash of white teeth in the dark features. "Is there anything you wish?"

At the question, Dasein's stomach knotted in a pang of hunger. He hesitated on the point of asking for breakfast. What might be in any food served here? he asked himself.

Hunger is more than an empty stomach, Dasein thought. *I can go without a meal*.

"What I wish," Dasein said, "is to know why you're here."

"The doctor thought I might be the safest one," Burdeaux said. "I, myself, was an outsider once. I can recall how it was."

"They tried to kill you, too?"

"Sir!"

"Well . . . did you have accidents?" Dasein asked.

"I do not share the doctor's opinion about . . . accidents," Burdeaux said. "Once . . . I thought— But I can see now how wrong I was. The people of this valley wish to harm no man."

"Yet, you're here because the doctor decided you'd be the *safest*," Dasein said. "And you haven't answered my question: Did you have accidents?"

"You must understand," Burdeaux said, "that when you don't know the ways of the valley, you can get into . . . situations which . . . "

"So you *did* have accidents. Is that why you asked for secret packages from Louisiana?"

"Secret packages?"

"Why else did you have them sent to Porterville?"

"Oh, you know about that." Burdeaux shook his head, chuckled. "Haven't you ever hungered for the foods of your childhood? I didn't think my new friends would understand."

"Is that what it was?" Dasein asked. "Or did you wake up one morning shaking with fear at what the Jaspers in the local food was doing to you?"

Burdeaux scowled, then: "Sir, when I first came here, I was an ignorant *nigger*. Now, I'm an educated Negro . . . *and* a Santarogan. I no longer have the delusions which I . . . "

"So you *did* try to fight it!"

"Yes . . . I fought it. But I soon learned how foolish that was."

"A delusion."

"Indeed; a delusion."

To remove a man's delusions, Dasein thought, *is to create a vacuum. What rushes into that vacuum?*

"Let us say," Burdeaux said, "that I shared your delusions once."

"It's normal to share the delusions of one's society," Dasein murmured, half to himself. "It's abnormal to develop private delusions."

"Well put," Burdeaux said.

Again, he wondered: *What rushed into the vacuum? What delusions do Santarogans share?*

For one thing, he knew they couldn't see the unconscious violence which created *accidents* for outsiders. Most of them couldn't see this, he corrected himself. There was a possibility Piaget was beginning to understand. After all, he'd put Burdeaux in here. And Jenny—*"Stay away from me! I love you!"*

Dasein began to see Santarogans in a new light. There was something decorously Roman about them . . . and Spartan. They were turned in upon themselves, unfriendly, insular, proud, cut off from exchange of ideas that might . . . He hesitated on this thought, wondering about the TV room at the Inn.

"The room you tried to hide from me," Dasein said. "At the Inn—the room with the television receivers . . . "

"We didn't really want to hide that from *you*," Burdeaux said. "In a way, we hide it from ourselves . . . and from chance outsiders. There's something very alluring about the sickness that's poured over TV. That's why we rotate the watchers. But we cannot ignore it. TV is the key to the outside and its gods."

"Its gods?" Dasein suddenly remembered his dream.

"They have very practical gods outside," Burdeaux said.

"What's a practical god?" Dasein asked.

"A practical god? That's a god who agrees with his worshipers. This is a way to keep from being conquered, you see."

Dasein turned away from Burdeaux to stare up at the green ceiling. *Conquer the gods?* Was that the dream's chronic frustration?

"I don't understand," he murmured.

"You still carry some of the outside's delusions," Burdeaux said. "Outside, they don't really try to understand the universe. Oh, they say they do, but that's not really what they're up to. You can tell by what they do. They're trying to conquer the universe. Gods are part of the universe . . . even man-made gods."

"If you can't beat 'em, join 'em," Dasein said. "To keep from being conquered, a practical god agrees with his attackers. Is that it?"

"You're just as perceptive as Jenny said you'd be," Burdeaux said.

"So outsiders attack their gods," Dasein said.

"Anything less than abject submission has to have some attack in it," Burdeaux said. "You try to change a god? What's that except accusing the god of not agreeing with you?"

"And you get all this from the TV?"

"All this from . . . " Burdeaux broke into a chuckle. "Oh, no, Doctor Gil . . . You don't mind if I call you Doctor Gil?"

Dasein turned to stare at the questioning look on Burdeaux's face. *Doctor Gil.* To object would be to appear the stiffnecked fool. But Dasein felt that agreement would be a step backward, the loss of an important battle. He could see no way to object, though.

"Whatever you wish," Dasein said. "Just explain this about the TV."

"That's . . . our *window* on the outside," Burdeaux said. "That whole world of the permanent expediency out there, that whole world is TV. And we watch it through . . ."

"Permanent expediency?" Dasein tried to raise himself on his elbows, but the effect set his burned arms to throbbing. He sank back, kept his gaze on Burdeaux.

"Why, of course, sir. The outside works on the temporary expedient, Doctor Gil. You must know that. And the temporary always turns into the permanent, somehow. The temporary tax, the necessary *little* war, the temporary brutality that will cease as soon as certain conditions end . . . the government agency created for the permanent *interim* . . ."

"So you watch the news broadcasts and get all this from . . ."

"More than the news, Doctor Gil. All of it, and our watchers write condensed reports that . . . You see, it's all TV out there—life, everything. Outsiders are spectators. They expect everything to happen *to* them and they don't want to do more than turn a switch. They want to sit back and let life happen to them. They watch the late-late show and turn off their TVs. Then they go to bed to sleep— which is a form of turning themselves off just like the TV. The trouble is, their late-late show is often later than they think. There's a desperation in not being able to recognize this, Doctor Gil. Desperation leads to violence. There comes a morning for almost every one of those poor people outside when they realize that life hasn't happened to them no matter how much TV they've watched. Life hasn't happened because they didn't take part in it. They've never been onstage, never had anything real. It was all illusion . . . delusion."

Dasein absorbed the intensity of the words, their meaning and what lay under them. There was a terrifying sense of truth in Burdeaux's words.

"So they get turned off," Dasein murmured.

"It's all TV," Burdeaux said.

Dasein turned his head, looked out the window.

"You really ought to eat something, Doctor Gil," Burdeaux said.

"No."

"Doctor Gil, you're a wise man in some things, but in others . . ."

"Don't call me wise," Dasein said. "Call me experienced."

"The food here is the very best," Burdeaux said. "I'll get it and serve you myself. You don't have to fear a . . ."

"I've been burned enough times," Dasein said.

"Fire won't crack a full pot, Doctor Gil."

"Win, I admire you and trust you. You saved my life. I don't think you were supposed to, but you did. That's why Doctor Piaget sent you in here. But an *accident* could happen—even with you."

"You hurt me to say that, Doctor Gil. I'm not the kind feeds you with the corn and chokes you with the cob."

Dasein sighed. He'd offended Burdeaux, but the alternative . . . It occurred to Dasein abruptly that he was sitting on a special kind of bomb. Santaroga had abated its attack on him, probably in part because of his present helplessness. But the community was capable of returning to the manufacture of *accidents* if and when he should ever want something not permitted here.

At the moment, Dasein wanted nothing more than to be far away from here. He wanted this desperately despite the certain knowledge this desire must be on the proscribed list.

The door beside Burdeaux opened. A nurse backed into the room pulling a cart. She turned. Jenny!

Dasein ignored his burns, lifted himself on his elbows.

Jenny stared at him with an oddly pained expression. Her full lips were thrust out almost in a pout. The long black hair had been tied back in a neat bun. She wore a white uniform, white stockings, white shoes—no cap.

Dasein swallowed.

"Miss Jenny," Burdeaux said. "What do you have on that cart?"

She spoke without taking her gaze from Dasein. "Some food for this madman. I prepared it myself."

"I've been trying to get him to eat," Burdeaux said, "but he says no."

"Would you leave us for a while, Win?" she asked. "I want . . ."

"The doctor said I wasn't to let . . ."

"Win, please?" She turned toward him, pleading.

Burdeaux swallowed. "Well . . . since it's you . . ."

"Thank you, Win."

"Twenty minutes," Burdeaux said. "I'll be right out in the hall where you can call me if you need."

"Thank you, Win." She turned her attention back to Dasein.

Burdeaux left the room, closed the door softly.

Dasein said: "Jen, I . . ."

"Be quiet," she said. "You're not to waste your strength. Uncle Larry said . . ."

"I'm not eating here," Dasein said.

She stamped a foot. "Gil, you're being . . ."

"I'm being a fool," he said. "But the important thing is I'm alive."

"But look at you! Look at . . ."

"How's Harry Scheler?"

She hesitated, then: "He'll live. He'll have some scars, and for that matter so will you, but you . . ."

"Have they figured out what happened?"

"It was an accident."

"That's all? Just an accident?"

"They said something about the line from the fuel pump being broken . . . a bad electrical connection to one of the lights and . . ."

"An accident," Dasein said. "I see." He sank back into his pillow.

"I've prepared you some coddled eggs and toast and honey," Jenny said. "You've got to eat something to keep up . . ."

"No."

"Gil!"

"I said no."

"What're you afraid of?"

"Another accident."

"But I prepared this myself!"

He turned his head, stared at her, spoke in a low voice: "Stay away from me. I love you."

"Gilbert!"

"You said it," he reminded her.

Her face paled. She leaned against the cart, trembling. "I know," she whispered. "Sometimes I can feel the . . ." She looked up, tears streaming down her face. "But I *do* love you. And you're hurt now. I want to take care of you. I *need* to take care of you. Look.'' She lifted the cover from one of the dishes on the cart, spooned a bite of food into her mouth.

"Jenny," Dasein whispered. The look of hurt on her face, the intensity of his love for her—he wanted to take her in his arms and . . .

A wide-eyed look came over Jenny's face. She reached both hands to her throat. Her mouth worked, but no sound came forth.

"Jenny!"

She shook her head, eyes staring wildly.

Dasein threw back the covers of his bed, winced as movement increased the pain along his arms. He ignored the pain, slid his feet out to a cold tile floor, straightened. A wave of dizziness gripped him.

Jenny, hands still at her throat, backed toward the door.

Dasein started toward her, hospital nightshirt flopping around his knees. He found movement difficult, his knees rubbery.

Abruptly, Jenny slumped to the floor.

Dasein remembered Burdeaux, shouted: "Help! Win! Help!" He staggered, clutched the edge of the cart. It started to roll.

Dasein found himself sitting helplessly on the floor as the door burst open. Burdeaux stood there glaring at him, looked down at Jenny who lay with her eyes closed, knees drawn up, gasping.

"Call the doctor," Dasein husked. "Something in the food. She ate some . . ."

Burdeaux took one quick breath of awareness, whirled away down the hall, leaving the door open.

Dasein started to crawl toward Jenny. The room wavered and twisted around him. His arms throbbed. There was a whistle in Jenny's gasping breaths that made him want to dash to her, but he couldn't find the strength. He had covered only a few feet when Piaget rushed in with Burdeaux right behind.

Piaget, his round face a pale blank mask, knelt beside Jenny, motioned toward Dasein, said: "Get him back in bed."

"The food on the cart," Dasein rasped. "She ate something."

A blonde nurse in a stiff white cap wheeled an emergency cart in the door, bent over Piaget's shoulder. They were cut from Dasein's view as Burdeaux scooped him up, deposited him on the bed.

"You stay there, Doctor Gil," Burdeaux said. He turned, stared at the action by the door.

"Allergenic reaction," Piaget said "Throat's closing. Give me a double tube; we'll have to pump her."

The nurse handed something to Piaget, who worked over Jenny, his back obscuring his actions.

"Atropine," Piaget said.

Again, he took something from the nurse.

Dasein found it difficult to focus on the scene. Fear tightened his throat. *Why am I so weak?* he wondered. Then: *Dear God, she can't die. Please save her.*

Faces of more hospital personnel appeared at the door, wide-eyed, silent.

Piaget glanced up, said: "Get a gurney."

Some of the faces went away. Presently, there was a sound of wheels in the corridor.

Piaget stood up, said: "That's as much as I can do here. Get her on the gurney—head lower than her feet." He turned to Dasein. "What'd she eat?"

"She took . . . " Dasein pointed to the food cart. "Whatever it is, she took the cover off. Eggs?"

Piaget took one stride to the cart, grabbed up a dish, sniffed at it. His movement opened the view to the door for Dasein. Two orderlies and a nurse were lifting Jenny there, carrying her out the door. There was one glimpse of her pale face with a tube dangling from the corner of her mouth.

"Was it a poison?" Burdeaux asked, his voice hushed.

"Of course it was a poison!" Piaget snapped. "Acts like aconite." He turned with the dish, rushed out.

Dasein listened to the sound of the wheels and swift footsteps receding down the hall until Burdeaux closed the door, shutting out the sound.

His body bathed in perspiration, Dasein lay unresisting while Burdeaux eased him under the blankets.

"For one moment there," Burdeaux said, "I . . . I thought you'd hurt Jenny."

She can't die, Dasein thought.

"I'm sorry," Burdeaux said. "I know you wouldn't hurt her."

"She can't die," Dasein whispered.

He looked up to see tears draw glistening tracks down Burdeaux's dark cheeks. The tears ignited an odd anger reaction in Dasein. He was aware of the anger swelling in him, but unable to stop it. Rage! It was directed not at Burdeaux, but at the disembodied essence of Santaroga, at the collecting *thing* which had tried to use the woman he loved to kill him. He glared at Burdeaux.

"Doctor Larry won't let anything happen to Jenny," Burdeaux said. "He'll . . . "

Burdeaux saw the expression in Dasein's eyes, instinctively backed away.

"Get out of here!" Dasein rasped.

"But the doctor said I was to . . . "

"Doctor *Gil* says you get the hell out of here!"

Burdeaux's face took on a stubborn set. "I'm not to leave you alone."

Dasein sank back, What could he do?

"You had a very bad shock reaction last night," Burdeaux said. "They had to give you blood. You're not to be left alone."

They gave me a transfusion? Dasein wondered. *Why didn't they kill me then? They were saving me for Jenny!*

"You all care so much for Jenny," Dasein said. "You'd let her kill me. It'd destroy her, but that doesn't make any difference, does it? Sacrifice Jenny, that's your verdict, you pack of . . . "

"You're talking crazy, Doctor Gil."

As quickly as it had come, the anger left Dasein. Why attack poor Win? Why attack any of them? They couldn't see the monkey on their back. He felt deflated. Of course this was crazy to Burdeaux. One society's reason was another's unreason.

Dasein cursed the weakness that had seized his body.

Bad shock reaction.

He wondered then what he would do if Jenny died. It was a curiously fragmented feeling—part of him wailing in grief at the thought, another part raging at the fate which had shunted him into this corner . . . and part of him forever analyzing, analyzing . . .

How much of the shock had been a Jaspers reaction? Had he become sensitized the way Santarogans were?

They'll kill me out of hand if Jenny dies, he thought.

Burdeaux said: "I'll just sit here by the door. You be sure to tell me if you need anything."

He sat down facing Dasein, folded his arms—for all the world like a guard.

Dasein closed his eyes, thought: *Jenny, please don't die.* He recalled Piaget telling how Harry Scheler had known of the brother's death.

An empty place.

Where do I sense Jenny? Dasein asked himself.

It bothered him that he couldn't probe within himself somewhere and be reassured by Jenny's presence. That kind of reassurance was worth any price. She had to be there. It was a thing any Santarogan could do.

But I'm not a Santarogan.

Dasein felt that he teetered on the razor's edge. One side held the vast unconscious sea of the human world into which he had been born. On the other side—there, it was like the green waters of a lake—serene, contained, every droplet knowing its neighbors.

He heard a door open, felt a storm begin in the unconscious sea, sensed a breeze stirring the surface of the lake. The sensation of balancing receded. Dasein opened his eyes.

Piaget stood in the middle of the room. He wore a stethoscope around his neck. There was a feeling of fatigue around his eyes. He studied Dasein with a puzzled frown.

"Jenny?" Dasein whispered.

"She'll live," Piaget said. "But it was close."

Dasein closed his eyes, took a deep breath. "How many more *accidents* like that can we take?" he asked. He opened his eyes, met Piaget's gaze.

Burdeaux came up beside Piaget, said: "He's been talking crazy, Doctor Larry."

"Win, would you leave us for a bit?" Piaget asked.

"You sure?" Burdeaux scowled at Dasein.

"Please," Piaget said. He pulled up a chair, sat down beside the bed, facing Dasein.

"I'll be right outside," Burdeaux said. He went out, closed the door.

"You've upset Win and that's rather difficult to do," Piaget said.

"Upset . . . " Dasein stared at him, speechless. Then: "Is that your summation of what's happened?"

Piaget looked down at his own right hand, made a fist, opened it. He shook his head. "I didn't mean to sound flippant, Gilbert. I . . . " He looked up at Dasein. "There must be some reasonable, rational explanation."

"You don't think the word *accident* explains all this?"

"An accident prone . . . "

"We both know there's no such thing as an accident prone in the popular sense of that label," Dasein said.

Piaget steepled his hands in front of him, leaned back. He pursed his lips, then: "Well, in the psychiatric view . . . "

"Come off that!" Dasein barked. "You're going to fall back on the old cliché about 'a neurotic tendency to inflict self-injury,' a defect in ego-control. Where did I have any control over the work on that bridge? Or the boy with the bow and arrow or . . . "

"Boy with a bow and arrow?"

Dasein thought to hell with his promise, told about the incident at the park, added: "And what about the garage hoist or the fire? For that matter, what about the poison in the food Jenny . . . Jenny, of all people! the food that she . . . "

"All right! You have grounds to . . . "

"Grounds? I've an entire syndrome laid out in front of me. Santaroga is trying to kill me. You've already killed an apparently inoffensive young man. You've almost killed Jenny. What next?"

"In heaven's name, why would we . . . "

"To eliminate a threat. Isn't that obvious? I'm a threat."

"Oh, now really . . . "

"Now, really! Or is it perfectly all right if I take Jenny out of this crazy valley and blow the whistle on you?"

"Jenny won't leave her . . . " He paused. "Blow the whistle? What do you mean?"

"Now, who's making the angels weep?" Dasein asked. "You protest that you love Jenny and won't have her hurt. What more terrible thing is there than to have her be the instrument of my death?"

Piaget paled, drew two ragged breaths. "She . . . There must be . . . What do you mean blow the whistle?"

"Has a Labor Department inspector ever looked into the child labor situation out at your *school*?" Dasein asked. "What about the State Department of Mental Hygiene? Your records say no mental illness from Santaroga."

"Gilbert, you don't know what you're talking about."

"Don't I? What about the antigovernment propaganda in your newspaper?"

"We're not antigovernment, Gilbert, we're . . . "

"What? Why, I've never seen such a . . . "

"Allow me to finish, please. We're not antigovernment; we're anti-*outside*. That's a cat of quite different calico."

"You think they're all . . . insane?"

"We think they're all going to eat themselves up."

Madness, madness, Dasein thought. He stared at the ceiling. Perspiration bathed his body. The intensity of emotion he'd put into the argument with Piaget . . .

"Why did you send Burdeaux to watch over me?" Dasein asked.

Piaget shrugged. "I . . . to guard against the possibility you might be right in your . . . "

"And you picked Burdeaux." Dasein turned his eyes toward Piaget, studied the man. Piaget appeared to be warring with himself, nervously clenching and unclenching his fists.

"The reasons should be obvious," he said.

"You can't let me leave the valley, can you?" Dasein asked.

"You're in no physical condition to . . . "

"Will I ever be?"

Piaget met Dasein's gaze. "How can I prove to you what we really . . . "

"Is there any place here where I can protect myself from accidents?" Dasein asked.

"Protect yourself from . . . " Piaget shook his head.

"You want to prove your honorable intentions," Dasein said.

Piaget pursed his lips, then: "There's an isolation suite, a penthouse on the roof—its own kitchen, facilities, everything. If you . . . "

"Could Burdeaux get me up there without killing me?"

Piaget sighed. "I'll take you up there myself as soon as I can get a . . . "

"Burdeaux."

"As you wish. You can be moved in a wheelchair."

"I'll walk."

"You're not strong enough to . . . "

"I'll find the strength. Burdeaux can help me."

"Very well. As to food, we can . . . "

"I'll eat out of cans picked at random from a market's shelves. Burdeaux can shop for me until I'm . . . "

"Now, see here . . . "

"That's the way it's going to be, doctor. He'll get me a broad selection, and I'll choose at random from that selection."

"You're taking unnecessary . . . "

"Let's give it a try and see how many accidents develop."

Piaget stared at him a moment, then: "As you wish."

"What about Jenny? When can I see her?"

"She's had a severe shock to her system and some intestinal trauma. I'd say she shouldn't have visitors for several days unless they . . . "

"I'm not leaving that isolation suite until I've convinced you," Dasein said. "When can she come to see me?"

"It'll be several days." He pointed a finger at Dasein. "Now, see here, Gilbert—you're not going to take Jenny out of the valley. She'll never consent to . . . "

"Let's let Jenny decide that."

"Very well." Piaget nodded. "You'll see." He went to the door, opened it. "Win?"

Burdeaux stepped past Piaget into the room. "Is he still talking crazy, Doctor Larry?"

"We're going to conduct an experiment, Win," Piaget said. "For reasons of Dr. Dasein's health and Jenny's happiness, we're going to move him to the isolation suite." Piaget jerked a thumb toward the ceiling. "He wants you to move him."

"I'll get a wheelchair," Burdeaux said.

"Dr. Dasein wants to try walking," Piaget said.

"Can he do that?" Burdeaux turned a puzzled frown on Dasein. "He was too weak to stand just a little . . . "

"Dr. Dasein appears to be relying on your strength," Piaget said. "Think you can manage?"

"I could carry him," Burdeaux said, "but that seems like a . . . "

"Treat him with the same care you'd treat a helpless infant," Piaget said.

"If you say so, Doctor Larry."

Burdeaux crossed to the bed, helped Dasein to sit on the edge of the bed. The effort set Dasein's head to whirling. In the fuzzy tipping and turning of the room, he saw Piaget go to the door, open it and stand there looking at Burdeaux.

"I'll take my evil influence elsewhere for the time being," Piaget said. "You don't mind, do you, Gilbert, if I look in on you shortly—purely in a medical capacity?"

"As long as I have the final say on what you do to me," Dasein said.

"It's only fair to warn you your bandages have to be changed," Piaget said.

"Can Win do it?"

"Your trust in Win is very touching," Piaget said. "I'm sure he's impressed."

"Can he . . . "

"Yes, I'm certain he can—with my instruction."

"All right then," Dasein said.

With Burdeaux's help, Dasein struggled to his feet. He stood there panting, leaning on Burdeaux. Piaget went out, leaving the door open.

"You sure you can manage, sir?" Burdeaux asked.

Dasein tried to take a step. His knees were two sections of flexing rubber. He would have fallen had it not been for Burdeaux's support.

"Do we go by elevator?" Dasein asked.

"Yes, sir. It's right across the hall."

"Let's get on with it."

"Yes, sir. Excuse me, sir." Burdeaux bent, lifted Dasein in his arms, turned to slip through the door.

Dasein glimpsed the startled face of a nurse walking down the hall. He felt foolish, helpless—stubborn. The nurse frowned, glanced at Burdeaux, who ignored her, punched the elevator button with an elbow. The nurse strode off down the hall, heels clicking.

Elevator doors slid open with a hiss.

Burdeaux carried him inside, elbowed a button marked "P."

Dasein felt his mouth go dry as the elevator doors closed. He stared up at a cream ceiling, a milky oblong of light, thinking: *They didn't hesitate to sacrifice Jenny. Why would they have a second thought about Burdeaux? What if the elevator's rigged to crash?*

A faint humming sounded. Dasein felt the elevator lift. Presently, the doors opened and Burdeaux carried him out. There was a glimpse of a cream-walled entrance foyer, a mahogany door labeled "Isolation" and they were inside.

It was a long room with three beds, windows opening onto a black tar roof. Burdeaux deposited Dasein on the nearest bed, stepped back. "Kitchen's in there," he said, pointing to a swinging door at the end of the room. "Bathroom's through that door there." This was a door opposite the foot of Dasein's bed. There were two more doors to the right of this one. "Other doors are a closet and a lab. Is this what you wanted, Doctor?"

Dasein met a measuring stare in Burdeaux's eyes, said: "It'll have to do." He managed a rueful smile, explained the eating arrangements.

"Canned food, sir?" Burdeaux asked.

"I'm imposing on you, I know," Dasein said. "But you were . . . like me . . . once. I think you sympathise with me . . . unconsciously. I'm counting on that to . . . " Dasein managed a weak shrug.

"Is this what Doctor Larry wants me to do?"

"Yes."

"I just pick cans from the shelves . . . at random?"

"That's right."

"Well, it sounds crazy, sir . . . but I'll do it." He left the room, muttering.

Dasein managed to crawl under the blankets, lay for a moment regaining his strength. He could see a line of treetops beyond the roof—tall evergreens—a cloudless blue sky. There was a sense of quiet about the room. Dasein took a deep breath. Was this place really safe? A Santarogan had picked it. But the Santarogan had been off balance with personal doubts.

For the first time in days, Dasein felt he might relax. A profound lassitude filled him.

What is this unnatural weakness? he wondered.

It was far more than shock reation or a result of his burns. This was like an injury to the soul, something that involved the entire being. It was a central command to all his muscles, a compulsion of inactivity.

Dasein closed his eyes.

In the red darkness behind his eyelids Dasein felt himself to be shattered, his ego huddled in a fetal crouch, terrified. One must not move, he thought. To move was to invite a disaster more terrible than death.

An uncontrollable shuddering shook his legs and hips, set his teeth chattering. He fought himself to stillness, opened his eyes to stare at the ceiling.

It's a Jaspers reaction, he thought.

There was a smell of it in the room. The aroma gnawed at his senses. He sniffed, turned toward a metal stand beside the bed, a partly-opened drawer. Dasein slid the drawer all the way out to a stop, rolled onto his side to peer at the space he'd exposed.

Empty.

But there'd been a Jaspers *something* in the drawer—and that recently.

What?

Dasein swept his gaze around the room. Isolation suite, Piaget had said. Isolation of what? From what? For what?

He swallowed, sank back on the pillow.

The deliciously terrifying lassitude gripped him. Dasein sensed the green waters of unconsciousness ready to enfold him. By a desperate effort of will, he forced his eyes to remain open.

Somewhere, a cowering, fetal *something* moaned.

Faceless god chuckled.

The entrance door opened.

Dasein held himself rigidly unmoving, afraid if he moved his head to one side his face might sink beneath the upsurging unconsciousness, that he might drown in . . .

Piaget came into his field of vision, peering down at him. The doctor thumbed Dasein's left eyelid up, studied the eye.

"Damned if you aren't still fighting it," he said.

"Fighting what?" Dasein whispered.

"I was pretty sure it'd knock you out if you used that much energy at this stage," Piaget said. "You're going to have to eat before long, you know."

Dasein was aware then of the pain—a demanding hollow within him. He held onto the pain. It helped fight off the enfolding green waves.

"Tell you what," Piaget said. He moved from Dasein's range of vision. There came a scraping, a grunt. "I'll just sit here and keep watch on you until Win gets back with something you'll stuff into that crazy face of yours. I won't lay a hand on you and I won't let anyone else touch you. Your bandages can wait. More important for you to rest—sleep if you can. Stop fighting it."

Sleep! Gods, how the lassitude beckoned.

Fighting what?

He tried to frame the question once more, couldn't find the energy. It took all of his effort merely to cling to a tiny glowing core of awareness that stared up at a cream-colored ceiling.

"What you're fighting," Piaget said in a conversational tone, "is the climb out of the morass. Mud clings to one. This is what leads me to suspect your theory may have a germ of truth in it—that some stain of violence still clings to us, reaching us on the blind side, as it were."

Piaget's voice was a hypnotic drone. Phrases threaded their way in and out of Dasein's awareness.

". . . experiment in domestication . . . " ". . . removed from ex-stasis, from a fixed condition . . . " ". . . must reimprint the sense of identity . . . " ". . . nothing new: mankind's always in some sort of trouble . . . " ". . . religious experience of a sort—creating a new order of theobotanists . . . " ". . . don't shrink from life or from awareness of life . . . " ". . . seek a society that changes smoothly, flowingly as the collective need requires . . . "

One of the faceless gods produced a thundering whisper in Dasein's skull: *"This is my commandment given unto you: A poor man cannot afford principles and a rich man doesn't need them."*

Dasein lay suspended in a hammock of silence.

Fear of movement dominated him.

He sensed a world-presence somewhere beneath him. But he lay stranded here above. Something beckoned. Familiar. He felt the familiar world and was re-pelled. The place seethed with disguises that tried to conceal a rubble of preten-sions, devices, broken masks. Still, it beckoned. It was a place in which he could fit, shaped to him. He sensed himself reaching toward it with a feeling of exuberant self-gratification, drew back. The rubble. It was everywhere, a blanket over life, a creamy ennui—soothing, cajoling, saccharine.

Still, it beckoned.

The lure was inexhaustible, a brilliant bag of pyrotechnics, a palette flooded with gross colors.

It was all a trick.

He sensed this—all a trick, a mass of signal clichés and canned reflexes.

It was a hateful world.

Which world? he asked himself. *Was it Santaroga . . . or the outside?*

Something grabbed Dasein's shoulder.

He screamed.

Dasein awoke to find himself moaning, mumbling. It took a moment to place himself. Where were the faceless gods?

Piaget leaned over him, a hand on Dasein's shoulder.

"You were having a nightmare," Piaget said. He took his hand away. "Win's back with the food—such as it is."

Dasein's stomach knotted in pain.

Burdeaux stood at his right next to the adjoining bed. A box piled with canned food rested on the next bed.

"Bring me a can opener and a spoon," Dasein said.

"Just tell me what you want and I'll open it," Burdeaux said.

"I'll do it," Dasein said. He raised himself on his elbows. Movement set his arms to throbbing, but he felt stronger—as though he had tapped a strength of desperation.

"Humor him," Piaget said as Burdeaux hesitated.

Burdeaux shrugged, went out the door across from the bed.

Dasein threw back the blankets, swung his feet out. He motioned Piaget back, sat up. His feet touched a cold floor. He took a deep breath, lurched across to the adjoining bed. His knees felt stronger, but Dasein sensed the shallowness of his reserves.

Burdeaux reappeared, handed Dasein a twist-handle can opener.

Dasein sat down beside the box, grabbed a fat green can out of it, not even looking at the label. He worked the opener around the can, took a proffered spoon from Burdeaux, lifted back the lid.

Beans.

An odor of Jaspers clamored at Dasein from the open can. He looked at the label: "Packed by the Jaspers Cooperative." There was a permit number, a date of a year ago and the admonition: "Not for sale in interstate commerce. Exposed Dec. '64."

Dasein stared at the can. *Jaspers?* It couldn't be. The stuff didn't ship. It couldn't be preserved out of . . .

"Something wrong?" Piaget asked.

Dasein studied the can: shiny, a glistening label.

"Beans with meat sauce and beef," read the yellow letters.

Dasein ignored the lure of the aroma from the can, looked in the box. He tried to remember whether the can had given off the characteristic hiss of a vacuum seal breaking as it had been opened—couldn't remember.

"What's wrong?" Piaget insisted.

"Can't be anything wrong," Burdeaux said. "That's all private stock."

Dasein looked up from the box. All the cans he could see bore the Co-op's label. *Private stock?*

"Here," Piaget said. He took can and spoon from Dasein's hands, tasted a bite of beans, smiled. He returned the can and spoon to Dasein, who took them automatically.

"Nothing wrong there," Piaget said.

"Better not be," Burdeaux said. "It came from Pete Maja's store, right off the private stock shelf."

"It's Jaspers," Dasein rasped.

"Of course it is," Piaget said. "Canned right here for local consumption. Stored here to preserve its strength. Won't keep long after it's opened, though, so you'd better start eating. Got maybe five, ten minutes." He chuckled. "Be thankful you're here. If you were *outside* and opened that can, wouldn't last more'n a few seconds."

"Why?"

"Hostile environment," Piaget said. "Go ahead and eat. You saw me take some. Didn't hurt me."

Dasein tested a bit of the sauce on his tongue. A soothing sensation spread across his tongue, down his throat. They were delicious. He spooned a full bite into his mouth, gulped it down.

The Jaspers went thump in his stomach.

Dasein turned, wide-eyed toward Burdeaux, met a look of wonder, dark brown eyes like African charms with butter-yellow flecks in them. The can drew Dasein's attention. He peered into it.

Empty.

Dasein experienced a sensation of strange recall—like the fast rewind on a tape recorder, a screech of memory: his hand in a piston movement spooning the contents of the can into his mouth. Blurred gulpings.

He recognized the *thump* now. It had been a thump of awareness. He no longer was hungry.

My body did it, Dasein thought. A sense of wonder enfolded him. *My body did it*.

Piaget took the can and spoon from Dasein's unresisting fingers. Burdeaux helped Dasein back into bed, pulled the blankets up, straightened them.

My body did it, Dasein thought.

There'd been a trigger to action—knowledge that the Jaspers effect was fading . . . and consciousness had blanked out.

"There," Piaget said.

"What about his bandages?" Burdeaux asked.

Piaget examined the bandage on Dasein's cheek, bent close to sniff, drew back. "Perhaps this evening," he said.

"You've trapped me, haven't you?" Dasein asked. He stared up at Piaget.

"There he goes again," Burdeaux said.

"Win," Piaget said, "I know you have personal matters to take care of. Why don't you tend to them now and leave me with Gilbert? You can come back around six if you would."

Burdeaux said: "I could call Willa and have her . . . "

"No need to bother your daughter," Piaget said. "Run along and . . . "

"But what if . . . "

"There's no danger," Piaget said.

"If you say so," Burdeaux said. He moved toward the foyer door, paused there a moment to study Dasein, then went out.

"What didn't you want Win to hear?" Dasein asked.

"There he goes again," Piaget said, echoing Burdeaux.

"Something must've . . . "

"There's nothing Win couldn't hear!"

"Yet you sent him to watch over me . . . because he was special," Dasein said. He took a deep breath, feeling his senses clear, his mind come alert. "Win was . . . *safe* for me."

"Win has his own life to live and you're interfering," Piaget said. "He . . . "

"Why was Win *safe*?"

"It's your feeling, not mine," Piaget said. "Win saved you from falling. You've shown a definite empathy . . . "

"He came from *outside*," Dasein said. "He was like me . . . once."

"Many of us came from outside," Piaget said."

"You, too?"

"No, but . . . "

"How does the trap really work?" Dasein asked.

"There is *no* trap!"

"What does the Jaspers do to one?" Dasein asked.

"Ask yourself that question."

"Technically . . . doctor?"

"Technically?"

"What does the Jaspers do?"

"Oh. Among other things, it speeds up catalysis of the chemical transmitters in the nervous system—5 hydroxytryptamine and serotonin."

"Changes in the Golgi cells?"

"Absolutely not. Its effect is to break down blockage systems, to open the mind's image function and consciousness formulation processes. You *feel* as though you had a better . . . an *improved* memory. Not true, of course, except in effect. Merely a side effect of the speed with which . . . ''

"Image function," Dasein said. "What if the person isn't capable of dealing with all his memories? There are extremely disagreeable, shameful . . . dangerously traumatic memories in some . . . ''

"We have our failures."

"Dangerous failures?"

"Sometimes."

Dasein closed his mouth, an instinctive reaction. He drew a deep breath through his nostrils. The odor of Jaspers assailed his senses. He looked toward the box of cans on the adjacent bed.

Jaspers. Consciousness fuel. Dangerous substance. Drug of ill omen. Speculative fantasies flitted through Dasein's mind. He turned, surprised a mooning look on Piaget's face.

"You can't get away from it here in the valley, can you?" Dasein asked.

"Who'd want to?"

"You're hoping I'll stay, perhaps help you with your failures."

"There's certainly work to be done."

Anger seized Dasein. "How can I think?" he demanded. "I can't get away from the smell of . . . ''

"Easy," Piaget murmured. "Take it easy, now. You'll get so you don't even notice it."

Every society has its own essential chemistry, Dasein thought. *Its own aroma, a thing of profound importance, but least apparent to its own members.*

Santaroga had tried to kill him, Dasein knew. He wondered now if it could have been because he had a different smell. He stared at the box on the bed. Impossible! It couldn't be anything that close to the surface.

Piaget moved around to the box, tore a small, curling strip of paper from it, touched the paper to his tongue. "This box has been down in storage," he said. "It's paper, organic matter. Anything organic becomes impregnated with Jaspers after a certain exposure." He tossed the paper into the box.

"Will I be like that box?" Dasein asked. He felt he had a ghost at his heels, an essence he couldn't elude. The lurking presence stirred in his mind. "Will I . . . ''

"Put such thoughts out of your mind," Piaget said.

"Will I be one of the failures?" Dasein asked.

"I said stop that!"

"Why should I?"

Dasein sat up, the strength of fear and anger in him, his mind crowded by suppositions, each one worse than its predecessor. He felt more exposed and vulnerable than a child running from a whipping.

With an abrupt shock of memory, Dasein fell back to the pillow. *Why did I choose this moment to remember that?* he asked himself. A painful incident from his childhood lay there, exposed to awareness. He remembered the pain of the switch on his back.

"You're not the failure type," Piaget said.

Dasein stared accusingly at the odorous box.

Jaspers!

"You're the kind who can go very high," Piaget said. "Why do you really think you're here? Just because of that silly market report? Or because of Jenny? Ah, no. Nothing that isolated or simple. Santaroga calls out to some people. They come."

Dasein looked sidelong at him.

"I came so you people could get the chance to kill me," Dasein said.

"We don't want to kill you!"

"One moment you suspect I may be right, the next you're denying it."

Piaget sighed.

"I have a suggestion," Dasein said.

"Anything."

"You won't like it," Dasein said.

Piaget glared at him. "What's on your mind?"

"You'll be afraid to do it."

"I'm not . . ."

"It's something like a clinical test," Dasein said. "My guess is you'll try not to do it. You'll look for excuses, anything to get out of it or to discontinue it. You'll try to misunderstand me. You'll try to break away from . . ."

"For the love of heaven! What's on your mind?"

"You may succeed."

"Succeed in what?"

"Not doing what I suggest."

"Don't try to crowd me into a corner, Gilbert."

"Thus it starts," Dasein said. He held up a hand as Piaget made as though to speak. "I want you to let me hypnotize you."

"What?"

"You heard me."

"Why?"

"You're a native," Dasein said, "thoroughly conditioned to this . . . consciousness fuel. I want to see what's under there, what kind of fears you . . ."

"Of all the crazy . . ."

"I'm not some amateur meddler asking to do this," Dasein said. "I'm a clinical psychologist well versed in hypnotherapy."

"But what could you possibly hope to . . ."

"What a man fears," Dasein said. "His fears are like a 'homing beacon.' Home in on a man's fears and you find his underlying motivations. Under every fear, there's a violence of no mean . . ."

"Nonsense! I have no . . ."

"You're a medical man. You know better than that."

Piaget stared at him, silently measuring. Presently, he said: "Well, every man has a death fear, of course. And . . ."

"More than that."

"You think you're some kind of god, Gilbert? You just go around . . ."

"Doth the eagle mount up at thy command, and make her nest on high?" Dasein asked. He shook his head. "What do you worship?"

"Oh . . . religion." Piaget took a deep breath of relief. "Thou shalt not be afraid for the terror by night; nor for the arrow that flieth by day; nor for the pestilence that walketh in darkness; nor for the destruction that wasteth at noonday. Is that it? What do . . ."

"That is *not* it."

"Gilbert, I'm not ignorant of these matters, as you must realize. To stir up the areas you're suggesting . . ."

"What would I stir up?"

"We both know that cannot be predicted with any accuracy."

"You're doing things as a community . . . a group, a society that you don't want me digging into,'' Dasein said. ''What does that society really worship? With one hand, you say: 'Look anywhere you like.' With the other hand, you slam doors. In every action of . . . ''

''You really believe some of us tried to . . . kill you . . . for the community?''

''Don't you?''

''Couldn't there be some other explanation?''

''What?''

Dasein held a steady gaze on Piaget. The doctor was disturbed, no doubt of that. He refused to meet Dasein's eyes. He moved his hands about aimlessly. His breathing had quickened.

''Societies don't believe they can die,'' Piaget said. ''It must follow that a society, as such, does not worship at all. If it cannot die, it'll never face a final judgment.''

''And if it'll never face judgment,'' Dasein said, ''it can do things as a society that'd be too much for an individual to stomach.''

''Perhaps,'' Piaget muttered. ''Perhaps.'' Then: ''All right, then. Why examine me? I've never tried to harm you.''

Dasein looked away, taken aback by the question. Out the window he could see through a frame of trees a stretch of the hills which enclosed Santaroga. He felt himself enclosed by that line of hills, entangled here in a web of meanings.

''What about the people who have tried to kill me?'' Dasein asked shortly. ''Would they be fit subjects?''

''The boy, perhaps,'' Piaget said. ''I'll have to examine him anyway.''

''Petey, the Jorick boy,'' Dasein said. ''A failure, eh?''

''I think not.''

''Another *opening person* . . . like me?''

''You remember that?''

''Then, you said societies die, that you'd cut yourselves off here . . . with Jaspers.''

''We had a speaking then, too, as I recall it,'' Piaget said. ''Have you really opened now? Are you seeing? Have you become?''

Dasein abruptly remembered Jenny's voice on the telephone: ''Be careful.'' And the fear when she'd said: ''They want you to leave.''

In this instant, Piaget became for him once more the gray cat in the garden, silencing the birds, and Dasein knew himself to be alone yet, without a group. He remembered the lake, the perception of perception—knowing his own body, that communal knowledge of mood, that sharing.

Every conversation he'd had with Piaget came back to Dasein then to be weighed and balanced. He felt his Santaroga experiences had been building—one moment upon another—to this instant.

''I'll get you some more Jaspers,'' Piaget said. ''Perhaps then . . . ''

''You suspect I'm fluttery behind the eyes?'' Dasein asked.

Piaget smiled. ''Sarah clings to the phrases of the past,'' he said, ''before we systematized our dealings with Jaspers . . . and with the outside. But don't laugh at her or her phrases. She has the innocent eye.''

''Which I haven't.''

''You still have some of the assumptions and prejudices of the non-men,'' Piaget said.

''And I've heard too much, learned too much about you, ever to be allowed to leave,'' Dasein said.

"Won't you even try to become?" Piaget asked.

"Become what?" Piaget's crazy, almost-schizophrenic talk enraged him. *A speaking! A seeing!*

"Only you know that," Piaget said.

"Know what?"

Piaget merely stared at him.

"I'll tell you what I know," Dasein said. "I know you're terrified by my suggestion. You don't want to find out how Vina's roach powder got into the coffee. You don't want to know how Clara Scheler poisoned her stew. You don't want to know what prompted someone to push me off a float. You don't want to know why a fifteen-year-old boy would try to put an arrow through me. You don't want to know how Jenny poisoned the eggs. You don't want to know how a car was set up to crush me, or how my truck was rigged as a fire bomb. You don't want to . . . "

"All right!"

Piaget rubbed his chin, turned away.

"I told you you might succeed," Dasein said.

" *'Iti vuccati'* " Piaget murmured. " 'Thus it is said: Every system and every interpretation becomes false in the light of a more complete system.' I wonder if that's why you're here—to remind us no positive statement may be made that's free from contradictions."

He turned, stared at Dasein.

"What're you talking about?" Dasein asked. Piaget's tone and manner carried a suddenly disturbing calmness.

"The inner enlightenment of all beings dwells in the self," Piaget said. "The self which cannot be isolated abides in the memory as a perception of symbols. We are conscious as a projection of self upon the receptive content of the senses. But it happens the self can be led astray—the self of a person or the self of a community. I wonder . . . "

"Stop trying to distract me with gobbledygook," Dasein said. "You're trying to change the subject, avoid . . . "

"A . . . void," Piaget said. "Ah, yes. the void is very pertinent to this. Einstein cannot be confined to mathematics. All phenomenal existence is transitory, relative. No particular thing is real. It is passing into something else at every moment."

Dasein pushed himself upright in the bed. Had the old doctor gone crazy?

"Performance alone doesn't produce the result," Piaget said. "You're grasping at absolutes. To seek any fixed thing, however, is to deal in false imagination. You're trying to strain soap from the water with your fingers. Duality is a delusion."

Dasein shook his head from side to side. The man was making no sense at all.

"I see you are confused," Piaget said. "You don't really understand your own intellectual energy. You walk on narrow paths. I offer you new orbits of . . . "

"You can stop that," Dasein said. He remembered the lake then, the husky feminine voice saying: "*There's only one thing to do.*" And Jenny: "*We're doing it.*"

"You must adapt to conditional thought," Piaget said. "In that way, you'll be able to understand relative self-existence and express the relative truth of whatever you perceive. You have the ability to do it. I can see that. Your insight into the violent actions which surround . . . "

"Whatever you're doing to me, you won't stop it, will you?" Dasein asked. "You keep pushing and pushing and . . . "

"Who pushes?" Piaget asked. "Are you not the one exerting the greatest . . . "

"Damn you! Stop it!"

Piaget looked at him silently.

"Einstein," Dasein muttered. "Relativity . . . absolutes . . . intellectual energy . . . phenomenal . . . " He broke off as his mind lurched momentarily into a speed of computation very like what he had experienced when deciding to hurdle the gap in the bridge.

It's sweep-rate, Dasein thought. *It's like hunting submarines—in the mind. It's how many search units you can put to the job and how fast they can travel.*

As quickly as it had come, the sensation was gone. But Dasein had never felt as shaken in his life. No immediate danger had triggered this ability . . . not this time.

Narrow paths, he thought. He looked up at Piaget in wonder. There was more here than fell upon the ears. Could that be the way Santarogans thought? Dasein shook his head. It didn't seem possible . . . or likely.

"May I elaborate?" Piaget asked.

Dasein nodded.

"You will have remarked the blunt way we state our relative truths for sales purposes," Piaget said. "Conditional thought rejects any other approach. Mutual respect is implicit, then, in conditional thought. Contrast the market approach of those who sent you to spy upon us. They have . . . "

"How fast can you think?" Dasein asked.

"Fast?" Piaget shrugged. "As fast as necessary."

As fast as necessary, Dasein thought.

"May I continue?" Piaget asked.

Again, Dasein nodded.

"It has been noted," Piaget said, "that sewer-peak-load times tend to match station breaks on TV—an elementary fact you can recognize with only the briefest reflection. But it's only a short step from this elementary fact to the placement of flow meters in the sewers as a quite accurate check on the available listening units at any given moment. I've no doubt this already is being done; it's so obvious. Now, reflect a moment on the basic attitudes toward their fellowmen of people who would do this sort of thing, as opposed to those who could not find it in themselves to do it."

Dasein cleared his throat. Here was the core of Santaroga's indictment against the *outside*. How did you use people? With dignity? Or did you tap their most basic functions for your own purposes? The *outside* began to appear more and more as a place of irritating emptiness and contrived blandishments.

I'm really beginning to see things as a Santarogan, Dasein thought. There was a sense of victory in the thought. It was what he had set out to do as part of his job.

"It isn't surprising," Piaget said, "to find the 'N-square' law from warfare being applied to advertising and politics—other kinds of warfare, you see—with no real conversion problem from one field to the other. Each has its concepts of concentration and exposure. The mathematics of differentials and predictions apply equally well, no matter the field of battle."

Armies, Dasein thought. He focused on Piaget's moving lips, wondering suddenly how the subject had been changed to such a different field. Had Piaget done it deliberately? They'd been talking about Santaroga's blind side, its fears . . .

"You've given me food for speculation," Piaget said. "I'm going to leave you alone for a while and see if I can come up with something constructive. There's a call bell at the head of your bed. The nurses are not on this floor, but one can be here quite rapidly in an emergency. They'll look in on you from time to time. Would you like something to read? May I send you anything?"

Something constructive? Dasein wondered. *What does he mean?*

"How about some copies of our valley newspaper?" Piaget asked.

"Some writing paper and a pen," Dasein said. He hesitated, then: "And the papers—yes."

"Very well. Try to rest. You appear to be regaining some of your strength, but don't overdo it."

Piaget turned, strode out of the room.

Presently, a red-haired nurse bustled in with a stack of newspapers, a ruled tablet and a dark green ballpoint pen. She deposited them on his nightstand, said: "Do you want your bed straightened?"

"No, thanks."

Dasein found his attention caught by her striking resemblance to Al Marden.

"You're a Marden," he said.

"So what else is new?" she asked and left him.

Well, get her! Dasein thought.

He glanced at the stack of newspapers, remembering his search through Santaroga for the paper's office. They had come to him so easily they'd lost some of their allure. He slipped out of bed, found his knees had lost some of their weakness.

The canned food caught his eye.

Dasein rummaged in the box, found an applesauce, ate it swiftly while the food still was redolent with Jaspers. Even as he ate, he hoped this would return him to that level of clarity and speed of thought he'd experienced at the bridge and, briefly, with Piaget.

The applesauce eased his hunger, left him vaguely restless—nothing else.

Was it losing its kick? he wondered. Did it require more and more of the stuff each time? Or was he merely becoming acclimated?

Hooked?

He thought of Jenny pleading with him, cajoling. *A consciousness fuel. What in the name of God had Santaroga discovered?*

Dasein stared out the window at the path of boundary hills visible through the trees. A fire somewhere beneath his field of view sent smoke spiraling above the ridge. Dasein stared at the smoke, feeling an oddly compulsive mysticism, a deeply primitive sensation about that unseen fire. There was a spirit signature written in the smoke, something out of his own genetic past. No fear accompanied the sensation. It was, instead, as though he had been reunited with some part of himself cut off since childhood.

Pushing back at the surface of childhood, he thought.

He realized then that a Santarogan did not cut off his primitive past; he contained it within a membranous understanding.

How far do I go in becoming a Santarogan before I turn back? he wondered. *I have a duty to Selador and the ones who hired me. When do I make my break?*

The thought filled him with a deep revulsion against returning to the *outside*. But he had to do it. There was a thick feeling of nausea in his throat, a pounding ache at his temples. He thought of the irritant emptiness of the *outside*—piecemeal debris of lives, egos with sham patches, a world almost devoid of anything to make the soul rise and soar.

There was no substructure to life *outside*, he thought, no underlying sequence to tie it all together. There was only a shallow, glittering roadway signposted with flashy, hypnotic diversions. And behind the glitter—only the bare board structure of props . . . and desolation.

I can't go back, he thought. He turned to his bed, threw himself across it. *My duty—I must go back. What's happening to me? Have I waited too long?*

Had Piaget lied about the Jaspers effect?

Dasein turned onto his back, threw an arm across his eyes. What was the chemical essence of Jaspers? Selador could be no help there; the stuff didn't travel.

I knew that, Dasein thought. *I knew it all along*.

He took his arm away from his eyes. No doubt of what he'd been doing: avoiding his own responsibility. Dasein looked at the doors in the wall facing him—kitchen, lab . . .

A sigh lifted his chest.

Cheese would be the best carrier, he knew. It held the Jaspers essence longest. The lab . . . and some cheese.

Dasein rang the bell at the head of his bed.

A voice startled him coming from directly behind his head: "Do you wish a nurse immediately?"

Dasein turned, saw a speaker grill in the wall. "I'd . . . like some Jaspers cheese," he said.

"Oh . . . Right away, sir." There was delight in that feminine voice no electronic reproduction could conceal.

Presently, the red-haired nurse with the stamp of the Marden genes on her face shouldered her way into the room carrying a tray. She placed the tray atop the papers on Dasein's nightstand.

"There you are, doctor," she said. "I brought you some crackers, too."

"Thanks," Dasein said.

She turned at the doorway before leaving: "Jenny will be delighted to hear this."

"Jenny's awake?"

"Oh, yes. Most of her problem was an allergenic reaction to the aconite. We've purged the poison from her system and she's making a very rapid recovery. She wants to get up. That's always a good sign."

"How'd the poison get in the food?" Dasein asked.

"One of the student nurses mistook it for a container of MSG. She . . ."

"But how'd it get in the kitchen?"

"We haven't determined yet. No doubt it was some silly accident."

"No doubt," Dasein muttered.

"Well, you eat your cheese and get some rest," she said. "Ring if you need anything."

The door closed briskly behind her.

Dasein looked at the golden block of cheese. Its Jaspers odor clamored at his nostrils. He broke off a small corner of the cheese in his fingers, touched it to his tongue. Dasein's senses jumped to attention. Without conscious volition, he took the cheese into his mouth, swallowed it: smooth, soothing flavor. A clear-headed alertness surged through him.

Whatever else happens, Dasein thought, *the world has to find out about this stuff*.

He swung his feet out of bed, stood up. A pulsing ache throbbed through his forehead. He closed his eyes, felt the world spin, steadied himself against the bed.

The vertigo passed.

Dasein found a cheese knife on the tray, cut a slice off the golden brick, stopped his hand from conveying the food to his mouth.

The body does it, he thought. He felt the strength of the physical demand, promised himself more of the cheese . . . later. First—the lab.

It was pretty much as he'd expected: sparse, but sufficient. There was a good centrifuge, a microtome, a binocular microscope with controlled illumination, gas burner, ranks of clean test tubes—all the instruments and esoteria of the trade.

Dasein found a container of sterile water, another of alcohol, put bits of the cheese into solution. He started a culture flask, made a control slide and examined it under the microscope.

A threadlike binding structure within the cheese leaped into vision. As he raised magnification, the threads resolved into spirals of elongated structure that resembled cells which had been blocked from normal division.

Dasein sat back, puzzled. The thread pattern bore a resemblance to fungoid mycelium spawn. This agreed with his early surmise; he was dealing with a type of fungus growth.

What was the active agent, though?

He closed his eyes to think, realized he was trembling with fatigue.

Easy does it, he thought. *You're not a well man.*

Some of the experiments required time to mature, he told himself. They could wait. He made his way back to bed, stretched out on the blankets. His left hand reached out to the cheese, broke off a chunk.

Dasein became aware of his own action as he swallowed the cheese. He looked at the crumbled specks on his fingers, rubbed them, felt the oily smoothness. A delicious sense of well-being spread through his body.

The body does it, Dasein thought. *Of itself, the body does it. Could the body go out and kill a man? Very likely.*

He felt sleep winding about his consciousness. The body needed sleep. The body would have sleep.

The mind, though, built a dream—of trees growing to gigantic size as he watched them. They leaped up with swift vitality. Their branches swept out, leafed, fruited. All basked under a sun the color of golden cheese.

12

SUNSET WAS burning orange in the west when Dasein awoke. He lay, his head turned toward the windows, looking out at the blazing sky, his attention caught in a spell akin to ancient sun worship. The ship of life was headed down to its daily rest. Soon, steel darkness would claim the land.

A click sounded behind Dasein. Artificial light flooded the room. He turned, the spell broken.

Jenny stood just inside the door. She wore a long green robe that reached almost to her ankles. Green slippers covered her feet.

"It's about time you woke up," she said.

Dasein stared at her as at a stranger. He could see it was the same Jenny he loved—her long black hair caught in a red ribbon, full lips slightly parted, dimple showing in her cheek—but furtive smoke drifted in her blue eyes. There was the calm of a goddess about her.

Something eternally of the past moved her body as Jenny stepped farther into the room.

A thrill of fear shot through Dasein. It was the fear an Attic peasant might have experienced before a priestess at Delphi. She was beautiful . . . and deadly.

"Aren't you going to ask how I am?" she asked.

"I can see you're all right," he said.

She took another step toward him, said: "Clara brought Jersey Hofstedder's car over and left it for you. It's down in the garage."

Dasein thought of that beautifully machined automobile—another bauble to attract him.

"And what have you brought—this time?" he asked.

"Gil!"

"There's no food in your hands," he said. "Is it a poisoned hatpin, perhaps?" Tears flooded her eyes.

"Stay away from me," he said. "I love you."

She nodded. "I do love you. And . . . I've felt how dangerous I could be . . . to you. There've been . . . " She shook her head. "I knew I had to stay away from you. But not any more. Not now."

"So it's all over," he said. "Let bygones be bygones. Wouldn't a gun be quicker?"

She stamped a foot. "Gil, you're impossible!"

"*I'm* impossible?"

"Have you changed?" she whispered. "Don't you feel any . . . "

"I still love you," he said. "Stay away from me. I love you."

She bit her lip.

"Wouldn't it be kindest to do it while I'm asleep?" he asked. "Never let me know who . . . "

"Stop it!"

Abruptly, she ripped off the green robe, revealing a white, lace-edged night-gown beneath. She dropped the robe, pulled the gown over her head, threw it on the floor, stood there naked, glaring at him.

"See?" she said. "Nothing here but a woman! Nothing here but the woman who loves you." Tears ran down her cheeks. "No poison in my hands . . . Oh, Gil . . . " His name came out as a wail.

Dasein forced his gaze away from her. He knew he couldn't look at her—lovely, lithe, desirable—and retain any coolness of judgment. She was beautiful and deadly—the ultimate bait Santaroga offered.

There was a rustling of cloth near the door.

He whirled.

She stood once more clothed in the green robe. Her cheeks were scarlet, lips trembling, eyes downcast. Slowly, she raised her eyes, met his stare.

"I have no shame with you, Gil," she said. "I love you. I want no secrets between us at all—no secrets of the flesh . . . no secrets of any kind."

Dasein tried to swallow past a lump in his throat. The goddess was vulnerable. It was a discovery that caused an ache in his chest.

"I feel the same way," he said. "Jen . . . you'd better leave now. If you don't . . . I might just grab you and rape you."

She tried to smile, failed, whirled away and ran out of the room.

The door slammed. There was a moment's silence. The door opened. Piaget stood in the opening looking back into the foyer. The sound of the elevator doors closing came clearly to Dasein. Piaget came in, closed the door.

"What happened with you two?" he asked.

"I think we just had a fight and made up," Dasein said. "I'm not sure."

Piaget cleared his throat. There was a look of confidence in his round face, Dasein thought. It was not a judgment he could be sure of, however, in the unmapped land of concentration. At any rate, the look was gone now, replaced by a wide-eyed stare of interest in Dasein.

"You're looking vastly improved," Piaget said. "You've a better color in your face. Feeling stronger?"

"As a matter of fact I am."

Piaget glanced at the remains of the cheese on the nightstand, crossed and sniffed at it. "Bit stale," he said. "I'll have a fresh block sent up."

"You do that," Dasein said.

"Care to let me look at your bandages?" Piaget asked.

"I thought we were going to let Burdeaux work on my bandages."

"Win had a small emergency at home. His daughter's getting married tomorrow, you know. He'll be along later."

"I didn't know."

"Just getting the new couple's house built in time," Piaget said. "Bit of a delay because we decided to build four at once in the same area. Good location—you and Jenny might like one of them."

"That's nice," Dasein said. "You all get together and build a house for the newlyweds."

"We take care of our own," Piaget said. "Let's look at those bandages, shall we?"

"Let's."

"Glad to see you're being more reasonable," Piaget said. "Be right back." He went out the lab door, returned in a moment with a supply cart, stationed the cart beside Dasein's bed, began cutting away the head bandages.

"See you've been puttering around the lab," Piaget said.

Dasein winced as air hit the burn on his cheek. "Is that what I've been doing, puttering?"

"What have you been doing?" Piaget asked. He bent, examined Dasein's cheek. "This is coming along fine. Won't even leave a scar, I do believe."

"I'm looking for the active agent in Jaspers," Dasein said.

"Been several attempts along that line," Piaget said. "Trouble is we all get too busy with more immediate problems."

"You've had a try at it?" Dasein asked.

"When I was younger."

Dasein waited for the head bandage to be tied off before asking: "Do you have notes, any summary of . . ."

"No notes. Never had time."

Piaget began working on Dasein's right arm.

"But what did you find out?"

"Got a broth rich in amino acids," Piaget said. "Yeastlike. You're going to have a scar on this arm, nothing alarming, and you're healing rapidly. You can thank Jaspers for that.''

"What?" Dasein looked up at him, puzzled.

"Nature gives; nature takes away. The Jaspers change in body chemistry makes you more susceptible to allergenic reactions, but your body will heal five to ten times faster than it would *outside*.''

Dasein looked down at his exposed arm. Pink new flesh already covered the burned area. He could see the scar puckering Piaget had noted.

"What change in body chemistry?" Dasein asked.

"Well, mostly a better hormone balance," Piaget said. "Closer to what you find in an embryo.''

"That doesn't square with the allergy reactions," Dasein protested.

"I'm not saying it's a simple thing," Piaget said. "Hold your arm out here. Steady now.''

Dasein waited for the bandage to be completed, then: "What about structure and . . .''

"Something between a virus and a bacteria," Piaget said. "Fungusoid in some respects, but . . . ''

"I saw cell structure in a sample under the microscope.''

"Yes, but no nucleus. Some nuclear material, certainly, but it can be induced to form virusoid crystals.''

"Do the crystals have the Jaspers effect?''

"No. They can, however, be introduced into the proper environment and after suitable development they will produce the desired effect.''

"What environment?''

"You know what environment, Gilbert.''

"The Co-op's cave?''

"Yes." Piaget finished exposing Dasein's left arm. "Don't think you'll have as much scar tissue on this side.''

"What's unique about the cave environment?" Dasein asked.

"We're not certain.''

"Hasn't anybody ever tried to . . . ''

"We do have a great many *immediate* problems just to maintain ourselves, Gilbert," Piaget said.

Dasein looked down, watched Piaget finish the bandage on the left arm. *Maintain themselves?* he wondered.

"Is there any objection to my looking into it?" Dasein asked.

"When you find time—certainly not." Piaget restored instruments and material to the cart, pushed it aside. "There. I think we'll be able to take the bandages off tomorrow. You're progressing beautifully.''

"Am I really?''

Piaget smiled at him. "Insurance from the garage will take care of paying for your new car," he said. "I presume Jenny told you about the car.''

"She told me.''

"We're also replacing your clothing. Is there anything else?''

"How about replacing my freedom of choice?''

"You have freedom of choice, Gilbert, and a broader area from which to choose. Now, I have some . . . ''

"Keep your advice," Dasein said.

"Advice? I was about to say I have some rather interesting information for you.

Your suggestion that I look into the people you accuse of trying to kill you has borne some . . . ''

"My suggestion that *you* look?"

"I took the liberty of going ahead with your suggestion."

"So you hypnotized some of them," Dasein said. "Did you prepare a Davis chart on their suscept . . . ''

"I did *not* hypnotize them," Piaget snapped. "Will you be silent and listen?"

Dasein sighed, looked at the ceiling.

"I've interviewed several of these people," Piaget said. "The boy, Petey Jorick, first because he's a primary concern of mine, having just been released from . . . school. An extremely interesting fact emerges."

"Oh?"

"Each of these persons has a strong unconscious reason to fear and hate the *outside*."

"What?" Dasein turned a puzzled frown on Piaget.

"They weren't attacking you as Gilbert Dasein," Piaget said. "You were the *outsider*. There's a strong unresolved . . . ''

"You mean you consider this good and sufficient . . . ''

"The reasons are unconscious, as you suspected," Piaget said. "The structure of motivation, however . . . ''

"So Jenny both loves me and hates me . . . as an *outsider?*"

"Get one thing straight, Gilbert. Jenny did not try to harm you. It was a student nurse who . . . ''

"Jenny told me herself she prepared . . . ''

"Only in the broadest sense is that true," Piaget said. "She did go to the diet kitchen and order your food and watch while it was prepared. However, she couldn't keep an eye on every . . . ''

"And this . . . this hate of *outsiders*," Dasein said, "you think this is why some of your people tried to get me?"

"It's clearly indicated, Gilbert."

Dasein stared at him. Piaget believed this—no doubt of it.

"So all I have to watch out for as long as I live in Santaroga is people who hate outsiders?" Dasein asked.

"You have nothing to fear now at all," Piaget said. "You're no longer an outsider. You're one of us. And when you and Jenny marry . . . ''

"Of all the nonsense I've ever heard," Dasein said. "This takes all the honors! This . . . this kid, Petey, he just wanted to put an arrow through me because . . . ''

"He has a pathological fear of leaving the valley for college outside," Piaget said. "He'll overcome this, of course, but the emotions of childhood have more . . . ''

"The roach powder in the coffee," Dasein said. "That was just . . . ''

"That's a very unhappy case," Piaget said. "She fell in love with an outsider at college—much as Jenny did, I might add. The difference is that her friend seduced her and left her. She has a daughter who . . . ''

"My god! You really believe this crap," Dasein said. He pushed himself against the head of the bed, sat glaring at Piaget.

"Gilbert, I find this far easier to believe than I do your wild theory that Santaroga has mounted a concerted attack against you. After all, you yourself must see . . . ''

"Sure," Dasein said. "I want you to explain the accident at the bridge. I want to see how that . . . ''

"Easiest of all," Piaget said. "The young man in question was enamored of Jenny before you came on the scene."

"So he just waited for the moment when . . ."

"It was entirely on the unconscious level, that I assure you, Gilbert."

Dasein merely stared at him. The structure of rationalization Piaget had built up assumed for Dasein the shape of a tree. It was like the tree of his dream. There was the strong trunk protruding into daylight—consciousness. The roots were down there growing in darkness. The limbs came out and dangled prettily distracting leaves and fruit. It was a consistent structure despite its falsity.

There'd be no cutting it down, Dasein saw. The thing was too substantial. There were too many like it in the forest that was Santaroga. *"This is a tree, see? Doesn't it look like all the others?"*

"I think when you've had time to reflect," Piaget said. "you'll come to realize the truth of what . . ."

"Oh, no doubt," Dasein said.

"I'll, uh . . . I'll send you up some more fresh cheese," Piaget said. "Special stock."

"You do that," Dasein said.

"I quite understand," Piaget said. "You think you're being very cynical and wise right now. But you'll come around." He strode from the room.

Dasein continued to stare at the closed door long after Piaget had gone. The man couldn't see it, would never be capable of seeing it. No Santarogan could. Not even Jenny despite her love-sharpened awareness. Piaget's explanation was too easy to take. It'd be the official line.

I've got to get out of this crazy valley, Dasein thought.

He slipped out of bed just as the door opened and a hatless, chubby young student nurse entered with a tray.

"Oh, you're out of bed," she said. "Good."

She took the old tray off the nightstand, put the new one in its place, set the old one on a chair.

"I'll just straighten up your bed while you're out of it," she said.

Dasein stood to one side while she bustled abut the bed. Presently, she left, taking the old tray with her.

He looked at what she had brought—a golden wedge of cheese, crackers, a glass and a bottle of Jaspers beer.

In a surge of anger, Dasein hurled the cheese against the wall. He was standing there staring at the mess when a soothing sensation on his tongue made him realize he was licking the crumbs off his fingers.

Dasein stared at his own hand as though it belonged to another person. He consciously forced himself not to bend and recover the cheese from the floor, turned to the beer. There was an opener behind the bottle. He poured it into the glass, drank in swift gulps. Only when the glass was drained did he grow aware of the rich bouquet of Jaspers in the remaining drops of beer.

Fighting down a fit of trembling, Dasein put the glass on the nightstand, crawled into the bed as though seeking sanctuary.

His body refused to be denied. People didn't take Jaspers, he thought. Jaspers took people. He felt the expanding effect within his consciousness, sensed the thunder of a host jarring across the inner landscape of his psyche. Time lost its normal flow, became compressed and explosive.

Somewhere in a hospital room there were purposeful footsteps. The toggles of a switch slammed away from their connections to create darkness. A door closed.

Dasein opened his eyes to a window and starshine. In its illumination he saw a fresh wedge of cheese on his nightstand. The mess had been cleaned from wall and floor. He remembered Jenny's voice—soft, musical, rippling like dark water over rocks, a plaintive tremor in it.

Had Jenny been here in the dark?

He sensed no answer.

Dasein groped for the call buzzer at the head of his bed, pressed it.

A voice sounded from the speaker: "Do you wish a nurse?"

"What time is it?" Dasein asked.

"Three twenty-four a.m. Do you want a sleeping pill?"

"No . . . thanks."

He sat up, slid his feet to the floor, stared at the cheese.

"Did you just want the time?" the speaker asked.

"What does a full round of Jaspers cheese weigh?" he asked.

"The weight?" There was a pause, then: "They vary. The smaller ones weigh about thirty pounds. Why?"

"Send me a full round," he said.

"A full . . . Don't you have some now?"

"I want it for lab tests," he said, and he thought: *There! Let's see if Piaget was being honest with me.*

"You want it when you get up in the morning?"

"I'm up now. And get me a robe and some slippers if you can."

"Hadn't you better wait, doctor. If . . . "

"Check with Piaget if you must," Dasein said. "I want that round now."

"Very well." She sounded disapproving.

Dasein waited sitting on the edge of the bed. He stared out the window at the night. Absently, he broke off a chunk of the cheese on his nightstand, chewed it and swallowed.

Presently, the foyer door produced a wedge of light. A tall, gray-haired nurse entered, turned on the room's lights. She carried a large wheel of golden cheese still glistening in its wax sealer.

"This is thirty-six pounds of prime Jaspers cheese," she said. "Where shall I put it?" There were overtones of outrage and protest in her voice.

"Find a place for it on one of the lab benches," he said. "Where are the robe and slippers?"

"If you'll be patient, I'll get them for you," she said. She shouldered her way through the lab door, returned in a moment and crossed to a narrow door at the far end of the room, opened it to reveal a closet. From the closet she removed a green robe and a pair of black slippers which she dumped on the foot of Dasein's bed.

"Will that be all—sir?"

"That'll be all, for now."

"Hmmmph." She strode from the room, shut the foyer door with a final-comment thump.

Dasein took another bite of the cheese from his nightstand, put on the robe and slippers, went into the lab. The nurse had left the lights on. The round of cheese lay on an open metal bench at his right.

Alcohol won't kill it, he thought. *Otherwise, it couldn't be incorporated in the local beer. What does destroy it? Sunlight?*

He recalled the dim red light of the Co-op's cave.

Well, there were ways of finding out. He rolled back the sleeves of his gown, set to work.

Within an hour he had three-fourths of the round reduced to a milky solution in a carboy, set about feeding it through the centrifuge.

The first test tubes came out with their contents layered in a manner reminiscent of a chromatograph. Near the top lay a thin silver-gray band of material.

Dasein poured off the liquid, burned a hole in the bottom of a test tube and removed the solids intact by blowing into the hole he'd created. A bit of the gray material went on a slide and he examined it under the microscope.

There was the mycelium structure, distorted but recognizable. He smelled the slide. It was redolent of Jaspers. He put a hand to the microscope's variable light control, watched the specimen while rotating the control. Abruptly, the specimen began to shrivel and crystallize before his eyes.

Dasein looked at the light control. It was the spectrum-window type and, at this moment, was passing light in the Angstrom range 4000–5800. It was cutting off the red end, Dasein noted.

Another look through the microscope showed the specimen reduced to a white crystalline mass.

Sunlight, then.

What would do the job? he wondered. A bomb to open the cave? A portable sunlamp?

As he thought this, Dasein felt that the darkness outside the hospital parted to reveal a shape, a monster rising out of a black lake.

He shuddered, turned to the carboy of milky solution. Working mechanically, he put the rest of the solution through the centrifuge, separated the silver-gray band, collected the material in a dark brown bottle. The solution produced almost a pint of the Jaspers essence.

Dasein smelled the bottle—sharp and definite odor of Jaspers. He emptied the bottle into a shallow dish, caught a bit of the substance on a spatula, touched it to his tongue.

An electrifying sensation of distant fireworks exploded from his tastebuds through his spine. He felt he could see with the tip of his tongue or the tip of a finger. Dasein sensed his core of awareness becoming a steely kernel surrounded by desolation. He concentrated his energy, forced himself to look at the dish of Jaspers essence.

Empty.

What had destroyed it? How could it be empty.

He looked at the palm of his right hand. How close it was to his face! There were specks of silver gray against the pink flesh.

Tingling pulses of awareness began surging out from his throat and stomach, along his arms and legs. He felt that his entire skin came alight. There was a remote feeling of a body slipping to the floor, but he felt that the floor glowed wherever the body touched it.

I ate the entire dish of essence, he thought.

What would it do—the active agent from more than thirty pounds of Jaspers cheese? What would it do? What was it doing? Dasein felt this to be an even more interesting question.

What was it doing?

As he asked the question of himself, he experienced anguish. It wasn't fear, but pure anguish, a sense of losing his grip on reality.

The steely kernel of selfdom! Where was it?

Upon what fundament of reality did his selfdom sit? Frantically, Dasein tried to extend his awareness, experienced the direct sensation that he was projecting his own reality upon the universe. But there was a projection *of* the universe simultaneously. He followed the lines of this projection, felt them sweep through him as though through a shadow.

In this instant, he was lost, tumbling.

I was just a shadow, he thought.

The thought fascinated him. He remembered the shadow game of his childhood, wondered what forms of shadows he could project by distorting the core of self. The wondering produced the effect of shapes. Dasein sensed a screen of awareness, a shapeless outline upon it. He willed the shape to change.

A muscled, breast-beating hero took form there.

Dasein shifted his emphasis.

The shadow became a bent-shouldered, myopic scientist in a long gown. Another shift: It was naked Apollo racing over a landscape of feminine figures.

And again—a plodder bent beneath a shapeless load.

With a gulping sensation of *deitgrasp* Dasein realized he was projecting the only limits his finite being could know. It was an act of self-discovery that gave birth to a feeling of hope. It was an odd sort of hope, unfixed, disoriented, but definite in its existence—not a hope of discernment, but pure hope without boundaries, direction or attachments.

Hope itself.

It was a profound instant permitting him to grasp for a fleeting instant the structure of his own existence, his possibilities as a being.

A twisted, dented and distorted *something* crossed the field of Dasein's awareness. He recognized the kernel of selfdom. The thing had lost all useful shape. He discarded it, chuckling.

Who discarded it? Dasein wondered.

Who chuckles?

There was a pounding sound—feet upon a floor.

Voices.

He recognized the tones of the gray-haired nurse, but there was a tingling of panic in the sounds she made.

Piaget.

"Let's get him on the bed," Piaget said. The words were clear and distinct.

What was not distinct was the shape of a universe become blurred rainbows, nor the pressures of hands which blotted out the glowing sensation of his skin.

"It's difficult to become conscious about consciousness," Dasein muttered.

"Did he say something?" That was the nurse.

"I couldn't make it out." Piaget.

"Did you smell the Jaspers in there?" The nurse.

"I think he separated the essence out and took it."

"Oh, my god! What can we do?"

"Wait and pray. Bring me a straight-jacket and the emergency cart."

A straight-jacket? Dasein wondered. *What an odd request.*

He heard running footsteps. How loud they were! A door slammed. More voices. Such a rushing around!

His skin felt as though it were growing dark. Everything was being blotted out.

With an abrupt, jerking sensation, Dasein felt himself shrivel downward into an infant shape kicking, squalling, reaching outward, outward, fingers grasping.

"Give me a hand with him!" That was Piaget.

"What a mess!" Another male voice.

But Dasein already felt himself becoming a mouth, just a mouth. It blew out, out, out—such a wind. Surely, the entire world must collapse before this hurricane.

He was a board, rocking. A teeter-totter. Down and up—up and down.

A good run is better than a bad stand, he thought.

And he was running, running—breathless, gasping.

A bench loomed out of swirling clouds. He threw himself down on it, became the bench—another board. This one dipped down and down into a boiling green sea.

Life in a sea of unconsciousness, Dasein thought.

It grew darker and darker.

Death, he thought. *Here's the background against which I can know myself.*

The darkness dissolved. He was shooting upward, rebounding into a blinding glare.

Dark shapes moved in the glare.

"His eyes are open." that was the nurse.

A shadow reduced the glare. "Gilbert?" That was Piaget. "Gilbert, can you hear me? How much Jaspers did you take?""

Dasein tried to speak. His lips refused to obey.

The glare came back.

"We'll just have to guess." Piaget. "How much did that cheese weigh?"

"Thirty-six pounds." The nurse.

"The physical breakdown is massive." Piaget. "Have a respirator standing by."

"Doctor, what if he . . . " The nurse apparently couldn't complete the statement of her fear.

"I'm . . . ready." Piaget.

Ready for what? Dasein wondered.

By concentrating, he found he could make the glare recede. It resolved momentarily into a tunnel of clarity with Piaget at the far end of it. Dasein lay helplessly staring, unable to move as Piaget advanced on him carrying a carboy that fumed and smoked.

Acid, Dasein thought, interpreting the nurse's words. *If I die, they'll dissolve me and wash me away down a drain. No body, no evidence.*

The tunnel collapsed.

The sensation of glare expanded, contracted.

Perhaps, I can no longer be, Dasein thought.

It grew darker.

Perhaps, I cannot do, he thought.

Darker yet.

Perhaps, I cannot have, he thought.

Nothing.

13

"IT WAS kill or cure," the yellow god said.

"I wash my hands of you," said the white god.

"What I offered, you did not want," the red god accused.

"You make me laugh," said the black god.

"There is no tree that's you," the green god said.

"We are going now and only one of us will return," the gods chorused.

There was a sound of a clearing throat.

"Why don't you have faces?" Dasein asked. "You have color but no faces."

"What?" It was a rumbling, vibrant voice.

"You're a funny sounding god," Dasein said. He opened his eyes, looked up into Burdeaux's features, caught a puzzled scowl on the dark face.

"I'm no sort of god at all," Burdeaux said. "What're you saying, Doctor Gil? You having another nightmare?"

Dasein blinked, tried to move his arms. Nothing happened. He lifted his head, looked down at his body. He was bound tightly in a restraining jacket. There was a stink of disinfectants, of Jaspers and of something repellent and sour in the room. He looked around. It was still the isolation suite. His head fell back to the pillow.

"Why'm I tied down like this?" Dasein whispered.

"What did you say, sir?"

Dasein repeated his question.

"Well, Doctor Gil, we didn't want you to hurt yourself."

"When . . . when can I be released?"

"Doctor Larry said to free you as soon as you woke up."

"I'm . . . awake."

"I know that, sir. I was just . . . " He shrugged, began unfastening the bindings on the sleeves of the jacket.

"How long?" Dasein whispered.

"How long you been here like this?"

Dasein nodded.

"Three whole days now, and a little more. It's almost noon."

The bindings were untied. Burdeaux helped Dasein to a sitting position, unlaced the back, slipped the jacket off.

Dasein's back felt raw and sensitive. His muscles responded as though they belonged to a stranger. This was an entirely new body, Dasein thought.

Burdeaux came up with a white hospital gown, slipped it onto Dasein, tied the back.

"You want the nurse to come rub your back?" he asked. "You've a couple of red places there don't look too good."

"No . . . no thanks."

Dasein moved one of the stranger's arms. A familiar hand came up in front of his face. It was his own hand. How could it be his own hand, he wondered, when the muscles of the arm belonged to a stranger?

"Doctor Larry said no one ever took that much Jaspers ever before all at once," Burdeaux said. "Jaspers is a good thing, sir, but everybody knows you can get too much."

"Does . . . is Jenny . . . "

"She's fine, Doctor Gil. She's been worried sick about you. We all have."

Dasein moved one of the stranger's legs, then the other until they hung over the edge of the bed. He looked down at his own knees. It was very odd.

"Here, now," Burdeaux said. "Best you stay in bed."

"I've . . . I . . . "

"You want to go to the bathroom? Best I bring you the bedpan."

"No . . . I . . . " Dasein shook his head. Abruptly, he realized what was wrong. The body was hungry.

"Hungry," he said.

"Well, why didn't you say so? Got food right here waiting."

Burdeaux lifted a bowl, held it in front of Dasein. The rich aroma of Jaspers enveloped him. Dasein reached toward the bowl, but Burdeaux said, "Best let me feed you, Doctor Gil. You don't look too steady."

Dasein sat patiently, allowed himself to be fed. He could feel strength gathering in the body. It was a bad fit, this body, he decided. It had been draped loosely on his psyche.

It occurred to him to wonder what the body was eating—in addition to the Jaspers, which surrounded him and pervaded him with its presence. Oatmeal, the tongue said. Jaspers honey and Jaspers cream.

"There's a visitor waiting to see you," Burdeaux said when the bowl was empty.

"Jenny?"

"No . . . a Doctor Selador."

Selador! The name exploded on Dasein's conscience. Selador had trusted him, depended on him.

Selador had sent a gun through the mails.

"You feel up to seeing him?" Burdeaux asked.

"You . . . don't mind if I see him?" Dasein asked.

"Mind? Why should I mind, sir?"

Burdeaux's not the you *I meant*, Dasein thought.

There arose in Dasein then an urge to send Selador away. Such an easy thing to do. Santaroga would insulate him from the Seladors of the world. A simple request to Burdeaux was all it would take.

"I'll . . . uh, see him," Dasein said. He looked around the room. "Could you help me into a robe and . . . is there a chair I could . . . "

"Why don't I put you in a wheelchair, sir? Doctor Larry had one sent up for when you awakened. He didn't want you exerting yourself. You're not to get tired, understand?"

"Yes . . . yes, I understand. A wheelchair."

Presently, Dasein's bad-fit body was in the wheelchair. Burdeaux had gone to bring Selador, leaving the chair at the far end of the room from the foyer door. Dasein found himself facing a pair of French doors that opened onto a sundeck.

He felt he had been left alone in a brutally exposed position, his soul naked, wretched with fear. There was a heavy load on him, he thought. He felt embarrassment at the prospect of meeting Selador, and a special order of fright. Selador saw through pretense and sham. You could wear no mask before Selador. He was the psychoanalysts' psychoanalyst.

Selador will humiliate me, Dasein thought. *Why did I agree to see him? He will prod me and I will react. My reaction will tell him everything he wants to know about me . . . about my failure.*

Dasein felt then his sanity had been corroded into a pitted shell, a thing of tinsel and fantasy. Selador would stamp upon it with the harsh, jolting dynamics of his aliveness.

The foyer door opened.

Slowly, forcing himself to it, Dasein turned his head toward the door.

Selador stood in the opening, tall, hawk-featured, the dark skin and wildness of India encased in a silver-gray tweed suit, a touch of the same silver at the temples.

Dasein had the sudden blurred sensation of having seen this face in another life, the lancet eyes peering from beneath a turban. It had been a turban with a red jewel in it.

Dasein shook his head. Madness.

"Gilbert," Selador said, striding across the room. "In the name of heaven, what have you done to yourself now?" The precise accents of Oxford hammered each word into Dasein's ears. "They said you were badly burned."

And thus it starts, Dasein thought.

"I . . . my arms and hands," Dasein said. "And a bit about the face."

"I arrived only this morning," Selador said. "We were quite worried about you, you know. No word from you for days."

He stopped in front of Dasein, blocking off part of the view of the sundeck.

"I must say you look a fright, Gilbert. There don't appear to be any scars on your face, though."

Dasein put a hand to his cheek. It was his cheek suddenly, not a stranger's. The skin felt smooth, new.

"There's the damnedest musky smell about this place," Selador said. "Mind if I open these doors?"

"No . . . no, go right ahead."

Dasein found himself wrestling with the feeling that Selador was not Selador. There was a shallowness to the man's speech and mannerisms all out of character with the Selador of Dasein's memory. Had Selador changed in some way?

"Lovely sunny day," Selador said. "Why don't I wheel you out on this deck for a bit of air. Do you good."

Panic seized Dasein's throat. That deck—it was a place of menace. He tried to speak, to object. They couldn't go out there. No words came.

Selador took the silence for agreement, wheeled Dasein's chair out the door. There was a slight jolt at the sill and they were on the deck.

Sunlight warmed Dasein's head. A breeze almost devoid of Jaspers washed his skin, cleared his head. He said: "Don't you . . . "

"Doesn't this air feel invigorating?" Selador asked. He stopped at a shallow parapet, the edge of the roof. "There. You can admire the view and I can sit on this ledge."

Selador sat down, put a hand on the back of Dasein's chair. "I would imagine that ward is wired for sound," Selador said. "I do not believe they can have listening devices out here, however."

Dasein gripped the wheels of his chair, afraid it might lurch forward, propel him off the roof. He stared down at a paved parking area, parked cars, lawn, strips of flowers, trees. The sense of Selador's words came to him slowly.

"Wired . . . for . . . " He turned, met amused inquiry in the dark eyes.

"Obviously, you're not quite yourself yet," Selador said. "Understandable. You've been through a terrible ordeal. That's obvious. I'll have you out of this place, though, as soon as you're able to travel. Set your mind at rest. You'll be safe in a *normal* hospital at Berkeley before the week's out."

Dasein's emotions boiled, an arena of dispute. *Safe!* What a reassuring word. *Leave?* He couldn't leave! But he had to leave. *Outside? Go to that hideous place?*

"Have you been drugged, Gilbert?" Selador asked. "You appear . . . so . . . so . . . "

"I've . . . I'm all right."

"Really, you're behaving rather oddly. You haven't asked me once what we found on the leads you provided."

"What . . . "

"The source of their petrol proved to be a dud. All quite normal . . . provided you appreciate their economic motives. Cash deal with an independent producer. The State Department of Agriculture gives their cheese and the other products of their Cooperative a clean bill of health. The real estate board, however, is interested that no one but Santarogans can buy property in the valley. It may be they've violated antidiscriminatory legislation with . . . "

"No," Dasein said. "They . . . nothing that obvious."

"Ah, ha! You speak in the fashion of a man who has discovered the closeted skeleton. Well, Gilbert, what is it?"

Dasein felt he'd been seized by a vampire of duty. It would drain the blood from him. Selador would feed on it. He shook his head from side to side.

"Are you ill, Gilbert? Am I wearying you?"

"No. As long as I take it slowly . . . Doctor, you must understand, I've . . . "

"Do you have notes, Gilbert? Perhaps I could read your report and . . . "

"No . . . fire."

"Oh, yes. The doctor, this Piaget, said something about your truck burning. Everything up in smoke, I suppose?"

"Yes."

"Well, then, Gilbert, we'll have to get it from your lips. Is there an opening we can use to break these people?"

Dasein thought of the greenhouses—child labor. He thought of the statistical few Santarogans Jaspers had destroyed. He thought of the narcotic implications in the Jaspers products. It was all there—destruction for Santaroga.

"There must be something," Selador said. "You've lasted much longer than the others. Apparently, you've been given the freedom of the region. I'm sure you must have discovered something."

Lasted much longer than the others, Dasein thought. There was naked revelation in the phrase. As though he had participated in them, Dasein saw the discussions which had gone into choosing him for this project. *"Dasein has connections in the valley—a girl. That may be the edge we need. Certainly, it gives us reason to hope he'll last longer than the others."*

It had been something like that, Dasein knew. There was a callousness in it that repelled him.

"Were there more than two?" he asked.

"Two? Two what, Gilbert?"

"Two other investigators . . . before me?"

"I don't see where that . . . "

"Were there?"

"Well . . . that's very discerning of you, Gilbert. Yes, there were more than two. Eight or nine, I suspect."

"Why . . . "

"Why weren't you told? We wanted to imbue you with caution, but we saw no need to terrify you."

"But you thought they were murdered here . . . by Santarogans?"

"It was all exceedingly mysterious, Gilbert. We were not at all sure." He studied Dasein, eyes open wide and probing. "That's it, eh? Murder. Are we in peril right now? Do you have the weapon I . . . "

"If it were only that simple," Dasein said.

"In heaven's name, Gilbert, what is it? You must have found something. I had such high hopes for you."

High hopes for me, Dasein thought. Again, it was a phrase that opened a door on secret conversations. How could Selador be that transparent? Dasein found himself shocked by the shallowness of the man. Where was the omnipotent psychoanalyst? How could he have changed so profoundly?

"You . . . you people were just using me," Dasein said. As he spoke, he recalled Al Marden's accusation. Marden had seen this . . . yes.

"Now, Gilbert, that's no attitude to take. Why, just before I left to come here, Meyer Davidson was inquiring after you. You recall Davidson, the agent for the investment corporation behind the chain stores? He was very much taken with you, Gilbert. He told me he was thinking of making a place for you on his staff."

Dasein stared at Selador. The man couldn't be serious.

"That would be quite a step up in the world for you, Gilbert."

Dasein suppressed an urge to laugh. He had the odd sensation of being detached from his past and able to study a pseudoperson, a might-have-been creature who was himself. The other Dasein would have leaped at this offer. The new Dasein saw through the offer to the true opinion Selador and his cronies held for "*that useful, but not very bright person, Gilbert Dasein.*"

"Have you had a look at Santaroga?" Dasein asked. He wondered if Selador had seen Clara Scheler's used car lot or the advertisements in the store windows.

"This morning, while I was waiting for visiting hours with you, I drove around a bit," Selador said.

"What did you think of the place?"

"My candid opinion? An odd sort of village. When I inquired directions of a native—their language is so brusque and . . . odd. Not at all like . . . well, it's not English, of course, full of Americanisms, but . . . "

"They have a language like their cheese," Dasein said. "Sharp and full of tang."

"Sharp! A very good choice of word."

"A community of individuals, wouldn't you say?" Dasein asked.

"Perhaps . . . but with a certain sameness to them. Tell me, Gilbert, does this have something to do with why you were sent here?"

"This?"

"These questions. I must say, you're talking like . . . well, damned if you don't sound like a native." A forced laugh escaped his dark lips. "Have you gone native?"

The question, coming from that darkly eastern face, couched in that Oxford accent, struck Dasein as supremely amusing. Selador, of all people! To ask such a question.

Laughter bubbled from Dasein.

Selador misinterpreted the response. "Well," he said. "I should hope you hadn't."

"Humanity ought to be the first order of interest for humans," Dasein said.

Again, Selador misinterpreted. "Ah, and you studied the Santarogans like the excellent psychologist you are. Good. Well, then—tell it in your own way."

"I'll put it another way," Dasein said. "To have freedom, you must know how to use it. There's a distinct possibility some people hunt freedom in such a way they become the slaves of freedom."

"That's all very philosophical, I'm sure," Selador said. "How does it apply to finding justice for our sponsors?"

"Justice?"

"Certainly, justice. They were lured into this valley and cheated. They spent large sums of money here and got no return on it whatsoever. They're not people to take such treatment lightly."

"Lured?" Dasein said. "No one would sell to them, that I'm sure. How were they lured? For that matter, how did they acquire a lease on . . . "

"This isn't pertinent, Gilbert."

"Yes, it is. How'd they get a lease on Santaroga land?"

Selador sighed. "Very well. If you insist. They forced a competitive bid on some excess State property and put in a bid . . . "

"One they were sure no one else would match," Dasein said. He chuckled. "Did they have a market survey?"

"They had a good idea how many people live here."

"But what kind of people?"

"What're you trying to say, Gilbert?"

"Santaroga's very like a Greek *polis*," Dasein said. "This is a community of individuals, not a collectivity. Santarogans are not anthill slaves to grubs and grubbing. This is a *polis*, small enough to meet human needs. Their first interest is in human beings. Now, as to justice for . . . "

"Gilbert, you're talking very strangely."

"Hear me, please, doctor."

"Very well, but I hope you'll make some sense out of this . . . this . . . "

"Justice," Dasein said. "These sponsors you mention, and the government they control, are less interested in justice than they are in public order. They have stunted imaginations from too-long and too-intimate association with an ingrown system of self-perpetuating precedents. Do you want to know how they and their machinations appear to a Santarogan?"

"Let me remind you, Gilbert, this is one of the reasons you were sent here."

Dasein smiled. Selador's accusatory tone brought not a twinge of guilt.

"Raw power," Dasein said. "That's how the *outside* appears to a Santarogan. A place of raw power. Money and raw power have taken over there."

"Outside," Selador said. "What an interesting emphasis you give to that interesting word."

"Raw power is movement without a governor," Dasein said. "It'll run wild and destroy itself with all about it. That's a civilization of battlefields out there. They have special names: market area, trade area, court, election, senate, auction, strike—but they're still battlefields. There's no denying it because every one can invoke the full gamut of weaponry from words to guns."

"I do believe you're defending these Santaroga rascals," Selador said.

"Of course I'm defending them! I've had my eyes opened here, I tell you. I lasted much longer, did I? You had such high hopes for me! How can you be so damn' transparent?"

"Now you see here, Gilbert!" Selador stood up, glared down at Dasein.

"You know what gets to me, really gets to me?" Dasein asked. "Justice! You're all so damned interested in putting a cloak of justice and legality on your frauds! You give me a . . . "

"Doctor Gil?"

It was Burdeaux's voice calling from the doorway behind him. Dasein yanked back on his chair's left wheel, pushed on the right wheel. The chair whirled. All in the same instant, Dasein saw Burdeaux standing in the French doors, felt his chair hit something. He turned his head toward Selador in time to see a pair of feet disappear over the edge of the roof. There was a long, despairing cry terminated by the most sickening, wet thud Dasein had ever heard.

Burdeaux was suddenly beside him, leaning on the parapet to peer down at the parking area.

"Oh my goodness," Burdeaux said. "Oh, my goodness, what a terrible accident."

Dasein lifted his hands, looked at them—*his* hands. *I'm not strong enough to've done that*, he thought. *I've been ill. I'm not strong enough.*

14

"A MAJOR contributing factor to the accident," Piaget said, "was the victim's own foolishness in standing that close to the edge of the roof."

The inquest had been convened in Dasein's hospital room—"Because it is at the scene of the accident and as a convenience to Doctor Dasein, who is not fully recovered from injuries and shock."

A special investigator had been sent from the State Attorney General's office, arriving just before the inquest convened at ten a.m. The investigator, a William Garrity, obviously was known to Piaget. They had greeted each other "Bill" and "Larry" at the foot of Dasein's bed. Garrity was a small man with an appearance of fragility about him, sandy hair, a narrow face immersed in a mask of diffidence.

Presiding was Santaroga's Coroner, a Negro Dasein had not seen before this morning—Leroy Cos: kinky gray hair and a square, blocky face of remote dignity. He wore a black suit, had held himself apart from the preinquest bustle until the tick of ten o'clock when he had seated himself at a table provided for him, rapped once with a pencil and said: "We will now come to order."

Spectators and witnesses had seated themselves in folding chairs brought in for the occasion. Garrity shared a table with an Assistant District Attorney who, it developed, was a Nis, Swarthout Nis, a man with the family's heavy eyelids, wide mouth and sandy hair, but without the deeply cleft chin.

In the two days since the tragedy, Dasein had found his emotions embroiled with a growing anger against Selador—*the fool, the damned fool, getting himself killed that way.*

Piaget, seated in the witness chair, summed it up for Dasein.

"In the first place," Piaget said, a look of stern indignation on his round face, "he had no business taking Doctor Dasein outside. I had explained Doctor Dasein's physical condition quite clearly."

Garrity, the State's investigator, was permitted a question: "You saw the accident, Doctor Piaget?"

"Yes. Mr. Burdeaux, having noted Doctor Selador wheel my patient onto the sundeck and knowing I considered this a physical strain on my patient, had summoned me. I arrived just in time to see Doctor Selador stumble and fall."

"You saw him stumble?" Swarthout Nis asked.

"Definitely. He appeared to be reaching for the back of Doctor Dasein's wheelchair. I consider it fortunate he did not manage to grab the chair. He could have taken both of them over the edge."

Selador stumbled? Dasein thought. A sense of opening relief pervaded him. *Selador stumbled! I didn't bump him. I knew I wasn't strong enough. But what did I bump? A loose board on the deck, perhaps?* For an instant, Dasein recalled his hands on the wheels of the chair, the firm, sure grip, the soft bump. *A board could feel soft,* he told himself.

Burdeaux was in the witness chair now corroborating Piaget's testimony.

It must be true then.

Dasein felt strength flow through his body. He began to see his Santaroga experience as a series of plunges down precipitous rapids. Each plunge had left him weaker until the final plunge had, through a mystic fusion, put him in contact with a source of infinite strength. It was that strength he felt now.

His life before Santaroga took on the aspects of a delicate myth held fleetingly in the mind. It was a tree in a Chinese landscape seen dimly through pastel mists. He sensed he had fallen somehow into a sequel, which by its existence had changed the past. But the present, here-and-now, surrounded him like the trunk of a sturdy redwood, firmly rooted, supporting strong branches of sanity and reason.

Garrity with his sleepy questions was a futile incompetent. "You ran immediately to Dr. Dasein's side?"

"Yes, sir. He was quite ill and weak. I was afraid he might try to get out of the wheelchair and fall himself."

"And Dr. Piaget?"

"He ran downstairs, sir, to see what he could do for the man who fell."

Only the Santarogans in this room were fully conscious, Dasein thought. It occurred to him then that the more consciousness he acquired, the greater must be his unconscious content—a natural matter of balance. That would be the source of Santaroga's mutual strength, of course—a shared foundation into which each part must fit.

"Doctor Dasein," the Coroner said.

They swore Dasein in then. The eyes in the room turned toward him. Only Garrity's eyes bothered Dasein—hooded, remote, concealing, *outsider eyes.*

"Did you see Dr. Selador fall?"

"I . . . Mr. Burdeaux called me. I turned toward him and I heard a cry. When I turned back . . . Doctor Selador's feet were going over the edge."

"His feet?"

"That's all I saw."

Dasein closed his eyes, remembering that moment of electric terror. He felt he was using a tunnel-vision effect in his memory, focusing just on those feet. An accident—a terrible accident. He opened his eyes, shut off the vision before memory reproduced that descending wail, the final punctuating thud.

"Had you known Dr. Selador for a long time?"

"He was . . . yes." What was Garrity driving at from behind those hooded eyes?

Garrity produced a sheet of paper from a briefcase on his table, glanced at it, said: "I have here a page from Dr. Selador's journal. It was forwarded to me by his wife. One passage interests me. I'll read it to . . . "

"Is this pertinent?" Coroner Cos asked.

"Perhaps not, sir," Garrity said. "Again, perhaps it is. I would like Dr. Dasein's views. We are, after all, merely trying to arrive at the truth in a terrible tragedy."

"May I see the passage?" That was Swarthout Nis, the Assistant District Attorney, his voice suavely questioning.

"Certainly."

Nis took the paper, read it.

What is it? Dasein asked himself. *What did Selador write that his wife would send to a State investigator? Is this why Garrity came?*

Nis returned the paper to Garrity. "Keeping in mind that Dr. Selador was a psychiatrist, this passage could have many interpretations. I see no reason why Dr. Dasein shouldn't have the opportunity to throw light upon it, however—if he can."

"May I see this?" the Coroner asked.

Garrity stood, took the paper to Cos, waited while the Coroner read it.

"Very well," Cos said, returning the paper to Garrity. "The passage you've marked in red pencil presumably is what concerns you. You may question the witness about that passage if you wish."

Garrity turned, the paper held stiffly before him, faced Dasein. With occasional glances at the page, he read: "Dasein—a dangerous instrument for this project. They should be warned."

He lowered the paper. "What project, Dr. Dasein?"

There was a hush in the room as thick as fog.

"I . . . when did he write this?"

"According to his wife, it's dated approximately a month ago. I repeat: what project?"

Dasein groped in his memory. *Project . . . dangerous?*

"The . . . only project . . . " He shook his head. The passage made no sense.

"Why did you come to Santaroga, Dr. Dasein?"

"Why? My fiancée lives here."

"Your fiancée . . . "

"My niece, Jenny Sorge," Piaget interposed.

Garrity glanced at Piaget, who sat now in the front row of chairs, looked back to Dasein. "Didn't you come here to make a market survey?"

"Oh, that—yes. But I don't see how I could be dangerous to that . . . " Dasein hesitated, weighing the time nicely. " . . . unless he was afraid I'd have my mind too much on other things."

A soft rustle of laughter whispered through the room. The Coroner rapped his pencil, said: "I remind you this is a serious occasion. A man has died."

Silence.

Garrity looked once more to the page in his hand. The paper seemed to have gained weight, pulling down.

"What else is on that page from his journal?" Dasein asked. "Doesn't it explain what . . . "

"Who are the *they* who should be warned?" Garrity asked.

Dasein shook his head. "I don't know—unless it could be the people who hired us for the market study."

"You have prepared such a study?"

"I'll complete it as soon as I'm well enough to be released from the hospital."

"Your injuries," Garrity said, a note of anger in his voice. "Something was said about burns. I'm not at all clear about . . . "

"Just a moment, please," the Coroner said. "Dr. Dasein's injuries are not at issue here in any way other than how they bear on his being in a particular place at a particular time. We have had testimony that he was very weak and that Dr. Selador had wheeled Dr. Dasein's wheelchair out onto the sundeck."

"How weak?" Garrity asked. "And how dangerous?"

The Coroner sighed, glanced at Piaget, at Dasein, back to Garrity. "The facts surrounding Dr. Dasein's injuries are common knowledge in Santaroga, Mr. Garrity. There were more than a dozen witnesses. He was severely burned while saving a man's life. Dr. Dasein is somewhat of a hero in Santaroga."

"Oh." Garrity returned to his seat at the table, put the page from Selador's journal on the briefcase. He obviously was angry, confused.

"I permit a considerable degree of informality in an inquiry such as this," Cos said. "Dr. Dasein has asked a question about the surrounding contents of that page. I confess the entries make no sense to me, but perhaps . . . " The Coroner left his question hanging there, his attention on Garrity.

"My office can add little," Garrity said. "There's an entry which obviously is a population figure; it's so labeled. There's a line . . . " He lifted the page. " 'Oil company checked out. Negative.' There's a rather cryptic: 'No mental illness.' Except for the one entry referring to Dr. Dasein . . . "

"What about the rest of the journal?" the Coroner asked. "Has your office investigated it?"

"Unfortunately, Mrs. Selador says she obeyed her husband's testamentary wishes and burned his journal. It contained, she said, confidential data on medical cases. This one entry she preserved and sent to us . . . " Garrity shrugged.

"I'm afraid the only man who could explain it is no longer living," the Coroner said. "If this was, however, a journal of medical data with reference to Dr. Selador's psychiatric practice, then it would seem the entry in question might be explained easily in rather harmless terms. The word *dangerous* can have many interpretations in a psychiatric context. It may even be that Dr. Dasein's interpretation is the correct one."

Garrity nodded.

"Do you have any more questions?" the Coroner asked.

"Yes. One more." Garrity looked at Dasein, a veiled, uncertain look. "Were you and Dr. Selador on friendly terms?"

Dasein swallowed. "He was . . . my teacher . . . my friend. Ask anyone at Berkeley."

A blank look of frustration came over Garrity's face.

He knows, Dasein thought. And immediately he wondered what it was Garrity *could* know. There was nothing to know. An accident. Perhaps he knew Selador's suspicions about Santaroga. But that was foolishness . . . unless Garrity were another of the investigators looking into things that were none of his business.

Dasein felt his vision blur and, staring at Garrity, saw the man's face become a death's-head skull. The illusion vanished as Garrity shook his head, jammed Selador's journal page into the briefcase. A rueful smile appeared on his face. He glanced at the Coroner, shrugged.

"Something amuses you, Mr. Garrity?" the Coroner asked.

The smile vanished.

"No, sir. Well . . . my own thought processes sometimes. I've obviously allowed an unhappy woman, Mrs. Selador, to send me on a wild goose chase."

The investigator sat down, said: "I've no more questions, sir."

Abruptly, Dasein experienced a moment of insight; Garrity's thoughts had frightened the man! He'd suspected a vast conspiracy here in Santaroga. But that was too fantastic; thus the smile.

The Coroner was closing his inquiry now—a brief summation: all the facts were in . . . an allusion to the pathologist's gory details—"massive head injuries, death instantaneous"—a notation that a formal inquest would be held at a date to be announced. Would Mr. Garrity wish to return for it? Mr. Garrity thought not.

It dawned on Dasein then that this had been a show for Garrity, something to set his mind at ease. Tiny bits of Piaget's preinquest conversation with Garrity returned to Dasein, fitted into a larger pattern. They'd been in school together—*outside!* Of course: old friends, Larry and Bill. One didn't suspect old friends of conspiracy. Reasonable.

It was over then—death by misadventure, an accident.

Garrity was shaking hands with Coroner Cos, with Piaget. Would Piaget be coming out to their class reunion? If his practice permitted . . . but Garrity certainly must know how it was with country doctors. Garrity understood.

"This was a terrible thing," Garrity said.

Piaget sighed. "Yes, a terrible tragedy."

Garrity was pausing at the foyer door now. There were knots of people behind him waiting for the elevator, a buzz of conversation. He turned, and Dasein thought he saw a look of angry speculation on the man's face.

Piaget bent over Dasein then, shutting off the view of the door. "This has been a strain on you and I want you to get some rest now," Piaget said. "Jenny's coming in for a minute, but I don't want her staying too long."

He moved aside.

The foyer doorway stood open and empty.

"Understand?" Piaget asked.

"Yes . . . Jenny's coming."

What was that look in Garrity's eyes? Dasein asked himself. A black savage in Africa might have peered that way into a white man's shiny city. Strange . . . angry . . . frustrated man. If Meyer Davidson and his crew chose Garrity for an investigator—there'd be a dangerous one. That'd be a bridge to cross in its own time, though . . . if at all. Many things could happen to a man out there in the wide-wide world. Dasein could feel it—Santaroga was preparing itself to reach out there.

That's why I was chosen, he thought. *And Burdeaux . . . and the others . . . whoever they are. The only good defense is a good offense.*

This was a disturbing thought that sent trembling agitation through Dasein's stomach and legs.

Why am I trembling? he wondered.

He tried to recapture the thought that had disturbed him, failed. It was brief unimportant disturbance, a momentary ripple on a lake that otherwise was growing calmer and calmer. Dasein allowed the sensation of calm green waters to flow over and around him. He grew aware he was alone in the room with Jenny.

There was calmness personified: blue eyes with laugh wrinkles at their edges, full lips smiling at him. She wore an orange dress, an orange ribbon in her dark hair.

Jenny put a package on his nightstand, bent over and kissed him—warm lips, a deep sense of peace and sharing. She pulled away, sat down beside him, held his hand.

Dasein thought she had never looked more beautiful.

"Uncle Larry says you're to rest this afternoon, but you can be released from the hospital by Saturday," she said.

Dasein reached out, ran his fingers through her hair—silky-smooth, sensuous hair. "Why don't we get married Sunday?" he asked.

"Oh, darling . . ."

Again, she kissed him, pulled back, looked prim. "I better not do that anymore today. We don't want to weaken you." The dimple flickered in her cheek. "You want to be fully recovered and strong by Sunday."

Dasein pulled her head down against his neck, stroked her hair.

"We can have one of the houses in the new section," she whispered. "We'll be near Cal and Willa. Darling, darling, I'm so happy."

"So am I."

She began describing the house to him, the garden space, the view . . .

"You've chosen one of them already?"

"I was out there—dreaming, hoping . . ."

The house was everything she'd ever longed for—it was important for a woman to have the right house in which to begin life with the man she loved. There was even a big garage with room for a shop . . . and a lab.

Dasein thought of Jersey Hofstedder's car sitting in the garage she described. There was a sense of continuity in the thought, a peasant complacency involving "good things" and "vintage crops."

His attention focused on the package Jenny had put on his nightstand.

"What's in the package?"

"Package?"

She lifted her head, turned to follow the direction of his gaze. "Oh, that. The gang at the Co-op—they put together a 'get-well' package for you."

"Jaspers?"

"Of course." She sat back, straightened her hair.

Dasein had a sudden vision of himself working in the wrapping line at the Co-op.

"Where will I work?" he asked.

"Uncle Larry wants you in the clinic, but we'll both get a month of honeymoon leave. Darling—it's going to be so long until Sunday."

In the clinic, Dasein thought. *Not as a patient, thank God.* He wondered then which god he was thanking. It was an odd thought, without beginning and without end, a bit of string hanging in the green lake of his mind.

Jenny began unwrapping the package on the nightstand—a wedge of golden cheese, two bottles of beer, dark wheat crackers, a white container that sloshed when she moved it. He wondered when they had been exposed.

Dasein had the sudden feeling that he was a moth in a glass cage, a frantic thing fluttering against his barriers, lost, confused.

"Darling, I'm tiring you." Jenny put her hand on his forehead. It soothed him, calmed him. The moth of his emotions settled on a strong green limb. The limb was attached to a tree. He felt the trunk of the tree as though it were himself—strong, an infinite source of strength.

"When will I see you?" he asked.

"I'll come by in the morning."

She blew him a kiss, hesitated, bent over him—the sweet fragrance of Jaspers about her breath, a touch of lips.

Dasein stared after her until the foyer door closed.

A momentary anguish touched him, a fleeting sense that he'd lost his grip on reality, that this room was unreal without Jenny in it. Dasein grabbed a chunk of the golden cheese, stuffed it in his mouth, felt the soothing Jaspers presence, his awareness expanding, becoming firm and manageable.

What's reality, anyway? he asked himself. *It's as finite as a bit of cheese, as tainted by error as anything else with limits.*

He settled his mind firmly then onto thoughts of the home Jenny had described, pictured himself carrying her across the threshold—his wife. There'd be presents: Jaspers from 'the gang,' furniture . . . Santaroga took care of its own.

It'll be a beautiful life, he thought. *Beautiful . . . beautiful . . . beautiful . . .*

SOUL CATCHER

For Ralph and Irene Slattery,
without whose love and guidance this book
would never have been

WHEN THE boy's father arrived at Six Rivers Camp, they showed him a number of things which they might not have revealed to a lesser person. But the father, as you know, was Howard Marshall and that meant State Department and VIP connections in Washington, D.C.; so they showed him the statement from the professor and the interviews with the camp counselors, that sort of thing. Of course, Marshall saw the so-called kidnap note and the newspaper clippings which some of the FBI men had brought up to the camp that morning.

Marshall lived up to expectations. He spoke with the measured clarity of someone to whom crises and decisions were a way of life. In response to a question, he said:

"I know this Northwest Coast country very well, you understand. My father was in lumber here. I spent many happy days in this region as a child and young man. My father hired Indians whenever he could find ones who would work. He paid them the same wages as anyone else. Our Indians were well treated. I really don't see how this kidnapping could be aimed at me personally or at my family. The man who took David must be insane."

STATEMENT OF Dr. Tilman Barth, University of Washington Anthropology Department:

I find this whole thing incredible. Charles Hobuhet cannot be the mad killer you make him out to be. It's impossible. He could not have kidnapped that boy. You must not think of him as criminal, or as Indian. Charles is a unique intellect, one of the finest students I've ever had. He's essentially gentle and with a profoundly subtle sense of humor. You know, that could just be our situation here. This could be a monstrous joke. Here, let me show you some of his work. I've saved copies of everything Charles has written for me. The world's going to know about him someday. . . .

FROM A news story in the Seattle *Post-Intelligencer:*

The most intensive manhunt in Washington history centered today on the tangled rain forest and virtually untouched wilderness area of the Olympic National Park.

Law enforcement officials said they still believe Charles Hobuhet, the Indian militant, is somewhere in that region with his kidnap victim, David Marshall, 13, son of the new United States Undersecretary of State.

Searchers were not discounting, however, the reports that the two have been seen in other areas. Part of the investigation focused on Indian lands in the state's far northwest corner. Indian trackers were being enlisted to assist in the search and bloodhounds were being brought from Walla Walla.

The manhunt began yesterday with the discovery at the exclusive Six Rivers boys' camp that young Marshall was missing and that a so-called kidnap note had been left behind. The note reportedly was signed by Hobuhet with his pseudonym ''Katsuk'' and threatened to sacrifice the boy in an ancient Indian ceremony.

THE NOTE left at Cedar Cabin, Six Rivers, by Charles Hobuhet-Katsuk:

I take an innocent of your people to sacrifice for all of the innocents you have murdered. The Innocent will go with all of those other innocents into the spirit place. Thus will sky and earth balance.

I am Katsuk who does this to you. Think of me only as Katsuk, not as Charles Hobuhet. I am something far more than a sensory system and its appetites. I am evolved far beyond you who are called hoquat. I look backward to see you. I see your lives based on cowardice. Your judgments arise from illusions. You tell me unlimited growth and consumption are good. Then your biologists tell me this is cancerous and lethal. To which hoquat should I listen? You do not listen. You think you are free to do anything that comes into your minds. Thinking this, you remain afraid to liberate your spirits from restraint.

Katsuk will tell you why this is. You fear to create because your creations mirror your true selves. You believe your power resides in an ultimate knowledge which you forever seek as children seek parental wisdom. I learned this while watching you in your hoquat schools. But now I am Katsuk, a greater power. I will sacrifice your flesh. I will strike through to your spirit. I have the root of your tree in my power.

ON THE day he was to leave for camp, David Marshall had awakened early. It was two weeks after his thirteenth birthday. David thought about being thirteen as he stretched out in the morning warmth of his bed. There was some internal difference that came with being thirteen. It was not the same as twelve, but he couldn't pin down the precise difference.

For a time he played with the sensation that the ceiling above his bed actually fluttered as his eyelids resisted opening to the day. There was sunshine out in that day, a light broken by its passage through the big-leaf maple which shaded the window of his upstairs bedroom.

Without opening his eyes, he could sense the world around his home—the long, sloping lawns, the carefully tended shrubs and flowers. It was a world full of slow calm. Thinking about it sometimes, he felt a soft drumbeat of exaltation.

David opened his eyes. For a moment, he pretended the faint shadow marks in the ceiling's white plaster were a horizon: range upon range of mountains dropping down to drift-piled beaches.

Mountains . . . beaches—he'd see such things tomorrow when he went to camp.

David turned, focused on the camp gear piled across chair and floor where he and his father had arranged the things last night: sleeping bag, pack, clothing, boots. . . .

There was the knife.

The knife stimulated a feeling of excitement. That was a genuine Russell belt knife made in Canada. It had been a birthday gift from his father just two weeks ago.

A bass hum of wilderness radiated into his imagination from the knife in its deer-brown scabbard. It was a man's tool, a man's weapon. It stood for blood and darkness and independence.

His father's words had put magic in the knife:

"That's no toy, Dave. Learn how to use it safely. Treat it with respect."

His father's voice had carried subdued tensions. The adult eyes had looked at him with calculated intensity and there had been a waiting silence after each phrase.

Fingernails made a brief scratching signal on his bedroom door, breaking his reverie. The door opened. Mrs. Parma slid into the room. She wore a long blue and black sari with faint red lines in it. She moved with silent effacement, an effect as attention-demanding as a gong.

David's gaze followed her. She always made him feel uneasy.

Mrs. Parma glided across to the window that framed the maple, closed the window firmly.

David peered over the edge of the blankets at her as she turned from the window and nodded her awareness of him.

"Good morning, young sir."

The clipped British accent never sounded right to him coming from a mouth with purple lips. And her eyes bothered him. They were too big, as though stretched by the way her glossy hair was pulled back into a bun. Her name wasn't really Parma. It bagan with Parma, but it was much longer and ended with a strange clicking sound that David could not make.

He pulled the blankets below his chin, said: "Did my father leave yet?"

"Before dawn, young sir. It is a long way to the capital of your nation."

David frowned and waited for her to leave. Strange woman. His parents had brought her back from New Delhi, where his father had been political adviser to the embassy.

In those years, David had stayed with Granny in San Francisco. He had been surrounded by old people with snowy hair, diffident servants, and low, cool voices. It had been a drifting time with diffused stimulations. *"Your grandmother is napping. One would not want to disturb her, would one?"* It had worn on him the way dripping water wears a rock. His memory of the period retained most strongly the whirlwind visits of his parents. They had descended upon the insulated quiet of the house, breathless, laughing, tanned, and romantic, arms loaded with exotic gifts.

But the chest-shaking joy of being with such people had always ended, leaving him with a sense of frustration amidst the smells of dusty perfumes and tea and the black feeling that he had been abandoned.

Mrs. Parma checked the clothing laid out for him on the dresser. Knowing he wanted her to leave, she delayed. Her body conveyed a stately swaying within the sari. Her fingernails were bright pink.

She had shown him a map once with a town marked on it, the place where she had been born. She had a brown photograph: mud-walled houses and leafless trees, a man all in white standing beside a bicycle, a violin case under his arm. Her father.

Mrs. Parma turned, looked at David with her startling eyes. She said: "Your father asked me to remind you when you awoke that the car will depart precisely on time. You have one hour."

She lowered her gaze, went to the door. The sari betrayed only a faint suggestion of moving legs. The red lines in the fabric danced like sparks from a fire.

David wondered what she thought. Her slow, calm way revealed nothing he could decipher. Was she laughing at him? Did she think going to camp was a foolishness? Did she even have a geographical understanding of where he would go, the Olympic Mountains?

He had a last glimpse of the bright fingernails as she went out, closed the door.

David bounced from bed, began dressing. When he came to the belt, he slipped the sheathed knife onto it, cinched the buckle. The blade remained a heavy presence at his hip while he brushed his teeth and combed his blond hair straight back. When he leaned close to the mirror, he could see the knife's dark handle with the initials burned into it: DMM, David Morgenstern Marshall.

Presently, he went down to breakfast.

STATEMENT OF Dr. Tilman Barth, University of Washington Anthropology Department:

The word *katsuk* is very explicit in Hobuhet's native tongue. It means "the center" or the core from which all perception radiates. It's the center of the world or of the universe. It's where an aware individual stands. There has never been any doubt in my mind that Charles is aware. I can understand his assuming this pseudonym.

You've seen those papers he wrote. That one where he compares the Raven myth of his people to the Genesis myth of Western civilization is very disturbing. He has perceived the link between dream and reality—how we seek to win a place in destiny through rebellion, the evil forces we built up only to destroy, the Great

Conquests and Great Causes to which we cling long after they've been exposed as empty glitter. Here . . . notice his simile for such lost perceptions:

". . .the fish eyes like gray skimmed milk that stare at you out of things which are alive when they shouldn't be."

This is the observation of someone who is capable of great things, as great as any achievements in our Western mythology.

IT HAD begun when his name still was Charles Hobuhet, a good *Indian* name for a *Good Indian*.

The bee had alighted, after all, on the back of Charles Hobuhet's left hand. There had been no one named Katsuk then. He had been reaching up to grasp a vine maple limb, climbing from a creek bottom in the stillness of midday.

The bee was black and gold, a bee from the forest, a bumblebee of the family Apidae. It's name fled buzzing through his mind, a memory from days in the white school.

Somewhere above him, a ridge came down toward the Pacific out of the Olympic Mountains like the gnarled root of an ancient spruce clutching the earth for support.

The sun would be warm up there, but winter's chill in the creek bottom slid its icy way down the watercourse from the mountains to these spring-burgeoning foothills.

Cold came with the bee, too. It was a special cold that put ice in the soul.

Still Charles Hobuhet's soul then.

But he had performed the ancient ritual with twigs and string and bits of bone. The ice from the bee told him he must take a name. Unless he took a name immediately, he stood in peril of losing both souls, the soul in his body and the soul that went high or low with his true being.

The stillness of the bee on his hand made this obvious. He sensed urgent ghosts: people, animals, birds, all with him in this bee.

He whispered: "Alkuntam, help me."

The supreme god of his people made no reply.

Shiny green of the vine maple trunk directly in front of him dominated his eyes. Ferns beneath it splayed out fronds. Condensation fell like rain on the damp earth. He forced himself to turn away, stared across the creek at a stand of alders bleached white against heavy green of cedar and fir on the stream's far slope.

A quaking aspen, its leaves adither among the alders, dazzled his awareness, pulled his mind. He felt abruptly that he had found another self which must be reasoned with, influenced, and understood. He lost clarity of mind and sensed both selves straining toward some pure essence. All sense of self slipped from his body, searched outward into the dazzling aspen.

He thought: *I am in the center of the universe!*

Bee spoke to him then: "I am Tamanawis speaking to you. . . ."

The words boomed in his awareness, telling him his name. He spoke it aloud: "Katsuk! I am Katsuk."

Katsuk.

It was a seminal name, one with potency.

Now, being Katsuk, he knew all its meanings. He was Ka-, the prefix for everything human. He was -tsuk, the bird of myth. A human bird! He possessed roots in many meanings: bone, the color blue, a serving dish, smoke . . . brother and soul.

Once more, he said it: "I am Katsuk."

Both selves flowed home to the body.

He stared at the miraculous bee on his hand. A bee had been the farthest thing from his expectations. He had been climbing, just climbing.

If there were thoughts in his mind, they were thoughts of his ordeal. It was the ordeal he had set for himself out of grief, out of the intellectual delight in walking through ancient ideas, out of the fear that he had lost his way in the white world. His native soul had rotted while living in that white world. But a spirit had spoken to him.

A true and ancient spirit.

Deep within his innermost being he knew that intellect and education, even the white education, had been his first guides on this ordeal.

He thought how, as Charles Hobuhet, he had begun this thing. He had waited for the full moon and cleansed his intestines by drinking seawater. He had found a land otter and cut out its tongue.

Kuschtaliute—the symbol tongue!

His grandfather had explained the way of it long ago, describing the ancient lore. Grandfather had said: "The shaman becomes the spirit-animal-man. God won't let animals make the mistakes men make."

That was the way of it.

He had carried *Kuschtaliute* in a deer scrotum pouch around his neck. He had come into these mountains. He had followed an old elk trail grown over with alder and fir and cottonwood. The setting sun had been at his back when he had buried *Kuschtaliute* beneath a rotten log. He had buried *Kuschtaliute* in a place he never again could find, there to become the spirit tongue.

All of this in anguish of spirit.

He thought: *It began because of the rape and pointless death of my sister. The death of Janiktaht . . . little Jan.*

He shook his head, confused by an onslaught of memories. Somewhere a gang of drunken loggers had found Janiktaht walking alone, her teen-aged body full of spring happiness, and they had raped her and changed her and she had killed herself.

And her brother had become a walker-in-the-mountains.

The other self within him, the one which must be reasoned with and understood, sneered at him and said: "Rape and suicide are as old as mankind. Besides, that was Charles Hobuhet's sister. You are Katsuk."

He thought then as Katsuk: *Lucretius was a liar! Science doesn't liberate man from the terror of the gods!*

Everything around him revealed this truth—the sun moving across the ridges, the ranges of drifting clouds, the rank vegetation.

White science had begun with magic and never moved far from it. Science continually failed to learn from lack of results. The ancient ways retained their potency. Despite sneers and calumny, the old ways achieved what the legends said they would.

His grandmother had been of the Eagle Phratry. And a bee had spoken to him.

He had scrubbed his body with hemlock twigs until the skin was raw. He had caught his hair in a headband of red cedar bark. He had eaten only the roots of devil's club until the ribs poked from his flesh.

How long had he been walking in these mountains?

He thought back to all the distance he had covered: ground so sodden that water oozed up at each step, heavy branches overhead that shut out the sun, undergrowth so thick he could see only a few body lengths in any direction. Somewhere, he had come through a tangled salmonberry thicket to a stream flowing in a canyon, deep and silent. He had followed that stream upward to vaporous heights . . . upward . . . upward. The stream had become a creek, this creek below him.

This place.

Something real was living in him now.

Abruptly, he sensed all of his dead ancestors lusting after this living experience. His mind lay pierced by sudden belief, by unending movement beneath the common places of life, by an alertness which never varied, night or day. He knew this bee!

He said:"You are Kwatee, the Changer."

"And what are you?"

"I am Katsuk."

"*What* are you?" The question thundered at him.

He put down terror, thought: *Thunder is not angry. What frightens animals need not frighten a man. What am I?*

The answer came to him as one of his ancestors would have known it. He said: "I am one who followed the ritual with care. I am one who did not really expect to find the spirit power."

"Now you know."

All of his thinking turned over, became as unsettled as a pool muddied by a big fish. *What do I know?*

The air around him continued full of dappled sunlight and the noise and spray from the creek. The mushroom-punk smell of a rotten log fiilled his nostrils. A stately, swaying leaf shadow brushed purple across the bee on his hand, withdrew.

He emptied his mind of everything except what he needed to know from the spirit poised upon his hand. He lay frozen in the-moment-of-the-bee. Bee was graceful, fat, and funny. Bee aroused a qualm of restless memories, rendered his senses abnormally acute. Bee. . . .

An image of Janiktaht overcame his mind. Misery filled him right out to the skin. Janiktaht—sixty nights dead. Sixty nights since she had ended her shame and hopelessness in the sea.

He had a vision of himself moaning beside Janiktaht's open grave, drunk with anguish, the swaying wind of the forest all through his flesh.

Awareness recoiled. He thought of himself as he had been once, as a boy heedlessly happy on the beach, following the tide mark. He remembered a piece of driftwood like a dead hand outspread on the sand.

Had that been driftwood?

He felt the peril of letting his thoughts flow. Who knew where they might go? Janiktaht's image faded, vanished as though of its own accord. He tried to recall her face. It fled him through a blurred vision of young hemlocks . . . a moss-floored stand of trees where nine drunken loggers had dragged her to . . . one after another, to. . . .

Something had happened to flesh which his mind no longer could contemplate without being scoured out, denuded of everything except a misshapen object that the ocean had cast up on a curve of beach where once he had played.

He felt like an old pot, all emotion scraped out. Everything eluded him except the spirit on the back of his hand. He thought:

We are like bees, my people—broken into many pieces, but the pieces remain dangerous.

In that instant, he realized that this creature on his hand must be much more than Changer—far, far more than *Kwatee.*

It is Soul Catcher!

Terror and elation warred with him. This was the greatest of the spirits. It had only to sting him and he would be invaded by a terrible thing. He would become the bee of his people. He would do a terrifying thing, a dangerous thing, a deadly thing.

Hardly daring to breathe, he waited.

Would Bee never move? Would they remain this way for all eternity? His mind felt drawn tight, as tense as a bow pulled to its utmost breaking point. All of his emotions lay closed up in blackness without inner light or outer light—a sky of nothingness within him.

He thought: *How strange for a creature so tiny to exist as such spirit power, to be such spirit power—Soul Catcher!*

One moment there had been no bee on his flesh. Now, it stood there as though flung into creation by a spray of sunlight, brushed by leaf shadow, the shape of it across a vein, darkness of the spirit against dark skin.

A shadow across his being.

He saw Bee with intense clarity: the swollen abdomen, the stretched gossamer of wings, the pollen dust on the legs, the barbed arrow of the stinger.

The message of this moment floated through his awareness, a clear flute sound. If the spirit went away peacefully, that would signal reprieve. He could return to the university. Another year, in the week of his twenty-sixth birthday, he would take his doctorate in anthropology. He would shake off this terrifying wildness which had invaded him at Janiktaht's death. He would become the imitation white man, lost to these mountains and the needs of his people.

This thought saddened him. If the spirit left him, it would take both of his souls. Without souls, he would die. He could not outlast the sorrows which engulfed him.

Slowly, with ancient deliberation, Bee turned short of his knuckles. It was the movement of an orator gauging his audience. Faceted eyes included the human in their focus. Bee's thorax arched, abdomen tipped, and he knew a surge of terror in the realization that he had been chosen.

The stinger slipped casually into his nerves, drawing his thoughts, inward, inward. . . .

He heard the message of Tamanawis, the greatest of spirits, as a drumbeat matching the beat of his heart: "You must find a white. You must find a total innocent. You must kill an innocent of the whites. Let your deed fall upon this world. Let your deed be a single, heavy hand which clutches the heart. The whites must feel it. They must hear it. An innocent for all of our innocents."

Having told him what he must do, Bee took flight.

His gaze followed the flight, lost it in the leafery of the vine maple copse far upslope. He sensed then a procession of ancestral ghosts insatiate in their demands. All of those who had gone before him remained an unchanging field locked immovably into his past, a field against which he could see himself change.

Kill an innocent!

Sorrow and confusion dried his mouth. He felt parched in his innermost being, withered.

The sun crossing over the high ridge to keep its appointment with the leaves in the canyon touched his shoulders, his eyes. He knew he had been tempted and had gone through a locked door into a region of terrifying power. To hold this power he would have to come to terms with that other self inside him. He could be only one person—Katsuk.

He said: "I am Katsuk."

The words brought calm. Spirits of air and earth were with him as they had been for his ancestors. He resumed climbing the slope, His movements aroused a flying squirrel. It glided from a high limb to a low one far below. He felt the life all around him then: brown movements hidden in greenery, life caught suddenly in stop-motion by his presence.

He thought: *Remember me, creatures of this forest. Remember Katsuk as the whole world will remember him. I am Katsuk. Ten thousand nights from now, ten thousand seasons from now, this world still will remember Katsuk and his meaning.*

FROM A wire story, Seattle dateline:

The mother of the kidnap victim arrived at Six Rivers Camp about 3:30 P.M. yesterday. She was brought in by one of the four executive helicopters released for the search by lumber and plywood corporations of the Northwest. There were tearstains on her cheeks as she stepped from the helicopter to be greeted by her husband.

She said: "Any mother can understand how I feel. Please, let me be alone with my husband."

AN IRRITANT whine edged his mother's voice as David sat down across from her in the sunny breakfast room that overlooked their back lawn and private stream. The scowl which accompanied the whine drew sharp lines down her forehead toward her nose. A vein on her left hand had taken on the hue of rusty iron. She wore something pink and lacy, her yellow hair fluffed up. Her lavender perfume enveloped the table.

She said: "I wish you wouldn't take that awful knife to camp, Davey. What in heaven's name will you do with such a thing? I think your father was quite mad to give you such a dangerous instrument."

Her left hand jingled the little bell to summon the cook with David's cereal.

David stared down at the table while cook's pink hand put a bowl there. The cream in the bowl was almost the same yellow as the tablecloth. The bowl gave off the odor of the fresh strawberries sliced into the cereal. David adjusted his napkin.

His mother said: "Well?"

Sometimes her questions were not meant to be answered, but *"Well?"* signaled pressure.

He sighed. "Mother, everyone at camp has a knife."

"Why?"

"To cut things, carve wood, stuff like that."

He began eating. One hour. That could be endured.

"To cut your fingers off!" she said. "I simply refuse to let you take such a dangerous thing."

He swallowed a mouthful of cereal while he studied her the way he had seen his father do it, letting his mind sort out the possible countermoves. A breeze shook the trees bordering the lawn behind her.

"Well?" she insisted.

"What do I do?" he asked. "Every time I need a knife I'll have to borrow one from one of the other guys."

He took another mouthful of cereal, savoring the acid of the strawberries while he waited for her to assess the impossibility of keeping him knifeless at camp. David knew how her mind worked. She had been Prosper Morgenstern before she had married Dad. The Morgensterns always had the best. If he was going to have a knife *anyway*. . . .

She put flame to a cigarette, her hand jerking. The smoke emerged from her mouth in spurts.

David went on eating.

She put the cigarette aside, said: "Oh, very well. But you must be extremely careful."

"Just like Dad showed me," he said.

She stared at him, a finger of her left hand tapping a soft drumbeat on the table. The movement set the diamonds on her wristwatch clasp aflame. She said: "I don't know what I'll do with both of my men gone."

"Dad'll be halfway to Washington by now."

"And you in that awful camp."

"It's the best camp there is."

"I guess so. You know, Davey, we all may have to move to the East."

David nodded. His father had moved them to the Carmel Valley and gone back into private practice after the last election. He commuted up the Peninsula to the city three days a week. Sometimes Prosper joined him there for a weekend. They kept an apartment in the city and a maid-caretaker.

But yesterday his father had received a telephone call from someone important in the government. There had been other calls and a sense of excitement in the house. Howard Marshall had been offered an important position in the State Department.

David said: "It's funny, y'know?"

"What is, dear?"

"Dad's going to Washington and so am I."

She smiled. "Different Washingtons."

"Both named for the same man."

"Indeed they were."

Mrs. Parma glided into the breakfast room, said: "Excuse me, madam. I have had Peter put the young sir's equipage into the car. Will there be anything else?"

"Thank you, Mrs. Parma. That will be all."

David waited until Mrs. Parma had gone, said: "That book about the camp said they have some Indian counselors. Will they look like Mrs. Parma?"

"Davey! Don't they teach you *anything* in that school?"

"I know they're different Indians. I just wondered if they, you know, looked like her, if that's why we called our Indians. . . ."

"What a strange idea." She shook her head, arose. "There are times when you remind me of your grandfather Morgenstern. He used to insist the Indians were the lost tribe of Israel." She hesitated, one hand lingering on the table, her gaze focused on the knife at David's waist. "You *will* be careful with that awful knife?"

"I'll do just like Dad said. Don't worry."

SPECIAL AGENT Norman Hosbig, Seattle Office, FBI:

Yes, in answer to that, I believe I can say that we do have some indications that the Indian may be mentally deranged. Let me emphasize that this is only a possibility which we are not excluding in our assessment of the problem. There's the equal possibility that he's pretending insanity.

HANDS CLASPED behind his head, Katsuk had stretched out in the darkness of his bunk in Cedar Cabin. Water dripped in the washbasin of the toilet across the hall. The sound filled him with a sense of rhythmic drifting. He closed his eyes tightly and saw a purple glow behind his eyelids. It was the spirit flame, the sign of his determination. This room, the cabin with its sleeping boys, the camp all around—everything went out from the center, which was the spirit flame of Katsuk.

He drew in the shallow breaths of expectation, thought of his charges asleep in the long barracks room down the hall outside his closed door: eight sleeping boys. Only one of the boys concerned Katsuk. The spirits had sent him another sign: the perfect victim, the Innocent.

The son of an important man slept out there, a person to command the widest attention. No one would escape Katsuk's message.

To prepare for this time, he had clothed himself in a loincloth woven of white dog hair and mountain goat wool. A belt of red cedar bark bound the waist. The belt held a soft deerhide pouch which contained the few things he needed: a sacred twig and bone bound with cedar string, an ancient stone arrowhead from the beach at Ozette, raven feathers to fletch a consecrated arrow, a bowstring of twisted walrus gut, elk-hide thongs to bind the victim, a leaf packet of spruce gum . . . down from sea ducks . . . a flute. . . .

A great aunt had made the fabric of his loincloth many years ago, squatting at a flat loom in the smoky shadows of her house at the river mouth. The pouch and the bit of down had been blessed by a shaman of his people before the coming of the whites.

Elkhide moccasins covered his feet. They were decorated with beads and porcupine quills. Janiktaht had made them for him two summers ago.

A lifetime past.

He could feel slow tension spreading upward from those moccasins. Janiktaht was here with him in this room, her hands reaching out from the elk leather she had shaped. Her voice filled the darkness with the final screech of her anguish.

Katsuk took a deep, calming breath. It was not yet time.

There had been fog in the evening, but it had cleared at nightfall on a wind blowing strongly from the southwest. The wind sang to Katsuk in the voice of his grandfather's flute, the flute in the pouch. Katsuk thought of his grandfather: a beaten man, thick of face, who would have been a shaman in another time.

A beaten man, without congregation or mystery, a shadow shaman because he remembered all the old ways.

Katsuk whispered: "I do this for you, grandfather."

Each thing in its own time. The cycle had come around once more to restore the old balance.

His grandfather had built a medicine fire once. As the blaze leaped, the old man had played a low, thin tune on his flute. The song of his grandfather's flute wove in and out of Katsuk's mind. He thought of the boy sleeping out there in the cabin—David Marshall.

You will be snared in the song of this flute, white innocent. I have the root of your tree in my power. Your people will know destruction!

He opened his eyes to moonlight. The light came through the room's one window, drew a gnarled tree shadow on the wall to his left. He watched the undulant shadow, swaying darkness, a visual echo of wind in trees.

The water continued its drip-drip-drip across the hall. Unpleasant odors drifted on the room's air. Antiseptic place! Poisonous! The cabin had been scoured out with strong soap by the advance work crew.

I am Katsuk.

The odors in the room exhausted him. Everything of the whites did that. They weakened him, removed him from contact with his past and the powers that were his by right of inheritance.

I am Katsuk.

He quested outward in his mind, sensed the camp and its surroundings. A trail curved through a thick stand of fir beyond the cabin's south porch. Five hundred and twenty-eight paces it went, over roots and boggy places to the ancient elk trace which climbed into the park.

He thought: *That is my land! My land! These white thieves stole my land. These* hoquat! *Their park is my land!*

Hoquat! Hoquat!

He mouthed the word without sound. His ancestors had applied that name to the first whites arriving off these shores in their tall ships. *Hoquat—something that floated far out on the water, something unfamiliar and mysterious.*

The hoquat had been like the green waves of winter that grew and grew and grew until they smashed upon the land.

Bruce Clark, director of Six Rivers Camp, had taken photographs that day—the *publicity* pictures he took every year to help lure the children of the rich. It had amused Katsuk to obey in the guise of Charles Hobuhet.

Eyes open wide, body sweating with anticipation, Katsuk had obeyed Clark's directions.

"Move a little farther left, Chief."

Chief!

"That's good. Now, shield your eyes with your hand as though you were staring out at the forest. No, the right hand."

Katsuk had obeyed.

The photographs pleased him. Nothing could steal a soul which Soul Catcher already possessed. The photographs were a spirit omen. The charges of Cedar Cabin had clustered around him, their faces toward the camera. Newspapers and magazines would reproduce those pictures. An arrow would point to one face among the boys—David Marshall, son of the new Undersecretary of State.

The announcement will come on the six-o'clock news over the rec room's one television. There will be pictures of the Marshall boy and his mother at the San Francisco airport, the father at a press conference in Washington, D.C.

Many hoquat would stare at the pictures Clark had taken. Let them stare at a person they thought was Charles Hobuhet. The Soul Catcher had yet to reveal Katsuk hidden in that flesh.

By the moon shadow on the wall, he knew it was almost midnight. *Time.* With a single motion, he arose from the bunk, glanced to the note he had left on the room's tiny desk.

"I take an innocent of your people to sacrifice for all the innocents you have murdered, an innocent to go with all of those other innocents into the spirit place."

Ahhh, the words they would pour upon this message! All the ravings and analysis, the hoquat logic. . . .

The light of the full moon coming through the window penetrated his body. He could feel the weighted silence of it all along his spine. It made his hand tingle where Bee had left the message of its stinger. The odor of resin from the rough boards of the walls made him calm. Without guilt.

The breath of his passion came from his lips like smoke: "I am Katsuk, the center of the universe."

He turned and, in a noiseless glide, took the center of the universe out the door, down the short hall into the bunk room.

The Marshall boy slept in the nearest cot. Moonlight lay across the lower half of the cot in a pattern of hills and valleys, undulant with the soft movement of the boy's breathing. His clothing lay on a locker at the foot of the cot: whipcord trousers, a T-shirt, light sweater and jacket, socks, tennis shoes. The boy was sleeping in his shorts.

Katsuk rolled the clothing into a bundle around the shoes. The alien fabric sent a message into his nerves, telling of that mechanical giant the hoquat called civilization. The message dried his tongue. Momentarily, he sensed the many resources the hoquat possessed to hunt down those who wounded them.

Alien guns and aircraft and electronic devices. And he must fight back without such things. Everything hoquat must become alien and denied to him.

An owl cried outside the cabin.

Katsuk pressed the clothing bundle tightly to his chest. The owl had spoken to him. In this land, Katsuk would have other powers, older and stronger and more enduring than those of the hoquat.

He listened to the room: eight boys asleep. The sweat of their excitement dominated this place. They had been slow settling into sleep. But now they slept even deeper because of that slowness.

Katsuk moved to the head of the boy's cot, put a hand lightly over the sleeping mouth, ready to press down and prevent an outcry. The lips twisted under his hand. He saw the eyes open, stare. He felt the altered pulse, the change in breathing.

Softly, Katsuk bent close, whispered: "Don't waken the others. Get up and come with me. I have something special for you. Quiet now."

Hesitant thoughts fleeing through the boy's mind could be felt under Katsuk's hand. Once more, Katsuk whispered, letting his words flow through his spirit powers: "I must make you my spirit brother because of the photographs." Then: "I have your clothes. I'll wait in the hall."

He felt the words take effect, removed his hand from the boy's mouth. Tension subsided.

Katsuk went into the hallway. Presently, the boy joined him, a thin figure whose shorts gleamed whitely in the gloom. Katsuk thrust the clothing into his hands, led the way outside, waiting for the boy at the door, then closing it softly.

Grandfather, I do this for you!

FRAGMENT OF a note by Charles Hobuhet found at Cedar Cabin:

Hoquat, I give you what you prayed for, this good arrow made clean and straight by my hands. When I give you this arrow, please hold it in your body with pride. Let this arrow take you to the land of Alkuntam. Our brothers will welcome you there, saying: "What a beautiful youth has come to us! What a beautiful hoquat!" They will say to one another: "How strong he is, this beautful hoquat who carries the arrow of Katsuk in his flesh." And you will be proud when you hear them speak of your greatness and your beauty. Do not run away, hoquat. Come toward my good arrow. Accept it. Our brothers will sing of this. I will cover your body with white feathers from the breasts of ducks. Our maidens will sing your beauty. This is what you have prayed for from one end of the world to the other every day of your life. I, Katsuk, give you your wish because I have become Soul Catcher.

DAVID, HIS mind still drugged with sleep, came wide awake as he stepped out the door into the cold night. Shivering, he stared at the man who had awakened him—*the Chief.*

"What is it, Chief?"

"Shhhh." Katsuk touched the roll of clothing. "Get dressed."

More from the cold than any other reason, David obeyed. Tree branches whipped in the wind above the cabin, filled the night with fearful shapes.

"Is it an initiation, Chief?"

"Shhh, be very quiet."

"Why?"

"We were photographed together. We must become spirit brothers. There is a ceremony."

"What about the other guys?"

"You have been chosen."

Katsuk fought down sudden pity for this boy, this Innocent. *Why pity anyone?* He realized the moonlight had cut at his heart. For some reason, it made him think of the Shaker Church where his relatives had taken him as a child—hoquat church! He heard the voices chanting in his memory: *"Begat, begat, begat. . . ."*

David whispered: "I don't understand. What're we doing?"

The stars staring down at him, the wind in the trees, all carried foreboding. He felt frightened. A gap in the trees beyond the porch revealed a great bush of stars standing out against the night. David stared into the shadows of the porch. Why wasn't the Chief answering?

David tightened his belt, felt the knife in its sheath at his waist. If the Chief were planning something bad, he'd have removed the knife. That was a real weapon. Daniel Boone had killed a bear with a blade no bigger than this one.

"What're we going to do?" David pressed.

"A ceremony of spirit brotherhood," Katsuk said. He felt the truth in his words. There would be a ceremony and a joining, a shape that occurred out of darkness, a mark on the earth and an incantation to the real spirits.

David still hesitated, thinking this was an Indian. They were strange people. He thought of Mrs. Parma. Different Indian, but both mysterious.

David pulled his jacket close around him. The cold air had raised goose pimples on his skin. He felt both frightened and excited. An Indian.

He said: "You're not dressed."

"I'm dressed for the ceremony."

Silently, Katsuk prayed: *"O Life Giver, now that you have seen the way a part of your all-powerful being goes. . . ."*

David sensed the man's tensions, the air of secrecy. But no place could be safer than this wilderness camp with that cog railroad the only way to get here.

He asked: "Aren't you cold?"

"I am used to this. You must hurry after me now. We haven't much time."

Katsuk stepped down off the porch. The boy followed.

"Where are we going?"

"To the top of the ridge."

David hurried to keep in step. "Why?"

"I have prepared a place there for you to be initiated into a very old ceremony of my people."

"Because of the photographs?"

"Yes."

"I didn't think Indians believed in that stuff anymore."

"Even you will believe."

David tucked his shirt more firmly into his belt, felt the knife. The knife gave him a feeling of confidence. He stumbled in his hurry to keep up.

Without looking back, Katsuk felt the boy's tensions relax. There had been a moment back on the porch when rebellion had radiated from the Innocent. The boy's eyes had been uncertain, wet and smooth in their darkness. The bitter acid of fear had been in the air. But now the boy would follow. He was enthralled. The center of the universe carried the power of a magnet for that Innocent.

David felt his heart beating rapidly from exertion. He smelled rancid oil from
the Chief. The man's skin glistened when moonlight touched it, as though he had
greased his body.

"How far is it?" David asked.

"Three thousand and eighty-one paces."

"How far is that?"

"A bit over a mile."

"Did you have to dress like that?"

"Yes."

"What if it rains?"

"I will not notice."

"Why're we going so fast?"

"We need the moonlight for the ceremony. Be silent now and stay close."

Katsuk felt brass laughter in his chest, picked up the pace. The smell of newly
cut cedar drifted on the air. The rich odor of cedar oils carried an omen message
from the days when that tree had sheltered his people.

David stumbled over a root, regained his balance.

The trail pushed through mottled darkness—black broken by sharp slashes of
moonlight. The bobbing patch of loincloth ahead of him carried a strange dream
quality to David. When moonlight reached it, the man's skin glistened, but his
black hair drank the light, was one with the shadows.

"Will the other guys be initiated?" David asked.

"I told you that you are the only one."

"Why?"

"You will understand soon. Do not talk."

Katsuk hoped the silence brought by that rebuke would endure. Like all hoquat,
the boy talked too much. There could be no reprieve for such a one.

"I keep stumbling," David muttered.

"Walk as I walk."

Katsuk measured the trail by the feeling of it underfoot: soft earth, a dampness
where a spring surfaced, spruce cones, the hard lacery of roots polished by many
feet. . . .

He began to think of his sister and of his former life before Katsuk. He felt the
spirits of air and earth draw close, riding this moonlight, bringing the memory of
all the lost tribes.

David thought: *Walk as he walks?*

The man moved with sliding panther grace, almost noiseless. The trail grew
steep, tangled with more roots, slippery underfoot, but still the man moved as
though he saw every surface change, every rock and root.

David became aware of the wet odors all around: rotting wood, musks, bitter
acridity of ferns. Wet leaves brushed his cheeks. Limbs and vines dragged at him.
He heard falling water, louder and louder—a river cascading in its gorge off to the
right. He hoped the sound covered his clumsiness but feared the Chief could hear
him and was laughing.

Walk as I walk!

How could the Chief even see anything in this dark?

The trail entered a bracken clearing. David saw peaks directly ahead, snow on
them streaked by moonlight, a bright sieve of stars close overhead.

Katsuk stared upward as he walked. The peaks appeared to be stitched upon the
sky by the stars. He allowed this moment its time to flow through him, renewing the

spirit message: *"I am Tamanawis speaking to you. . . ."*

He began to sing the names of his dead, sent the names outward into Sky World. A falling star swept over the clearing—another, then another and another until the sky flamed with them.

Katsuk fell silent in wonder. This was no astronomical display to be explained by the hoquat magic science; this was a message from the past.

The boy spoke close behind: "Wow! Look at the falling stars. Did you make a wish?"

"I made a wish."

"What were you singing?"

"A song of my people."

Katsuk, the omen of the stars strong within him, saw the charcoal slash of path and the clearing as an arena within which he would begin creating a memory maker, a death song for the ways of the past, a holy obscenity to awe the hoquat world.

"Skagajek!" he shouted. "I am the shaman spirit come to drive the sickness from this world!"

David, hearing the strange words, lost his footing, almost fell, and was once again afraid.

From Katsuk's announcement to his people:

I have done all the things correctly. I used string, twigs, and bits of bone to cast the oracle. I tied the red cedar band around my head. I prayed to Kwahoutze, the god in the water, and to Alkuntam. I carried the consecrated down of a sea duck to scatter upon the sacrificial victim. It was all done in the proper way.

The immensity of the wilderness universe around David, the mystery of this midnight hike to some strange ritual, began to tell on him. His body was wet with perspiration, chilled in every breeze. His feet were sopping with trail dew. The Chief, an awesome figure in this setting, had taken on a new character. He walked with such steady confidence that David sensed all the accumulated woods knowledge compressed into each movement. The man was Deerstalker. He was Ultimate Woodsman. He was a person who could survive in this wilderness.

David began dropping farther and farther behind. The Chief became a gray blur ahead.

Without turning, Katsuk called: "Keep up."

David quickened his steps.

Something barked "Yap-yap!" in the trees off to his right. A sudden motion of smoky wings glided across him, almost touched his head. David ducked, hurried to close the gap between himself and that bobbing white loincloth.

Abruptly, Katsuk stopped. David almost ran into him.

Katsuk looked at the moon. It moved over the trees, illuminating crags and rock spurs on the far slope. His feet had measured out the distance. This was the place.

David asked: "Why'd we stop?"

"This is the place."

"Here? What's here?"

Katsuk thought: *How is it the hoquat all do this? They always prefer mouth-talk to body-talk.*

He ignored the boy's question. What answer could there be? This ignorant Innocent had failed to read the signs.

Katsuk squatted, faced the trail's downhill side. This had been an elk trail for centuries, the route between salt water and high meadows. The earth had been cut out deeply by the hooves. Ferns and moss grew from the side of the trail. Katsuk felt into the growth. His fingers went as surely as though guided by sight. Gently, gently, he pulled the fronds aside. Yes! This was the place he had marked out.

He began chanting, low-voiced in the ancient tongue:

"Hoquat, let your body accept the consecrated arrow. Let pride fill your soul at the touch of my sharp and biting point. Your soul will turn toward the sky. . . ."

David listened to the unintelligible words. He could not see the man's hands in the fern shadows, but the movements bothered him and he could not identify the reason. He wanted to ask what was happening but felt an odd constraint. The chanted words were full of clickings and gruntings.

The man fell silent.

Katsuk opened the pouch at his waist, removed a pinch of the consecrated white duck down. His fingers trembled. It must be done correctly. Any mistake would bring disaster.

David, his eyes adjusting to the gloom, began to make out the shadowy movement of hands in the ferns. Something white reflected moonlight there. He squatted beside the man, cleared his throat.

"What're you doing?"

"I am writing my name upon the earth. I must do that before you can learn my name."

"Isn't your name Charlie something?"

"That is not my name."

"Oh?" David thought about this. Not his name? Then: "Were you singing just now?"

"Yes."

"What were you singing?"

"A song for you—to give you a name."

"I already *have* a name."

"You do not have a secret name given between us, the most powerful name a person can have."

Katsuk smoothed dirt over the pinch of down. He sensed *Kuschtaliute*, the hidden tongue of the land otter, working through his hand upon the dirt, guiding each movement. The power grew in him.

David shivered in the cold, said: "This isn't much fun. Is this all there is to it?"

"It is important if we are to share our names."

"Am I supposed to do something?"

"Yes."

"What?"

Katsuk arose. He sensed tensions in his fingers where Kuschtaliute still controlled his muscles. Bits of dirt clung to his skin. The spirit power of this moment went all through his flesh. *"I am Tamanawis speaking to you. . . ."*

He said: "You will stand now and face the moon."

"Why?"

"Do it."

"What if I don't?"

"You will anger the spirits."

Something in the man's tone dried David's mouth. He said: "I want to go back now."

"First, you must stand and face the moon."

"Then can we go back?"

"Then we can go."

"Well . . . okay. But I think this is kind of dumb."

David stood. He felt the wind, a foreboding of rain in it. His mind was filled suddenly with memories of a childish game he and his friends had played among the creekside trees near his home: *Cowboys and Indians.* What would that game mean to this man?

Scenes and words tumbled through David's mind: *Bang! Bang! You're dead! Dead injun cowboy injun dead.* And Mrs. Parma calling him to lunch. But he and his friends had scratched out a cave in the creek bank and had hidden there, suppressing giggles in the mildew smell of cave dirt and the voice of Mrs. Parma calling and everything stirring in his head—memory and this moment in the wilderness, all become one—moon, dark trees moved by the wind, moonlit clouds beyond a distant hill, the damp odor of earth. . . .

The man spoke close behind him: "You can hear the river down there. We are near water. Spirits gather near water. Once, long ago, we hunted spirit power as children seek a toy. But you hoquat came and you changed that. I was a grown man before I felt Tamanawis within me."

David trembled. He had not expected words of such odd beauty. They were like prayer. He felt the warmth of the man's body behind him, the breath touching his head.

The voice continued in a harsh tone:

"We ruined it, you know. We distrusted and hated each other instead of our common foe. Foreign ideas and words clotted our minds with illusion, stole our flesh from us. The white man came upon us with a face like a golden mask with pits for eyes. We were frozen before him. Shapes came out of the darkness. They were part of darkness and against it—flesh and antiflesh—and we had no ritual for this. We mistook immobility for peace and we were punished."

David tried to swallow in a dry throat. This did not have the sound of ritual. The man spoke with an accent of education and knowledge. His words conveyed a sense of accusation.

"Do you hear me?" Katsuk asked.

For a moment, David failed to realize the question had been directed at him. The man's voice had carried such a feeling of speaking to spirits.

Katsuk raised his voice: "Do you hear me?"

David jumped. "Yes."

"Now, repeat after me exactly what I say."

David nodded.

Katsuk said, "I am Hoquat."

"What?"

"I am Hoquat!"

"I am Hoquat?" David could not keep a questioning inflection from his voice.

"I am the message from Soul Catcher," Katsuk said.

In a flat voice, David repeated it: "I am the message from Soul Catcher."

"It is done," Katsuk said. "You have repeated the ritual correctly. From this moment, your name is Hoquat."

"Does it mean something?" David asked. He started to turn, but a hand on his shoulder restrained him.

"It is the name my people gave to something that floats far out on the water, something strange that cannot be identified. It is the name we gave to your people because you came that way to us from the water."

David did not like the hand on his shoulder, but feared saying anything about it. He felt that his being, his private flesh, had been offended. Opposing forces struggled in him. He had been prepared for an event which he could almost see, and this ritual failed to satisfy him.

He asked: "Is that all there is to it?"

"No. It is time for you to learn my name."

"You said we could go."

"We will go soon."

"Well . . . what's your name?"

"Katsuk."

David fought down a shudder. "What's that mean?"

"Many, many things. It is the center of the universe."

"Is it an Indian word?"

"Indian! I am sick with being Indian, with living out a five-hundred-year-old mistake!"

The hand on David's shoulder gripped him hard, shook him with each word. David went very still. Suddenly, he knew for the first time he was in danger. *Katsuk.* It had an ugly sound. He could not understand why, but the name suggested deadly peril. He whispered: "Can we go now?"

Katsuk said: "Mamook memaloost! Kechgi tsuk achat kamooks. . . ."

In the old tongue, he promised it all: *I will sacrifice this Innocent. I will give him to the spirits who protect me. I will send him into the underplaces and his eyes will be the two eyes of the worm. His heart will not beat. His mouth. . . ."*

"What're you saying?" David demanded.

But Katsuk ignored him, went on to the end of it.

"Katsuk makes this promise in the name of Soul Catcher."

David said: "I don't understand you. What was all that?"

"You are the Innocent," Katsuk said. "But I am Katsuk. I am the middle of everything. I live everywhere. I see you hoquat all around. You live like dogs. You are great liars. You see the moon and call it a moon. You think that makes it a moon. But I have seen it all with my good eye and recognize without words when a thing exists."

"I want to go back now."

Katsuk shook his head. "We all want to go back, Innocent Hoquat. We want the place where we can deal with our revelation and weep and punish our senses uselessly. You talk and your world sours me. You have only words that tell me of the world you would have if I permitted you to have it. But I have brought you here. I will give you back your own knowledge of what the universe knows. I will make you know and feel. You really will understand. You will be surprised. What you learn will be what you thought you already knew.''

''Please, can't we go now?''

''You wish to run away. You think there is no place within you to receive what I will give you. But it will be driven into your heart by the thing itself. What folly you have learned! You think you can ignore such things as I will teach. You think your senses cannot accept the universe without compromise. Hoquat, I promise you this: you will see directly through to the thing at its beginning. You will hear the wilderness without names. You will feel colors and shapes and the temper of this world. You will see the tyranny. It will fill you with awe and fear.''

Gently, David tried to pull away from the restraining hand, to put distance between himself and these terrifying words of almost-meaning. Indians should not speak this way!

But the hand shifted down to his left arm, held it painfully.

No longer trying to conceal his fear, David said: ''You're hurting me!''

The pressure eased, but not enough to release him.

Katsuk said: ''We have shared names. You will stay.''

David held himself motionless. Confusion filled his mind. He felt that he had been kicked, injured in a way that locked all his muscles. Katsuk released his arm. Still David remained fixed in that position.

Fighting dryness in his mouth, David said: ''You're trying to scare me. That's it, isn't it? That's the initiation. The other guys are out there waiting to laugh.''

Katsuk ignored the words. He felt the spirit power grow and grow. *''I am Tamanawis speaking to you. . . .''* With slow, deliberate movements, he took an elkhide thong from his pouch, whipped it over the boy's shoulders, bound his arms tightly to his body.

David began twisting, struggling to escape. ''Hey! Stop that! You're hurting me!''

Katsuk grabbed the twisting hands, pinioned the wrists in a loop of the thong.

David struggled with the strength of terror, but the hands tying him could not be resisted. The thong bit painfully into his flesh.

''Please stop it,'' David pleaded. ''What're you doing?''

''Shut up, Hoquat!''

This was a new and savage voice, as powerful as the hands which held him.

Chest heaving, David fell silent. He was wet with perspiration and the moment he stopped struggling, the wind chilled him. He felt his captor remove the knife and sheath, working the belt out with harsh, jerking motions, then reclasping the belt without putting it into its loops.

Katsuk bent close to the boy, face demoniac in the moonlight. His voice was a blare of passion: ''Hoquat! Do what I tell you to do, or I will kill you immediately.'' He brandished David's knife.

David nodded without control of the motion, unable to speak. A tide of bitter acid came into his throat. He continued to nod until Katsuk shook him.

''Hoquat, do you understand me?''

He could barely manage the word: ''Yes.''

And David thought: *I'm being kidnapped! It was all a trick.*

All the horror stories he'd heard about murdered kidnap victims flooded into his mind, set his body jerking with terror. He felt betrayed, shamed at his own stupidity for falling into such a trap.

Katsuk produced another thong, passed it beneath David's arms, around his chest, knotted it, and took the free end in one hand. He said: ''We have a long way to go before daylight. Follow me swiftly or I will bury your body beside the trail and go on alone.''

Turning, Katsuk jerked the rope, headed at a trot toward the dark wall of trees across the bracken clearing.

David, the stench of his own fear in his nostrils, stumbled into motion to keep from being pulled off his feet.

STATEMENT OF Bruce Clark, chief counselor at Six Rivers Camp:

Well, the first night we make the boys write a letter home. We don't give them any dinner until they've written. We hand them paper and pencil there in the rec room and we tell them they have to write the letter before they can eat. They get their meal cards when they hand in the letter. The Marshall boy, I remember him well. He was on the six-o'clock news and there was a kind of hooraw about it when his father's picture came on and it was announced that the father was the new Undersecretary of State. The Marshall boy wrote a nice long letter, both sides of the paper. We only give them one sheet. I remember thinking: There's probably a good letter. His folks'll enjoy getting that.

ABOUT AN hour after sunrise, Katsuk led Hoquat at a shambling trot to the foot of the shale slope he had set as his first night's goal. The instant they stopped, the boy collapsed on the ground. Katsuk ignored this and concentrated on studying the slope, noting the marks of a recent slide.

At the top of the slope a stand of spruce and willow concealed a notch in the cliff. The trees masked a cave and the spring which fed the trees. The cliff loomed as a gray eminence behind the trees. The slide made it appear no one could climb to the notch.

Katsuk felt his heart beating strongly. Vapor formed at his mouth when he breathed. The morning was cold, although there would be sunlight here below the cliff later. The sharp smell of mint scratched at his awareness. Mint fed by the runoff of the spring protruded from rocks at the bottom of the slide. The odor reminded Katsuk that he was hungry and thirsty.

That would pass, he knew.

Even if the searchers used dogs, Katsuk did not believe they would get this far. He had used a scent-killer of his own making many times during the night, had broken trail four times by wading into streams, starting one way, killing the scent, then doubling back.

The low light of morning set the world into sharp relief. Off to his right at the edge of the rockslide red fireweed plumes swayed on the slope. A flying squirrel glided down the slope into the trees. Katsuk felt the flow of life all around him, glanced down at Hoquat sprawled in a bracken clump, a picture of complete fatigue.

What a hue and cry would be raised for this one. What a prize! What headlines! A message that could not be denied.

Katsuk glanced up at the pale sky. The pursuers would use helicopters and other aircraft, of course. They would be starting out soon. Just about now, they would be discovering at the camp what had been done to them. The serious, futile hoquat with their ready-made lives, their plastic justifications for existence, would come upon something new and terrifying: a note from Katsuk. They would know that the *place of safety* in which their spirits cowered had been breached.

He tugged at the thong that linked him to Hoquat, got only a lifted head and questioning stare from eyes bright with fear and fatigue. Tear streaks lined the boy's face.

Katsuk steeled himself against sympathy. His thoughts went to all the innocents of his own people who had died beneath guns and sabers, died of starvation, of germ-laden blankets deliberately sold to the tribes to kill them off.

"Get up," Katsuk said.

Hoquat struggled to his feet, stood swaying, shivering. His clothes were wet with trail dew.

Katsuk said: "We are going to climb this rock slope. It is a dangerous climb. Watch where I put my feet. Put your feet exactly where I have. If you make a mistake, you will start a slide. I will save myself. You will be buried in the slide. Is this understood?"

Hoquat nodded.

Katsuk hesitated. Did the boy have sufficient reserves of strength to do this? The nod of agreement could have been fearful obedience without understanding.

But what did it matter? The spirits would preserve this innocent for the consecrated arrow, or they would take him. Either way, the message would be heard. There was no reprieve.

The boy stood waiting for the nightmare journey to continue. A dangerous climb? All right. What difference did it make? Except that he must survive this, must live to escape. The madman had called him Hoquat, had forced him to answer to that name. More than anything else, this concentrated a core of fury in the boy.

He thought: *My name is David. David, not Hoquat. David-not-Hoquat.*

His legs ached. His feet were wet and sore. He felt that if he could just close his eyes right here he could sleep standing up. When he blinked, his eyelids felt rough against his eyes. His left arm was sore where a long red abrasion had been dragged across his skin by the rough bark of a tree. It had torn both his jacket and shirt. The madman had cursed him then: a savage voice out of darkness.

The night had been a cold nightmare in a black pit of trees. Now he saw morning's rose vapors on the peaks, but the nightmare continued.

Katsuk gave a commanding tug on the thong, studied the boy's response. Too slow. The fool would kill them both on that slide.

"What is your name?" Katsuk asked.

The voice was low, defiant: "David Marshall."

Without change of expression, Katsuk delivered a sharp backhand blow to the boy's cheek, measuring it to sting but not injure. "What is your name?"

"You *know* my name!"

"Say your name."

"It's Dav—"

Again, Katsuk struck him.

The boy stared at him, defiant, fighting back tears.'

Katsuk thought: *No reprieve . . . no reprieve. . . .*

"I know what you want me to say," the boy muttered. His jaws pulsed with the effort of holding back tears.

No reprieve.

"Your name," Katsuk insisted, touching the knife at his waist. The boy's eyes followed the movement.

"Hoquat." It was muttered, almost unintelligible.

"Louder."

The boy opened his mouth, screamed, "Hoquat!"

Katsuk said, "Now, we will climb."

He turned, went up the shale slope. He placed each foot with care: now on a flat slab jutting from the slide, now on a sloping buttress which seemed anchored in the mountain. Once, a rock shifted under his testing foot. Pebbles bounded down into the trees while he waited, poised to jump if the slope went. The rocks remained in place, but he sensed the trembling uncertainty of the whole structure. Cautiously, he went on up.

At the beginning of the climb, he watched to see that Hoquat made each step correctly, found the boy occupied with bent-head concentration, step for step, a precise imitation.

Good.

Katsuk concentrated on his own climbing then.

At the top, he grasped a willow bough, pulled them both into the shelter of the trees.

In the shaded yellow silence there, Katsuk allowed the oil-smooth flow of elation to fill him. He had done this thing! He had taken the Innocent and was safe for the moment. He had all the survival seasons before him: the season of the midge, of the cattail flowering, of salal ripening, of salmonberries, the season of grubs and ants—a season for each food.

Finally, there would be a season for the vision he must dream before he could leave the Innocent's flesh to be swallowed by the spirits underground.

Hoquat had collapsed to the ground once more, unaware of what waited him.

Abruptly, a thunderous flapping of wings brought Katsuk whirling to the left. The boy sat up, trembling. Katsuk peered upward between the willow branches at a flight of ravens. They circled the lower slopes, then climbed into the sunlight. Katsuk's gaze followed the birds as they swam in the sky sea. A smile of satisfaction curved his lips.

An omen! Surely an omen!

Deerflies sang in the shadows behind him. He heard water dripping at the spring.

Katsuk turned.

At the sound of the ravens, the boy had retreated into the tree shadows as far as the thong would allow. He sat there now, staring at Katsuk, and his forehead and hair caught the first sunlight in the gloom like a trout flashing in a pool.

The Innocent must be hidden before the searchers took to the sky, Katsuk thought. He pushed past the boy, found the game trail which his people had known here for centuries.

"Come," he said, tugging at the thong.

Katsuk felt the boy get up and follow.

At the rock pool where the spring bubbled from the cliff, Katsuk dropped the thong, stretched out, and buried his face in the cold water. He drank deeply.

The boy sprawled beside him, would have pitched head foremost into the pool if Katsuk had not caught him.

"Thirsty," Hoquat whispered.

"Then drink."

Katsuk held the boy's shoulder while he drank. Hoquat gasped and sputtered, coming up at last with his face and blond hair dripping.

"We will go into the cave now," Katsuk said.

The cave was a pyramidal black hole above the pool, its entrance hidden from the sky by a mossy overhang which dripped condensation. Katsuk studied the cave mouth a moment for sign that an animal might be occupying it, saw no sign. He tugged at the thong, led Hoquat up the rock ledge beside the pool and into the cave.

"I smell something," the boy said.

Katsuk sniffed. There were many old odors—animal dung, fur, fungus. All of them were old. Bear denned here because it was dry, but none had been here for at least a year.

"Bear den last year," he said.

He waited for his eyes to adjust to the gloom, found a rock spur too high up on the cave's wall for the boy to reach with his tied hands, secured the end of the thong on the spur.

The boy stood with his back against the rock wall. His gaze followed every move Katsuk made. Katsuk wondered what he was thinking. The eyes appeared feverish in their intensity.

Katsuk said: "We will rest here today. There is no one to hear you if you shout. But if you shout, I will kill you. I will kill you at the first outcry. You must learn to obey me completely. You must learn to depend on me for your life. Is that understood?"

The boy stared at him, unmoving, unspeaking.

Katsuk gripped the boy's chin, peered into his eyes, met rage and defiance.

"Your name is Hoquat," Katsuk said.

The boy jerked his chin free.

Katsuk put a finger gently on the red mark on Hoquat's cheek from the two blows at the rockslide. Speaking softly, he said: "Do not make me strike you again. We should not have that between us."

The boy blinked. Tears formed in the corners of his eyes, but he shook them out with an angry gesture.

Still in that soft voice, Katsuk said: "Answer to your name when I ask you. What is your name now?"

"Hoquat." Sullen, but clear.

"Good."

Katsuk went to the cave mouth, paused there to let his senses test the area. Shadows were shortening at the end of the notch as the sun climbed higher. Bright yellow skunk cabbages poked from the shadowed water at the lower end of the spring pool.

It bothered him that he had struck Hoquat, although strong body-talk had been required then.

Do I pity Hoquat? he wondered. *Why pity anyone?*

But the boy had showed surprising strength. He had spirit in him. Hoquat was not a whiner. He was not a coward. His innocence lay within a real person whose center of being remained yet unformed but was gaining power. It would be easy to admire this Innocent.

Must I admire the victim? Katsuk wondered.

That would make this thing all the more difficult. Perhaps it would occur, though, as a special test of Katsuk's purpose. One did not slay an innocent out of casual whim. One who wore the mantle of Soul Catcher dared not do a wrong thing. If it were done, it must fit the demands of the spirit world.

Still, it would be a heavy burden to kill someone you admired. Too heavy a burden? Without the need for immediate decision, he could not say. This was not an issue he wanted to confront.

Again, he wondered: *Why was I chosen for this?*

Had it occurred in a way similar to the way he had chosen Hoquat? Out of what mysterious necessities did the spirit world act? Had the behavior of the white world become at last too much to bear? Certainly that must be the answer.

He felt that he should call out from the cave mouth where he stood, shouting in a voice that could be heard all the way to the ocean:

"You down there! See what you have done to us!"

He stood lost in reverie and wondered presently if he might have shouted. But the hoard of life all around gave no sign of disturbance.

If I admire Hoquat, he thought, *I must do it only to strengthen my decision.*

FROM THE speech Katsuk made to his people:

Bear, wolf, raven, eagle—these were my ancestors. They were men in those days. That's how it was. It really was. They celebrated when they felt happy about the life within them. They cried when they were sad. Sometimes, they sang. Before the hoquat killed us, our songs told it all. I have heard those songs and seen the carvings which tell the old stories. But carvings cannot talk or sing. They just sit there, the eyes staring and dead. Like the dead, they will be eaten by the earth.

DAVID SHUDDERED with aversion to his surroundings. The gray-green gloom of the cave, the wet smoothness of rock walls at the sunlit mouth which his thong leash would not permit him to reach, the animal odors, the dance of dripping water outside—all tormented him.

He was a battleground of emotions: something near hysteria compounded of hunger, dread, shuddering uncertainty, fatigue, rage.

Katsuk came back into the cave, a black silhouette against the sunlight. He wore the Russell knife at his waist, one hand on the handle.

My knife, David thought. He began to tremble.

"You are not sleeping," Katsuk said.

No answer.

"You have questions?" Katsuk asked.

"Why?" David whispered.

Katsuk nodded but remained silent.

The boy said: "You're holding me for ransom, is that it?"

Katsuk shook his head. "Ransom? Do you think I could ransom you for an entire world?"

The boy shook his head, not understanding.

"Perhaps I could ransom you for an end to all hoquat mistakes," Katsuk said.

"What're you. . . ."

"Ahhh, you wonder if I'm crazy. Drunk, maybe. Crazy, drunken Indian. You see, I know all the clichés."

"I just asked why." Voice low.

"I'm an ignorant, incompetent savage, that's why. If I have a string of degrees after my name, that must be an accident. Or I probably have white blood in me, eh? Hoquat blood? But I drink too much. I'm lazy. I don't like to work and be industrious. Have I missed something? Any other clichés? Oh, yes—I'm blood-thirsty, too.

"But I just—"

"You wonder about ransom. I think you have made all the mistakes a hoquat should be permitted."

"Are you . . . crazy?"

Katsuk chuckled. "Maybe, just a little."

"Are you going to kill me?" Barely whispered.

"Go to sleep and don't ask stupid questions." He indicated the cave floor, clumps of dry moss which could be kicked into a bed.

The boy took a quavering breath. "I don't want to sleep."

"You will obey me." Katsuk pointed to the floor, kicked some of the moss into position at the boy's feet.

Every movement a signal of defiance, Hoquat knelt, rolled onto his side, his tied hands pressed against the rock wall of the cave. His eyes remained open, glaring up at Katsuk.

"Close your eyes."

"I can't."

Katsuk noted the fatigue signs, the trembling, the glazed eyes. "Why can't you?"

"I just can't."

"Why?"

"Are you going to kill me?" Stronger that time.

Katsuk shook his head.

"Why are you doing this to me?" the boy demanded.

"Doing what?"

"Kidnapping me, treating me like this."

"Treating you like what?"

"You know!"

"But you have received ordinary treatment for an *Indian*. Have our hands not been tied? Have we not been dragged where we would rather not go? Have we not been brutalized and forced to take names we did not want?"

"But why me?"

"Ahhhh, why you! The cry of innocence from every age."

Katsuk pressed his eyes tightly closed. His mind felt damned with evil sensations. He opened his eyes, knew he had become that *other person*, the one who used Charles Hobuhet's education and experiences, but with a brain working in a different way. Ancient instincts pulsed in his flesh.

"What'd I ever do to you?" the boy asked.

"Precisely," Katsuk said. "You have done nothing to me. That is why I chose you."

"You talk crazy!"

"You think I have caught the hoquat disease, eh? You think I have only words, that I must find words to pin down what cannot be cut into word shapes. Your mouth bites at the universe. You give tongue to noises. I do not do that. I send another kind of message. I draw a design upon the emotions. My design will rise up inside people where they have no defenses. They will not be able to shut their ears and deny they heard me. I tell you, they will hear Katsuk!"

"You're crazy!"

"It is odd," Katsuk mused. "You may be one of the few people in the world who will not hear me."

"You're crazy! You're crazy!"

"Perhaps that's it. Yes. Now, go to sleep."

"You haven't told me why you're doing this."

"I want your world to understand something. That an innocent from your people can die just as other innocents have died."

The boy went pale, his mouth in a rigid grimace. He whispered: "You're going to kill me."

"Perhaps not," Katsuk lied. "You must remember that the gift of words is the gift of illusion."

"But you said. . . ."

"I say this to you, Hoquat: Your world will feel my message in its balls! If you do as I tell you, all will go well with you."

"You're lying!"

Anger and shame tore at Katsuk. "Shut up!" he shouted.

"You are! You're lying—you're lying." The boy was sobbing now.

"Shut up or I'll kill you right now," Katsuk growled.

The sobs were choked off, but the wide-open eyes continued to stare up at him.

Katsuk found his anger gone. Only shame remained. I *did lie*.

He realized how undignified he had become. To allow his own emotion such wild expression! He felt shattered, seduced into the word ways of the hoquat, isolated by words, miserable and lonely.

What men gave me this misery? he wondered.

Barren sorrow permeated him. He sighed. Soul Catcher gave him no choice. The decision had been made. There could be no reprieve. But the boy had learned to detect lies.

Speaking as reasonably as he could, Katsuk said: "You need sleep."

"How can I sleep when you're going to kill me?"

A reasonable question, Katsuk thought.

He said: "I will not kill you while you sleep."

"I don't believe you."

"I swear it by my spirits, by the name I gave you, by my own name."

"Why should I believe that crazy stuff about spirits?"

Katsuk pulled the knife partly from its sheath, said: "Close your eyes and you live."

The boys eyes blinked shut, snapped open.

Katsuk found this vaguely amusing but wondered how he could convince Hoquat. Every word scattered what it touched.

He asked: "If I go outside, will you sleep?"

"I'll try."

"I will go outside then."

"My hands hurt."

Katsuk took a deep breath of resignation, bent to examine the bindings. They were tight but did not completely shut off circulation. He released the knots, chafed the boys wrists. Presently he restored the bindings, added a slip noose to each arm above the elbows.

He said: "If you struggle to escape now, these new knots will pull tight and shut off the circulation of blood to your arms. If that happens, I will not help you. I'll just let your arms drop off."

"Will you go outside now?"

"Yes."

"Are you going to eat?"

"No."

"I'm hungry."

"We will eat when you waken."

"What will we eat?"

"There are many things to eat here: roots, grubs. . . ."

"You'll stay outside?"

"Yes. Go to sleep. We face a long night. You will have to keep up with me then. If you cannot keep up, I will be forced to kill you."

"Why're you doing this?"

"I told you."

"No, you didn't."

"Shut up and go to sleep."

"I'll wake up if you come back."

Katsuk could not suppress a grin. "Good. I know what to do when I want to awaken you."

He stood up, went down to the spring pool, pushed his face into the water. It felt cold and fresh against his skin. He squatted back on his heels, allowed his senses to test the silences of this place. When he was sure of his surroundings, he made his way out to the edge of the trees where the shale slope began. He sat there for a time, quiet as a grouse crouching in its own shadow. He could see the trail his people had beaten down for centuries. It skirted the trees far down below the slide. The trail remained quite visible from this height, although forest and bracken had reclaimed it.

He told himself: *I must be strong now. My people have need of me. Our trails are eaten by the forest. Our chilren are cursed and slaughtered. Our old men do not speak to us anymore in words we can understand. We have withstood evil heaped upon evil but we are dying. We are landless in our own land.*

Quietly, to himself, Katsuk began singing the names of his dead: *Janiktaht . . . Kipskiltch. . . .* As he sang, he thought how all of the past had been woven into the spirit of his people's songs and now the songs, too, were dying.

A black bear came out of the trees far below him, skirted the slide, and went up the fireweed slope eating kinnikinnick. It gave the shale a wide berth.

We need not hurry here, Katsuk thought.

Presently, he crept under the wide skirt of a fat spruce, deep into the shadows of the low boughs. He lay down facing the shale slope and prepared to sleep with the smell of the forest floor in his nostrils.

Soon, he thought, *I must replace the hoquat knife with a proper blade, one that is fit to touch the bow and arrow I will make.*

FROM A letter to his parents by David Marshall:

Dear Mother and Dad: I am having a lot of fun. The airplane was early in Seattle. A man from camp met me there. We got on a small bus. The bus drove for a long time. It rained. It took us to a thing they call a cogwheel train. The train comes up the mountain to the camp. They chased a bear off the tracks. My counselor is a Indian, not like Mrs. Parma. He was born by the ocean he said. His name is Charles something. We call him Chief. We do not have tents to sleep in. Instead, we sleep in cabins. The cabins have names. I am in Cedar Cabin. When you write, put Cedar Cabin on the letter. One of the guys in my cabin was here last year. He says the Chief is the best counselor. Mr. Clark is the camp director. He took our picture with the Chief. I will send you one when he gets them. Eight of us sleep in our cabin. The chief has his own room at the back near the toilet. Please send me six rolls of film and some insect repelent. I need a new flashlight. My other one got broken. A boy cut his hand on the train. There are lots of trees here. They have good sunsets. We will go on a two day hike Sunday. Thanks for the package of goodies. I found them on the train. After I passed my cookies around to all my friends half of them were gone. I haven't opened the peanuts yet. We are waiting for dinner right now. They are making us write before we eat.

DAVID AWAKENED.

For a moment his only awareness was of hunger cramps and the dry, hot thirst rasping his throat. Then he felt the thongs around his wrists and arms. He experienced surprise that he had slept. His eyes felt rough and heavy. Katsuk's warning against fighting the thongs came back to him. The cave light was a green grayness. He had scattered the cushioning moss. Coldness from the rock beneath him chilled his flesh. A moment of shivering overcame him. When it passed, his gaze went up the thong to the loop secured around the rock spur. It was much too high.

Where was that crazy Katsuk?

David struggled to a sitting position. As he moved, he heard a helicopter pass across the rock slope directly opposite the cave's mouth.

He recognized the sound immediately and hope surged through him. Nothing else made quite that sound: *Helicopter!*

David held his breath. He remembered the handkerchief he had dropped below the slide. He had carried the handkerchief for miles during the nightmare journey, wondering where to drop it. The handkerchief carried his monogrammed initials—a distinctive *DMM*.

He had wormed the handkerchief from his pocket soon after thinking about it, wadded the cloth into a ball, and held it—waiting . . . waiting. There had been no sense dropping it too soon. Katsuk had led them up and down streams, confusing their trail. David had thought of tearing the cloth into bits, dropping the pieces like a paper chase, but the monogram occupied only one corner and he had felt certain Katsuk would hear cloth ripping.

At the rock slope, David had been moved as much by fatigue and desperation as any other motive. Katsuk was sure to hide them during daylight. The ground below the slope was open to the sky. No trail crossed that area. A handkerchief in an unusual place *could* attract attention. And Katsuk had been so intent on the slide, so confident, he had not been watching his back trail.

Surely, the men in the helicopter out there now had seen the handkerchief.

Again, the noisy racket of rotors swept across the mouth of the notch and its concealed cave. What were they doing? Would they land?

David wished he could see the slope.

Where was that crazy Katsuk? Had he been seen?

David's throat burned with thirst.

Again, the helicopter passed the notch. David strained to hear any telltale variation in sound. Was rescue at hand?

He thought of the long night's march, the fears which had blocked his thoughts, the dark paths full of root stumbles. Hunger and terror cramped him now, doubled him over. He stared down at the cave's rock floor. The bear smell of the place came thickly into his nostrils.

Again, the machine sound flooded the cave.

David tried to recall the appearance of the slope. Was there a place for a helicopter to land? He had been so tired when they had emerged from the trees, so thirsty and hungry, so filled with desperation about where to leave the telltale handkerchief, he had not really seen the area. The blind feelings of the night with its stars cold and staring clogged his memory. He recalled only the confused surge of bird cries at dawn, falling upon senses amplified by hunger and thirst.

What were they doing in that helicopter? Where was Katsuk?

David tried to recall riding in a helicopter. He had traveled with his parents to and from airports in helicopters. That sound had to be a helicopter. But he had never paid much attention to what landing place a helicopter required, except to know it could land on a small space. Could it land on a slope? He didn't know.

Perhaps the rockslide kept the machine from landing. Katsuk had warned about that danger. Maybe Katsuk had a gun now, he could have hidden one here and recovered it. He could be out there waiting to shoot down the helicopter.

David shook his head from side to side in desperation.

He thought of shouting. No one in the helicopter would hear him above that engine noise. And Katsuk had warned that death would follow any outcry.

David recalled his own knife in its sheath at Katsuk's waist—the Russell knife from Canada. He imagined that knife being pulled from its sheath by Katsuk's dark hand—one hard thrust. . . .

He'll kill me sure if I shout.

The clatter of the machine circling in and out of the clearing around the rockslide confused David. The cave and its masking trees baffled the sound. He could not tell when the helicopter flew low into the slope or when it hovered above the cliff—only that it was out there, louder sometimes than at other times.

Where was Katsuk?

David's teeth chattered with cold and terror. Hunger and thirst chopped time into uneven bits. The dusty yellow light outside the cave told him nothing. No matter how hard he listened, straining to identify what was happening, he could not interpret the sounds into meaning.

There was only the single fact of the helicopter. The sound of it filled the cave once more. This time it came as an oddly distorted noise building slowly into a rumbling roar louder than thunder. The cave trembled around him.

Had they crashed?

He held his breath as the terrifying noise went on and on and on . . . louder, louder. It built to a climax, subsided. The noise of a raven flock became audible. The helicopter had faded to a distant background throbbing.

He could still hear the machine, though. The rotors' *beat-beat-beat* mingled with drifts of cold green light within the cave to dominate David's awareness. He swallowed dry terror, listened with an intensity which began in the middle of his back. The sound of the helicopter faded . . . faded . . . vanished. He heard ravens calling and the dull clap of their wings.

The arch of the cave mouth was filled by Katsuk's black silhouette, its edges blurred by dusty light from outside. Katsuk advanced without a word, removed the thongs from the rock, untied the boy's wrists and arms.

David wondered: *Why doesn't he say something? What happened out there?*

Katsuk felt David's hip pocket.

David thought: *The handkerchief!* He tried to swallow, stared at his captor, begging for a clue to what was happening.

"That was very clever," Katsuk said, his voice conversational. He began massaging the boy's wrists. "Very, very clever; so very clever."

The sound of Katsuk speaking low, a voice like smoke in the cave, filled David with more fear than if the man had betrayed rage.

If he calls me Hoquat, David thought, *I must remember to answer and not anger him*.

Katsuk released David's wrists, sat down facing the boy. He said: "You will want to know what happened. I will tell it."

I am Hoquat, David reminded himself. *I must keep him calm.*

David watched Katsuk's lips, eyes, listened for any change of tone, any sign of emotion. Words came slow cadence from Katsuk's mouth: "Raven . . . giant bird . . . devil machine. . . ."

The words carried odd half-meanings. David felt he was hearing some fanciful story, not about a helicopter but about a giant bird called Raven and Raven's victory over evil.

Katsuk said: "You know, when Raven was young, he was the father of my people. He brought us the sun and the moon and the stars. He brought us fire. He was white then, like you, but fire smoke blackened his feathers. It was that Raven who came back today and hid me from your devil machine—black Raven. He saved me. Do you understand?"

David trembled, unable to comprehend or to answer.

Katsuk's eyes reflected cobalt glints in the cave's half-light. The sunlight pouring in the entrance behind him put a honey glow on his skin, made him appear larger.

"Why are you trembling?" Katsuk asked.

"I . . . I'm cold."

"Are you hungry?"

"Y-Yes."

"Then I will teach you how to live in my land. Many things are provided here to sustain us—roots, sweet ants, fat grubs, flowers, bulbs, leaves. You will learn these things and become a man of the woods.''

"A w-woodsman?"

Katsuk shook his head from side to side. "A man of the woods. That is much different. You are sly and have a devil in you. These make the man of the woods.''

The words made no sense to David, but he nodded.

Katsuk said: "Raven said to me we can travel by daylight. We will go now because the hoquat will be sending men on foot. They will come to this place because of your sly handkerchief.''

David ran his tongue over his lips. "Where are we going?"

"Far into the mountains. We will find the valley of peace, perhaps, where my ancestors put all the fresh water once.''

David thought: *He's crazy, pure crazy.* And he said: "I'm thirsty.''

"You can drink from the spring. Stand up now.''

David obeyed, wondered if the thongs would be tied on his wrists. His side hurt where he had slept on the rock floor of the cave. He looked at the light flaring outside. *Travel by daylight . . . with a helicopter out there somewhere?*

Was pursuit close on their heels? Was crazy Katsuk running in daylight because searchers were near?

Katsuk said: "You think your friends will fly to us in their devil machine and rescue you.''

David stared at the cave floor.

Katsuk chuckled. "What is your name?"

"Hoquat.'' Without looking up.

"Very good. But your friends will not see us, Hoquat.''

David looked up into staring dark eyes. "Why not?"

Katsuk nodded at the cave mouth. "Raven spoke to me out there. He told me he will conceal us from all searchers in the sky. I will not even bind you. Raven will keep you from running away. If you try to escape, Raven will show me how to kill you. Do you understand me, Hoquat?''

"Y-Yes. I won't try to escape.''

Katsuk smiled pleasantly. "That is what Raven told me.''

GENESIS ACCORDING to Charles Hobuhet, from a paper for Anthropology 300:

And therefore a man shall leave his father and shall leave his mother and he shall cling to the spirit which binds him to his flesh, being naked before this flesh as he can be naked before no other. And were he not ashamed before this nakedness, aware of this bone from his bones, then shall his flesh be closed and made whole. Then the heavy sleep shall fall upon this man, though he built a god. And finding no other helper, all the names of man shall be his. And his god shall cause the heavens to fall that every beast of the field might call the man, seeking a soul. A living soul is its name. All the cattle, all the fowl, every creature shall be brought unto the man to see what was formed from the primal substance into a living soul. And man, to his separation from that which formed him, will say only its name, thinking this his helper of helpers. But Alkuntam has said: "Not being good, thou shalt die. And all things that live shall become flesh of your flesh, and a separation from the heavens—and therefore a man.''

THE NOISE of a helicopter had awakened Katsuk shortly after noon. He lay motionless in the shadow of the spruce, locating the sound before he lifted his head. Even then, he moved slowly, as an alerted animal, aware that the low limbs concealed him, but avoiding any disturbance to attract a searcher's attention.

The helicopter came in over the trees below the rock slope, climbed to circle above his hiding place, went out and around once more. The *thwock-thwock* of its rotors dominated all other sounds around Katsuk as the machine circled over the cliff above him and back over the open ground of the slope.

Katsuk peered upward through the concealing limbs. Sunlight flashed from the helicopter's bubble canopy. The machine was green and silver with Park Service markings on its sides. Under the sound of its rotors it made a greedy hissing noise which set perspiration flowing in Katsuk's palms.

Why did they keep circling? What attracted them?

He knew the spruce hid him, but the abrasive presence of the searchers sank into his nerves, sent his mind leaping to escape.

Around and around the helicopter went, circling the open slope with its boundaries of cliff and trees.

Katsuk thought of the boy in the cave. The men in the helicopter would have to land and shut down their machine before they could hear a shout. They could not land atop the cliff, though: Stunted trees grew from the rocks up there. And the slope below the slide was too steep.

What were they doing here?

Katsuk tore his attention from the circling machine, scanned the slope. Presently, his gaze focused on something out of place. Far down the slope below the slide, in the narrow strip of grass and bracken before the trees, something unnaturally white glistened.

Where all else should be gray and green an odd whiteness lay draped in the bracken. A sharp woodsman's eye in that helicopter had seen it.

Katsuk studied the white thing as the helicopter made another pass. What was it? The wind of the rotors disturbed the thing, set it fluttering.

Awareness exploded in him: *Handkerchief!*

Hoquat had slipped a handkerchief out of his pocket and let it fall there. Again, the wind from the helicopter stirred the square of cloth, betrayed its alien nature.

The thing shouted to an observer that something man-made lay there in the wilderness, far off the usual trails. Such a thing would arouse a searcher's curiosity.

Once more, the helicopter came in over the trees below the rock slope. It flew dangerously low, tipped to give the man beside the pilot an opportunity to study the white object through binoculars. Katsuk saw sunlight flash from the lenses.

If the searcher aimed his binoculars into the shadows beneath the spruce, he might even detect a human shape there. But experience worked against the men in the aircraft. They had recognized the nature of the rockslide. They could see wind from their craft raising dust in the shale. They would see the slide as a barrier to a man on foot, especially to a man encumbered by an inexperienced boy. They would *know* a man could not climb that slope.

The pilot tried to hover his craft over the slope, giving his observer a steady platform, but a strong wind beat across the cliff in turbulent eddies. The helicopter bounced, slipped, drifted close to the treetops. The engine roared as the machine climbed out over the rocks. It skidded in a gust of wind, went around for another circuit.

Katsuk crept farther back into the trees.

The pilot obviously was daring, but he would know the perils of attempting a landing near the white object which had attracted him. He must have radio, though. He would have reported the strange thing he had seen. Searchers on foot would be coming.

Again, the helicopter skimmed in low over the trees, dipped across the slope. Engine sound filled the air.

A slow, grinding rumble came from the rocks below Katsuk. The slide began to move as the helicopter's thunderous vibration loosed a key rock in that delicate balance on the slope. The movement of the slide built momentum with ponderous inevitability. Tufts of dust puffed in the tumbling gray. The rocks gathered speed, raised a storm noise that drowned out the mechanical intruder. The machine climbed out of the clearing just above a rising cloud of dust that lifted into the wind. The odor of burnt flint drifted into the notch past Katsuk.

Abruptly, a flock of ravens that had perched silently in the grove behind Katsuk through all the disturbance took flight. Their wings beat the air. Their beaks opened. But no sound of them could be heard above the avalanche.

The entire slope was in motion now. A great tumbling maelstrom of rock roared downward into the trees, buried the bracken, hurled bark chips from the trunks. Smaller trees and brush snapped and were smothered beneath the onslaught.

As slowly as it began, the slide ended. A few last rocks bounded down the slope, leaped through drifting dust, crashed into the trees. The ravens could be heard now. They circled and clamored against this outrage in their domain.

From a circling path high over the clearing, the helicopter played background to the ravens.

Katsuk peered up through the limbs at all the motion.

The helicopter drifted out to the right, came in for another pass over the subsiding dust of the rockslide. The handkerchief was gone, buried beneath tons of rocks. Katsuk distinctly saw one of the men in the bubble canopy gesture toward the ravens.

The flock had opened its ranks, whirled, and called raucously around the intruder.

The machine slid across Katsuk's field of vision. It climbed out over the trees and its downdraft sent the birds skidding.

Some of the ravens settled into the trees above Katsuk while their mates continued dipping and feinting around the helicopter.

The machine climbed out westward, set a course toward the ocean. The sound of its engines faded.

Katsuk wiped wet palms on his loincloth. His arm brushed the knife at his waist, made him think of the boy in the cave.

A handkerchief!

The ravens had protected him—and the rockslide. The spirits might even have started the slide.

As certainly as if he had heard the man's voice, Katsuk knew the searcher who had gestured at the ravens had explained that the birds were a sure sign no human was around. The aircraft had gone elsewhere to search. Its occupants were secure in the message of the ravens.

Head bowed, Katsuk silently thanked Raven.

This is Katsuk who sends gratitude to Thee, Raven Spirit. I speak Thy praise in a place where Thy presence was made known. . . .

As he prayed, Katsuk savored appreciation of the ignorant hoquat beliefs. Whites did not know *The People* had sprung from Raven. Raven always guarded his children.

He thought about the handkerchief. There had been one in Hoquat's pocket. Surely, that was the one on the slope.

Instead of angering him, the defiant gesture ignited a sense of admiration. *Daring . . . clever . . . little Hoquat devil!* Even the most innocent remained sly and resourceful. Hands tied behind him, terror in his heart, he still had thought to leave a sign of his passage.

Awareness growing within him, Katsuk studied the small seed of admiration he now held for Hoquat. Where could such a feeling lead? Was there a point of admiration that might prevent Hoquat's death? How much were the spirits willing to test Katsuk?

The boy had almost succeeded with that handkerchief.

Almost.

This then was not the real test. This was a preliminary skirmish, preparation for something greater to come.

Katsuk felt wild awareness telling him why the boy had failed. Something was tempering them here—both of them. Katsuk sensed that his own thinking had changed once more, that these events had been anticipated. The blur of black wings, that waterfall of ravens, had seized upon his awareness. He was being watched and guarded.

Fear had searched all through him and left him clean.

What had it done to the boy?

The blue-gray panting of the rockslide, the dust cloud rising like steam, had set the wilderness in motion, had given it a new voice which Katsuk could understand.

Tamanawis, the being of his spirit power, had been reborn.

Katsuk rubbed the place on his hand where Bee had marked him. His flesh had absorbed that message and much more: a power that would not be stopped. Let the searchers send their most sophisticated machines against him. He was the Bee of his people, driven by forces no hoquat machine could conquer. All that lived wild around him helped and guarded him. The new voice of the wilderness spoke to him through every creature, every leaf and rock.

Now, he could remember Janiktaht with clarity.

Until this moment, Janiktaht had been a dream-sister: disheveled, drowned, eyes like torches among treacherous images. She had been a tear-clouded mystery, her perfume the rotting sea strand, her soul walled in by loneliness, a graceless memory, accusing, united with every witch enchantment of the night.

Now his fears lay buried in the rockslide. He knew the eyes of Charles Hobuhet had seen reality: Janiktaht dead, sodden and bloated on a beach, her hair tangled with seaweed, one with a welter of lost flotsam.

As though to put the seal on his revelation, the last of the raven flock returned from pursuit of the helicopter. They settled into the trees above Katsuk. Even when he emerged boldly from the spruce shadows and climbed to the cave where Hoquat lay captive, the ravens remained, talking back and forth.

FRAGMENT OF a note left at the Sam's River shelter:

Your words perpetuate illusion. You clot my mind with foreign beliefs. My people taught that Man is dependent upon the goodwill of all other animals. You forbade the ritual which taught this. You said we would be punished for such thoughts. I ask you who is being punished now?

AS THEY picked their way down the remnants of the rockslide and walked openly into the forest, David told himself the helicopter was sure to return. The men in it had seen his handkerchief. Katsuk as much as admitted that. What did all his insane talk about ravens have to do with anything real? The men had seen the handkerchief; they would return.

David looked over his shoulder at the cliff, saw a thin cloud above it clinging like a piece of lint to the clear-blown sky.

The helicopter would return. People would come on foot.

David strained to hear the sound of rotors.

KATSUK HAD led him into solid shadows under trees, and David prayed now that the aircraft would come only when they were in a clearing or on a trail not shielded by trees.

Crazy Indian!

Katsuk felt the pressure of the boy's thoughts, but he knew the two figures in this forest gloom were not people. No people passed this way. They were primal elements who snagged their essence upon bits of time like animal fur caught on thorns. His own thoughts went as wind through grass, moving this world only after they had passed. And when they had passed, everything behind them resolved itself into silence, almost-but-not-quite the way it had been before their intrusion.

Yet—something changed.

They changed something essential that could be felt on the farthest star.

Once Katsuk stopped, faced the boy, and said:

"Therefore the flight shall perish from the swift, and the strong shall not strengthen his force, neither shall the mighty deliver himself. That's what it says in your hoquat book. It says he that is courageous among the mighty shall flee away naked in the day. You hoquat had some wise men once, but you never listened."

Another time, they rested and drank at a spring that bubbled from a ledge. A green river roared in its chasm below them. High clouds rippled the sky and there were hill shadows on gray rocks across the river.

Katsuk pointed down to the river. "Look."

David whirled, stared down, and in the quick rhythm of light flung by the river into the canyon's gloom he saw a brown deer swimming, its head thrusting at the far shore. The light and sound and animal movement roaring together dazzled his mind.

There was a dark chill in the wind, and as they left the spring David sensed the quick silence of the forest birds. More clouds had accumulated. A deerfly crouched on his arm. He watched it pause and take flight. He had long since given up hope that Katsuk would produce food from this wilderness. It had been talk, just talk—all those words about food in this place. Katsuk had said it himself: Words fooled you.

David's eyes were caught by the venturesome racing of a squirrel's feet along a high limb. He wondered only if the creature could be caught and eaten.

The day wore on. Sometimes Katsuk talked about himself and his people, fanciful stories indistinguishable from reality. They moved through damp woods, through sunlit clearings, beneath clouds, beneath dripping leaves. Always, there was the sound of their own footsteps.

David forgot about his hunger in the presence of great weariness. Where were they going? Why were there no more aircraft?

Katsuk did not think of a destination, saying, "Now we are here, and we will go there." He felt himself changing, sensed the ancient instincts taking over. He sensed blank places growing in his memory, things he no longer knew in the ways this hoquat world accepted.

Where would the changes in him lead?

The answer unfolded in his mind, the spirits revealing their wisdom: The workings of his brain would go through a deep metamorphosis until, at last, his mind lay like a drunk within his driven self. He would be Soul Catcher entirely.

There was a spring shadowed by a giant cottonwood. Deer tracks led up to it and all around. Katsuk stopped and they drank. The boy splashed his face and collar.

Katsuk watched him, thinking: *How powerful, this young human, how strange, drinking from that spring with his hands. What would his people think of such a lad in such a pose?*

There was a new grace in things the boy did. He was fitting himself into this life. When it was time for silence, he was silent. When it was time to drink, he drank. Hunger came upon him in its proper order. The spirit of the wilderness had seeped into him, beginning to say that it was right for such a one to be here. The rightness of it had not yet become complete, though. This was still a hoquat lad. The cells of his flesh whispered rebellion and rejection of the earth around him. At any moment he might strike out and become once more the total alien to this place. The thing lay in delicate balance.

Katsuk imagined himself then as a person who adjusted that balance. The boy must not demand food before its time. Thirst must be quenched only in the rhythm of thirst. The shattering intrusion of a voice must be prevented by willing it not to happen.

Bees weighted with pollen were working in fireweed on the slope below the spring. Katsuk thought: *They watch us. They are the spirit eyes from which we never escape.*

He stared through leaf-tattered light at the working creatures. They were fitted into the orderliness of this place. They were not many creatures, but one single organism. They were Bee, the spirit messenger who had brought him here.

The boy finished drinking at the spring, sat back on his heels, watchful, waiting.

For a glimmering instant, something in the set of the boy's head opened for Katsuk a glimpse of the man who had fathered this human. The adult peered out of youthful eyes, weighing, judging, planning.

Momentarily, it unnerved Katsuk to think of that man-and-father here. The father was no innocent. *He* would have all of the hoquat vices. *He* would have the powers, evil and good, which had given the hoquat dominion over the primitive world. That one must be kept in the background, suppressed.

How could it be done? The boy's flesh could not be separated from that which gave it life. A spirit power must be invoked here. Which spirit power? How? Could the man-father be driven away with his own guilt?

Katsuk thought: *My father should come to help me now.*

He tried to call up a vision of his father, but no face came, not even a voice.

Katsuk felt the seeds of panic.

There had been a father. The man had existed. He was back there walking the beaches, fishing, breeding two children. But he had taken the path of drink and inward rage and a death in the water. Were the hoquat to blame for that?

Where was his face, his voice? He was Hobuhet, the Riverman, whose people had lived on this land for twice a thousand years. He had fathered a son.

And Katsuk thought: *But I am no longer Charles Hobuhet. I am Katsuk. Bee is my father. I have been called to do a terrible thing. The spirit I must call upon is Soul Catcher.*

Silently, he prayed then, and saw at once how the boy's eyelids blinked, how his attention wandered. No power stood against Soul Catcher in this wilderness. Once more, Katsuk felt calm. The greatest of the spirits could not be doubted. The hoquat father had been driven back into the flesh. Only the Innocent remained.

Katsuk arose and strode off along the slope, hearing the boy follow. There had been no need for words of command. Soul Catcher had created a wake in the air which drew the boy into it as though he were caught on a tow line.

Now, Katsuk left the game trail he had been following and struck off through moss-draped hemlocks. There was a granite ledge up above them somewhere hemming in the river valley. Without ordering his feet to seek that place, Katsuk knew he could find it.

He came on the first outcroppings within the hour and moved out of the trees, climbing a slope of stunted huckleberry bushes toward rock shade. The boy followed, panting, pulling himself up by the bushes as he saw Katsuk doing. They emerged presently on a bald rock and there was the river valley spread out southward with sweet grass and elk grazing in a meadow.

A string of fat quail stuttered through sun-splashed shadows below him, catching Katsuk's attention. The quail reminded him of a hunger which he knew his body would feel if it were time for that sensation. But he sensed no hunger, knowing by this that his flesh had accommodated itself to primitive ways.

The boy had sprawled out on sun-warmed rock. Katsuk wondered if Hoquat felt hunger or denied it. The lad also was accommodating to primitive ways. But how was he doing it? Was he immersed so deeply in each moment that only the needs of the moment called out to his senses? The climb had tired him and thus he rested. That was the correct way. But what else had changed in the hoquat flesh?

Carefully, Katsuk studied his captive. Perspiration had left damp darkness in the hair at the boy's neck. Stains of brown dirt marked the legs of his trousers. Streaks of mud were drying on his canvas shoes.

Katsuk smelled the boy's sweat, a youthful, musky sweetness in it which called up memories of school locker rooms. He thought:

It is a fact that the earth which marks us on the surface also leaves its traces within us.

There would come a moment when the boy was tied so firmly to this wilderness that he could not escape it. If the link were forged in the right way, innocence maintained, there would be a power in it to challenge any spirit.

I was marked by his world; now he is marked by mine.

This had become a contest on two levels—the straightforward capture of a victim and the victim's desire to escape, but beneath that a wrestling of spirits. The signs of that other contest were all around.

Katsuk looked out across the valley. There was an old forest on the far slope, fire dead, burned silver hacking the green background into brittle shapes.

The boy turned onto his back, threw a hand across his eyes.

Katsuk said: "We will go now."

"Can't we wait just a minute?" Without removing the hand from his eyes.

Katsuk chuckled. "You think I don't know what you've been doing?"

The boy took the hand away, looked up at Katsuk. "What do you. . . ."

"You slow down when we're crossing a meadow. You trip when we ford the river, then you want me to build a fire. You think I don't know why you complained when we left the elk trail?"

Blood suffused the boy's cheeks.

Katsuk said: "Look where we are now, eh?" He pointed skyward. "Wide open to searching devil machines, huh? Or men could see us from the valley. They could identify us with binoculars."

The boy glared at him. "Why do you say *devil machines* instead of helicopters? You know what they are."

"True, I know what you think they are. But different people see things differently."

David turned away. He felt stubborn determination to prolong this moment in the open. Hunger and fatigue helped him now. They sapped his physical strength but fed his rage.

Abruptly, Katsuk laughed, sat down beside him.

"Very well, Hoquat. I will demonstrate Raven's power. We will rest here while it's warm. Stare at the sky all you wish. Raven will hide us even if a devil machine flies directly over us."

David thought: *He really believes that!*

Katsuk rolled onto his side, studied his captive. How strange that Hoquat didn't understand about Tamanawis. The boy would wait and wait, hoping, praying. But Raven had spoken.

The rock felt warm and soothing beneath him. Katsuk rolled onto his back, glanced around. A quaking aspen grew from the sunward side of their aerie. The quickness of the bright sun pulsing on the aspen's leaves made him think of Hoquat's life.

Yes, Hoquat is like that: trembling in every wind, now glittering bright, now shadowy, now innocent, now evil. He is the perfect Hoquat for me.

The boy said: "You don't really believe that raven stuff."

Katsuk spoke softly: "You will see."

"A guy at camp said you went to the university. They must teach you at the university how stupid that stuff is."

"Yes, I went to the hoquat university. They teach ignorance there. I could not learn ignorance, although everyone was studying it. Maybe I'm too stupid."

Katsuk grinned at the sky, his gaze aimlessly following an osprey which soared and circled high above them.

David watched his captor covertly, thinking how the man was like a big cat he'd seen at the San Francisco zoo—supine on the rock, reclining at ease, the tawny skin dulled by an overlay of dust, eyes blinking, flaring, blinking.

"Katsuk?"

"Yes, Hoquat."

"They're going to catch you and kill you."

"Only if Raven permits it."

"You were probably so stupid they wouldn't let you stay at the university!"

"Haven't I admitted it?"

"What do you know about anything?"

Katsuk heard the rage and fear in the boy's voice, wondered what kind of a son this one had been. It was easy to think of that stage in the boy's life as past—all done. This one would never live to a ripe and wrinkled fulfillment. He had accepted too many lies, this one. Even without a Katsuk he would never have made it to a rich old time of quiet.

"You don't know anything!" the boy pressed.

Katsuk shrugged himself into a new position, selected a stem of grass growing from a crack in the rock. He slipped the grass free of its sheath, began to chew the sweet juices.

David tasted the sourness at the back of his throat, muttered: "You're just stupid!"

Slowly, Katsuk turned his head, studied the boy. "In this place, Hoquat, I am the professor and you are the stupid."

The boy rolled away, stared into the sky.

"Look up there all you wish," Katsuk said. "Raven hides us from searchers." He extracted another grassblade from its green sheath, chewed it.

"Professor!" the boy sneered.

Katsuk said: "And you are slow to learn. You are hungry, yet there is food all around us."

The young eyes jerked toward the grass in Katsuk's mouth.

"Yes, this grass. It has much sugar in it. Back when we crossed the river, you saw me take the roots of those reeds, wash them, and chew them. You saw me eat those fat grubs, but you only wondered out loud how we could catch fish."

David felt the words burn into his consciousness. Grass grew from the rock near his head. He yanked a stem. It came up by its roots.

Katsuk chuckled, selected a supple young shoot, showed how to draw out the tender stem—slowly, firmly—without disturbing the roots.

David chewed the grass, experimentally at first. Finding it sweet, he ground the stem in his teeth. Hunger knotted his stomach. He pulled another stem, another. . . .

Katsuk interrupted: "You've learned one lesson. Come. We will go now."

"You're afraid your raven can't hide us."

"You want a conclusive scientific test, eh? Very well, just stay where you are."

Katsuk turned away, cocked his head to one side, listening.

The pose primed David's senses. He felt the sound of an engine in the air, realized Katsuk must have been hearing it for some time. So that was why he'd wanted to go!

Katsuk said: "You hear it?"

David held his breath. The sound grew louder. He felt his heart beating wildly.

Katsuk lay back without moving.

David thought: *If I jump up and wave, he'll kill me.*

Katsuk closed his eyes. He felt sheet lightning in his brain, an inner sky filled with fire. This was an ultimate test. He prayed for the inner sense of power. *This is Katsuk.* . . . The sound of the helicopter weighed upon his senses.

David stared southwest across the aspen which shaded their rock. The sound was coming from there. It grew louder . . . louder.

Katsuk lay motionless, with his eyes closed.

David wanted to shout: "Run!" It was insane. But Katsuk would be caught if he stayed there. Why didn't he get up and run into the trees?

A fit of trembling overcame David.

Movement flickered in the sky above the aspen.

David stared, frozen.

The helicopter was high but in plain sight. His gaze followed its passage: a big helicopter flying through a patch of blue sky between clouds. It flew from right to left in the open sky perhaps a mile away. An occupant would only have to glance this way to see two figures on the high rock escarpment.

The big machine crossed the far ridge of the river valley. High trees there gradually concealed it. The sound diminished.

As it disappeared, a single raven flew over the rock where David lay, then another, another. . . .

The birds flew silently, intent upon some private destination.

Katsuk opened his eyes in time to see the last of them. The sound of the helicopter was gone. He looked at the boy. "You did not try to attract their attention. Why? I would not have stopped you."

David's glance flicked across the knife at Katsuk's waist. "Yes, you would."

"I would not."

David sensed an impulse in the words, a confidence that spoke of truth. He reacted with bitter frustration. It made him want to run and cry.

Katsuk said: "Raven hides us."

David thought of the birds which had flown overhead. They had arrived after the helicopter was gone. It made no real sense to him, but David felt the flight of birds had been a signal. He had the eerie sensation that the birds had spoken to Katsuk in some private way.

Katsuk said: "I don't have to kill you while Raven protects. Without Raven's protection . . . well. . . ."

David whirled away. Tears stung his eyes. *I should've jumped up and waved! I should've tried!*

In one supple motion, Katsuk arose, said: "We go now."

Without a backward glance to see if the boy followed, Katsuk crossed the open rock, plunged into the trees on the next slope. He sensed rain in that southwest wind. Tonight it would rain.

FROM AN editorial submitted to the University of Washington *Daily* by Charles Hobuhet:

In terms of the flesh, you whites act upon fragmented beliefs. You fall therefrom into loneliness and violence. You do not support your fellows, yet complain of being unsupported. You scream for freedom while rationalizing your own self-imposed limitations. You exist in constant tension between tyranny and victimization. Through all your fraudulent pretensions and roundabout self-trickery, you say you would risk anything to achieve equal happiness for all. But your words risk nothing.

DAVID FINGERED the two small pebbles in his pocket—one for each day. The second day with this madman. They had slept and dozed through the night beneath a ledge which sheltered them from the rain. Katsuk had refused to build a fire, but he had gone alone into the forest and returned with food: a gray mush in a bark bowl. David had wolfed it, savoring an acrid sweetness. Katsuk had explained then that it was lily roots chopped with grubs and sweet red ants.

At the look of revulsion on David's face, Katsuk had laughed, said: "Squeamishness can kill you out here as fast as anything else. That is good food. It has everything in it that you need."

The laughter had silenced David's objections more than any other argument. He had eaten the gray mush again as dawn glared over the trees.

He had been following Katsuk two hours this morning before his clothes dried.

There were hemlocks overhead now. Ancient blaze marks formed pitch-ringed scars on some of the tree trunks. Katsuk had recognized the marks and explained them: This was a way his ancestors had traveled. Ferns and moss lay in a tangled miniature wilderness under the trees, obscuring the ancient track, but Katsuk said this was the way.

The sky darkened. David wondered if it was going to rain again.

Up ahead, Katsuk paused, studied his surroundings. He turned, watched the boy plunging along behind—over mossy logs, around great clumps of fern.

Katsuk stared down the slope ahead of him. The ancient elk trail his people had used ran somewhere down there. He would cross it soon and follow the path of his wild brethren.

The boy came up to him, stood panting.

Katsuk said: "Stay closer to me."

He set out once more, skirted a mossy log, noted beneath it a tiny dewed spiderweb. All around him lay a forest of mossy limbs—every limb draped with moss like green wool hung out to dry. The light, now bright and now dull as clouds concealed the sun, alternately flattened the colors and then filled the world with green jeweled glowing. At one passage of muted green, the sun suddenly emerged and sent a rope of light plunging through the trees to the forest floor.

Katsuk walked through the light, then ducked under dark boughs. He heard

495

limbs catching at the boy behind him, scratching, slithering.

Beyond the dark passage, Katsuk stopped, reached out a hand, and caught the boy from stepping past. The trail was directly in front of them about two feet down a steep bank. It sloped down to the left. Tracks of hiking boots marked the soft earth.

David saw the tension in Katsuk, listened for the sound of the hikers. The tracks appeared fresh. Water trickled down the trail but had not yet filled the tracks.

Katsuk turned, glanced at the boy, motioned flatly with one hand—back up the way they had come.

David shook his head: "What?"

Katsuk stared up the hill behind them, said: "That big log we came over. Go back there and hide behind it. If I hear or see any sign of your presence, I will kill you."

David stepped backward, turned, and climbed back to the log. It was a cedar, its bark hidden beneath moss, but live limbs climbed skyward along its length. Katsuk had pointed out another such fallen tree, calling it a nurse log. The limbs would be trees some day. David climbed back over the nurse log.

He sank to his heels there, stared through the shadows. His eyes looked for color, for movement. In his own silence, he grew aware of the constant sound of water dripping all around. He felt the dampness of this place. His feet were sopping and his trousers were dark with water almost to the waist. It was cold.

Katsuk stepped down to the trail, turned left in the direction of the hiker's tracks. He glided down the trail, moving with a wraith quality—brown skin, the white loincloth tugging at David's gaze.

The trail switched back to the right. Katsuk turned with it. Only his head and shoulders remained visible to the watching boy.

Abruptly, far down the hillside David saw color and movement—a group of hikers. As though vision opened the air to sound, he heard their voices then: no distinguishable words, but sudden laughter and a shout.

David sank farther down behind the log, peered out between a tangle of dead limbs. As he did it, he wondered: *Why am I hiding? Why don't I sneak around Katsuk and get to those hikers? They'd protect me from him.*

But he sensed his own destruction in any movement. Part of Katsuk remained focused on his captive, some inner sense. There might even be ravens around.

David crouched, tense and quivering.

Katsuk had stopped, head and shoulders visible above the trail embankment. He stared up toward David, then looked up the trail.

David heard noise up the trail then, tried to swallow in a dry throat. More hikers?

He thought: *I could shout.*

But he knew any outcry would bring Katsuk and the knife.

Slogging, heavy footsteps became audible.

A bearded young man came down the trail. A green pack rode high on his shoulders. His long hair was bound at the forehead by a red bandanna. It gave him a curiously aboriginal look. The hiker glanced neither right nor left but kept his attention on the trail. He walked with a stiff, heel-first stride that jarred the ground.

David felt giddy with fear. He no longer could see Katsuk but knew the man lay in wait down there somewhere. He would be watching the hiker from some hidden spot below.

David thought: *All I have to do is stand up and shout.*

The other hikers might not hear it, but this one would. He was just passing David's hiding place. The other hikers were a long way down there though. There was a stream down in that canyon. Its noise would hide any sound from up here.

David thought: *Katsuk would kill this guy . . . and then me. He told me what he'd do . . . and he meant it.*

The bearded hiker was at the switchback. He would see Katsuk momentarily, or pass right by without noticing anything.

What was Katsuk doing?

For several minutes, Katsuk had felt a test of purpose building to a climax. In that dark passage before he had reached the trail, he had felt an odd fear that he would find his secret name carved some place—on a tree or stump or log.

At the few open places, he had stared up at the sky—now gray, now bright as blue-green glass. It was a crystal without form, but ready to take any shape. Perhaps his name would be written there.

A bulbous gray quinine canker on an old stump had filled him with foreboding. He had thought of Hoquat following him like a pet on a leash. Then, wonderingly: *Soul Catcher has given me power over Raven, but that is not enough.*

He wondered if there were any *thing* in these mountains with the power to set his universe in perfect order once more. A vision of Janiktaht filled his mind: a head with sand on its cheeks, a head turned to seaweed shadows, the face broken upon its imperfections. The ghost of Janiktaht could not set things right.

Now he heard the voices and laughter of the hikers below and thought it was people taunting him. He heard the lone straggler coming.

The forest was a dull green-gray world suddenly, lidded by a lead sky. The wind had gone down under the trees, and in that new silence of birds and a storm building, Katsuk thought he heard his own heart beating only when he moved, that it stopped when he stopped.

Hatred formed in him then. What right had these hoquat to play in his forest? He felt all the defeats of his people. Their sobs and oaths and lamenting echoed within him, a swarm of unavenged shadows.

The bearded hiker came around the switchback, his head down, the many signs of fatigue in his stride. The pack was too heavy, of course, filled with things he did not need here.

With a dull shock, Katsuk realized he had seen that bearded face before—on the university campus. He could put no name to the face, only a vague recognition that this was a student he had seen. It bothered him that he could not name the face.

In that instant, the hiker saw Katsuk crouched on the trail and jarred to a stop.

"Wha. . . ." The young man shook his head, then: "Hey, It's Charlie the Chief! Hey, man, what're y' doing out here in that getup? You playing Indians and settlers?"

Katsuk straightened, thinking: *The fool doesn't know. Of course he doesn't. He's been in my forest without a radio.*

The hiker said: "I'm Vince Debay, remember? We were in that Anthro Three-hundred class together."

Katsuk said: "Hello, Vince."

Vince leaned his pack against the trail's uphill embankment, took a breath. His face betrayed the questions in his mind. He could not help but recognize the strangeness of this encounter. He might recognize the face, but he must know this was not the same Charlie the Chief of that Anthro 300 class. He must know it! Katsuk felt hate covering his face with a stale mask as dry and wrinkled as a discarded snakeskin. Surely, Vince could see it.

Vince said: "Man, am I tired. We've been all morning coming from the Kimta.

We were hoping to make it to Finley Shelter by tonight, but it doesn't look like we're going to make it." He waved a hand. "Hey, I was just joking, you know—about Indians and settlers. No offense."

Katsuk nodded.

"You see the other guys?" Vince asked.

Katsuk shook his head.

Vince said: "Why the loincloth bit, man? Aren't you cold?"

"No."

"I stopped to blow a little grass. The other guys must be almost to the bottom by now." He peered around Katsuk. "I think I hear them. Hey, guys!" The last came out in a shout.

Katsuk said: "They can't hear you. They're too close to the river."

"I guess you're right."

Katsuk thought: *I must kill him without anger, an act of irony. I must cut a malignant and venomous thing from my forest. It will be an event in which the world may see itself.*

Vince said: "Hey, Chief, you're awfully quiet. You're not mad or anything."

"I am not angry."

"Yeah . . . well, good. You want a little grass? I got half a lid left."

"No."

"It's high-grade stuff, man. I got it in Bellingham last week."

"I do not smoke your marijuana."

"Oh. What *are* you doing out here?"

"I live here. This is my home."

"Come on! In that getup?"

"This is what I wear when I search for a deformity of the spirit."

"A what?"

"A thing by which men may know sanity."

"You're putting me on."

Katsuk thought: *I must end it. He cannot be allowed to go and report that he has seen me.*

Vince rubbed his shoulder beneath a pack strap. "This pack sure is heavy."

Katsuk said: "You have not yet discovered that having too much is not better than having enough."

Nervous laughter jerked in Vince's throat. He said: "Well, I gotta catch up with the others. See you, Chief." He hunched his shoulders into the straps, taking the weight of it off the embankment, stepped past Katsuk. There was obvious fear in his movements.

Katsuk thought: *I cannot pity. That would make the earth fall away from beneath my feet. My knife must go cleanly into this walking youth.* He pulled the knife from its sheath, moved after Vince. *The knife must pay homage to his blood and break open the time of death. Birth must end with death, with eyes gone dull, memory gone, heart gone, blood gone, all the flesh gone—the miracle ended.*

As he thought, he moved: left hand into Vince's hair, yanking the head back, right hand whipping the knife around and across the exposed throat.

There was no outcry, just the body slumping back, guided by the hand in the long hair. Katsuk dropped to one knee, caught the weight of the pack on it, held the jerking figure upright. A jet of red gushed from the slashed throat, the lucid color of a young life spurting in a bright fountain onto the trail—a rose petal spurting, ebbing, softly now and now frothing, resurgent, the body twitching, then still.

It was done.

Katsuk felt that this moment had been following him all his life, now to catch up with him.

An ending and a beginning.

He continued to support the body, wondered how old this young man had been. Twenty? Perhaps. Whatever his age, it was ended here—the pleasure and the time passing, all a dream now. Katsuk felt his mind whirling with what he had done. Strange visions captured his awareness: all a dream, black and hidden, an evil profile, clouds under water, limbs of air moving with jade ripples, a green crystal, fluid carving traces in his memory.

This earth had green blood.

He felt the weight of the sagging body. This flesh had been a minor pattern in an overlarge universe. Now it faded. He allowed the body to fall on its left side, stood, and peered uphill toward the log where Hoquat lay hidden. It was a hillside suddenly full of green light as clouds exposed the sun.

Deep within himself, Katsuk prayed: *Raven, Raven, keep the edge on my hate. O Raven, keep me terrible in revenge. This is Katsuk, who lay three nights in thy forest, who heeded no thorn, but did thy bidding. This is Katsuk, thy torch, who will set this world afire.*

SPECIAL AGENT Norman Hosbig, Seattle Office, FBI:

Just because we suspect he may have gone to some city doesn't mean we stop searching that wilderness. As of today, we have almost five hundred people in all phases of the search over there. We have sixteen aircraft still in the park—nine of them helicopters. I read in the morning paper where they are calling it a strange kind of contest, modern against primitive. I don't see it that way at all. I don't see how he could be walking those trails unseen with all the people we have searching.

DAVID HAD watched the killing, standing up from his hiding place, his mind raddled by terror. That young hiker who had been so alive—nothing but a carcass now. Katsuk's eyes were fearful things, their gaze hunting through the gloom of the hillside. Were they seeking another victim?

David felt that Katsuk's eyes had been hidden in some far depth, coming now to the surface—brown and terrible and so deep from where they had been.

On trembling legs, David crept up the hill behind his hiding place. He knew his face was contorted with terror, his breathing all out of pace, coming fast and shallow. But he had little control over his muscles.

All he wanted was release.

Slowly, he started, moving parallel with the trail. He had to find those other hikers! At last, he turned downhill, stumbling over logs and limbs. Movement restored some of his muscle control. He began to run, emerging from the trees onto a lower section of the trail.

There was no sight or sound of the other hikers or of Katsuk.

He was running all out now. There was nothing left to do but run.

In a trick of light, Katsuk saw the running boy—hair flying, a winged head, a slow-motion being of solid light: ivory with inner brilliance, splendid and golden, swimming upon the green field of the forest and the air.

Only then did Katsuk realize that he, too, was running. Straight down the slope he went in great gulping strides. He burst out upon the switchback trail as Hoquat rounded a corner above him, caught the running boy in full stride, and swept him to the ground.

Katsuk lay there a moment, catching his breath. When at last he could speak, his words came out in a wild drumbeat with little meaning outside the angry syllables pounding.

"Damn! Damn! Damn! I told you! Stay down earth. . . ."

But Hoquat had been knocked unconscious, his head striking a log beside the trial.

Katsuk sat up, grinning, his anger evaporated. How foolish Hoquat had appeared—the stumbling flight of a recent nestling. Raven had, indeed, anticipated everything in the universe.

There was a bloody bruise on the side of Hoquat's head. Katsuk put a hand to the boy's breast, felt the heart beating, saw vapor form as the boy breathed. The heart, the breath . . . the two things were one.

Sadness overcame him. Those loggers on the La Push road! Look what they had done. They had killed Janiktaht. They had killed this boy beneath his arm here. Not this moment, perhaps . . . but eventually. They had killed Vince, growing cold up there on the trail. There would be no sons of Vince's making. No daughters. No laughter ringing after him. Not now. All killed by those drunken hoquat. Who knew how many they had killed?

How could the hoquat not understand these things they did with their own violence? They remained blind to the most obvious facts, unwilling to see the consequences of their behavior. An angel-spirit could come down from heaven and show them the key to their actions and they would deny that spirit.

What would the nine drunken hoquat say if they saw Vince's dead flesh up there on the trail? They would become angry. They would say: *"We didn't do that!"* They would say: *"We just had a little innocent fun."* They would say: *"Christ! It was just a little klooch! When did a bit of tail ever hurt one of them?"*

Katsuk thought of Vince walking on the campus—not innocent enough to satisfy Soul Catcher, but naïve in the rightness of his own judgments. A preliminary sacrifice, one to mark the way.

Vince had judged his own people harshly, had shared the petty rebellions of his time, but had never sent his thoughts ahead to seek out a way in his world. He had merely *reacted* his way into sudden death.

Katsuk climbed to his feet, threw the unconscious boy over his shoulder, trudged back up the hill. He thought:

I must not pity. I must hide Vince's body and then go on.

Hoquat stirred on Katsuk's shoulders, muttered: "My head. . . ."

Kastuk stood the boy on his feet, steadied him. "You can walk? Very well. We will go on."

PSALM OF Kastuk: written on the backs of trail registry blanks and left at Cedar Cabin:

You brought your foreign god who sets you apart from all other life. He presents you with death as His most precious gift. Your senses are bedazzled by His illusions. You would give His death to all the life that exists. You pursue your god with death, threatening Him with death, praying to take His deadly place.

You stamp the crucifix across the earth's face. Wherever it touches, there the earth dies. Ashes and melancholy shall be your lot all the rest of your days.

You are a blend of evil and magnificence. You torture with your lies. You trample the dead. What blasphemy resides in your deadly pretensions of love!

You practice your look of sincerity. You become a mask, transparent, a grimace with a skull behind it. You make your golden idols out of cruelty.

You disinherit me in my own land.

Yea, by the trembling and fear of my people, I blight you with all of the ancient curses. You will die in a cave of your own making, never again to hear birdsong or trees humming in the wind or the forest's harp music.

DAVID AWOKE in pale dawn light. He was trembling with cold and damp. Katsuk's hand gripped his shoulder, shaking, shaking. Katsuk wore clothes taken from the dead hiker's pack: jeans that were too tight for him over the loincloth, a plaid shirt. He still wore moccasins and the band of red cedar bark around his head.

"You must awaken," Katsuk said.

David sat up. A cold, gray world pressed around him. He felt the damp chill of that world all through his body. The clothing on Katsuk made him think of the hiker's death. Katsuk had murdered! And so swiftly!

That memory conveyed a deeper chill than anything in the creeping gray fog of this wilderness.

"We will go soon," Katsuk said. "You hear me, Hoquat?"

Katsuk studied the boy, seeing him with an odd clarity, as though the dull gray light around them were concentrated into a spotlight which illuminated every movement in the young face.

Hoquat was terrified. Some part of the boy's awareness had translated the hiker's death correctly. One death was not enough. The ritual sacrifice must be carried through to its proper end. Hoquat must not let this awareness rise into his consciousness. He must know it while denying it. Too much terror could destroy innocence.

The boy shuddered, a sudden, uncontrollable spasm.

Katsuk squatted back on his heels, felt a sudden inward chill, but kept a hand on Hoquat's arm. The flesh pulsed with life beneath Katsuk's fingers. There was warmth in that life, a sense of continuity in it.

"Are you awake, Hoquat?" Katsuk pressed.

501

David pushed the man's hand away, flicked a glance across the sheathed knife at Katsuk's waist.

My knife, David thought. *It killed a man.*

As though his memory had a life of its own, it brought up the picture of his mother warning him to be careful with "that dreadful knife." He felt hysterical laughter in his throat, swallowed to suppress it.

Katsuk said: "I will be back in a few minutes, Hoquat." He went away.

David's teeth chattered. He thought: *Hoquat! I am David Marshall. I'm David Morgenstern Marshall. No matter how many times that madman calls me Hoqaut, that won't change a thing.*

There had been a sleeping bag in the hiker's pack. Katsuk had made a ground cover of moss and cedar boughs, spread the bag over them. The bag had been pushed aside during the night and lay now in a damp wad. David pulled it around his shoulders, tried to still the chattering of his teeth. His head still ached where he had bruised it when Katsuk had hurled him to the ground.

David thought then about the dead hiker. After he had regained consciousness and before they crossed the river, Katsuk had forced his captive back up the trail to that bloody body, saying: "Hoquat, go back to where I told you to hide and wait there."

David had been glad to obey. As much as he had wanted *not* to look at the dead youth, his eyes kept coming back to the gaping wound in the neck. He had climbed back to the mossy nurse log, hidden his face behind it, and lost himself to dry sobs.

Then Katsuk, who had called him after a long time, was carrying the pack. There had been no sign of body or bloody marks of a struggle on the trail.

They had stayed off the elk track for a time after that, climbing parallel to it, returning to the trail on the other side of a high ridge.

At dusk, Katsuk had built a crude cedar-bark shelter deep in trees above a river. He had brought five small fish from the river, cooked them over a tiny fire in the shelter.

David thought about the fish, tasting them in memory. Had Katsuk gone for food now?

They had crossd the river before building the shelter. There had been a well-marked hiking trail, a bridge above a flood-scoured bar. The boards of the bridge had been soft wet with a pocking of slush on the downstream lip, the air all around full of smoky spray.

Had Katsuk gone down there to get more fish?

There was a sign by the bridge: FOOT OR HORSE USE ONLY.

Game was thick along the river trail. They had seen two does, a spotted fawn, a brown rabbit running ahead of them for a space, then darting into the wet greenery.

David thought: *Maybe Katsuk put out a rabbit snare.*

Hunger knotted his stomach.

They had climbed under a drizzle of rain. It had come down in thin plumes from catch-basin leaves to bend the ferns flat. There was no rain now though.

Where *was* Katsuk?

David peered out of the shelter. It was a dawn world of cold and dampness with the sound of ducks quacking somewhere. It was a ghostly world, a dark dawn. No bright cords of light, just a twisted, incoherent gray.

He thought: *I must not think how that hiker was killed.*

But there was no escaping that memory. Katsuk had done it in full view of his captive. A splash of light on steel and then that great gout of blood.

David felt his chest shaking at the memory.

Why had Katsuk done that? Because the hiker had called him Chief? Surely not. Why then? Could it be the spirits Katsuk kept referring to? Had they commanded him to murder?

He was crazy. If he listened to spirits, they could order him to do anything. Anything.

David wondered if he could escape in this foggy morning. But who knew where Katsuk was now? The hiker had tried to leave. Katsuk could be waiting even now for his captive to run.

After the murder, all during that day, David's mind had rattled with unspoken questions. Something had told him not to ask those questions of Katsuk. The death of the hiker must be put behind them. To recall it was to invite more death.

They had come a long way from that terrible place of murder. David's legs had ached with fatigue and he had wondered how Katsuk could keep up such a pace. Every time David had lagged behind, Katsuk had motioned with the hand which had wielded the knife.

David remembered how he had welcomed nightfall. They had stopped perhaps a half hour before dark. It had been raining. Katsuk had ordered the boy to wait beneath a cedar while the shelter was built. The river valley had filled with liquid darkness that flowed into it from shadowed hills. The sodden woods had fallen silent. At dark, the rain had stopped and the sky had cleared. Sounds had grown in the darkness. David had heard rocks laboring in the river bottom, the noises of a world become chaos.

Every time he had closed his eyes, his memory had filled with that blood-wet, gaping neck, the knife in its brittle flashing.

For a long time, he had kept his eyes open, peered out of the shelter into the bower of darkness. A gray bulk of rock had emerged, hanging on the river's far slope, released from the night by moonlight. David had stared at it. Somewhere in that fearful staring, he had gone to sleep.

What was Katsuk doing?

Dragging the sleeping bag around him, David crawled to the shelter's opening. He poked his head out: cold, drifting fog everywhere. There was only one thing outside, a bulk of surrounding gray, wet and full of dull shapes, as though the fog tried to hold onto the night.

Where had Katsuk gone?

The man materialized then out of one of the dull shapes. He walked from the fog as though brushing aside a curtain, thrust a rolled bark cone into David's hand, and said: "Drink this."

David obeyed, but his hands trembled so that he spilled part of the cone's milky liquid onto his chin. The stuff smelled of herbs and tasted bitter. He gasped as it went down. It was cold in his mouth at first, then burned. He gulped convulsively, almost vomited.

Shuddering, David held out the cup of bark, demanded: "What was that?"

Katsuk pulled the sleeping bag from David's shoulders, began rolling it. "That is Raven's drink. I prepared it last night." He stuffed the sleeping bag into the pack.

"Was it whiskey?" David asked.

"Hah! Where would I get the hoquat drink?"

"But what. . . ."

"It is made from roots. One of the roots is devil's club. It gives you strength."

Katsuk slipped the pack straps over his shoulders, stood up. "We go now."

David crawled out of the shelter, got to his feet. As he cleared the entrance, Katsuk kicked a supporting limb for the shelter. The Bark structure fell with a clatter, sending up a puff of ashes from the their fire pit. Katsuk took up a limb, went to an animal burrow above the shelter, scattered dirt over the area. When he was through, he had created the effect that the animal had moved the dirt.

A ball of heat radiated from the drink in David's stomach. He felt wide awake and full of energy. His teeth had stopped chattering.

Katsuk threw aside the digging stick, said: "Stay close behind me." He climbed around the animal burrow into the fog.

David, stopping to pick up a pebble—his third, to make the third day—thought of putting his footprints in the raw dirt. But Katsuk had stopped above him and was watching.

Skirting the burrow, David climbed toward his captor. Katsuk turned, resumed the climb.

Why do I just follow him? David wondered. *I could run away and hide in this fog. But if he found me, he'd kill me. He still has that knife.*

A vision of the slain hiker filled his mind.

He'd kill me sure. He's crazy.

Katsuk began reciting something in a language strange to David. It was a low chant that went over the same syllables again and again.

"Crazy Indian," David muttered.

But he spoke in a low voice which would not carry to Katsuk.

CHIEF PARK Ranger William Redek:

Well, you have to realize how big and wild this country really is, especially in the Wilderness Area. For example, we know there are at least six small aircraft crashed somewhere in there. We've never found them, although we've searched. Have we *ever* searched! Not even a clue. And those aircraft aren't actively trying to hide from us.

"WHY DO you pick up those rocks?" Katsuk asked.

David held up four pebbles in his left hand. "To count the days. We've been gone four days."

"We count by nights," Katsuk said.

And Katsuk wondered at himself, trying to teach this essential thing to a hoquat. Four pebbles for the days or four pebbles for nights, what difference could it make for a hoquat? Night and day were only separations between degrees of fear for this young man's people.

They sat in another bark shelter Katsuk had built, finishing off the last morsels of a grouse Katsuk had snared. The only light was from the fire in the center of the shelter. It cast ruddy shadows on the crude structure over them, glistened on the knots tied in rope made from twisted willow which supported the framework.

It was full dark outside and there was a pond which had reflected molten copper in the sunset. Now it was a haunted pond full of captured stars.

Katsuk had taken the grouse from a giant hemlock near the pond. He had called it a roosting tree. The ground beneath it was white with grouse droppings. The grouse had come sleepily to the hemlock branches at dusk and Katsuk had snared one with a long pole and a string noose.

David belched, sighed, put the last of the grouse bones into the fire pit as Katsuk had instructed him. Pit and bones would be covered up and disguised in the morning.

Katsuk had spread cedar boughs under the sleeping bag. He stretched out under the bag with his feet toward the dying fire, said: "Come. We sleep now."

David crawled around the fire, slid under the bag. It felt clammy from not being hung to dry in the sun. There was an acid smell to it which mingled with the smoke and burned grease, perspiration, and cedar.

The fire burned itself down to a few coals. David felt the night close in around him. Sounds took on fearful shapes. He felt the cedar needles scratching. This was a place so utterly foreign to the sounds, sights, and smells of his usual life that he tried to recall things from other times which would fit here. All he could bring to mind were the tire-humming whine of a car crossing a steel bridge, the city's smoke, his mother's perfume . . . nothing fitted. One place rejected the other.

Softly, he slipped across the border of awareness and into sleep, there to dream. A giant face leaned over him. It was a face much like Katsuk's—broad, prominent cheekbones, a mane of thick black hair, wide mouth.

The mouth opened, said: "You are not yet ready. When you are ready, I will come for you. Pray then, and a wish will be granted you." The mouth closed, but the voice continued: "I will come for you . . . come for you . . . for you . . . you!" It reverberated in his skull and filled him with terror. He awoke trembling, sweating, and with a feeling that the voice continued somewhere.

"Katsuk?"

"Go to sleep."

"But I had a dream."

"What kind of dream?" There was alertness in the man's voice.

"I don't know. It scared me."

"What did you dream?"

David described it.

His voice oddly withdrawn, Katsuk said: "You have a spirit dream."

"Was it your god?"

"Perhaps."

"What does it mean, Katsuk?"

"You are the only one who can tell."

Katsuk struggled with an empty feeling in his breast. *A spirit dream for Hoquat!* Was it Soul Catcher playing an evil game? There were stories about such things. What a disturbing dream! Hoquat had been granted the right to a wish—any wish. If he wished to leave the wilderness, Hoquat could do it.

"Katsuk, what's a spirit dream?"

"That's where you get a spirit guide for your other soul—in the dream."

"You said it could be a god."

"It can be a god or a spirit. He tells you what you must do, where you must go."

"My dream didn't tell me to go anywhere."

"Your dream told you that you aren't yet ready."

"Ready for what?"

"To go anywhere."

"Oh." Silence, then: "That dream scared me."

"Ahhh, you see—the hoquat science doesn't liberate you from the terror of the gods."

"Do you really believe that stuff, Katsuk?"

His voice low and tense, Katsuk said: "Listen to me! Every person has two souls. One remains in the body. The other travels high or low. It is guided by the kind of life you lead. The soul that travels must have a guide: a spirit or a god."

"That isn't what they teach in church."

Katsuk snorted. "You doubt, eh? Once, I doubted. It almost destroyed me. I no longer doubt."

"Did you get a guide?"

"Yes."

"Is Raven your guide?"

Katsuk felt Soul Catcher stirring within him, said: "You do not understand about guides, Hoquat."

David scowled into the darkness. "Can only Indians get—"

"Don't call me Indian!"

"But you're—"

"Indian is a fool's name. You gave it to us. You refused to admit you hadn't found India. Why must I live with your mistake?"

David recalled Mrs. Parma, said: "I know a real Indian from India. She works for us. My parents brought her from India."

"Everywhere you hoquat go, the natives work for you."

"She'd be starving if she stil lived in India. I've heard my mother talk about it. People starve there."

"People starve everywhere."

"Do real Indians get guides?"

"Anyone can get a guide."

"Do you do it just by dreaming?"

"You go into the forest and you pray."

"We're in the forest. Could I pray now?"

"Sure. Ask Alkuntam to send you a guide."

"Is Alkuntam your name for God?"

"You could say that."

"Did Alkuntam give you your guide?"

"You don't understand it, Hoquat. Go to sleep."

"But how does your spirit guide you?"

"I explained that. It speaks to you."

David recalled the dream. "Right in your head?"

"Yes."

"Did your spirit tell you to kidnap me?"

Katsuk felt the boy's questions as a pressure, stirring up wild powers within him. Soul Catcher moved there, stretching.

David pressed the question: "Did your spirit tell you?"

Katsuk said: "Be silent or I will tie and gag you." He turned away, stretched his feet toward the warmth remaining in the rocks around the fire pit.

"I am Tamanawis speaking to you. . . ."

Katsuk heard the spirit so loud he wondered that the boy could not hear it.

"You have been given the perfect innocent."

David said: "When does your spirit speak to you?"

"When there is something you need to know," Katsuk whispered.

"What do I need to know?"

"How to accept my sharp and biting point," Katsuk whispered.

"What?"

"You need to know how to live that you may die correctly. First, you need to live. Most of you hoquat do not live."

"Does your spirit make you talk crazy like that?"

Katsuk felt hysterical laughter in his throat, said: "Go to sleep or I will kill you before you have lived."

David heard intensity in the words, began to tremble. The man was crazy. He could do anything. He had murdered.

Katsuk felt the trembling, reached back, and patted the boy's shoulder. "Do not worry, Hoquat. You will yet live. I promise it."

Still the boy's trembling continued.

Katsuk sat up, took the old flute from his belt pouch, blew softly into it. He felt the song go out, smoke-yearning sounds in the shelter.

For a few moments, Katsuk imagined himself in some old, safe place with a friend, with a brother. They would share music. They would plan the hunt for the morrow. They would preserve the dignity of this place and of each other.

David listened to the low music, lulled by it.

Presently, Katsuk stopped, restored the flute to its pouch. Hoquat breathed with the even rhythm of sleep. As though it were a thing of reality which could be seen and touched, Katsuk felt a bond being created between himself and this boy. Was it possible they were really brothers in that other world which moved invisibly and soundlessly beside the world of the senses?

My brother, Hoquat, Katsuk thought.

FROM A paper by Charles Hobuhet for Philosphy 200:

Your language is filled with a rigid time sense which denies the plastic fluidity of the universe. The whole universe represents a single organism to my people. It is the raw material of our creation. Your language denies this with every word you utter. You break the universe into lonely pieces. My people recognize immediately that Whitehead's "bifurcation of nature" is illusion. It is a product of your language. The people who program your computers know this. They say: "Garbage In—Garbage Out." When they get garbage out, they look to the program, to the *language*. My language requires that I participate with my surroundings in everything I do. Your language isolates you from the universe. You have forgotten the origin of the letters in which your language is written. Those letters evolved from ideographs which stood for movements in the surrounding universe.

IN THE low light of morning, David stood beneath a tall cedar, fingered the five pebbles in his pocket. There was dew on the grass outside the cedar's spread, as though each star from the night had left its mark upon the earth. Katsuk stood in the grass adjusting the straps of the pack. Morning's red glow remained on the peaks beyond him.

David asked: "Where are we going today?"

"You talk too much, Hoquat."

"You're always telling me to shut up."

"Because you talk too much."

"How'm I going to learn if I don't talk?"

"By opening your senses and by understanding what your senses tell you."

Katsuk pulled a fern frond from the ground, set off through the trees. He swung the fern against his thigh as he walked, listened to the world around him—the sounds of the boy following, the animals. . . . Quail ran through an opening off to his left. He saw the yellow-brown patch of an elk's rump far off through the moss-green light of the morning.

They were climbing steadily now, their breath puffing out in white clouds. Presently, they came to a saddleback filled with old-growth hemlock and went down into a gloomy valley where lichen grew like scabs on the trees.

Water ran down their trail, filling the deep elk tracks, exposing small rocks, splashing off the downhill side wherever a channel formed. The dominant sound around them was the fall of their own footsteps.

Once, they passed a squirrel's head left on a log by a predator. The head was being picked at by birds with black topknots and white breasts. The birds continued their feeding even when the two humans walked within a pace of them.

At the foot of the valley, they came out of the trees to the reed fringe of a small lake. There was a dun-blue skyline full of haze beyond the lake; wax-green trees came down to the far shore. A stretch of mud indicated shallows off to the right. Bird tracks were written in the mud, crisscrossing from food to food. Mergansers fed alertly along the far shore. As Katsuk and the boy emerged from the screening trees, the ducks fled, beating the water with a whistling in their wings, gaining flight at the last moment and circling back above the intruders.

David said: "Gosh. Has anybody ever been here before?"

"My people . . . many times."

Katsuk studied the lake. The ducks had been wary. That was not a good sign.

A windfall hemlock lay across the reeds into the lake. Its back was scarred by the passage of many hooves. Katsuk dropped the pack, stepped out onto the log. It trembled beneath him. He wove his way between upthrusting limbs to a flat space near the open water, hesitated. A black feather floated beside the log. Katsuk knelt, plucked the feather from the water. He shook away clinging moisture.

"Raven," he whispered.

It was a sign! He thrust the feather into his headband, steadied himself with one hand on a limb, immersed his face to drink from the lake. The water was cold.

The log trembled under him and he felt the boy approach.

Katsuk stood up and once more studied his surroundings. The boy made noisy splashings drinking. There was a marsh at the lake's upper end and a meadow beyond the marsh with a stream slashing through it. He felt the boy leave the log, turned.

The pack was an alien green mound beyond the reeds. He thought of the food in it: a package of peanuts, two chocolate bars, tea bags, a bit of bacon, some cheese.

Katsuk considered these things, thought: *I am not yet hungry enough to eat hoquat food.*

The boy stood waiting beside the pack, staring at it.

He is hungry enough, Katsuk thought.

A grasshopper went "Chrrrk! Chrrk!" in the reeds.

Katsuk returned to the boy, picked up the pack.

David said: "I thought you were going to fish."

"You would never survive alone in this country," Katsuk said.

"Why?"

"There is something wrong about this place and you do not even feel it. Come."

Katsuk settled his shoulders into the pack straps, went back into the trees to the game trail which ran parallel to the shore.

David followed, thinking: *Something wrong about this place?* He sensed only the biting cold, the way every leaf he touched left its deposit of moisture on him.

Katsuk turned left on the game trail, fell into a stalking pace—slow, alert, every motion fitted into the natural tempo of his surroundings. He felt himself caught up in the supernatural world of Soul Catcher, a movement of ecstasy within him, an ancient religious ritual described by every step he took.

The wilderness was too wakeful. Something had slipped out of place here . . .a broken pattern, a special quality to the silences. It all focused on that meadow at the head of the lake.

David tried to match his movements to Katsuk's, thinking: *What's he seen?* The oppressive caution of their movements filled the forest around him with danger.

They passed a salmonberry patch, the fruit still hard and unripe. David watched Katsuk pause, study the bushes, saw how the leaves went swaying as though they were tongues telling him of this place: voices from the bushes, from the trees, from the lake—conversation all around but intelligible only to Katsuk.

Is it more hikers?

David stumbled on a root, finding himself possessed by both hope and dread.

The trail slanted up the hill beyond the salmonberry bushes. Katsuk heard the boy stumble, recover his balance, heard the crouched silence of the forest, a creek running in shallows down to the left. Trail dew had left streaks of moisture along the sleeves of the dead hiker's shirt he wore. He felt the damp chill against his skin, thought how it would be to have a sheepskin coat.

The thought shocked him to stillness, as though the forest had sent him a warning. *A hoquat coat!* He knew he never again would see a sheepskin coat or feel its warmth. That was hoquat nonsense. And he realized the essence of the warning: hoquat clothing weakened him. He would have to discard it before long or be destroyed.

Slowly, he resumed the stalking climb, heard the boy following. The trees were too thick below him for a view of the meadow, abut he knew the danger lay there. He slid under a low branch, shifting the pack to prevent its rasping on wood.

The trail branched. One arm went down the hill toward the meadow. The trees were thinner below him, but still no vista of the meadow. Katsuk eased himself down the trail, around a thick spruce, and there was the meadow. The bright light of it was like a collision after the forest shadows. The creek sent a straight black gash through tall grass and patches of blue camas and bog laurel. Elk had beaten tracks across the lush pasture and had carved out a muddy ford across the stream.

Katsuk felt the boy ease up behind him. He studied the meadow. Abruptly, he clutched the boy's arm to hold them both frozen. A dead elk calf lay in the meadow, steam still rising from it. The calf's head was twisted under its body, the neck broken. Great claw marks flowed along its flanks, red against the brown.

Katsuk moved only his eyes, searching for the big cat that had done this. It was not like a cat to leave such a meal. What had frightened it? He stared across the meadow, abruptly conscious of the discordant potential in the crouched boy beside him. Hoquat was not trained in silence. He could attract whatever had frightened away the cat. Katsuk felt his stomach as tight as a drumhead with tension.

Softly, as though without beginning, a wave motion traversed tall grass at the far side of the meadow. Katsuk sensed the cat shape within the grass. He felt his heart rolling, a stone beat in his breast. The wave of grass moved diagonally toward the upper end of the meadow where the creek emerged from a wall of trees.

What had frightened the beast?

Katsuk felt anger. Why was there no sign to specify the danger? He gripped Hoquat's arm tightly, began to drift backward up the trail, pulling the boy with him, heedless of the occasional snapped branch.

A grouse began to drum somewhere far up the hill behind him. Katsuk fixed his hearing on that sound, moved toward it. They were partly screened from the meadow by the trees now. He no longer could see the wave of grass. Katsuk's thoughts were one long pang of uncertainty: something wrong in that meadow, so wrong it shrieked at him. His lips felt cold to hs tongue, cracked and cold.

David, frightened by Katsuk's silent probing and the sudden retreat, moved as quietly as he could, allowing himself to be hauled up the hill toward the drumming grouse. A bramble scratched his arm. He hissed with pain. Katsuk only tugged at him, urging more speed.

They glided around the uplifted root tangle of a nurse log, a long hemlock studded with young trees feeding on it.

Katsuk pulled the boy into a crouch behind the log. They peered over the log.

"What is it?" David whispered.

Katsuk put a hand over the boy's mouth to demand silence.

David pushed the hand away, and as he moved, the sharp crack of a rifle shot in the meadow sent echoes rolling back and forth across the lake valley.

Katsuk pulled the boy flat behind the nurse log, lay tense and listening, breathing in an even, shallow rhythm. *Poacher! It has to be a poacher. There is no hunting allowed in here.*

A hazelnut tree shaded the hiding place behind the log. Its yellow-green leaves filtered the sunlight, glistened on a spider casting its net between two ferns beside Katsuk's head. The nimble hunter with its silken web spoke to him of this place. *Poacher.* In this valley, the poacher would be one of his own people. Who else would know of the supplies hidden in buried steel drums, of the camouflaged huts, the cave that had been a mine?

Why were his people here? He had honored all the principal spirits. His deed was ready to be sung. The design of it lay in his mind where Soul Catcher had imprinted it. The thing was a tattoo needle to impress its shape upon the entire world!

Would his people try to stop him?

There could be no stopping. The hiker had been killed. His blood was a promise to this forest. The body might never be found, but Hoquat had seen the blood flow, had seen the young man die. Hoquat could not live now.

Katsuk shook his head, moving his eyes through the dappled light, seeing-but-not-seeing the silver wheel of the spiderweb.

No!

He could not think of the boy as a witness to the killing. Witness? That was hoquat thinking. What was a witness? Vince's death had not been murder. He had died because he was part of a larger design. His death was an imprint upon the *Perfect Innocent,* to prepare the way for the sacrifice.

A deep sigh shook Katsuk. He sensed Hoquat shivering beside him—a small forest creature caught in the web and almost resigned to its fate.

SHERIFF MIKE Pallatt:

Look, this Indian lost his kid sister a couple months ago. He adored that kid. He was her family, understand? After their parents died he raised her almost by himself. She was raped by a gang of drunken bastards and went out and killed herself. She was a good kid. I'm not surprised Charlie went off his nut. This is what comes of sending an Indian to college. He studies how we've been giving his people the shitty end of the stick. Something happens . . . he reverts to savage.

DAVID JERKED upright into empty blackness. He shivered with fear and cold. He hugged himself to still the trembling, searched for something to place him in a world, any abrasive edge to convey reality. Where was he?

He knew why he had awakened. A dream had taken him, loping along the edge of wakening. It had confronted him with a black stone, then green water and rippling glass. The smell of rancid oil had tickled his awareness. Something had chased him. Something still ran close behind him, singing softly of things he knew but did not want to hear. Even the awareness that the song contained a meaning terrified him.

David exhaled a sobbing breath. Fear shimmered over him with a bass hum of sweat and running and the remembered dream. He felt the white gold pulsebeat of gods and firelight. The thing with meaning pressed close. It was right behind him. He felt his muscles wanting to run. His mouth tasted of rusty iron. He felt his throat jerking with sounds he could not make. The thing behind him was going to catch him! The words of its song draped over his mind, a white-gray whispering, smooth as glass, promising happiness while it presented him with terror.

The dream singing persisted.

David heard it and tasted bitter acid in this throat. The dream terror washed around him in that faint tide of sound. He shuddered, wondering if he still dreamed, if the sensation of awakening was illusion.

A spark of orange light formed in the darkness. He heard movement near the light. Cautiously, he reached up with his left hand. His fingers encountered a rough wood surface.

Memory filled him—a dungeon cave with moldering plank walls. Katsuk had brought them here at dusk, searching out the way, exploring ahead while the boy crouched in shadows. This was a secret place used by his people when they broke the hoquat law and hunted game in these mountains.

The orange light was a remnant of the tiny fire Katsuk had built in the cave mouth. Movement of shadowy arms flickered across the light—Katsuk!

But the singing continued. Was it Katsuk? No . . . it seemed far away and full of words he could not understand—a whistling flute and a slow, walking rhythm on a drum. Katsuk had played his flute one night and this sounded like a distant parody of that playing.

David's fear ebbed. That was real singing, a real drum, and a flute like Katsuk's. There were several voices.

The poachers!

Katsuk had crept away in the first dark, returning much later to say he recognized the people camped in the trees at the edge of the meadow.

A groan came from near the fire. Was that Katsuk? David strained to hear what Katsuk was doing. He wondered: *Should I let him know I'm awake? Why did he groan?*

Again, the groan sounded.

David cleared his throat.

"You are awake!" Katsuk hurled the words at him from the cave's mouth.

David recoiled at the madness in Katsuk's voice, was unable to answer.

"I know you are awake," Katsuk said, calmer now and nearer. "It will be daylight soon. We go then."

David sensed the presence over him, blackness in blackness. He tried to swallow in a dry throat, managed: "Where will we go?"

"To my people."

"Is that them . . . singing?"

"There is no singing."

David listened. The forest outside the cave gave off only the soughing of wind in trees, faint drippings, stirrings, and rustlings. Katsuk pressed something hot beneath the boughs beside David: another heated rock.

"I heard singing," David said.

"You dreamed it."

"I heard it!"

"It is gone now."

"What was it?"

"Those of my people who have eaten spirits."

"What?"

"Try to sleep a little longer."

David remembered the dream. "No." He pressed against the moldering boards beside him. "Where are your people?"

"Everywhere around us."

"In the forest?"

"Everywhere! If you sleep, the spirit eaters may come to you and explain their song."

With sudden realization, David asked: "You're trying to tell me it was ghosts singing!"

"Spirits."

"I don't want to sleep."

"Have you prayed for your spirit?"

"No! What was that song?"

"It was a song asking for power over that which no human can defeat."

"It was a song asking for power over that which no human can defeat."

David groped in the darkness for the sleeping bag, pulled it around him. He leaned over the place where Katsuk had placed the heated rock. *Crazy Katsuk! He makes no sense.*

"You will not sleep?" Katsuk asked.

"How soon will it be daylight?" David countered.

"Within the hour."

Katsuk's hand came out of the dark, pressed David toward the warm rock. In a soothing tone, Katsuk said: "Go to sleep. You dreamed an important dream and ran from it."

David stiffened. "How do you know?"

"Sleep," Katsuk said.

David stretched out over the rock. His body drank the warmth. The musky, falling, swimming attraction of sleep radiated from the warmth. He did not even feel it when Katsuk's hand released him.

He lapsed into a state with no sharp edges. Magic and ghosts and dreams: They were gauze in an orange wind. Nothing completed a sensation of touch. Everything blended, one blur into another: warmth into the cedar boughs beneath him, Katsuk returning to the cave's mouth, the dream into the chill where the rock's warmth failed to reach him. Vagueness everywhere.

All blurred and faded.

He felt his childhood fading, thought: *I am becoming a man.* Memory treasures stored up against just such an awakening receded into gray impressions—pictures he recalled pasting in a book, the rungs of a staircase where he had peered through to watch guests arriving, being tucked into bed by a benign figure whose face was lost in a halo of silver hair.

David sensed warm orange firelight. Katsuk had built up the fire at the cave's mouth. He felt damp cold under his back. A night bird screamed twice. Katsuk groaned.

The groan sent a shock all through David.

Vagueness vanished, taking sleep and the dreams of his childhood. He thought: *Katsuk is sick. It's a sickness no one can heal. Katsuk has caught a spirit and eaten it. He has the power no human can defeat. That's what he meant about the song! The birds obey him. They hide us. He has gone into some place where humans can't follow. He has gone where the song is . . . where I'm afraid to go.*

David sat up, wondered at such thoughts coming all unbidden into his mind. Those were not the thoughts of childhood. He had thought real things, penetrating things. They were thoughts from immediate pressures of life and death.

As though his thoughts had called it into being, the song started up once more. It began out of nothing, the words still unintelligible, even it's direction undefined . . . somewhere outside.

"Katsuk?" David said.

"You hear the singing?" He spoke from near the fire.

"What is it?"

"Some of my people. They hold a sing."

"Why?"

"They try to call me out of the mountains."

"Do they want you to turn me loose?"

"They have eaten a small spirit, Hoquat. It is not as powerful as my spirit."

"What're you going to do?"

"When it is daylight, we will go to them. I will take you to them and show them the power of my spirit."

FROM KATSUK'S speech to his people, as reported by his Aunt Cally:

This is the way it is with me. My mind was sick. My mind suffered the sickness of the hoquat. I lost my way without a spirit to guide me. Therefore, I had to beg medicine from anyone who would give it to me. I begged it from you, my people. I begged it from my grandfathers, my father's brothers, all the people we came from, all our ancestors, my mother's grandmothers and grandfathers, all the people. Their medicine words poured down upon me. I felt them within me. I feel them now. They are a fire in my breast. Raven leads me. Soul Catcher has found me.

IN THE darkness, Katsuk stood outside the cave which was an ancient mine shaft high on the hillside above the lake. He saw lights flickering in the branches below him, campfires beneath the fog that veiled the valley. The lights glowed and swam as though they were moving phosphor in water, shapes blurred in fog ripples.

He thought: *My people.*

He had crept close and identified them in the night, not by their hoquat names but by their tribal names which were shared only with those who could be trusted. They were Duck Woman, Eyes on Tree, Hates Fish, Elk Jumping, One-ball Grandfather, Moon Water. . . . In his own tongue now, he said their names:

"Tchukawl, Kipskiltch, Ishkawch, Klanitska, Naykletak, Tskanay. . . ."

Tskanay was there, thinking of herself as Mary Kletnik, no doubt. He tried to summon a Charles Hobuhet memory of Mary Kletnik. Nothing came into his mind. She was there, but behind a veil. Why was she hiding? He sensed a lithe shape naked in firelight, a voice murmuring, fingers touching flesh, a softness which demanded dangerous things of him.

She was a threat.

He understood this now. Tskanay had been important to Charles Hobuhet. She might strike through to the center which was Katsuk. Women had powers. Soul Catcher must deal with her.

The sun came over the edge of the valley. Katsuk looked beyond the bowl of fog to the mountain suspended in the dawn. Black splotches of rock stood out against snow as white as a goat-hair blanket. The mountain was an ancient shape pressed hard against the sky and left hanging there.

Katsuk prayed then: *Soul Catcher protect me from that woman. Guard my strength. Keep my hatred pure.*

He went into the mine-cave then, awakened the boy, and fed him chocolate and peanuts from the pack. Hoquat ate hungrily, unaware that Katsuk was not eating.

The boy said nothing of his dream, but Katsuk recalled it, sensing the dangerous forces being gathered against him.

Hoquat had dreamed of a spirit who would grant any wish. The spirit had said he was not yet ready. Ready for what? For the sacrifice? It said something that Hoquat had a spirit in his dream. That didn't happen to everyone. That was a sign of real powers. How else could this be, though? The sacrifice must be a great thing to have any meaning. The *Innocent* must go into the spirit world with a great voice which could not be denied. Both worlds must hear him or the death would be meaningless.

Katsuk shook his head. It was disturbing, but this was no morning for dreams. This would be a day for testing the realities of the fleshly world.

He went back outside then and saw that the sun had burned part of the fog from the valley. The lake was a mirror catching the bright flare of sunlight. It filled the valley with pale clarity. A black bear came out into the meadow above the lake, drank the air with its tonuge hanging like a dog's. It caught the scent of humans, whirled, and loped back into the trees.

Katsuk stripped off the hoquat clothing, stood in only the loincloth and the moccasins Janiktaht had made, the medicine pouch hanging at his waist.

The boy came out. Katsuk handed the hoquat clothing to him, said: "Put this in the pack. Stuff the sleeping bag on top, and hide the pack beyond where we slept."

"Why?"

"Do it and come back here."

David shrugged, obeyed. Presently, he returned, said: I'll bet you're cold."

"I am not cold. Come. We go to my people now." He led the way at a fast walk which had the boy trotting to keep up.

They went down across a bracken slope, acid green with red-leaved vines creeping through the green. A gray prow of rock jutted from the slope. They went around the rock and plunged into a dark trail through trees.

David was panting by the time they splashed across rocky shallows in the creek. Katsuk seemed unaware of exertion, keeping up that steady, long stride. There were cottonwoods by the creek—pale, yellow-green moss on their trunks. The trail went through wet salal, emerged on a narrow ledge thick with spruce and cedar, a few tall hemlocks. Four crude huts, one of them as large as all the other three together, were spaced among the trees about fifty feet apart. All had been built of split cedar boards dug into the needle duff of the ground and lashed to a pole framework. David could see the lashings of twisted willow rope. The largest hut had a low door curtained by raw elk-hide.

As Katsuk and the boy came in sight of the door, the curtain lifted and a young woman emerged. Katsuk stopped, held his captive with a hand on the boy's shoulder.

The young woman came fully outside before she saw them. She stopped then, put a hand to her cheek. Recognition was obvious in her stare.

David stood locked under Katsuk's grip. He wondered what was in Katsuk's mind. Katsuk and the young woman just looked at each other without speaking. David studied the woman, his senses abnormally alert. Her hair was parted in the middle, hanging loosely over her shoulders. The ends were braided, tied with white string. Pockmarks disfigured her left cheek, showing around the hand she held there. Her cheeks were broad. They glistened, and her eyes were set deeply into the flesh. Her figure was full and slender beneath a red-purple dress which stopped just below her knees.

All the way down the mountain, David had told himself Katsuk's people would end this nightmare. The old days of Indians and white captives were gone forever.

These people had come here as part of the search for Katsuk. Now David saw fear in the young woman's eyes and began to doubt his hopes.

She dropped her hand, said: "Charlie."

Katsuk gave no response.

She looked at David, back to Katsuk. "I didn't think it would work."

Katsuk stirred, said: "Didn't think *what* would work?" His voice sounded strained.

"The sing."

"You think I came because they sang me in?"

"Why not?"

Katsuk released David's shoulder, said: Hoquat, this is Tskanay . . . an old friend."

Coming toward them, she said: "My name is Mary Kletnik."

"Your name is Tskanay," Katsuk said. "Moon Water."

"Oh, stop that nonsense, Charlie," she said. "You—"

"Do not call me Charlie."

Although he spoke softly, his tone stopped her. Again, she put a hand to her pockmarked cheek. "But. . . ."

"I have another name now: Katsuk."

"Katsuk?"

"You know what it means."

She shrugged "The center . . . kind of."

"Kind of," he sneered. He touched the boy. "This is Hoquat, the Innocent who will answer for all of our innocents."

"You don't really. . . ."

"The reality I show you, it will be the only reality."

Her glance went to the knife at his waist.

"Nothing that simple," Katsuk said. "Where are the others?"

"Most of them went out before dawn . . . searching."

"For me?"

She nodded.

David's heart leaped at her response. Katsuk's people *were* here to help. They were searching. He said: "My name is David Marshall. I—"

A stinging backhand blow sent him reeling.

Tskanay put both hands to her mouth, stifled a scream.

In a conversational tone, Katsuk said: "Your name is Hoquat. Do not forget again." He turned to the young woman. "We spent the night in the old mine. We even built a fire. Why did your searchers not search there?"

She lowered her hands, did not answer.

Katsuk said: "Do you still think your pitiful sing brought me in?"

Her throat convulsed with swallowing.

David, his cheek burning from the blow, glared angrily at Katsuk, but fear kept him rooted.

"Who is still in camp?" Katsuk asked.

Tskanay said: "Your Aunt Cally and old Ish, that I know of. Probably one or two of the younger boys. They don't like to go out in the cold too early."

"The story of our lives," Katsuk said. "Do you have a radio?"

"No."

The elkhide curtain behind her lifted. An old man emerged—long nose, gray hair to his shoulders, a crane figure. He wore bib overalls and a green wool shirt that flopped loosely on his thin frame. Caulked boots covered his feet. He carried a lever-action rifle in his right hand.

David, seeing the rifle, allowed his hopes to grow once more. He studied the old man: pale face full of wrinkles, eyes sunken above high cheeks. A dark, elemental spirit lay in the eyes. His hair was twisted together like old kelp that had dried and rotted on a beach.

"Been listening," the old man said. His voice was high and clear.

Katsuk said: "Hello, Ish."

Ish came fully out of the door, let the curtain drop. He moved with a limp, favoring his left foot. "Katsuk, eh?"

"That is my name." Katsuk spoke with a subtle air of deference.

"Why?" Ish asked. He advanced to a position beside Tskanay. A distance of about ten feet separated them from Katsuk and the boy.

David sensed the contest between these two, looked at Katsuk.

"We both know what opens the mind," Katsuk said.

"Solitude and suffering," Ish said. "So you think you're a shaman."

"You use the correct word, Ish. I'm surprised."

"I've had a *little* education, boy."

Katsuk said: "I sought the old ways. I suffered with hunger and cold in the high mountains. I gained a spirit."

"You're a woods Indian now, eh?"

In a cold, hard voice, Katsuk said: "Do not call me Indian."

"Okay," Ish said. He shifted his grip on the rifle.

David looked from the rifle to Katsuk, hardly dared to breathe, afraid he might call attention to himself.

Ish said: "You really think you got a spirit?"

Tskanay said: "Oh, this is idiot talk!"

Katsuk said: "I will not be disinherited by my own people in my own land. I know why you are here. My spirit tells me."

"Why are we here?" Ish asked.

"You used the excuse of hunting for me to *poach* in your own land. You came to break the hoquat laws, to kill game your families need to survive and which is ours by right!"

The old man grinned. "Didn't need a spirit to tell you that. You think we weren't really hunting for you?"

"I heard the sing," Katsuk said.

"It brought you in, too!" Tskanay said.

"Sure did," Ish agreed.

Katsuk shook his head. "No, uncle of my father, your sing did not bring me in. I came to show you my rank."

"You didn't even know I was here," Ish protested. "I heard you ask Mary."

"Tskanay," Katsuk corrected him.

"Mary, Tskanay—what's the difference?"

"You *know* the difference, Ish."

David realized suddenly that, despite his glib tone, the old man was terrified and trying to hide it. Why was he afraid? He had a rifle and Katsuk only had the knife. The fear was there, though—in the pallor, in the stiffness of his grin, the tension in his old muscles. And Katsuk knew it!

"So I know the difference," Ish muttered.

"I will show you," Katsuk said. He spread his arms, lifted his face to the sky.

"Raven," he said, his voice low, "Show them that my spirit is all powerful."

The old man sighed, said: "That sure as hell isn't why we sent you to the university."

"Raven," Katsuk said, louder this time.

"Stop calling your damned bird," Tskanay said. "Raven's been dead for a hundred years at least."

"Raven!" Katsuk screamed.

A wooden door banged in one of the huts off to the left. Two boys about David's age emerged, stood staring at the scene in the clearing.

Katsuk lowered his head, folded his arms.

David said: "I saw him bring the birds once." Immediately, he felt foolish. The others ignored him. Did they doubt him? "I *did*," he insisted.

Tskanay was looking at him now. She shook her head sharply. David saw that she, too, was fighting down terror. She was angry, also. Her eyes flashed with it.

Katsuk said: "I accept what Raven gives." He began singing, a low chant with harsh, clicking sounds.

Ish said: "Stop that!"

Tskanay looked puzzled. "That's just names."

"Names of his dead," the old man said. His eyes glittered as he glanced around the clearing.

Katsuk broke off his chant, said: "You felt them last night during your sing!"

"Don't talk nonsense," the old man growled, but there was fear in his voice. It trembled and broke.

"Felt *what?*" Tskanay demanded.

Cold gripped David's chest. He *knew* what Katsuk meant: There were spirits in this place. David sensed a dirge humming in the trees. He shivered.

"While you sang, I heard them here," Katsuk said. He touched his chest. "They said: 'We are the canoe people, the whale people. Where is our ocean? What are you doing here? This lake is not our ocean. You have run away. The whales taunt us. They spout only a spear's throw from the beach. Once, they would not have dared this.' That is what the spirits told me."

Ish cleared his throat.

Katsuk said: "Raven protects me."

The old man shook his head, started to lift the rifle. As he moved, a single raven flew in through the trees from the lake. Its pinions clattered in the clearing. It alighted on the ridge of the largest hut, tipped its head to stare at the people below it.

Ish and Tskanay had turned their heads to follow the flight. Tskanay turned back immediately. Ish took longer to study the bird before returning his attention to Katsuk.

David kept his attention on Katsuk. What a thing that was—to summon the raven.

Katsuk stared into the old man's eyes, said: "You will call me Katsuk."

Ish took a deep, shuddering breath, lowered the rifle.

Tskanay put both hands to her cheeks, lowered them guiltily when she saw David glance at her. Her eyes said: "I don't believe this and neither do you."

David felt sorry for her.

Katsuk said: "You, of all our people, Ish, must know what I am. You have seen the spirits work in men before this. I know it. My grandfather told me. You might have been a *shichta*, you, a great leader of our people."

Ish coughed, then: "Lot of damned nonsense. That bird's just a coincidence. I haven't believed in that stuff for years."

Softly, Katsuk asked: "How many years?"

Tskanay said: "Do any of you *really* believe he called that bird in here?"

David whispered: "He did."

"How many years?" Katsuk insisted.

"Since I saw the light of reason," Ish said.

"Hoquat reason," Katsuk said. "Ever since you fell for the hoquat religion."

"By God, boy. . . ."

"That's it, isn't it?" Katsuk demanded. "You swallowed the hoquat religion like a halibut eating the bait. They pulled you right in. You swallowed it, even though you knew it took you out of all touch with our past."

"That's blasphemy, boy!"

"I am not *boy!* I am Katsuk. I am the center. I say *you* blaspheme! You deny the powers that are ours by right of inheritance."

"That's damned nonsense!"

"Then why don't you shoot me?" He screamed it, leaning toward the old man.

David held his breath.

Tskanay backed away.

Ish hefted the rifle. As he moved, the raven on the roof squawked once. Ish almost dropped the rifle in lowering it. His eyes reflected terror now, peering at Katsuk as though he were trying to see inside the younger man.

"Now, you know," Katsuk said. He waved his right arm.

At the gesture, the raven leaped into the air, flew back toward the lake.

"What is my name?" Katsuk demanded.

"Katsuk," the old man whispered. His shoulders sagged. The rifle dragged at his arm as though he wanted to drop it.

Katsuk gestured at David. "This is Hoquat."

"Hoquat," the old man agreed.

Katsuk strode between Ish and Tskanay, went to the elkhide curtain. He lifted the curtain, turned back to the girl. "Tskanay, you will keep watch on Hoquat. See that he doesn't try to run away. It is too soon for him to die." He went into the hut, droppig the curtain.

"He's crazy," David whispered. "He's wild crazy."

Tskanay turned on the old man. "Why did you cave in like that? The boy's right. Charlie's—"

"Shut up!" Ish snapped. "He's lost to you, Mary. Understand me? You'll never have him. I know. I've seen it before. He's lost to all of us. I've seen it."

"You've seen it," she sneered. "Why, you old fool, you just stood there with that rifle while he—"

"You saw the bird!"

"The bird!"

"It could just as well have been lightning to strike us dead!"

"You're as crazy as he is!"

"Are you blind, girl? I was just talking to keep up my nerve. I dind't even have to see him call that bird. You can feel the power in him. He didn't come in because of our sing. He came to show us his power."

She shook her head. "Then what're you going to do?"

"Going to wait for the others and tell them."

"What're you going to tell them?"

"That they better watch out before they go up against Katsuk. Where's Cally?"

"She went out before I did . . . about ten minutes."

"When she gets back, tell her to fix the house for a big meeting. And don't let that kid there get away from you. You do, Katsuk'll kill you."

"And you'd just stand there and let him!"

"Damned right I would. Don't catch me going up against a real spirit. Soul Catcher's got that one."

SPECIAL AGENT Norman Hosbig, FBI:

Look, I told you media guys how much we appreciate your cooperation. We're giving you everything we can. I know how big a story this is, for Christ's sake. We're in complete charge and the sheriff is talking out of turn. We consider that note Hobuhet left to be a ransom note. As soon as that comes up, we automatically take jurisdiction. We're operating on the rebuttable presumption that the kid has been transported in interstate or foreign commerce. I know what the sheriff says, but the sheriff doesn't know everything. We're going to get another ransom demand before long. Hobuhet was a university student and we've reason to believe he was an Indian militant. He's going to demand that we cede Fort Lawton or Alcatraz or set up an independent Indian Territory somewhere else. Now, for God's sake, don't print any of this.

DAVID WAS perplexed. He knew he had a stake in what had just happened in this woods clearing. He had a life-and-death problem with Katsuk, but the contest between Katsuk and old Ish had gone beyond any question of a captive's fate. It had gone into another world, into the place of the spirit dreams. David knew this. It no longer was a problem of the world in which he lived with his body.

He wondered: *How do I know this?*

It went against everything he had been taught to believe before Katsuk. There were two problems, or one problem with two shapes. One involved his need to escape from the crazy Indian, to get back with people who were sane and could be understood. But there was another part of this thing—a force which tied together two people called Katsuk and Hoquat.

He thought: *I'm David, not Hoquat.*

But just by answering to Hoquat he knew he had formed a link of some kind. If he were to escape, he had to break both bonds. Ish had understood this, but Tskanay had not.

Tskanay still stood where Katsuk had left her. There was a worried look on her face as she studied the boy who had been put in her care. A wind from the lake ruffled her hair. She brushed a lock from her forehead. There was anger in the movement and frustration.

Ish had gone off into the forest with a purposeful, long-legged stride. It was her problem now.

Tskanay stood firmly in this world, David realized. She held only half the vision. It was like being blind. Ish was another matter. He could see both worlds, but he was afraid. Perhaps Ish felt fear *because* he could see both worlds.

David stilled a spasm of trembling.

Tskanay's long silence bothered David. He looked away from her toward the lake, disturbed by the steady pressure of those dark eyes. What was she thinking? The sun stood high over the hills now, throwing dappled light onto the floor of the clearing. Why was she staring like that? Why didn't she say something? He wanted to shout at her to say something or go away.

She was thinking about Katsuk.

He knew this as surely as though she had said it. She wanted to talk about Katsuk.

It was dangerous to talk to her about Katsuk. He knew this now. But it had to be done. *The problem with Katsuk.* The danger had something to do with the spirit dream which Katsuk had experienced but refused to describe in detail. It had been a powerful dream. That was obvious. David wondered suddenly if his Hoquat-self had been caught up in Katsuk's dream. Could that happen? Could you take another human being into your dream and hold that person captive there?

With a chill shock of awareness, he realized that he had favored Katsuk over Ish in their contest. How could that be? The realization filled him with guilt. He had abandoned himself! He had weakened the David part. Somewhere, he had made a colossal mistake.

His mouth opened in dismay. What power had commanded that he strengthen the Hoquat-Katsuk bond?

Tskanay stirred, said: "Are you hungry?"

David wondered if he had heard her correctly. What did hunger have to do with anything real? Hungry? He thought about it for a moment.

"Have you eaten?" Tskanay insisted.

David shrugged. "I guess so. I had some peanuts and a chocolate bar."

"Come with me." She led the way across the clearing to a gray mound of ashes outside the end hut.

David, following her, noted there were several such ash mounds in the clearing. Some of them were smoking. Tskanay had chosen one that smoked. It had a charred log behind it and a pile of bark at one side.

As Tskanay walked, David noted the edges of her skirt were damp from dew. She had been out in the tall grass already this morning. The skirt showed dirt and stain marks all around the hem. She squatted by the ashes.

David asked: "What do I call you?"

"M—" She glanced at the hut where Katsuk had gone. "Tskanay."

"It means Moon Water," David said. "I heard him."

She nodded, picked up small branches from a stack beneath the bark, scraped coals into view, and piled the branches over them.

David moved around the charred log. "Have you known Katsuk very long?"

"Since we were kids." She leaned close to the coals, blew them into life. Flame climbed through the piled branches. She put bark around the flame.

"Do you know him very well?" David asked.

"I thought I was going to marry him."

"Oh."

She went into the end hut, returned wth two old enamel pots. Water sloshed in one of them. Huckleberry leaves floated on the water. The other contained a gray-blue mush.

"Salal berries, tule roots, and tiger-lily bulbs," she told him when David asked what was in the mush.

David squatted by the fire, enjoying its warmth.

Tskanay put both pots into the coals. She went into the hut, returned with an enamel plate and cup, a tinned spoon. She wiped them on her skirt, served up the mush and a steaming cup of huckleberry-leaf tea.

David sat on an end of the charred log to eat. Tskanay sat on the other end, watched him silently until he had finished. He found the mush sweet and filling. The tea was bitter but left his mouth feeling clean.

"You like that food?" Tskanay asked. She took the utensils from him.

"Yes."

"That's Indian food."

"Katsuk doesn't like you to say Indian."

"Too hell with Katsuk! Has he hit you very much?"

"No. Are you going to marry him?"

"Nobody's going to marry him."

David nodded. Katsuk had gone into a world where people didn't marry.

Tskanay said: "He was never cruel before."

"I know."

"He calls you his Innocent. Are you?"

"What?"

"Innocent!"

David shrugged. This trend in the conversation embarrassed him.

"I'm not," she said. "I was his woman."

"Oh." David looked away toward the lake.

"You know why he named you Hoquat?" she asked.

"Because I'm white."

"How old are you?"

"Thirteen." David looked toward the big hut. "What happened to Katsuk?"

"He hates."

"I know, but why?"

"Probably because of his sister."

"His sister?"

"Yeah. She committed suicide."

David looked at Tskanay. "Why'd she do that?"

"A bunch of white guys caught her alone out on the Forks road and raped her."

David read the hidden enjoyment in Tskanay's recital, wondered at it. He asked: "Is that why Katsuk hates whites?"

"I guess so. You never raped anyone, huh?"

David blushed, felt anger at himself for this betrayal of his feelings. He turned away.

"You know what it means, though," Tskanay said.

"Sure." His voice sounded too gruff.

"You really are innocent!"

"Yes." Defiant.

"You never even felt under a girl's skirt?"

Again, David felt his cheeks flame hot.

Tskanay laughed.

David turned, glared at her. "He's going to kill me! You know that? Unless you people stop him!"

She nodded, face suddenly sober. "Why don't you run away?"

"Where would I go?"

She pointed toward the lake. "There's a creek goes out the other end of the lake. Follow it. Lots of game trails. You come to a river. Turn left, downstream. You come to a regular park trail and a bridge. Go over the bridge. Got a sign there. Trail goes to a campground. That's where we left our cars."

Cars! David thought. The image of a car represented safety to him, release from this terrifying bondage.

"How far?"

She considered, then: "Maybe twenty miles. Took us two days coming in."

"Where would I rest? What would I eat?"

"If you hold to the north side of the river, you'll find an abandoned park shelter. Ish and some of his friends buried a steel drum in it. Got some blankets, beans, stuff to make fire. It's in the northeast corner of the shelter, I heard him say."

David stared out at the lake. *Shelter . . . blankets . . . bridge . . . cars . . .* He glanced at the hut where Katsuk had gone.

"He'll kill you if I escape."

"No, he won't."

"He might."

"He'll scream for his damned Raven!"

David thought: *He'll send his birds after me!*

"He won't hurt me," Tskanay said. "Don't you want to escape?"

"Sure."

"What're you waiting for?"

David got to his feet. "You're sure?"

"I'm sure."

David looked once more at the lake. He felt elation grow. *Follow the creek to the river. Go downstream to the park trail. Cross a bridge.*

Without a backward glance or thought for Tskanay, he strolled down to the lake, making it casual in case Katsuk was watching. At the lake, he found a flat stone. He skipped it into the reeds to make it appear he had just come down to the water to play. Another stone went into the reeds. It startled a drake frim hiding. The duck went squawking out of the reeds, beating the water with its wings, settled at the far end of the lake. It shook its feathers, stretched.

David swallowed, forced himself not to look back at the camp. The drake had made a lot of noise and it had made him bird-conscious. Watching for ravens, he skirted the meadow, found a game trail with water running across a low spot. The wet grass around him was waist high. His knees and feet already were sopping. He hesitated at the edge of the trees. Once he entered the trees he was committed.

A raven called.

David whirled left, looked down the lake. A whole flock of ravens sat in a tall silver snag beside the lake. The trail would go directly under them!

He thought: *If I go close to them, they'll fly up. They'll make a big fuss and call Katsuk.*

Through the trees in front of him, he could see the hillside above the lake: no trail, a tangle of closely packed spruce and hemlock, roots, mossy logs.

Anything was preferable to the ravens.

David moved straight into the trees, up the hill. It was hard climbing—over logs, slipping on moss, falling between logs, getting himself caught on brush and broken limbs. He lost sight of the lake within two hundred steps. Once, he confronted a moss-topped stump with a grouse sitting atop it, blinking at him.

The bird twisted its head around to watch him pass.

Except for the constant sound of dripping, the forest felt silent to him. He thought: *When I get to the top of this hill, I'll turn left. That way, I'll come back to the lake or the creek.*

His feet hurt where the wet socks chafed them.

The hill was steeper now, trees smaller and thinner. There were blackberry vines to catch at his clothing. He came out into a small clearing with twisted black roots ahead of him. They snaked down over the foundations of a granite steeple—straight up! No way to climb it.

David sat down, panting. Roots and rock formed a cup, blocking his way to the left, but a narrow deer trail angled up to the right. He thought: *When I get to the top, then I can turn left.*

Taking a deep breath, he got up, climbed into the deer trail. Before he had climbed one hundred steps, he was confronted by a thick wall of brush. The wall ran up to his left toward the rock steeple, curved away from him on the downhill side. He tried to press into the brush, saw it was useless. Fur on a limb above the brush told him the deer had leaped this barrier.

Winded, frightened, he studied his surroundings. Downhill to the right was back to Katsuk . . . unless he crossed the valley above the Indian encampment. That way, he could go down the left side of the lake, away from the ravens. There was a trail there, too: He and Katsuk had come up that way.

Decision restored some of his hope. He angled downhill, trying to move with the caution he'd learned from watching Katsuk. It was no use: He continued to step on dead branches which broke with loud snappings; he continued to stumble through limbs and brush.

The trees were bigger now, more of them, more windfalls. He was thirsty and felt the beginnings of pangs of hunger.

Presently, he stumbled onto another deer trail. Within a few steps, it divided sharply. One arm went almost straight up the hill to his left, the other plunged steeply into green gloom.

David stared around him. He knew he was lost. If he went uphill, he felt sure he would come face to face with another part of that rock cliff. Downhill was the only way. He would find water to quench his thirst at least. He plunged into the green gloom. The trail switched back and forth, went almost straight down in places, avoided a tall curve of roots at the base of a fallen tree.

He went around the roots, found himself face to face with a black bear. The bear backed up, snorting. David leaped off the deer trail, downhill to his right, straight through brush and limbs, panic driving him in great, gulping strides. A low limb cut his forehead. He stumbled on a mossy log, fell hard into a narrow rivulet tinkling across black rocks. He got up, mud and water dripping from him, stared around. No sign of the bear. His chest and side ached where he had fallen.

He stood, listening, heard only wind in the trees, the sound of the tiny stream, his own gasping breaths. The sound of water recalled him to his thirst. He found a hollow in the rocks, stretched out and sank his face into the water to drink. His face dripped when he sat up, but he could find no dry part of his clothes to wipe away the water. He shook his head, scattering droplets.

There was a breeze blowing across the hillside. It chilled him. David felt his muscles trembling. He got up, followed the tiny stream downhill. It ran under logs, over shallows, dropped in miniature cataracts, growing larger and larger. Finally, it came out on flat, marshy ground, ran directly into a tangle of devil's club.

David stopped, looked at the sharp white spines of the thicket. No way to get through there. He looked to the right: That way must lead to the camp. He turned to the left, moved out across ground so spongy it sloshed and squirted with each step. The devil's club gave way to a stand of salal higher than his head. The ground became more solid.

A deer trail entered the salal. David stopped, examined his surroundings. He guessed he had been gone at least three hours. He was not even sure he still was in the valley of the lake. There was a trail. He peered into the dark hole through the salal. The ground was gray mud, pocked with deer tracks.

Fear crept through him. His teeth chattered with the cold.

Where did that trail go? Back to Katsuk?

The constant sound of water dripping from leaves wore on his nerves. His feet ached. He sensed the silent, fearful warfare of the plants and animals around him. His whole body shook with chill.

A distant cawing of ravens came to his ears. David turned his head, searching for the direction of the sound. It grew louder, a great clatter of wings and calling directly over him, hidden by the thick tree cover.

They could see him even through the trees!

In a panic even greater than when he had seen the bear, David sprinted into the salal, slipped, almost fell. He regained his balance, ran gasping and crying to himself through the heavy shadows. The trail twisted and turned. David skidded, burst from the thicket, desperate, incoherent, his mind filled with confusion, his body teetering.

Ish stood directly in front of him. The old man put out a hand to steady the boy.

"You lost, boy?"

David, his mouth open, panting, could only stare up at the wrinkled old face, the glittering birdlike eyes. There was a clearing behind Ish, a wide circle of trees all around. Sunlight poured into it. David blinked in the brightness.

Ish said: "Kind of figured you were lost when I heard you crashing down the hill a while back." He dropped his hand from David's shoulder, stepped back to get a full view. "You *are* a mess. Had you a time out there."

"I saw a bear," David managed. Even as he said it, he felt that was a stupid thing to say.

"Did you, now?" There was laughter in Ish's voice.

David blushed.

Ish said: "Came looking for you because of Tskanay."

"Did he hurt her?"

"Cast a spirit into her. Gave her a cramp and she fell down in a faint."

"He hit her!"

"Maybe so."

"I told her he would."

"You shouldn't run away, boy. Get yourself killed."

"What's the difference?"

Ish said: "Well, you had yourself a good walk. I'll show you the short way back to camp. Katsuk's expecting you." He turned, strode off across the clearing, a limping old man with the sun beating onto his gray head and shoulders.

David, too tired to cry, trailed after the old man like a puppy on a leash.

FROM KATSUK'S ''Red Power'' letter to the United Indian Council:

You call yourselves Indians! Every time you do that you deny that you are People. Nehru was an Indian. Gandhi was an Indian. They knew what it was to be People. If you cannot listen to me, listen to Gandhi. He said: ''Immediately the subject ceases to fear the despotic force, its power is gone.'' Do you hear that, you fearful subjects? Choose your own name!

AN OLD woman stood just outside the curtained doorway of the big hut. She was talking to Katsuk as Ish and the boy entered the clearing. Ish held out a hand to stop the boy and they waited there just into the clearing.

''That's Cally, his aunt on his mother's side,'' Ish said.

She was a head shorter than Katsuk, heavy and solid in a black dress that stopped halfway between knees and ground. Low black socks and tennis shoes covered her feet. Her hair was shiny black streaked by gray, pulled tight and tied with a blue ribbon at the back. Below the ribbon, her hair sprayed out to her shoulder blades. She had a high forehead, cheeks that puffed out round and fat and dark. When she looked across the clearing at David, he saw remote brown eyes that told him nothing.

Cally motioned with her head for Ish to bring the boy closer. Katsuk turned at the gesture and a smile moved from his lips to his eyes.

''Come on, boy,'' Ish said. He led David to the pair at the doorway.

''You have a good walk, Hoquat?'' Katsuk asked. And he thought: *It is true and real—the Innocent cannot escape me. Even when he runs away he is brought back.*

David looked at the ground. He felt miserable and lost.

There were other people around, squatting at the lake edge of the clearing, standing clustered in the door of another hut. David felt only a cold curiosity from them. He thought:

This can't be happening. These aren't wild Indians out of a history book. These people have gone to school and to church. They have cars. They have TV.

He felt his mind trying to draw points of similarity between himself and the people around him. It was a growing-up effort, a stretching of himself out of desperation. He focused on the tennis shoes that covered Cally's feet. Those shoes came from a store. She had been to a city and a store. Ish had a rifle. He wore clothes which came from a store . . . just like Cally's shoes did. They were people, not wild Indians.

And they were all afraid of Katsuk.

Katsuk glanced at the old woman, said: ''Hoquat is tied to me, you understand? He cannot escape.''

"You're talking crazy," she said, but there was no force in the words.

To David, Katsuk said: "This is Cally, my mother's sister. I don't expect you to understand that, Hoquat, but it is from my mother's people that I got my first power."

David thought: *He's talking to impress her, not me.*

David shot a penetrating glance at the old woman's face to gauge her reaction, found only a withdrawn measuring in remote brown eyes. With breath-choking realization, David saw that Cally was proud of Katsuk, proud of what Katsuk was doing, but had not admitted it to herself. She would never admit it.

Cally asked: "Are you all right, boy?"

David shrugged, still caught in realization of the power Katsuk held over this woman. She was proud.

What can I do? David wondered. He blinked back tears. His shoulders sagged with despair. Only then did he realize how desperately he had hoped this woman would help him. He had thought a woman would have softness for a boy in trouble.

But she was proud . . . and afraid.

Cally put a hand on David's shoulder, said: "You got yourself all soaking and cut up out in that brush. Ought to get those clothes off you and dry them."

David peered up at her. Was she softening? No. She was only going through the motions. This would keep her from admitting how proud she was.

She glanced sideways at Katsuk, said: "What're you *really* going to do with him, son? Are you going to potlatch them?"

Katsuk frowned. "What?" He didn't like this tone in his aunt's voice. There was slyness in her now.

Cally said: "You tell me he's tied to you and you're the only one can cut him loose. Are you going to give him back to them?"

Katsuk shook his head, seeing his aunt's fear for the first time. What was she trying to do? She wasn't talking to Katsuk. She was trying to revive Charles Hobuhet! He put down a surge of rage, said: "Be quiet!" Even as he spoke, he knew it was pointless. He had brought this upon himself with his own thoughtless arrogance. He had said this was his aunt. Katsuk had no relatives. It was Charles Hobuhet who had been related to this woman.

"That'd be about the biggest gift anyone could give," Cally said. "They'd owe you."

Katsuk thought: *How sly she is. She appeals to the ancestors in me. Potlatch! But those aren't my ancestors. I belong to Soul Catcher.*

"What about it?" Cally demanded.

David tried to swallow in a dry throat. He sensed the struggle between Katsuk and this woman. But she wasn't trying to save a captive. What was she trying to do?

Katsuk said: "You want me to save my life by saving his."

It was an accusation.

David saw the truth in Katsuk's words. She was trying to save her nephew. She didn't care about any damned hoquat. David felt like kicking her. He hated her.

"Anything else doesn't make sense," Cally said.

David had heard enough. He screamed at her, fists clenched at his sides: "You can't save him! He's crazy!"

Unnervingly, Katsuk began to laugh.

Cally turned on the boy, said: "Be still!"

Katsuk said: "No, let him talk. Listen to my Innocent. He knows. You cannot save me." He stared across David's head at Ish. "Did you hear him, Ish? He knows me. He knows what I have done. He knows what I must do yet.''

The old man nodded. "You've got a bloody look on you.''

David felt himself frightened into stillness. His own actions terrified him. He had almost told about the hiker's murder. Katsuk had realized this. *"He knows what I have done.''* Did all of these people know about the murder? Was that why they were afraid? No. They feared Katsuk's power from the spirit world. Even while some of them didn't admit it, that was what they feared.

Katsuk stared at Cally, asked: "How could we make the hoquat owe us more than they do already?''

David saw that she was angry now, fighting against the realization of her own pride. She said: "There's no sense crying over the past!''

"If we don't cry over it, who will?'' Katsuk asked. He felt amusement at her weakness.

"The past is dead!'' she said. "Let it be!''

"As long as I live it is not dead,'' Katsuk said. "I may live forever.''

"That boy's right,'' she snapped. "You're crazy.''

Katsuk grinned at her. "I don't deny it.''

"You can't do this thing,'' she argued.

His voice low and reasonable, Katsuk asked: "What thing?''

"You know what I mean!''

Katsuk thought: *She knows and cannot say it. Ahhh, poor Cally. Once our women were strong. Now they are weak.* He said:

"There is no human being who can stop me.''

"We'll see about that,'' she said. Anger and frustration in every movement, she turned away, grabbed David's arm, hustled him down the line of huts to the end one. "Get in there,'' she ordered. "Take off your clothes and pass them out.''

Katsuk called after her: "Indeed, we will see, Cally.''

David said: "Why do you want my clothes?''

"I'm going to dry them. Get in there now. There're blankets in there. Wrap up in blankets until your things are dry.''

The split plank door squeaked as David opened it. He wondered if Cally might yet try to save him—out of anger. There were no windows in the hut. Light came in the door. He stepped inside onto a dirt floor. The place smelled of fish oil and a wet mustiness that came from the fresh hide of a mountain lion pegged to the wall opposite the door. Thin strips of something dark hung from the rafters. There were a jumble of nets, burlap bags, rusty cans, and boxes on the dirt floor. A pole frame in one corner held a crumpled pile of brown-green blankets.

"Get a wiggle on,'' Cally said. "You'll catch your death in them wet clothes.''

David shuddered. The hut repelled him. He wanted to run outside and beg the people there to save him. Instead, he stripped down to his shorts, passed the clothing out the door.

"Shorts, too,'' she said.

David wrapped up in one of the blankets, stripped off the shorts, and passed them out the door.

"These'll take a couple of hours,'' she said. "Wrap up warm and get some rest.'' She closed the door.

David stood in the sudden darkness. Tears began running down his cheeks. All the alien strangeness of people and place weighed in upon him. The young woman had wanted him to escape. Old Cally seemed to want to help him. But none of them would really stand up to Katsuk. Katsuk's spirit was too powerful. David wiped his face on a corner of his blanket, stumbled through the confusion on the floor to the pole bed. Putting the blanket tightly around him, he sat down on the bed. It creaked.

As his eyes adjusted to the gloom, he saw that the door did not shut completely. There were cracks and holes all around to admit light. He heard people moving outside, low voices. At one point, there was a sound like young boys playing—the sound of a stick hitting a can.

Tears continued running down David's cheeks. He stifled a sob. Anger at his own weakness overcame him. He thought: *I couldn't even escape!*

Katsuk had power over birds and people and his spirits all through the forest. There was no place to hide. Everything in the forest spied for crazy Katsuk! The people in this camp knew it and were afraid.

Now they held Katsuk's captive trapped without clothes.

David smelled smoke, meat cooking. There came a shout of laughter outside, quickly silenced. He heard wind in the trees, people moving about, low conversations with the words unintelligible. The blanket around him smelled of old perspiration. It was rough against his skin. Tears of despair ran down his cheeks. The sounds of activity outside gradually diminished. There came longer and longer silent periods. What were they doing out there? Where was Katsuk? He heard footsteps approaching his hut. The door squeaked open. Tskanay entered with a chipped bowl in one hand. There was an angry furtiveness about her movements.

As the door opened wide and she stepped inside, the light revealed a blue bruise down her left jaw. She closed the door, sat down beside him on the pole bed, and offered the bowl.

"What's that?"

"It's smoked trout. Very good. Eat it."

David took the bowl. It was smooth and cold against his fingers. He stared at her bruised jaw. Light coming through the cracks in the wall drew stripes down across the mark on her skin. She appeared restless and uncomfortable.

David said: "He hit you, didn't he?"

"I fell down. Eat the trout." There was anger in her voice.

David turned his attention to the fish. It was hard and chewy with a light and oily fish flavor. At the first bite, he felt hunger knot in his stomach. He ate a whole trout before speaking, then: "Where're my clothes?"

"Cally's drying them in the big house. Be another hour at least. Charlie and Ish and some of the others have gone out hunting."

David heard her words and wondered at them. She seemed to be saying one thing but trying to tell him something else. He said: "He doesn't like you calling him Charlie. Is that why he hit you?"

"Katsuk," she muttered. "Big deal." She looked toward the door as she spoke.

David ate another of the trout, licked his fingers. She was acting uncomfortable, shifting on the pole bed, picking at the blankets beneath them. He said:

"Why're you all afraid of him?"

"I'll show him," she whispered.

"What?"

Without answering, she took the bowl from David's hands, tossed it aside. He heard the clatter of it in the shadowy center of the hut.

"Why'd you do that?"

"I'm going to show that *Katsuk!*" She made the name sound like a curse.

David felt a surge of hope, quickly extinguished. What could Tskanay do? He said:

"None of you are going to help me. He's crazy and you're afraid of him."

"Crazy wild," she said. "He wants to be alone. He wants death. That's crazy. I want to be with someone. I want life. That's not crazy. I never thought he'd be a stick Indian."

Katsuk doesn't like you to call him Indian."

She shook her head, setting the string-tied braids in motion. "Fuck Katsuk!" It was low and bitter.

David sat in shocked silence. He'd never heard an adult say that openly before. Some of his more daring friends said it, but never anyone such as this young woman. She was at least twenty years old.

"Shocks you, huh?" she asked. "You're an innocent, all right. You know what it means, though, or it wouldn't shock you."

David cleared his throat.

Tskanay said: "Big mean, crazy Indian thinks he has an innocent, huh! Okay. We'll show him." She got up, went to the door, closed it.

David heard her moving, the slither of clothing. He whispered: "What're you doing?"

She answered by sitting down beside him, finding his left hand and pressing it against her bare breast.

David hissed in surprise. She was naked! As his eyes adjusted to the gloom, he could see her beside him.

"We're going to play a game," she said. "Men and women play this game all the time. It's fun." She slid a hand beneath his blanket, caressing, touched his penis. "You got hair. You're man enough for this game."

David tried to push her hand away. "Don't."

"Why not?" She kissed his ear.

"Because."

"Don't you want to get away from Charlie-Katsuk?"

"Sure." Her skin was soft and exciting. He felt a strange eagerness in his loins, a hardness. He wanted to stop her and he did not want to stop her.

"He wants you innocent," she whispered. She was breathing fast now.

"Will he let me go?" David whispered. There was an odd milky smell about her that sent his pulse racing.

"You heard him." She guided his left hand, pressed it into the tangle of hair between her legs. "Doesn't that feel good?"

"Yes. But how do you know he'll. . . ."

"He said he wants you innocent."

Frightened and fascinated, David allowed her to pull him down onto the pole bed. It creaked and stretched. Eagerly now, he did what she told him to do. They were showing that Katsuk! Crazy damned Katsuk.

"Right there," she whispered. "There! Ahhhhh. . . ." Then: "You've got a good one. You're good. Not so fast. There . . . that's right . . . that's right . . . ahhhh. . . ."

It seemed to David much later. Tskanay rubbed him down with a blanket while he stretched out, tingling and excited, but calm and relaxed, too. He thought: *I did it!* He felt alive, in direct contact with every moment. *Pretty Tskanay.* He reached up boldly, touched her left breast.

"You liked that," she said. "I told you it was fun." She stroked his cheek.

"You're a man now, not a little innocent Katsuk can push around."

At the sound of Katsuk's name, David felt his stomach tighten. He whispered: "How will Katsuk know?"

She giggled. "He'll know."

"He's got a knife," David said.

She stretched out beside him, caressed his chest. "So what?"

David thought about the murdered hiker. He pushed her hand away, sat up. "He's crazy, you know." And he wondered if he could tell Tskanay about the murder.

She spoke languidly: "I can hardly wait to see his face when he—"

The door banged open, cutting her off and bringing a gasp from David.

Katsuk stepped inside, his face in black shadows from the back lighting. He carried David's shoes and clothing in a bundle. As the light from the doorway revealed the two naked figures on the pole bed, Katsuk stopped.

Tskanay began to laugh, then: "Hey, Charlie-boy! He's not your little innocent anymore! How about that?"

Katsuk stared at them, consternation tightening his throat. His hands went to the knife at his waist and he almost drew it. Almost. But the wisdom of Soul Catcher whispered to him and he saw the trickery in her woman power. She wanted the knife! She wanted death and the end of him by that death. She wanted the ancient ritual defeated. Ahhhh, the slyness of her. He threw the clothing at David, took one step forward, his face still in shadows and unreadable.

"You going to kill us, Charlie-boy?" she asked.

David sat frozen with terror. He expected the knife. It was the logical thing to happen—the *right* thing. His chest ached. His body felt even more exposed than its nakedness of flesh. There was no way to prevent the knife.

Katsuk said: "Don't think you will steal my spirit *that* way, Tskanay."

"But he's not your innocent little hoquat anymore." She sounded puzzled. Katsuk wasn't reacting the way she had expected. She wasn't sure precisely what she had expected, but certainly not this quietness. He should be raging and violent.

Katsuk glanced at the terrified boy. *Innocent?* Could sex make the difference? No. The quality of innocence was something else. It was tangled with intent and sensitivity. Was there selfishness in this hoquat? Was he indifferent to the fate of others? Was he capable of self sacrifice?

"Are you sure he's not innocent?" Katsuk asked.

She slid off the pole bed, stood up, angrily defiant in her nakedness, taunting him with it. "I'm damned sure!"

"I am not," Katsuk said.

"You want another performance for proof?" she demanded.

Slowly, David got his knees beneath him on the bed. He sensed that Katsuk was not completely in this room, that the man listened to voices from another world. Tskanay still could not see this. Katsuk was obeying his spirits or he would have struck out with the knife. He might hit Tskanay again if she continued to taunt him, but he wouldn't use the knife.

David said: "Katsuk, don't hurt her. She was only trying to help me."

"You see," Katsuk said. "You tried to use him against me, Tskanay, and still he doesn't want you hurt. Is that not innocence?"

"He's not!" she raged. "Damn you, he's not!"

His voice oddly soft, Katsuk said: "I know, Hoquat. Get dressed now. There is your clothing all dry and clean and mended by Cally."

Tskanay whispered: "He's not, I tell you. He's not."

"But he is," Katsuk said.

David touched the clothing Katsuk had thrown onto the bed. Why couldn't Tskanay shut up? It was a stupid argument. He felt defiled, tied to Katsuk even more strongly than before. She hadn't been trying to help. She'd been trying to get back at Katsuk, but she couldn't reach that part of him in the spirit world.

Tskanay stood trembling now, her fists clenched, her face immobile. Her whole body spoke of failure. She had tied herself to something lost in this place and would carry the mark of it for the rest of her life and she knew it.

Katsuk said: "Hoquat, we are truly bound together now. Perhaps we are brothers. But which of us is Cain and which Abel?" He turned away, went out, leaving the door open.

In the clearing, Katsuk stood a moment thinking.

Innocence is not taken by being used.

He looked at his right hand, the hand that had struck Tskanay earlier in anger. *It was wrong to strike her. There was a small bit of Charles Hobuhet remaining in me. That's who struck her. Now she has cleansed me of that. It was a hoquat thing to strike her. She has cleansed that away, too, and proved the innocence of my chosen victim. I am Katsuk who can smile at what she did and appreciate its value to me.*

In the hut, Tskanay said: "Damn him! Damn him! Damn him!" She was crying.

David put a hand on her calf, said: "Don't cry."

She put her hands to her face, sobbing harder.

David pleaded: "Please don't cry, Tskanay."

She jerked away, dropped her hands. "My name is Mary!"

Still crying, she found her clothes, pulled them on, not bothering to straighten the garments. She went to the door and, without looking back, said: "Well, you heard him. Get dressed!"

HARLOW B. WATTS, teacher at Pacific Day School, Carmel, California:

Yes, David is one of my students. I'm very shocked by all this. He's a very good student, considerably ahead of most in his form. We use the British system here, you know. David is very sensitive the way he studies things. His reports and other papers often reveal this. He sometimes says odd things. He once remarked that Robert Kennedy had tried too hard to be a hero. When I questioned David about this, he would only say: "Well, look, he didn't make any mistakes." Don't you think that's an odd thing for a boy to say?

IN THE afternoon, the sky darkened with a heavy overcast. A cold, raw wind began blowing from the southwest. It chilled David where he stood at the lake margin below the huts. He rattled the six pebbles in his pocket. Six days!

Most of the people in the camp, more than twenty of them, had gone into the big hut and built a fire there. They had two haunches of elk turning on a spit over the fire.

David felt that everyone in the camp must know what he and Tskanay had done. His cheeks felt hot every time he thought about it.

Two youths squatted at the timber's edge watching him unobtrusively. Tskanay was no longer his guard. He had not seen her since she had left the little hut. The two youths were his guards now. David had tried to talk to them. They had refused, turned away when he insisted. He heard them talking in low voices.

Barren frustration permeated him. Again, he thought of Tskanay. She had not changed a thing. Even worse, she had bound him tighter to Katsuk.

"Perhaps we are brothers now."

Katsuk had said that.

By forgiving, by denying anger, Katsuk had put a new burden on his captive. A link had been forged between them.

David tried to imagine Katsuk and Tskanay making love. It had happened. Tskanay admitted it. Katsuk as much as admitted it. David could not imagine them doing it. They had been two other people then—Mary and Charlie.

It was growing darker. Sunset conjured a bloody lake at the edge of the forest's green darkness. The wind was blowing hard up on the ridges, sweeping the clouds away. The moon emerged and David saw it as Katsuk would: the moon eaten, a curve of it gnawed out by Beaver. The moon was in the lake, too. He watched it there as it drifted against the reeds and was gone. But the reeds remained.

One of the youths behind him coughed. Why wouldn't they talk to him? David wondered. Was it Katsuk's command?

He heard distant aircraft engines. An airplane's green wing light moved off to the north. The engines flowed with the light, a cold, far sound in the sky. Sound and light gathered up David's hopes, bore them away. He chewed his lower lip. He could feel himself falling into emptiness, the whole sky opening to take him. That plane, the warmth, the light, the people—all vanished into another dimension.

Katsuk was speaking in the big hut, his voice rising and falling. The curtain had been thrown back. Light spilled into the clearing. David turned away from the lake, went toward the firelight. He passed the two youths in the dark, but they gave no indication of noticing him. David squatted just outside the range of the firelight, listened.

Katsuk, his powerful body clad in the loincloth and moccasins, wore the red cedar band around his head, a single raven feather stuck into the band at the back. He stood with his back to the open door. The fire drew glowing outlines of his movements, his skin now amber, now bloody.

"Have I found this innocent in my belly like a woman?" Katsuk demanded. "Look you! I am Katsuk. I am the center, yet I live everywhere. I can wear the chief beads. What do you fear? The hoquat? They did not conquer us. Gun, steel, knife, hatchet, needle, wheel—these conquered us. Look you! I wear the chilkat cloth and moccasins made by a woman of our people."

He turned slowly, staring at each face in turn.

"I can see in your faces that you believe me. Your belief strengthens me, but that is not enough. We were the Hoh people. What are we now? Does any among you call himself a Christian man and sneer at me?"

His voice grew louder: "We lived on this coast more than fifteen thousand years! Then the hoquat came. Our cedar plank houses are almost gone from this land. We hide a few pitiful huts in this forest! Our salmon rivers are dying. I must tell you these things mostly in English because all of you do not speak our tongue."

He turned, stared out into the dark, whirled back.

"Ours is a beautiful tongue! English is simple beside it. Things have reality in our tongue! I go from one condition to another in my tongue and feel each condition. In English, I feel very little."

He fell silent, stared into the fire.

A woman shifted closer to the fire at the right and David thought at first it was Tskanay, youth and grace in her movements. But she turned, the light flaring briefly, and he saw it was the old aunt, Cally. Her face was a gaunt mask. The illusion shook him.

Katsuk said: "Look you at the preparations you made for me. You brought body paints and a Soul Catcher rattle. Why do these things unless to honor me?"

He touched the knife at his waist. "I am Drukwara. I make war all around the world. I have only two dances. One of them is Bee."

Someone in the circle around the fire coughed.

Cally said: "Ish, answer him. A man must answer him."

Ish stood up directly across the fire from Katsuk. The old man's gangling frame appeared taller in the low light. His eyes reflected firelight.

He said: "You talk of old times, but these are not old times." Diffident voice, fear in it.

Katsuk said: "You mean we no longer bang a log drum until moonrise." He pointed to the ground beside Ish. "But you bring a flute and that wood rattle dressed with eagle feathers. Why?"

"Some of the old ways work," Ish said. "But those tribes were wild."

"Wild?" Katsuk shook his head. "They had their loyalties. Their world had shape. They worked it so."

"But they were wild."

"This is a hoquat word! Our woods, our animals, our people had loyalties and shape!"

"Shape," Ish said, shaking his head.

Katsuk said: "You came up the Hoh road. In cars, by damn! You parked your cars beside those of the hoquat and walked in here. You saw the signs of the new shapes: WATCH FOR TRUCKS. RANGE AREA—WATCH FOR LIVESTOCK. Whose trucks? Whose livestock? We drive their trucks to help destroy our land! That shingle mill down there at tidewater where they let you work . . . sometimes! That's the shape now!"

Ish said: "That what you learned at the university?"

"You're more right than you imagine, uncle. I am the last chosen of my mother's clan. Once were were strong and could withstand any strain. We supported our people in their troubles. Now. . . ."

"Now, you bring trouble on all of us," Ish said.

"Do I? Or do we merely live in hoquat trouble we have come to accept?" Katsuk pointed to the west. "The dragways of our whaling canoes, dug deep for those thousands of years, line the beaches down there. Yet we must petition a hoquat congress to tell us we can use one little piece of that land! Our land!"

"If you're talking about the old village at the beach," Ish said, "we'll get it back. The whites are beginning to understand our problems. They have—"

"Pity!" Katsuk shouted. "They throw us a bone out of pity—a tiny corner of all this that once was ours. We don't need their pity! They deprive us of the experience and responsibility of being human!"

Ish said: "Who cares why the whites do what we—"

"I care!" Katsuk touched his chest. "They come into our land—*our* land! They cut the underbrush to decorate their flower arrangements. They pile the logs high that should be left as trees. They take fish for sport that should feed our families. All the while, these hoquat do the one thing we must not forgive: They reamin complacent in their evil. They are so satisfied that they are doing right. Damn these fiends!"

"Some of them were born here," Ish protested. "They love this land."

"Ahhhh," Katsuk sighed. "They love our land even while they kill it and us upon the land."

Guilt filled David. He thought: *I am Hoquat.*

His people had stolen this land. He knew Katsuk was speaking the truth.

We stole his land.

That was why the two youths set to guard him wouldn't speak to him. That was why the room full of people around Katsuk showed their sympathy with him even while they voiced fears and objections.

David felt himself hostage for all the sins of his kind. He had even sinned as his ancestors had, with a woman of these people. Thought of Tskanay weighed him down. He felt shattered, broken by the ruin of a life that once had seemed sweet and constant. He stared into the hut: ruddy shadows on rafters there, firelight in the crossbeams . . . all the people—honey-red skin, the sleek black hair, the gray hair, the old and tangled hair. He suddenly saw Tskanay almost directly behind Ish in the third row: round face, a purple blouse, fawn red of her skin in the firelight. David swallowed convulsively, remembering the slither of her clothing in the dark hut, the tangle of shadows.

Katsuk said: "You will not stop me. No one will stop me."

Cally stood up. She moved with slow stiffness now. She faced Katsuk. "We won't stop you. That's true. But if you kill that boy, you'll be like the worst of them. I won't want to live with that in my family." She turned away, walked into the shadows.

Ish said: "What's past is past." He sat down.

Katsuk straightened, glanced left and right. He did not appear to be looking at his audience but to be showing them his face.

He said: "All the past is in my words. If those words die, you will have forgotten the moaning and misery in our houses. You will forget what the hoquat did to us. You will forget what we were. But I will not forget. This is all I must say."

He turned, strode out of the house.

Before David could move, Katsuk was upon him. Katsuk grabbed the boy's arm, dragged him along. "Come, Hoquat. We go now."

SHERIFF MIKE Pallatt:

Sure I think old Cally has seen her nephew. Why else would she come in with all that warning stuff? She and her gang were in the Wilderness Area. That's where I'm concentrating my men. I listened to her real good. Got a head on her shoulders, that old woman. She says we should call him Katsuk, we call him Katsuk. There's no more Charlie Hobuhet. Somebody calls him Charlie at the wrong moment, that could blow the whole show.

IT BEGAN to rain intermittently soon after they left the clearing of the huts: rain, then moonlight, rain, moon. It was raining steadily and hard before they reached the old mine shaft. There was distant lightning and thunder. David, allowing himself to be dragged along in the darkness, wondered if Katsuk was creating the trail one step at a time out of his magic. Katsuk could not possibly see his way in the wet blackness.

All the way up the hill, Katsuk chanted and raged.

David, his heart palipitating, heard the word-ravenings and understood only the rage. Wet branches clawed at him. He tripped on roots, slipped in mud. He was drenched by the time they reached the shaft.

Katsuk's mind was in turmoil. He thought: *It was the truth. They know I told them truth. Still they fear. They do not give me all their thoughts. My own people are lost to me. They do not want the powers I could give them. My own people!*

He pulled Hoquat into the shelter of the mine shaft, released him. Water ran from them. Katsuk pressed his hands against the chilkat loincloth. Rivulets ran down his legs. He thought: *We must rest, then go on. Some of my people are fools. They could tell the hoquat where I am. There must be a reward. Some have the hoquat sickness. They could do it for money. My own people deny me a home in their thoughts. There is no home. My own people turn away. No one will come to meet me. I am truly homeless.*

How could he rest here? Katsuk wondered. He could feel his own people down there by the lake—restless, disturbed, divided, arguing. They had heard his words had felt his meaning, but all in a language which blasphemed what he held sacred.

No darkness will ever rest me. I will be a ghost spirit. Not even Tskanay supports me.

He thought of how Tskanay had looked at him. Her eyes had seen him and found him alien. She had given her body to the boy, trying to swallow innocence. She had thought to make Hoquat unfit. She had failed. Hoquat's shame reinforced his innocence. He was more innocent now.

Katsuk stared into the black emptiness of the old mine shaft. He sensed the dimensions of it with his memory, with his skin, his nose, his ears. There were ghost spritis here, too. The boy's teeth chattered. Hoquat's fear could almost be touched.

The boy whispered: "Katsuk?"

536

"Yes."

"Where are we?"

"In the cave."

"The old mine?"

"Yes."

"Are y-you g-going t-to b-build a f-f-fire?"

Lightning gave a brief flicker of illumination: the cave mouth, dripping trees, rain slanting down. Thunder followed, close, a crash that made the boy gasp.

Katsuk said: "Perhaps we have too much fire."

The world suddenly was shattered by a barren plume of lightning so close they smelled the hell fragrance of it as the thunder shook them.

The boy whirled, clung to Katsuk's arm.

Again, lightning flickered against wet blackness, this time near the lake. The thunderclap came like an echo of the one before it.

The boy trembled and shook against Katsuk.

"That was Kwahoutze," Katsuk said. "That was the god in water, the spirit of all the regions brought together by water."

"It was s-so close."

"He tells us this is still his land."

Again, the lightning flashed—beyond the lake now. Thunder followed, rumbling.

The boy said: "I don't want to steal your land."

Katsuk patted his shoulder. "And *I* was going to over-proud my enemies. This land does not know who owns it."

David said: "I'm sorry we stole your land."

"I know, Hoquat. You are truly innocent. You are one of the few who feel why this land is sacred to me. You are the immigrant invader. You have not learned how to worship this land. It is my land because I worship it. The spirits know, but the land does not know."

Silence fell between them. Katsuk freed himself from the boy's grip, thinking: *Hoquat depends upon me for his strength, but that can be dangerous for me. If he takes strength from me, I must take strength from him. We could become one person, both of us Soul Catcher. Who could I sacrifice then?*

David listened to the sound of falling rain, the distant progression of lightning and thunder. Presently, he said: "Katsuk?"

"Yes."

"Are you going to kill me . . . like your aunt said?"

"I use you to send a message."

David chewed his lower lip. "But your aunt said. . . ."

"Unless you tell me to do it, I will not kill you."

Relief flooded through David. He drew a deep breath. "But I'd never tell you to—"

"Hoquat! Why do you prefer mouth-talk to body-talk?"

Katsuk moved into the shaft.

Rebuked, David stood trembling. The old madness had returned to Katsuk's voice.

Katsuk found the pack by smelling the mustiness of it. He squatted, felt the fabric, removed matches, a packet of tinder. Presently, he had a small fire going. Smoke drifted in a gray line along the ceiling. The flame cast raw shadows on old beams and rock.

David approached, stood close to the fire, trembling, holding his hands out to the warmth.

Katsuk gathered the cedar boughs of their bed, spread the sleeping bag. He stretched out on the bag with his back against a rotting beam.

The boy stood with his head just beneath the smoke. The gray line above him was like a spirit essence drifting toward the dark entrance into the world.

Katsuk withdrew the willow flute from his waistband, touched it to his lips. He blew softly. The clear sound circled upward into the smoke, carrying his mind with it. He played the song of cedar, the song to placate cedar when they took bark for mats and clothing, for rope and net string. He blew the song softly. It was a bird singing deep in the shade of cedar boughs.

Sweetly on the song, he sensed a vision: Janiktaht carrying a basket piled with curling shreds of cedar bark. And he thought: *This is better for Janiktaht. I should not be forever seeking her face among the faces of strangers.*

The words of the song echoed in his mind: "Life maker cedar . . . fire maker cedar. . . ."

The vision of Janiktaht moved within him. She grew larger, larger, older, uglier. The basket of cedar bark shriveled.

Sweat broke out on his forehead. His mind stumbled. He dropped the flute.

David asked: "Why did you stop?"

Katsuk sat up, stared at the evil flute beside him. He shook his head. The movement was like wind swaying cedar boughs. The cedar band around his head pressed into his skull. He knew it might crush his head. He could not remove the band.

"Keep that sickness away from me," he muttered.

"What?"

"I don't want to be killed by that sickness."

"What's wrong?"

Katsuk glared across the fire at the boy. "What had made me so unlucky?"

"Are you unlucky?" David didn't understand the conversation but felt his participation being demanded.

"I am overcome by it," Katsuk said. "I have been found by Short-Life-Maker."

"Katsuk, you're talking awfully funny."

"Evil words have been sent against me!"

"What words?"

"I have enemies. They have cursed me. They wish me to die quickly. My own people! They have no mercy."

David moved around the fire, squatted beside the sleeping bag. He touched Katsuk's flute. "I liked the music. Will you play some more?"

"No!"

"Why?"

"Because I have discovered my omen tree."

The boy stared at him, puzzled.

Katsuk closed his eyes. He pictured a cedar, a great cedar with bulging roots, glossy needles, a cedar deep in the forest, sucking at the earth's belly and piling its boughs high, a skirt of long boughs at the bottom that leaned outward into a thick bed of leaf mold.

"My omen tree," Katsuk whispered.

"What's an omen tree?" David asked.

Katsuk said: "I was my mother's firstborn." He opened his eyes, stared upward into the ruddy smoke. "Her brother carved a little canoe for me. He made a tiny fish spear. He made a rattle box. He made all of these things from cedar."

"That makes an omen tree?"

Katsuk spoke in a distant voice: "My parents were in a cedar canoe when they died. Janiktaht stole a cedar canoe when she. . . . The splinter! I was very sick that time with the splinter in my knee. They said I could lose the leg. It was a cedar splinter. All this is very clear, Hoquat. Someone in my family has offended cedar. That is the end of me, then."

"Do you really believe that stuff?"

"Don't tell me what I believe!" He glared at the boy.

David recoiled. "But. . . ."

"We have burned cedar, carved her. We have made rafts of cedar, kindling wood, long planks, and shakes to keep off the rain. But we did not show how thankful we were to her. Cedar's heart aches. We have stepped on her roots, bruised them, and never thought about it. I rest on cedar right now! How stupid!"

He leaped off the sleeping bag, jerked it aside, began gathering up the boughs. He carried them outside, stacked them in the rain. His skin glistened with water when he returned. He squatted, gathered the fallen needles, sweeping them together, searching out every one. When he had them all, he took them out into the rain, scattered them.

"Cedar!" he shouted. "I give you back what I took! I beg forgiveness! I ask my spirits to give you this message. I did not mean to harm you. Cedar, forgive me!"

David squatted by the fire, watched wide-eyed. Katsuk was insane!

Katsuk returned to the fire, put a damp spruce limb into the flame. "See," he said, "I do not burn cedar."

David stood, pressed his back against the rock wall.

Katsuk nodded his head to the flames. Falsetto whines came out of his throat, monotone grunts.

David said: "Are you praying?"

"I need a language to explain how I feel. I need a language that has never been heard before. Cedar must hear me and know my prayer."

David listened for words, heard none. The sounds were hypnotic. He felt his eyelids drooping. Presently, he went to the sleeping bag, wrapped himself in it, stretched out on the hard ground.

Katsuk went on with his odd noises, groaning, whining. Even after the fire had reduced itself to a glowing, orange eye, the sound went on and on and on. The boy heard it occasionally as he half awoke from sleep.

FROM A note left by Katsuk in the abandoned shelter at Sam's River:

Hoquat is an innocent without father and mother. He says his father will pay me. But how can people who do not exist make payment? Besides, I do not ask ransom. I have the advantage over you. I understand your economics. You do not understand mine. My system goes by vanity, prestige, and ridicule, the same as the hoquat. But I see the vanity. I see the prestige. I see the ridicule. This is how my people made potlatch. The hoquat do not have potlatch. I know the names and shapes of everything I do. I understand the spirit powers and how they work. That is the way it is.

THE FIRST thing David saw when he awoke was thin pillars of rain slanting across the mine entrance. The world outside was full of dawn's broken light, misty gray-white. Katsuk was nowhere to be seen, but ravens clamored somewhere outside.

David trembled at the sound.

He slid out of the sleeping bag, stood up. It was cold. Moisture filled the air. He went to the mouth of the shaft, stared around him, shivering.

The rain slackened.

David turned, peered into the shaft. Not likely Katsuk had gone back deeper into there. Where was he?

The ravens called from the trees down by the lake. Mist hid them. David felt hunger grip his stomach. He coughed.

The wind remained strong. It blew from the west, pushing clouds against the peaks beyond the lake valley. Branches whipped in the wind atop the ridge, chopped the light.

Should I go down to the huts? David wondered.

He could see the game trail they had climbed in the night. The rain stopped, but water dripped from every leaf he could see.

David thought of the huts, the people. They had allowed Katsuk to take his captive away. They wouldn't help. Cally had said as much.

He heard splashing on the game trail, grunting.

Katsuk climbed into view. He wore a loincloth and moccasins. The sheathed knife flopped against his side with every step. His body glistened with wetness, but he seemed unaware of water or cold. He climbed onto the ledge at the mouth of the mine and David saw that he carried a package. It was wrapped in dirty cloth.

Katsuk thrust the package toward the boy, said: "Smoked fish. Cally sent it."

David took the package, opened it with cold-stiffened fingers. The fish was bright red, oily, and hard. He broke off a piece, chewed. It tasted salty and sweet. He swallowed and imediately felt better.

He took another mouthful of fish, spoke around it: "You went down to see your friends?"

"Friends," Katsuk said, his voice flat. He wondered if a shaman ever had friends. Probably not. You went outside human associations when you gained spirit powers. Presently, he glanced at the boy, said: "You didn't try to escape again."

"I thought about it." Defiant.

"Why didn't you try?"

"I heard the ravens."

Katsuk nodded. It was logical. He said: "That lightning last night—it hit the big spruce beside the house where my *friends* were talking. They were arguing whether to turn me over to the hoquat police when pieces of the tree smashed through the roof.'' He smiled without mirth.

David swallowed a bite of fish. "Was anybody hurt?"

"A fish rack fell on Tskanay. It bruised her arm. Ish was burned. He tried to jump across the fire. They were not hurt much, but they no longer discuss what to do with me."

David chewed silently, studying his captor, trying not to betray awe at this revelation. It was one more thing to confirm the powers Katsuk controlled. He could bring down the lightning.

Katsuk said: "They don't want me to send more lightning."

David sensed something cynical and doubting in Katsuk's tone, asked: "Did you make the lightning?"

"Maybe. I don't know. But that's what they think."

"What did you tell them?"

"I told them an owl's tongue will bring rain. I told them Raven can create fire. They know this, but they've been taught the hoquat ways of doubting their own past. Have you had enough of that fish?"

"Yes." David nodded numbly. To have lightning silence those who could harm you! To know what would bring rain and fire! What powers those were.

Katsuk took the package of fish from the boy's hand, wrapped it tightly, thrust it into his pouch. He said: "Will you follow, or will you try to escape?"

David swallowed a lump in his throat. Escape? Where could he run that Katsuk's powers would not follow? But there had to be some way out of this nightmare. There must be some way to break free of Katsuk.

"Answer me," Katsuk ordered.

David thought: *He'll know if I try to lie to him.* He said: "If I find a way to get away from you, I will."

The honesty of innocence, Katsuk thought. Admiration for this hoquat youth rose in him. What a magnificent sacrifice Hoquat would make. Truly, this was the Great Innocent, one to answer for all of those the hoquat had slain.

Katsuk asked: "But will you follow me now?"

"I'll follow." Sullen. "Where're we going?"

"We will climb today. We will go over the mountain into another valley where there are no man trails."

"Why?"

"I am pulled in that direction."

"Shall I get the pack and the sleeping bag?"

"Leave them."

"But won't we. . . ."

"I said leave them!" There was wildness in his voice.

David backed up into the mine.

Katsuk said: "I must discard hoquat things. Come."

He turned to his right, went up around the mine shaft on a deer trail. David darted into the open, followed.

Katsuk said: "Follow close. You will get wet. Never mind that. The climb will keep you warm."

They stayed on the deer trail until the sun began to break through the overcast. Tiny cones like deer droppings covered the trail. Ferns blanketed the ground on both sides. Moss obscured all the downed trees. The trail dipped and climbed. Water ran in the low spots.

As the sun came out, Katsuk took to the ferns and moss, climbing straight up a steep ridge side to another trail. He turned right on this and soon they encountered snow on the ground. It had collected along the hill margins of the trail but had melted away on the downhill side. They walked the thin strip of open ground. Urine-colored lichen poked through the snow in the thinner places.

Once, they heard an aircraft flying low under the broken clouds. It could not be seen through the heavy tree cover.

As they climbed, the trees began to thin. The deer track crossed a park trail with a signboard. The sign pointed left: KIMTA PEAK.

Katsuk turned right.

They began encountering long stretches of snow on the trail. There were old footprints in the snow. The flat inner surfaces of the prints had almost lost their foot shape. Rain pocked the prints. Some of them showed mud stains.

Once, Katsuk pointed to the prints, said: "They were going over Kimta Peak. It was last week."

David studied the tracks. He couldn't tell toe from heel. "How do you know?"

"Do you see how we leave mud in the snow? It is always after we cross open ground. They left mud on the downhill side. The tracks have melted for at least a week."

"Who was it, do you suppose?"

"Hoquat searching for us, perhaps."

David shivered as the wind gusted. The air carried the chill of snow and ice. Even the effort of keeping up with Katsuk failed to warm him. He wondered how Katsuk could endure it in only loincloth and moccasins. The moccasins were dark with water. The loincloth appeared soggy. David's tennis shoes sloshed with each step. His feet were numb with cold.

They came to another sign: THREE PRUNE SHELTER. It pointed downhill to the right.

Katsuk left the park trail there, took to a deer path that went straight up the hill. David was pressed to keep up.

Whenever he could see up through the trees, the sky showed blue patches. David prayed they would come out into warm sunshine. The backs of his hands were wet and cold. He tried to put them into his jacket pockets, but the jacket was soaking.

They came to a rocky ridgetop. Katsuk followed it, climbing toward a mountain which lifted itself against clouds directly ahead. Trees on both sides of the ridge were gnarled, stunted, wind-bent. Wrinkled patches of lichen marked the rocks.

Katsuk said: "We are near timberline. We will go down soon."

He spoke above the sound of water roaring in a deep gorge to the right. They came to an elk trail which angled down toward the sound. Katsuk scrambled down onto the elk trail. David followed, slipping, avoiding snow where he could. Katsuk was covering the ground in great long strides. David ran to catch up, almost overran Katsuk. An outthrust arm stopped him.

"Dangerous to run down such a hill," Katsuk said. "You could run right off a cliff."

David nodded, shivered. He felt the cold seep through him. It was that way every time they stopped. How coud Katsuk stand it?

"Come," Katsuk said.

Again, they went down the trail. Presently, they came out on a granite ledge above the river. The roaring milky water below them filled the air with cold mist.

Katsuk turned left, upstream. Soon, the stunted trees gave way to tiny clumps of huckleberry bushes. They encountered smaller and smaller bushes until there were none. Lichen lay on the bare rocks. Tufts of greenery speared through snow patches. The river became narrower, gray rocks thrusting out of it. The sound of it was loud beside them. The water was gray-green with snowmelt, no more than six feet across. Patches of vapor drifted on its surface.

Katsuk came to the place he had been seeking—rocks like stepping stones across the river. Water piled high against the upstream sides of the rocks. He looked upstream. There was the ice wall from which this tumbling water flowed. He stared at the cold, dirty-white fountainhead of all that water. Ice . . . ice. . . .

The boy stood behind him, huddled up, shivering with the cold. Katsuk glanced at Hoquat a moment, then peered down to the right where the river plunged into the trees—far, far down there. The sun came through the clouds. He saw a deep pool in the river's middle distance: scintillant water, its current pulled taut against the deep unrest beneath. He felt the river ceaselessly churning in its depth. Who counted that water or cut it into bits? The water was bound together, one end connected to the other.

''Why're we waiting?'' David asked.

Katsuk did not hear him. He thought: *All things start downstream from this place. Here is the beginning.*

There were river spirits here. The spirits permitted no leisure for this torrent of water or the torrent in his own breast. Each would run until it broke its energy into other forms. All was movement, energy, and currents—never ceasing.

He found a deep, calming, enjoyment in this thought. His mind had taken a leap, not asking why, but how?

How?

The spirits told him: ''Never ceasing, one energy into another.''

''Come,'' he said, and crossed the stream, jumping from rock to rock.

The boy followed.

SHERIFF PALLATT:

Hell, I know the FBI thinks he's gone underground in some city. That's nuts! That twisty-minded, goddamned Indian's in there someplace. I'm sure he crossed the Hoh. I saw tracks. Could've been a man and a boy. Right up near the middle fork. How they got across there, though, with the river that high, I'll never know. Maybe he's a woods devil. I guess if you're crazy enough you do impossible things.

A VINE maple shadow stretched out into the river below Katsuk. The maple leaves above his head shone as though polished. He squatted beside an old elk trail whose edges had tumbled into the water, stared at the tree shadow, thinking.

The boy lay stretched out, belly down, on a thin strip of grass upstream. The grass blended gradually into a moss-covered ledge of rock which the elk trail skirted. The inevitable blade of grass protruded from the boy's mouth and he was picking red ants out of the grass, nipping off their heads, and eating them. He had told Katsuk he was going to try *not* thinking.

David thought: *That's a very strange thing. How do you get a nonthought into your head?*

Katsuk had started this queer train of thinking. He had accused the boy of thinking too much in words and had said this was a failing of all hoquat.

David glanced at Katsuk. The man obviously was thinking right now—squatting there, thinking. Did Katsuk use words?

They had spent most of a day coming down into the lowlands after crossing the high ridge and the river. There were seven pebbles in David's pocket—seven days, a week. They had spent the night in an abandoned park shelter. Katsuk had dug up a poacher's cache of blankets and tallow-dipped cans of food. He had built a small fire in the shelter and they had eaten beans and slept on spruce boughs over the ashes.

It had been a long hike from the shelter. David glanced up at the sun: early afternoon. Not too long, then. He hadn't really thought about the time.

The trail into the lowlands had followed a watercourse. It had plunged through salal thickets, forded the river, followed dry sloughs. Once, they had surprised a cow elk poking her nose from an alder copse. Her fur had glistened.

David gave up attempting to not-think. He began mouthing "David" silently to himself. He wanted to say his name aloud but knew this would only excite the craziness in Katsuk.

He thought: *I'm David, not Hoquat. I'm a hoquat, but my name is David, not Hoquat.*

The thought rolled through his mind: *David-not-Hoquat, David-not-Hoquat. . . .*

The trail from the high ridge had crossed well-traveled park trails twice. One of the trails had carried a pattern of recent boot tracks in mud. Katsuk had avoided the mud, had taken them up a game trail that angled across an old burn. They had crossed another river beyond the burn and Katsuk had said there would be no more man trails now.

Katsuk seemed to go on and on without tiring. There was a nervous, sweaty energy in him even now as he squatted beside the river. He had brought the blankets from the poacher's cache, one of them rolled and tied at his waist, the other carried loose over his shoulders. He had discarded the blankets when he had squatted beside the river. His dark, flat-cheeked face remained immobile in thought. His eyes glistened.

David thought: *I am David-not-Hoquat.*

Was that another name? he wondered. Was it a halfway identity, David-not-quite-Hoquat? He recalled that his mother had called him Davey. His father had occasionally called him *Son*. Grandmother Morgenstern had called him David, though. Names were odd. How could he be Hoquat in his own mind?

He thought: *What's Katsuk thinking?*

Was it possible Katsuk knew how to not-think?

David raised himself on his elbows, pushed the chewed blade of grass from his mouth with his tongue, said: "Katsuk, what're you thinking?"

Without looking up from the river, Katusk said: "I am thinking how to make a bow and arrow in the old way. Do not disturb my thinking."

"The old way? What's that?"

"Be still."

David heard the edge of insanity in Katsuk's voice, lapsed into sullen silence.

Katsuk studied the river, a milky-green surge. He noted the shadows on a tumbling twig.

An uprooted stump came twisting through the current which boiled under the vine maple shadow. The stump was an old one with dark, red-brown punk wood in the root end. It turned slowly, end over end, roots up like clutching hands, then falling over, sinking beneath the slick water, the cut end rising into the afternoon sunlight. Water drained from it and the whole cycle started once more as it passed.

The stump made a sound in its turning—*klug-slumk-hub-lub*.

Katsuk listened, wondering at the language of the stump. He felt the stump was talking to him, but it was no language he understood. What could it be saying? The cut end was gray with age. It was a hoquat scar. The stump did not seem to be talking about its own travail. It went downstream, turning and talking.

He felt the presence of the boy with disturbing intensity. That was flesh back there with all of its potential for good or evil . . . for both at once. Goodevil. Was there such a word?

Katsuk felt that he and the boy had fallen into a new relationship. Almost friendly. Was that Tskanay's doing? He felt no jealousy. Charles Hobuhet might have been jealous, but not Katsuk. Tskanay had given the boy a moment of life. He had lived; now he must die.

It was correct to feel friendship toward a victim. That subdued the enemy soul. But this new association went beyond such friendship.

How did we get into this new relationship?

It could change nothing, of course. The Innocent must ask for death and be killed.

Katsuk felt sadness twist in his breast. There could be no stopping this thing. There had been no stopping it from the beginning. It had come out of the ice. Bee's message had been cold. And Raven's. It must end with the Innocent slain.

The boy stood up, walked upstream off the grass, sat down with his back against the cathedral pillar of a rotten stump. He began searching for grubs in the rotten wood.

Katsuk refused to look at him.

Let Hoquat escape . . . if Raven would permit it.

The vine maple shadow lay black on the river. The water appeared calm on its surface, but Katsuk felt the wild power underneath. He felt himself being driven by such a power—Soul Catcher within. Soul Catcher moved like the water, deep and strong underneath.

Katsuk found one of the blankets beside him, wiped his eyes.

David cast an occasional sidelong glance at his captor. Why was Katsuk so changeable? The man hovered between friendliness and violence. One minute, he would explain a legend of his people. The next second, he could scream for silence. Katsuk had been very different since he had played the flute in the old mine shaft.

For the moment, the boy felt a strange happiness. He watched the river, the waning sun. He was aware of movements and patterns. For a time, he dozed. Katsuk would catch a fish soon and they would eat. Or Katsuk would find another poacher's cache, or make a bow and arrow and kill game. Katsuk had said he was thinking how to make a bow and arrow.

David's eyes snapped open. He felt no passage of time but knew he had slept. The sun had moved toward the horizon.

A long sandbar protruded into the current downstream. The river turned there in a wide arc against a thick stand of hemlocks. A matchstick pile of silver and gray logs lay stranded on the sand. The sun, about two log-widths above the hemlocks, colored the tops of the stranded logs yellow-orange.

The light and color reminded David of Carmel Valley and his home. He wondered what had brought that memory. He decided it was the heat waves dancing over the logs. This day had been so bone-cold when they had walked through the forest shadows, but the sun-warmed ground beneath him induced a comfortable drowsiness.

As they had come down from the high country, the land had grown increasingly wild and rugged. The steeper mountainsides and narrower canyons had given way to a broad valley thick with trees. Just before coming to this place, they had crossed a long, narrow benchland covered with stunted fir, pine, and spruce. An ancient storm had twisted the trees together, some fallen and dead, some leaning and still alive.

Katsuk continued to stare at the river.

David sighed, feeling hunger pangs. He searched for more grubs in the stump. They were juicy and sweet.

As he ate the grubs, he had a sudden vision of his mother delicately plucking hors d'oeuvres from a tray held by a maid. He imagined what his mother would say if she could see him now. She would be frantic and hysterical even when he told her about this. Her eyes would go wide. Gasps of shock would escape her. She would cry. David had no doubt these events would occur. Katsuk had promised: There would be no killing unless the victim asked for it.

David felt no special worry. It was a time for storing up memories. A wonderful curiosity drove him. This would end in time and he would have a glorious adventure to tell. He would be a hero to his friends—kidnapped by a wild Indian! Katsuk was wild, of course . . . and insane. But there were limits to his insanity.

The light on the stranded logs had become like sunshine on autumn grass. David watched Katsuk and the hypnotic flow of the river. He came to the decision this might be one of the happiest days of his life: Nothing was demanded of him; he had been cold, now he was warm; he had been hungry and had eaten. . . . Soon, they would eat again.

A long orange-brown deerfly landed on his left wrist. He slapped it reflexively, wiped the dead insect from his hand on a clump of grass.

Katsuk began singing: low-voiced. It was a chant oddly in tune with the river and the golden sunlight. His voice rose and fell, full of clicks and coughing sounds.

The thought in Katsuk's mind was that he desperately needed a sign. He needed an omen to guide him from this place. Swaying, he chanted his prayer song, appealing to Bee and Raven, to Kwahoutze and Alkuntam. Soul Catcher stirred within him. Gusts of wind began to blow along the river—the wind that came before dark. Katsuk sensed a barrier, an obstruction to his prayer. Perhaps it was Hoquat blocking the way. Katsuk recalled Hoquat's dream. That was a powerful dream. The boy could have a wish—any wish. When he was ready. There was a powerful spirit waiting in that boy.

The wind chilled Katsuk's cheek.

A glacier filled the river source up there and the wind of evening blew down the valley toward the sea.

Katsuk sensed that he had left pursuit far behind in the upper reaches of the Wilderness Area. Not even a helicopter crossed the sky here, although earlier there had been a jet soundlessly drawing its white plume high over the peak that dominated the eastern skyline.

As he thought these things, Katsuk continued chanting. The memory of Hoquat's dream troubled him. It lay festering in his awareness. It was a thing which might defy Soul Catcher. How could the boy have dreamed a powerful spirit? He was a hoquat! But that was a warning dream, a thing to spread disquiet all around. And Hoquat appeared content. Had he wished the thing which would not be denied him?

Movement on the river stirred Katsuk from his reverie. A long, smooth limb, pearl gray, and glistening, drifted on the current. Katsuk's gaze followed the limb. It appeared to glide downstream independent of the current. It was headed with a sure inward direction toward the figure squatting beneath the vine maple. The limb pierced the vine maple's shadow like an arrow penetrating its target. The shadow moved along the length of the limb. Katsuk felt shadow darkness penetrating the wood.

He broke off his chant, breathed a long "Ahhhhhh."

The limb surged across a dark upswelling of current. It came directly at him. One end drove into the muddy embankment at Katsuk's feet. He knelt, lifted the limb from the water with a feeling of reverence. He sensed something powerful struggling in the wood.

Gently, he examined what the river had sent him. The wood felt smooth and vibrant beneath his fingers. Alive! Water dripped from it. One end had been burned, the other broken. The wood had not been long in the water. It was not soaked. Not a deformity or twisting of grain marked its smooth length—almost as long as he was tall. At its thickest end, it was larger than his clenched fist. The tapering was almost indiscernible, less than a finger's width.

How supple and alive it felt!

Katsuk stood up, put one end on the ground, his hand in the center, and tried to flex it. He felt the wood fighting him. It quivered with hidden power. It was the wood of a god-bow!

The feeling of reverence strong in him, Katsuk lifted Hoquat's knife from its sheath to test the hardness of this wood. A large black bee darted across his line of vision—another, another.

He hesitated, the knife gripped tightly in his hand. Sweat broke out on his forehead.

Ahhhhhh, that had been close!

One touch of hoquat steel on this wood! Just one and the spirit power would leave it. His prayer had brought the wood of a god-bow and he had almost defiled it.

Katsuk's throat was dry from the nearness of the defilement. He returned the knife to its sheath, slipped the sheath from his waist, hurled the hated instrument into the river. Only when the blade had sunk beneath the current did he feel free from deadly peril.

How close that had been!

He glanced to where the boy sat, eyes closed, drowsing. The spirit had been strong in Hoquat, but not strong enough. That evil spirit with its subtle persuasions had almost tempted Katsuk into an act of defilement. Who knew where such an act could have led? It might even have given Hoquat the upper hand here. When two beings were bound together this way, captor and captive, the tie that bound them could be pulled in either direction.

Katsuk grasped the limb in both hands, held it high over his head. How beautiful it was! He sang the song of dedication. He dedicated it to Bee. Bee had sent this omen wood.

The whole course of what he must do came into his mind as he prayed. He must find obsidian and fashion a knife from it to work this omen wood into a bow. That was how it must be done: a bow fashioned in the ancient way, then an arrow tipped with the stone point from the ocean beach of his ancestors at Ozette. From ancient times to this time, it would all be connected.

Katsuk lowered the limb, relaxed.

He sensed his ancestors singing within him.

This is how the Innocent must die!

Carrying the omen wood reverently in his left hand, Katsuk went to where Hoquat lay asleep against the stump. The boy awoke when he felt Katsuk's shadow, stared up at his captor, smiled.

The smile heartened Katsuk. He returned it. Hoquat's dream spirit had been subdued.

The boy yawned, then: "What're you going to do with the stick? Are you going to fish?"

"This?" Katsuk lifted the limb. His whole arm throbbed with the power in the omen wood. "This was sent by my spirits. It will do a great thing."

FROM A story in the Seattle *Post-Intelligencer:*

Sheriff Pallatt said he is concentrating his searchers in the virtually untracked Wilderness Area of the park (see map at right) and that he is instructing them to move with extreme caution. He said: "This is no ordinary kidnapping. This is a crime of revenge against the white race by an embittered young man who may be temporarily deranged. I am convinced Hobuhet knows what he is doing and is acting according to a plan. He's still in those mountains with that boy."

KATSUK LAY stretched face down on a shale ledge, staring along his own arm immersed to the elbow in clear, cold river water. The omen wood for the bow was beside him. His hand in the water appeared wavery and distorted against the mossy rock. He could feel the pulse at his elbow. Intense awareness of the world around him permeated his being.

He saw two long gray logs high on the flood-scoured bar at the river bend across from him. Their shadows mingled in a staggering track across the bar, long, flat shadows in the low afternoon sun.

A scuffling sound behind him told Katsuk the boy had moved. Katsuk glanced back. Hoquat squatted beneath a big-leaf maple juggling his day-counting pebbles. There were eight pebbles now: eight days. A limb above the boy was strung with fuzzy moss, dirty green and straggling. It dangled above the blond head like wool on a sheep's belly. The boy was sucking on a grass stem.

Katsuk turned away, concentrated once more on his hand in the water.

The river was clear and deep here. He could see periwinkles on the bottom: irregular black marks against the varicolored rocks. For some time now, he had been observing the progress of a big fish as it worked its way along the mossy side of the ledge. It was a native whitefish—*kull t' kope*.

Katsuk mouthed its name under his breath, praying to the fish spirit and the water spirit.

Kull t' kope's tail wriggled spasmodically as it concentrated on eating insects from the moss.

Katsuk felt the presence of the fish and the river all through him. The river was called Sour Water in his own tongue. A strange name, he thought. The water was sweet to the taste, clean, and with a musty edge of snow in it.

The chill water made his arm numb from the elbow down, but Katsuk remained motionless, waiting. He allowed his thoughts to contain only friendliness toward the fish. That was an old way, older than memory—from First Times. He had learned it as a boy from his Uncle Okhoots.

The fish encountered the barrier presence of Katsuk's arm, swam gently around it, nosed the moss beside it. Gently, slowly, Katsuk raised his hand. He stroked the fish along its belly. Motion set his hand tingling painfully and he felt the cold softness of the fish—stroking slowly, softly, gently. . . .

It was slow work . . . slow . . . slow. . . .

His opened fingers went under the flexing gills.

Now!

Grabbing and lifting in one motion, Katsuk leaped backward, hurled the fish over his shoulder, whirling to watch where it landed.

It was a big fish, almost as long as a man's arm, and it hit the boy full in the chest, sent him sprawling. Boy and fish went down in one big, writhing tangle on the riverbank—legs, arms, flopping tail.

Katsuk was on them in a scrambling, bounding dash. He pinned the fish with both hands over the back of its head, thumb and fingers of one hand in its gills.

The boy rolled away, sat up, demanding: "Did we get it? Did we get it?"

Katsuk lifted the still struggling fish, broke its neck.

The boy exhaled wordlessly, then: "Wow! It's a big one!"

Katsuk took the fish in one hand, helped the boy to his feet, leaving a smear of fish blood across the jacket.

The boy stared at the dead fish, eyes wide and fixed. His arms, hands, and the front of his jacket presented a splotched mess of fish slime, scales, sand, mud, and leaves from the mad scramble on the riverbank.

"You're a mess," Katsuk said. "Go splash that stuff off you while I clean the fish."

"Are we going to eat it right away?"

Katsuk thought: *Trust the hoquat to think only of his stomach, and not of the spirit in what we have killed.*

He said: "We will eat at the proper time. Go clean yourself."

"Okay."

Katsuk retrieved his omen wood. He searched among the beach rocks until he found a large one with a slim, jagged edge. He went to the shallows, sawed the head off the fish, pulled away the gills. He reached into the fish then, pulled the entrails out, cleaned the cavity in running water. A sharp stick through there and *kull t' kope* could be cooked over coals.

As he worked, Katsuk mouthed the prayer to Fish, asking pardon that this thing must be done. He heard the boy splashing below him.

The boy shouted: "Hey! This water's cold."

"Then wash faster."

Katsuk picked up fish and omen wood, started back to the ledge. The boy scrambled across the rocks, trotted beside him. He was dripping, shivering, and there was an odd look on his face.

"What are you thinking?" Katsuk asked.

"Did you mean for that fish to hit me?"

"No. I was just making sure we didn't lose it."

The boy grinned. "Did I look funny?"

Katsuk chuckled, felt oddly relieved. "You looked funny. I couldn't tell which was fish and which was boy."

They came to the rim of the ledge where grass and moss began. Katsuk put the fish on moss, placed the omen wood gently beside it. He thought how it must have been for Hoquat—a big flash of silver as the fish tumbled through the air.

What a shock!

Katsuk began to chuckle.

The boy closed his eyes, remembering. Katsuk had said he was fishing, but it had looked stupid: just waiting there . . . waiting . . . waiting . . . Who could expect a fish to come from such inactivity? No pole, no line, no hook, no bait—just a hand in the water. Then: whap!

Katsuk was laughing now.

David opened his eyes. His stomach began to shake with laughter. He couldn't suppress it. The cold, flopping surprise of that sudden fish!

In a moment, boy and captor were facing each other, laughing like idiots. The noise brought a flock of gray jays, black-crowned camp robbers. They circled overhead, alighted in a stand of alders high up on the riverbank. Their querulous calls made a wild background for the laughter.

Katsuk doubled over with mirth. His mind held the entire compass of that scene: boy, legs, fish, the brown-green riverbank with its overhanging moss, that insane tangle of feet and fish. It was the funniest thing Katsuk could remember in all of his life.

He heard the boy laughing, trying to stop, then laughing more.

The boy gasped: "Oh . . . please! I . . . can't . . . stop . . . laughing."

Katsuk tried to think of something to stop the laughter. *The pursuers!* He thought of searchers coming upon the pair of them at this moment. He thought of the puzzlement this scene would create. How ludicrous it was! He laughed all the harder. His sides ached from laughter. He struggled up the mossy bank, flopped on his back, sent great peals of laughter at the sky.

The boy scrambled up to sprawl beside him.

Man and boy—they lay there, spending themselves on laughter until fatigue overcame them, not daring to speak then lest it release new mirth.

Katsuk thought of the laughing game he had played as a boy, as the boy Charles Hobuhet. Make each other laugh, that was the game. Whoever could not control his laughter lost the game.

A spasmodic chuckle shook him.

The boy lay silent. Hoquat had won this game.

For a long while after the joy of that laughter had subsided, they lay on the warm ground, catching their breath.

Katsuk grew aware that the sky was darkening. Clouds covered the low sun. The clouds moved upriver on a cold, raw wind. Katsuk sat up, stared at the clouds. They hung above the trees, unsupported, mysterious gray turrets with the last glowing strip of day beneath them.

He slapped the boy's arm. "Come. We must make a fire and dry you out."

The boy scrambled to his feet. "And cook the fish?"

"Yes—and cook the fish."

FROM A scrap of note left at the Sam's River shelter:

When I am confused I listen with as much of my being as I can allow. This was always what my people did. We fell silent in confusion and waited to learn. The whites do a strange thing when they are confused. They run around making much noise. They only add to the confusion and cannot even hear themselves.

FOR A long while that night, Katsuk lay awake in their shelter thinking. Hoquat, breathing beside him with the even rhythm of sleep, remained a disturbing presence. Even asleep, there was a spirit in the boy. It was like the times when the hoquat first arrived and some said they must be the descendants of Seagull, who had owned the daylight. Grandfather Hobuhet had recounted the tale often. The hoquat squawked and ran around like Seagull; so the confusion was understandable. This boy, though, no longer ran around and squawked. He remained silent for long periods. At such times, the spirit could be sensed growing within him.

The spirit grew even now.

Katsuk sensed the spirit speaking to the boy. The spirit stood there in the darkness in place of the man this youth would never become. It was a thing of excitement and peril.

The spirit of the boy spoke then to Katsuk:"You see this, Katsuk? In this flesh there are good eyes and a mind that has seen something you have not."

Katsuk felt that he must weep, must punish his senses for this recognition of Hoquat's spirit. But the revelation demanded that he deal with it.

"This is flesh that made something happen," the spirit said.

Katsuk fought to remain silent. He shuddered. If he answered this spirit, he knew it would gain power over him. It might pick him up and shake him. Katsuk would rattle in the Hobuhet flesh like a stick in a basket.

"What folly to think you can ignore me," the spirit said.

Katsuk clenched his teeth tightly. What a seductive spirit this was. It reminded him of the hoquat world.

"I give you back your own knowledge of what the world knows," the spirit said.

Katsuk groaned.

"I make you really know what you only thought you knew," the spirit said. "You think there is no place in you to receive this? Whether you say aye, or nay, something is driven into your heart by the thing itself. This boy's hand and your eye have met. He has said something and part of you listened . . . without compromise. If you have as good an eye as his, you can look directly through his flesh and see the man he would become. He has shared this with you, do you understand?"

Katsuk rolled his head in the darkness, holding fast to his link with Soul Catcher.

"Where does such a thing begin?" the spirit asked. "What made you believe you could master this matter? Do you not see the wonder of this youth? Bring your sight back to the surface and observe this being. How do you dignify yourself in this?"

Katsuk felt sweat drench his flesh. He was chilled inside and out. The temper of this hoquat spirit was emerging. It was looking far back into deeper things. It was primitive and tyrannous. Its concepts spanned all time. There was no greater tyranny. It struck through to the ultimate human. He felt vibrations of color in the night, sensed something wonderful and terrifying about these moments. The spirit had netted a piece of the universe and shaken it out for observation. The thing had been said without decision and without any concern for Katsuk's desire to hear. It was merely said. The spirit invited him to do nothing except listen. The message was brought to him as though painted on wood. In a time of madness, it said a simple thing:

"If you carry out your purpose, it must be done as a man to a man."

Trembling and awed, Katsuk remained awake in the darkness.

Hoquat rolled over, mumbled, then spoke quite clearly: "Katsuk?"

"I am here," Katsuk said.

But the boy was only talking in his sleep.

FROM A paper by Charles Hobuhet for Philosophy 200:

The fallacies of Western philosophy fascinate me. No "body English." Words-words-words, no feelings. No flesh. You try to separate life and death. You try to explain away a civilization which uses trickery, bad faith, lies and deceit to make its falsehoods prevail *over* the flesh. The seriousness of your attack on happiness and passion astounds the man in me. It astounds my flesh. You are always running away from your bodies. You hide yourselves in words of desperate self-justification. You employ the most despotic rhetoric to justify lives that do not fit you. They are lives, in fact, not lived. You say belief is foolish, and you believe this. You say love is futile and you pursue it. Finding love, you place no confidence in it. Thus, you try to love without confidence. You place your highest verbal value on something called security. This is a barricaded corner in which you cower, not realizing that to keep from dying is not the same as "to live."

"ABOUT THIRTY thousand years ago," Katsuk said, "a lava flow pushed its way out of a vent in the middle slope up there." He hooked a thumb over his shoulder. "Some of it fell out in great lumps which you stupid hoquat called Indian tears."

David peered up at the mountain, which he could see shining in the morning sun beyond a stand of hemlocks. The mountain was a series of rock pillars. Cloud shapes drifted over it. There was an avalanche scar on a slope to the south. A river ran somewhere under that slope, but the sound of it lay hidden beneath the wind soughing in the trees.

"What time is it?" David asked.

"By hoquat time?"

"Yes."

Katsuk glanced over his shoulder at the sun. "About ten o'clock. Why?"

"You know what I'd be doing at home right now?"

Katsuk glanced at Hoquat, sensing the boy's need to talk. Why not? If Hoquat talked here, that would keep his spirit silent. Katsuk nodded, asked: "What would you be doing?"

"Taking my tennis lesson."

"Tennis lesson," Katsuk said. He shook his head.

Katsuk squatted on the slope. He held a length of brown-black obsidian in hs left hand. He steadied the obsidian on his thigh and chipped at it with a piece of flint. The sound of chipping rang sharply in the clear, high air. It produced a pungent smell which David sniffed.

"Tennis lesson," Katsuk repeated. He tried to imagine the boy as a grown man—rich and pampered, a romper man first class in the playboy army. No longer innocent. Black and white dress uniform for night. Black tie. A crew-cut, nightclub smoke-blower. Or whatever would pass for that in his time of maturity. It was a kindness to prevent that. It was a kindness to preserve Hoquat's innocence forever.

"Then I'd go swimming in our pool," David said.

Katsuk asked: "Do you want to swim in the river down there?"

"It's too cold. Our pool is heated."

Katsuk sighed, went on chipping. The obsidian was beginning to take shape. It would be a knife soon.

For some time now, David had been trying to plumb his captor's mood. There had been increasingly long silences between them while walking around the mountain slope. It had taken a full day. There were ten pebbles in David's pocket—ten days. Katsuk's few responses during the long hike had been more and more moody, snappish, and short. Katsuk was troubled by some new awareness. Was Katsuk losing his spirit powers?

David did not allow himself to think yet of escape. But if Katsuk's powers were weakening. . . .

A large chip flew off the obsidian. Katsuk held it up, turned it, examining the shape.

"What're you making?" David asked.

"A knife."

"But you've got . . . my knife." David glanced at Katsuk's waist. The Russell knife had been missing all during the walk around the mountain, but he had guessed it was in the deerhide pouch Katsuk wore.

Katsuk said: "I need a special kind of knife."

"Why?"

"To make my bow."

David accepted this, then: "Have you been here before?"

"Many times."

"Did you make knives here?"

"No. I guided hoquat in here to find pretty rocks."

"Did they make knives out of the rocks?"

"I don't think so."

"How do you know what kind of rock will make a knife?"

"My people made knives from these rocks for thousands of years. They used to come up here at least once a year—before you hoquat came with steel. You call this rock obsidian. We call it black fire—*klalepiah*.

David fell silent. Where was the Russell knife? Would Katsuk give it back?

Katsuk had caught a rabbit and two small quail in snares during the night. He had cleaned them with a sharp piece of the brown-black rock, cooked them in an earth oven heated by pitch balls. The pitch had made a hot fire with almost no smoke.

David found a remnant of rabbit leg, sat down, and chewed on it while he watched Katsuk work. The gray striking rock in Katsuk's right hand had one narrow end. Katsuk struck sharply and steadily at the obsidian, using the narrow end of the flint. Sparks flew. The sulfurous odor grew strong in the still air.

Presently, David summoned his courage, asked: "Where's my knife?"

Katsuk thought: *Ahhh, the sly, clever hoquat!* He said: "I must make my bow in the ancient way. Steel cannot touch this wood."

"Then where's my knife?"

"I threw it in the river."

Outraged, David hurled the gnawed rabbit bone to the ground, leaped to his feet. "That was my knife!"

"Be still," Katsuk said.

"My father gave me that knife," David said, his voice tight with fury. Angry tears began running down his cheeks.

Katsuk peered up at him, weighing the boy's passion. "Could your father not buy you another knife?"

"That one was for my birthday!" David shook tears off his cheeks. "Why'd you have to throw it away?"

Katsuk looked at the obsidian and flint in his hands.

A birthday gift, father to son: a man's gift to a man.

Katsuk experienced emptiness at the certainty that he would never have a son to receive the gift of manhood. The obsidian felt heavy in his hand. He knew he was experiencing self-pity and it angered him.

Why pity anyone? There could be no reprieve.

"Damn you!" David raged. "I hope your Cedar sickness kills you!"

Awareness blazed in Katsuk. There lay the source of the curse! The Innocent had found a spirit to work his curse. Where had Hoquat found this spirit? Had he received it from Tskanay? Then, where had she found it?

Katsuk said: "I was warned by Bee to throw away that steel knife."

"Stupid Bee!"

Katsuk jerked his chin up, glared at the boy. "Careful what you say about Bee. He might not let you live out this day!"

The glazed look of madness in Katsuk's eyes cooled David's anger. He felt only the loss now. The knife was gone, thrown into a river by this madman. David tried to take a deep breath, but his chest pained him. The knife would never be found again. He thought abruptly of the murdered hiker. That knife had killed a man. Was that why it had been thrown away?

Katsuk went back to his chipping.

David said: "Are you sure you didn't hide my knife in that pouch?"

Katsuk put down obsidian and flint, opened the pouch, exposed the interior to the boy.

David pointed: "What's that little package?"

"It's not your knife. You can see I do not have the knife."

"I see." Still angry. "What's that package?"

Katsuk sealed the pouch, went back to chipping his obsidian. "It is the down of sea ducks."

"Down?"

"The soft feathers."

"I know that. Why do you carry a stupid thing like that?"

Katsuk noted how anger spoke in the boy, thought: *The down is to sprinkle on your body when I have slain you.* He said: "It is part of my spirit medicine."

"Why'd your spirit tell you to throw away my knife?" David asked.

Katsuk thought: *He is learning to ask the right questions.*

"Why?" the boy demanded.

"To save me," Katsuk whispered.

"What?"

"To save me!"

"You told Cally nothing can save you."

"But Cally does not know me."

"She's your aunt."

"No. She had a nephew named Charles Hobuhet. I am Katsuk."

And Katsuk wondered: *Why do I explain myself to my victim? What is he doing that I must defend myself? Is it the knife I threw away? That was a link with his father, the father he had before he became Hoquat. Yes. I threw away his past. It is what those drunken loggers did to Janiktaht . . . and to me.*

"I'll bet you've never even been in a heated pool," David said.

Katsuk smiled. Hoquat's anger darted here and there. It was like a creature in a cage. *Tennis lessons, a swimming pool.* Hoquat had lived a sheltered life, a life of preserved innocence in the fashion of his people. Despite Tskanay, he remained in that delicate transition place: part man-part boy. Innocent.

Sorrow permeated David. His mouth felt dry. His chest ached. He felt tired, frustrated, lonely. Why was crazy Katsuk making a stone knife? Why was he *really* making it? Had Katsuk lied?

David remembered reading that Aztecs had killed their sacrificial victims with stone knives. Aztecs were Indians. He shook his head. Katsuk had promised.

"Unless you tell me to do it, I will not kill you." The stone knife had another purpose. Perhaps it was just to make the stupid bow.

Katsuk said: "You are no longer angry with me?"

"No." Still sullen.

"Good. Anger blocks the mind. Anger does not learn. There is much for you to learn."

Anger does not learn! David thought. He climbed deliberately close to Katsuk, went short way up the slope, and sat down with his back against the bole of a hemlock. Bits of obsidian littered the ground around him. He picked up a handful, began throwing them past Katsuk at brush and trees down the slope.

The bits of obsidian made a clattering sound when they hit a tree. They went flick-flick in salal leaves on the forest floor. It was a curious counterpoint noise to Katsuk's chipping. David felt his anger pouring out in the exertion of throwing the rocks. He threw harder, harder.

Katsuk said: "If you wish to throw a rock at me, throw it. Do not play games with your feelings."

David leaped up, anger flaring. He held a sharp-edged piece of obsidian the size of a quail's egg in his hand. He gritted his teeth, hurled the rock at Katsuk with all his strength. The rock struck a glancing blow on Katsuk's cheek, left a red slash from which blood oozed.

Terrified by what he had done, David stepped backward. Every muscle was in readiness to flee.

Katsuk put a finger to the wound, brought it away, examined the blood. Curious. The cut did not hurt. What could it mean that such a blow caused no pain? There had been a brief sensation of pressure, but no pain. Ahhh, Bee had blocked off the pain. Bee had interposed a magic to make the blow ineffective. It was a message from Bee. The Innocent's spirit would not prevail.

"I am Tamanawis speaking to you. . . ."

David said: "Katsuk? Katsuk, I'm sorry."

Katsuk looked up at him. Hoquat appeared ready for flight, his eyes wide and bright with fear. Katsuk nodded, said: "Now, you know a *little* of how I felt when I took you from the hoquat camp. What a hate that must be to want to kill an innocent for it. Did you ever think of that?"

Kill an innocent! David thought. He said: "But you promised. . . ."

"I will keep that promise. It is the way of my people. We do not tell hoquat lies. Do you know how it is?"

"What?"

"When we were whalers, whale had to demand the harpoon. Whale asked us to kill him."

"But I'd never. . . ."

"Then you are safe."

Katsuk returned to his chipping.

David ventured a step closer to Katsuk. "Does it hurt?"

"Bee will not let it hurt. Be quiet. I must concentrate."

"But it's bleeding."

"The bleeding will stop."

"Shouldn't we put something on it?"

"It is a small wound. Your mouth is a bigger wound. Be quiet or I will put something in your mouth."

David gulped, wiped his mouth with the back of his hand. He found it difficult not to look at the dark scratch on Katsuk's cheek. The bleeding stopped, but coagulation formed a ragged lower edge to the wound.

Why didn't it hurt?

It outraged David that the wound did not hurt. He had wanted it to hurt. Cuts always hurt. But Katsuk had spirit protectors. Maybe it really didn't hurt.

David turned his attention to the obsidian knife taking shape under Katsuk's hands. The blade, about four inches long and sharply wedged, was held flat against Katsuk's thigh. With quick, glancing blows, Katsuk broke tiny flakes from the edges.

The knife did not appear long or slim enough to stab anyone. The cutting edges were serrated. But it could cut an artery. He thought again of the hiker Katsuk had killed. That hiker had not asked to be killed. But Katsuk had murdered him anyway.

David found his mouth suddenly dry. He said: "That guy . . . you know, on the trail . . . the guy you . . . well, he didn't ask you to. . . ."

"You hoquat always think mouth-talk is the only talk." Katsuk spoke without looking up from his work. "Why can't you learn body-talk? When Raven made you, did he leave that ability out of you?"

"What's body-talk?"

"It is what you do. A thing you do can say something about what you want."

"That's crazy talk about Raven."

"God made us, eh?"

"Yes!"

"It depends on what you're taught, I guess."

"Well, I don't believe that about body-talk and Raven."

"You don't believe Raven keeps you tied to me?"

David could not answer. Raven *did* do what Katsuk wanted. The birds went where Katsuk ordered them to go. To know where the birds would go—what a power that was.

Katsuk said: "You are quiet. Did Raven take your tongue? Raven can do that. Your stupid hoquat world does not prepare you to deal with Raven."

"You always say *stupid* when you talk about my people," David accused. "Isn't there anything good about our world?"

"Our world?" Katsuk asked. "*Your* world, Hoquat."

"But nothing good in it?"

"I see only death in it. The whole world dies of you."

"What about our doctors? We have better doctors than you ever had."

"Your doctors are tied to illness and death. They make as much illness and death as they cure. An exact balance. It's called a transactional relationship. But they are so blind, they do not see how they are tied to what they do."

"Transactional . . . relationship? What's that?"

"A transaction is where you trade one thing for another. When you buy something, that's a transaction."

"Ahhh, that's just big words that don't mean anything."

"They are words from your world, Hoquat."

"But they don't mean anything."

"They mean doctors don't know they do it, but still they do it: They maintain a level of illness to justify their existence. Police do the same thing with crime. Lawyers keep up the legal confusions. Body-talk, Hoquat. No matter what they say they want, or how hard they work to overcome their defects, things work out in a way that keeps them busy and justifies their existence.''

"That's crazy!''

"Yes, it is crazy, but it is real. It is what you see when you understand body-talk.''

"But my world does lots of good things. People don't go hungry anymore.''

"But they do, Hoquat. In Asia, they—''

"I mean people in this country.''

"Aren't they *people* in the other countries?''

"Sure, but. . . .''

"Even in this country—in the moutains of your East, in the South, in big cities, people are hungry. People die of hunger every year. Old people, young people. My people die that way, too, because they try to live like hoquat. And the world gets hungrier and hungrier. . . .''

"What about our houses? We build better houses than you ever saw.''

"And you destroy the earth to plunge your houses into it. You build where no house should be. You are insensitives. You live *against* the earth, not *with* it.''

"We have cars!''

"And your cars are smothering you.''

David quested in his mind for something Katsuk could not strike down. Music? He'd sneer the way adults always did. Education? He'd say it didn't prepare you to live out here. Science? He'd say it was killing the world with big bombs, big machines.

"Katsuk, what do you mean by body-talk?''

"What your actions say. You say with your mouth: 'That's too bad.' Then you laugh. That means you're really happy while you're saying you're sorry. You say: 'I love you.' Then you do something to hurt that person's feelings. Body-talk is what you *do*. If you say, 'I don't want that to happen,' and all the while you are making it happen, which thing are we to believe? Do we believe the words or do we believe the body?''

David thought about words. He thought about church and sermons, of all the words about "eternal life.'' Were the words true, or did the preacher's body say something different?

"Katsuk, do your people understand body-talk?''

"Some of them. The old ones did. Our language tells me this.''

"How?''

"We say eat while eating, shit while shitting, fuck while fucking. The words and body agree.''

"That's just dirty talk.''

"It is innocent talk, Hoquat. Innocent.''

FROM A note left by Katsuk in the abandoned park shelter at Sam's River:
   My body is a pure expression of myself.

KATSUK PUT down the chipping stone, examined his obsidian knife. It was done. He liked the way the smooth end fitted his hand. It made him feel close to the earth, part of everything around him.

The sun stood straight overhead, beating down on his shoulders. He heard Hoquat breaking twigs behind him.

Katsuk placed the omen wood from Bee across his knees, examined it once more for flaws. The wood appeared to have no irregularities. Every grain ran straight and clean. He took the smooth handle of his knife in his right hand, began scraping the wood. Long, curly shavings peeled back. He worked slowly at first, then faster, whispering to himself.

"A little bit here. More there. Some here. Ahhh, that's a good one. . . ."

David came and squatted beside him. Presently, he said: "May I help?"

Katsuk hesitated, thought about the purpose of this bow—to drive a consecrated arrow into the heart of the youth beside him. Was Hoquat asking now to be slain? No. But this showed Soul Catcher at work, preparing the boy for that final moment.

"You may help," Katsuk said. He handed the knife and the omen wood to the boy, indicated a bulge to be scraped. "Remove this high place. Work slowly, just a little bit at a time."

David held the limb as Katsuk had, resting it across his knees. "This place here?"

"Yes."

David put the knife to the wood, pulled. A curl of wood formed over the blade. Another. He scraped energetically, intent on the bulge. Perspiration ran down his forehead, into his eyes. Lengths of shaving curled away, dropped around his knees.

"No more," Katsuk said. "You have fixed that place." He took back the wood and knife, resumed his careful shaping of the bow.

"More here . . . and over here . . . that's right . . . now, in here. . . ."

David tired of watching the wood curl away from the bow. Chips and shavings were all around Katsuk. Light, reflected from the newly cut wood, played glowing patterns against Katsuk's skin.

Up the slope above them, a granite chimney climbed toward a sky of blue patches in bulging, fleecy clouds. David stood up, examined the slope, the outcropping of volcanic glass below the granite. He turned, looked down into the forest—dark down there: old-growth fir, hemlock an occasional cedar. A game trail angled into the trees through heavy undergrowth of salal and wild huckleberries.

Katsuk's voice as he talked to himself carried a hypnotic quality. "Lovely wood . . . a bow of the old times. . . ."

Old times! David thought. *Katsuk certainly lives in a strange dream.*

David picked up an obsidian chip, hurled it into the trees. He thought: *If you go downstream, you come to people.*

The rock made a satisfying clatter which Katsuk ignored.

David hurled another rock, another. He worked his way down the slope to the game trail, picking up rocks, tossing them—a boy at play.

He threw my knife away! He killed a man.

Once, David paused to slash a mark in a tree trunk peering back at Katsuk. The

559

murmuring voice did not change pitch. Katsuk still paid no attention to his wandering captive.

He thinks his damned Raven is guarding me.

David searched the sky all around: no sign of the birds. He ventured about fifty feet down the game trail, pulling off salal leaves, sampling a sour berry. He could see Katsuk through the brush and trees. The sound of the obsidian knife on the bow remained clear: a slithering that noised its way oddly into the woods. Katsuk's murmurous conversation with himself remained audible.

''Ahhh, beautiful bow. Here's a beautiful bow for the message. . . .''

''Crazy Indian,'' David whispered.

Katsuk hummed and chanted and mumbled at his work.

David broke off a huckleberry twig, studied his situation. No ravens. Katsuk distracted. An open trail, all downhill. But if Katsuk caught him trying to escape again. . . . David took a trembling breath, decided he wouldn't really try to escape, not yet. He'd just explore this trail for a ways.

Casually, he wandered down into the trees. The neatly collected flight of a flicker dipping through the forest caught his attention. He heard deerflies singing. A dusty sunshaft spread quiet light on the brown floor of the woods, illuminating a delight of greenery. David saw it as an omen. He still felt anger at Katsuk. The anger might break the spirit spell.

David ventured farther down the trail. He crossed two fallen trees, went under a low passage of moss-draped limbs. The trail forked at the brink of a steep hill. One track plunged straight down. The other angled off to the left. He chose the steep way, went down through the trees to a long slope scarred by an avalanche. David studied the open area. A single cedar had survived the slide, sheltered by a prow of granite directly above it. Part of the tree had been shattered, though—one side half stripped away. Great shreds of wood had been left dangling.

Deer tracks led straight across the scarred area.

David stayed on the mossy, fern-patched forest floor, skirted the open area. Several times, he glanced around, searching out his back trail for signs of pursuit.

Katsuk was nowhere to be seen.

He listened, could not hear the scraping of the obsidian knife on the bow. There was only the wind in the trees.

The avalanche had lost itself in a small, gently rounded valley, leaving a tangle of trees and earth which dammed a small stream. The stream already had cut a narrow way across the slide. Water tinkled over rocks below the scarred earth.

David broke his way through a salal thicket above the water, surprised a spotted fawn which splashed through the shallows.

For a moment, David stood trembling in the aftermath of the shock at the way the fawn had burst from the thicket. Then, he went down to the stream, pushed his face into cold water to still his trembling.

He thought: *Now, I'm escaping.*

SHERIFF PALLATT:

There's a goddamned lot of horseshit around about who's going to get the credit in this case—us or the FBI. All I want is to save that kid—and the Indian, if I can. I'm tired of playing sheriff! Me'n Dan Gomper, my chief deputy, is gonna take our own crew in there and find that pair. A couple of old boar woodsmen like us can do it if anyone can. We're gonna camp cold so's the Indian don't see smoke and know we're trailing him. Gonna be outrageous hard work, but we'll do 'er.

KATSUK LOOKED up from the completed bow. It was a lovely bow, just right for the walrus-gut string in his pouch. He felt the notches for the string.

His chest ached and there were sharp pains in his back from bending so long in one position. He coughed. Why was it cold now? He looked up. The sun stood low over the trees.

Katsuk got to his feet, sought his captive.

"Hoquat!" he called.

Forest silence mocked him.

Katsuk nodded to himself.

Hoquat thinks to escape.

Again, Katsuk studied the sky. No sign of Raven.

He thought: *Raven invites everyone to go with him and be his guest, but on the new day, Raven turns against his guests and wants to kill them. So the guests flee into the woods. Now, I am Raven. I have the bow; I need only the arrow.*

Again, Katsuk coughed. The spasm sent pain shooting through his chest.

It was clear where Hoquat had gone. Even from up on the slope, Katsuk saw the scar the boy had carved on the tree beside the game trail.

Is it a new test? Katsuk wondered. *Do my spirits test me now that the bow is completed? Why would they not wait for the arrow?*

He took the walrus-gut string from his pouch, fitted it to the bow, tried the pull. His grandfather had taught him to make such a bow and use it. He felt his grandfather beside him as he pulled the bow to its fullest arc.

It was a great bow, truly a god-bow.

Katsuk lowered the weapon, stared down into the forest. Sweat drenched his neck and waist. He felt suddenly weak. Had Hoquat cast a spell upon him?

He glanced over his shoulder at the snow peaks. He thought of the long night: Death lurked up there, calling to him with Soul Catcher's rattle. It was a spell, for sure.

Once more, Katsuk studied the forest where Hoquat had gone. The trail beckoned him. He measured the way of it in his memory: by shadows of trees and passages of moss. He sensed the way that trail would feel beneath his feet: thinly flowing dampness of springs, the roots, the rocks, the mud.

Janiktaht's moccasins were growing thin. He could feel the raw ground through them.

The trees—Hoquat had gone that way, trying to escape.

Katsuk spoke aloud to the trail: "I am Katsuk, he who buried Kuschtaliute, the land otter's tongue. My body will not decompose. Boughs of the great trees will not fall upon my grave. I will be born again into a house of my people. There will be many good things to eat all around me."

Deadly whirlwinds of thought poured thorugh his mind, shutting off his voice.
He knew he must go after Hoquat. He must plunge down that trail, but lethargy
gripped him. It was a spell.

An image of Tskanay filled his mind.

Tskanay had cast this spell, not Hoquat! He knew it. He felt her eyes upon him.
She had looked upon him and found him alien. She stood this moment amidst the
perfume of burning cedar needles, reciting the ancient curse. Evergreens arose all
around her, a green illusion of immortality.

"Raven, help me," he whispered. "Take this sickness from me." He looked
down at the cinnamon leather of the moccasins Janiktaht had made for him.
"Janiktaht, help me."

The vision of Tskanay left him.

He thought: *Has the curse been taken away?*

Far away, with inner ear and eye, he heard and saw a vaporous river speaking
with its primitive tongues. He saw dead trees, wind-lashed, sparring with eternity.
Amidst the dead, he saw one live tree, torn and scarred but still standing, a cedar,
straight and tall, straight as an arrow shaft.

"Cedar has forgiven me," he whispered.

He stepped out onto the trail Hoquat had taken then, strode down it until he saw
the tree standing alone on the scarred earth—exactly as his vision had shown it to
him.

Cedar for my arrow, he thought. *And already consecrated.*

The hullabaloo of a raven caucus sounded over the forest. They came over the
avalanche scar, settled into the cedar.

Katsuk smiled. *What more omen do I need?*

"Katlumdai!" he shouted.

And the sick spirit of the curse left him as he called it by name. He went down
into the scarred earth then to make his arrow.

CHARLES HOBUHET'S dream, as recounted by his aunt:

When I was small I dreamed about Raven. It was the white Raven I dreamed
about. I dreamed Raven helped me steal all of the fresh water and I hid it where
only our people could find it. There was a cave and I filled it with water. I dreamed
there was a spirit in the cave who told me about creation. The spirit had created my
cave. There were two entrances, a way to enter and a way to leave. there was a
beach in the cave and waves on it. I heard drums there. My dream spirit told me
there really is such a place. It is clean and good. I want to find that place.

KATSUK SAT with his back against a tree, praying for the earth to forgive him. The
bow lay in his lap with the arrow and it was dark all around him, a cold wind

blowing dampness onto his skin. The bow was not as well made as those of the ancient people. He knew this, but he knew also that the spirit in the wood of this bow would compensate for the way he had hurried the making of it. The arrow in his lap had been fitted with the stone tip from the beach village where his people no longer were permitted to live. The ancient times and the present were tied together.

Clouds hid the stars. He felt the nearness of rain. The cold wind made his flesh tremble. He knew he should feel the chill of that wind, but his body possessed no sensation except the loss of Hoquat.

Hoquat had run off. Where?

Katsuk's mind slipped into the spirit chase of which his ancestors had spoken. He would search out Hoquat's spirit. That would lead him to the boy.

Katsuk stared into the darkness. There was a small fire somewhere and he could not tell if he saw it with the inward vision or outwardly. Flames from the fire cast ruddy light on raw earth and a tangle of roots. There was a figure at the edge of the firelight. It was a small figure. Now, Katsuk knew he was having the spirit vision.

Where was that fire?

Katsuk prayed for his spirit to guide him, but nothing spoke to him from Soul Catcher's world. It was another test then.

A small animal ran across Katsuk's outstretched legs, fled into the darkness. He felt the tree behind him growing, its bark searching upward. The damp earth and the cold wind moved all through him and he knew he would have to fight a spirit battle before he could reclaim Hoquat.

"Alkuntam, help me," he prayed. "This is Katsuk. Help me send my message. Lead me to the innocent one."

An owl called in the night and he sensed its tongue bringing rain. It would rain soon. He was being called to an ordeal within an ordeal.

Slowly, Katsuk got to his feet. He felt his body as a remote thing. He told himself: *I will begin walking. I will find Hoquat in the light of day.*

FROM AN interview with Harriet Gladding Morgenstern in the San Francisco *Examiner:*

My grandson is a very brave lad. He was never afraid of the dark or any such nonsense as that, even as a small child. He was always thoughtful of his elders. We taught him to be respectful and considerate of those around him, no matter who they were. I'm sure these are the qualities which will bring him through his present trial.

SHORTLY BEFORE nightfall, David found a sheltered place where a tree had been uprooted by a storm. The tree had fallen almost parallel to a small stream and its roots formed an overhang whose lip had been taken over by moss and grass.

David crouched in the shelter for a moment, wondering if he dared build a fire. Katsuk had made a fire bow and showed the captive how to use it as a diversion, but David wondered if smoke and fire might lead Katsuk here.

It was late, though. And there was a cold wind. He decided to risk it.

Bark had been ripped from the tree by its fall. David found lengths of bark and leaned them in an overlapping row against his shelter to make a heat pocket. He collected a pitch deposit from beneath a rotten log as Katsuk had taught him. A dead cedar lay along the slope above him. David slipped on wet salal and bruised his forehead getting to the cedar, but found, as he had hoped, that the tree's fall had splintered it, leaving long dry sections underneath which could be torn off by hand. He assembled a store of the dry cedar under the roots, brought in dead limbs and more small pieces of bark, then went in search of a short green limb for a fire bow. It would have to be short to fit a shoestring.

"Preparation, patience, persistence," Katsuk had told him in explaining this way to make fire.

David had wanted to give up in his first attempt with Katsuk's fire bow, but the man had laughed at "hoquat impatience." Goaded by that laughter, David had persisted, running the bow back and forth across its driver stick until friction made a spark in the dry grass tinder. Now he knew the careful way of it.

With a slab of cedar notched by pounding with a stone, with a shoestring bow to drive the tinder stick, with pitch and cedar splinters ready at hand, he persisted until he had a coal, then gently blew the coal into flame which he fed with pitch and cedar. When it was going well, he thought: *Katsuk should see me now.*

The thought frightened him, and he peered out of his shelter at the forest. It would be dark soon. He wondered if he would be safer from Katsuk in the night. The man had strange powers. Hunger gripped his stomach. He looked down at the stream. There would be trout in that stream. He had seen Katsuk build a weir. But the night would be cold and he knew he would get wet trying to trap a trout. He decided to forego the trout. Tomorrow . . . tomorrow there might be hikers or the people he knew must be searching for him. They would have food.

It was a long night.

Twice, David went out to replenish his firewood, dragging back dead limbs, bark. It was raining lightly the second time and the wood sizzled when he put it on the fire. His shelter turned the rain and most of the wind, though, and it was warm by contrast with the night outside.

Several times he dozed, sitting up with his back against the earth which had been exposed by the upheaval of roots. Once, he dreamed.

In the dream, he was running away, but there was a long brown string trailing behind him. It was tied around his forehead the way Katsuk wore the braided cedar around *his* head. David sensed the string trailing him wherever he ran. The string went up the mountain to Katsuk and the man up there spoke along its length. Katsuk was calling for help. "Hoquat, help me. Help me. Hoquat, I need you. Help me."

David awoke to find dawn breaking and his fire almost out. He covered the coals with dirt to extinguish them and prevent telltale smoke. An attack of shivering overcame him when he went out into the misty dawn.

I'll keep following the stream down, he decided. *There have to be people downstream.*

As he thought this, he stared upstream, searching for any sign of pursuit. Where was Katsuk now? That had been a crazy dream about string. Was Katsuk really in trouble up there? He could have fallen in the night or broken a leg or something. Crazy Indian.

Still shivering, David set off down the watercourse.

SHERIFF PALLATT:

Sure, some of these Indians can do strange things. Make your hair stand on end, some of them. I tell myself that if you live close to something like this wilderness you get a feeling for it that others don't have. I guess that's it. Maybe.

IN LATE afternoon David worked his way through a stand of big-leaf maples in a creek bottom. His little stream had become a torrent more than ten feet across. A thick carpet of moss covered the ground beneath the maples. David thought how soft a bed the moss would make. He had found a few berries to eat and he drank water frequently, but hunger was a persistent ache now. It had moved from his stomach to a tight band around his head. David wondered if the ache in his head could be real. Was it really that brown string he had dreamed about? Was Katsuk up there somewhere holding the other end of that string? He was tired and the moss invited, but when he pressed his hand into it, water ran up between his fingers.

He noted then that his feet were soaking wet.

The wind had turned to the southwest. That meant rain. Patches of blue showed in the sky, but gunmetal clouds were scudding toward the peaks behind him.

He paused beside a beaver-downed cottonwood, studied his surroundings: trees, trees, trees . . . the river, a black pier of rocks buffeted by gray current . . . a squirrel running on a log. Was Katsuk out in that forest nearby, silently watching? It was a thing he might do. He could be there.

David put this fear out of his mind. That wouldn't help. He plunged on, masking his passage wherever he could in ways he had learned from watching Katsuk: walking on rocks, on logs, avoiding muddy places.

For a time, he wondered if he had used sufficient care in putting out his fire. If Katsuk found that fire. . . . Would Katsuk know his escaping captive was following the watercourse? David considered leaving the stream, striking out over the hills. But the hills went up. They might go right back to Katsuk.

A small stream entered the larger one he was following. It came in from a ravine and barred his way with a thick growth of salal and devil's club along the watercourse. David worked his way up the small stream, found a green hole through the barbed thicket, a footlog scarred by the passage of many hooves. He peered across the footlog at the water, saw fish flicker in the current. They reminded him of his hunger, but he knew he dared not take the time to try catching one.

He crossed the footlog, skirted a nettle patch. The trail branched upstream and downstream. David went downstream, avoided the upthrust and twisting roots of a recently fallen tree. Brown dirt there to take his footprints. He climbed the steep hillside above the tree to conceal his passage.

David began to wonder at his escape. It didn't seem possible, but he was daring to hope. He knew he was in a place called the Wilderness Area. Katsuk had described it in general terms. There were park trails at the edge of the area. If he found park trails, there would be signs to tell him he was going in the right direction.

There would be hikers.

There would be food.

He paused to drink from the stream before going on.

There was the smell of mint along the stream and many patches of nettles. The back of his left hand burned from brushing the leaves. The game trail he was following twisted away from the stream and back to it, up the hill to avoid trees on the bank, back down to mossy rocks in the water. He could see no farther than fifty feet down the watercourse. Bright yellow skunk cabbages glistened in shadows downstream. The water would be slower there.

David found himself preoccupied with the many things he could sense about his surroundings, things he had learned from being with Katsuk: where a stream would run slower and deeper, where to seek a footlog, how to avoid leaving signs of his passage.

Just beyond the skunk cabbages, he returned to the larger stream he had been following earlier. A muddy elk trail ran parallel to the stream, fresh tracks on it. Some of the tracks had not yet filled with water. A patch of elk droppings still steamed on the trail.

He studied the trail ahead, the hillside, looking for the yellow patches of elk rumps. No sign of them, except the trail with its tracks and droppings.

David stayed in the trees just off the trail, moved downstream, keeping the water in sight. Trees and undergrowth became thicker. He caught occasional glimpses of the opposite shore, strips of gray water. His feet were wet and cold. His toes ached.

How far have I come from Katsuk? he wondered.

David knew Katsuk must be seeking him by this time. The question was how? Was Katsuk tracking the fugitive? Was there another way to find him?

He stopped to rest beside a cottonwood whose base had been partly chewed out by a beaver. Yellow chips covered the ground. They were at least a week old from the color of the wood. A thick spruce towered into the sky across the muddy elk trail from him. He looked down, saw the puddles in the trail reflecting the spruce's brown bark, the sky painted with branches, his own wet feet. The vision filled him with a sense of his own smallness in all of this immensity.

Where was Katsuk?

David wondered if he dared build another fire to dry his feet. They throbbed with the cold. There was plenty of dry cedar around, lots of dry wood under the fallen trees. The cottonwood chips would burn easily. But Katsuk might see the smoke. Others could see it, too—but who would arrive first?

He decided against a fire. It was too much of a gamble even for the sake of warm feet.

Movement helped him to stay warmer, he knew. David resumed his cautious passage through the trees. There was a blister forming on his left heel and he tried to ignore it.

Once, he heard a raven call. He cowered for five minutes under the sweeping limbs of a cedar before daring to go on. Even so, he kept a cautious outlook on the sky, wondering if those were Katsuk's ravens.

The elk trail turned, angled up a steep hill.

David chose to stay with the river and abandon the trail. He leaped across the trail to avoid leaving tracks, forced his way through underbrush along the river, worked his way around a thin rock ledge above a waterfall taller than himself. Logs left by the last high water lay in a red-brown tangle across from him, swept up onto a muddy beach beneath an alder copse.

Below the waterfall, the rock barrier forced him to cross the stream. He got wet to the waist doing it, almost lost his footing. He floundered through a pool, frightened a big trout from beneath a cutbank. The trout went arrowing downstream, half of its back exposed across a rocky shallows before it plunged into deeper water.

David followed the trout across the shallows, the river loud in his ears, climbed into the forest on the other side, and found a game trail there.

He estimated three hours to nightfall. The stream down which he moved now was a wide and roaring river, its edges lost in the shadows of steep banks. Hemlocks and cedars on both banks hid the upper ridges. Vine maples bowered the water in places.

For a time, he found relatively easy passage along a dry slough back from the stream. Bleached-white alders lined the slough, scrawling sharp lines against the evergreen background. He came on a logjam at the lower end of the slough. There were rough gray trunks of long-dead trees to cross, another maple bottom on the far side of the jam.

Fatigue and hunger forced him to a stop before crossing the logjam. He sat on a log. His chest heaved. Beneath his fear and fatigue, he felt the growth of elation. All during the night he had nurtured his hope as he nurtured the tiny fire. All through this day, he had lived in the shadow of signs and portents. But there had been no evidence of Katsuk except that brief flurry of ravens, and even they were gone. The sounds all around him were dominated by the river working its way under the edge of the logjam.

Katsuk had said that this river sound was the voice of Water Baby, a monster who could take human form. The man's words had given a sense of reality to the monster which David had found it hard to discount. Water Baby trapped your soul by getting you to tell it your name. David shuddered at the memory, listened to the water. There were voices in the water, but no words.

David looked up at the sky. It was getting darker. The light had dropped markedly and the wind possessed a new chill. Rain began to fall—big drenching drops. David got up, looked for shelter. There was only the steep hill behind the maples, the logs. He was soaked to the skin in a minute, shivering with cold.

As swiftly as it had come, the rain passed.

Blue patches could be seen in the scudding gray clouds.

Once more, David set off downstream. He longed for shelter, despaired of finding it. The river ran beside him, flowing noisily in its canyon. There were more patches of blue sky, but he felt no sunlight.

An osprey took off from a gray snag ahead of him. It climbed out over the watercourse, circled. David stared up at the bird, letting his mind fly high, but his feet still blundered through the rocks beside the river.

Osprey.

David recalled Katsuk describing a tribal chief of the old times: blanket of dog wool, raven's beak headdress, osprey feathers in his headband.

The river made a wide curve to the left, debauched from a spruce copse into a meadow full of blue camas.

David stopped within the tree shadows.

The river grew wider out there, moved slow and meandering through the meadow before it plunged into thick green darkness of brush and trees at the far side. A flood-scoured bar marked the nearest river bend. Milky wavelets clawed at · sand there.

David let his gaze traverse the meadow's rim, right to left, gasped as he saw a sign. He saw the park trail then, off to the left. A small stream came down into the meadow there, reaching out to the river. A man-made footbridge crossed the small stream. Big letters on the sign beside the bridge read KILKELLY SHELTER 2 MI.

Shelter!

David felt his heart beating faster. He and Katsuk had stayed in shelters. One had been in a deep stand of cedar, water running down the trail beside it. There had been a wet smell of ashes, a fire pit under an overhanging porch. The shelter's lower logs had been rotten, chipped out at the bottom by hikers in search of dry fuel.

The arrow on the sign pointed to the right, downstream.

David thought: *There may be hikers!*

He stepped from the tree shadows, stopped in confusion at a great flapping of wings and bird cries overhead. A flock of ravens had leaped into the sky at sight of him, filling the air with their uproar. David stared up at them, terrified.

Ravens! Hundreds of them!

They darkened the sky, wheeling and calling.

As though the birds had summoned him, Katsuk emerged from the trees across the meadow on the far side of the river. He stood a moment beside a great spruce, his headband dull red, a black feather in the back. He came straight then toward the river, one arm brushing aside silken green leaves at the bank. He stopped only when he was thigh deep in the water. The river around him ran milky with snowmelt.

David stared at Katsuk, unable to move.

The ravens continued to wheel and call.

Katsuk waited in the water, holding his bow and arrow high, staring up at the birds.

Why is he waiting? David wondered.

At the river's near shore, David saw the silvery white of raindrops on reeds, then gray rocks, then the river, and Katsuk standing in the water like an animal startled into stillness, undecided which way to turn, waiting.

Why!

The ravens whirled out over the trees beyond the meadow, went away with diminishing noise, grew abruptly silent. They had settled down.

As the birds fell silent, Katsuk plunged into motion, crossed the river, climbed dripping into the meadow. He came straight on to where David stood, walking with slow, deliberate steps. The strung bow was carried in his left hand, a single arrow clutched to it with two fingers. He wore the obsidian knife in a loop of his rope belt near the pouch. His loincloth was stained with brown earth. Water ran from it down his legs.

Katsuk stopped a pace from David, stood staring into the boy's face.

David trembled, not knowing what to do or say. He knew he could not outrun Katsuk. And there was that bow with an arrow ready for it.

"Raven told me where you would be," Katsuk said. "I came straight here after I had made my arrow. You followed the river as Raven told me. That is the long way here."

David's teeth chattered with cold and fear. There was an oddly deliberate pacing to Katsuk's words.

Katsuk held up the bow and the arrow. "You see—they are finished." He nodded. "But I did not feel it when you lured me to that arrow tree. I thought the arrow wood was a gift and took it. I thanked Cedar. But you tricked me. It was a trick."

Katsuk coughed, deep and racking. When the spasm passed, he stood trembling. The skin of his jaws and cheeks was pale.

What's wrong with him? David wondered.

"You have put the Cedar sickness upon me," Katsuk said. "You and Tskanay."

David thought: *He really is sick.*

Katsuk said: "I am cold. We must find a place to be warm. Cedar takes the heat of my body and sends it to the sky."

David shook his head, tried to still the chattering of his teeth. Katsuk had been waiting here at the meadow with his birds. But he sounded so . . . strange. The sickness had changed him.

"Take this sickness from me," Katsuk said.

David bit his lip, seeking pain to help stop the chattering of his teeth. He pointed to the sign. "There's a shelter. We could—"

"No! We cannot go that way. People come." Katsuk peered at the spruce copse from which David had emerged. "There is a place . . . in there."

"I've just come that way," David said. "There's no—"

"There is a place," Katsuk said. "Come."

Walking with that odd, stiff-legged stride, Katsuk stepped past the boy, moved into the trees. David followed, feeling that he had moved into Katsuk's delirium.

Again, Katsuk coughed, deep and racking.

At the logjam where David had rested, Katsuk paused. He studied the water hurtling against the logs: dark, blue-gray river crossed by smoky driftwood. Yes, this was the place.

He stepped up onto the jam, crossed the river, jumping from log to log. David followed.

On the far shore, David saw what he had missed earlier: an abandoned park shelter, part of its roof caved in. The logs and shakes were mottled with moss and lichen. Katsuk entered the shelter. David heard him digging in there.

David hesitated on the riverbank, looked downstream.

People coming! Katsuk had said it.

The air was cold. He felt an added chill of madness. Katsuk is sick. I could run back to the meadow. But he might catch me, or shoot me with that arrow.

The sky was dark over the trees downstream. Rain walked on a black line up the river, that hard sky behind it, clouds crouched over the sunset, the wind floating the leaves, whipping night before it.

Katsuk called from the shelter. "Hurry up. It is going to rain."

Again, Katsuk coughed.

David entered the shelter, smelling raw earth, the damp fungus odors of rot.

Katsuk had dug a hole in one corner. He pulled a small metal drum from it. The lid popped with a rusty creaking. Katsuk extracted two blankets and a small, tightly wrapped package.

"Fire tinder," Katsuk said, tossing the package at the boy.

Katsuk turned, moved toward the shelter's entrance. David saw that the man was almost staggering.

"You thought to kill me with Cedar sickness," Katsuk said. "I will yet do what I must do. Raven will give me the power."

CHIEF PARK Ranger William Redek:

It's cold in there for this time of year, been more snow and rain than usual. Snow line's lower than I can remember for years. I hear Indian fakirs have a trick for keeping warm without lots of clothes or fire, but this Hobuhet is a different kind of Indian. Doubt if he knows that trick. If he and that boy are in there, they have to be in shelter of some kind, and with fire. That, or they're dead. You lose enough body heat and that country kills you.

KATSUK LAY on moss between two logs, his mind howling in a fevered nightmare. There was a wood path, an arrow. The arrow must balance just right. He had found the wood for the arrow in the avalanche scar of a tall cedar. It had been a trick, all a trick. He held the arrow and the arrow held him. He led a cortege up the wood path from the most ancient times to the present. His mind was drunk with all the lives it held.

A spirit shouted in his mind: "The earth does not know who owns it!"

Katsuk groaned.

Delirium moved his feet on the wood path. He sang the names of his dead, but each new name brought a change in the nightmare. When he sang Janiktaht's name, he saw Hoquat running, hair flying like a wind-whipped bush.

Another name: *Okhoots.*

He was in a field embroidered with yellow flowers, a bubbling spring beside the field. He drank at the spring, but the water failed to slake the dry burning of his throat.

Another name: *Grandfather Hobuhet.*

He was confronted by wave tops blown white in a gale, a sorrel weaving in green water. A dead whale rose out of the water, said: "You dare disturb me!"

Another name: *Tskuldik.*

Father . . . father . . . father!

He called a nameless name in a canyon, was back on the nightmare trail of his ordeal. He heard the woods' dirge, felt wet bracken at his waist. He was marching upcountry from the hoquat places. There was a dirty yellow logging rig parked beside the road, heavy green of second-growth fir behind it. Side roads poked out into the tree wall. Dead snags thrust up through the green.

There was an alder bottom, a stump ranch glimpsed through the bleached-white maze of trunks. He saw platform notches on old stumps, ragged bark dangling. There was a corrugated culvert with arsenic-yellow skunk cabbages on one side of a rutted road, water trickling out the other side. He saw the open scar of a logged-off hillside, a sign: WARNING: UNDERGROUND POWER AND TELEPHONE CABLES.

As he read the sign, Katsuk felt his mind plunge into a cold river. He saw moss-covered boughs vibrating in the water. He became one of the boughs.

He thought: *I have become a water spirit.*

In his delirium, he screamed for Raven to save him. Raven swam by him under the water, became a fish, *kull t' kope!*

Katsuk awoke, trembling with terror. Cramps contorted his body. He felt weak, drained. Dawnlight glared gray through the shelter's open entrance. Sweat bathed him. He shivered with chill. Blankets had been tucked around him, but he had thrown them off in his nightmare thrashing.

Painfully, his knees trembling with Cedar sickness, he managed to stand, forced himself to the entrance. He leaned against a log upright, shivered, half conscious of some ultimate necessity which he could not name.

Where was Hoquat?

A piece of wood broke with a clear snapping off to his right. The boy came around the shelter there, his arms loaded with firewood. He dumped the wood beside the gray ashes of the fire pit.

Katsuk stared at the boy, at the fire pit, trying to put the two together in his thoughts.

David saw the weakness in Katsuk, said: "I found a can of beans in that little barrel and heated them. I left most of them for you."

He used a split length of green wood to lift the can from the ashes and place it at Katsuk's feet. A flat piece of wood for a spoon protruded from the can.

Katsuk squatted, ate greedily, hungry for the warmth more than for the food. The beans tasted of ashes. They burned his tongue, but he gulped them, felt heat radiate from his stomach.

The boy, working to restore the fire, said: "You had a nightmare. You yelled and tossed around all night. I kept the fire going most of the night."

Flame began to climb through the wood the boy had placed in the coals beneath the ashes.

Katsuk nodded dumbly. He heard water dashing on stones only a few steps from the shelter but could not find the strength to go to it. A burning dryness filled his throat.

"Wa-ter," he croaked.

The boy stood up from the fire, took the empty bean can to the river.

The way the leaf-broken sunlight dappled the boy's hair made Katsuk think of a lion he had seen in a zoo: a lion draped in sunlight and shadows. The memory caged him. He thought: *Does Hoquat have a new spirit? Is it Lion? I do not know that spirit.*

David returned from the river with the can slopping icy water. He saw the glazed look in Katsuk's eyes. Katsuk clutched the can with both hands, drained it, said: "More."

The boy brought another can of water. Katsuk drank it.

A distant engine sound came into the valley, rising above the noise of the river. It grew louder: a plane flying low over the ridge above them. The sound went away upcountry.

David stood, stared through the trees, hoping for a glimpse of the aircraft. He failed to see it.

Katsuk ignored the sound. He seemed to have lapsed back into his dream-sleep, squatting in the shelter's doorway, occasionally shuddering.

David put more wood on the fire, piled rocks around the flames to heat them. He said: "It's going to rain again."

Katsuk stared through slitted eyes at the boy. He thought: *The victim is here, but he must desire my arrow. The Innocent must ask for death.*

Low-voiced in the ancient tongue, Katsuk began chanting:

"*Your body will accept the consecrated arrow. Pride will fill your soul at the touch of my sharp and biting point. Your soul will turn toward the sun and people will say to one another: 'How proudly he died!' Ravens will alight beside your body, but they will not touch your flesh. Your pride will send you outward from your body. You will become a great bird and fly from one end of the world to the other. This is how you will accept the arrow.*"

David listened until the low chanting stopped, said: "There are more beans in that barrel. Do you want some?"

"Why do you not run away?" Katsuk asked. "You have given me the Cedar sickness. I could not stop you."

The boy shrugged, said: "You're sick."

Katsuk felt at his waist for the obsidian knife. It was gone! He stared around him, wild-eyed. His pouch with the consecrated down to place on the sacrificed body—that, too, was gone. Katsuk lurched to his feet, clutching at the boy, fell heavily beside the fire pit.

David jumped up, then hurried to kneel beside Katsuk.

"Knife," Katsuk whispered.

"Your knife? I was afraid you'd cut yourself tossing around on it. I hung the knife and your pouch in the corner back there where you put the bow and arrow." He gestured into the shelter.

Katsuk tried to turn his head, but his neck ached.

David put an arm under Katsuk's shoulders, said: "You should be in the bed. I'm heating rocks. Come on." He helped Katsuk back to the moss between the logs, pulled the blankets over him.

Katsuk allowed himself to be tucked into the blankets, asked: "Why do you help me? It was you who put the sickness on me."

"That's crazy."

"It is not! I know you did it. I saw you in my dream. You put it into these blankets."

"Those are *your* blankets! You took them out of that barrel!"

"You could have changed the blankets. You hoquat have used sickness blankets on us before. You gave us the smallpox with your blankets. You killed us with hoquat sickness. Why do you do this to me?"

"Do you want more beans or don't you?"

"Hoquat, I have had my death dream. I have dreamed the way it will be."

"That's crazy talk."

"No! I have dreamed it. I will go into the sea and become a fish. You hoquat will catch me."

The boy shook his head, went back to the fire. He put more wood on it, felt the outsides of the rocks around the flames.

It grew suddenly dark under the trees and began to rain. Cold wind blew up the river canyon. It drove big wet droplets before it, drummed rain into the trees and onto the mossy roof of the shelter. Water ran from the eaves and blew in across the fire. It hissed on the rocks.

Katsuk felt a nightmare take him. He tried to scream but could make no sound. *Water baby has me!* he thought. *How did it learn my name?*

After what seemed only a few seconds, Katsuk awoke to find warm stones piled on the blankets around his feet. A smell of scorched wool drifted on the damp air. Rain still fell from a dark sky.

The boy came then, replaced a stone on the blankets. He used a bent green limb of alder to handle the stone. Katsuk felt the warmth.

"You've been asleep all day," the boy said. "Are you hungry? I heated more beans."

Katsuk's head felt light. His throat was a dry patch of sand. He could only nod and croak.

The boy brought him a can of water. Katsuk drank it greedily, then permitted himself to be fed. He opened his mouth like a bird for each bite.

"More water?"

"Yes."

The boy brought it. Katsuk drank, fell back.

"More?"

"No."

Katsuk felt himself returning to the middle of his own being, but it was all wrong. It was himself where he had come into this primitive world, but pieces had been snipped away, the lines changed. If he could see his own face in a mirror, he knew it would be unfamiliar. He might reject that face. The eyes would be those of a stranger. He longed for restful sleep but felt nightmares lurking. The spirits waited with their willy-nilly purpose, unreasonable and demanding. He tipped his head back, stretching his neck. His mind rang like a bell.

He thought: *I am being overwhelmed by the spirits!*

The boy came with a can of water. Katsuk lifted his head to drink. Part of the water spilled down his chin. He lay back. The drink weighed on him, made his body torpid.

Katsuk thought: *He has poisoned me!*

The rain beat on the roof over him, a drum sound, whispering at first, then louder. He thought he heard a flute with the drum: pitiful music but marvelous. His life danced on the flute song, a summer moth, about to die.

I have become the soul of this place, he thought. *Why has Soul Catcher brought me here?*

He awoke in darkness. The silence was resonant, the silence after a drum. The rain had stopped. Faint, unrhythmic drips came from the eaves. The fire had burned low. A shadow near the fire revealed itself as the boy asleep curled up beside the warm rocks. As Katsuk stirred, the boy sat up, stared into the shelter's darkness.

"Katsuk?"

"I am here."

"How do you feel?"

Katsuk felt the clarity in his head. Cedar sickness had left him. He sensed his weakness, but the dry juice of his fear had been squeezed into oblivion.

"The sickness has gone from me," Katsuk said.

"Are you thirsty?"

"Yes."

The boy brought a can of water. Katsuk drank it, his hand steady.'

"More?"

"No."

Katsuk sensed the multiplicity of his universe, knew the spirits remained within him. He said: "You drove the sickness from my body, Hoquat. Why?"

"I couldn't just leave you. You were sick."

"I was sick, yes."

"May I come in there now and sleep under the blankets?"

"You are cold?"

"Yes."

"It is warm here." Katsuk opened the blankets.

The boy scrambled over the logs that contained the moss bed, crawled under the blankets. Katsuk felt the thin body trembling.

Presently, Katsuk said: " Nothing has changed, Hoquat."

"What?"

"I still must create a holy obscenity."

"Go to sleep, Katsuk." The boy sounded exhausted.

"We have been gone thirteen nights," Katsuk said.

The boy made no response. His trembling had stilled. Soft, even breathing betrayed sleep.

Katsuk thought: *Nothing has changed. I must produce for this world a nightmare they will dream while awake.*

SHERIFF PALLATT:

They only give me thirty-five men and one helicopter to cover the whole goddamned Wilderness Area. It's a goddamned mess. My feet hurt. Look how swollen they are! But I'm gonna find that pair. They're in there and I'm gonna find 'em.

DAVID OPENED his eyes into white darkness, a collision of sight. It was several heartbeats before he realized he was staring at the moon, another arc of it eaten away by Beaver. It was cold. A moon river glowed through the trees outside the shelter. The river whispered to him, reminding him of rain and silence. A mountain slowly revealed itself through the trees. It had been there all along, but now it showed itself to him: moon-drenched, awash with snow. A star mantle wound through the sky beyond the mountain.

With a sudden shock, David realized Katsuk was not beside him.

"Katsuk?" he ventured, voice low.

No answer.

Katsuk had added more wood to the fire. Coals glowed brightly in the fire pit.

David pulled the blankets more tightly around himself. Smoke from the fire pit blurred the moon's pale witchery. The sky was full of stars! He recalled Katsuk saying the stars were holes in a black deerhide. Crazy Katsuk! Where was he?

Katsuk had prayed: *Net of stars, Deer and Bear in the sky—I take care for thee!*
"The moon is the eye of Kwahoutze!"

Again, David called: "Katsuk?"

But there was no answer to the call—only the wind in the trees, the voices of the river.

David peered into the darkness, searching. Where was Katsuk?

In the remembered green of the night, a shadow moved. Katsuk stood beside the fire pit, flung there by his own movement.

"I am here, Hoquat."

Katsuk stared into the shelter's blackness, seeing the boy there and not seeing him. It was as though he stared at the boy's dream and the spirit talking:

"You are not yet ready. When you are ready, I will come for you. Pray then, and a wish will be granted you."

Those were the spirit's words.

David asked: "Where have you been?" He said it accusingly, aware of a change in Katsuk's manner, but unable to identify that change.

Katsuk heard the question like a voice calling within his skull and wondered: *Should I tell him where I've been? Is that what the spirit demands of me now?*

The question disturbed Katsuk, setting up currents within him that left his mind in turmoil. He recalled how Raven had awakened him in the night, speaking from a dream that bridged the two worlds. Raven had ordered him to go downstream to the big meadow, warning him of danger there. Searchers were camped there now, a big party of them with tents and rifles and radios.

Katsuk recalled his stalking approach to the camp. He had crawled through the tall grass to within a few yards of the searchers, close enough to hear the men awakening in the dark and preparing for their day of hunting for human quarry. Their mouths full of sleep, the men had talked. Their words had revealed much. The smoke from the fire in the abandoned shelter on Sam's River had been seen by an aircraft searcher just before dark last night. Could Hoquat be blamed for building up that fire? Had it been a breach of innocence? Katsuk thought not. The boy had been concerned with his captor's illness and with the need for warmth.

With that fire as their goal, though, the men from the meadow would be here soon. Even now, they could be in the hills around the shelter, waiting for dawn before moving.

"Where were you?" the boy pressed.

"I've been walking in my forest."

David sensed evasion in the answer, asked: "Will it be dawn soon?"

"Yes."

"Why did you go walking, Katsuk?"

"Raven called me."

David heard the remoteness in Katsuk's voice, realized the man stood half in the spirit world, in the place of his dreams and his visions.

"Are we going to stay here today?" David asked.

"We are going to stay."

"Good. You should rest after your sickness."

And David thought: *Maybe if I just talk to him calmly he'll come out of it and be all right.*

Katsuk sensed then that the boy had also developed another self which must be reasoned with, influenced, and understood. The immobility in the surface of this youth was not to be mistaken for peace. Hoquat's spirit was no longer hiding. And Katsuk asked himself: *Why shouldn't this happen to Hoquat as it happened it me?*

Why else had Hoquat nursed his captor through the Cedar sickness? Logic said the boy should flee while Katsuk was weak, yet he stayed.

David felt the pressure of Katsuk's silence, asked: "Do you need anything? Shall I get up now?"

Katsuk hesitated, then: "There is no need for you to get up. We have a little time left us yet."

Katsuk thought then of the bow and its single arrow hidden in a tree behind him. The past and the present were tied together, but the great circle had yet to be completed. He felt the pouch at his waist, the packet with the down from the sea ducks in it to scatter on the slain victim as it had been done through all time. He knew his mind grazed above its old levels. He sensed Soul Catcher speaking to him and through him. The passionate simplicity of Bee had caught him up in full awareness of death and world-silence. The spirit power of his realization reached all through him. He felt death not as negation but as the assignment of his life. It was why he stood in this place. It was why he had made the bow, touching the wood only with a stone knife. It was why he had fitted the old arrowhead from the ocean beach into its new wodden pocket, preparing it for the death to come.

Spirits had energized him. They were spirits without shape or smell or sound— yet they moved this world. They moved it! They moved the aircraft and machines engaged in this primitive contest. They moved the Innocent who must die. They moved Katsuk, who had become more spirit than man.

Katsuk thought: *I must do this thing to the perfection which the old gods have ordered. It must have the unmistakable spirit pattern that all men may understand it: good and evil bound one to the other by unbreakable form, the circle completed. I must keep faith with my past. Goodevil! One thing. That is what I do.*

With inward vision, he sensed elk horn lances in the dark all around him. Their shafts were trimmed with tufted bear fur. They were held by people from the past. Those people came from the time when men had lived with the land and not against it. He dropped his gaze to his hand. The shape of it was there, but details were lost in shadow. Memory provided the image: Bee's slug-white accusation in his skin.

Katsuk thought: *Any man may emulate the bee. A man may sting the entire universe if he does it properly. He must only find the right nerve to receive his barb. It must be an evil thing I do, with the good visible only when they turn it over. The shape of hate must be revealed in it, and betrayal and anguish and the insanities we all share. Only later should they see the love.*

David sensed undercurrents in the silence. He found himself afraid *for* Katsuk and *of* him. The man had become once more that wild creature who had bound his captive's arms and half dragged him to the cave a night's march from Six Rivers Camp.

What's he thinking now? David wondered. And he said: "Katsuk, shouldn't you come back to bed?"

Katsuk heard two questions in the boy's words, one on the surface and one beneath. The second question asked: *"What can I do to help you?"*

"Do not worry about me, Hoquat," Katsuk said. "It is well with me."

David heard a softness in Katsuk's voice. Sleep lay at the edge of the boy's awareness like a gray cloud. Katsuk was concerned for his captive now. The boy readjusted the blankets around him, shifted closer to the coals in the fire pit. The night was cold.

Katsuk heard the movement as a demonstration of life. He thought in sudden fearful awareness of the thing he had to do in this world of flesh and time. Would people misinterpret his actions?

The spirits had summoned him to perform an artistic act. It would be a refinement of blood revenge, a supreme example to be appreciated by this entire world. His own people would understand this much of it. His own people had blood revenge locked into their history. They would be stirred in their innermost being. They would recognize why it had been done in the ancient way—a mark upon raw earth, an incantation, a bow untouched by steel, a death arrow with a stone head, the down of sea ducks sprinkled upon the victim. They would see the circle and this would lead them to the other meanings within this act.

What of the hoquat, though? Their primitive times lay farther back, although they were more violent. They had hidden their own violence from their surface awareness and might not recognize Katsuk's ritual. Realization would seep upward from the spirit side, though. The very nature of the Innocent's death could not be denied.

"I have in truth become Soul Catcher," Katsuk said, realizing he had spoken aloud only after the words were uttered.

"What'd you say?" The boy's voice was heavy with sleep.

"I am the creature of spirits."

"Are you sick again, Katsuk?" The boy was coming back from sleep, his tone worried.

"I no longer have the Cedar sickness, Hoquat."

His flesh gripped by anguish, Katsuk thought: *Only one thing remains. The Innocent must ask me for the arrow. He must show that he is ready. He must give me his spirit wish.*

Silently, Katsuk prayed: *"O, Life Giver, now that you have seen the way a part of your all-powerful being goes, put all of you that way. Bring the circle to completion."*

Somewhere down the river behind Katsuk, a man shouted. It was a hoarse sound, words unintelligible but full of menace.

David started from sleep. "What was that?"

Katsuk did not turn toward the sound. He thought: *It must be decided now.* He said: "The searchers have found us."

"People coming?"

"Your people are coming, Hoquat."

"Are you sure?"

"I am sure. That was where I went walking in my forest, Hoquat. I went down to the meadow. There was a camp in the meadow. The people from that camp will be here by daylight."

David heard the words with mounting panic. "What're we going to do?"

"We?"

"You've gotta run, Katsuk!" Even as he spoke, David felt the mixture of reason and unreason in his words. But the demand for flight was larger than any other consideration.

"Why must we run?" Katsuk asked. He sensed the spirit guiding the boy's reason through a maze of panic.

"You can't let them catch you!"

Katsuk spoke with the calming presence of his vision: "Where would I run? I am still weak from the Cedar sickness. I could not go far."

David dropped the blankets from his shoulders, jumped up. The man's serenity outraged him. "I'll help you!"

"Why would you help me?"

"Because . . . because they. . . ."

"Because they will kill me?"

How could the man be so calm? David asked himself. And he blurted: "Katsuk! You've gotta run!"

"I cannot."

"You've just gotta!" The boy clutched up the blankets, thrust them across the glowing fire pit at Katsuk. "Here! Take the blankets and go hide on the hill. There must be someplace to hide up there. I'll tell 'em you left yesterday."

"Why would you do such a thing?"

Katsuk's patience filled David with panic. He said: "Because I don't want you caught . . . and put in jail."

"Hoquat, Hoquat," Katsuk reasoned, "until these past few weeks I've lived all my life in cages."

The boy was frantic now. "They'll put you in jail!"

"No. They will kill me."

David immediately saw the logic of this. Katsuk had murdered a man. David said: "I won't tell them about that guy."

"What . . . guy?"

"You know! The hiker, the guy you . . . You know!" How could Katsuk be this stupid?

"But they will kill me because I kidnapped you."

"I'll tell 'em I came of my own free will."

"Did you?"

"Yes!"

Katsuk thought: *Now, the spirits guide us both.* The Innocent had not yet asked for the consecrated arrow. He was not yet ready. But the circle was closing. Katsuk said: "But what about my message?"

"What message?" *There he went, talking crazy again!*

"The spirit message I must send to the whole world," Katsuk explained.

"I don't care about your message! Send it! Just don't let them catch you!"

Katsuk nodded. Thus it went. He said: "Then it is your wish—your *spirit* wish, that I send my message?"

"Yes! Only hurry. I can hear them coming."

Katsuk sensed the calmness of his vision sweep upward through his body from the soles of his feet. He spoke formally, as one did to the properly prepared sacrificial victim. "Very well, Hoquat. I admire your courage, your beauty, and your innocence. You are admirable. Let no man doubt that. Let all men and all spirits. . . ."

"Hurry, Katsuk," David whispered. "Hurry."

"Let all men and all spirits," Katsuk repeated, "learn of your qualities, Hoquat. Please sit down and wait here. I will go now."

With a sigh of relief, the boy sank to a sitting position on one of the bed logs beside the shelter's entrance. "Hurry," he whispered. "They're close. I can hear them."

Katsuk cocked his head to listen. Yes, there were voices shouting directions in the dark, a movement seen only by its noises. Still in the formal tone, he said: "Hoquat, your friend Katsuk bids you good-bye."

"Good-bye, Katsuk," the boy whispered.

Quickly now, because he could feel the predawn stillness in the air and see the flashlights of searchers coming through the trees across the river, Katsuk faded back in the shadows to the young spruce where he had secreted the bow and arrow. Murmuring his prayers, he set the bowstring, that hard line of walrus gut. The bow trembled in his hands, then steadied as he felt the power of it. Truly, it was a god-bow. He nocked the arrow against the bowstring. Now, his vision focused down to the infinity of this instant.

A bird whistled in the trees overhead.

Katsuk nodded his awareness. The animals of this forest knew the moment had come. He felt the spirit power surge all through his muscles. He turned toward the shelter, sensed the morning world begin to glow all around him, all platinum and gray movement. The boy could be seen behind the fire pit, sitting wrapped in a blanket, head bowed, a primordial figure lost to the world of flesh.

Although he heard no sound ot if, Katsuk knew the boy was crying. Hoquat was shedding spirit tears for this world.

Steadily, Katsuk drew the bow taut, sighted as his grandfather had taught him. His thumb felt the fletching of the arrow. His fingers held the unpolished cedar of the arrow. All of his senses were concentrated upon this moment—river, wind, forest, boy, Katsuk . . . all one. In the magic instant, feeling the bow become part of his own flesh, Katsuk released the arrow. He heard the *whang* of the walrus gut. The sound flew straight across the clearing with the arrow. Straight it went and into the boy's chest.

Hoquat jerked once against the log post at the shelter's entrance. The post held him upright. He did not move again.

For David, there was only the sharp and crashing instant of awareness: *He did it!* There was no pain greater than the betrayal. Hunting for a name that was not *Hoquat*, the boy sank into blackness.

Katsuk felt anguish invade his breast. He said: "Soul Catcher, it is done."

Carefully measuring out each step, Katsuk advanced upon the shelter. He stared at the arrow in Hoquat's breast. Now, the circle was complete. It had been a clean and shattering stroke, straight through the heart and probably into the spine. Death had come quickly to the Innocent.

Katsuk felt the ancient watchers of the spirit world departing then. He stood alone, immobile, fascinated by his own creation—this death.

In the growing daylight, the folds of the boy's clothing took on a semblance of the mossy post behind the body. Part of the body appeared ready to dissipate into the smoke winding upward from the fire pit. It created an illusion of transparency about Hoquat. The boy was gone. The Innocent had left this place in company with the ancient watchers. That was as it should be.

Katsuk heard the searchers then. They were climbing onto the logs which crossed the river. They would be here within minutes. What did it matter now?

Tears coursed down Katsuk's cheeks. He dropped the bow, stumbled forward across the fire pit, fell to his knees, and gathered up the small body.

When Sheriff Pallatt and the search party entered the clearing at the shelter, Katsuk sat with Hoquat's body in his arms, cradling the dead boy like a child, swaying and chanting the death song one sang for a friend. The white down of the sea ducks floated in the damp air all around them.